Praise for Juilene Osborne-McKnight

I Am of Irelaunde

"Osborne-McKnight beautifully portrays the intricacies of faith, love, and humanity in this novel."   —*Booklist*

"WHAT a lovely book! Not only first-rate storytelling, but a feel for the yearning for mystery and belief that lie at the roots of the soul. I think both Osian and Patrick would be more than pleased with this re-creation of their lives and stories."   —Diana Gabaldon

"A wonderful, magical story; it whipped me up into the air right from the first page and took me soaring to places I had never visited or imagined before. . . . The book is an enchantment, nothing less."   —Jack Whyte

Daughter of Ireland

"Osborne-McKnight has spun a spellbinding fable of love and loyalty in the land of poets and kings."   —*Booklist*

"Juilene Osborne-McKnight reveals Irish history through a mixture of fiction and fact, magic and realism, love and hate, forgiveness and redemption. The effect is a captivating story that will entrance and leave the reader yearning for more."   —*Romance Reviews Today*

Bright Sword of Ireland

"Warm, playful, and eloquent, *Bright Sword of Ireland* is a welcome addition to the genre."   —*Publishers Weekly*

"Osborne-McKnight continues to retell mystical Irish folktales in spellbinding fashion."   —*Booklist*

Forge Books by Juilene Osborne-McKnight

Daughter of Ireland
I Am of Irelaunde
Bright Sword of Ireland
Song of Ireland

SONG OF IRELAND

Juilene Osborne-McKnight

TOR®

A TOM DOHERTY ASSOCIATES BOOK
NEW YORK

SONG OF IRELAND

Copyright © 2006 by Juilene Osborne-McKnight

Map by Jonathan Bennett

A Tor Book
Published by Tom Doherty Associates, LLC
175 Fifth Avenue
New York, NY 10010

www.tor-forge.com

Tor® is a registered trademark of Tom Doherty Associates, LLC.

The Library of Congress has cataloged the hardcover edition as follows:

Osborne-McKnight, Juilene.
 Song of Ireland / Juilene Osborne-McKnight—1st ed.
  p. cm.
 "A Tom Doherty Associates Book."
 ISBN 978-0-7653-1243-3 (hardcover)
 ISBN 978-1-4668-2374-7 (e-book)
  1. Mythology, Celtic—Fiction. 2. Celts—Ireland—Fiction. 3. Fairies—Fiction.
 4. Ireland—Fiction. I. Title

 PS3565.S455S66 2006
 813'.6—dc22

                                                                2005044637

ISBN 978-0-7653-3680-4 (trade paperback)

Tor books may be purchased for educational, business, or promotional use. For information on bulk purchases, please contact Macmillan Corporate and Premium Sales Department at 1-800-221-7945, extension 5442, or write specialmarkets@macmillan.com.

First Edition: April 2006
First Trade Paperback Edition: February 2014

This one is for Ireland, for the gift of story.

I have wandered through the ring forts at Kenmare Bay,
passed through the dolmens on the Burren,
stood in the singing wind at Tara,
pondered the ancient moon maps at Knowth.
Because Amergin gave dwelling places to the others,
magic still remains in Ireland, shimmering in the world.
May it never leave you on a wind of change.

ACKNOWLEDGMENTS

First, I would like to thank Father Caoimhin O'Neill, Father Conn O'-Maoldhomhnaigh, Dr. James Heaney, Ms. Cheri Conlon, and all of St. Patrick's Carlow College, Ireland, for reading to me in Irish, for singing to me in Irish, for hiking us to the tops of the mountains and taking us to the fairy mounds and the monasteries, for dancing, for the singing pubs, for Jameson's with red lemonade, for looking just like himself, a throwback, for adding such a layer to my life that both the book and I were reimbued with magic. Also, to Michael Norris, who got us to the ring fort on Kenmare Bay, and to Dr. Ellie Wymard of Carlow University in Pittsburgh, the Great Organizer, who is the person I would like to be when I grow up.

At Tor/Forge, I would like to thank Claire Eddy, the best editorial eye in the business, and Deborah Wood for all of her help and organizational assistance. At Curtis Brown, ongoing thanks to Maureen Walters, Dave Barbor, and Josie Schoel.

I would also like to thank my students at DeSales University, who see it all fresh, and make me laugh out loud.

Mostly I would like to thank my family and friends, who never abandon me, even though I dwell for most of each year in another time, in another language, in another world, with people who are just as real as me, but who never ever go with me to book signings, offer to do the dishes, take me out for coffee milkshakes, or pretend to be interested in hearing the stories just one more time.

Ah, now, just one more time.

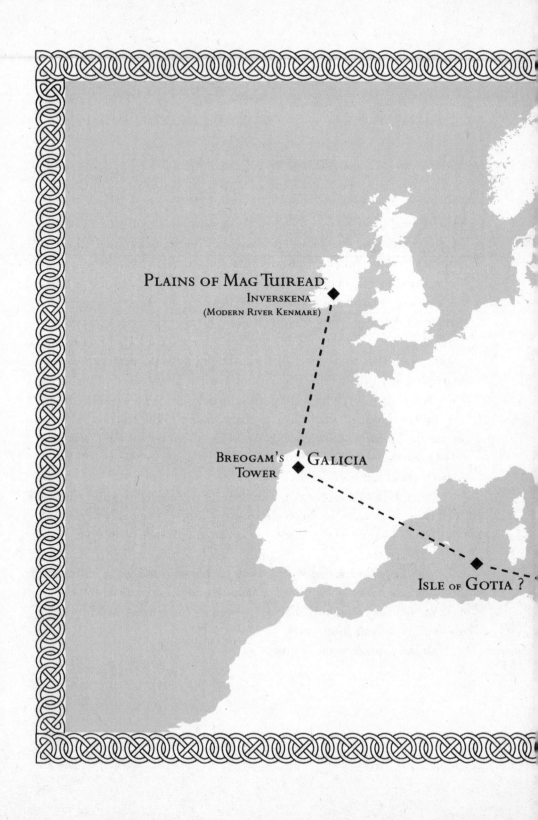

PLAINS OF MAG TUIREAD
INVERSKENA
(MODERN RIVER KENMARE)

BREOGAM'S
TOWER

GALICIA

ISLE OF GOTIA ?

The Journey of the Milesians

ISLE OF IRENA ?

EGYPT

GLOSSARY AND PRONUNCIATIONS

A DANU CHARACTER AND PLACE-NAME GLOSSARY

Airmid (Air vid) Daughter of Dian Cecht in the ancient Celtic myths. He was so angry over her restoration of Nuada's arm that, in the myths, he destroyed her herb gardens, which would have healed all the illnesses of the world.

Bres (Bresh) half Fomorian, half Danu king, called "the Beautiful" for his physical appearance. One of the original traitors in Irish mythology.

Dagda (as spelled) Called the "good god" in later versions of the myth, "good" meaning provider. In many versions of the myth, Dagda is a giant who drags a huge club behind him and possesses a giant cauldron sunk into the earth and constantly replenished with food so that the Danu will never go hungry.

Danu (Da noo) This is the tribe of the goddess Danu. They are also called the **Danaan** of the **Tuatha de Danaan** (Too a ha day dan an), or the tribe of the Danaan. They became both the panoply of gods in ancient Celtic Ireland and the **sidhe** (shee), or "others," who are also called the "little people."

Dian Cecht (Deean Kecht) Original physician of the Danu, he killed his son Miach and destroyed the herb garden of his daughter Airmid in his anger over their restoration of Nuada's biological arm.

Fir Bolg (as spelled) One of the five original races of Ireland, supposedly a Stone Age hunter-gatherer people who were the ancestors of Connachtsmen.

Fomor (Fovor) Also Fomorians. Supposedly these dark and terrifying sea raiders had their stronghold on an island off the coast of Ireland called Tor Mor (Great Rock) or Tober Mor. No one knows who they were.

Lugh (Loo) Lugh is the son of the Sun, the all-powerful male god figure of the Danaan myths. His origins are unclear; some versions of the myth have him as the son of the Dagda, others of a half-human, half-Danaan liaison. **Lamfhada** (Lam fa da) is his "Long-Arm" designator, evidently from his skill with a spear. **Ildanach** (Ill da nok) is his "All-Craftsman" appellation, from the myth in which he wins over the Danaan by being good at everything.

Mag Tuiread (Moy Teera) Three battles take place on the Plains of Mag Tuiread, and a variety of places in Ireland claim themselves as the location. (See "Historical and Mythological Background"). Wherever these battles took place, there must have been multiple monoliths and sarsen circles there, because the name means Many Towers.

Miach (mee ak) Son of Dian Cecht and a physician himself, he restores Nuada's biological arm. Some versions of the myths say that his father killed him because he was jealous of his son's higher medical skills.

Morrigu (Mor ee goo) The Morrigu is a triad, a form that seemed to be essential to the ancient Celtic myths. Each of the three sisters of this triad performs a specific function.

> **Macha** (Ma ha) is the shape-shifter and evidently the intellect of the triad.

> **Banbh** (Ban ev) is the carrion crow. She encourages war so that she can feed on the dead from the battlefield.

> **Nemhain** (Nev in or Ne whain) She is the sower of chaos and panic.

Nuada Argetlamh (Noo a da Ar get lav) First "king" of the Danu, his arm was hacked off in battle with the Fir Bolg, replaced by a Silver Arm, and restored as a biological arm in time for the battle with the Fomor in which Nuada was killed.

The Three Sisters In the ancient myths, pre–Milesian Ireland was ruled over by triads, first three men—Mac Cuill, Mac Cecht, and Mac Grene—and then three sisters—**Banba** (as spelled), **Fodla** (as spelled), and **Eriu** (air ee oo). The sisters encounter the sons of Mil; Eriu predicts that they will rule in Ireland forever, the sons of Mil name the island Eire in honor of her.

A GALAECI CHARACTER AND PLACE-NAME GLOSSARY

An Scail (an skel) While it means the Shadow or the Ghost, An Scail represents the druidic presence among the ancient Celts. Druids were highly learned professorial characters who kept the history, knowledge, and theology of the tribes. Many sources say that druids existed at three levels: those who were essentially priests, those who were what we would term professors, and those who served as poets or bards, keeping, telling, and passing the history of the tribes from one generation to another. At any of these levels, druids could be considered **ollamh** (ol lam) or master. Once the Milesians were settled in Ireland, poets possessed particularly high status, second only to that of the king.

Breogam (broc em) The ancestor of the sons of Mil, who built the first lighthouse on the seacoast of Galicia in Spain. Although a Roman tower stands in this location now, Breogam was supposedly the founder of the Celtic city of Brigantia, that is now called La Coruña, on the northwest coast of Spain.

Galaeci/Galicia The Galaeci were a tribe, clan, or collection of clans in northwestern Celtic Spain, around 500 BC. That region, known today as Galicia, is still Celtic in its topography, archaeology, climate, and mind-set.

Inisfail (as spelled) The Galaeci name for Ireland; they translate it as Isle of Destiny. In actual translation from the Irish it means something like Island of Getting or Finding.

Ith (as spelled) In the legends, Ith is the brother (or uncle) of Mil, who serves as the scouting party for the Milesians on the first trip to Ireland.

Skena (skee na) Supposedly the first wife of Amergin; she drowned en route to Ireland.

Sons of Mil Mil is variously known as Milesios, Mile Easpain, and Golamh (his original Galician Celtic name). He was married first to Seang, with whom he had two sons, and later to Scota, daughter of the pharaoh of Egypt, with whom he had five to seven sons. These legendary travelers are the Jason and the Argonauts of Celtic mythology. Some versions of the legend list them as nine sons, some as seven.

> **Amergin** (A ver geen) Probably originally spelled Amhairghin. The most famous of the sons of Mil, he was bard, poet, or **ollamh** (master). To be ollamh (ol lam) in a Celtic tribe was to be

13

master of the word. Such a person had tremendous power in the tribe and could rule on matters of war and battle. There are hundreds of translations of his poems, of which we have two or possibly three, depending on the translations.

Airioch Feabhruadh (Air ee ok Fev roo ahd) Mentioned in some of the versions of the myth as being one of the two sons of Mil by his first wife, Seang of Scythia.

Bile (Beel ya) In some of the myths listed as a son of Mil, in others, variously, as Mil's brother, uncle, father, or grandfather.

Colpa (as spelled).

Eber Donn (Ever Don) Son of Mil by his first wife, Seang of Scythia.

Eber Finn (Ever Fin) In the legends, went to war against his brother Eremon because his wife wanted Eremon's land.

Eremon (Air e mon) First king of Ireland, who supposedly began the construction of the Hill of Tara, although, in terms of artifacts, the hill probably dates to about 95 BC.

Ir (eer).

GAELIC TERMINOLOGY

Aither (a her) father.

An Corr (as spelled) Also called the **corrguinecht** (cor gwee nect), it means the "crane-wounding." Evidently it is some kind of martial art in which the warrior stands on a single leg and then launches forward.

Buiochas le cruthú (bwee e has le croo hoo) Blessed be Creation.

Ceolas (kee yol as) Music maker or song maker.

Coracle (as spelled) A round boat made of hide stretched on a wickerwork frame. Extremely difficult to maneuver because it is round.

Curragh (cur a) Long hide boats still used in Ireland today.

Eistigi (esh te gi) The command form of Listen!

Erbe ndruad (as spelled) A druid fence. Once pronounced by a poet, this imaginary fence could not be crossed, even in battle.

Fanacht le solas (as spelled) Wait upon the light. Ancient Celtic myth is replete with references to the light, sometimes as in the Sun, sometimes in a much larger concept that seems to signify the All-Good or the All-Knowing or the Source.

Fidchell (fid kell) Ancient Celtic chess.

Fulacht fiadh (foo lact fee ahd) A pit lined with hot stones in which the ancient Celts cooked both meat and fish. Remnants of these pits have been found in many Celtic locations, including Ireland.

Gaeilge (gale ge) There are six Gaelic languages: Irish, Scots, and Manx, called q-Goidelic and believed to be the older form of Gaelic; and Welsh, Cornish, and Breton, called p-Goidelic, or Brythonic Gaelic and believed to be a later alteration of the language. There was, of course, an original Proto-Celtic language, and many scholars now see links between that language and Proto–Indo-European or Italic, the precursor to Latin. Other scholars claim links between Celtic and ancient Hindu-Sanskrit.

Gaimred (gaiv roo) Cold season, November 1 to May 1.

Gaita (ga ta or guy ta) Spanish bagpipes. Listen to Carlos Nunez.

Gutruatri (goo troo a tree) A Milesian Celtic druid who is a singer of praise to God.

Keltoi (kel toy) This is the Greek name for the ancient Celts. The Romans called them the **Gauls** or the **Gaels.**

Lughnasa (loo na sa) The Celtic summer festival, which took place on August 1. A celebration of the warm season, of crops being in the ground, of life in general. This festival may actually have been named for Lugh.

Maither (ma her) mother.

Mo ghra (mow graw) my beloved.

Na biodh eagla ort (Na viod egla ort) Be not afraid.

Ogham (om) The Ancient Celtic stick language. It consists of a horizontal or vertical bar over which sticks are incised in various combinations. Evidently, it was a language used primarily by initiates, i.e., druids.

Ollamh (ol lam) master. Used to refer to a variety of druids, also physicians, judges, and lawyers who had achieved the top of their profession.

Samhain (sau win) The evening of October 31, the turning from the warm part of the year to the cold season. This was considered the beginning of the New Year and was an extremely dangerous time in the Celtic world because, the Celts believed, the doorway between this world and the otherworld is very thin on this night. Samhain eventually became All Hallows' Eve or Halloween.

Samhradh (sau roo) The warm season, May 1 to November 1. Summer.

Tir Nan Og (teer na nog) Variously called Mag Mell, the Island of the Ever Young, the Country of the Young, and in later myths, Avalon. This concept pervades the Celtic world; ships of light will carry the departing soul into the west, where he will be young and happy in a place of feasting and music, until he is ready to return, or is asked to return.

pROLOGUe

Near the water's edge, where the sea had thrown up round, speckled stones, Eriu halted. Behind her, her sisters stopped, Banba at her right shoulder, Fodla at her left. Mist from the sea dusted through the air, fell in crystalline drops on Eriu's long copper curls, lighted like flickering gems on the black thickness of Banba's hair, vanished into the white-gold mane of Fodla. Eriu sighed. The stones, the mist, the long green sweep to the sea. How she would miss it all. She sighed again, a long, deep exhalation. Nothing would stop what was to come.

"I will look for them now," she said to her sisters.

Without even turning, she felt them close in behind her, form the perfect triangle, heard the soft reedy chant that issued from deep in their throats.

Eriu held her arms before her, formed her fingers in the triangle, symbol for the Journey. Next, she raised both hands with fingers spread, for the children of Maker in infinite variety. Finally, she placed her hands upright and palm to palm, then interlaced the fingers, turning her hands in opposite directions to symbolize the Braid.

"Mother," she whispered, "clear my sight that I may see, clear my mind that I may understand, clear my spirit that I may choose wisely for my people."

She closed her eyes, placed her palms together parallel to the ground, then thrust them forward like the prow of a ship. She followed their line in her mind, out, out, over the waters and south.

Nothing.

Not even the vision of the coastline of the great continent came to mind. She drew her hands back in, repeated her gesture, tried again.

Still nothing.

Eriu opened her eyes.

"What do you see?" asked Banba, impatient as always.

"Nothing."

"But how can that be? You saw them when Ith first came among us."

"I do not know. I thought that I saw them once again, after Ith departed from us, but now their ships are obscured in mist. Now I cannot see anything at all."

"Well, what on the Green Orb is wrong with you? Your vision never fails you! The Danu rely upon it. Upon you."

"Banba, when Ith came among us more than a year ago, I had not used my Journey vision for more than five hundred years. How should we know if it fails me or not? Ith promised us that he would try to persuade them not to return once he understood clearly who we were and from whence we came; I took him to be a man of his word. I sent his people the message of his return with its veiled warning. Why would I need my Journey vision for a people who promised us that they would not return? That is why I asked you to help me. Perhaps I only imagined a returning fleet, or dreamed it, an anomaly of vision that has seen nothing but the sea for centuries of their time. Perhaps there are no ships on the water, or, if there are, it is a fleet of some other country, going somewhere else and not to the Green Isle after all."

She sighed and sat down hard on the bank. Oh, if only that could be true.

From behind her Fodla spoke in her voice like soft wind.

"There is another possibility, Sisters."

Eriu turned toward her sisters, who now sat opposite her, forming a triangle. Fodla was, as always, the voice of quiet reason.

"The Council recommended that all of us adopt the Metaphor again, as we did with Ith and the brothers. And so we have. Perhaps the Metaphor prevents the vision from congealing, because in it, we are not our true selves."

Banba shook her head impatiently. "For Danu's sake, Fodla. We have used the Metaphor for five centuries when we have approached the Fir Bolg who dwell here in the western bogs. Have we ever frightened the Fir

Bolg? And they are known for being easily frightened. The bogs in which they dwell may well describe their entire thought process. Has the Metaphor ever prevented us from interacting with them?"

"You do not hear me, Banba," said Fodla quietly. "I do not say that the Metaphor is a bad choice. All who dwell on the Green Orb would be frightened by our true appearance. And the Fir Bolg are known for being easily frightened. But we have never attempted vision in the Metaphor. Perhaps it blocks our ability to see."

Eriu nodded. "I think Fodla is wise. How can we look out into the future if we are not who we are?"

Banba shook her head emphatically. "We dare not abandon it. The Council has said that we must all practice the Metaphor until we can keep it in place, until no slipping occurs. These who come will be travelers, the clan of Ith. Unlike the Fir Bolg, they will have gone beyond the bogs. These new travelers may be more sophisticated. They may well know the Greeks!"

Fodla laughed. "Admit it, Sister. You find the Greek Metaphor beautiful. You like to look like a tall Greek woman with sweeping hair. You liked the one who came among us who looked like a Greek. Airioch Feabhruadh. Speak the Truth. You like the appearance of the humans."

Banba snorted, but she cast a sidelong smile at Fodla. "They are beautiful, these creatures, with their long limbs and their thick hair and their eyes like interior rainbows."

"You are beautiful too, Sister, just as you are."

"Fodla, you love the humans too. I have seen your gentle care of the Fir Bolg."

"They are like little children, so trusting, their sweet gratitude for the smallest binding of wounds, the simplest medicaments for their children. How do they see us, do you suppose?"

"As gods," said Eriu.

Banba and Fodla gasped as one.

"I mean no sacrilege, Sisters. This is how they speak of us. We are the gods of the place. Illyn has told me this."

"Then Danu forgive us," said Fodla. "For there is only one Weaver of the Braid."

"But how would we explain that to children such as these? These are not the Greeks."

"Ah," said Banba. "You see, Fodla. Eriu loved the Greeks as well."

"I did love them," Eriu said, lifting her chin. "How well their spirits contended citizenship, the nature of the state, the purpose of man, the choices of good and evil. Their minds turned on all the great questions, and so often they came right to the core of the argument. They were minds of great sophistication, spirits of great striving. And we could not have chosen a better place than the Greek Isles for our first dwelling place when we arrived here on the Green Orb."

"And yet when the Metaphor slipped and some of the Greeks saw us as we truly are, all their sophistication left them. They were as terrified as these Fir Bolg would be," said Banba.

"Illyn says that the Fir Bolg might be less terrified to see us true. She makes a good point that the Greeks were so sophisticated that they had an expectation for the behavior of the world. Our appearance violated that expectation. Hence their terror. But the Fir Bolg think in small bursts and dwell in darkness and superstition. Our true appearance might be less frightening to them."

"And what of these new ones who come?" asked Fodla.

"I know not," Eriu answered. "I saw ships. Greek biremes. Accompanied by cargo ships. Hired ships for traveling great distances. I did not see those who manned them. Nor those who visited us before."

"Still, we raise interesting questions Sisters," Banba interrupted. "Where shall we tell them we are from? Metaphor or no, our appearance here, the apparent sophistication of our civilization, will surprise them."

"We shall say we are from Greece," said Fodla.

Eriu nodded. "It is not untrue, after all. It was the most recent stop on our journey. And the Metaphor emulates the people of that country."

"And what of those like Illyn? How shall we explain them?" Banba raised her fingers, one at a time. "First these were human. Then we altered their braiding. Now they are Hybrids. No human in all the history of the Green Orb could comprehend such a thing."

Fodla shook her head. "Banba, what would you have had us do? When the Fir Bolg left their cripples and their sickling infants on the hills to die, should we have walked past them in the darkness, shrugged our shoulders? All life is of the Braid, and our physicians have the knowledge to make them well and whole. Sometimes that required rebraiding. The Hybrids who resulted are a joy among us."

"And what of our own Raveners? How shall we explain them?"

"Their darkness came within them, surely," said Fodla. "As it will undoubtedly come with the Invaders. Perhaps they will understand our Raveners best of all."

Eriu sighed. "Sisters, you debate well, and as always I thank you for your clear articulation. But we will not answer all of these questions today."

Banba and Fodla grew silent, knowing that Eriu was about to choose.

"I think that perhaps Fodla was right. It is the Metaphor which stops the vision. To see well and truly we must stand before Maker as she made us."

No argument ensued. The sisters simply stood together and turned toward the sea, forming again the triangle with Eriu at its prow.

"Sisters, remove the Metaphor," Eriu commanded softly.

As one, the three sisters touched the luminous crystal triangles with their twining spiral vines, that dangled as pendants around their necks.

There was a flashing snap of blue light. The air around the threesome congealed and grew viscous. Tiny sparkles of light and color coalesced and then dispersed. Standing on the shore were three beings who could never be mistaken for human. Their slender bodies did not look strong enough to support the weight of their large heads, of their huge oval eyes colored the deep blue-gray of the sea. Their warm golden skin was luminous, as if an aura of soft blue and gold light, constantly changing and sparkling, surrounded their little frames. Their ears folded back and up in a shape like the feathers of a bird's wing. Soft tufts of silver hair grew from each sharp triangle of bone. Around their skulls, a cloudy cap of silver-white curls seemed to catch the light in blue and gold, no more substantial than a mist upon the sea. Their mouths were their most human feature, for their lips were full and rosy and seemed curved into a permanent expression of joy. An observer might have guessed at gender, but their own people would have known them as female by their long, slender hands and delicate fingers, by the soft feathering at their ears.

From Banba and Fodla issued the deep sustained sound of the chant, the base note for Vision. Again, Eriu made the signs, Triangle, Children, Braid. Again she placed her palms parallel to the ground and sent them before her like the prow of a ship. Over the water. South and south.

And there! Seven great ships with sails unfurled. Greek biremes with the forward square sails. Cargo ships. Not hugging the coast as the non-seafaring people did but dipping and heaving, fearless in the open sea.

Destination, she must find destination.

Ith had said that they would not return; she had known him to be a man of honor. So who were these approaching travelers?

With her hands she navigated, deck to deck. Huge men, more than six feet tall. Long, braided hair. Bearded and laughing. Shouting to each other. Weapons at their belts. Women, tall and broad of shoulder, their braided hair festooned with bells. How lovely the sound in the wind! And on their backs, great swords, tall and broad. Swords down the backs of the women! No, these were not the Greeks, these loud and massive voyagers. Nor were these like the simple Fir Bolg who dwelled in the stony boglands of the Green Island. These were warrior people. Eriu shuddered. Warrior people. Against her people, who had not made war for five hundred years. Who had put away Nuada's Silver Arm. She searched among the voyagers. Was Ith among them? Or Airioch, who had made her so wary with his wandering and his watchful eyes? Was there anywhere a sign that her Green Isle was their destination? What made her think it so?

Again she navigated her hands, back to the last large ship of the fleet. Seated in the stern, a huge man, unbearded, dark hair spilling behind him in the wind. Alone. Upon him the mark of the outsider, the dreamer. Before him a map. Crudely drawn and raw, but clearly marked. The starting point on the peninsula in the south, the long coast, the island to their east, the Green Isle.

Eriu closed her eyes. There was no mistaking the map. Would her people die? Where would they go? Would any choose for war, call for the use of Nuada's Silver Arm? O Weaver of Worlds! The children of the Braid should not make war! So great grew her terror that it began to affect the chant of her sisters. It raced among the ships; some of the sailors, always superstitious, looked behind them or shaded their eyes at the sea ahead. Eriu drew a deep breath. She must not make them aware; they must not sense the presence of the Danu here on the Green Isle. Her people must have time to prepare.

Eriu opened her eyes. The one with the map was looking in her direction.

No!

She pulled her hands back, began the slow withdrawal of the vision.

He stood, stepped forward. His dark eyes fastened on her own.

By the Danu!

This one could see her. And not in Metaphor. He kept his eyes locked to hers. He lifted the map, pointed to the Green Isle. He was waiting for her to nod, to confirm, to tell him that yes, they were here, waiting. Her heart beat so fast that it felt as if it would burst out of her chest wall.

Another man approached across the deck of the ship.

"Amergin! What are you staring at now?"

It was Airioch Feabhruadh, he who had come with Ith! Then this was Amergin, the nephew Ith had spoken of with such obvious love.

Amergin broke gaze with her. "Staring?"

"We need you to watch the sea, look for the coastline, interpret the map. This is not the time for one of your strange fugues. There will be plenty of time for that on the Green Isle."

Amergin nodded.

Eriu blessed the Danu for the distraction. She withdrew her hands, navigated backward toward safety, toward the sweet ground beneath her feet. She brought her palms in against her chest, cradled them in a gesture of thanks to Maker, closed her eyes, and dropped to the ground.

"Resume the Metaphor," Banba commanded.

"Sister, she cannot. She trembles and is weak as a child." Fodla rushed to cradle Eriu in her arms. "Hush now, hush."

Banba knelt next to them. "Tell us what you saw. Now."

"There are seven ships. Airioch Feabhruadh is with them. The nephew of Ith."

"He who tried to enter our cities?"

"The very one."

"Was Ith among them?" asked Fodla.

"I did not see him."

"Then surely we are doomed," said Banba.

"Doomed I cannot say, but surely we must consider it an invasion force. They are garbed as warriors."

Eriu fell silent; her eyes were thoughtful and clouded.

"There is more," said Fodla.

"There is," said Eriu, "but I do not know what to make of it."

"Tell us, and we will bring the wisdom of three upon it."

"There was one who saw me."

"Saw you? In vision? Not possible," said Banba.

"Yet it was so, Sisters. It was Amergin, he of whom Ith so often spoke."

"He saw you this way, without Metaphor?"

"So he did, and that was the strangest thing of all. He looked directly into my eyes. He saw me true and he did not look away."

PART ONE

AM GA'ETH
TAR NA BHFARRAIGE

I AM THE
WIND ON THE SEA

I am the stag of seven tines...
I am a flood on the plain...
I am a wind on deep water...
I am a tear from the sun...
I am a hawk on a cliff...
I am the fairest of flowers...
I am the god who fires the mind...
I am the spear of battle...
I am the lake of the salmon...
I am a hill where poets walk...
I am a wild boar...
I am the roar of the sea...
Who but i knows the secrets of the dolmen?

THE SONG OF AMERGIN

1

My father was ever a wanderer. Even in my earliest, unformed memories of him, he is always standing on some parapet or framed in the embrasure of a tower of Egypt. Even now, I see his cloak blowing back in the wind, his gaze fixed west and north, the long thickness of his chestnut mane twisting against the bunched cloak as he pondered the distance. I can hear the dry rattle of the palm fronds and feel the constant friction of the wind-borne sand of Egypt, gritty against my skin.

Though I was my father's fifth son of two wives, with more still to brood in my mother's womb cradle, it was with me that he shared his vision of a magical journey. He would hold me up to the window, close his eyes to the breeze.

"Inisfail," he would say. "The Isle of Destiny. I smell her on the breeze, lad. I see her in my dreams."

"How do you know of her?"

"She is in the legends of my people. The people of Galicia. Inisfail, the Isle where dwell the Magic People. They say that he who finds her will be gifted with their magic. But in all my wanderings, I have never found her."

Usually, his dreams of Inisfail were the sure sign that soon we would be wandering again, so that by the time I reached my fifteenth year, I had been already to Rhatokis on our north coast, to the Greek democracy more than once, and even to the newly minted republic of Rome, though my father was not of any of those countries.

My father had begun his life as Golamh, son of Bile, the great chief of the Galaeci. Our tribe dwelled in the town of Brigantia in the far west of

Spain, in the region called Galicia for the people of our tribe. My father had described it to me as a soft and rainy country, itself green. I must admit that when the sands of Egypt blew against the sky, I often longed for Galicia, though perhaps it was only my father's love of the place and my worshipful love of him. The tales said that our people had wandered there to the edge of the sea centuries before. Perhaps our ancestors too were searching for the Isle of Destiny, but knew not how to find it when they reached the edge of the water.

For them, my grandfather, Breogam, had built the tall, slender broch that stood by the sea and placed into it the Eternal Flame. My father referred to it always as Breogam's Light Tower. Though my father had grown up in Galicia, even my elder brothers had never seen the place at all, though truly we had all caught the wandering disease.

For my older brothers Eber Finn and Eremon, it took the form of land longing.

"When I have my own parcel," Eber Finn would say, and Eremon would chime in, "I will fill it with grazing cattle as far as the eye can see."

For my eldest brother, Eber Donn, the sickness took the form of acquisition. What he needed or what he wanted he took, be it women or wine, land or weapons. To be truthful, women seemed to sense the hunger in him and rushed to fill it. By the time I had a mere eight years, he was possessed of three handsome wives whom he pleasured together and separately, much to the envious jesting of Eber Finn and Eremon, who possessed only one wife each.

Eber Donn was the son of my father's first wife, the long departed Seang, daughter of the king of Scythia. There my father had first taken service when he was a young man. So powerful a soldier was he, so vital to the king, that he became known as Mile Easpain, Soldier of Spain, and he captained the armies of that country.

But when Seang died in the birthing of my second brother, Airioch Feabhruadh, the king of Scythia was racked with grief and took against my father for the womb-death of his daughter. My father fled to Egypt and there took service with the army of the Pharaoh Mesuti Ra. There, he met my mother Scota, daughter of Pharaoh. Though my mother was a strong and beautiful woman, she was no woman of Egypt. Mesuti Ra, my grandfather, began his life as Cambysis of Persia. Never satisfied with single conquest, Cambysis resigned his position as king of Babylon to invade and conquer Egypt and to name himself after the sun god Ra. He died before my birth, leaving my father to serve his cousin Darius, ruler of Persia and Egypt.

Though my mother seemed always to be bearing, as fertile as the delta of the Nile, she was ever a warrior woman and so beautiful. Her hair was glossy and dark, her skin smooth, her black eyes huge, and her body strong. From her, my father had first Eber Finn, then Eremon, then me. One brother died soon after his birth when I had but six years. When I had ten years, she gave birth to my little brother Bile in the dark hours of the night. Though she had women aplenty to assist her, she rose and washed both herself and the babe and suckled him. Before she slept, she handed him not to her women, but to me. In the dark of the night, rocking my baby brother, something fierce and loving arose in me for the first time. In the morning, she dressed them both, slung Bile into a hip bag, and went about the business of the day. My father called her fearsome strong, and that was so. For me, I longed for the babe all day, and though I was only ten, felt sick with shame that a man should be so besotted of a child. I knew that my warrior brothers and even my father would pay him no mind until he could fight, until he could take to horse and ride.

In me, the wandering sickness had taken a stranger form than in my brothers, a great, vast longing that would not be satisfied by land or palaces or having. I eschewed them all. Sometimes I felt that the things of this world could all pass away, but I would still be present, my eyes looking, my ears listening.

So I looked in the eyes of everyone I met, seeking something, I knew not what. A port? A tower and a light? Magical people on a fabled isle? Perhaps it was simply belonging I sought, for I knew myself to be different, surely, from my brothers. I could not have said myself what I sought. I became a watcher of humanity. I knew that I made people fearful, that the directness of my probative gaze made them squirm. Among our people, some came to believe that I could read them, could see the tale inside. Since many of them had secrets they wished to hide, many avoided me. They should not have worried; what I looked for I found in no one. Though I tried to train myself away from staring, I could not, and eventually it came to pass that I did indeed find myself reading their stories, their jealousies and hopes, their aggravations, in the tilt of a head, in the woman their eyes followed, in the cross of the arms, in the sighs or laughter which coalesced around them. There was no magic to it, only the wisdom that one who watches and listens accrues.

Even my own brothers, though they would clap me on the shoulder or grasp my forearm in the soldiers' way, would not look at my eyes. Only little Bile saw to the core of me, and by the time I was twelve he was my constant companion, swinging up into my arms, laughing aloud when he met my eyes, placing his chubby hands against my cheeks.

So, in my awkwardness, I became like the sponges that the Greek sailors would bring us from the sea. I listened to the words that everyone spoke around me, learned the languages of Greeks and Phoenicians, of Romans and Egyptians, badgered my father and mother for the languages of their homelands. I collected people through their stories and their be-haviors and told myself the tales of their travels. In the stories, I be-longed.

At last my father must have realized my strangeness, and in my twelfth year he put me into the bardic training with his brother Ith, the druid, who was a teacher and a gutruatri, a singer of praise to God.

Ith taught me how to drift on the pool of silence, how to dwell in the great stillness that permitted me to hear, to reflect, to sink into deep knowing. From him too I learned the language of our homeland and all its tales and poems. It was Ith who gave me my first and most beloved clarsach, the harp I called Ceolas, the Song, and Ith who taught me the mournful gaita, the bagpipe of our people.

Still, in all my training, I never once saw what I sought, never once met the eyes of anyone who reflected either my music or my stillness back to me. Only my little brother Bile seemed to me to be tethered to my soul by an invisible rope. I came to think of myself as dwelling in the great alone; only the poems and the tales filled the well of my longing. So I took to the bardic life as the wind takes to the sea, pouring out stories until the stories became my coin; all demanded them of me; all took delight in them despite my seeming strangeness.

And then I began to have the dream. I was standing at the prow of a ship, a Greek bireme, laden with cargo. I looked out to the north. It was as if I sped across the water then, my own body a sail. There in the sea rose a blue and green land, the rain misting across it, high cliffs spilling to the sea. I looked into the eyes of something, someone, I know not what. They were ovoid and huge, gray as the water, deep as the sea. I saw nothing else but the eyes. A voice said, "Poet, we of the Braid have been expecting you," but it was no voice, no language that I knew. Still, it centered me, like the polestar the sailors follow.

And then I would awake, words threading and weaving in my head for weeks, composing in the darkness, trying to capture the voice and the place of the dream, trying to move the poem into the deep stream of memory. At last, with much trying and rewording, I captured it, the elusive country my father had spoken of so often. My song would be my gift to him. I had thought that would be the end of it then, that my mind would move to other subjects, begin to compose new tellings, as it had always done before. I was wrong.

It was the month when the light grows short and we were sailing on the Nile, on one of my father's rare holidays from duty. The green fields stretched away from the broad, flat river, and the sunlight splintered the water into stars. I was in my fifteenth year then. My brothers, all but Bile, had been left behind for this trip, all of them being men about their business, so I would not be subjected to their constant jibes about their strange brother, dreaming words into the world. I was glad of that, for on this day, I would give my father the gift of the poem of Inisfail. Bile wandered the boat on his sturdy five-year-old legs, occasionally stopping to smile sweetly when I played some song that he particularly loved, placing his chubby hands on my knees.

I remember that the breeze danced across the deck as I tuned up Ceolas. Strangely, the wind smelled like rain. And I began to sing.

CEOLAS SINGS OF INISFAIL
Green is my longing, Inisfail
Isle of Destiny, northern diadem.
Why do you call to me?
How shall I sing them,
sloe-eyed creatures at your shore?
Do you await me, Inisfail?
Country of my dreams;
I am Amergin, son of Mil,
warrior, wanderer.

Dream of the father now become
the harpsong of the son.
Inisfail, land of mystery,
Sing to me.

I got no further. My father stood abruptly in the boat. He stared into the sky. I followed his gaze.

The sun had begun to darken, a wedge of it obscured by a crescent of darkness.

My mother screamed aloud. She rushed for Bile, pressed his head against her shoulder. He began to cry in terror.

"Do not look at it!" she cried. "Do not look! I have heard tales of this; to see the darkness will make you blind."

We dropped to the deck of the boat, curled in upon ourselves. My father wrapped his body around my mother and Bile. Our sailman began to weep aloud and to call up Ra, the sun god, to deliver us. He released the tiller and fell to the deck, repeatedly touching his head to the boards. Our little boat slewed wildly, the wind filling the sails, no hand on the tiller.

I leaped to the tiller and trimmed the sail, but I took my mother's advice and kept my eyes on the deck. Darkness came across it like a shadow; my heart filled with dread. For a few moments, I sailed on what seemed to me the river of death, no light, no color, and then a wedge of color reappeared upon the water.

"Look!" I cried. "The light returns!"

My father looked up; he rose and glanced into the sky, albeit obliquely.

"We will journey," he said to my mother. "We will leave Egypt."

She did not hesitate, nor did she argue.

Though she barely crested five feet and though she was heavy with bearing yet again, I remember that she stood and tilted her chin, all the way to my father's six-foot height.

"To Inisfail?" she asked, and her voice was soft with something that sounded like wonder. I remember thinking that the idea was not new to her, not strange or unwanted.

But my father shook his head.

"No. First we go home. Across the mountains to Galicia. First we must gather the clans."

The light returned to its full strength, dancing across the water. My father nodded in certainty.

"Amergin has sung us to it. Did you say north, boy?"

I nodded.

"How do you know this?"

"It is what I dreamed. It is what Ceolas permitted me to sing."

He shook his head. "North. All these years. North. I thought that I would find them in the Internal Sea." He seemed to muse for a moment, then shook his head. "Perhaps that is why my grandfather built the tower. I have been a fool then. All the while it was before me." He shrugged, then nodded. "The sun was the sign. We go first to Galicia. From there we sail north. Amergin has sung it." He clapped me on the shoulder.

Bile must have sensed the adventure. He ran between Scota and Mil, and when they paid him no mind, he dashed to me and lifted up his arms. I scooped him up.

Father turned toward our oarsman.

"Make to the shore, Aknet," he called. "We must prepare our horses and our wagons."

Perhaps I should have been afraid at all that we were leaving, afraid of the loss of all that I had known. But I was not. Instead I felt a surge of joy as visceral as light.

Perhaps at last I would find the place that I could belong.

2

"Why does our brother Airioch's shadow grow large?" asked Bile.

I looked up from where I was working with my uncle Ith, memorizing star maps. Far below, my brother Airioch was climbing the hill toward us, his cloak billowing around him in the island wind.

"It is large because he is so tall." I turned to my uncle Ith. "See where he comes. Perhaps he brings news that we will depart again."

My uncle looked toward the approaching figure of my half brother. His face, which had been rapt on the star maps, shuttered a little and seemed to grow cautious. He sucked in at the sides of his cheeks.

"Perhaps," he answered.

We were on the isle of Gotia, in the second year of our journey.

Though we had traveled on Greek cargo ships, though we were burdened with horses and wagons, with women and squalling children and shamefaced soldiers who were green with the sickness of the sea, the two years of our journey had for me the feel of great wandering, an epic of the Galaeci.

CEOLAS WANDERS
Who dwelled here
on the isles of the Inner Sea
among the stone pillars
in the shimmering temples?
It was the ancient ones,

the keepers of the white city
beneath the sea.

I plucked gently at Ceolas and considered the journey. In truth, it should not have taken us two years to cross the great sea that the Romans call the Internum Mare, the Inner Sea. My father scornfully called it the Little Water and kept telling us to prepare ourselves for the great Atlantic Sea, but we had no comparison. To us it was sea enough and more.

Fortunately for the stomachs of the soldiers, our journey was broken up by Scota's pregnancies.

We stopped first at the island of Irena near Thrace so that my mother could give birth to my brother Ir. There we set up camp and lived in our circled wagons with their curved tops; though they were minuscule compared to the palaces of Egypt, we were happy. At night by the fires, I sang the stories of our journey, and all of my brothers and their wives would call out the additions to the tales.

Little Bile would stay beside me, and one night he surprised all of us by taking up the harmony and singing with me in counterpart. From that night forward, my brothers' wives would have none but that he should sing with me, and he flourished happily under the attention of all the women.

We took to sea again when six weeks' time had passed, but before long my mother was with child again and sick of a morning, so we spent the whole of her pregnancy on the isle of Gotia, where my brother Colpa was born.

We were nearing Spain by then and isles grew greener, their stands of forest thicker. This filled my uncle Ith with joy, for as all the Keltoi well know, forests are the sacred places of the gods. There on Gotia, at the crest of a great hill, my uncle had found a sort of temple made of circled stones and surrounded by great cedar trees. He pronounced it to be one of the sacred circles of our Old Ones, the StarWise Druii. In the center of that ancient circle he had set up our traveling pole of oak with its carvings of birds and leaping deer, of animals that those of us who had been born in Egypt and Scythia had never seen.

Daily Uncle Ith and I began the mornings there, his arms outstretched in prayer, a look of sublime joy on his face as he tilted his visage upward with the rising light. There he began to train me in star maps and the movement of light across the pairs of stones, in the families of the gods, in more stories of our tribe. I could see in him the great joy of anticipation, the gladness that he would soon be home.

Little Bile accompanied us to the stone-and-cedar circle, my mother being occupied with Ir and with the suckling of her newest babe. To distract Bile and his seven years while we worked on our lessons, Uncle Ith had given him Egyptian parchment, with a little collection of paints and pots. He had become an artist of some little skill, capturing ships and sails, birds, and even the faces of our clan.

Now my uncle Ith looked up at the approaching form of Airioch and then down at the drawing by my little brother. Though Bile had well captured Airioch's tall, rangy form, the golden hair that fell constantly forward over his eyes, Airioch's form was surrounded by a smudgy nimbus of gray.

"This is what he does," I whispered to Ith. "His humans . . . billow, in various colors. Their edges are never sharp."

"Hmm." Ith looked down the hill at the approaching form of Airioch. "Bile," he said, sharply.

My little brother looked up at him.

"What mean you with the shadow of Airioch? I see his shadow before him on the ground, long and thin, the morning sun behind him."

Bile smiled happily. "Not his sun-shadow, Wise One. His other shadow. The one that comes from his body. It grows larger than once it was."

Ith regarded Bile seriously. "Can you describe it to me?"

"It is not the same as yours."

"As mine?"

"Yours is gold, like firelight." Bile smiled in delight.

"So. So. And gold is a color that you favor?"

"I favor you because of it. You are always warm."

"That we all know well enough," I interjected.

"Hush!" Ith held his hand up toward me. He was entirely focused on Bile. "And your brother Amergin here?"

"Oh, his is blue and green and sometimes silver. Like the sea or the bending trees in wind or rain." He smiled up at me. "Your shadow is most beautiful, Brother. When I see it, I feel . . ." He tapered off, looking off into the distance. "Forever."

"What does this mean?"

Bile shrugged. He returned to his drawings, Ith and me forgotten.

I looked toward my uncle; Ith was staring down the hill at Airioch, who would be upon us momentarily. I regarded his face, felt surprise course through me.

"You like him not! He is my brother, your nephew. He is clan!"

"Clan is all of creation!" Ith snapped. "Have you not been listening to my teachings?"

"Do not avoid me, Uncle. You are my teacher. You have taught me to question all of creation, all of life."

Ith looked at me directly. "What do you know of this brother of Scythia?"

"But little. He is the son of my father's first wife. She died in his birthing. He is more than twenty years older than I." I shrugged. "I know little else; like my father he is a soldier. He pays me no mind. What do you know?"

Ith looked at Bile, at his little drawings. "This little one sees well; we will begin to train him in his drawings."

"That is no answer."

"Men choose their destinies, Amergin; remember this. A man's character is his destiny. We are not born to our character; we choose it with each small action of each day, accruing light or darkness to us, putting light or darkness into the world. That is my answer. Now Airioch is upon us." I watched as my uncle composed his face, smoothing out his features, dropping into a practiced smile. It was the first time that I had ever seen anything duplicitous in my uncle. Surely my own astonishment must have made me slack-jawed.

"Welcome, Airioch, son of Mil. What news do you bring us?"

Airioch made a formal inclination of his head and shoulders. The golden brown hair dropped across his eyes, as always. He regarded all three of us.

"Well, brother Amergin. You seem surprised to see me."

I felt a flush begin to rise in my cheeks.

"I am indeed surprised, Brother. Though not by you. For Uncle has just told me that the star maps change their faces in the southern part of the world. So he has learned from the Phoenicians and the Greeks."

Why had I lied?

"Is that so?" Airioch asked, his voice utterly uninterested. "Well, our uncle has much knowledge. But I bring news. Your mother is well and walking, her newest spawn fit now to travel. Our father says to set aside your studies and prepare. We will journey within the week."

He turned, his cloak swirling around him. He began to lope down the hill, his stride tipping left and right for the angle of descent. We three were silent. When he had gone far enough away, Bile drew a deep breath and exhaled.

I turned to my uncle.

"I would know," I said.

He pointed at the top of Bile's head and pressed his finger to his lips. Later.

"We have much to do," said Ith.

Bile looked up and smiled at us both. He held up his little drawing. He had begun to sketch a ship in full sail.

3

Most of the stories of my life I have learned from my uncle Ith, who had learned the great tradition of the seanchaie of the Keltoi and knew how to keep even a great crowd rapt with his telling.

Once, though, when I was young, my mother told me a story.

We had gone to Rhatokis on the great Internal Sea. I loved the sea, the wash of the waves against the rocks, the smell of far traveling places, and I told my mother that we should move our household here beside the sea.

"Oh no, my dreaming boy," Scota replied. "You do not wish to live by the sea. She can rise and overwhelm the land with no warning at all."

"Not so, for see the gentleness of these waves upon the shore."

My mother smiled.

"When I was much upon the age that you are now, my father, your grandfather, told me a tale." Here she turned to look at me. "I wish that you had known your grandfather. He was an emperor in Persia, where we come from in the long ago."

"I remember well," I said, more anxious to hear the tale than to speak of him. In truth, he had been dead before my birth and I thought of him not at all.

"Good," said my mother, smiling. "I should not wish him to be forgotten." She wrapped an arm around my shoulders—even then, I remember, my head was nearly level with her own—and pointed out across the water. "My father said that long, long ago, the gods grew tired of the ways of men, so tired that they created a great flood. The seas rose up and overwhelmed the world." She pointed at the vast body of water before us.

"This sea itself stretched across all the lands around us, they say. My father swore that there are ancient cities drowned beneath the sea. The rage of the gods was so great that all of humanity was destroyed."

Though I had not yet begun my training with Uncle Ith, I fancied myself a budding philosopher, so I applied my child's logic to the tale.

"This cannot be," I said. "For surely if the gods destroyed all humans, you and I would not be here."

"Ah, my little Greek," said my mother, ruffling my hair. "But the story goes that one of the gods had grown fond of these human creations. That god chose a man named Atra-hasis, who was wise and soft of speech. To him, the god gave the warning of the waters. He told him to build a great ship and to put in it his own family and two of every creature on the earth. Thus did they ride out the flood of the world, and thus, slowly, was mankind restored. For his work in saving all the creatures of the world, Atra-hasis was rewarded with immortality."

"What god would destroy its own creation?" I demanded.

"I am not a philosopher like you, Amergin," she answered, smiling, "but it seems to me that if the gods indeed created humans, they created also trees and earth, river and sea, and even the great crocodiles of the Nile. Surely mankind is the most difficult of the creations of the gods, for do not the Egyptians call us the tears of Ra? Why should the gods protect mankind above all their other creations, for surely they must be proud of all that they created?"

I remembered thinking about her answer for days afterward, turning it over in my head, seeking out the idea of what the gods themselves might hold sacred. Or disposable.

And I thought of that story again as we fought to load our wagons and our wretched, balking horses onto our Greek cargo ship for the final leg of our journey to Spain. Immortality did not seem gift enough for Atra-hasis, if this was what he had to endure with all of the creatures of the world. The horses kicked and snorted, their eyes wild, their ears drawn back. They stamped their hooves among the wagons and pulled on their leads as we tried to drag them to the cargo holds.

Oh, you gods! Why did I not see then what would befall? Where were my powers of observation when the horses shifted their weight in fear? Had I known what was to come, I would have stayed on the island of Gotia forever, never again to think of Inisfail.

We made landfall well enough, our ships coming into a quiet harbor on the far eastern coast of Spain. Our mother disembarked with the two babies and her waiting women. We brothers and our retainers stayed on board to move the horses and the wagons.

We managed to get the kicking, snorting beasts onto the deck, but from that point chaos reined.

I saw my brother Airioch sidling among the horses, looking busy enough, but doing nothing to hold them. My uncle Ith called out to him, "You know they like you not, Nephew. Go ashore and there await the wagons!"

I saw the look that Airioch returned, full of disdain. Who was he to take direction from our uncle, never mind a druid? He moved among the horses swiftly and they snorted back from him. I saw my brothers Eber Donn and Eremon try to calm the beasts, blowing into their nostrils and talking softly. But just when the horses began to calm, the boat shifted on the incoming tide. One of the wagons was standing at the head of the gangway, awaiting the horses to draw it to shore. With a creak, it began to plunge down the gangway, then to tilt toward the water. This spooked the horses further. Three who were not tethered reared up in fear, then plunged toward the selfsame gangway, manes tossing and eyes wild. They divided around the wildly tilting wagon the way the crowds parted for the pharaoh of Egypt. Two careened to its port side, thundered down the gangway beside the wagon. One veered stupidly to the side nearest the edge. He slipped and dropped over the side, rear legs landing in the water, forelegs hammering a terrified staccato rhythm on the boards as he tried to drag himself back up to safety. Other horses witnessing the scene began to buck and scream, to tear their harnesses loose from the hands who held them. A wild parade of hooves and manes pushed against the shifting wagon as all cascaded toward the docks.

And standing just below the onrush, his mouth agape, his eyes wide, was Bile.

I knew then what would come.

"Bile," I screamed. "Bile!" But by then it was too late.

The stampede roared over him like a tide. I watched in horror as he was trapped beneath them, hooves and wagon wheels, flopping like a whitened fish out of its element against the shore. Finally his cloak caught in the rear wheel spoke of the wagon. The wagon thumped over him, then rolled him up in his cloak like a shroud, like a mummy of the Egyptians, tipped to its side, and fell.

Strangely, because the cloak had caught the outside edge of the wheel, the wagon did not fall on Bile. Rather, it pulled him up into the air, onto the surface of the wheel, and, still spinning, wound in his cloak like a shroud, he circled endlessly as the assembled company grew still.

I heard my mother's wail split the silence at the same time that some fool began to scream. I saw my uncle Ith approach me and say something, but I could not hear his words for the caterwauling of the fool. His hands came up suddenly beside my face and he clapped me on both sides of the head. The screaming stopped.

I launched myself toward Bile in the selfsame moment that I realized the screaming had been my own.

I halted the wheel and examined him.

The cloak had wrapped itself tight around my little brother, and his face had a grayish cast. I pulled my close dagger from its sheath and began to slice away at the plaid. Immediately, his face regained some color, but it began to swell and distort, like the face of a bloated fish. He coughed and sputtered.

One of his legs was bent and broken in several places. Though his body was tightly wound in the cloak, blood had begun to seep through the fabric. I placed my hand at the side of his neck, where the heartsounds are strong, but could not find the rhythm.

"Physicians!" I cried, looking around wildly.

I saw my weeping mother straighten, hope moving over her face. In the tongue of Egypt she called for the healers who had accompanied us, but Skena, the meiga, a midwife healer of my father's people, reached us first.

She was young, only some five years my senior, and her knowledge would be for the birthing of babies and of elixirs and tisanes for cough or wounds. I could see the panic in my mother's eyes.

"Where is Mehmet?" my mother demanded, searching the crowd for the surgeon of Egypt who journeyed with us.

"In the hold," Skena replied, "caring for those who did not voyage well. Fear not, Scota; I will hold your child's life as mine until he comes." She moved toward Bile.

"Send for Mehmet!" my mother cried commandingly, pointing to her household staff. "Tell him Scota, daughter of Pharaoh, commands him. Now!"

They scurried to do her bidding while Skena bent above my brother. She turned to me and spoke softly.

"Cut him away from the wheel, Amergin. We will lift him to the ground."

I did as she bid me and together we laid him gently behind the tumbled wagon. At Skena's command, I cut away his cloak and peeled it back from him, thinking all the while of the death bandages of Egypt. My screaming had given way to silence, and I could not speak at all. When we had cut away all of the strips of cloak, I looked upon a sight the likes of which I have never seen in my life.

My baby brother's body was a pulpy mess, bruised and bloody. His leg was broken in three places and his face was swollen and bruised. One of his eyes had disappeared into the pulpy mass of flesh that was his face. And oh, his arm! His right arm dangled just below the elbow, from a single bloody thread, the forearm and hand hanging loose into the air. Blood gushed everywhere.

To her credit, Skena was efficient and quick. She grabbed strips of the bloody cloak and tied them just above his elbow, stopping only to command me.

"Break me a spoke of the wagon, Amergin. Now twist it tight until all the bleeding stops. Now raise his little legs. Higher. Good. The blood must go to his heart and his brain."

Mehmet arrived accompanied by my father, who had stayed behind to see to the unloading.

"What has happened?" my father demanded. "Will it hold up the journey long? We have been delayed enough!" He pushed around the cluster of my brothers and their wives. When he saw Bile, he fell silent.

Mehmet knelt beside Skena, his white tunic shrouding my brother. Skena bent her head before him.

"The leg and arm are beyond my skill, Physician. And the rest." She gestured at her own head.

Gently Mehmet examined my brother with his long, thin hands. Then he turned his full gaze on Skena, his huge dark eyes with their kohl rings taking her in. "You have saved his life, Meiga," he said. He turned to my mother. "Her speed and skill have let your son live to fight the day. Now we must work to bring him through the night."

He turned back to Skena. "You will assist me. Who else?"

She pointed at me. "Amergin will do well for his brother."

Mehmet nodded. He scanned the crowd until he saw my uncle Ith. When their eyes met, Mehmet raised his two bloody hands and held them up at either side of his head. Ith came immediately among us and knelt. He held his own hands at either side of Bile's head and began to chant. I will remember his words all of my days.

"Eistigi, eistigi," he began.

"Hear me, hear me.
Here is the soul of Bile
Do not hide it from us
O Maker of the world
Return his spirit to us
Full of song.
Here is the body of Bile
Our brother and our child
Do not return it to earth, O Maker
Give us the skill to heal
Come you now to Bile
O come you now
O come you now."

Over and over he chanted, and while he sang, Mehmet worked. He instructed our men to build a tent over us. They did so, attaching canvas to the wagons and shoving poles into the ground. At the edge of the tent he requested fire and water and sent his apprentices to find a cold stream with fresh water.

The hours of day passed into night. Ith chanted, his face a mask of worry, while Mehmet and Skena wrapped my brother's head again and again in cold compresses, set the leg against strips of polished wood, cleaned and washed the wounds. All the while Bile uttered no protest, made no sound.

"Why does he not protest at the pain?" I asked once. "Surely, we wound him with our ministrations."

Mehmet shook his head, his hands never stopping. "His head was injured, whether by wagon or horses we know not. You see how swollen it is?"

I nodded.

"To protect the spirit encased there, all around it has swollen like a pillow. The mind itself, so fragile in its casing, has retreated, to allow the healing to occur."

I shook my head, not understanding.

"His spirit travels," said my uncle Ith. "It departs so that the healing of the body will not affect the spirit."

Mehmet nodded at this explanation, evidently finding it satisfactory.

I took the nod to bode well. "So he will return to us as he was before."

Mehmet sighed and leaned back on his heels.

"We cannot know that yet. The brain inside its casing of skull is fragile and soft." He cast around for a comparison. "You have been to the sea and seen the jellyfish that sometimes wash up on the shore."

I nodded.

"Just so the human mind. Smash or dent a piece of the brain and other systems in the body may not work."

"Such as?"

He shrugged. "I have seen those who could not walk, though their limbs were whole. I have seen those who could not talk or feed."

"And Bile?"

"We will not know for a time. Perhaps for some time." He sighed. "And there is yet more sorrowful news." He gestured at the dangling thread of arm. "This arm must go. I have no skill to patch so torn and shredded a limb."

I suppose something in me must have known the conclusion of it all. The arm dangled shriveled and useless from its thread, but the idea revulsed and terrified. My gorge rose, and I rushed from the tent and vomited. Not all the blood of the day had brought me to this, until the thought of my brother, crippled and maimed, all his life reduced to the awkward stares and muttered sorrow of the tribe.

My love for him and my terror welled up in me and I curled myself against the ground and let out a single sob. Then I rose, knowing that my little brother would need my strength.

Mil and Scota were waiting outside the tent, surrounded by the ebb and flow of my brothers and their wives, by endless cups of wine and murmured words of hope and sympathy. My mother cradled the newest babe in her arms, as if she could sustain her hope in the holding.

They regarded me as I wiped my mouth on the fold of my cloak. Their bodies had gone rigid and still.

"What is it?" my mother whispered.

"The arm must come off. It cannot be saved."

She made no sound, pressing her hand against her mouth, but my father rose and swept into the darkness.

"It would be better if he had died!" he called aloud as he vanished.

And though I wanted to hate him for the saying, I could not. I had thought the thought myself and was ashamed.

CEOLAS PRAYS FOR BILE
Take my arm, this poet's arm.
I offer it as payment, gift
for the arm of Bile,
child of sweetness,
best of all brothers.
Take my life, the poet's life.
I offer it as payment, gift,
against the life of Bile,
child of sweetness.
For if he is gone,
surely there can be
no more song
no more song.

4

The sickness of a loved one is itself like a sea; we lose ourselves upon it, we ride its tides and currents like a ship, adrift on hope and sorrow.

The hours of Bile's recovery grew to days. We placed him on a raised sleeping platform and covered him with the finest linens of Egypt. Twice he rose and broke in fevers. My mother's servants fanned him during the day with huge straw fronds, and my mother herself once bathed his forehead and his wrists with cool water. My father did not visit him at all. Mehmet changed the dressings on his arm and put poultices against the wounded stump, all the while sharing with Skena the medical skills of Egypt. Three times a day, Ith chanted for my brother, and through all of it Bile did not move. He uttered no sound; beneath his eyelids, his eyes did not move as those of a proper dreamer should.

Mehmet insisted that my brother's stillness was a blessing.

"Let him be," he warned. "While he journeys, as you of the Keltoi call it, he feels no pain, nor fear. His body has time to heal itself, free of his own fight against it."

Each night I slept beside him, stretching my body against the ground. Each morning, Skena arrived to awaken me, to spell me that I might bathe and eat. After a week, she no longer needed to touch me, for deep in my dreams I would smell the perfume of her long auburn hair as it cascaded toward me. I began to awaken each morning to those silken strands as they brushed my forearm, tickled the back of my hand. I began to feel that I needed them, as one who has wandered in the desert needs water.

On the eighth day of my brother's journey, I returned to the tent after my morning rituals. Skena's back was toward me and she did not hear my approach.

"Ah, little Bile," I heard her say. Her voice was cheerful and singsong. "When the leg is healed up well, we shall set Amergin to teaching you to ride and to fight with that strong left arm. How wonderful you will be, the left-handed warrior of the tribe!"

Joy leaped up in me! My brother was awake. Bile had returned to us!

I shouldered in beside Skena and looked down at his little form. Nothing had changed. My brother lay still and silent, a one-armed sarcophagus. I turned on Skena, bewildered.

"Why do you speak to him thus?"

For answer, she placed her fingers on her lips and led me outside the silken tent. Her hand never released mine. She answered in a soft whisper.

"Just because he travels does not mean that he cannot hear us. Your uncle Ith will tell you this as well. The journeyer moves above the world, swift as wind. We cannot let him become confused about his dwelling, for during this time, his spirit dwells wide in the world. So we speak to him. We remind him of the dwelling of the body. We call him back to us."

A sense of wonder overtook me.

"You love my brother," I said.

Skena's eyes met mine.

"Of course I love him, Amergin. I am his healer; a healer mends the spirit as well as the body. The truest healers pour out their love with their skill; we healers of the Keltoi know this to be true."

And that was the moment that I fell in love with Skena. Deeply. Irrevocably. The difference was clear to me immediately. My brothers fell for their women for beauty or sensuality or warrior skills or wit. I had fallen in love with Skena's spirit. Now I saw her whole, the silken skeins of her hair, the wide gray eyes, each soft motion of her slender hands; all were the mirrors of that great and generous spirit. My heart was overwhelmed with gratitude that she, of all the Galaeci, should be my little brother's healer, for in that moment, I was certain that only she, among all humans, could return him to us. I was awestruck.

Of course I did not tell her. I was a stripling lad of seventeen summers, and though seventeen is the year of manhood among the Galaeci, she had five years upon me and was a healer's apprentice. She thought of me in the same way she thought of Bile. I was a boy. But in her reflection, I knew the man that I wanted to become.

Heeding her words, I began each night to sit beside Bile's bed on a small camp stool. I would hold his good hand in my own, stroking at the long fingers, and while I did, I would tell him stories. I told him of our grandfather's people, the warriors of Persia, and of the Galaeci, the history of our father's tribe. I spun him wondrous stories of Inisfail, the Isle of Destiny, of the wide-eyed and magical people of that island, of hidden waterfalls and forests of fairy ferns. Of course I knew nothing of the place, but I invented, drawing out the stories of our father from childhood, spinning upon the fanciful tales of Greek and Roman sailors and soldiers. But as I spun them I came to believe them, came to think of Inisfail as the green and magical land of my own invention.

Finally there came a night when I thought that perhaps our little traveler might enjoy Ceolas. I tuned her to sweet perfection and began to sing. The song was a long and complex one, another story of the journey to Inisfail, and I closed my eyes and began to sing Bile on the journey with me. I was some way into the song when I noticed that a soft, harmonious humming accompanied me. Thinking that perhaps Skena had joined me in the tent, I opened my eyes. I was alone!

I looked around and behind me and finally down at my little brother. His eyes were wide open and his mouth was slightly pursed as he hummed along with me!

CEOLAS SINGS JOY
Here you are returned to us
Bile my brother,
child of my heart
journeyer returned.
What stories you will tell us,
what far countries you will draw.
Here is our joy at your return
that these strings quiver to hear you.

I did not dare stop. I wanted to set Ceolas down, to call aloud to Skena and Ith and Mehmet, to send for my mother, but I could not. I feared that if I stopped, Bile would disappear again, would fold back down into his travels and disappear forever. So I kept on singing, Ceolas thrumming beneath me, my own harp quivering with so much joy at the return of my little brother that my legs trembled beneath her. On and on we went. I sang of the journey on the sea and Bile hummed the tune. I took us to the far green island and Bile hummed the tune.

At last, outside in the darkness, Skena must have awakened from her rest, must have realized that my evening song had gone on far too long. She came into the tent softly, her hair undone and tousled, her white sleeping gown billowing around her in the torchlight. I could see her long-limbed shape beneath its diaphanous folds.

She looked at me, a query, and then followed my eyes to Bile. She started back, then dropped to her knees beside him. Gently, gently, she kissed his little cheeks, his forehead.

"Welcome back, my little traveler," she whispered. He watched her with his great eyes and kept humming.

Skena stood and came before me. She lifted my chin in her hand. "How great a spirit you have, Amergin, that you have called him back from his journeys. How magical is your song."

She dropped her hand and the place burned.

"I shall call the others."

She swept from the tent, and I turned back to my little brother. His eyes watched me, huge and luminous, and I knew that he had learned much on his journeys. I was filled with anticipation to hear the stories he would tell.

5

In three days' time, Bile made rapid progress. Mehmet and Skena assisted him to sit up, and he took some soup and drank cool water from a cup. My mother came in to cool his brow and hands with her own hands again and to elevate Skena to the position of Healer of the Household, an honor that Skena accepted with her head bowed humbly. Her only response was, "I thank you that I shall be able to spend more time with my boys." Here she gestured at both Bile and me, and though I was glad to be included in her regard, I felt deflated to know that she did indeed think of me as a boy.

Even my father swept into the tent; although he blustered and cried out a welcome, he would not look at Bile's arm.

By the evening of the third day Bile was sitting up on his own, propped against pillows. My uncle Ith came and held Bile's remaining hand and sang a chant of thanks for his return while Bile hummed softly in accompaniment.

Bile did not ask about the arm, nor venture any words on any subject. He watched the company with wide luminous eyes that seemed to me now much older than his seven years.

I wanted desperately to hear him speak, to learn the wisdoms of his journey, to see if he remembered aught of the accident. But Mehmet cautioned me against conversation.

"Let his mind and his speech return as they will," he said. "Remember the fragility we spoke of? The mind must heal slowly, as it will."

So I contented myself with singing for my brother and listening to his sweet accompaniment. Indeed, his spirit, which had always seemed to me to be made of sweetness, seemed now large with joy.

He smiled when our brothers swept in and out, looked upon our father and mother with both pity and love, laid his hand in Skena's whenever she arrived.

That was the scene that Airioch encountered when at last he made an appearance by Bile's bed.

Skena was kneeling by our brother's side, her left hand enfolding his remaining little hand. Her auburn hair was unpinned; it tumbled forward over her shoulders and spilled like water into the folds of the blue tunic she was wearing. Her feet were bare, as they always were in the tent. She was talking to Bile softly as she bathed his face in cool water. I sat behind them, Ceolas in my lap.

Airioch paid little attention to Bile and none to me. Beyond his perfunctory welcome back to our little brother, all of his attention was focused on Skena.

"So . . . ," he said. "This is the exquisite creature who has been elevated to Healer of the Household. It is no wonder my brothers never leave this tent." Here he looked significantly at Bile and then winked at me, as though we were little children, privileged to be made part of his jest.

Skena came to her feet before him and bowed her head, but she was silent.

"I like a silent woman," Airioch said, smiling. He boldly reached out a hand and lifted her chin. When her face came up, I could see that her eyes were blazing, whether with anger or fear, I knew not. I stepped up beside her and drew my arm around her. She did not resist, instead folding herself into my shoulder in a way that she had never done.

"This is Skena, she who has healed our brother."

Airioch regarded me in surprise, as if, for the first time, he had heard speech from a tree. Then he lifted her arm and pressed his lips to the back of her hand. It was a courtly Galaeci custom, nothing more, but something about the way his lips lingered on her hand turned my stomach in its hasp.

I knew not what to do. My hand itched toward my dagger, my mind reminding me that this was my brother, son of my father, a warrior of more than thirty-five years.

We were saved by Bile. He began to gabble, to make noises that sounded like speech trapped below water. "Agghh, arrww, waahn, ah waahn."

All three of us relaxed our postures and turned toward him, Skena dropping immediately to her knees beside him.

Bile turned the huge luminous eyes on Airioch. He kept voicing, the inarticulate sounds of cattle or yard fowl issuing from his mouth. His eyes never left Airioch's face. Airioch regarded him for a moment and spoke, his tone surprised.

"I did not know that the accident had made him both fool and cripple. He were best to stay mute. Does our father know this?"

The anger that flooded me was white-hot and dangerous. "He would be neither dumb nor crippled had you not stirred the horses on the day of disembarking."

Airioch turned his full regard on me then, scrutinizing me as one would a new species of bug. "Think you so, little poet brother?" He turned. His cloak swirled in a dark arc around him. "Well, our father shall hear of it."

"Shall hear of what?" Our father himself stormed into the tent, wafting in the smell of horses and warm metal. In a single glance he took in Bile and the kneeling Skena, my angry stance and Airioch's intention. It was when he looked on Airioch's face that I saw something I had not expected to see: my father's face shuttered, just as my uncle Ith's had done; it grew wary, hidden, closed. I could not have been more surprised if serpents had risen, speaking, from the sea.

"What shall I hear?" he said again, his tone testy.

"It is nothing," said Airioch, sulky as a child. "Or nothing that you shall not know soon enough."

He swept from the tent.

"Never mind," said Mil, his hand waving Airioch away. "I come with good news. Now that Bile is back among us, we make ready the wagons and strike the camp. We will journey in three days' time."

Skena came to her feet, her eyes wide, one hand upraised. I saw that she would plead for waiting, to allow her little patient time to heal. But I looked beyond her to Bile. He made no sound at all, but when he met my eyes, he winked!

I spoke before Skena could say anything. "We will be ready," I said. "Bile is anxious to go!"

I did not miss the look that Skena turned on me, nor relish the wrath that would follow the look.

6

She dragged me outside the tent and out of Bile's earshot, eyes blazing with anger. "He cannot travel yet. He has returned to us from his journeys only three days past! Are you daft to tell your father he can go?"

"Bile is ready to go."

"Bile is a child. By the gods, you also are a just a boy! I am arguing with children."

I could see the speckled heat of her anger against her neck. I feared making her angrier still if I could not stop my gaze from returning again and again to the red pattern on the white skin.

She followed the path of my eyes. "What do you regard?"

"Your anger blotches your skin. I fear that you would not be good at secrets."

She tried to look at her own neck, abandoned the effort. She sighed. "I sometimes think that Mil and his sons are too good with secrets. Give me instead a man who speaks his mind."

"I like it not that Airioch approaches you so. There is my mind."

She looked at me in surprise. "Should I fear him, Amergin?"

I squirmed. "I know not," I said. "He is not for you. Be cautious of him, Skena."

I sounded like the lame and foolish child she thought me. She sighed. "You see. You speak no more clearly than the rest. Your father will not look at his broken child, your brother threatens to tell him——what? That his little son no longer speaks? What does he hope from such a pearl of wisdom? That your father will send Bile away? I do not understand you sons of Mil."

"We are a family of brothers, men all. When have you known men to speak themselves clearly, Skena? Is that not why so many judges of the Galaeci are female? And as for Bile, you must not mistake his speech for his mind itself! The leg is healing and we can do nothing for the arm. But my brother Bile is there inside that broken, speechless body!" I grabbed her upper arms. "Do I speak clearly enough for you there?"

She looked down at my hands upon her arms. "Oh my," she said softly, and I saw the red speckling begin again across her throat. I dropped my hands.

"I am sorry. Healer, accept my apology. I did not mean to hurt you or to frighten you."

"You did not," she said, softly, but she would not meet my eyes.

"Please, Skena. Do not be angry with me. I could not bear that. Nor your disappointment."

For answer, she simply turned her back on me and headed back toward the tent. Oh, I could have kicked myself for a gangling fool. I did not know whether to follow her like a dog or to turn and run away in shame. She solved the problem for me.

"Come, Amergin," she called over her shoulder. "We have three days to prepare your brother for the rigors of travel."

CEOLAS SINGS OF JEALOUSY AND DESIRE
Even in her anger I desire her,
the sweet whiteness of her skin,
the lightning of her eye,
her spirit like great water.
Rigid am I; quivering with desire,
my own anger turned against my brother,
against his ways with women,
his winning ways, his courtly ways,
his ways that I despise.

I suppose that they thought we three the most disposable of the tribe, but no matter. We were given our own wagon and no duties but to see to

Bile. By day, we sang silly songs and took turns propping him against us by the rear opening so that he could see the countryside unfold behind him. When we stopped to set up camp, we got him walking around the circle on a little wooden crutch that our mother's craftsmen had made; by a few weeks into the journey, he needed only a cane.

He did not speak of the arm, or speak at all. Each time he tried, the sounds came out as a series of animal utterances, unintelligible as human speech. Skena and I took to interpreting his vocal clues and learned that "Ah" meant yes. For no, he simply shook his head; for all other wants he took to gesturing, eventually creating a language with his hand and face that only Skena and I could read. We two knew instantly when he was hungry or ready to walk. Sometimes when we were camped, I brought him his papers and his chalk. Bile would mime to me the things he would wish to draw; I would steady his left hand in my own right hand and let him guide our sketching. The sketches became more complex as our journey progressed, and eventually he was capturing the mountains and rivers, the trees and campfires of our journey.

At night the three of us slept together in the wagon, Skena and I on sleeping platforms attached to the walls of the wagon, Bile between us on his little silken bed. I took to watching Skena as she slept, waiting for the moonlight to slip across her cheeks and illuminate the pale skin. I loved the way she shifted in her sleep and the soft noises that she made in her dreams.

One night as I was watching her I looked down to see Bile, eyes wide open, watching me from his little bed.

"I love her," I whispered.

"Ah." He nodded simply, as if he had known all along, and I wondered if she knew as well, if she was aware of my longing stares, if she suspected that the poems I wrote and sang on Ceolas were all for her. I felt a great fool, until Bile patted my hand gently with his own little hand. From the moment that he returned to us, I had felt that he was, after all, the older brother, an ancient spirit made wise by its journeys, and I took comfort in his approval.

But the next evening I returned to our wagon to the sound of my brother Airioch, making wry and pungent observations about our journey to gales of laughter from Skena. I had taken Bile to visit with Uncle Ith; the two of them were happily absorbed in Bile's drawings when I returned to the wagon. I will admit it honestly, I hoped to spend the evening there with Skena, helping her with the simple domesticities of the wagon, engaging in conversation as we worked. But instead, there was Airioch, propped on one arm.

I stopped outside the wagon and listened.

"So the horse reared up and caught my brother in the chin. You should have seen him then; his eyes wept like a girl!"

I could hear Skena's laugh in response and then a murmured comment I could not understand. For a moment I felt a flash of jealousy that my older brothers were riding to horse on the journey, while I rode the wagon like a child. Airioch spoke again.

"In truth I am not much better, Healer. All this jostling by horse and wagon makes the bones ache. That is why I have come."

I heard her murmur again, concern in the tone.

"It is this shoulder, and my rein arm; they ache. Do you have a poultice you could rub in for me?"

A pause.

"Here, allow me to remove my tunic."

I came around the corner of the wagon and launched up the steps like a cat. Airioch was stretched out on my sleeping platform, his boots grinding dust into the linens of my bed. He was shirtless and propped on one elbow, his long, muscled body gleaming in the lamplight of the wagon. Skena was busy rubbing one of her salves into the exposed shoulder and down his arm.

Rage pulsed through me as hot as coals. Jealousy. I wanted to stab his heart, to strike her down for her hands upon his skin.

Airioch did not stir when I entered. He looked up, lazy and satisfied, a big cat before the kill. "Little brother," he said. "Your good healer ministers to my aches. Already I feel better."

He took his large hand and closed it over hers where it worked on his shoulder.

"I thank you, Healer," he said. He brought the hand to his lips and kissed it, his eyes locked with hers. Something seemed to be working around her mouth, but she said nothing. Airioch stood, long and lean and shirtless.

"I shall return," he said, his voice fraught with significance.

Skena nodded, saying nothing; she caught her bottom lip between her teeth.

Airioch disappeared into the darkness. Skena dropped to her knees on the wagon floor, holding her stomach, absolutely silent.

My anger was replaced by fear and I dropped beside her and lifted her face in my hand. Tears were streaming down her face.

"Did he hurt you?"

She placed her finger on her lips, then drew my head down until my ear tickled against her lips.

"The salve," she whispered. "It was fire salve. To warm the muscles. He kissed my hand. His lips will burn for days."

Then she dropped to the floor and, stuffing her face into Bile's pillow, laughed until she had no wind left to her.

All my anger left me, but I did not tell her that the place where her lips had touched my ears burned too. And yes, for days.

All the way, in fact, to Galicia.

7

There! I had heard it again.

From my perch in the top of the tower I heard soft laughter.

For a fortnight now, when Bile had drifted off to sleep, I had climbed Breogam's Tower to look out over the moonlit sea, longing for the north, for Inisfail.

I did not know how soon my father would choose to depart, but for me it could not be soon enough.

Here in Galicia, I was a stranger.

I do not know what I had expected from my father's country. I had lived in Egypt, traveled in Greece and Rome. Perhaps I had expected the alabaster palaces of Greece with their white colonnades, or the billowing silks of the Nile River palaces with their white light.

Perhaps I had expected the worldliness of all those places, where all the citizens of the world contended together.

Galicia was none of those.

The countryside was rainy and green, swards of green hills down to the roiling sea. My kinsmen dressed in braichs, a kind of baggy belted trouser, and plaid cloaks, and dwelled in conical huts that reminded me of the slave huts of Egypt. They scattered brochs—huge stone towers with many levels—around the countryside and used them for both meeting places and storage holds for grain and supplies. Though their villages were well fortified, surrounded with circles of stone walls and laid out on a well-defined street system, they were not the great cities of Egypt and Greece. And though my kinsmen were prosperous, mining, herding cattle, farming the sea and the land and trading beautiful artwork to the Greeks, I missed the scrolls and libraries, the rich learning of Greece and Egypt—and was ashamed of myself for missing it. Here, the Galaeci spoke my father's tongue, but in a rapid and inflected way that he had evidently forgotten, so that all his teaching of us was for naught. We sounded like foreign fools, stumbling over the language of our ancestors.

Here in Galicia I was a stranger, but I wondered often if this was why my father had departed Galicia, the search for Inisfail an excuse merely, a ruse for venturing into the wider world. For surely my father's restless spirit was too large for this place, for the repetitive days and nights, for the clans who had all known each other for generations and who now excluded us from the small borders of their world.

Oh, they welcomed us well enough, my father's cousins exclaiming over the return of Mile Easpain, the great warrior of Scythia and Egypt, but we were strangers among them. In truth, I could understand their suspicion of us. We traveled with Egyptian servants and Roman plateware, Persian cousins and fine silk garments. Never mind that we traveled in the same curved wagons as our kinsmen; our horses were fine Greek warrior beasts; our wagons were swathed in silks. Our women and our physician wore kohl around their eyes. We brothers were not all of the same mother, the same clan, or even the same country. And then, of course, there was Bile.

They took great pains to avoid Bile, making small signs with their hands when they encountered him, but in truth, even my own father and my brothers avoided him as well. Only my mother visited him; Skena and I were his constant companions. Because of this, I too was exiled in their midst, and my heart grew hard at the treatment of my brother.

To fit in with the Galaeci, my little mother abandoned her Egyptian ways. She took to braiding her hair with bells, and she wore the tunic and leathers of the women of the Galaeci. She learned to fight with shortsword and dagger from one of their warrior teachers—all women—and began to speak the language of the Keltoi exclusively, to the frustration of my father and older brothers, who had taken pains to learn the tongues of Persia, Egypt, Greece, and, in Airioch's case, even Rome.

Our attendant strangeness had made me even more reclusive than I had been in Egypt.

And so I came to love this tower with its night fire encased in stone and its long views out to the heaving sea. Here Ceolas and I would sing, seated at the stone window, gazing out over the northern sea. Here my loneliness, my sense of belonging nowhere and to no one, grew, mitigated only by my time with Skena and Bile.

From far below me came the sound again, giggling and then the low murmur of a male voice. A man and woman then, coupling. Well who was I to disturb them at their play? My loins tightened up at the thought. What man of my people and eighteen years of age had never bedded a woman? I felt suddenly ashamed of my own inexperience. Suddenly the woman cried out, as if in pain. Her cry was followed by the sound of a slap.

I took the tower stairs two at a time. Outside in the darkness I made my way around the tower until I saw them. Airioch and a woman of the Galaeci. He was sitting on a patch of sand, leaning back against one of the great rocks which line the shore, and she was kneeling before him, riding him hard. Periodically he smacked her flank, and his teeth and tongue worked at her dark nipples, which were rigid with desire. Though I had never lain with a woman I felt my own manhood swell to bursting with need. I saw my brother arch against her, then sigh with satisfaction.

"Go," he said, smacking her flank again.

She moaned and leaned into him, evidently not finished with her pleasure, but he set her off from him and pointed up the path.

"Go! I am finished."

She said something unintelligible and angry and strode away, pulling clothing over her head as she went.

My brother sat back and let the moonlight stream over him. He sighed with satisfaction. "Did you enjoy watching, little brother?"

The hot shame burned up into my face.

"Come out here."

I stepped into the clearing, my eyes downcast. "I heard her scream and I thought that someone was hurting her," I mumbled. "I did not mean to intrude."

"You did not intrude. I knew that you were in the tower and I knew that you would hear us. Did it give you pleasure?" He stared hard at my braichs. "I see that it did not and I am sorry. I would have called her back to share her with you. It greatly enhanced my pleasure that you were watching."

"Enhanced?"

"Of course. To know that you were watching me perform. I would have liked to watch you take her. You have never had a woman, have you?"

I said nothing, not sure if I burned with my own lack or at his offer to share.

"Too much time with our baby brother, I suppose."

"I love Bile," I said defensively.

"Obvious enough," he said. "But he is not much draw for women. But for that glorious red woman, the healer. Oh, I do so like women."

"You seemed to like this one well enough."

He grinned at me. "She was willing. In truth, I like them all."

"You have bedded many?" I was ashamed of wanting to know.

"Hundreds. All shapes and sizes and ages. Boys as well. Does that shock you?"

"I know it is the Greek and Roman way."

"Very good, for that is where I learned my habits. You know little about me, Brother. I spent much time in Greece and Rome. There are many ways to pleasure, and I have tried them all. Galicia offers me new delicacies from the table, and a man should take his pleasures where he will."

"What of her pleasure?" I found that I truly wanted to know.

He opened his eyes and regarded me coolly. "Ah, I hear the makings of a connoisseur. A woman can be pleasured. They are slow creatures, though, and it is only worth the effort if there is something to be gained."

"To be gained?"

He smiled. "Yes. For example, once when I was soldiering in Greece there was a woman—much older than I, but married to a wrinkled ancient Greek near twice her age. I knew that if I could pleasure her, she would give me anything. So I took my time and did it well." Here, he flicked his tongue at me. "And more than once so that she was besotted. And then I began to ask for things. Fine tunics and gold and a deed of land. All of these she gave. And when I had them and more, I asked for her handmaids to join us, and then her houseboys, and at last I could sate myself with her and with any person or thing of her household. I was sorry to be posted away from that little treasure trove." He shook his head.

I thought for a while about what he had said. "Does our father—cavort—as you do?"

"Our father seems to have eyes only for Scota. And she for him. Even

Eber Donn seems to have all that he can do to pleasure his three wives. But perhaps that is all that his paltry tool can do. You see what gifts I have been given." He stroked himself once or twice and looked with affection at the huge shaft. "My soldier. Always at attention. And I like the games of seduction; I like best to win them."

He leaned back against the rock in the moonlight, sighing with satisfaction, content in his naked splendor. As I looked at him there, I realized that he looked like a statue of the Greeks, and then I knew, suddenly and certainly, why my father's face shuttered each time he saw this brother. I tried to turn toward the sea to hide the knowledge, so that he would not see it in my face, but it was too late.

"You are thinking," he said, "that I was sired by a Greek. Do not fear to say it; I believe it to be so. Much better that than the little Gael you call your father."

"My father has given you a home, has treated you as his own son."

He inclined his head. "Well, he has given me a home, that much is so."

"What of Skena?" I blurted out suddenly.

"Oh, I would love to bed that one. All that auburn hair and those eyes. And I think she is a virgin, although . . ." He fixed me with a stare. "Have you bedded her, little brother?" His tone was teasing. He met my eyes directly. "No, of course you have not. Well, then, fresh fruit. Though it would be much work to win her." He sighed again. "All this talk of mating matters. I am ready again. I must go look among the willing. I did enjoy this conversation, little brother. It was, I think, our first as men."

He pulled on his braichs and sauntered off into the moonlight.

I remained on the beach, deeply troubled, rigid with desire and shame, fearful that I would be just like him, not sure if it was a source of fear or of pride.

CEOLAS SINGS DESIRE
I burn.
In the dark of the night I burn.
Rigid with longing, I burn.
Red woman, cailin rua,
I am on fire for you.

I sought out my uncle Ith. Since we had returned to Galicia he had taken to living among his fellow druids in the oak groves and the small stone dwellings that perched like mushrooms on the ground among the great oaks. Of all of us, he was most content among his brother and sister druids.

I found him seated in a circle of sages, the wind lifting the sleeves of their white robes, all of them conversing on the nature of the soul.

I stood at the fringe of the grove, waiting in silence, but he called to me, "Come sit among us, Nephew."

Again I felt a fool. Twice in the same week to be caught out as I lurked near the activities of my elders. I felt like a gawky, stripling boy of no experience, loud and awkward. I vowed at least to learn to move as the forest cat moves, silent on the ground.

I came in among them. For two days, since my conversation with Airioch, I had been feeling confused and ashamed, half of me filled with longing; but now, in this oak grove, my curiosity lifted me out of my miasma.

Here was the brother-sisterhood of the druii, the wisest elders of the Galaeci. All my life my uncle Ith had spoken of them. I studied their faces.

The oldest of their company was a woman of indeterminate age, older than my uncle. Her hair, though thick with gray, cascaded around her shoulders in long waves of alternating dark and silver. Her eyes were luminous and deep, of some strange color that moved between gray and silver, so that the orbs seemed to catch and hold the light. I found myself staring at her, and she returned my look with such intensity that I could not look away.

"Brothers and sisters," she said. Her voice, though soft, was commanding. "Our little brother needs the company of his uncle. Shall we depart?"

They seemed almost to vanish then, like blowing leaves of snow, their white robes billowing toward the trunks of the huge trees, fading into the forest and gone.

Uncle Ith gestured to me. "Come sit, lad; it is obvious that you are troubled."

I sat before him, unsure of how to begin, nearly squirming with shame.

"You wish to speak to me about a matter of the body." Uncle Ith spoke kindly and without preamble.

"How do you know?"

"It is a subject that preoccupies the young and fills them with confusion. Your body shouts confusion, so I have concluded a mating matter."

"I watched Airioch at the mating," I blurted. "I did not mean to, but I thought that he was hurting her." I raised my hand at the look on Uncle Ith's face. "He was not, but I watched them. Airioch knew that I was watching, so he called me out."

"He was angry?"

"No. He was . . . pleased. He said that it . . . that I . . . that he . . . enjoyed it more for knowing I was watching. He said that women are difficult to pleasure. He said that he would like to bed Skena. He said that he was sired by a Greek. . . ." I trailed off and lifted my hands helplessly.

Uncle Ith sighed. "Well, it's all a bit much at once, isn't it?"

"Yes." In Uncle Ith's presence, I no longer felt like a stupid child. "I am overwhelmed, I guess. I need help to sort it out."

"As do we all. Let's begin with the Greek."

"Is it true?"

"It may be. Surely Airioch does not resemble either your father or his mother. It is why your father kept him."

"I don't understand."

"Seang was the daughter of the king of Scythia. She died giving birth to Airioch. This turned the king's wrath against your father."

"All of this I know."

"Well consider further, then. If Airioch were to have remained in Scythia when your father departed and if he were to have grown up there, eventually the day would have come when the king also would have seen the Greek in Airioch. Where would his rage for the loss of his daughter have turned then?"

"Oh, you gods! So my father protected him even if Airioch is not his own."

"He did."

"This is a most noble act on the part of my father."

"Your father is a most noble and honorable warrior. I would say this of him even if he were not my brother."

"But his treatment of Bile?"

"To move in the world is difficult. To move in the world with no speech and one arm and the fear and strangeness of those who encounter you is nigh to impossible. Your father weeps for Bile, and it hurts him to the core to see his little child so maimed. He has told me more than once that he is proud and grateful for your care of Bile."

"He has said this of me?"

"He has."

I turned this over in my mind, felt a gladness of heart in knowing it. "But then why does not he himself spend more time with Bile?"

"He feels responsible."

"Why should he?"

"Because the wagons and the horses were his charge."

"But not his fault. It was Airioch who disturbed them."

"You cannot blame Airioch for Bile's misfortune. Airioch riles the horses by virtue of what they sense in him, but he bore no ill will toward your little brother."

"Does Airioch bear ill will toward me?"

"Perhaps. Perhaps he only craves your woman."

"He has said that he would like to bed her. She is not my woman." I ached to say that she was.

"What if I told you that what will pass between you and Skena goes far beyond bedding?"

I hung my head. In his usual subtle way, Uncle Ith had seen straight to the heart of my shame.

"I would also like to bed her." I mumbled it out.

"Of course you would."

I looked up in surprise. "Then how am I different from Airioch?"

"We of the Galaeci and, in fact, all of the Keltoi believe that woman is the mother of the world."

I nodded. This was obvious to anyone who saw the world.

"Therefore, if woman is mother of the world, we men must treat her with respect. We must honor her, learn from her, heed her counsel, and yes, mate with her, but always with her consent and desire."

"Airioch had the consent of the woman with whom he mated."

Even as untried as I was, I knew that clearly enough.

"And did he respect that consent?"

"Well, he . . ." I squirmed under Uncle Ith's direct gaze. "He did not pleasure her."

"He pleasured himself?"

"Yes."

"So he did not respect her."

"So the mating is always good if it is done with mutual respect and pleasure and consent."

"Yes."

"Now I see, Uncle. And thank you." I started to rise.

He held up his palm. "As of yet, you see nothing. Airioch is a man of many desires. He sates most of them. A man who accrues to himself all of the things of this world cannot lighten himself of their burden unless he gives something away."

"This I do not understand."

Ith sighed. "Here is what we druii know. We are not of this world. Not really. We are here and gone and then return again. But what is true of us is this spirit that moves between the worlds." He placed his hands on either side of my head, surrounding my soul. "The things of this world have weight. They tie us to this world. They do not allow the spirit to travel well and lightly. And a man like Airioch, a man who sates so many desires, weights himself down with a kind of darkness, a heaviness of spirit. That is the darkness that Bile sees around him, the darkness of so much accrual, of so many choices for the self and not the other."

"Is this the nature of evil, then?"

"No. Evil occurs when the darkness begins to spill off onto others, when the bearer of darkness chooses to do harm to sate his own desires. It is a process of small choices, little decisions that grow larger over time."

"Is Airioch a servant of darkness?"

"Right now he is a servant of the self. We do not know the way that he will choose, so we are cautious."

"We?"

"Your father and I. We watch him."

"I would not like him to choose for Skena."

"Then do not let him do so."

"I am a lad of eighteen years; he is a warrior of some thirty-five years. And Skena is five years my senior."

"Have you not listened to me?" Ith's voice was angry. I started back, for he had never been angry with me before.

"You are a spirit, as ageless and timeless as I. The body is young, but the spirit is old and wise. You have before you a great gift, a gift that is given to few on Earth."

"I wish to be wise," I said. "Teach me."

"You have before you the gift of anam cara, the gift of the beloved soul. It is the gift that travels through time, through lifetimes, through distance and age and death. Very few ever receive it, Amergin; too many pass it by or throw it away. But I see in you a man capable of wisdom, a man capable of knowing the Light. Do not let that slip from you for foolishness or youth."

"You speak of love as if you know."

"You have met my beloved."

I gasped aloud. "The woman with the silver eyes."

"An Scail. The Shadow."

"You were parted from her for forty years!"

"Yes," he said simply. "And no. Your father needed my counsel. His family needed their druid. She and I agreed that I must go. Love . . . travels. It sustains. It endures. Be wise, Amergin, for few are offered so priceless a gift."

8

CEOLAS SINGS OF ANAM CARA
The longing of my body
is the longing of my soul.
Selfsame the desires,
that all of your mysteries
will open to me.
I will treasure them
as spirit gifts
dwell in you complete,
belonging.

S kena, come walking with me."
It had taken but little time after I talked with Uncle Ith to decide, to know that my soul had chosen for Skena and would move to win her despite our ages.

Over Skena's shoulder, Bile met my eyes. He must have sensed my new urgency, for his eyes widened.

Skena's back was to me, her fingers firmly placed on either side of his little cheeks. For all the weeks of Skena's working, Bile could utter no more than "Ah" and a sound that resembled "New, new, new," like the mewling of a kitten.

It seemed to me that we were better to leave him be, to let him express himself with his eyes and his humming tunes and, best of all, with his drawings, which grew more complex and expressive as he learned to manipulate his chalks with his left hand.

Now he nodded at me enthusiastically and pointed to his chalks and papyri.

"Do you wish to draw?" Skena asked, beginning to gather his materials.

"Ah," he answered, pointing toward the door.

She shook her head, not comprehending. He snatched a papyrus and made a rapid-fire sketch of a tower.

"Oh, you wish to go to the tower?"

He shook his head, frustration specifying every gesture.

I smiled at her gently. "He wishes for you to go to the tower with me so that he can have some time to draw alone."

"Oh!" Skena clapped her hand over her mouth. "I am frustrating you, little brother! I am so sorry."

His eyes filled with laughter and he held out his good arm. She dropped toward him and he threw the arm around her neck and kissed her cheek gently.

I felt an odd surge of envy that she would embrace him so freely, immediately felt ashamed of myself for so selfish a thought.

"New," he said, and pointed at the door.

"Go?" I asked. Bile nodded with delight, well pleased with both of us for finally understanding our lessons. When I looked back at him he was bent above his drawings, already absorbed in the detail.

Skena threaded her arm through mine and we walked across the edge of the cattle pasturage to the forest that lined the crest of the hill. From deep inside the trees, we could hear the soft rhythm of the sea. I loved this moment, the moment when I would emerge from the trees to the insistent pounding of the surf, when the soft hint of the forest became the urgent tumble of the shore. From all my years in Egypt, I was unused to the deep green of the forest giving way to the sea, and the walk had a magical aspect, more so that she was beside me, her arm resting in mine.

I thought of Airioch and drew my other hand over her fingers, entwining them with mine. She did not remove them, let them remain in the braidwork they made.

We threaded our way to the top of the tower, me bounding the stairs, she puffing a little and stopping to place her hand over her heart, then swatting me playfully.

"You are a warrior and young, Amergin. Go more gently for an old lady."

"No old lady you, nor warrior I," I protested. "Only a man of songs and dreams. From here I can see them."

"From the tower?" she asked. "All the way to Inisfail?"

We had reached the tower platform with its wide embrasures overlooking the sea, its central fire banked and untended until darkness.

I did not look out to sea, but kept my back to the wall, regarding her. I did not take my eyes from hers.

"No," I said. "Not from the tower. From here."

For a moment she looked confused. Then her face suffused with color and she lowered her head, hid behind the waterfall of auburn hair.

"Skena," I whispered. "I dream of you in the darkness and the day."

What happened next I shall not forget. Though I grow old and foolish, though I journey to the Country of the Young, it shall remain in my memory like an ember, like the light that burns forever in that tower by the sea.

Skena stepped forward until her face was tipped up inches from mine.

"Then awaken, dreamer," she said, softly. And in that moment I knew that she, too, had chosen for me.

My arms were around her so swiftly that even I was surprised. I moaned aloud when my lips covered hers. She whimpered, a soft, girlish sound that made my legs feel weak beneath me. I found that I needed to feel my hands on her skin, her skin against mine. She helped me with the fumbling and I drew her down upon me, the curtain of her auburn hair dropping over our kisses and our sighs. And then there was the rhythm of the waves and the rhythm that we made, one heartbeat at the center of the world.

When at last we had crossed our own vast sea, she raised up on her elbow beside me, her hair curling over the curve of an impossibly white breast, her legs still entwined with mine.

"Amergin," she whispered softly, "I shall remember this day with joy for all of the days of my life."

"Remember?" I said, bewildered. "Shall we not wish this day again and yet again? Oh, sweet my love, you sound as though you will part from me."

Her eyes filled with tears. "Your brother Airioch will speak for my hand; I fear that it will come at the Beltaine feis."

"You fear it?"

Her face had tightened until her eyes seemed to fill the orb. She nodded.

"You are a woman of the Galaeci. Say him nay."

"If I say him nay, I will wound his pride. He will see to it that Bile is removed from my keeping."

"But this would be beyond all cruelty—to both you and Bile."

"See him clearly, Amergin."

I thought about what my uncle Ith had said and of Airioch himself. Would he speak for her hand to win her? Would it be to best me, his young half brother? Would it be just a play in his game of seduction?

"But why would he speak for you? He knows you not at all."

She said nothing. And then I understood.

"Because he could not have you any other way."

She nodded. "Your brother is twelve years my senior; most of the women of the Galaeci are married. He does not have as wide a pool to choose from as once he did, and I am . . . I was . . . untried . . . until to-day. He thinks of me as a prize to be won." Her neck speckled with color. I brushed my fingers across the blushing whiteness, felt desire rise in me again. I cupped my hand around the back of her head, leaned toward her. She pressed her fingers gently against my lips. She spoke softly. "Amergin, I cannot be removed from Bile. I love him as if he were my child."

"He cannot remove you if you are wife to another."

She shook her head, the auburn hair skimming across the milky skin so that I could feel my desire ignite my body again.

"Oh no. No. I could not ask that of you, though I have thought it often."

"You have thought it?"

She nodded, her face a mask of shame. "But such a thought was selfish of me. You are poet and bard, apprenticed. The time will come when your tribe will rely upon your judgment, when you may be required to journey as your uncle Ith did. Besides, you are a young man. I have more than five years upon you. You have never married, nor had another love. You deserve to be a young man, to explore all the worlds before you."

"You are saying that you would want me? As husband?"

She silenced. Looked away.

"Look at my eyes."

She looked up, locking her eyes with mine.

"Tell me that you look into the eyes of a boy," I commanded.

"I look into the eyes of him that I have loved for so long," she whispered, fear welling up in the words.

"You love me?" Joy surged through me then, unlike any that I had felt before in my life.

"Of course," she said softly. "I have loved you from the first moment that I saw you tune your harp for your brother."

"I thought that you would not love me because I am too young."

"And I thought the same because I am too old."

"See what fools our thoughts have made of us."

She lifted a shoulder, said nothing. When her eyes met mine, they shone with water.

"I shall speak for you at tonight's meal if you will have me," I said softly. "Now. Before anyone else can speak."

She hesitated for a moment only, and then her eyes lit with determined radiance. "Then, I will have you, beloved."

I lifted my hand tentatively to her breast. "Do you wish me to love you again?" I whispered.

She raised to me a face of complete joy and trust. "I am your Ceolas," she whispered.

For the rest of that afternoon, we sang in a language that would be ours and ours alone for all of time.

9

The time has come for the sons of Mil to depart for Inisfail! All of the Galaeci are welcome to accompany us. This will be the journey of our destiny!"

The clans gathered around the fire erupted in a babble of voices.

Why my father had chosen this feast, this night of all nights, to announce our departure, I knew not. Some inner mechanism of his longing, some sundial, seemed to tell him that the hour was upon us. Selfishly, I was glad that I had spoken for Skena at the start of the evening, and that my request had been accepted with a nod and my mother's quick "Of course, dear." Even Airioch had raised his fist to me in the soldier's sign of victory and grinned his most suggestive grin.

Perhaps I should not have been surprised; our care of Bile had made us inseparable. Perhaps the clans already saw us as a mated pair. The knowledge of it filled me with quiet joy. I kept turning toward her where she sat with Bile on her lap, certain that I had imagined it all. Each time she looked back at me, her face was suffused with love. Bile even winked at me once, as though he had always known it.

For a moment it struck me that all along, I had been wishing for our journey to Inisfail, and now that it had come, I no longer needed to go. My Inisfail was wherever Skena and Bile were; the journey of my life would be made with them.

Though my father, too, had decided on his journey, his announcement among the clans had not produced the result that he desired. Women shouted that they would not part from their homelands; some of the Galaeci warriors called my father crazy.

"You have wandered far from us, Mile Easpain," one cried. "You are more Greek or Roman than Galaeci. They are the wanderers of the world. We are the clans of Galicia and here we shall remain."

My father looked stunned, never mind that he had never served in either Greece or Rome. He had just discovered the sad truth that he was a stranger among his own people. My heart moved in sympathy.

Now my mother stood and moved into the firelight. She made an imposing figure with her sturdy little body clad in warrior leathers, her long black hair cascading down past her waist, her eyes ringed for the occasion with the precious kohl of Egypt. I wondered if she knew how strange her little darkness seemed among her husband's huge clansmen or if she felt that she had truly become one of them. She answered my questions immediately.

"I am none of your clan!" she cried. "I am daughter of pharaoh of Egypt, king of Persia. Yet all of my life with my warrior husband, I have heard of the great deeds of the Galaeci, of your fearless, nomadic spirit. I have journeyed far in your wagons to reach you here, and I have chosen to become one of you for the journey. Where is your wandering spirit now?"

"The wife of Mil speaks well," cried one of the clan mothers. "I and my clan will journey!"

"Nay," cried another. "You will divide the clans; how shall we stay related when the sea separates our children one from the other?"

It seemed to me that all of the arguments made sense. Though I was poet by training and knew that my words would hold weight, I kept silent, knowing myself also for young. Perhaps too there was some selfishness in me, for here in the firelight with Skena and Bile, I had no wish to test the whims of the great heaving sea beyond Breogam's Tower. For the first time in my life, I was full of belonging and needed no journey to explore what was here within my grasp.

Into the void around the fire came An Scail, the Shadow. She wore her long white robes, embroidered with gold and silver, enhanced with little bells at hem and cuff. At her neck was a lunula of hammered gold in the shape of the crescent moon. Her long white hair cascaded behind her, at one with her robe. Though she was most ancient, I had the fleeting thought that it was obvious to me why my uncle Ith had loved her alone through all the years of his exile.

An Scail circled the fire once, those odd silver eyes catching the firelight, mesmerizing the company. Silence fell down upon us like the sea fog.

When only the crackling of the logs could be heard, she spoke, so softly that all the company leaned in to hear her.

"My brothers and sisters. Hear me well, for my wisdom is old. Here at the edge of the sea we have dwelled for more than a hundred years. Here did our ancestor Breogam build the great stone lighthouse and command that it cleave the night's darkness with fire. Here did we first hear the tales of Inisfail.

"Who among you has not climbed those stony stairs and looked out to the north? Who among you has not whispered, 'Inisfail, I will come to you, Isle of Destiny'?"

The crowd shifted and murmured, for surely it was ritual among them.

"In Mile Easpain, that ancient journey is more than ritual. It is an imperative."

I knew what she meant. For my father, this journey was his polestar, the fixed constant of his wandering life, the final place of his journey.

"Still," she continued, "the best journeyer is the wise journeyer. And we of the Galaeci would be wise before we send our children to the sea."

Again, nods and murmurs.

"So we of the Druii offer to you our services as emissaries. From among us Ith, brother of Mil, will take to the sea with two of our own druii. Together, they will petition the Greeks for passage. They will journey to Inisfail and return to us with the wisdom of the place.

"Mile Easpain, will you allow us to choose from among the company three warriors who will best serve us on the journey?"

I do not know if my father had been aware of their plan. If he had not, none of the company could have known it from his response, for he stood among the druids as if the idea had been known to him all along.

"I salute my brother and his companions, bravest of our wisdom keepers. I will abide by the knowledge they return. To them the choice of fellow journeyers from among my sons and the clans of the Galaeci."

I knew him well enough to see the look of hope upon his face, his wish to journey to Inisfail, but I knew with certainty that it was me my uncle Ith would choose. The impending separation from Skena and Bile sat in my stomach like a stone. Had she not said to me only yesterday when she was cradled in my arms that I would be called upon to travel. She turned toward me now, her face pale in the firelight, her eyes large.

Ith came forward with two young druids by his side. He embraced my father, clapping him on both shoulders, clasping arms from elbow to hand.

"I shall be the faithful ears and eyes for our people," Uncle Ith cried. "The safety of our journey shall be my sacred trust. I shall return to you the knowledge of my going and my coming home. I choose as my warrior companion"—here I drew myself up and let out a long, ragged breath— "Airioch Feabhruadh, son of Mile Easpain."

The shock on my father's face was mirrored only by the shock in my own heart. I barely heard as the second druid chose his own brother, a man of the clans that I did not know, and the third my own elder brother Eber Donn.

10

"Why not me? Why not my father? Not Airioch! Uncle Ith, I plead with you to change your mind."

In the low conical hut amid the towering pines, Uncle Ith was packing his hide bag for the journey. Behind him I saw An Scail wrap a long crescent of wood incised with markings in a tanned and waterproof hide. She slipped it into his bag.

She saw me watching and smiled. "We are the Oak People," she said. "It bears our sacred name."

"How could you let him do this?" I asked, my anger making my respect for her slip.

"Let? One does not let fate, Amergin. Fate is; to be his brother's eyes and ears has been Ith's fate for all his life. Your father is an impetuous man, a strong warrior who acts first and thinks second. Your uncle is his wisdom; they are two halves of one being. I do not 'let,' I accept."

"But why Airioch?" I turned back to Ith. "He will not serve you. Airioch serves himself. This you know."

"It will serve my purpose to have him with me."

"What purpose could that be?"

"The purpose is you, boy," said An Scail. Her voiced sounded frayed, irritable.

"Me?"

"Can you see nothing?" Her silver eyes challenged me from across the dwelling.

Uncle Ith sighed. "Sweeting," he said softly. "Did we not agree?"

"We did," she answered. But her voice broke on the saying.

Uncle Ith smiled. "All life is duality, Amergin. Learn this well. Action is followed by reflection. Journey is followed by remembrance. Learning is followed by teaching. You have a new family; Bile needs your strong arms, and Skena your love and protection."

"My own selfishness has told me this. But you will need me on the journey. I can protect you. I can sing the truth of what we see."

"This I know to be true, but I need other things from you. You are a poet in training. That position will bear much responsibility to the clan; a poet must be well schooled and wise. I will not live forever, lad. You must follow me. I do have a mission to ask of you, and I ask that you perform it well."

"Ask anything of me and I will give it. This you know."

He looked at me long then, and his eyes filled with unshed water.

"I know it well," he said softly. "You are the son of my heart. In our journeys together, I have taught you all that I know. But there is one whose knowledge is deeper and older than mine. I would have you learn from her before this journey begins."

I knew he spoke of An Scail; I am ashamed to say that the knowledge made my stomach curl with fear.

"While I am gone, I wish you to study with her. You must learn the deep knowledge, the workings of the universe. You must study every day. Will you promise me that?"

For my uncle I swallowed my fear for him and my pride. I spoke humbly to An Scail. "If you will have me, Wise Teacher, I will prove an apt pupil."

Her face registered surprise.

"Do you see?" asked Ith. "There is wisdom here beyond his years."

"I do see," she said softly. "I thought that he would argue."

"Then let me argue Airioch," I said. "Any other of my brothers would be a wiser choice."

"Which is why our apprentice has chosen Eber Donn," said An Scail. "He is your father's twin, an impulsive warrior, but loyal as the trees."

I saw then that they had planned it carefully: my warrior brother and two men not of our clan, all but Airioch loyal to Uncle Ith.

"O you gods. You take him away because you fear what trouble he might cause. For my father. For me. For Skena and Bile."

Ith acknowledged the truth of my words with a single nod. "But also, a man like Airioch has a singular eye. Because he sees what will benefit him, he sees what will benefit the tribe. You will have much to do here, Amergin. Your father must prepare all of his clan for this great journey, their goods and their gear. You must prepare their spirits."

"I will do as you have asked," I said.

"This I have known from the first," said Uncle Ith. He exchanged a long look with An Scail, full of unspoken sorrow for their impending separation.

CEOLAS SINGS OF CHANGE
Even the wind sings change.
The very seasons
wear it as a cloak.
All souls journey into the West
and all return.
Do not fear change, my kinsmen.
Stand strong before it.
For it will come upon us
whether we will it, or no.

We came down to the sea, to the inlet where the Greeks had anchored the bireme that would take our scouting party north. I clasped Uncle Ith hard by his arms and did all that I could not to weep like a stripling child. Bile did weep, the "Ah, ah" sounds ripping me to the heart.

"Return to us safely," I whispered.

He put me back at arm's length. "I am never gone from you, lad. Never. Learn well from An Scail."

My father approached, and he and Ith bent heads together in whispered conversation as I had seen them do since childhood, then clasped each to the other. I realized suddenly and for perhaps the first time that my father loved Ith as I did.

I clasped arms with Airioch in the soldier's way. "Care for him," I urged him. "He is old and more frail than he seems." I would not release him until he answered.

"Why, what else would I do for our uncle?" Airioch replied lightly. "And you care well for her." He pointed at Skena. "Ride once or twice for me; I should have liked it well." He grinned his most wolfish grin and bounded toward the ship. "Come, Uncle," he cried. "The sea waits for no man, druid or no!"

I saw Uncle Ith place his hand against An Scail's cheek. I saw her tip the silvery eyes toward his own. I do not know what words passed between them, but I saw her nod once.

And then they were gone, the square sail of the bireme dipping and rising as it led them out to sea, away to the north. To Inisfail.

11

The full moon crested the horizon, luminous and orange, its resident rabbit tilted forward toward the bowl of the sea. I made my way through the forest softly, rolling inward from the sides of my feet, making no sound at all, just as An Scail had taught me to do.

My heart hammered like a bodhran as I shifted through the dark trees. Samhain.

Tonight I would stand among the druids as they ushered out the old year and chanted in the new. There in the sacred oak grove, I would stand in the Sacred White Circle for the first time. More than six months had passed since my uncle and my brothers departed on the sea. Tonight we would know what message Ith had sent us from across the sea.

Had I known what studying with An Scail would entail, I might not have agreed so readily to Uncle Ith's request to be her student. Hours of standing first on one leg, then the other, my arms encircled, in a move that An Scail called An Corr, the Heron, were followed by the study of star charts drawn on the forest floor, each with its own story.

"We believe," An Scail said softly, "that there are Star People out there, for would the Creator waste so vast a sky as this?"

Each morning there was warrior study. The druids of the martial arts taught me to run in the forest in absolute silence, even to still my breathing to the breath of the leaves. I could throw a spear and hit the smallest target, leap into the air and twist down, stabbing sword in hand.

I memorized hundreds of poems and songs, the entire history of the Galaeci and of the greater Keltoi who wandered across the world. I learned the cycles of the earth and the cycles of the people, we whose souls go across the water and then return again and yet again. I learned that the Creator of the world is a maker of superfluous abundance.

"We must acknowledge that abundance with both solemnity and joy," An Scail taught me. "It is a gift worthy of the gratitude of the Galaeci."

And then at last, after many months, the Dreaming—three days of fasting without food or water, alone in the far forest on a high cliff overlooking the sea.

But no vision came.

On the third night the moon had been full and white, a knowing eye in a sky spangled with stars. I was seated in the Sacred Circle, staring out at the sea. I felt drowsy and cold, almost empty, a vessel awaiting water. I looked out at the geese-wing path the moonlight made on the water. At the apex of the V was an island, a small stone outcropping that the Galaeci knew to be deserted but for cormorants and water seals.

Suddenly I saw a white light followed by a strange blue ovoid. Moments later, a flame flared up at its crest, sending red sparks toward the night sky.

I did not dream it. I know well enough that to deprive the body of food and water is to open the door to vision. We Keltoi have practiced such rituals for centuries. This was fire, real and red and warm, like the hill-to-hill signal fires of Samhain Eve. It was followed soon after by a flash in the sky, a sudden whiteness followed by blue light, something shimmering, viscous like a waterfall, through which I could see the attenuated stars. Then darkness. The fire had been extinguished. The night sky was as it had been: moon and pinprick stars.

I remember that I tried to rise but my body, folded so long into its waiting position, would not come up with me. My legs had fallen asleep. I crawled from the circle and threw myself on my back, massaging the blood back into the limbs. When at last they stopped tingling, I rose and ran through the midnight forest all the way to the hut of An Scail.

"Coracle or curragh, it does not matter. If I have to swim, I will go. Someone was on that island. Something is there!"

An Scail held up her hand.

"I believe you, Amergin. This is the strength of vision, that the veil between this world and the next separates, and we see what is there. You have had a powerful vision, a parting of the veil. You are most fortunate."

"No. Honored Teacher, there is a quality of vision that was not present at that moment. No vision came to me in the Dreaming. I sat hungry and tired, my legs asleep, and nothing came. And then I saw fire on the Isle of Seals. Real fire."

She tipped her head, and the strange silvery blue eyes regarded me. At last she spoke. "We will need the largest of the curraghs and several men to row. The water between here and the stone is rough."

"We?"

"Do you think that a good teacher would let her pupil go alone?"

And so we went, the ancient woman, her student, the rowers who would not venture from the boat, who turned it beetle-backed upon the rocky shore and made the sign against the evil while we scrabbled our way to the crest of the treeless rock, at the last, me dragging and pulling a weary An Scail up the stony scree.

We were not disappointed. There at the crest, wrapped carefully in its waterproof hide, was Uncle Ith's curved oaken stick. Between us, An Scail and I turned it all ways, face up and face down, toward the light and toward the shadow. She ran her hands over it delicately again and again. It was precisely the stick that he had taken with him. It said exactly what it had said when Uncle Ith departed—"The Oak People"—carefully incised in ogham letters on its face. It was alone, wrapped in hide, at the top of a hill on a deserted island. And that was all. Nothing more.

For a long time we sat there at the crest of the hill, amazement rendering us silent. At last I ventured what we both were thinking.

"How did it come here? And why? And if it says what last we saw, what message more?" I also feared for Uncle Ith's safety, though I did not say so to my teacher.

"Ith is well," she said simply, having read the question in my mien or perhaps in my heart of hearts. I no longer questioned the well of her knowledge, which was ancient and most deep.

"And of the message?"

"I try to think as Ith thinks. Samhain approaches. He will know that we are strongest then, that the druii in the Sacred Circle speak directly to the gods themselves. It is then that he will speak to us. He must want you among us, boy, to have sent the message at this very time." She nodded.

"You will stand with us in the Sacred Circle. We must prepare your lunula and your robes."

And so the orange moon rising into white by slow degrees, my heart beating beneath the soft wool of my new robes, the small golden circlets of the male druii clicking at the hem of my robe as I nervously shifted side to side. While other druids had been sent to the village to perform the Samhain rituals there, this was the circle of High Druids, the most ancient and wisest among the priesthood. I felt humbled and more than a little afraid to be among them, and my legs trembled. Each druid was flanked by two tall oaks so that we formed a perfect forest circle, the dark oaks, the druii in their white cloaks tinted orange, awaiting full moonrise.

On the neck of each was a lunula, a huge hammered crescent of gold or silver that represented the moon, the Keeper of Time. As the moon rose higher and whitened in its arc, the lunula reflected her face, so that a dark crescent winked and flickered between each oak.

I stilled myself, inhaled the breath of the forest—oak leaves and pine needles, mint and onion, fecund life, wet with promise. Here was the smell of abundance, the pungent odor of forever. Awe caught at my breath.

Just at that moment, the moon approached zenith. The drum began, one of the acolytes beating on the bodhran in deep, measured tones. Another drum answered from the far side of the circle. Back and forth the drums spoke.

We began to chant with them, the deep thrumming of the male druii counterparted with the light voices of our sisters.

"Give thanks to Creation.
Buiochas le cruthú.

Oh, be not afraid.
Na' bi'odh eagla ort.

Give thanks to Creation.
Buiochas le cruthú.

Wait upon the Light.
Fanacht le Solas."

Back and forth we chanted as the moon crested. Now An Scail approached the eldest of the druii, a lighted pine-pitch torch in her hand. I saw her ancient brother limned in firelight as she tipped the torch toward his own. It caught and flared with a whooshing sound. One by one she moved among us; one by one the torches lighted. As they did, I could see clearly each druid, white-haired and dark, male and female, standing small between the ancient, towering trees, a pail of water by each priestly side as precaution for protecting the wise old oaks, who bore our prayers skyward.

"Buiochas le cruthú," An Scail whispered to each acolyte, who whispered in repeat as the torches lighted. She reached me last, her torch tipping forward to ignite mine. "Buiochas le cruthú," she whispered, and I repeated the chant. Suddenly, her ancient hand reached out, and I felt her delicate fingers on my cheek.

"Ah, wondrous, Amergin," she whispered. "Most wondrous. You weep at the presence of the Sacred. Here in the Sacred White Circle, you are truly blessed among us, for Creation has made its full Wonder known to you and you have wept for the Presence of God."

I bowed my head in awe.

Silence moved around the circle then. Drums and chanting stopped. A wind picked up and whispered through the forest top. Far beyond the grove I could hear the wash and drum of the sea. Our torches burned and tiny sparks ascended toward the stars. We were silent for a long time, until the moon passed zenith and began its retreat to the horizon.

An Scail led us in procession out of the Sacred Circle to the Druid Broch, a stone tower just beyond the trees. There we extinguished our torches and sat in a circle around the lodge fire, the sacredness of the moment still holding us in silence.

At last, An Scail stepped forward with Uncle Ith's oak curve in her hand.

"We have received a message from our brother Ith," she said, "who has journeyed for many months to Inisfail. We ask the gods for wisdom that we might unlock that message on this most sacred night.

"Amergin." She beckoned in my direction.

I stepped to the center of the circle and took the proffered curve in hand.

I tipped it toward the firelight, first the plain side, then the side with its ogham incisings. There, among the stick words, was something new, something that had not been there when An Scail and I rowed out to sea. It looked like a triangle, slightly raised from the wood. Deep in its surface were spirals, twined together as vines.

"Here, Honored Teacher," I said, handing the curve toward her.

"Tell us what you see," she commanded.

"I see a raised shape, three-sided, like the pyramids of Egypt." It crossed my mind that perhaps the druii did not know the pyramids, but they said nothing, and I remembered that their wisdom was old and well traveled.

"And it was not there when first we found the ogham stick?"

"It was not."

"Stand before the fire then and press upon the shape."

I turned and faced the fire. I pressed the little shape with my thumb. There was a slicing of the air, sharp and white. It mimicked what I had seen from the vision circle. For a moment, the fire looked viscous behind the white light, slow and gleaming like a waterfall. Then, suddenly, there was a woman, most beautiful. She stood encased in blue light at the center of the flame; it seemed she stood upon the flames themselves. Her hair was copper, long, curling in wave after wave. Her skin was milky white. Only her eyes seemed somehow unlike ours, huge, almond-shaped orbs, blue and gray as the wild sea beneath the cliffs. Though she looked at us directly, I had the strange impression that she did not see us at all.

"I send greetings to An Scail, the Shadow, and to Amergin, son of Mil, from Ith of the Sacred Circle. He dwells among us here in . . . Inisfail and is well." Her voice was mellifluous and low.

There was a pause; the form of the woman dipped and seemed to shrink; it crackled out of shape and then re-formed itself. Her voice began again as though it echoed, as though it came from a deep well.

"I am Eriu of the Three Sisters."

Behind her, two other forms shifted into place, female, though they seemed shadowy and insubstantial, as if they stood in a place of little light.

"These are my sisters Banba and Fodla. We are of the Tribe of the Danu, the Children of the Braid.

"Ith has been among us and has told us of the desire of the Galaeci to journey to Inisfail. We are not a warrior race, though, like you, we are journeyers. We have spoken of Ith. Of us, Ith alone will tell you. You must trust the story he brings you. He has treated us with honor. We return him to you with honor. May he come safely back to you."

The woman sputtered like a candle in wind. Her form seemed to shrink and thin until it looked like a single blue flame. With a popping sound, she vanished.

I stared at the place where she had been. I pressed the little triangle with my thumb again but no form emerged. I stared down at the little pyramid shape on Ith's oak crescent.

"Honored Teacher," I whispered. "The pyramid is fading."

"She has said what she came to say," said An Scail. "Obviously, she expects we of the druii to remember her warning."

"Warning?"

"We will be welcome only as long as we come in peace."

"She must already have met Airioch," I muttered, unthinking. One or two of the druids hid their mouths behind their hands.

An Scail did not reply. She seemed deep in thought.

"You and Skena will move with Bile into Breogam's Tower," she said suddenly. "We must begin the watch for Ith's return. We will be most curious to hear of the Journey of these Children of the Braid, for something went unsaid. I will go to speak to your father."

One of the druids spoke from the circle. "Will you need my arm, Honored One? It is a night of much strangeness."

"Amergin will accompany me," she said. "I thank you. I will fetch my cloak."

When she left the room for her lodge, the druid approached me. "Support her well, younger brother. The Samhain Circle wearies her vision, and we fear that her Sight will be much taxed by the events of the evening."

"The torches trouble her eyes?" I asked. "Or was it the message from the ogham wand?"

"Neither," said the druid, his head tilted sideways. He seemed to be eyeing me in surprise. "It is her vision that is taxed. An Scail is blind."

*   *   *

I held to her hard in the dark forest, all my months of study, all my pride in my hard-won knowledge, shaken to the core. How had I not known? All this time; the strangeness of the silvery owl eyes. Why had I not seen?

An Scail sensed the difference in the way I guided her. "They have told you that I am blind, have they not?"

"I should have seen . . . should have known."

"And how?"

"I don't know. You asked me to describe the oak crescent. On the hill, you kept running your hands over it. I don't know." I shook my head helplessly.

"I could have seen it perfectly well myself, Amergin. I asked you to describe it for the group."

"How would you have seen it?"

"With my hands. I hear more than you hear. My hands can see more than most people see with their eyes. I can smell and identify the way our wolfhounds do."

"So you have always been blind?"

"No. My sight left me more than ten years ago. I could actually see the first eye go milky in my mirror, but even before then I knew that my vision was departing when I could not see the stars."

I stopped suddenly on the path, struck by a thought so sad that it took my breath from me. "Oh, An Scail. You could not see Ith when he returned."

She was silent for a long moment and her hand patted my supporting arm gently. "I see why Ith loves you so, Amergin. You think with the soul of the poet. You speak with your compassion. But do not trouble yourself. I have seen Ith's face with my hands, but perhaps I have been given a gift, for my mind's eye sees him as he was when he departed with your father so long ago, young and strong with his hawk nose and his long dark hair."

I thought of my uncle now, the thin ring of white hair, the bald pate. I said nothing at all.

After a moment, An Scail chuckled gently.

"You are becoming a wise man, Amergin. But now we must go to your father. There will be many preparations, and first among them, we must keep the tower light at full fire. Now be careful, for there is a great root here on the path and it will trip us both."

"How do you know that?" I asked in awe.

An Scail laughed aloud. "Because it was here yesterday. And last week. And the year before."

12

Scota had us seated in family groups around the fire: Eber Donn's three wives and their children, all crying and babbling incessantly; Eber Finn and Eremon and their clans, quieter by virtue of fewer wives; Skena and Bile; Ir and Colpa.

An Scail and me she had seated in the position of honor at the front of the room, a place which made me very uncomfortable surrounded by my elder brothers and their families.

Scota's servants moved among us with warm mead. They served the traditional meal of the new year, wild boar and haunch of deer steamed in fulacht fiadh, the wood- and stone-lined cooking pits that made the meat so tender that it fell from the bone; a rich seaweed soup heated in leather bags by hot stones; and a salty seaweed laver bread. Finally, they brought sticky, delicious honey-cakes, all designed to fuel us for the cold and dark half of the year—the Gaimred—that we had entered at the turning of last night's moon.

When the feast was finished my father stood before the company. In his blunt and soldierly way, he went directly to the heart of the matter.

"What does it mean?" He turned his attention to An Scail and to me with a look that was as trusting as Bile's face when he regarded Skena. For the first time, I realized that my father was a man completely composed of action, a man who acted and reacted to everything with no wavering—sudden decision, complete movement. I realized that it was no real wonder that he had wandered the world, made his decision to return to Galicia based upon the darkening of the sun. It was as though a wind shifted inside him and he turned in the way that it blew. I realized that his ability to act quickly was probably what made him so masterful a soldier that emperors and pharaohs trusted his actions. I also realized that I was cut from completely different cloth.

An Scail stood before the company; I knew that she sensed my diffidence, my awkwardness before the whole assemblage of my clan, and I was grateful to her for assuming the burden of telling.

Mothers hushed the children; by degrees, the central chamber of the dwelling grew quiet.

"We have had a message," she said; "Ith returns to us."

My father shouted aloud. "This is well!" he cried. "Lads, we must begin the preparations. The ships. The horses. Which of the clans will accompany us?"

An Scail held up her hand. "There is more." Her tone was ominous, quiet.

Even my father sat instantly.

"The island . . . Inisfail . . . is already occupied."

"That will not impede us," said my father, cheerful and sure of himself.

"It may," said An Scail. "I hear in them some difference from us. Their voices sound . . . reedy, somehow . . . like the bone flutes of the cattle herders."

I looked up in surprise. She was right. I had not noticed the sound, because I had been so occupied with their appearance, with the strange vessel for the message. An Scail turned her attention to me.

"Amergin," she said quietly. "You must tell your clan what you have seen."

I stood and cleared my throat, bringing Ceolas up with me. I had begun the tale on that night when I had seen the flash of light on the Isle of Seals. All day my mind had been composing it further: the moonlight among the oaks, the druids, the little triangle on the oaken curve, the beauty of the woman in the blue sphere of light, her sisters, the warning, the message that Ith had been treated with honor. I chanted it to them, Ceolas moving warm beneath my fingers, and when I was done, there was silence.

CEOLAS SINGS OF STRANGENESS

How has she sprung from the oak wand
her gray eyes upon us,
her very presence in the room
but not among us?
On this night of moonlight
our wisdom keepers see her, hear her,
though she be worlds away.
Who is the woman in the oak wand,
she who returns our uncle to us,
who sends her message to Seal Isle,
wings it to us in a flash of light?
Return, Uncle, for we would know
the origin of strangeness,
the tale of these,
who travel in the wood.

At last, it was my brother Eber Finn who broke the silence. "What should we do, Amergin?" he asked.

I felt a strange lightness spin through me, a kind of giddy surprise, followed by a weight that settled on my shoulders like a heavy woolen cloak. I cleared my throat.

"An Scail has asked that Skena and I move into the tower. She requests that we keep the tower fires burning high that Ith and our brothers can see their way home. Beyond that, I think that we should wait. The woman Eriu said that Ith alone would bring us the knowledge of her people, of their journey. We must hear that knowledge before we decide to journey to Inisfail."

"This is wise," said Scota. "Mil, I think that we should do as our son has suggested."

My father nodded. "Thank you for your wisdom, Amergin," he said. He came to where I was standing and clapped me on the shoulder. "Good man."

"Amergin?"

"Mmm?"

I came up from a deep slumber, to the long threads of her hair fanned across my chest, to her lips tickling the side of my ear. I turned toward her, as I did each morning, traced my hand along the sweet curve of her cheek, the soft whiteness of her breast. I loved the sound of her breath catching at my smallest touch.

"The night watch has left the tower and Bile has descended to fetch the breakfast. We have a little time."

"Ah, really? Time for what? What do you suggest, red woman?"

She laughed and swatted at me. "I suggest that you love me."

"You suggest that every morning."

Her face flushed. "I am emboldened, then, because you take my suggestion every morning."

I rolled up then and over her, bracing myself on my arms. She stroked them gently, her hands sliding down from my shoulders.

"I must be easily suggestible."

"Well, you are a poet after all. The smallest words suggest large purpose." She smiled, veiled her eyes. I watched the delicate lashes fan against her cheeks.

"Large purpose is it, love? Who is the poet now?"

She laughed and pushed against me, but her back was already arching.

We had moved into Breogam's Tower, Skena and Bile and I. And though I had but nineteen years, I was at last fully a man. Wisdom singer for the clan. Husband to Skena. Father for all purposes to Bile. Skena and I kept the fire in the lightkeeper's room just above our own chamber burning so high that our room below was warm, even though it was winter. On the nights when the watch was mine, she kept me company, humming along to my harpsongs, sometimes joining me at the window, our arms twined around each other, our faces illumined by the light from the sea, our watch punctuated by small kisses and sweet sighs until at last we could bear it no more and wrapped ourselves together for the briefest of couplings before resuming the watch.

On nights when others of the tribe took the watch, we slept folded together in our chamber below. Though it was furnished simply with a sleeping platform wide enough for two, a smaller platform for Bile, a table, and four curved Roman chairs that some long ago Galaeci had acquired in a trade, for me that chamber in the tower was and will remain forever the room of complete abundance.

Even when we were apart, tending to the business of the clan or to

Bile, we remained tethered to each other by an invisible thread of shared knowledge.

As for Bile, he ran up and down the tower stairs like the mountain goats of Greece, climbing and descending so many times a day that his legs grew strong and tireless.

He took to playing with our baby brother Ir, who had upon him now four years. This made Bile, with his own nine years, the big brother. No matter to Ir that Bile possessed only one arm and could speak only three sounds. To Ir, Bile was an object of worship. For his part, Bile was tirelessly patient in helping the baby to run and to learn to draw. In Ir's adoring gaze, Bile grew confident and happy. When Ir began to imitate Bile's speech, articulating his own wants as "Ah, ah, ah," Bile stopped vocalizing entirely and taught Ir his own system of gestures and signs. Somehow, Bile's strong body, his silence, and his obvious care for his brother made him much less terrifying to the clan, and I noticed that one or two of them began to learn his signs and to return his conversations with their own hands.

For me, when I did not watch for Ith's return, I studied with An Scail. I wrote songs for Ceolas and played my gaita at the window while I kept the watch for Ith. The songs became beloved of the Galaeci. In the evenings, Bile and I would sing them by the fire, and in his humming accompaniment, the people ceased to fear Bile. By firelight they would call for us by name and Skena would push us forward, whispering, "Sing well, my boys."

I had loved my Skena so often, by day and by night, by the fire in the lightkeeper's room, on the end of the rocky shore, that when she told me that her courses no longer came, it seemed to me inevitable perfection. So much great love could only serve to produce another being, to call back a spirit from the Country of the Young. I began to sing to the womb-child on my harp, and when the moon was full, I sang my praises to Creation with a heart more full than all its whiteness.

CEOLAS SINGS A LULLABY
Come to us, returning child.
Here is the hand of your mother,
she who rocks the womb-cradle,
softly, softly, little one, beloved one,

here is your beautiful mother.
Here is the song of your father
that you might know his voice,
the love he will bear you always.
Come, little journeyer,
swiftly among us.
Grateful our hearts
that we are chosen.
Great the love between us
who will keep you safe from harm.

And at last the morning came when I was standing at one of the windows of the tower looking down at the village spread below us and it came to me that I no longer wanted to leave Galicia, that somehow this place and its people had become home. And soon I would have to leave them.

Too soon, for our idyll lasted for only two full turnings of the moon.

We began the month that bore my brother Airioch's name with a wild storm at sea. Not for the first time, my father fretted that Ith had chosen to return on winter seas. On the sixth morning of that month, when Bile and I were keeping watch at the window, we saw Ith's ship undulating toward the harbor.

I sounded the alarm on the long curved war horn that hung by the tower window for just this purpose and raced for the shore, hand in hand with Skena, Bile and Ir behind us.

By the time I reached the curved bay, the ship was coming into harbor and my father and mother and half of the clan of the Galaeci were assembling.

My father grinned when he saw me and slapped me on the shoulder. "Inisfail, lad. At last, I see our destiny!"

So it was to my father's face that I first looked when they carried my uncle Ith down the gangplank on a litter, Eber Donn and Airioch beside him.

My father ran toward them. The bearers lowered the litter to the ground and we pushed in toward my uncle.

The Ith who returned to us was not the uncle who had left us. Drool coursed from one side of his mouth, and like our brother Bile, Ith had to him no speech. His arm on that same side was useless and flopped about like a fish. Only his one eye seemed to hold any awareness of his surroundings, and it swung wildly from side to side as if it searched for someone or something.

Our father dropped to his knees beside him and gave out such a heartrending cry that I thought my own heart would break. Scota knelt behind him and put her hands against his shoulders. When she looked up to meet my eyes, her face bore a look of piteous supplication, as if she thought that someone, I or Skena, could somehow nurse Ith back to health as we had done with Bile.

I turned to Eber Donn. "He was injured on the sea journey?"

Eber Donn's face twisted with rage. "No. It is they who did this to him, the treacherous Danu, the Children of the Braid."

"The Danu? But they sent us greetings, said that they returned him to us with honor. They indicated that perhaps they would welcome us if we were people of peace."

"We will not give them peace. We will go among them and slaughter them for the treacherous, dangerous creatures that they are."

This Eber Donn shouted, raising his arm in the air and screaming it to the assembled Galaeci as if he bore aloft an imaginary sword.

"Hush!" I commanded. "You frighten our uncle Ith." And indeed, Uncle Ith was twisting on his pallet, mewling and wagging his head from side to side.

Eber Donn heeded my wisdom, pulled me aside. "Hear me, Brother. They are dangerous, duplicitous folk, these Danu. Their women are beautiful but strange. . . . Their eyes, I do not know. They possess magical powers beyond anything even our druii have seen. They seem to disappear and reappear in all hours and in all places with no signs of journey upon them. They are keepers of dark secrets. There are places on the island from which they warn us away, even taking to charging some of their most sacred doorways with lightning bolts. Can you imagine?"

Airioch had sidled over to us and now nodded his head vigorously. "It is true, Brother. I tried to penetrate one of their secret spaces!" He whispered it and then turned his back on the assembled company gathered around Ith.

"Why did you try to do so?"

"They keep treasure," he said. "Vast treasure. They wear ancient jewels and diadems."

I waved my hand at this. "I care not for treasure. Return to Ith. How was he injured?"

"I know not," said Eber Donn. "I was preparing our ships for departure. Ith had decided, he said, that we would not return to Inisfail."

"Why did he decide this?"

"I know not. He said that he would speak to our father of what he had learned. I will tell you that it suited me well enough, for I like them not; they keep impenetrable secrets. On the morning of departure, I went to his hut to fetch him and I found him thus."

Airioch broke in. "They were with him before departure. All of the evening before. The Sisters!" He spat the word. "Banba, Fodla, and Eriu. They did this; they cast some spell upon him."

I returned and leaned over my uncle Ith. Skena was bending to him, wiping the spittle from his cheeks.

"I do not see a spell here," I said. "We will send for Mehmet."

Mehmet, surgeon of Egypt, had become much valued among the Galaeci of all the region, traveling from village to village where his medical expertise could right many wrongs. Eber Donn dispatched a rider to find him.

We carried Ith to the village and made him comfortable in one of the conical dwellings. We placed him on soft furs and pillows, built up the fire. My father refused to leave his side. He wept and apologized over and over for sending him to Inisfail, and rubbed constantly at his own left arm, so agitated that I began to fear that he worsened Uncle Ith's condition.

The druids brought An Scail; her presence seemed to calm Ith greatly as she sat beside him and gently stroked his good hand.

When he was calm, Skena bathed him and fed him sweetened porridge and water.

At last Mehmet arrived and hurried into the dwelling. He examined Ith with care, then spoke directly to Ith himself.

"I have seen this before, old friend. You suffered a great shock, did you not?" Ith slowly closed and opened the one good eye.

"Should I take that to be yes?"

Again the blink.

Mehmet nodded. "Sometimes when the body is old and it suffers a great shock, the mind cannot sustain it. It closes all the pathways that it can. Was it accompanied by a blinding headache?"

Again the blink.

"Pain in the arm."

Blink.

"I *have* seen this before," Mehmet repeated. "But the mind is beyond the practice of medicine, as we have seen with Bile. I have seen the brain that dwells inside the skull. It is carved like a river, with streams and channels that flow in all directions. Sometimes I have seen its pathways reroute themselves. Other times, as with Bile, it is as if the mind has put a dam in its own river. I cannot tell you what your fate will be. Only time will tell that. I am sorry."

The mention of Bile seemed to awaken something in Ith. He began to gesticulate with his good hand, and at last I realized that he was speaking in Bile's finger language.

"Do you wish me to fetch him?"

Ith blinked.

I ran for our little brother, who came into the dwelling, his eyes wide with fright.

"Uncle Ith would speak, but his voice will not work. Only his hands work. Only you can speak to him now."

Bile drew himself up, and I was proud of the way his little body girded itself for the work.

Uncle Ith's hands began to work, and Bile turned to me. He made the sign for his papers and chalks. I ran all the way to the tower, took the stairs two at a time, clutched everything to me, and returned at a run.

Ith gestured to all of us but An Scail, Mil, and Bile that we should depart. Though I was wounded to be sent from the bedside of my beloved uncle, I complied, waiting outside the hut.

Half of an hour passed.

My father staggered from the hut, his eyes wide. He clutched his own arm and reeled against the wall of the hut in an agony of grief. He cried aloud. Sure that Uncle Ith had crossed, I ducked beneath the lintel. Ith was still alive, his eyes turned toward the door through which my father had departed, his face sorrowful. He gestured to me and I knelt beside him. He placed his hand on my head. He shook his own head gently.

"What has happened?"

"Bile has drawn something," said An Scail. "It has greatly upset your father."

I looked down at Bile's sketch. "But it is nothing. It is simply a sketch of lightning, a storm at sea perhaps. Or perhaps the lightning Airioch has spoken of."

Again Ith blinked.

"Is that it, Uncle? Airioch has told us that they guard their doorways with bolts of lightning."

My uncle became agitated again at that, moaning and thrashing from side to side.

"Leave us!" An Scail commanded. "Let me try to calm him."

From outside the hut I heard a piercing cry. I raced to the door. My mother was kneeling beside my father. He had collapsed in the dust; his skin was the color of the winter ground. He was dead. Ith followed before morning.

The sparks rose skyward from the headland.

We had built their biers side by side, lighted the torches beneath them at precisely the same moment. At their heads, we placed the urns that would contain their ashes.

An Scail had been given the honor of lighting the bier of Ith. As eldest, Eber Donn lighted my father's bier, and though he was a warrior, he could barely steady his hand for the strength of his weeping.

Eber Finn and Eremon stood side by side in silence, as much a pair as Ith and Mil had been in life. When the grief threatened to shake them, each fastened an arm over the shoulder of the other, and so they stood, a bulwark against sorrow.

Bile clung to Skena on one hand and held hard to Ir on the other. Someone of the tribe had taken Colpa from my mother. I knew not who quieted him.

Only An Scail seemed well, moving back and forth between the biers, chanting to the brothers, the red fire reflected in her lunula and in the sightless silver eyes.

In the darkness of the sacred moon, their spirits rose from their bodies and drifted toward the stars. I could see the path of the twin fires reflected in the sea far below.

My mother clung to me, barely able to stand alone, so shaken by sobs that I thought they would wrench apart her bones. From time to time, she would cry out, "Inisfail my love, Inisfail." I do not know if she mourned his failure to go to the place of his dreams or blamed the place for his passing. At last, when the fires had burned to nothing, she simply crumpled to the ground like ash. I liftted her up; it was the first time I ever realized how very small she was. I carried her back to her dwelling, and Skena brought a draught that at last allowed Scota to sleep.

Skena and I returned to our tower with Bile and Ir. She curled the children into her arms, until at last the three of them slept. I stood late and long at the tower window, watching away to the north, hollow with the loss of Ith and my father, feeling strangely orphaned in the world.

The night had gone well past the turning time when the breeze carried the sound of weeping, muffled, from the shore below.

I took the tower steps by rolling inward, soundless as the air.

He was curled up below the rocks, his head dropped onto his knees. He was wrapped in his cloak like a shroud; already, its neck was wet from the tears he had wept. He lifted his head and stared out to sea. It was Airioch.

For a moment, I considered departing, returning to my tower. But he was my brother. Or so my father had behaved. And so I came up soundlessly beside him and knelt upon the shore.

He must have sensed my presence. His head snapped up, swift and angry, his eyes wide. He regarded me for a moment and his expressions softened.

"Amergin," he said. "I thought that you were Eber Donn."

"And that angered you?"

He shrugged. "He is my brother. We are sometimes angry with each other."

"I am your brother as well."

Something about the statement brought fresh tears to his eyes; they spilled down his cheeks, silver in the moonlight.

"What have I said to bring you such sorrow?"

He shook his head. "You sounded, then, like Mil."

"Our father?" A wave of loss swept over me again to think him gone.

"Your father. But he never said so, Amergin. Never once. He must have known that I was not his own. Just look at me. But all my life he called me as his son. He treated me no differently than he did Eber Donn. Than he did any of you."

"And this has made you weep?"

"I was not grateful enough. I . . . Why do you think he died, Amergin?"

I sighed. "Sometimes I thought that he and Ith were two halves of the same soul. Mil the warrior and Ith the philosopher, Mil the man of action and Ith the thinker. Perhaps he did not know how to live without Ith."

"O you gods," said Airioch. The sound wrenched up from his soul. "Ith knew me for a bastard, Amergin."

"Ith would not have judged you for your mother's weakness."

"Ith watched me for weaknesses of my own."

It was true enough. I thought for a moment.

"All of us have watched you, Airioch. You keep your feelings close within. Until tonight, I thought you saw our father with disdain. You seem always to have some hidden purpose, some plan that is all your own. And your appetites are large."

My assessment seemed to agitate him. He shifted his position, punched his fist into his hands.

"O you gods," he said. "O you gods."

He turned toward me, his eyes meeting mine. I realized with a start that it was the first time that Airioch had ever looked me directly in the eyes.

"Ith loved you like a son," he said.

It was not what I had expected. The full loss of Ith hit me in the chest and I flattened back against the rock. A sob shook up from my core and I pressed my hand over my mouth that it might not carry to the tower and wake Skena, Bile, and Ir.

Airioch's eyes never left my face. I watched as some decision formed on his face. He nodded once.

"I am your brother, Amergin," he said. "Just as I am Eber Donn's. Know this. You have nothing to fear from me, ever. I am your brother."

He stood and looked out to sea, turned, and walked away. We did not see him for two fortnights.

CEOLAS WEEPS
We have lost a brace of fathers.
What cruelty is this O gods?
What whimsy, that you take from us
our wisdom and our strength
not separate, but together?
How shall we live

Without Ith, without Mil?
How shall we journey
In the hollow world
Without them?

On the night that Airioch Feabhruadh returned, my mother called a Council of the clans.

"I say that we shall go! The sons of Mil shall avenge him in Inisfail!" My mother stood among the assembled company, her dark eyes flashing. She was dressed not in mourning, but as a warrior of the Celts, in leather and war boots, her dagger at her belt, her shortsword at her side.

In the month since my father had died, Scota had mobilized her sorrow to such rage that she had brought my brothers with her, so that Eber Donn, who knew of Uncle Ith's wishes, shouted also for revenge.

Across the fire, my eyes met those of Skena and Bile. I stood among the company. I raised my hands.

Silence moved across the assembly like a wind; even my mother sat down in the circle. When had such a thing occurred? When had I become poet and bard, wisdom keeper and sage? I felt it not as a joy, but as a weighty burden with Ith and my father both gone.

I cleared my throat.

"People of the Galaeci. Let us reason past our grief. First we must consider history. All our lives we have thought of Inisfail as the place of destiny; our legends speak of it for ten generations past."

A general nod moved around the circle.

"Yet in any of those legends, did we hear of those who dwelled there?"

"A well-thought point, Amergin," An Scail called from the fireside.

"And our own brother Eber Donn has told us that Ith did not wish us to return among them. Speak, Eber Donn!"

My brother stood, shamefaced, but determined not to lie.

"It is so. Ith told me that he would recommend to our father that we not go among them."

"And did you not tell me that you liked his decision well and found them fearsome?"

"Fearsome, no! They are little people and would be no match for the sons of Mil and the clan of the Galaeci!" Again he was screaming and raising his arms as if he wielded an imaginary sword.

"Eber Donn!" I shouted above the noise of the crowd. "Speak without the theatrics of war! What did you say of them?"

"I said that they are dangerous and duplicitous, keepers of secrets. And is that not borne out by the deaths of Ith and Mil? Perhaps it was one of their own lightning bolts which killed our uncle. Ask Airioch."

I turned toward Airioch Feabhruadh. "Brother?"

Airioch stood among the company like a stranger, clearing his throat and shuffling from side to side. He would not meet my eyes. It seemed to me that he had not returned from Inisfail, nor from his month of wandering, the bold and insouciant Airioch of old. I wondered how much of that had to do with the Children of the Braid. Had he angered them somehow? Been frightened by them?

"Tell us what you learned on Inisfail," I commanded.

"I tried to enter one of their secret doorways," he said. His voice was soft. A wave of chatter passed across the company but I kept my eyes on Airioch. A crafty and calculating look passed across his face. Here at last was the Airioch of old.

"They are keepers of great treasure, these Danu. They guard it well; they charge their doors with bolts of lightning. I told this to Uncle Ith, but he was not much interested in worldly goods, as well we know."

His statement had precisely the effect he desired. My brothers Eremon and Eber Finn stood at once.

"More reason still to go!" shouted Eremon.

"I agree," cried Eber Finn. "Donn has told us that there is land and cattle pasturage aplenty. Now Airioch tells us of treasure. And all of this in the possession of a people who have killed our uncle and our father, he who wished forever to journey to Inisfail."

"Then we shall take him with us!" cried our mother. She lifted my father's urn, which she would not allow from her sight. She held it into the firelight. "The sons of Mil shall take their father to Inisfail!! And their uncle Ith as well."

And so it was decided.

I returned to the tower with Skena. I folded myself down into her arms, and I allowed myself to weep like a lost child for my father, who had never seen his dream; and for my uncle, who had seen it and had not lived to tell the tale; and for myself, who had lost not one father but two, and who had not been able to dissuade or protect his clansmen, though I sensed great danger in the journey.

Eber Donn was dispatched to the south, to the people of the Arganthos, who traded silver with the Greeks, there to trade tin and other goods for the fleet that we would need to journey. In the end, we required only seven ships, for many of the people of the Galaeci declined to accompany us, based, I supposed, on the tales of Airioch and Eber Donn and on Ith's death, for he had been beloved of the Galaeci. Frankly, I thought them wise.

We departed in the month of April, with a fair wind and sunny skies, a fleet of three biremes and four cargo ships. Scota and our baby brother Colpa sailed on the first ship, with my brother Eber Donn and his three wives and children. They were followed by my brothers Eremon and Eber Finn, each in his own ship with wives and children and retinue.

My own ship consisted of myself and Skena, now four months heavy with our child, Bile, Ir, An Scail and the three druids who had chosen to accompany her to Inisfail, and various of the Galaeci. Airioch Feabhruadh commanded our ship, though many of the Galaeci who had chosen to accompany us seemed less than happy to have him as commander.

Most of the days of the journey were uneventful, though once I thought that I saw her, the woman of the message, when I was seated with my map across my knees. The vision slipped away when Airioch interrupted me with a reprimand.

The weather at that time of year was warm, and Skena and I slept each night on the open deck, the clouds scudding across the moon, the great veil of the cosmos throwing its diaphanous scarf across the night sky. My love for her, my adoration, grew as the child in her belly grew, and somehow I felt that something of Ith and Mil would be returned to us with the birth of our child.

Despite the deaths of my father and Ith, we were true Milesians, I suppose, for a spirit of adventure overtook the company as we moved north.

Skena and I whispered of it in the darkness.

"I wonder if we shall always be this way," she whispered, "the people of the Gaels, scattering ourselves before the wind, turning toward every curve in the road."

I had my arm wrapped around her and I whispered gently in her ear. "These are the only curves I wish to travel." I ran my hand gently over her swelling breasts and belly.

She giggled aloud. "Your babe will hear you," she whispered.

"Then she will know how much I love the mother who bears her."

"She, is it?"

"It is. And I think that she will be as beautiful as her mother with skeins of ruby hair."

"Such foolishness." She swatted at me, her eyes full of laughter.

"I am foolish for you," I answered, and she turned on her side toward me and pressed her lips to mine, making our little foolishness as vast as the stars sweeping by above the moonlit clouds.

We sighted land in the far distance on the day that tragedy struck. Oh, we were filled with high spirits! Even the sea-wise Greeks had caught some spirit of adventure from us and had taken to calling the island Inisfail. One of our Greek sailors had scurried up the rigging and cried the sighting aloud. I shaded my eyes and watched him from my position in the stern. "Three days hence," he called.

Excitement raced through the ship.

Far ahead, near the bow, Ir and Bile were dashing from railing to railing to see if they could spot their destination. Ir clambered up on the railing, in imitation of the sailor in the crow's nest. Skena was amidship and she called to him to climb down. I saw Ir's little body shifting forward like a seabird, too far forward on the railing. We ran for him, both of us at once. Skena was closer and reached him first. I saw her arms dart forward, saw her swipe at his little body where it tipped above the railing.

She had him! I saw her arms close tight around him. They would have been fine. But then the great ship plunged downward into the trough of a wave. I saw Skena lose her balance, tip forward at the prow.

I called her name aloud, ran toward them.

If only she had not been so heavy with child, her balance undone. If only we had begun the climb along the next crest! They would have been flung back to the deck. Instead, they were flung forward into the sea.

Her face turned toward me as they fell, on it a look of terror and sorrow.

By the time I reached the prow of the ship, both Ir and Skena were gone.

Behind me Bile began to wail his "Ah, ah, ah," and my own soul emptied into the sea and drowned.

NONE WILL KNOW US DARKLY SUNG

Am gaeth i m-muir
    is gaoth ar muir mé
Am tond trethan
    is tonn treathain na farraige
Am fuaim mara
    is glór na mara
Am torc ar gail
    is torc ar gail
Am he i l-lind
    is bradán i linn
Am loch i m-maig
    is loch i maigh
Am brí a ndai
    is briathair aindéithe

PART TWO

CINIOCHA FÁIN

WANDERING TRIBES

13

People of the Danu, we call this Council. May we seek wisdom in the Braid!"

The assembled Danu began to take their places, to move from the clusters of discussion in the room to the long, curving benches which lined the walls, their cushions and backs adorned with braiding in cobalt blue and red and emerald green.

The room was a soft blue-gray, the lighting muted so that it would not trouble the eyes of the Ancients. Curling all around the ceiling in purest silver and gold, inlaid with gems, was the unbroken symbol of her people, the woven knotwork that symbolized the Braid.

The acoustics in the chamber were perfect, the walls curved and arched and battened. Eriu would need only to speak in a normal voice. She sighed. The sound carried around the room. The people of the Danu began to silence themselves.

The Sisters stood before their assembled people in the Great Council Hall. Eriu stood at the prow and raised her arms high. She felt the hands of Banba and Fodla slip into hers. Not for the first time in her life, she experienced profound gratitude that she traveled through life in the company of these, her beloved sisters.

"We serve you as did the three brothers before us," said Banba. She referred to Mac Cuill, Mac Cecht, and Mac Grene, who had been the Triad of Brothers before them, and who had been also their three first husbands and teachers as the Sisters trained for their duties as Council Triad.

We serve you as Threeborn of One Mother," Fodla intoned, aware of their nearly miraculous status as triplet sisters.

"We serve you in the ancient Triad decreed by the Weaver of Worlds, she our mother, the Danu. Know in us that all of the creations of Danu are Mother, Child, and the Love that moves between them. See us now and know that you are seen and loved by the Maker of the Braid."

The room silenced, the people's upturned faces waiting. Eriu took a deep breath. She spoke.

"Now is the time to prepare, now when there is still a little time before the arrival of the Invaders. To remember is to prepare. Our own history will sustain us now; we will gather from it the wisdom to go forward. As we have done before." She paused.

"Speak to us of the Invaders," one of the people called out from the crowd.

Eriu nodded. "They come from the south, from a land they call Galicia in a country at the western edge of the Internum Mare." She paused, considered for a moment. Her people would know or remember the reference. It would need no explanation. "They call themselves the Galaeci. Of those who came with them, one was a priest, a druid called Ith. He was a man of great spirit and honor; when he learned of our doorways and saw our Hybrid children, he decided that his people would not return. Of this decision, he said that the Galaeci and the Danu would succeed only in frightening each other."

"And yet you say that they return? Where is honor?" one of the people called out.

Banba spoke. "To our great misfortune, he was not their only spokesman. With him were others of his priestly caste and three warriors. Of these, one was a massive, loud, and hairy being who tramped every field for miles and shouted about cattle and pasturage. The other was a tall and handsome Greek"—here the crowd chuckled, knowing Banba's preference for Greeks—"who was nonetheless far too curious. He asked many questions about our jewels and once tried to enter Tara through one of the portals."

A collective gasp went up from the company. Murmurs of "Fomor," "Just like the Fomor," ran through the room.

"How would you assess them?" asked one of the Ancients, her voice practical and competent. Her very tone seemed to quiet the room, to quell the impending panic.

Fodla stepped before the company. "From what we have been able to judge, they are brighter and more developed than Fir Bolg. Their civilization is complex; they have traveled well. Although we cannot yet know, they seem less brutal, less warlike than Fomor, but far more curious and perhaps as acquisitive. Obviously, they are stubborn or single-minded, as it seems they return against the advice of the wisdom keeper. If these who came here are an indicator, they are, as a race, quite large."

A collective murmur ran through the room.

"And so, what will they think of us?" asked one of the Danu.

Eriu sighed.

What would the Invaders think of them indeed, her diminutive race with its huge eyes and long fingers; what would the Invaders make of their nimbus of light, of their Ancients, of their Raveners?

Here, deep below the earth, in the great city of Tara beneath the great hill, it was not necessary to maintain the Metaphor. Eriu looked out over her people. The littlest children of the Danu dashed about laughing. Their laughter pierced Eriu's heart. Would they laugh again if they could not play on the surface, tumble in the long grasses, bathe in the lakes and waterfalls? How long could she and her people hide here below the surface? The subterranean cities were large and well supplied, but they were purposed to keep the surface pristine and green that all the people of the Danu might enjoy the upper world. And when they could no longer hide, where would they go? Worse, would they laugh again when they had heard the terrible story of the Journey of Exile?

The Ancients were already seated, their skin pale, almost gray, their eyes gone dark and cloudy. Some of them wore the dark lenses that covered their whole orb even here in the soft, subterranean chamber. They gestured slowly with their long, thin fingers. So few were left of the original Braided Ancients, these few who were not of the mixed race of Braided Danu who had married with the Penitents. Eriu herself was mixed, her eyes the soft blue-gray, her hair the curling silver that the Penitents had brought on the Journey. The day would come soon when there would be none of the First Journeyers, when all of the Danu would be those who had been born here on the Green Orb. The few remaining Ancients had lived for more than two millennia.

Some of the Hybrids moved among the Ancients, gentling, bringing libations. Among them she saw Illyn moving, directing. Her heart ached with love for this little daughter of the Bog People, the Fir Bolg.

Near the far wall, some of the Raveners were present, the black almonds of their eyes impenetrable as always. Even in Metaphor nothing could change those eyes, that darkness. Perhaps the Raveners were the inevitable result of the long-ago experiment that made them exiles. Or perhaps darkness simply found a way, as it always did, to sidle into the world. She wondered briefly if the coming Invaders were servants of the Braid or of the Unweaver. Perhaps they knew of neither. How should the Danu protect themselves?

"There is one more thing that you should see," said Eriu softly. The acoustics carried her voice around the room. The Danu stilled, looked up expectantly. From its velvet bag, Eriu took out the gift that Ith had given them. It was a wine cup in fine silver, its handles rendered as leaping stags. All around the rim of the cup was elaborate chasework, and endless series of braided knots.

"By the Braid!"

"O Danu, what does it mean?"

For the chasework on the cup and the braidwork at the ceiling of the room were nearly alike, an unending stream of ribbons and knots, complex, beautiful, eternal.

Before any of the people could render opinions on the meaning of the coincidence, one of the doors hidden in the wall made a soft swishing sound and opened. Morrigu entered. Around the room, the assembled company grew silent, then whispered their presence to each other.

The three sisters of Morrigu were clothed as always in unremitting black, their long slender fingers gesticulating as they talked, their black eyes deep and hungry. Eriu realized with a start that even when Morrigu had hidden herself in Metaphor, she could not hide the dark hunger of those eyes. Around their heads moved a cloudy nimbus of darkness. They formed themselves into a triangle, standing at the far end of the hall. Eriu felt Banba and Fodla move closer behind her, instantly moving into the protective triangle. Eriu held the cup behind her; before Morrigu could see it, Banba slid it into its velvet case, hid it under her skirts on the floor.

The triangle of the Braid faced the triangle of the Raveners, like the prows of two great ships. The room silenced. It had been five hundred years since last they had all gathered in this room for this purpose. For many children in the room it would be the first time that they had ever seen the Journey of Exile, the first time they had ever known themselves as Braided Children. Eriu ached for them at the knowledge. It was time to reopen the Journey of Exile.

The lights in the room dimmed to an ambient silver glow near the floor. To the left and right of Eriu, the walls grew viscous, like a waterfall made thick. Suddenly the room was filled with stars, a sky full of stars. They were not the stars that arched in the night sky over the Green Island.

Among the people, one or two of the Ancients cried out, as if they remembered these pathways, this night sky.

Eriu did not remember. Nor would her own parents have remembered. Not the sky, not the journey that had brought them through it.

The voice of the Teller issued through the walls. Not for the first time, Eriu wondered who he had been, his voice mellifluous and so sorrowful.

"This is the place you came from," he intoned. The stars blurred and swept through the arc of the sky, and they were on the Homeworld. The room filled with its sights and its smells—mint and water and something honey warm in a breeze. There were long green fields filled with flowers, huge trees, their limbs shifting from side to side in an emerald forest. By a great sea were cities of gleaming crystal and coral and turquoise, some of the shapes and colors mimicked even now in their own underground cities. Vehicles shaped like triangles of light moved through them in the air.

Eriu reflected that it seemed to be less bright there than here. The quality of the light seemed somehow softer, muted. She wondered if that was why the light so troubled the eyes of the Ancients, so that they always covered their eyes, wearing dark lenses over the whole eye. Another reason for their love of the Green Island, for it was often rainy here and soft. Eriu stifled another sigh, knowing that it would carry around the room.

"We were a learned people, as you can see. We had learned to preserve our world in pristine beauty. We educated our people. We had mastered the world of science and we bent its rules to our uses. All of these things we had learned over centuries. We believed that we had learned at last to value the ways of the Braid. We tried to emulate Her in all things. Our mistake was that we tried to take from her the power of Creation. Because we made many mistakes in the management of our world, many—no, most—of our people became infertile. Women were unable to bear. We tried to correct that problem with the best and brightest of our people."

The picture shifted again; it seemed to show some hall of science. Patients were receiving care. The Teller's voice resumed, weighty.

"We had become healers of great skill. The lame and the blind we healed, the paralytic and the diseased. We did this through PreBraiding and ReBraiding. Even now, we hope and believe that Danu, the Weaver, would be proud of us for the healing of her children. Among us now, even such healing as that has been banned. We take responsibility for that loss. In our great pride, we went beyond healing to try to usurp the right of Creation, the power of life and death. Over many generations of the Danu, you, the Children of the Braid, were created.

"You possessed intelligence and immense longevity, the power to heal your own diseases. But in the process of achieving that end, we destroyed hundreds"—his voice paused, wearied—"thousands of your people who were imperfect or deformed. Some of those imperfections were physical, some were mental. Some must surely have been imperfections of the spirit, but those we could not see. I fear that those creatures may be among you now."

Eriu thought of the Raveners, glanced toward the triangle of the Morrigu at the far side of the chamber. The ancient voice continued.

"We bear the weight of the murders of your people, for that is what we now know them to be. Even when, at last, we created you of the Braid, you were judged by the people of our world to be not of the Danu. You did not look as we looked, you lived much longer, your vast intelligence terrified our people. To keep you in control, you were granted no rights among us. You were placed in the holds, removed from the sight and thought of our people." Here the picture shifted to a kind of prison structure; though clean and well appointed, it was nonetheless an obvious camp surrounded by lightbolt-walls.

"Though they were few in number, your ancestors rose up. Who would blame them now? All creatures yearn toward freedom and respect. Your ancestors began the BraidRising.

"We had created a race of people who were self-healing, who would live to be most ancient, who were physically beautiful, intelligent beyond our own capacities, dangerous. We tried to repress, to exterminate, the very thing we had created.

"We are the authors of your exile. The result of the BraidRising was that you were granted freedom, but only in exile. From the four great cities of our world, we provisioned you for a distant journey. From Falias, they sent with you the Lia Fail, the Stones of History and Destiny. They speak to you now. From Gorias, they sent with you the Invincible Spear Arms so that you might protect yourselves. It is my hope that you have never had to use those weapons.

"Finias provisioned you with the Spear Ships in which you traveled. Murias provisioned you with food and the means to store and duplicate those stores. All shared in your provisions for all shared in the shame of what had been done to you.

"Here, in the time and place that you see now, we of science have been judged and found guilty. We have received the ultimate punishment for our pride. That punishment is death; we accept that judgment as fair for what was done to you.

"You, our brothers and sisters in the Braid, have been forced into exile by the very nature of your creation. To assist you on your journey, we have sent with you our own people, healers and lawgivers, wisdom keepers and historians, who have volunteered to accompany you into exile to right the wrongs that have been done you. They have called themselves the Penitents; they will live to right the wrong that has been done you."

The picture shifted now to her paternal ancestors, the solemn, tall Penitents with their copper skin and curling silver hair, their expressions of sorrowful solemnity. They were ranged up by the hundreds. She felt a surge of love for them, these ancient sacrificial people. How afraid they must have been! All had been dead for hundreds, thousands of years.

"With you we have sent the knowledge of the healing, of the PreBraiding and the ReBraiding. You may guard it or destroy it, but use it wisely. It must never fall into the wrong hands, for it could lead again to the knowledge of Braid creation. That knowledge will never again be used on this world.

"In the way of all creatures, time will pass and you of the Braid will marry and mate with those of the Penitents who accompany you. Some of you may well mate with the inhabitants of the worlds you will encounter.

You will form a new race. We cannot say what your attributes will be. Will you live forever or will you die? Will you be creatures of the light or servants of the dark? What we have set in motion, we will not see to fruition. But we ask that you retain the name Children of the Danu that our two races will be joined forever across the stars, that She, the Mother Weaver, will protect you. We offer this as our apology; we seek your forgiveness. We ask that you remember that within the Braid dwells the spirit of Creation; that spirit moves in all and every create thing. We send with you our profound shame that we did not remember such a thing before we usurped the powers of the Weaver."

Not for the first time, Eriu wondered about the Teller's people. How long had they lived? How wise had they become? Did they dwell out there still, among the far stars? Among her own people were none of them now, for all who had journeyed with them had died long, long ago. The Teller was right, though. There had been much intermarriage through the centuries, and now her own race was an admixture of Exiles and Penitents.

And now a new race would soon come into their midst.

Eriu sighed. It was the first time she had seen the history in hundreds of years, yet just as it had done the first time she viewed it, it had made her feel alien to herself and profoundly sad. She could hear soft weeping in the room and knew that it had had the same effect on some of her people. The Braided Ancients were silent, their eyes lowered, as if they were ashamed. The children in the room were silent.

Eriu moved to the front of the chamber. She lifted her hands. From behind her she felt the hands of Banba and Fodla close around hers.

"People of the Danu," she intoned, "braided we are unbreakable, braided all life is unbreakable, all one, all in the Braid." In the great room, her people linked hands, arm over arm, a physical representation of the Braid. She waited until all were linked.

"Shall we hear more?" She almost hoped that they would say her nay. It was a sad history; in her memory it terrified her still.

"We must!" An old and tremulous voice rose above the discussion. An Ancient couple arose from among the company and made their way toward the front.

Historians. The man a descendant of the Penitents, the woman one of the last of the living Ancient Creatures of the Braid.

Immediately, the Hybrids rushed to assist them, to raise them gently to the platform, to bring them chased stools with cushioned seats and soft backs, to attach the devices that would engage the Lia Fail. Not for the first time, Eriu blessed the Hybrids for the love and adoration they brought to the Ancients, for treating them as honored grandparents. When the Ancients were seated before the company, the woman spoke first, as was always the way of the Danu.

"Children, it may be that soon we will be exiled again. We must know our history to choose our future. Open the Walls of Wisdom!"

The walls of the room slid back to reveal a kind of museum. Suspended in midair were wavering, three-dimensional pictures, an island in the Internal Sea, the temples of the Greeks, the pyramids of Egypt, a city of lights encased in bubbles below the sea. In shimmering cases around the room were the gifts that the people had been given by those they had encountered, Egyptian necklaces of jade and gold, Greek diadems encrusted with jewels, beautiful chalices and dishes of chased silver and gold, finespun linens, musical instruments, gifts of gratitude for teaching and knowledge.

"When first we came to this place, we slid our ships into the sea. We built our cities below the water and there we hid for many years. The shame and terror of the BraidRising dwelt upon us still." She touched a button on the arm of her chair, and the Danu could see the city below the waters, its lights shimmering beneath the sea.

She stood, her mate rising to hold her on his arm. She was withered, her skin a dusty white, folded on itself in ridges and creases. Her eyes were rheumy gray, her head completely bald, her fingers overlong. She was tinier than Eriu and her sisters by almost a foot, standing only three feet off the ground. Her grandchildren must have towered over her. She continued.

"At last, however, some of our number ventured to the surface. They captured the images of those they encountered. They returned to us and learned to create Metaphor. The taught us to practice so that we could hold the image in place."

She touched the triangle at her neck with its braided vines. A rainbow shimmered within it. Suddenly she was more than five feet tall. Her black curly hair was swept back at the crown and cascaded in long ringlets down her back. Her eyes were dark and expressive. She wore a white gown, single-shouldered, attached to a necklet of gold. The children in the room laughed and applauded. Eriu wondered how many generations of children and grandchildren she had delighted with her multiple transformations.

She smiled. Pearly teeth glistened in a mouth that possessed none in its true form.

"With Metaphor we could travel. Some few of our people came north into the region of the world where we now dwell. Our own ancestors built a city on an island in the middle of the Internal Sea." Again she pressed a button. A city of curved white dwellings and huge gleaming columns arose on a mountainous island filled with light.

"We traveled among all of the people of that region, Egyptians, Greeks, Persians. We taught and we learned. We shared our skills for building and healing. Our island in the Internal Sea became known as a center for wisdom and learning. I fear that the Greeks began to think of us as gods. This filled us with terror, for those who perceived us as different had exiled us.

"But before the problem had time to grow, the Green Orb itself changed our circumstances."

She pressed a button on the arm again; a great volcano shimmered up in three dimensions, spewing hot red fire. The earth cracked apart. The people watched as the white-columned temples tumbled to the ground, as the island slipped beneath the sea. The ancient woman was silent, her eyes filled with sorrow. Her companion took up the tale.

"Many of our people were killed, both Ancients and Penitents. Our ancestors retreated to the sea. Those who remained, intermarried and gave birth to the new children of the Danu, the true ReBraid of our races. When enough time had passed, we searched for a new place where we could dwell. We remembered that some of our company had traveled to the north, and we decided to follow. We found the Green Isle. Imagine our joy when we found evidence of the Danu in the structures of the people, huge lunar circles, temples incised with the Braid of the Weaver. We found no evidence of our vanished brothers and sisters. We could find no sign that they had married with the people of the place. Did Metaphor fail them? Were they destroyed? We do not know.

"For a time we dwelled on the surface, but there came among us two great crises—the Fomorian sea raiders and the years of no summer. To be safe from those, we built our cities here"—he paused—"beneath the ground. Here we have dwelled for more than a thousand years. Now a new race will come among us, warlike and strong. It is time for the Danu to consider. Where shall we go?"

From the back of the room came three voices in succession, nasal and smoky, sure of their powers. It was the voice of Morrigu.

"We shall not go. We shall destroy the interlopers."

"We have the power. Did we not drive the Fomor back to the sea?"

"We shall unleash the power of the Silver Arms."

14

CEOLAS MOURNS
Forgive me, my beloved.
Oh, take me with you
into the dark sea, the cold sea,
that she may keep us both together.
I cannot live apart from you.
My heart is cold and dead.
My heart is a drowned vessel.

ush! Do you hear it?" Eriu pressed her hand against Banba's lips to still her sister's chatter, tilted her head toward the stone passageway that led to the surface.

The Sisters had secreted themselves in one of the wedge passages whose secret doors opened into the hidden city of Tara below. They were seated together in the circular chamber at the end of the long passage that descended into the earth. Together they had examined the chamber, made certain that none of their people were anywhere nearby. Particularly, they looked to see that the Morrigu had not followed them to the surface.

The command had been given that the people of the Danu were to remain below until they had decided what to do about the Invaders. The Sisters had violated their own order to enter the Chamber of Memory.

"Hear what?" Banba swatted the hand away. "Do you think they are among us already?"

Eriu shook her head. "I don't know. I thought I heard singing . . . or chanting . . . I don't know. It drifts in and out on the wind."

"I hear it too," said Fodla softly. "It is a most mournful sound, a cup full of sorrow."

Banba stilled at last and tipped her head.

Eriu shook her head again. "It is gone now. Finished. It made me want to weep."

"I think you are both imagining it," Banba snapped. "We have more important things to consider. Did you charge the doorway?" she added in a soft whisper.

"I did," said Eriu. "They have not yet come to shore, but if they do, their attempt to enter will bring them the same reward that Airioch Feabhruadh earned."

"Oh, if only we had not worn the jewels and diadems when first we met them!" said Fodla.

"We were trying to appear as Greeks," said Banba. "Their ships were Greek."

"Ith had no interest in jewels and gold!" said Eriu. "Even his interest in our crops and cattle pasturage faded to nothing when he learned from whence we truly came."

"But, Sister, Airioch Feabhruadh had much interest," said Banba. "As did the brother Eber Donn, though I think he too was more taken with the green fields and forests. And neither of them knows the dangers. There was too much here that called them back. Too much beckoned. Oh, we beckoned them." This last came out of her as a moan.

"What will become of our people?" Fodla whispered.

"Come now," said Eriu. "Do not give in to despair. We have lived long on the Green Orb and long on the Green Isle. We know that our ancestors did not have an easy way here in the beginning. Did we not lose Nuada Silver Arm in the war with the Fomor?"

"Do you remember aught of Nuada's Silver Arm?" Fodla asked.

"It was a thousand years ago." Banba shrugged. "We were children."

"I know that it was during the time when the Brothers presided over the Council. Mac Cuill, Mac Cecht, and Mac Grene," Eriu replied softly. "And the Morrigu said 'arms.' Plural."

"Well, there is only one way to know," said Banba.

Eriu nodded. "We will study our ancestors here in the Chamber of

Memory and reason how best we can defeat the newcomers. We are wisdom givers and gatherers. Throughout our history we have learned from those we encountered. We can reason our way out of this dilemma with our own history, Sisters."

"We should have studied our history earlier, Sisters," said Banba. "Why did the Brothers not teach us this when we were bonded to them?"

"You would not have studied it then," said Fodla. "You were too busy fondling your new husband to study. You would have paid no attention at all."

Banba grinned. "Oh yes, I remember it well. One of these dark chambers, a huge cozy chair, and a husband who had been bound to me for the sole purpose of teaching me everything. And besides, they had learned the history before us and did not seem much interested in passing that part of our heritage on."

"And the result is that we are deficient in history," said Fodla.

"Did you ask them to teach it to you?" Banba asked. Fodla shifted uncomfortably. Banba laughed aloud.

"Very well," said Eriu. "We were young and full of desire."

"You too? Our senior sister?" said Banba and Fodla in unison.

"The young should be full of desire," said Eriu. "And our bond husbands did not seem troubled that they had to them such young and . . . frolicsome . . . wives. I do not remember them calling us back to any of our lessons. When once I did ask to study the history, they simply shrugged me off and suggested a picnic instead. They were men, after all." She smiled at her sisters. "But now we are old and alone and our people are in danger." She sighed; the mood of all three sisters changed liked quicksilver. "Now we must learn the lessons and draw from them the answers. Our ancestors dealt with invaders. How did they protect the Danu? That is what we seek to know."

From deep inside her robe, she took a speckled stone the size of a hand.

Fodla gasped. "How did you get that? Is it the turnstone of the Lia Fail?"

"It is. I simply took it from its case in the room of the Walls of Wisdom." A single protrusion jutted from the great rock at the center of the room. She lowered the stone over the protrusion, placed her hand upon its jutting surface.

"Stop!"

A door slid open at the back of the chamber, seeming to open out of the unbroken stone wall. An Ancient entered, a tiny woman of only three feet, bald with gray skin and long, slender fingers.

All three sisters stood.

"Ancient!"

"Airmid, daughter of Dian Cecht!"

"We are honored that you have come among us, Great Physician."

"You will not be so pleased when I have spoken." The voice of the ancient woman was nasal, almost metallic, the words undergirded by a continuous soft, buzzing sound. "You must not use the Lia Fail."

"Ancient," said Eriu. "With respect, this is why the Lia Fail was sent with us, that we might accrue knowledge and disperse it, that we might learn from it the true way to go. We must immerse ourselves in Memory now. We no longer have husbands to carry that knowledge. We must learn from those who came before, those who forged truce and those who drove the Invaders away. We must choose the right way to go."

Airmid shook her head. "To experience the Lia Fail is to experience history as those before you lived it. It will be as if you are there, seeing, hearing, smelling what they encountered. That is why these chambers are . . . above the surface. They are a space between our world and their world, a place where history may be experienced out of its sequence of time."

Eriu nodded. "Then this is well. We will learn much."

"The experience will ask much from you. It will exhaust you, render you incapable of speech or movement for some time after you have returned."

"Very well, we will work independently then, each of us alone. The one who goes will teach the others."

"There is more." Airmid hesitated, then leaned her head back against the chair. "Have you never wondered why your husbands are no longer with you, why they did not live many millennia, as most of the Children of the Braid do, why they died younger than most?"

"They were much older than we, Ancient," said Banba. "We . . . assumed . . . oh, Mother, I begin to suspect what you will tell us."

Airmid nodded. "There is a price to pay for the access of memory. This is why the Brothers kept you from it. It is a price of time. We do not simply view the past; the Lia Fail allows us to relive it, to shift into that time with those people, to see as they saw, to know as they know. Such access requires a price. Such access changes us at the level of the Braid."

"And the price is a price of years," said Banba softly.

"It is. That is why the stone has remained under glass for all these years since the Brothers passed, why they asked me specifically to keep it from you."

"They protected us," said Fodla softly.

"How many years?" asked Eriu.

Airmid sighed. "I do not know. Oh, you will live long, surely, longer than the Fir Bolg, longer than these who come. But your lives will be shortened with this learning, with this traveling through time."

"We have no choice, Ancient. Invaders come to our shore. Our people require our wisdom. If that is the price, I will pay it." Eriu's hand rested on the speckled stone.

"No!" Banba raced forward, slapped her hand down upon Eriu's. Fodla followed, her eyes resting on those of each of her sisters. "We are a Triad. We live together and we die together. If there is a price, we pay it together," said Banba.

"Whatever it is," said Fodla softly.

Airmid stepped among them. She nodded. "I too have had just this dilemma, when my decision had upon it a cost too much to bear. Will you heed the wisdom of an old physician?"

"We will, Ancient," said Eriu softly.

"Then learn here in short bursts, in small snippets of time. Allow yourself recuperative time between the journeys. Think about what you have learned and how you may apply it to the Danu. In this way, you may minimize the damage, but hear me clearly. You will not stop it. Do you understand?"

"We do," said Eriu. "Leave us now that you may not also be affected."

The door in the rock shivered open, closed behind the Ancient.

Eriu pressed down upon the surface of the speckled green stone, twisted the stone to the right twice. A soft whirring sound arose from the great altar stone at the center of the chamber. All around the Sisters the walls shimmered and came to life. They were standing in a great forest, the trees towering above them like sentinels, a breeze moving the leaves. On the path before them were two men, still as paintings.

"Nuada Silver Arm!" Fodla exclaimed.

The little man with his cap of cloudy curls and his high curved ears was completely unaware of their presence, though the Sisters were standing on the path, the wind shifting their curls, the smell of the forest all around them. Beside Nuada was a much taller man, his features more like the dwellers of the Green Orb, his hair a deep red-gold.

"Bres the Beautiful. Why did our people not see his unlikeness to us from the first?" asked Banba. "He is as much like the Danu as these new arrivals."

"Because our people would have been the last to judge him by his appearance, that having been the standard by which we were judged. Among us was the safest place for his treachery."

"He was aptly named, wasn't he?" said Banba.

"How so?"

"The Beautiful. For is he not?"

Fodla chuckled softly. "You do like the look of these humans, Banba."

Banba shrugged. "I did not say that he was good. Only that he looked good."

"But look how small Nuada is; he cannot quite reach four feet."

"There had been less intermarriage then, Exiles to Penitents, and none yet with humans." They all looked at the two men side by side. "Well, almost none," Fodla amended.

"Sisters, shall I make the third turn?"

Banba and Fodla nodded solemnly.

Eriu twisted the speckled stone. The forest began to sigh and move. Before them, the two men ran softly along the path. The Sisters had stepped back in time a thousand years.

"Look where before us comes a man of the bags." The voice of Bres was sarcastic, nasal.

"You will treat him with respect, Bres. He is a man of the Braid, no matter his station." Though he was head and shoulders smaller than Bres, the voice of Nuada was commanding, confident. He walked toward the approaching stranger, held up his hand.

"Welcome, man of the Fir Bolg. We greet you as newcomers to the Green Isle. I am Nuada; my companion is Bres."

The man was taller than either of them, stocky and dark, his brows beetled together and heavy, his body covered with dark hair. He eyed them both, but the weight of his suspicion fell obviously on Bres.

"I am Sreng. I ask what you will demand of us. More corn? More cattle? The firstborn of our children?"

"Why would we want such thing?" Nuada's voice was puzzled.

"It is what the Fomor ask and more." He gestured toward Bres with his chin. "Are you not of them?"

"I am of the Danu," said Bres. "I do not know these Fomor."

"You will. They will ask the same of you. Your cattle, your women, your children. All in thirds. As if they think of thirds as fair." He snorted.

"They dwell here?"

"You really do not know?" asked the Fir Bolg. "Would that we did not. They are sea raiders from the north. But they maintain a stronghold just offshore on Tober Mor. A better location from which to fleece us naked, I suppose. They are a bottomless well of demands; the holds of their ships must be huge and hollow."

"This from a man who makes his boats of dirt bags." Bres spoke in heavy disdain.

"The leather of our bags is bog-tanned," Sreng said, his voice defensive. "Until you know the bog, do not ridicule its ways. The ships of our tribes do not sink."

"Tribes?"

"We are three clans, Fir Bolg, Fir Domnan, Fir Galioin. And you?"

"We are one. Children of the Danu. People of the Braid."

"Danu?"

"She is our Mother. Weaver of Worlds."

"How is it that you speak our language? I was told that you had come in cloud ships. I thought that we would not understand each other."

Nuada was silent. It would not do to mention the pulsing triangles beneath their tunics, rendering the languages intelligible. Nor would they speak of the cloud ships, those giant triangles, now carefully hidden in the lakes and under hollow hills. Even Bres did not know of them, his mother, Eri, having only returned to the tribe some years ago.

Nuada inclined his head politely. "We have learned your language that we might negotiate."

"Nego?" The Fir Bolg got lost in the word, stood staring.

"We come to you with a proposal for your people."

"Propose as you will." Sreng gave a shrug, as if the proposal were of no matter.

"We would share this green island with you. Your people would have the north and we the south."

"Why would we agree to such a thing?"

"We would provide three gifts: We have some skill at healing; that we would share with your people. We have some skill at defense; we would assist you in defending against these Fomor. Last, we have some skill with the land; we will assist you with provision."

"I shall take this to our people. Meet us tomorrow at the Plain of Mag Tuiread."

"This is not a place that we know."

"It is the Plain of Many Towers. There we will give answer." Sreng of the Fir Bolg turned and moved away into the forest, a lumbering, silent beast.

"How strangely he responds," Nuada said.

Bres smiled. "I did not know your Greeks, but I would venture to say he is not one of them."

"As different from them as night is from day."

Bres tapped the side of his head. "Very little up there, Nuada. Trust me. They will respond with force. That is what they know. He has looked at you. You are small and slight and weaponless. He will judge that you are defenseless as well."

The Chamber of Memory darkened; for a while the Sisters sat silent in the darkness.

At last Eriu sighed. "What have we learned, Sisters?"

"Bres was no fool," said Banba.

"No," said Eriu thoughtfully. "Perhaps in what we saw, there is wisdom for us."

"How so?" Fodla tilted her head toward her sisters.

"We agree that these new Invaders are warrior people?"

"They bristle with swords and daggers. It is the logical conclusion," said Banba.

"Then perhaps we should make a first show of force."

Fodla gasped.

"No, Sister, I do not mean to harm them. Only to show force, that they respect it and are wary. That they will think us many more in number than we are."

Fodla shook her head. "Force did not work for our ancestors. Do you not remember? Take us to the Plain of Mag Tuiread. Let us see."

"Perhaps we should wait a little," Banba said, her voice unsure.

"And if the Invaders come to shore while we are waiting?" asked Fodla.

Eriu nodded. She twisted the speckled stone.

15

Fog moved among the great megaliths on the plain.

"So this is what they meant by many towers," Nuada said. "These that were built by our ancestors."

"Or mimicked by these ponderous Fir Bolg? It is not likely, is it? Surely they must have seen our ancestors as gods," said Bres. He examined one of the great pairs of stones, then whispered, "Our ancestors, Nuada. See where they have left passage to the world below." He pointed at a raised triangle on the stone with its interlocked spiraling braids.

Bres was carrying a Scythian shortsword from the weapons horde deep below the earth. The piece was a museum piece, taken from the wall, but it suited his greater height. Nuada and his companions, diminutive men with caps of cloudy silver hair, carried replicas of Greek spears made shorter and lighter for their small size. They came up among the great stones, crossed under a lintel. Nuada raised his spear.

"I salute the Braid who binds us."

Bres snorted. "Your Braid won't bind you to these folks, I can tell you that with certainty." He gestured with the shortsword.

Ranged up on the plain were hundreds of Fir Bolg. They carried heavy broad spears. They were garbed in animal skins, the men covered with hair from their faces all the way to their feet. Many of them were toothless, heavy-lidded, and beetle-browed.

"Sreng!" called Nuada. "I return with our proposal." The sound bounced around the great circle of stones, echoed eerily between the linteled dolmens.

Sreng did not step forward from the crowd. There was a general shifting and moaning among the Fir Bolg. Behind him Nuada could hear the silver buzz of alarm as it passed among the Danu.

"Do they not remember you?" someone whispered in Danaan from behind Nuada.

"They seem not to wish to." Bres's voice was heavy with its usual sarcasm. "Or perhaps they are a race of folk whose memory lasts for less than a day; they do not look as if they could hold much, do they?"

His remarks brought a silver wave of laughter through the ranks of the Danu. As if the laughter were their signal, the Fir Bolg gave off a mighty roar and charged at the Danu.

What ensued next was almost impossible to follow, the cloudy curls of the Danu nearly obscured by the fog and by the hairy presence of the larger Fir Bolg. At times there was the sound of metal on stone, at times screams, though the watching Sisters could not have said from whom.

Suddenly there was a scream of rage and pain. The picture narrowed, rushed toward a dolmen, focused. Nuada. He stood with his head tilted back, an expression of agony on his delicate features. His right arm had vanished at the elbow. Blood was spurting everywhere in arterial streams.

One of the Fir Bolg raised the severed arm and lifted it high into the air. It dripped blood down into his hair and across his face. He shouted something in his guttural tongue. Behind him the Fir Bolg began to make an ululating sound, a warble that could only signal victory. Suddenly Bres was beside Nuada. He stripped off his cloak, wrapping it hard around the tiny leader.

"We go below!" he shouted.

"We cannot abandon our people!" Nuada screamed.

Bres yanked hard at the cloak, pulling Nuada with him into the dolmen space. His hand reached out to the rock and smacked it hard. There was a flash of white light, a shape like a blue ovoid that thinned and vanished. Where the two had stood, there was nothing.

On the Plain of Mag Tuiread the assembling Fir Bolg ceased their warbling. Many began to hold up their right hands, to make signs in the air, their eyes wide.

It was the opening the Danu required; they rushed among them with their sharp light swords. The screams of the Fir Bolg were now screams of pain.

Suddenly the snap of white light with its ensuing blue moved among two dolmens at the far side of the plain.

Bres and Nuada appeared between the standing stones. On his arm Nuada wore a silver appendage that resembled a hand on a long shining gauntlet of silver, covered with shimmering triangles and spirals of color. He held it forward; the silver fingers curled and unfurled. When they had reached full extension, one finger snapped forward an arc of blue light. A dozen Fir Bolg fell, stunned and wounded, to the ground.

The battle was over. Those Fir Bolg who were still of sound body, who were closest to the edge of the stone ring, ran for the forest, their high gabbling screams ringing behind them. Those who were wounded curled into themselves on the ground, clung each to the other. Hairy men sobbed and scrabbled backward on hands and knees as the Danu approached them.

Nuada stepped into the circle. He tapped the triangular crystal etched with twining vines at his neck. In its depths, a rainbow shimmered and coalesced.

"Hear me, men of the Fir Bolg," he called. "Fear us not. We will heal your wounds. Be still and unafraid."

Suddenly white light and blue ovoids snapped between every portal in the circle. The physicians appeared, the long white robes wafting in the breeze, their hands gloved, faces covered. They moved among the wounded, easing pain, their huge eyes assessing the wounds, slender fingers working. When the field surgery was organized, Nuada called again.

"Come before us three men, one each of the Fir Bolg, the Fir Domnan, and the Fir Galioin."

Sreng came forward then, accompanied by two companions.

Nuada said nothing for a moment, assessing the threesome.

Sreng bowed his head before Nuada. "You were so small, Nuada; I judged you weak. I did not know that we fought with gods."

"No gods, just men of the Danu, weary of exile."

A crafty look passed across Sreng's face.

"Then we will agree now to your proposal. We will divide the land with you north and south."

"It is too late for that, Sreng," said Nuada. He held up the silver arm. "You must now bargain for less, for you bargained falsely at the first."

Sreng was silent.

Nuada regarded the three men. "What is Sreng's territory?" he asked at last.

The second man spoke. "Sreng and his tribe bespeak Connacht. We call them the Tribe of the Bogs, for it is stony country and full of bog, though the fishing is good."

Nuada nodded. "Then that shall be the territory for all three of your tribes in perpetuity."

The three men eyed each other, their looks uneasy.

"You will have to learn to get along among your tribes," Nuada continued. Though it was easy enough to read their looks, even for the Sisters these many centuries later, the men of the Fir Bolg seemed surprised to be so easily read. The third chief, still silent, made a sign in the air.

"But this, we of the Danu, will promise you. We will not make war on you again as long as you keep to your territory, nor will we build our cities there. The hunting and the fishing will be yours. We will trouble none of your women, nor ask of you grain or children or cattle." Surprise ran over the faces of the three Fir Bolg chiefs, and they glanced at each other again. "Finally, when your children are sick or ailing, we will offer the services of our healers."

"Why would you do this for us, Nuada Silver Arm?" asked Sreng.

Nuada shifted his position, cradling the silver arm in his good hand. "You too are Children of the Braid," he said softly.

A long silence pervaded the chamber when the pictures had vanished. The Sisters were still. Fodla rested her head on the arm of her chair. At last Eriu stirred.

"And so he became forever known as Nuada Argetlamh," Eriu said. "Nuada Silver Arm."

"How noble he was and how wise," said Fodla.

"At last I have found my true love," Banba sighed.

At this all three sisters burst into laughter, hiding the sound behind their hands.

"When do you not find your true love?" hissed Fodla. "It is too bad that both of these have passed into the Braid."

At her statement, all three grew silent momentarily. Eriu sighed.

"There is no point in dreading what might befall us. We must think only of the safety of our people now. And we have learned much, Sisters."

"We have learned that Nuada tempered punishment with promise," said Fodla. "And that he required consequences for actions. There was a wise ruler indeed."

"And we have seen that Bres was a true friend and companion in arms," said Banba. "The histories have painted him as traitor."

"Well, whatever he later became, he saved the life of Nuada on that day. But I wonder at the arm," said Eriu.

"Wonder what? It looked to me as though the weapon operated on the same principal as Metaphor and Transport do, rearrangement of the molecules of matter, water, air." Fodla waved her hand in the air at her obvious and simple conclusion.

"That, yes, but what of history?" asked Eriu.

"Ah . . . I see what you mean." Banba closed her eyes. "The histories say that the physician Dian Cecht created the arm for Nuada after his had been lost in war. They say nothing of the arm being already created and ready."

"Precisely."

"And yet we have seen him using it on the Plain of Many Towers on that very day." Fodla shook her head. "How was it done?"

The Sisters fell into a long silence, curled into their chairs, deep in contemplation. Long moments passed. Then Eriu gasped.

"Sisters, hear me now. For our ancestors have given us the answer. They did not shift the molecules of matter, water, air. Not on that day. They shifted time!"

"By the Danu!" said Banba. "I see it too. They slowed it down."

"But how was it done?" Fodla shook her head.

"I know not, but I know that we must know. Somehow, in that timeshift is the answer to our problem."

"Then let us return to them," said Banba. "I welcome the task."

"You would," said Fodla.

"I think we must ask the Ancient. Airmid the Physician," said Eriu. "Perhaps she will know or remember."

Suddenly there was a soft, hissing sound in the wall and a door slid open. Illyn moved through, her slippered feet quiet on the stone floor. In her hand she held a tray filled with fruits and small crystal candies. Steam rose from three clay goblets bearing warm honeymead.

She set the tray on the surface of the rock.

"How did you know we were here?" Banba snapped the question at her. Illyn's eyes went wide.

"Have I done wrong? The Ancient wished for you to have libation. She said that it is time for you to rest from your labors."

"Banba." Eriu wheeled toward her sister. "You frighten our Daughter of the Braid."

Banba stood and threw her arms around the child. "I am sorry, truly. I am so sorry. I fear that the Morrigu will find us here. We try to prevent a war of the Silver Arm. Of course the Ancient knows that we are here. It was she who warned us. O Danu, I am babbling." She released the little girl, who stepped back immediately and hid her hand behind her back.

Eriu knew that she made her own people's ancient sign against the evil. Eriu sighed.

The child heard the sigh, pulled the hand forward from behind her back, guilt washing across her face. She twisted her hands together.

"No, child," said Eriu softly. "You need not hide it. These are troubled times; we are all filled with fear."

Illyn's huge dark eyes filled with tears. "They will not hurt my mother, will they?"

"The Morrigu or the Invaders?"

"I know that you will keep the Morrigu from her. But the Invaders. I think that they grow closer."

"Have you seen them?" Banba asked, her voice imperative. Tears sprung into the little girl's eyes.

"Sister!" said Fodla. "Surely the Chamber of Memory makes you more irritable than usual."

Banba hung her head.

Eriu sat and opened her arms. Illyn launched herself into the huge chair, snuggling up beside Eriu. She leaned her head on the little woman's shoulder. For a time, Eriu stroked Illyn's long, dark hair. She loved the silky feel of it between her fingers, remembered the days eight years ago when Illyn had first came among them, when Eriu had calmed her by washing and braiding and flowering the rich tresses. This child of the Fir

Bolg was the closest thing that Eriu had to a daughter, and she loved her as she would her own child.

"You have been on the surface, haven't you, sweeting?"

Guilt flashed across Illyn's face, but she nodded. "I was afraid for my mother. I thought that I would go to her, but when I got to the surface I thought that I heard music. It was sad and angry all at once and I grew afraid."

"Would you like to see your mother?" Eriu asked softly.

Illyn looked up, hope spreading across her features. "Will she know me?"

Eriu closed her eyes. They had let her return once, when she was eight years old. She had accompanied Illyn then, cloaked carefully in Metaphor. The child's mother would not come near her daughter, repeatedly making the sign against the evil in the air. At last Eriu led a weeping Illyn away. Only when they reached the edge of the village did the woman come dashing after them, slipping from tree to tree. Though she would not approach them, she called from hiding. "Woman of the Danu!"

"Eriu," she called back, thinking that a real name might calm the Fir Bolg woman. But the woman made no connection between Eriu and her name.

"Woman of the Danu! Do you keep my child safe inside her?"

"Inside Illyn?"

"Inside the girl that you call Illyn?"

Eriu understood then. The girl that the woman had left to die in the forest was not the girl that she saw now. That child of four years had had a clubfoot and a harelip. She had been mentally deficient and had possessed no speech. How could the woman recognize the fleet and beautiful Illyn with her quick speech and bright mind? So Eriu replied, "I do. I keep your child safe inside her. Illyn keeps her safe."

From behind the tree, she could hear the caught breath, the muffled sob.

"Then I thank you and I am in your debt."

Now Eriu stroked Illyn's hair. "I think," she said softly, "that she will see you as the bearer for Illyn, that she will believe that inside your beauty is the wounded child of the forest. She may not know you as Illyn, but she will revere you as keeper of Illyn."

Illyn sat up straight. "I do not wish to frighten her. That is how I will introduce myself. 'Keeper of Illyn,' so she will not be afraid."

Eriu felt the tears well up in her eyes. Not for the first time, she wondered if they had done the right thing in rescuing the abandoned children of the Fir Bolg, in using all of the skills of healing and ReBraiding to right them physically and mentally. Now they were children of no tribe, neither Fir Bolg nor Danu.

She felt Illyn's soft hands against her cheeks.

"We are the Children of the Braid, Eriu. Do not fear for us; we know that we belong among you and are loved."

"You are wiser than we are," said Banba. "I am sorry, little Braid sister, for my quick tongue today."

"How lucky we are that you are among us," said Fodla.

Eriu said nothing, used the sleeve of her gown to wipe away the copious tears that flowed from such large eyes.

"I will send three Danu with you, two warriors and one woman. All of them will go in Metaphor. You may take with you any other children who wish to see their tribe."

"You will not go with us?"

"No, we will watch by the sea while you are gone."

"You will look for the Invaders?"

Eriu nodded quietly.

"And may we warn the Fir Bolg of them?"

"I thought perhaps that was why you wished to go. Warn them, Illyn, but do not frighten them. The Invaders look for land or cattle or riches. Your people's country is stone and bog and far to the west and north. I do not think the newcomers will wish the harsh lands of the Fir Bolg. Only say that some are coming from the sea. And specify the south."

Illyn leaped to her feet, her twelve-year-old frame bursting with energy. "Lest they think the Fomorians have returned."

"Precisely," said Eriu.

It crossed her mind that the newcomers could prove to be as bad as the Fomor. Or worse.

16

ow long did it take to make the Silver Arm?"

Airmid, daughter of Dian Cecht, the most ancient physician of their created race, was one of the original children of the Braided Ancients.

Although she had lived now for almost three millennia and looked every day of her years, even at this great age she was busy in her lab, her eye glued to some instrument, searching out the patterns below the lens.

She leaned back and regarded the threesome for a long moment and then smiled, a toothless upfolding of the lips that seemed so reminiscent of an infant smile that Eriu turned her head to hide the answering laughter.

"Why don't you ask what you really want to know, Sisters? And did you rest as I asked you to do?" No trace of the infant in the acerbic directness of the question.

"We rested and partook of—" Eriu began, but Banba cut her off.

"We want to know if they somehow shifted time to create the arm," Banba said, ever blunt. Eriu realized with a start that a thousand years hence, Banba would be this very woman, looking infantile and cherubic, with speech as caustic and direct as a spear.

The old woman set down her instruments. "Not precisely. Why do you ask this question?"

"In the Chamber of Memory, we saw Nuada lose the arm, saw him return on the same day in the same battle with the Silver Arm upon his own." Eriu shrugged. "Biology alone would tell us that such a thing could not be possible."

"It was not; he was badly maimed. Even with all of our skills, the arm would have required some time to heal. So Dagda moved him to an alternate leaf, and Bres with him."

"Dagda himself?"

"An alternate leaf?"

The old woman sighed. "It is strange how the story of my life has become the history of your generation."

"Well it was more than three thousand years ago," said Banba.

Eriu glared at her for letting her acerbic tongue run away.

"Not to me," said Airmid. "To me, it all seems as present as you three. They were a threesome, you know. The first Council Triad. That is how they were created by the Makers, as a Threeclone. Dagda, Dian Cecht, Nuada. Like your husbands, like you, but create, not a natural birth. We say that they are the first sons of Danu, because they were the first to be created from the Braid."

"I apologize, Ancient One," said Banba, her eyes shifting to Eriu's glare. "It just seems so strange to hear them spoken of that way, as if they were present and alive. Dagda is the Father of Our Freedom; it is a large title."

"It was large work. It was Dagda who organized the people in the camps, who created the three-pronged attack. My father, Dian Cecht, coordinated the medical care so that we could be renewed and healed. Dagda was the provider, the great engineer. He created the Silver Arms. A dozen of them. Nuada, my uncle, was the chief warrior and negotiator. How he wrangled from the Creators ships and Penitents and provisions I do not know to this day. I do know that the Creators wanted to destroy the arms. As weapons they had been too effective in the BraidRising. But Dagda negotiated for those that remained. He argued that we would need them to protect ourselves in the new world and that the ancient world would be safer with them gone." She smiled again. "You have heard the Teller say that Gorias provisioned us with Invincible Spear Arms?" The Sisters nodded. "Well they did not provision. They relinquished. They gave up the arms. They did it to get rid of us."

"You were born on the ancient world?" asked Banba, hearing the tone of deep bitterness in Airmid's voice.

"I was. I was a child, I and my brother Miach, two of the Firstborn of Joining, natural births resulting from mating between two Braideds. That alone terrified the Makers, that we could reproduce all on our own apart from science. They feared that we would multiply and take over the world, long-lived, self-healing, intelligent. They feared that they had created a master race who would enslave them. They were right, of course, to fear the arms." She shook her head.

"And how many of the arms still exist?"

"Three. We never used any of them until Nuada, but we lost almost all of them. Only three remain."

"We lost them to the humans?" asked Eriu, a note of alarm in her voice.

"No, thank the Danu. When the great volcano destroyed our island in the Internal Sea, the entire armory was lost. We can only hope that it tumbled to the bottom of the sea and will never be found by humans. One can imagine what they would do with such a weapon."

"And those that remained?"

"Three arms. My father had been keeping them in his BraidRoom, had been working to alter them so that they would slip on like a glove, so that each finger would articulate a different purpose. Only those three remained, and it was one of those that Nuada used."

"But as to the alternate leaf?" said Banba, direct and hurried.

Airmid grinned. "I like you, girl. You remind me of me."

Eriu laughed aloud. "She reminds me of you as well."

"Never mind," said Airmid. She patted Eriu's hand. "You are triad leader. You are supposed to be the diplomatic one. As Nuada was. They can't all be like us." She winked at Banba, who made a face at Eriu.

"Now. The alternate leaf. Fetch me that silver spear," she said. She pointed at a thin silver needle stuck upright in a base of gold. Near the base, a series of small, bright leaves of silver and gold fluttered in the constant breeze of the recycled air.

"It was supposed to be a replica of the spear used in the Fir Bolg war. I thought it a particularly stupid thing to commemorate, so I use it to incise reminder notes to myself," said Airmid.

At this all three sisters laughed aloud.

Airmid pulled all of the bright leaves with their hieroglyphic markings up and over the top of the spear, their little rips increasing in size as she did so.

"Very well. Pay attention, girls; you may ask questions when I'm finished. Most people think of time the way you see this spear, a long straight line with a defined beginning and a defined end. That is a simplistic and inaccurate view of time."

She took a blank silver leaf from her table. On it, in the stick-letter language of their ancient world, she wrote the words "City of the Danu." She slid this slip down over the spear. A little tear increased in size as she lowered the leaf onto the spear. Next she took a golden leaf. On it she wrote, "Plain of Mag Tuiread." She slipped it down over the spear and lined it up so that it was precisely over the first slip.

"This is how it happened, is it not? At precisely the same time that we physicians were below the earth preparing for the wounded, Nuada and Bres were above the ground engaged in battle."

"Obvious enough," said Fodla.

"Now I ask you to alter your thinking. Pretend for a moment that the spear is all of the universe, all of life, all of time. On successive leaves she wrote "BraidRising," "Star Journey," "Greece." She slipped these down over the spear and fanned them so that they looked like the petals of an exotic gold and silver flower.

"What if these things are occurring always, at all times?"

"Not possible," said Banba.

"Not possible if you are standing on a single petal. But what if you could jump from petal to petal?"

Eriu shook her head. "I do not understand."

Gently Airmid reached down and caught at the bottom petal, the one she had labeled "City of the Danu." She pulled it so that it was out of alignment with the slip labeled "Plain of Mag Tuiread," so that they intersected only at the triangle of their base.

"O Danu, the monoliths." Eriu gasped it out.

Airmid clapped her hands. "My good wise girl; I am most proud of you."

"Call me stupid," said Banba

"But we still do not see," Fodla echoed.

"It works thus," Eriu began, but Airmid held up her hand.

"They are Danu; let their own good minds work upon it."

Banba and Fodla circled the spear with its bright petals. At last they looked up.

"Each petal exists in its own time, separate from the others," Fodla said slowly.

"Yet each intersects at the base in a . . . O Danu, in a triangle." Banba sounded excited now.

"And so," Eriu continued, "the wedge-shaped passage graves, the stone circles, the pyramids, the triangles we wear at our necks, all of these are doorways, or reminders of doorways, passages between . . . between what?"

"The time in which we dwell," said Airmid, "and the time as it moves here on the Green Orb."

"Why are we not taught this? Why do we not train in this timeshift?"

Airmid shrugged her shoulders. "Would you train the wind? The stars? This is how the universe is made. We discovered so on our travels across the stars. There are places out there"—she waved her hand skyward—"passages, if you will, where time shrinks and we can jump through space and time. Do you see the little tears in the paper?" The Sisters nodded in unison.

"In those passages are entrances and exits to worlds and times aplenty. Accidental doorways, if you will. We came here through one doorway to the Green Orb. It took us a very long time to harness the secret of those passages and doors. For a time we thought that Metaphor might be sufficient to protect us, but when it became clear that our knowledge and longevity were at least as frightening to the creatures here as our appearance, we knew that we would have to find a way to protect ourselves. You know that some of our brothers and sisters journeyed here to the north and built the monoliths, but they vanished. We suspect that they were destroyed because the locals feared them. And so we built these cities; we ourselves think that they are beneath the ground, but they are not; they simply rest on a different leaf of time.

"So that we might not be so alone here on the Green Orb, we opened doorways—the passage graves, the standing stones. The dwellers on the planet believe that we have armed our entrances with lightning bolts. We ourselves speak of arming the doors, but in truth we do no such thing. Instead we launch ourselves through miniature versions of the passages in space, time corridors, if you will. It is part of the reason we live so long. This petal of time in which we dwell grows slowly. Were you to live constantly among the surface folk, your life would be shortened. Just as it will be shortened by your use of the Chamber of Memory. You do not so much see our history there as reenter it. Through a tear in time. For that you will pay a price."

"We will live only as long as the humans do?" asked Banba in alarm. "They have to them only some forty of their years."

"No. No. Never so short as that. You are Braided; your biology is engineered for longevity. But shorter than now, yes."

"So . . ." Eriu moved one of the paper petals further out of alignment. "To protect our people, could we shift the timespread wider, move further out of alignment with the humans here? They would not see us or know us."

Airmid inclined her head. "Had we the knowledge, yes. We could do just that. But what we have here is the limit of what we know. We can shift in and out of times that are closely aligned. We cannot move time itself. And even then, even if we pulled the petals further out of alignment, we would be at risk at the doorways. If the invaders ever found their way through the doorways, they would find us still."

"So what you are saying is . . ." Eriu pondered for a moment. "To avoid them completely, we must close the doorways."

"Not just close, seal. Not just seal, destroy."

"And if we do, we will live all alone on this petal of time, while the humans live on theirs. There will be no contact between any of us and any of them again. Ever." Eriu's voice broke.

Airmid inclined her head. "It would be a terrible price," she said softly. "Just as there was a terrible price for the arm."

"For the Silver Arms?" asked Banba. "Where are they now? Have you hidden them?"

But Airmid's eyes had filled with tears. "Enough!" she said. She held up her hand. Then, with slow dignity, she simply left the chamber.

17

The Fir Bolg village in morning light looked worse than it had by torchlight and fire. The conical dwellings with their thatched roofs were small and squat; smoke drifted skyward through their central holes.

As the oldest Hybrid in their little group, Illyn spoke sharply to her companions. "Speak to them only in Fir Bolg! They will fear you if you address them in Danu. Do you hear me?"

The children nodded, their eyes wide.

"Do not speak of the cities or of the Danu. Do not tell them of our clothing or our food or our dwellings. All would frighten them. We are here to tell them that Invaders come from the southern sea. Reassure them that the Invaders are not Fomorians."

The children who had been allowed to make the journey were all close upon Illyn's age. The Danu had judged that children younger than nine years would not know what to say and what to keep. In truth, these children should be dead, or, if they had been kept, they would be the broken of the tribe, those who could not see or hear or speak or reason, those who had been left in the cold hills to die.

Illyn well knew that her people would perceive her as a changeling child. In truth, she was. Neither Fir Bolg nor Danu, neither human nor Braid. The Danu had been rescuing the Fir Bolg children for generations, long ago stealing healthy children away from the slave-hungry Fomorians, later rescuing the imperfect of the tribe.

In the beginning, the Fomor captives had simply returned to their tribes with fanciful tales of rescue by a race of golden-haired Fair Folk. But the Hybrids could never return. Some dwelled forever among the Danu. Others formed their own strange tribes on the Green Island, different by degrees from any humankind, and so considered strange. Illyn wondered briefly what choice she would make.

Beside her, her Danu companions untidied their hair, spread dirt on their faces and feet. They had chosen for Metaphor to look as much like the Fir Bolg as possible so as not to frighten them. Now they were attempting to look as if they had made a long overland journey, though they had simply stepped from a portal a half hour before dawn.

Illyn smiled. They were kind and careful to a fault, these Danu. She did not wish to disappoint them with the knowledge that their nuances of disguise would be lost on her people. She sighed. Sometimes she felt so lonely. A creature of no one and nowhere. An old, old mind in a young and ill-fitting body.

The village began to bustle.

"Come," said Illyn. "And remember your lessons."

They moved in among the villagers. The Fir Bolg were slow to react to the strangers among them. Then suddenly, buffeted by a wind of gutturals and shouts, the Danu were surrounded by Fir Bolg men, their heavy spears in hand. The men tilted their heads, assessing the group, trying to recognize those they could never recognize.

Illyn spoke.

"I am Keeper of Illyn, daughter of Degna. Call her to me." This she said in a voice that was at once commanding and kind.

Degna arrived between two warriors, her legs trembling with fear. She swallowed and nodded. "This is she; she keeps my Illyn safe inside her."

The warriors lowered the spears. "Why do you return to us?"

"These children are also keepers." Illyn gestured around her. "We live far south of here; it may be that we cannot return for a time; these . . . keepers would like to see their parents."

"Why will you not return?" Degna asked.

"We have seen raiders approaching from the sea."

A collective gasp arose from the Fir Bolg; they began to chatter in tones of fear.

"They are not Fomor," said Illyn, but her child's voice was lost in the deeper noise of the tribe. One of the Danu struck his spear on the ground. A spark of blue lightning shot from its point. The tribe stilled, moved back from the visitors and away.

"They are not Fomorians," said Illyn quietly.

"This you know?" asked Degna. She seemed to have gathered the courage to function as the speaker for the tribe. Illyn felt a little surge of pride.

"This we know."

"These that you dwell with." Degna gestured at the disguised Danu. Evidently she was not fooled by their Metaphor. "They are knowers of many things?"

"They know more things than you and I have ever known," said Illyn softly.

Degna nodded her head. "Long ago, they say, we went to war with them; they were Fair Folk. The stories say that they came among us from doorways in the stones."

Illyn said nothing at all.

"It is also said that long ago there was a great war with the Fomor. It is said that these folk defeated the Fomor and drove them to the northern sea. Is this true?"

One of the Danu spoke up. "It is true, woman of the Fir Bolg."

Degna cleared her throat. "Then we are in your debt not only for these keepers but for driving the dark ones from our shores. We will trust that you will do the same with these newcomers."

Degna looked around at her tribesmen as if making up her mind about something. Then she stepped forward. Gently, timorously, she drew Illyn into her embrace. A little gasp arose from the gathered Fir Bolg. While Illyn was in her embrace, Degna whispered in her ear. "That is why I left you there, between the stones wrapped in the warm pelts of wolves. I knew that they would find you there; I wished for them to take you among them. I could not bear it if you had been taken by the Fomor."

Illyn felt her eyes fill with tears. "For that I thank you . . . Maither," she whispered back.

"You will keep my Illyn safe?" Degna asked.

"Here, inside me." Illyn gestured at her heart.

"She was not . . . right," said Degna. "But she was mine. I did not want to give her away. She was not right."

"I know," said Illyn softly. "But she is now."

18

CEOLAS MOURNS

I am the sea for drowning
I am the dark night
I am a wave of sorrow
I am the cold, dark water
I weep more salt tears than the sea
I shall never cease weeping.

A strong wind moved across the headland and the full moon was threaded with clouds. The threesome stared out to sea, unencumbered by Metaphor. The moon slipped from behind its scarf; it made a silvery path along the water.

"I love this beautiful isle," Eriu sighed.

"Listen where they sing again," said Fodla softly.

"Some sorrow moves them," Eriu said thoughtfully. "Twice now we have heard their songs, and both were sad."

"Sorrow is what they deserve," said Banba. "They should have stayed in their homeplace."

"Banba! I do not wish ill on them; I wish only that change will not come. Though it always does."

"Sister, do not abandon hope. They may not be as the Fomor were," said Fodla.

"Or perhaps they will turn around and go back," said Banba. "Perhaps some sorrow has befallen them on the journey."

"Well then, let us look," said Eriu.

Eriu held her arms before her, formed her fingers: Journey, Children of the Braid, the Braid itself. She raised her hands, felt Banba and Fodla close hands around her own. She closed her eyes and drew a deep breath, opened them. She gazed out over the water in silence. Behind her Fodla and Banba chanted the deep sounds of vision.

The ships were within a day of landing. Eriu sped among them, searching for Ith. Under the moonlight on the deck of the last ship she found Amergin. He plucked at the strings of his harp. His face seemed hollowed out, empty. Dark bruised circles outlined his eyes. As before, he seemed to sense her once again. He looked up.

"Skena?" he whispered.

Eriu felt his pain wash over her. What tragedy had befallen these voyagers? This was not the Amergin of just a few days ago. Eriu filled with pity. She sighed aloud.

"You have seen them again?" asked Fodla.

"I have. Something terrible has befallen them."

"And still they progress toward us?"

Eriu nodded. "Unless they go down in the sea, they will make landfall within the next day or so," she said softly.

"And we are still unprepared," said Fodla.

"Well, we shall hope they go down in the sea," said Banba.

"Banba!" This time Eriu and Fodla spoke at once.

Banba waved her hand. "You know that we are all thinking it. Will they be warlike? What will they wish of us? Fear moves through the Danu like this light moves across the water. And to think that we invited them."

"We did not invite," said Fodla. "We sent the message that Ith asked us to send. We greeted them as we had greeted Greeks and Romans, Egyptians and Persians, with a message of peace and warning."

"Ith said that they would not come," said Eriu. "I took him to be a man of his word. And I can find him nowhere on the ships."

Banba shrugged. "He is an elder. Perhaps he is seasick below."

"Or perhaps there are warriors among them who overrode his word," said Banba softly.

"Then we, too, should be more warlike. Be fierce against them." The voice came from behind them, nasal and smoky.

The Sisters turned as one. Morrigu stood behind them, the three sisters cloaked in black, their gowns shifting and swaying in the sea wind, their huge black eyes reflecting the silver moonlight.

"Banbh, Nemhain, Macha." Eriu addressed them separately with a formal nod. "We of the Council Triad are willing to listen to your wisdom."

"Wisdom, is it?" said Macha. She smiled, her lips folding up into a rictus that looked almost painful. "When have any of the Danu considered us wise?"

Eriu resisted swallowing. She looked at them each in turn. Panic rose in her throat when she met the eyes of Nemhain, but she fought it back. Panic is what Nemhain engendered. Everywhere she went, she seemed able to draw upon any creature's worst fear, bring it to the surface, strengthen it until the poor victim gibbered in terror, made terrible decisions based upon that panic.

Panic was not what Eriu felt when she regarded Banbh; rather, she felt revulsion. It was rumored among her people that Banbh's favorite use of Metaphor was as carrion feeders, ravens and vultures, birds of darkness who fed on the blood of the fallen.

And then there was Macha, their primary sister. She was beautiful, although she in no way resembled the People of the Danu or the Penitents. She was taller even than her sisters. Her long black hair floated and shifted in the breeze, and her dark almond-shaped eyes gave away nothing, reflected everything. Eriu could see herself in them now, small and pale, her cap of cloudy curls ruffling in the wind, her eyes wide and startled.

Macha was the mistress of Metaphor. Even now, Eriu did not know if she looked upon the real creature or some image Macha wished her to see. Eriu herself had seen Macha disappear into the shapes of wolves or eagles and then lope away into the forest or soar above the earth. All in Metaphor, perfectly sustained.

"You can think of nothing else to say?" Macha asked, the smoky voice pouring from her. "Perhaps that is because you wonder what the Makers called into existence when they created us, when the Raveners emerged from the Braid."

Eriu decided that honesty would serve her best with this trio. She nodded. "I have wondered it often, Morrigu, what the Makers called from the Braid when they called forth the Raveners, for you are as unlike the Danu as are Fomor or Fir Bolg."

Morrigu shrugged as one. "We are what we are," said Macha. "But I do find your honesty . . . fearless and appealing, Eriu. Perhaps they called to some darkness in themselves. Some . . . hunger. For we are always hungry." She smiled. "Surely they amplified some fierceness in themselves, for the Raveners are fierce, and the Danu . . . well." She shrugged again, pitying them their weakness, Eriu supposed. She decided again on directness.

"So how would you deal with these Invaders?"

"Bring the Silver Arms from hiding. Confuse them while they are still at sea. Destroy the Invaders before they reach the shore. Or if they come to shore, destroy them all. Leave the cleanup to the Morrigu." She grinned her wolfish grin. "We have the preservation of the Danu to think of; all others must perish before that need."

"You have not destroyed the Fir Bolg."

She shrugged. "Well, they are like cats or dogs, are they not? Simple but domesticated. We enjoy dallying with them sometimes"—here Nemhain snickered—"but we do not harm them because there would be no point. Of these newcomers we know not. They could be like Fomorians."

"We remember the final battle with the Fomor," said Banbh. Her voice was harsh, deep, almost masculine. She actually licked her lips; the dark almond eyes flared suddenly, as if a fire had been lit deep within them.

"Hush!" Macha commanded. "You go too far as always."

Eriu was startled. It was the first time she had ever realized that Macha was keeping the sisters in check, holding them like the reins on a pair of horses. Something like pity arose in her.

Macha must have sensed it, must have felt it wafting toward her. She stepped toward Eriu.

"Take my hands," she whispered, softly, gently. Eriu put her hands into the long hands of the Macha. "Ravener and Danu," she whispered. "At last! This is how it should have been from the first, our two races linked in the Braid, no separation between us. See what we know."

Suddenly it all came pouring into Eriu's mind, the BraidRising, the smoking weapons, the maimed and the dead, the screams of both Danu and Makers, the long journey, the weeping of the Ancients at their exile, the tumble of the Danu into the sea when the volcano erupted, the Fir Bolg war, the agony of Nuada's severed arm.

She staggered back from the weight of it, held her hands up in the moonlight. They bore the marks of burning.

"This is what we contain," said Macha softly, her voice pitched low.

"It is a terrible burden," said Eriu. She stepped forward suddenly, compelled. She placed her long, slender hand against Macha's cheek. "I am sorry that you bear it."

The Morrigu gasped aloud.

"We revel in it," said Nemhain.

"It feeds us," said Banbh in her strange, masculine voice.

Only Macha said nothing, her eyes fixed on Eriu.

"You are the fulcrum," Eriu whispered. It was so suddenly clear that she wondered that she had never understood it before. Macha kept the other two in balance. She contained the dark; she repelled the dark. She caused sorrow; she kept sorrow at bay. She engendered evil; she kept evil at bay.

Macha blinked, nodded once. "We will assist you with these Invaders," Macha said.

"You will not destroy them."

"Until the time comes that you require their destruction. We will assist."

"Do you know where the arms are hidden?"

Macha made no reply. She touched the triangle at her neck with its spiraled vines. Wolf, eagle, darkness, light, void. Gone.

Eriu dropped to the ground.

"By the Danu!" Fodla rushed to her side.

"What was that? What just happened?" Banba kept batting at the air where they had been, as though she did not understand how they had vanished, had not been vanishing in just that way all of her life.

"That was one of the results our ancient Makers had not counted on. They called upon the Braid; they used its secrets. They did not know that to call upon the Braid is to also call the Antithesis into being."

"Terrifying. And they live among us."

"Usually silently and secretively. How often do you see them?"

"Almost never. Few Councils. No ceremonies or healings. I was shocked to see them at the Great Council."

Eriu nodded. "They are the Shadow."

"Of what?" asked Fodla.

"Of sorrow. Of war. Of darkness and evil. Of our ancestors. Of us. Of our own internal darkness."

"And now they propose to assist us?"

"They propose, I think, that we will need to bring battle against these Invaders. They will be there to simplify that process."

"To provide the darkness," said Fodla.

"And will we?"

"Will we what?"

"Call up darkness against the Invaders?"

"I do not know. Our ancestors surely were forced to war with the Fomor."

"Then we need to know how and why," said Fodla.

"And we need to check on Illyn's journey," said Eriu. The very mention of Illyn's name made her feel better, as though she were grounded in something simple and good.

She faced back out to sea, caught at her sisters' hands. Together, they touched the triangles at their throats.

At sea, off the southern coast of the island, a group of voyagers saw a flash of white light, followed by a blue ovoid.

"Heat lightning," said one of the Greek sailors, though the night was cold.

In the stern, Amergin looked up from the strings of Ceolas.

"Skena?" he whispered, his voice half strangled with sorrow.

19

"Why did the Fir Bolg give away their children?" asked Illyn. She was seated with the Sisters in a garden near a small water fountain, dipping apples into sweet sauces.

Eriu had known that this day would come, that Illyn would need to know why she had been abandoned so long ago. She had practiced her answer for many years.

"Long ago," she said softly, "long, long before you were born, there came a time when no summer came here to the island. The trees did not grow, nor give birth to leaves. No flowers budded forth in spring and no berries grew on the bushes. The animals grew thin; many of them died. There was nothing for the Fir Bolg to eat."

"Just one summer?" asked Illyn.

"No, sweeting; it lasted for eighteen summers. The Fir Bolg starved; it was cold all the time. In some summers, snow fell. So when they could no longer raise their children, the Fir Bolg began to select some to leave on the mountains and in the cold rivers, that the tribe might be thinned and those who were left could survive."

"But if it happened long before my birth, why are they still leaving the children?"

Eriu drew breath, felt her way carefully through the answer.

"The life of the Fir Bolg is hard. Sometimes children are born to them who are special—different from the other children of the tribe. The Fir Bolg have a memory of the cold years and so they leave their children for us so that we can care for them and keep them well."

"And so they save us."

"Yes," said Eriu. "Exactly."

"My mother saved me."

"She did."

Illyn pondered this for a moment. "Eriu, what would cause winter in summer? Did the Fir Bolg do something to anger the Mother?"

"No, child, surely not. The Mother loves her children. She does not punish them. Do you remember the story of the Journey of Exile of our people?"

Illyn nodded.

"Do you remember our first home on the island in the south?"

"Yes, the one that sank into the sea. Oh . . . I see . . . a volcano caused the winter."

"It may be so," said Eriu. "Or it may be that a . . . star . . . fell from the sky and scattered the cold into the air. After our own island was destroyed, the Danu have studied these things. Sometimes there is danger in the Green Orb itself."

"Is that why the Fir Bolg feared the Fomor so? Because they brought another kind of darkness?"

"Oh, you grow wiser by the day, little daughter. But we of the Danu feared them too. The Fomorians were the scourge of the Green Isle for many a year. They brought much grief to both Fir Bolg and Danu."

"How could they have any sway over the Danu?"

"Well, they had help from one of our own," said Banba as she worked a piece of apple.

"A traitor?" asked Illyn with a gasp.

"So we have always been told. But the histories have shown us a different picture," said Eriu. "Perhaps we should know more."

"Why?" asked Illyn.

"To know history is to profit from its lessons in this time. We learned of at least one way to deal with the Invaders just by watching the Fir Bolg war."

"You began the war on my people?" Illyn was on her feet gasping.

Banba shook her head at Eriu. "So I am not the only one with a loose and simple tongue."

Eriu sighed. She held out her hand to the little girl.

"Sweeting, we will watch the histories and we will tell you the truth of them ourselves. Then you can judge for yourself."

"Can I watch with you in the Chamber of Memory?" asked Illyn.

"You cannot," said Eriu, "for there are . . . dangers in the chamber that—"

"You are in danger?"

"Of course not," said Fodla.

"Do not be angry with us, Illyn," said Banba. "Eriu protects you only; she will not keep the truth from you."

"I know that," said Illyn. "Eriu only fears that she will disappoint me." She turned to Eriu. "You could not lose my love; you are my little mother."

All three sisters gaped openmouthed at Illyn. Banba walked to her and took the little face between her hands. "Where did you come from, Little Wisdom Mother?" She turned her around and around, then made a show of patting the air around her. "What doorway did you come through?"

Illyn giggled, a little girl again. "You are always silly, Banba. Call me for the memories when you are finished." She flounced away.

Eriu turned to her sisters. She arched her eyebrows in amazement and surprise. The gesture made her ears go up and down and the feathered tips looked as though they might take flight.

Banba and Fodla burst into laughter.

From the front of the group Illyn spoke again. "Don't make faces behind my back; it isn't nice."

A door opened in the wall and she disappeared up the hall.

"She enters that period in humans when they are most dangerous," said Fodla. "I have seen it before in Hybrid children."

"Nearly as dangerous as Morrigu," said Banba. "I certainly feel small and stupid."

"That is what they do," said Eriu.

"For how long?"

"For years."

"O Danu, spare us," said Banba.

The walls of the room shimmered and became viscous. From the northern sea a fleet of ships moved toward the land, their tall prows carved and dangerous, the rhythmic drop and rise of their oars the only sound on the water.

They drew up on the beaches. From them stepped the Fomor.

"By the Braid. Look at them!" Banba hissed.

From the boats stepped men larger than any of them in the chamber had ever seen, human or otherwise. Most of them were seven feet or taller, broad of shoulder, with thick, muscular legs. Their hair was long, red and gold, and they were bearded and mustached. Together they bore more hair upon their bodies than the Danu owned collectively. They wore worked leather tunics and they carried huge battleaxes in hand. Long broadswords cascaded down their backs, and their belts bristled with dirks and daggers.

"Each man his own army," breathed Banba.

"No wonder Illyn's people feared them," whispered Fodla. "I fear them, even now."

"Our people feared them as well," said Eriu.

"But for Bres the Beautiful," said Banba. "See where he comes."

The Fomorian Invaders had built a small fire on the beach, its flames hidden behind the cliff wall. There they were grilling fish on long skewers. Bres came into their midst.

"So. You return to us, little brother, king of the Danu."

Bres came into view, his face lighted by the flames.

"I do," he said softly. "Not king but Council Leader."

"To us, you are their king."

Bres preened a little in the praise.

"And you have asked your mother for the truth of the story?" one of the Fomor asked.

"I have wrested it from her. She admits that I am of you, just as you said. Danu and Fomor."

"A blind man could see the likeness. Balor himself could see that you are one of us, a handsome Fomor lad."

From the darkness came a huge, rumbling laugh. A shadow detached itself from the deeper darkness and unfolded. Taller and taller it grew. Ponderous and fearsome, it moved from the darkness into the firelight. It was a man, more than nine feet tall. His hair was black, the planes of his face hidden by a massive mustache and beard. One eye was hidden behind a patch. He approached Bres.

Though Bres was the tallest by far of the Danu, this giant was twice his size. He leaned down and down, peered into the face of Bres the Beautiful. Bres did not shrink back.

"I remember you, boy. The spawn of Eri."

"Eri's son."

"And ours, boy. And ours." The giant laughed. "We are proud of that boy. Proud of you. I am told you are king of the Danu."

"Only Council Leader. And I think they plot to take that from me."

"They did not like our Fomor boy?" The giant sounded angry at this, as if he were personally offended.

"I am not Danu. Some say I do not make decisions that befit their people."

"What decisions do you make?"

"I have asked them for chambers, for fine clothing, for some of the jewels of their travels."

"And they begrudge you these? We begrudge our kings nothing!" The giant shook his head. "I remember the Danu well. They came here long ago, built cities on the plains. They were a people full of themselves, truly. All self-importance and wisdom. This was long, long ago, before these boys here were born. When the Nemedians dwelled here. Weak fools those! A puny race of no numbers. We demanded of them their corn and their cattle and their children, and they gave them all. We were rich in both food and slaves. And then one day we came to raid and they were gone. They had a king—Britan, I think his name was. The rumor was that he went east." The giant shrugged. "No matter.

"So we needed more volunteers, and there were your mother's people, ripe for the picking. I did so love Danu slaves. My favorite of all the peoples we have raided. They knew how to do so much and they seemed so healthy. I suppose we overused them some; we were surprised that they died as easily as they did. And oh, those Danu women; so small and light that you could bounce them on your lap. I did it often, boy! I'll wager you do too. And then on one of our raiding parties your little mother escaped us. It was a great loss to us. A great loss." He shook the massive head.

"Danu women do not mate with me," Bres said.

"You are large enough. Simply take them."

"Danu women do not find my looks pleasing."

"How could this be?" said Banba. "I find his looks pleasing. I have said so."

Eriu shrugged. "This was long, long ago. Our ancestors had only just come here. When he was born among them, think how strange he looked. And Eri. Arriving from nowhere with a strange story of having lived among giants. At the very least Bres would have been regarded as suspect. From what he says, it seems that he became greedy soon after the Council Triad chose him."

"Nuada seemed to love him."

"Then why did he betray Nuada?"

"We shall see," said Eriu.

In the firelight, Bres shifted from foot to foot. He lowered his head. "What did you bring?" he asked.

"You liked what we brought you on our first visit?" asked the giant. "The jewels and the daggers?"

"I liked the woman."

"Oh, lad, we bring lavish gifts for those of our own. Lads!" he called. Some of the giant men stepped forward with bags. They spilled jewels and gold before him. One carried forward a sword, richly incised with symbols.

"I thank you," said Bres. "But these are not necessary." He kept looking toward the darkness.

"They are our gifts to the great king of the Danu," the giant said softly; "you will offend us if you do not take them." He jerked his head back toward the shadows. "Don't worry, boy. We have our special gift for you. Well, a pair of special gifts really."

"A pair?" said Bres. His eyes flicked toward the shadows. He licked his lips.

"Better than before, eh? We will provide more each time we come."

"What do you need in return?" So Bres had not lost his senses entirely.

From the darkness came the sound of feminine laughter, followed by a low, sweet moan. Bres closed his eyes.

"We need only the simplest thing, boy. When first we came among your people, they lived in villages on the land. We took slaves and children from them; such are necessary to manage our farms when we are at sea. Now these Danu have disappeared. Where did they go?"

"I will not give you slaves or children!" said Bres. He turned to go.

"Oh no no!" the giant said hastily. "You mistake me. We will find our servants elsewhere. But that requires money. Levy a tax on your people. You can explain to them why you do so; it will keep us from them. Let your mother speak to the assembly. She will tell them well. They will accept the tax, I think." He smiled, a slow baring of his yellow and scraggly teeth.

"And then you will go."

"We have a camp on Tober Mor. From time to time we will return to collect that tax and to bring gifts to you. After all, we are proud of our kinsman, the king of the Danu!"

Bres thought for a time; from the darkness came the soft sound of moans and giggles. At last he nodded. "A tax is fair; it is really all that I myself have asked for," he said.

The one-eyed giant slapped his knee. "Good lad." He signaled with his hand. From the shadows beyond the boats stepped two women, both Fomor, taller than Bres. As they approached they threw off their voluminous cloaks. They were naked but for two golden girdles that rode at their hips. Their breasts were large and pendulous. They wrapped their arms around each other and flicked their tongues as they approached. Then they surrounded Bres, nuzzling and undulating against him.

"The girdles are yours," said the giant, his voice teasing. "And of course what comes with them." He waved off toward the darkness. "Go and enjoy; they have many plans for you, these two. And we will bring more on our next visit. Just you tell us what you want."

"I will," said Bres. His arms were already encircling those of the girls. He was nuzzling at the white breasts.

"Well now we know how he was suborned." Eriu rested her hand on the stone; the picture froze on Bres, his arms around the pale women of the north, the giant looking on. She sighed. "We must blame ourselves, surely. Among the Danu, he was pariah."

"Blame his appetites; obviously they were large," said Banba, her voice caustic.

The door slid open and Illyn entered bearing a tray with steaming mugs of liquid. She gasped at the frozen picture; at her inattention the steaming mugs began to slide to the edge of the tray. Banba launched herself from her chair to catch the tray. She moaned aloud at the motion.

Her cry reminded Illyn of her burden; she righted the tray and lowered it carefully to the table.

"Banba!" said Fodla. "What ails?"

"It is my knees. They actually . . . ached . . . as I stood from the chair. I have never experienced such a thing."

"Time lies upon them like the damp, Sister," Eriu said carefully so that she would not frighten the little girl. "The . . . damp . . . of the room wears at your . . . bones, Banba."

Illyn nodded. "Airmid said that the damp of the chamber might give you aches and pains. She sends this tisane to ease them. She says to drink it all and right away." She handed a mug to each of the Sisters, but her eyes returned to the picture.

"Am I in danger to see it?" asked Illyn. "No, sweeting," said Eriu. "It no longer moves in time."

"Will I have those?" asked Illyn.

"Those . . . breasts?" asked Eriu. She drank the potion, sighed with relief as its warmth spread through her. Among her own people, the indicators of female gender were small and subtle. She had seen larger markings among humans. She looked at Illyn, took the question seriously.

"Stand before me," she said. Illyn complied. Eriu shook her head. "No," she said. "You are slight of bone. Remember your mother."

"She was slender and tall."

"Then so will you be."

"Good," said Illyn. "Those are . . ."

"Overwhelming," said Banba. "Like the mountains of the Green Isle. But obviously an interesting climb for Bres."

Illyn giggled. Mating was no secret among the Danu, nor was it among the Fir Bolg, but Banba made it all seem funny and dry.

"Well, Illyn, are we safe now?" asked Banba, seeking to distract the little girl.

"Safe from the Fomor?" asked Illyn.

The picture faded from the walls, returning the chamber to its stony appearance.

"No, safe from your tart tongue of earlier," Banba replied.

"As safe as we are from yours," Illyn answered innocently.

All three sisters burst into laughter.

"Oh, keep her with us always," Fodla said to Eriu. "She saves us the trouble."

Banba made a face. "Perhaps our little daughter just sees the wisdom of being just like me. She emulates her hero."

"What say you, Illyn?" asked Eriu. "Will your voice be Banba's voice?"

Illyn was quiet for a moment. Then a smile crept across her face. "I will take the sweetness of Fodla's voice and the wisdom of Eriu's voice and the bluntness of Banba's voice and I will speak in a voice all my own."

At this all three sisters applauded.

"By the Danu," said Banba. "I believe that you will!"

"My mother found a voice," said Illyn. "She told me that she wrapped me and placed me among the stones so you would find me."

"So she did," said Eriu, "for you were bundled into wolfskins and laid between the portals of a stone circle. And someone had surrounded you with stones, perhaps so the wolves would not find you."

"And which of you found me?"

"I did," said Eriu. "On the night of a full moon."

"She said that she had arranged it so that the Danu would find me. She called you the Fair Folk."

"Then I'm glad that we could return her gift to her."

"Gift?"

"You are my gift," said Eriu, seriously. "The gift your mother gave to me. The best gift of all my life."

Illyn kissed the tiny woman's cheek gently. "Thank you, Little Mother," she whispered.

Eriu drew her arms around Illyn and hugged her.

"My mother said that she did not wish the Fomorians to find me. What made them so terrible, Sisters?"

"Well, for one thing that they were tall and hairy with long beards, bad teeth, and great bouncing breasts," said Banba.

Illyn laughed aloud. "You make it sound like the beards and the breasts go together."

"Maybe they did; maybe that was what everyone found so scary."

"Banba!" said Eriu. She shook her head, then answered seriously. "From what we have seen of them, they took what they wanted—people, treasure, anything. And they were not above trickery and deceit."

163

"There is one thing we do not know," said Fodla.

"Why Nuada was rendered king again," said Banba.

"But I am willing to venture that we know one who knows," said Eriu quietly.

20

You restored Nuada's arm."

"My father refashioned the Silver Arm for Nuada. He fit it to the stump of Nuada's arm."

"No. You restored Nuada's arm. His biological arm. You have the knowledge of the Braid."

Airmid lifted her chin. "My brother restored his arm. Miach. I helped him; I hid them and I hid the work. I am proud that I did." Her eyes dropped in shame. "I am only sorry that Miach paid the price." She sighed, a sound full of old sorrows. "And Nuada."

"Nuada died because of the Silver Arm?" Banba shook her head. "I did not remember that from the memories."

"Why must you ask me? These memories are painful," the Ancient woman snapped.

Eriu placed her hand gently on the woman's arm. "We are looking for the way to protect our people from these Invaders. For the past two days we have done nothing but try to study and learn. We are young; forgive us."

"You are more than a thousand years old by human reckoning of time. You are only the third generation born on this world."

"Well for the first three hundred years we were children," said Banba in exasperation. "Then, in our adolescence we were married to the Triad of Brothers that they might . . . train us . . . in the duties of Council of the Braid."

"They did not train you very well, did they?"

"To be fair," said Eriu, "they trained us well in the Journey of Exile and the duties of Council. They paid little attention to the history of this island. By their time, the Danu and the Fir Bolg lived in peace and the Fomor had disappeared. What was to fear on this isle?"

"Well, they had the previous Triad to thank for that, didn't they? Dagda, Nuada, and my father, Dian Cecht."

Banba started to speak, but Eriu held up her hand. "And so we come to you to learn of that, Ancient," Eriu said gently. "Your wisdom and your memory contain it. But if the memories are too difficult for you, we can access them in Lia Fail Chamber."

"Have you begun to experience pain in the chamber?"

"We have," said Banba.

Airmid sighed. "I am a selfish old woman. The Brothers wished to protect you from the price that the Chamber of Memory exacts. Now I am trying to protect myself from the price that my memories exact when my telling will limit your time in the chamber. I will tell you what you want to know. Ask, Eriu."

"We are not sure what to ask, Ancient. We have a new set of Invaders approaching. Should we simply seal the doorways shut between us? Should we bring out the Silver Arms? How should we prepare? We look to history to teach us now. And to you, Ancient. But we do not wish to make you sad."

Airmid sighed, a great wafting of breath. "Oh, Eriu, I have been sad for more than a thousand years. I will tell you what I know; the rest you will have to see in Lia Fail. Perhaps what I know can help you to decide." She shrugged. She pressed a small triangle on her table, and a picture projected on the blank wall of her lab of three tiny men, pale and silver-haired with huge eyes and upspiraled ears.

"There they are: The First Council Triad. They were Braid-Men, a Threeclone. Dagda, the Father of Our Freedom; Nuada, the first chief of Council; Dian Cecht, physician and healer, my father. They called themselves Brothers in the Braid. They were like you three, inseparable and strong. Because of them, Council is always headed now by a triad in each generation."

She shook her head.

"When the Fir Bolg cut off Nuada's arm, my father affixed the Silver Arm to Nuada's stump. I remember well how bravely Nuada bore the pain! The stump was barely healed; even timeshift had not given it enough time, and the arm rubbed the skin until it was raw and bleeding. But back he went among the Fir Bolg. He fought and negotiated as though he were whole and strong. There was a man of the Danu! But when he returned among us, the stump made him ineligible to be Triad chief. That was the way. Physical imperfection was unnecessary and therefore unacceptable. The kingship was given to Bres the Beautiful, whose mother had returned to us after many months as captive of the Fomor."

"Why Bres?" asked Banba. "Why not Dagda or your father?"

"My father was a healer, unsuited to the job. As for Dagda, he bore a weakness that none of our people knew. In the BraidRising on the Homeworld, Dagda had been blinded in one eye. My father replaced the eye with one so realistic that you could not tell, but Dagda was unfit to rule and knew it well. So he . . . provided. Anything the Danu needed, he found it, made it, wheedled it, purchased it. That is why even now the people call him the Great Provider."

"But surely your father had knowledge of the ReBraiding. He was the Great Physician. Why did he not replace the eye with a real eye?"

"That was my father's weakness. Or perhaps his strength," said Airmid. "He believed that no ReBraiding should be permitted by the law. He said that by Braiding, UnBraiding, and ReBraiding, the Homeworld had brought upon itself its own downfall, creating a perfect race and then treating it with fear and loathing. He vowed that he would never UnBraid or ReBraid again."

"And Dagda and Nuada? They agreed?" asked Eriu.

"Dagda agreed. He had been the architect of the BraidRising. He had suffered greatly for being a Braided One."

"And Nuada?"

"We persuaded Nuada."

"We?"

"Miach and I. My brother." She tapped her console. The picture appeared of a handsome man of the Danu. Airmid stared at it for so long that Eriu began to suspect she had forgotten their presence.

"You persuaded him, Ancient?" she said gently.

"We had no choice," Airmid said in a broken voice. "The Fomor came below."

"Below?! Here into our cities?" The sisters were thunderstruck.

Airmid nodded. "Few know it now, and those who know are silent on the subject. Why terrify the Danu? The Fomor are gone."

"Bres showed them the way?"

"He did and more. He began by allowing them to tax us. The tax was not heavy, and he claimed that he had negotiated with them that the tax would be sufficient, that it would keep them from our door."

"This we have seen in the Lia Fail Chamber," said Fodla.

The Ancient shrugged. "Then you know that when the Danu first moved to the Green Isle we lived on the surface. We did not live in fear; the Fir Bolg war was over. We lived in peace with the Bog People. We offered them healing and food and knowledge of provision. They spoke often of the Fomor, but we had never seen them. Then one night, in darkness, the Fomor slipped among us. In the morning, dozens of our people were gone. Just gone. Men, women, and children. At first we suspected the Fir Bolg. We took a war party among them, but when we arrived we found them in chaos and disarray, women screaming for their vanished children, men brandishing spears and shouting vengeance for their missing women. That was when we knew that the Fomorians had come among them as well."

"And so we built our cities beneath the surface?" asked Banba.

"Or so it seems to us; they are on a different petal of time. But we left the doorways between the worlds open. By that time, we had some obligation to the Fir Bolg. We could not abandon them. The years of no summer had come; the Fir Bolg were starving, their children freezing to death. Oh, if only we could have closed the doors! Nuada would be among us still. And my brother Miach."

Eriu lifted her arm across the Ancient's shoulders. "Even we Danu cannot see far into what the future will bring."

"No," said the Ancient softly. "That is how the Mother protects us from sorrow, I suppose."

Banba had been quietly thinking over the story. "And so when Eri returned heavy with child and gave birth to that redheaded boy, you all knew that he was Fomor."

"We knew. But we decided that he was half Fomor, half Danu. We held him in our regard like the race of Penitents and Exiles, the ancestors of you three. We raised him in that way among us."

"And yet no Danu women would mate with him."

"No. Nor marry. Eri herself, his mother, had seen to that. For her stories of her Fomorian captors terrified her listeners, their immense size and the painful ways they had used their Danu women captives." Airmid shook her head. "She doomed her own boy to loneliness among us with the tales. Only Nuada truly loved him; to Nuada he was like a younger brother."

"And he betrayed Nuada."

"He did," the Ancient said softly. "That was when Miach and I decided. After he betrayed us, we knew that we had to do something, that the Fomorians would enslave or kill us all if we did not find a way. So we called Nuada to us. We proposed to ReBraid his arm, to grow for him a true arm. But we would need his cooperation to do that. He declined. But then the Fomor came below. On the next day Nuada came to us; he agreed to our work."

She began to weep in earnest now, her hands clutching her table, but she kept talking through her sobs.

"My brother put all of himself into that work. All of his love for the Danu. And when the arm was ready—I remember it well—he incanted, 'Let this be joined sinew to sinew and nerve to nerve so that there is movement and feeling in every joint.' We worked the arm then, exercising it, submerging it in water. And when it was ready, Nuada stood before the assembly, whole and complete, and the Danu named him as their king."

She was silent.

"And Bres? And your father, Dian Cecht? And Miach?"

"Go and see it, Daughters. Uncolored by my own beliefs or by the tricks of memory. See it as true history. And when you have seen it, tell me if I judged aright. If you say no, I request that I receive the same penalty as my brother. It is, perhaps, what I deserve."

21

Now you come up here," said Bres, drunkenly. He caught at the hair of one of the three Fomor women who were swarming over him and pulled her up. She started to put her lips to his, but he flicked his thumb and forefinger over her nipple and pulled it into his mouth. He licked and swirled at the breast and sighed in satisfaction.

"We've done all right by you then, lad?"

Bres turned lazily toward the side of the room where the giant Balor was bouncing a woman up and down on his lap. His head rested comfortably against the wall; his giant arms supported the woman as she bounced. He had removed the patch from his missing eye; the blue-white orb was grotesque in appearance.

"You have, Balor. The mead, the women, the gifts." Bres sighed lazily as one of the threesome bent to her labors. "I think I could never have enough of women."

"Boy, I say again that it's not right that these Danu women won't mate with you. And head of Council? What is that? You should be king."

He grunted with satisfaction and lifted the woman from his lap, pointed down at Bres. "Take care of our lad there; he needs more of you," he said, and she scurried to join the group.

Balor quaffed a giant tankard of mead. "They've paid their tax, but they've paid you no respect. You are Fomorian; they owe you respect."

"This mating is fine," Bres said. "They will never mate with me."

"It's a shame," said Balor softly. "The little Danu women." He shook his head. "Light as a feather. Bounce on the lap. You could even take one to wife;

she would be smaller than you and half like you. You deserve a Danu wife, lad. Or several Danu women if you wish. You deserve whatever you wish."

"Why should I need a Danu wife when I have all of these?" Bres ran his hands lazily over the flanks of one of the women, bounced the large breasts of another.

"These do my bidding," said Balor. He clapped his hands; the foursome sat up and moved away. Bres raised himself drunkenly on his elbows, his face suffused with lust and anger.

"But a little Danu woman or two," Balor continued, "now they would do your bidding. We would see to that, your brother Fomorians. We could take a selection of Danu, men, women, children. You would have wives, servants, slaves, all Danu. All saying 'Yes, my lord.' It's what they owe you, nothing less."

Bres closed his eyes, the look on his face greedy. "How could this be done?" he asked.

"Can you get us into their cities?"

"Easily," said Bres. "But I wouldn't want them harmed."

"No harm," said Balor. "Just a selection of ten or so. All for you. All yours to command. Consider what women you would want. We would collect them for you. As many as you need. We will build you a great lodge on Tober Mor. There you will rule your household."

"No harm?"

"None."

Bres watched the Fomor women, who had begun to nuzzle each other. He moaned a little.

"Lad, are the cities beautiful?" Balor asked.

"Most beautiful," Bres said distractedly. "Return these to me, Balor: I am full to bursting. Come; you said they were a gift."

"And treasure?"

"Great treasure. Now may I have them?"

Balor smiled. He gestured to the women. They descended on Bres, hands and tongues working busily. They fed him delicacies and poured mead down his throat. He moaned and leaned back on the pillows.

"You!" Bres gestured to the smallest of the girls. "Up on my lap. We will pretend you are one of my Danu women."

"There's my good lad," said Balor. "More Fomorian than Danu by any measure, boy."

*   *   *

"Well, it's an old enough story," said Eriu.

"Mead and meat and women and riches," said Banba dryly. "And slowly, by degrees, suborn the willing to your purpose. And the heart becomes dark. And greed grows. And each time the lost one is willing to give away more of his spirit."

"They also offered him acceptance," said Fodla quietly. "You are one of us. You belong with us. More important than all the rest."

"You are wise as always, Fodla," said Eriu. "I begin to see why Airmid and Miach made the choice they did."

"But the histories tell us that Nuada paid the price of his life. Did he defeat them? And if so, how?"

Eriu rested her hand on the speckled stone. "Sisters, shall we rest or shall we continue?"

"There is no time to waste," said Fodla. "In our hours here, the Invaders approach even closer on the sea."

"We shall see more," Banba said softly. "Now."

At the doorway into the passage, Bres pressed his triangle into the recess in the wall. White light snapped, and then a blue oval coalesced before them. Balor bent low.

Bres held him back. "You will not fit in the passages," he said softly. "The tallest of the Danu only reach five feet; even I have to crouch to reach the city."

With his giant forefinger, Balor pointed at ten men, each under six feet tall. "Will they suit?"

Bres grinned. "Even they are a little large. But they will be fine in the city below."

Balor's voice adopted a wheedling tone. "I should love a piece of treasure, boy. Something I could wear around my neck."

"That is easily done. I owe you that much at least."

Balor grinned, the yellowed teeth half obscured beneath the giant, shaggy mustache. "Good lad," he said. "Now go. And you need not stop at ten. Bring back as many as the group of you can gather. As many as you wish. Or wish to share."

The group disappeared into the passageway, bending low.

In the Chamber of Memory, Eriu spoke softly. "They do not know the price that they will pay, these Fomor. Our price is but small compared to theirs."

"No," said Banba. "They are not Braid or Hybrid. But this is what they deserved. I should laugh to see them tomorrow by their fire, young men gone gray and wrinkled, their eyes rheumy, their pates bald."

"I wonder what he will think," said Fodla, pointing toward Balor.

As if he had heard them, Balor watched the company go and shrugged. "And if he does not bring enough, we can always come back for more," he said. "The boy is mine. Slaves and treasure will follow."

He sat down against the wall; he belched in satisfaction and leaned his head back against the rock.

Deep below the passageway, an alarm began to sound, the deep thrum of bells and drum. The sound of screams echoed up the long walkway.

"Good lad," said Balor. "You'll make a fine Fomor when all of this is over."

The scene shifted.

The Sisters were now observing a surgery.

Under an arc of blue-white light, Nuada was stretched on a table. Around the table a nimbus of electricity crackled and sparked.

Airmid held up an instrument and read it. "The field is sterile, Miach."

From the table Nuada spoke softly. "Beloved Niece and Nephew. I ask you once more. Are you certain of this course of action? I should not wish for you to pay the price for this action. Dagda and most especially Dian Cecht will not approve of this course."

"The Danu have paid the price for our inaction. Even now our city smolders and mothers cry out for their missing children. We have no other choice," said Miach.

"How could he have done this thing?" asked Airmid. She was young, her wide eyes full of sorrow.

"We kept him apart from us. An honored guest. But not a brother."

"You did not."

"No," said Nuada. "I loved him well." His voice broke on the admission.

"We have no choice," said Miach again. "We must find our missing people. We cannot just abandon them. And we must ensure that the Fomor can never come into Tara again."

"The Council has changed the doorway arms," said Airmid softly. "The Fomor can no longer enter."

"They will find a new way," said Nuada. "They have seen our city and our treasures. They have stolen our people. What will stop them now?"

"True," said Miach. "And they cannot change the heart of a traitor. Sister, I say again. You need not remain with us here."

"I remain," she said quietly. "I am proud to defend my people with the Knowledge of the Braid."

"Then you must promise me that you will keep silent in Council, that you will not speak for us and our work here."

Airmid said nothing.

"Promise me or you must go now."

"I promise," she said in a small voice.

"Swear on the Danu," said Nuada from the table. "For I know of your love for us."

"I swear on the Braid, in the name of the Mother." Airmid choked it out.

Miach nodded. "Then with your permission, Uncle, we will remove your awareness of pain so that we can proceed."

Nuada nodded.

Carefully, Airmid affixed small ovoids to Nuada's forehead, behind his ears, and at the back of his neck. She activated a small device in her hand.

After a moment, she took a probe. "Uncle, I will touch the stump now. You must tell me the truth."

She inserted the probe into the uneven layers where Nuada's arm ended.

In the chamber, Fodla turned away and hid her eyes. "Tell me when it is finished," she said softly.

"We need not relive it all," said Eriu. "We know what choice they made." She depressed the stone and gently twisted it to the right. The scene shifted again to the Great Council Hall. Nuada stood before the company, his arm attached. He flexed his fingers before the assembled Danu.

"Restore him as Triad Leader!" cried the Danu.

Dagda stepped to the platform beside Nuada. "Speak to us, Nuada; tell us why this was done."

Nuada nodded. He spoke softly, and the entire company leaned forward to listen.

"It was done that I might save the Danu. Our people must be rescued from the Fomor. We must drive them from the shores of the Green Isle that they will no longer trouble the Danu or the Fir Bolg. The Fomorians are like a ship with a bottomless hold. This even the Fir Bolg told us long ago. No taxes, no slaves, no riches will ever satisfy them. More makes them want more."

Now Dian Cecht stepped forward. "Someone must pay the price for this action. The Braid has been used in defiance of the law. Who has used the Braid Knowledge?"

Miach stepped forward bravely. "I have done this, Father," he said quietly.

Dian Cecht's face blanched and he looked stunned. Miach continued.

"It is not just that the Danu should always hide from their enemies. Nor is it just that the best and brightest among us should be unable to serve as a result of physical imperfection. Hear me, People of the Danu. The laws of the Old World should not be the laws for this world. We are a different race. Our circumstances here are different. The laws of Braiding must change. Of course we should not do what the Homeworld did. The power of Creation belongs to the Braid, not to any of her children. But those who have been created by the Braid should be healed and made whole! This the Mother would expect of us, that we would heal her children."

Among the Danu there was murmuring and shouts of agreement.

"Still, the law is the law!" cried Dian Cecht. "The law must be obeyed. There is a price affixed to this transgression."

"No, brother," said Dagda. "Such a price is too high."

"I will pay whatever price the law requires," Miach shouted. "I have done what I believe is right and just."

Dian Cecht turned toward his son, his eyes wide and sorrowful. "My son," he said softly. "The penalty is death."

"No!" Airmid screamed. "No! Do not kill my brother."

Both Nuada and Miach whipped in her direction, their eyes fixing on her.

"Sister!" Miach cried. "By the Braid."

Airmid pressed her lips together. Slowly, as though her legs had turned watery beneath her, she crumpled to the floor. The people of the Danu rushed to assist her.

"It is too much," they cried.

"The penalty goes too far!"

"He has restored Nuada to us."

"We will defeat the Fomor and rescue our lost children."

On the platform Nuada and Dagda stared out over the crowd. Dian Cecht began to weep like a child in great gulping sobs until at last Miach enfolded his father in his arms.

"And so he was executed?" Eriu asked softly.

"He was," said Airmid.

"And you never spoke?" Banba addressed the Ancient quietly, with none of her usual blunt attack.

"Never," said Airmid softly. "I begged them to let me speak and they would not. 'Live,' they said. 'Work to change the law. Heal the Danu.' And that is what I did."

"It is because of you, then, that we can save the Hybrid children of the Fir Bolg," said Eriu softly.

"It is because the people of the Danu changed the law," Airmid said softly. "It is because of the courage of Miach and Nuada."

"You asked me to tell you if we thought you had done aright," said Eriu softly. "We believe that you and your brother chose well. We believe that the fear of the Braided Ones against the use of the Braid was over-done, based on their own experiences on the Homeworld. We believe that the change in the law was wise. Had you not restored Nuada, the Danu might well today be the slaves of the Fomor, and the abandoned children of the Fir Bolg would be freezing on the hillsides."

Airmid nodded quietly. "I thank you." She kept her head bent above her table, her hands clutching the edge.

"But our acknowledgment does not ease the pain, does it?"

"No." Airmid whispered the word, forced it from her. "I thought that it might, but it does not."

"Because you did not speak."

"I should have died with my brother. I should have spoken that day before the Council."

Banba brought a chair and placed it behind Airmid. The Ancient collapsed into it, her little frame shaken by weeping.

Eriu knelt before her. "You gave them your sacred vow."

Airmid nodded.

"Your brother was wise. Do you not see? He knew that the law must change and he knew that the First Triad could not change it. You were the only hope for change."

Airmid looked up. "You are saying what you truly believe?"

"I am. Did not Nuada defeat them in battle?"

"So I am told."

"You were not there?"

Airmid shook her head. "I buried my brother high in the hills overlooking the sea and then I ran away. I went far to the north, alone. I lived in a cave in a hillside, nor did I speak to anyone. I studied the herbs of this planet and the healing medicaments and I stayed alone for many months. Once my father journeyed to find me. He pleaded with me to return, but I turned my back to him and would not speak. In his rage and anger, he tore my herbs from the ceiling, scattered the contents of my medicine jars, tore through my gardens and ripped my plants out at the roots. This from the gentlest of fathers that ever a child had known. But still I would not look at him or speak. He returned to Tara; later he died, his heart broken by grief and guilt, but I did not know then. I think that I would never have returned among the Danu. Never."

"But you did. What changed?"

"Lugh," she said softly, and her face folded into a smile that looked almost like a girl's. "I met Lugh."

22

I remember Lugh!" said Banba. "I was a young girl—long before they married us to the Brothers. By Danu, he was a handsome man!"

"He was indeed," said Eriu.

"You too?" said Fodla. "Are you catching her disease?" She gestured at Banba.

"Do you think he was her beloved?" said Banba.

"By the look on her face, what else should we conclude?" said Fodla.

"It would have been rude to ask," said Eriu.

"If only we had not been betrothed to the Brothers," said Banba with a sigh.

"Banba!" said Fodla. "Those were happy days. The Fomor had departed and the Fir Bolg were in our care. There was no danger for the Danu. The six of us wandered the Green Isle, always laughing. They were to us as elder brothers."

"We did seem to be always laughing, didn't we?" said Eriu.

"Well, they were such great friends, to us and to each other," Fodla said softly. "How much longer do you think they might have lived, had it not been for the Lia Fail?"

"Do not think on it," said Eriu. "We do what we must."

Fodla nodded. "I think of them often. Mac Cuill, Mac Cecht, and Mac Grene. Handsome men and good."

Banba sighed. "But oh, Lugh. There was a man!"

"He was not Danu, you know," said Fodla.

"Surely he was," said Banba. "He possessed our light and our eyes."

"But not our hair or our height."

"Don't you mean our lack of height?" said Eriu.

The door slid open. The Sisters were surprised to see Airmid silhouetted in the passage, her tiny, bent frame leaning on the arm of Illyn.

"Ancient!" said Eriu. She leaped to her feet. "How may we assist you?" Illyn bowed from the room, and Eriu conducted Airmid to her own chair.

"The Invaders will make landfall on the morrow."

"How do you know this?"

"I have had a watch posted for these three days; at dusk they saw the lights in their top rigging. Our spear warriors have heard music from their ships."

"We have heard it too. It is most sorrowful."

Airmid nodded. "So they have said. Only I hope that they do not blame their sorrows on us."

Banba snorted. "Well, the Fomor always did. And the Fir Bolg as well, at least for a time. Why should these newcomers be any different?"

"What shall we do?" Eriu asked the Ancient. "Should we abandon our studies here and prepare?"

"In the past is the answer to the present, Sisters. You have very little time left for this work . . . and that is probably well." She regarded Banba, squinted her eyes. "It seems to take a toll on you."

Eriu turned to look at Banba. Banba looked weary; soft circles curved beneath her eyes.

Airmid seated herself and closed her eyes, resting her head on the back of the chair. "As for me, I know what I will do."

"Ancient, you cannot stay here with us," Eriu said, alarm in her tone.

"Have you seen him yet?"

"Seen who? Where?" asked Banba. She made a face at her Sisters as if the Ancient were crazy or mindless.

"I see that," said the Ancient, her long finger admonishing. "One day you will be as I am now and the youngsters will gesture behind your back and call you mindless."

"Or mean-tongued," said Fodla.

"It is likely that they already call her that," said Airmid, and all three sisters burst into laughter.

"True enough," said Banba. "I apologize, Ancient."

"Lugh Lamfhada," said Airmid. "Have you seen him yet? Here in the Chamber of Memory?"

"No."

"But you will return to the final battle, will you not?"

"We will," said Eriu. "But memory is difficult, Ancient, just as you warned us. Sights, smells, sounds, fears and joys. It is as if we were there among them. Even the immediate effects . . ." She glanced again at Banba.

"What should I fear, Eriu?" said Airmid, the infant smile creasing her face. "Old age? I have lived for three millennia. Weariness? I have been weary in my spirit since Miach died. Death? There is no death, as well you know. We return to the Braid who wove us, she who will weave us again. Only you three know my secret and you have forgiven my choices. With you I feel myself again. As I have not felt since . . . well, for a long time."

Banba snorted. "Since Lugh. You wish to see Lugh again."

"I wish to see Lugh again," said Airmid. And her voice was the voice of a young girl.

The Plain of Mag Tuiread shimmered into view, morning sunlight pouring down among the stones.

"So we come to battle here again," said Eriu. She was curled on the floor at Airmid's feet, resting on a pillow, her back against the chair in which the Ancient sat.

The Ancient tousled her curls. "Always here, girl. You know that history repeats; it is as true for us as for every culture we have ever known."

The Fomorian horde was gathered at the far side of the field, among them ten ancient, shrunken men dressed in the garb of much younger warriors. None of the other Fomor stood near them, as if they bore a disease that all could catch.

"So," said Airmid. "They paid the price for entering Tara."

"Rather for departing from it," said Eriu softly.

The giant Balor stood at the head of the Fomorian army. He bristled with war armor, a huge two-horned helmet on his head, a giant war ax in his right hand. He was all hair and beard, black like some ancient animal. He had removed the patch from his eye and the cloudy blue-gray orb appeared luminous and large, terrifying in the morning light.

Beside him was Bres, dressed in the war garb of the Fomorians.

"False king," he called out now, taunting Nuada. "A damaged man of the Danu. Ask to see his arm, Balor."

Nuada said nothing. Slowly, almost gently, he removed the silver gauntlet from his hand. He held up his arm, whole in the light. He clenched and unclenched his fingers.

"You betrayed us," he said. "I treated you ever as a brother." Though his voice was soft, it carried across the field. He replaced the silver gauntlet, pulling it on like a glove.

"No brother to those who did not want me."

"Bres is ours!" cried Balor.

"Bought and paid for!" cried Dagda. "What did it take, little halfling? Wine, women, treasure?"

Bres had the good grace to lower his eyes.

Dagda stepped from behind Nuada, his own arm clad in silver. The Danu ranged up beside the two, holding their Light Spears. "Know this, men of the north!" Dagda cried. "This day we will defeat you. This day you will sail to the north from whence you came. For a thousand years hence, you will whisper of the little people of the Danu. You will fear to return among us. This day you will return our people to us!"

"Do you mean these?" cried Balor. More than a dozen Fomorian warriors stepped forward. Each held a leash in his hand, dragging at its end a Danu captive. Men, women, children, some of them so small that they did not reach even to the knees of their Fomorian captors. The Fomor held the little people before them, using them as human shields.

An uneasy shifting moved through the Danu.

"Come, Nuada Argetlamh!" called Bres. "Unleash your weapons now."

"We will hit them," Nuada whispered to Bres. "What course now, Brother?"

Suddenly there was a blast of sound and light from the rear of the Fomor company, followed by an unearthly scream of pain. Fomorians began to run for the front of the line, pelting in front of Bres and Balor and their Danu captives.

"What has happened?" Dagda shouted at Nuada.

"I know not. But take the tide that turns for us. Let us rescue our people!"

Lightning began to stream from the thrown Light Spears, which hissed as they arced toward the enemy. The Silver Arms began to spit blue light, flame, concussions of noise. Fomor stiffened and fell, great clods of dirt exploding around their tumbling forms.

While the Sisters watched, the little Danu sped among the Fomor, appearing and disappearing, unleashing confusion and terror.

Balor came at a run toward Nuada and Dagda.

"Obscure the field!" screamed Nuada.

Suddenly, Balor swung his great club. It connected hard with Nuada's shoulder. The Danu gave out a cry of pain.

Dagda held forth his own Silver Arm. He pulsed it once toward the sky, once toward the earth. A high wind began to wail in the trees. Fog began to creep along the ground, threading through the great stone portals of the plain. In moments the battlefield was obscured by fog.

Suddenly, into the midst of the company rode a man on a great horse. He was tall and strong-limbed. His curly golden hair and wide eyes proclaimed him Danu, but he was a man of over six feet. He thundered in, straight at Nuada and Balor, who had raised his club for the death strike. Balor staggered back before the thundering hooves of the horse. The huge man leaned down and stretched out his arm to Nuada.

"Clasp it, brother!" he cried. "I will not play you false." Nuada reached up; the great man hauled him into the saddle and they thundered across the battlefield.

The big man deposited him at the edge of the field.

"Physician," he cried. Airmid came running from the edge of the field toward Nuada, her belt with its healing instruments and medicines bouncing at her waist.

"This is Nuada?" the big man asked.

"It is," she said. "Our captives, mo ghra. Save them." He turned and rode hard for the field.

Nuada looked up at her. "Welcome back, Airmid."

"Uncle," she said softly.

"It has been nearly seven years," said Nuada.

"I have been in the north."

"Your father has passed."

She nodded. "He could not bear that he was author of Miach's execution."

Nuada nodded toward the horseman. "And the rider?"

"Lugh."

"He is one of us?"

She nodded once.

"And who else? He is not Penitent."

"He knows not. He is Danu."

The big man rode back on his horse, a captive before him and two behind him. "Take them below," he called. He rode away.

"They will not readily accept him," said Nuada. He winced as she pressed a pulsing instrument into the shoulder. "Not after Bres."

She shrugged. "He is what he is. He does not need our acceptance. Nor theirs."

Nuada smiled. "And he has yours."

Airmid smiled. "You can return to battle, Uncle."

"So that was Lugh," Banba said softly.

Airmid was leaning back against the cushions, her eyes closed. She said nothing.

"Ancient," said Eriu. "You are well?"

"I am well, child. It has brought him back to me again in all his beauty."

"Did they accept him?"

"No. Not at first. Between Lugh and Nuada and Dagda, they rescued all the hostages. When the battle had ended, Lugh returned with us here to Tara. The people shunned him."

"Despite what he had done?"

"Perhaps because of it. They feared his purpose; they feared that he would be as false as Bres. None of it bothered Lugh. He simply laughed and said, 'They will come to know me.' And eventually they did."

"How did you come to know him?" Banba asked.

"When I was in the north. One day, there he was in the forest, hunting on foot, silent as wind." She shrugged. "Obviously Danu. Obviously something else as well."

"What did he say of that?"

"He did not know. Rumors swirled about him here at Tara. Some of the Danu said they had heard that Dagda had a son by a Fir Bolg woman. Others said that he was the son of Cian of the Danu, who had taken to wife Ethlim of the Fomor. For many years there had been a story, that Balor of the Fomor had a daughter, that he kept her locked in a tower that she might never be troubled by a man. Among the Danu, it was whispered that Cian had seen her and been smitten, that he had used Metaphor to transform himself into a woman. In that guise, he had visited her in her tower. Nine months later she gave birth to triplets."

"Triplets?" said Eriu.

"It does lend weight to the story, does it not?"

"It does. Where were his brothers, then?"

"Among the Fomor there was a legend that Balor of the One Eye would be killed by his own grandson."

"So there is the truth of why he walled his daughter up," said Banba. "He was not protecting her virtue."

"Well, when he saw the triplets, he knew that the tower had failed. The story was that he tried to drown them all. He succeeded with all but Lugh."

"Who raised him?"

"He was raised in the deep northern forest by a woman named Birog. She was a wise woman. Druii, he called her. She told him that he was Danu and that he should learn well, so that the Danu would know him as a wisdom keeper when at last they met. When he was seven, he was fostered to a blacksmith. It was the first of many apprenticeships."

"Did our people come to accept him?"

"At length," she said. "He simply worked his way into their hearts. I say this literally, daughters. He was a carpenter and a smith, a warrior, a poet and a harper, a physician . . ."

"That last thanks to you, I suppose," said Banba.

Airmid nodded. "He did whatever he was asked. Whenever. Without complaint and always in good spirits. He even taught the Danu to be horsemen. The Danu came to call him Lugh Ildanach, Lugh All-Craftsman. It was not possible not to love him."

"You called him Lugh Lamfhada," said Eriu.

Airmid nodded. "He earned that name in the battle."

"How?" asked Eriu.

"Why did Nuada not speak for him among the Danu?" asked Banba.

"So it was Lugh who began the battle from behind the lines?" asked Fodla.

"Too many questions, daughters," she said softly. "And the answers are troubling and sad. You must see them for yourselves."

She pointed to the speckled stone.

Nuada returned to the field, dashing in and out of the Danu, appearing and disappearing in the battlefield fog. Bolts of lightning emerged from the spears of the Danu, and Lugh on his white horse pounded across the field.

Suddenly there was a huge roar.

Balor had sighted Nuada. He heaved back his spear arm. The spear flew true, piercing Nuada through the heart.

In the chamber Airmid let out a sob.

Nuada fell to the ground lifeless, the Silver Arm falling hard across his chest. The people of the Danu began to scream.

"Nuada Argetlamh."

"Nuada! No! Nuada!"

Balor began to move inexorably toward the dead man, his huge frame leaning forward at a heavy run, his eye focused on the Silver Arm.

Suddenly Lugh rode toward the fallen Nuada. Without ever leaving his horse, he swept his arm down and snatched the Silver Arm, pulling it from Nuada's own. Holding it out in front of him like a spear, Lugh called out, "For Nuada."

He shifted the arm and it gave out a bolt of great light and noise. It pierced Balor, directly through the blind and rheumy eye. Balor fell.

A great cry arose from the Fomorians. The began to scatter, to flee between the lintels of the great stone circle and run for the forest below. It was not long before they fled for their sea boats, leaving the rest of the Danu captives behind.

The fog began to lift at the edge of the battlefield. In the trees at the far side of the circle, where once they would have been behind the Fomor lines, a shadow moved. The Morrigu stepped onto the Plain of Mag Tuiread. Macha wore a Silver Arm.

"Well begun, Sisters," said Macha softly.

"And well ended," said Banbh in her scratchy, masculine voice. "Let the Danu take our wounded and our dead. I will take the rest." She touched the triangle at her neck. Ravens began to circle the field, to dip to the grisly work below; Banbh flew among them.

In the chamber, Airmid wept softly.

"And so we lost Nuada?" said Eriu.

"And Lugh became known as Lugh Lamfhada, for the way he used the Silver Arm, as if it were a spear," said Fodla.

"And if the legend is true, Balor was indeed killed by his own grandson." Airmid nodded.

"And the Morrigu?" asked Banba.

"They are sowers of chaos," said Airmid quietly. "They make war very well indeed; they are the necessary evil."

"There is one thing I do not understand," said Eriu. "The fog that covered the field. It was not raining. Was it created by the Light Spears?"

Airmid smiled. "That is the beauty of the Silver Arms, child. They are not weapons only. Each finger of each arm is articulated to a specific purpose. Wind, fog, noise, lightning, images of warriors, even sweet music."

Eriu tried to stand from the floor, but her legs would not come up with her. She hissed in pain, pressed her palms to the floor to lift her own weight. When she was standing, she shifted gingerly from one leg to the other. Airmid watched from her chair.

"It will pass," Airmid said. "These are temporary effects only. The long-term costs will be assessed later, five hundred, a thousand years from now. And you are finished now with Lia Fail. Eriu has learned the answer from the history, have you not?"

Eriu nodded excitedly. "I have. Sisters, the answer was before us always. The Silver Arms. You must teach us, Airmid. All three arms."

"You will destroy the Invaders with them?" asked Banba.

"No. We will use them on their minds, not their bodies. We will make them wary of us and wise."

"Until now, our memory had shown me only three ways: we could hide from the Invaders, seal the doors to Tara—"

"Which would abandon the Fir Bolg," said Airmid.

"Precisely. No Danu wishes such a thing. Or we could destroy the Invaders."

Airmid sighed and shook her head. "We have seen what price our history paid for that choice."

"We have," said Eriu. "If these Invaders were enough like Fir Bolg, we might frighten them into submission."

"But they are far more sophisticated than Fir Bolg," said Banba. "Superstition will not keep them from the doors."

"We know not yet if they are more like Fir Bolg or Fomor," said Fodla.

"Oh, they are more like Fomor," said Banba.

"What makes you say so, child?" asked Airmid.

"Airioch Feabhruadh and the way he was eyeing the jewels we wore in Metaphor," Banba replied.

"When he was not eyeing the jewels your Metaphor created elsewhere," said Fodla.

"And Eber Donn, that great hairy beast who kept muttering about cattle pasturage." Banba shook her head. "Stupid but dogged. Small-minded but determined."

"So they are greedy," said Airmid quietly. "As Bres was. You could feed their greed with treasure."

"No," said Eriu. "Greed feeds on itself and grows larger. Think of Bres. He became all greed, all wanting. It destroyed him and nearly destroyed us."

"And so the arms?"

"Do you see?" she said. "If the arms are not destroyers alone, if they are many-purposed . . ."

"We could make a show of strength; we could seem to be more in numbers and to be more skilled and dangerous than we are," said Fodla.

"Yes," said Banba. "Now have we learned from our memory. We can appear to be as Lugh Lamfhada was—so skilled in all things . . ."

"That the Invaders will respect us," said Fodla, "and so let us be, or work with us in truce."

"Airmid," said Eriu, "will you take us to the hiding place of the Silver Arms?"

Airmid stood and held out her hand. "Come," she said. "This is a wise plan. It honors them all. Nuada, Lugh, Miach, all who protected the Danu.

"Braid hands," Airmid commanded. "I will stand in your midst. Encircle me; braid me into your Triad. I will press upon my triangle. You will see it pulse and grow warm. Do not touch me or stop me. Promise this."

"We promise, Ancient," said Eriu softly. "Begin the chant of vision."

Banba and Fodla issued the deep sounds, reed and chanter. Eriu began the chant. She watched as Airmid pressed her palm to her own triangle. She could smell the flesh of the Ancient's palm burning, burning. But she remembered her promise and did not break hands or cease chant.

All around them, the room grew viscous; lights pulsed within her frame of vision, then darkness. Complete darkness.

"Sisters, you may unbraid."

It was Airmid's voice.

"Ancient," Fodla whispered. "Are you well?"

"You need not whisper," said Airmid. "No one knows of this place. No one can hear you. We hid the arms here, Lugh and I. Not even Council knows where they are. Nor can they be discovered by any but a triad. After the battle was done and the Fomor departed for the cold north. This is how we hid them, that they could not be reached by one person alone. The Danu have not needed them since."

Eriu could hear her moving in the darkness. Suddenly the room began to illuminate with an eerie blue light. Airmid was standing to the side, her triangle pressed into a depression in the wall.

"How did you find it?" asked Banba.

"I can see it," said Airmid. "Have you not wondered why we of the Braided Ancients wear the dark lenses over our eyes? Our eyes are more sensitive than yours by a thousandfold. I see in darkness." She took small blue torches from a niche in the wall, each seeming to contain its own source of light. She handed one to each of the Sisters. Eriu stepped toward Airmid and looked at the Ancient's palm. It was burned and blistered. Airmid shook her off.

"A little salve will heal me. It is nothing."

"Where are we?" asked Eriu.

The light began to illuminate the walls, which seemed crystalline, almost opalescent. Clear crystal towers grew from the ceiling and the floor.

"Deep beneath the earth and sea," said Airmid. "Where these three would remain safe and untouched forever."

She turned her torch toward a depression in the wall. Before it shimmered a waterfall, softly descending, seeming to chime, small lights flickering within the viscous cascade. Airmid gestured to a triangular recess at each side of the waterfall. Eriu stepped up to one side of the cascade while Airmid pressed her triangle into the recess at the opposite side. The water ceased to fall. Behind the cascade, illuminated in soft light, were the clear tubular chambers that should have held the Silver Arms of the Danu.

The tubes gleamed in the ambient blue light.

They were empty.

23

By the Danu!" The Sisters rushed to catch Airmid, who swayed in place, her eyes riveted to the wall in horror. "Just so we left them, Lugh and I. I do swear it."

Banba nodded. "There is no mystery here, Ancient. You said they could be accessed only by a Triad. Who were the only ones who knew to use them in the battle other than Nuada and Dagda and Lugh?"

"The Morrigu." Airmid wailed it out into the cold cave. "But how did she find them here? We hid them well."

"Like darkness, she slips into the hollows of the world," said Eriu softly. "Oh, I fear the work that she will do. Does she know all of their powers?"

"I know not. Nuada knew, and Dagda. When Nuada had passed, Dagda taught their uses to Lugh. He became chief after the death of Dagda."

Eriu patted the shoulder of the Ancient. "It will be well. We will speak to the Morrigu."

"What leverage do we have? How can we bargain with her from a position of strength? We do not have the arms and we know nothing," said Banba.

"We will act as though we know. Airmid will teach us," Eriu replied.

"Except that I do not know their uses," said Airmid softly.

"How can that be?"

"Council Triad knew the weapons. My father, Nuada, Dagda. And after Dagda died, Lugh. No others."

"And Lugh is dead."

"There is no death," Airmid said.

Eriu sighed. "So I have heard the Ancients say. If only that could help us now."

"Then hear me," said Airmid. Her tone was urgent. The Sisters sat before her in Triangle.

"Speak, Ancient," said Eriu. "We are listening."

"What do we say of death?"

Eriu replied. "We say that the departed has gone into the west, that he dwells on Mag Mell, the Isle of the Ever Young. We say that when his time is right, he will return. We celebrate his departure, for that country is beautiful and devoid of sorrow. And when a child returns to us, we toll the bells and thank him for his sacrifice, his return to this world."

"And the Isle of the Ever Young? It is a place to which we can sail?" asked Banba.

"It is . . . an idea?" asked Eriu.

"A state of being in the Braid?" asked Fodla.

"Perhaps a leaf," Airmid responded.

For a moment the Sisters were still. Then they all answered at once.

"We see," said Fodla.

"Like the leaves of time," said Eriu.

"If only we could speak to them there," said Banba. "Then such knowledge would be useful."

"But you cannot. That is not your gift. Yet, among the Danu are those who do see and hear what is not there. We call them second-sighted." Airmid was silent.

"And you are one of those?"

She nodded simply. "It has always been a useful skill for a physician, a deeper way of knowing. I am very old and most of those I love have crossed to Mag Mell. There are places in this world which serve as doorways between this world and the next. At such a doorway I have spoken once to Miach. In the Chamber of Memory, when I said that you had returned Lugh to me?"

Eriu nodded.

"Now I will speak to Lugh again."

Eriu tilted her head and regarded the Ancient. "Why have you not done so before now, Ancient? Why not more often, for surely we can see how he resides in your heart."

"Like accessing memory, it takes much to do it," she said softly. "We ask much when we ask for this world and the next to intersect, for they are much different from each other. The . . . space . . . between this world and the next vibrates with voices, with presence, with all that comes and goes. It is more difficult than the Lia Fail because the Chamber of Memory shows us only selected . . . episodes. But to speak to those who have passed is to hear all of the voices who have crossed and then try to select from them. It is like standing in a forest in a great wind and listening for the sound of a single tree. And some of those voices come bearing a darkness."

"Then you shall not do it," said Eriu.

"But I shall," Airmid said softly. "How shall I do less than you have done, in immersing yourself in Lia Fail? I have told you that I have nothing to fear."

"It is we who fear," said Fodla.

"You are one of the last of our Ancients, one of so few remaining to us who were born on the Homeworld," said Banba. "If you die in trying to speak to Lugh, we will lose you."

"You will not lose me; I will always be here in memory for you. The very walls around me will remember me for you. But let me show you something." Carefully, she placed her memory triangle in the wall, pressed the stick language incised below it. Onto the walls came an image of a Danu of the Braid, a young woman, diminutive and pale, her huge dark eyes wide with wonder. She was laughing at the man beside her as they ran side by side along a windy beach.

"Come, Brother," she cried. "Just because this world is rainier and cold does not mean that I should beat you every time."

He put on a burst of speed and passed her at a run, a tiny pale man with a large childlike mouth.

"You let me win!" he cried.

She shrugged. "You are my brother Miach. We can run races together forever."

A silence prevailed in the room for a long time.

Then Eriu spoke softly. "Tell us what we must do to help you prepare."

*   *   *

In the deep forest at the top of a little rise, a huge flat rock rode unevenly across two great upright stones incised with whorls and spirals. Moonlight spilled across the surface of the rock, inched down its sides, making it looked like a giant ill-pitched table covered with a patchy tablecloth of white. Ivy had twined and curved around the uprights, hiding much of their carved surface in a moon-silvered profusion of leafy green triangles.

"It is a dolmen," said Airmid softly. "It is not like the doorways to our cities. Rather, it is a place of concentration; forces gather here. You must not enter it with me; stand here and wait. You will know when you can come for me."

The Sisters stopped at the foot of the hill, peering upward into the darkness. Airmid climbed carefully upward, leaning on her medical staff, her tiny body and her great age making her seem fragile and vulnerable in the darkness. She stepped beneath the great stone.

The space beneath the dolmen shimmered and wavered. In the sky beyond, the stars seemed to lengthen, the moon to stretch its shape from round to oval. A long time passed. An hour, perhaps two, by the reckoning of this world. And then he was there. Lugh Lamfhada, his huge frame silhouetted in the doorway.

"By the Danu," Banba whispered. "Surely we are seeing him there."

"Or so it would seem," Eriu whispered. "This is a fearsome thing; I am joyful and afraid at once. Oh, Sisters, we have learned much in these last days."

"And still we know but a single leaf on the vine of Airmid's knowledge," whispered Fodla.

In the dolmen, Airmid and Lugh stood apart, the air between them shimmering and thick. Once he turned his head toward the Sisters, who stood awestruck and still at the base of the hill. Collectively, they drew in their breath at his gaze.

A soft wind moved high in the trees above them; small animals skittered on the floor of the forest, as though a meeting between the living and the dead were ordinary, as though they should go about their business as they always did. Time seemed to slow, almost to still. Eriu felt heavy; her limbs, weighted and watery. And then Lugh was gone.

Airmid stepped from the dolmen and crumpled to the ground; the Sisters rushed to assist her. Eriu lifted her into her arms, gently poured drops of cool libation between her lips. For her part, Airmid smiled and smiled, though she was weak as a newborn Danaan.

"I did not see him leave," said Banba, "though I was watching him well."

"He did not leave," said Airmid. "He simply closed the door. But he is here still. The Braid contains us all at all times. We are sustained inside the Braid."

"Why do we weep their absence, Ancient? When all the while their presence is right here next to ours?"

"We weep their absence from their bodies in this time and in this place. We weep their incarnation. We see from a single leaf, Daughter. But do you see the vines that twine around these lintels?"

Eriu nodded.

"The Braid knows all of that; the beginnings and the endings, the intertwinings, the new and the old, the death and the reblossoming. She tries to show us; she weaves the worlds in Metaphor. Over and over again. But we are singled-minded and blind. We see a single leaf, we cannot see the pattern."

"It is all too much for me," said Banba, her reaction to the strange and the new being irritation, as always.

"You are young," said Airmid. "You will come to see it clearly. Lugh has told me what we need to know. You have much to learn, Daughters. Return me to Tara, for I have little time."

"This also Lugh has told you?" asked Eriu.

Airmid nodded. She kept smiling and smiling, touching her long fingers to her lips as though she held some wondrous secret.

"Hurry now. We have much to do."

Far out at sea, Amergin stood on the deck of the ship and looked toward the land, silhouetted in the moonlight. Airioch Feabhruadh slipped up beside him in the darkness.

"What do you see, Brother?"

"I see only the outline of the island in the moonlight. But the wind seems full of voices."

"And they all speak of treasure," said Airioch Feabhruadh. He clapped Amergin on the shoulder. "On the morrow, you will see. The treasure is bottomless." His face was flushed with excitement. Amergin regarded him in silence. Airioch returned across the deck and descended below.

Amergin remained on the deck.

"My treasure has vanished into the sea," he whispered. "Skena, do you hear me? Is our child within you still? And Ir? Do you care for them both? Oh, forgive me, love, that I did not reach the railing first."

Around him the wind twisted and grew, snapping at the sails, howling in the rigging. He leaned far forward over the railing.

"It would take so little, love, a shift forward, that is all. But then I would betray my father and Uncle Ith. My duty to the tribe. Always duty."

Amergin dropped his head to the railing and wept.

24

Sisters, I would speak to her alone!"

"You do not wish our presence?" Fodla's voice sounded at once wounded and surprised.

"And with, of all people, Morrigu?" Banba was incredulous and angry.

Eriu shook her head. "It has naught to do with you. It has to do with her sisters. I would meet with Macha alone, separate from Nemhain and Banbh."

"That I understand well enough," said Banba. "Those two make my very skin crawl."

Eriu nodded. "Precisely. We know now what we need to know of the functions of the arms. I stand a better chance of learning what the Morrigu knows and of negotiating a reasonable position if I meet with Macha alone. What she sows, she does with intelligence; the other two are all instinct, all base. But Macha will never meet with us in triad if she is alone. Her position would be too weak without her sisters."

"Well reasoned," said Banba.

"But still I like it not," said Fodla.

"And yet you see its wisdom?"

The Sisters nodded.

"But promise us that you will stay near the doorway."

"And that you will have your triangle at the ready should you need to return to Tara."

"I promise."

Yet now, sitting on the spring ground, her back against a sarsen stone, she felt no fear. A soft breeze blew up from the forest, and the stars, which had been spread across the sky like a veil, blurred and lightened as the soft gray of predawn paled their fire.

Eriu sighed. What she wished, just once, was to see what Airmid had seen in the dolmen, to see on the face of a beloved absolute recognition, a look of complete belonging.

The Brothers had been good men, funny and wise in the ways of the Danu. They had been good companions and gentle elder teachers for the mating. They had been friends. But they were interchangeable; the Sisters had been bonded to them because that was the way of the people—triad to triad, that the learning might be passed on, the duties of triad. And of course, there had been the hope that one of the matings would itself produce a triad.

But none had; the Brothers had passed from the world leaving no off-spring at all. Briefly, Eriu wondered again if that too had to do with the Brothers' long immersion in Lia Fail. She was filled suddenly with a terrible sorrow at the thought that neither she nor her sisters might bring children into the world.

Eriu wondered if her sisters sometimes felt lonely, if they too wished for a companion of the soul. Even when they were bonded to the Brothers, the Sisters had been bonded first to each other and to their duty to the Danu.

Eriu thought of Illyn, and a small smile crossed her face. In Illyn she had a daughter of the heart, but Banba and Fodla did not even have that. Her heart ached for all of them.

She began to feel panic rising in her. They would produce no triad, none of them. There would be no Council to serve the Danu. Chaos would reign; the Invaders would defeat them, would kill the Danu. Those who remained would be trapped below world, never to see the sun. . . . Eriu gasped. She stood.

"Nemhain, show yourself!"

Nemhain stepped into view from behind the stone, her face sulky, her black eyes beginning to lose their luster.

"You were causing my panic!"

"And I was feeding on it too." Nemhain smiled, her look almost ec-static, the white teeth gleaming in the moonlight. "You are not as good a subject as the Invaders, but you were doing well, racing down some path of self-destruction in much the same fashion that they do. The only difference is that they do not know me as the cause and I can feed on the mounting panic for hours, days, sometimes years." She actually ran her small, dark tongue over her lips.

"How do you know about the Invaders?"

"I have been on their ship. One of them I infected with such sorrow that he weeps on the railing and thinks of drowning himself in the sea. The other is so hard with his lust for treasure that he has to relieve himself whenever I am near."

"You disgust me," Eriu said bluntly. "I asked to meet with your sister."

"We did not approve of your meeting with her alone. So we came. But now I fear I have given myself away. Macha will be furious." She smiled again. "I can feed on fury, too."

Eriu felt a shiver run up her arms, drew her cloak closer around herself. "What are you?"

"We are that part of you that you do not acknowledge. We are the Antithesis. We dwell everywhere in all times. We plant ourselves and feed and wait for growth."

"Banbh is with you."

"She has shifted. There are dead in the water. She awaits them."

"What dead are in the water?"

"The Invaders have lost some of their own to drowning. Banbh will feed."

"Banbh!" Eriu called it out. A huge raven came spinning up from the direction of the sea and landed at the top of the sarsen stone. A moment later Banbh stepped from behind the stone. She was brushing her cloak into shape, dark iridescent feathers drifting from it. She turned on Nemhain immediately.

"So. You could not keep your presence hidden for a little hour, Chaos. I am hungry."

"I never keep my presence hidden, Feather. It is only that Eriu recognized my presence. Most do not recognize chaos or panic. They take it into themselves and let it grow." She smiled. "And then I feed. Have you fed tonight?"

"The dead have not washed to shore. Soon enough they will. I would be sated soon had you stayed hidden."

"Then I am somewhat sated and you are empty."

Banbh stepped toward her sister, her masculine, nasal voice low and threatening. "I can feed from you, Sister. Never forget that." In a flash, she raised a single finger with its long curved nail and swept it across her sister's throat. A thin trail of blood appeared.

"I will share," said Nemhain, softly, seductively. She tilted her head back in the moonlight.

Eriu backed against the stone; her hand went reflexively to the triangle at her neck. Her sisters had been right to tell her not to come alone.

Banbh looked at Eriu, her eyes glittering. She turned back to Nemhain.

"You will share because you know that our little ritual will repulse her and throw her sweet vision of the world into chaos and then you can feed again."

Nemhain chuckled. Blood was trickling now down into the neck of her gown.

"But then," said Banbh, "we both win, do we not, Sister? I feed and you feed."

"We do," said Nemhain. "Come, Sister."

Banbh bent her head toward Nemhain's neck, her long black tongue flicking. Eriu turned toward the stone, raised her triangle.

"Stop!" The word was so commanding, the sound thundering across the clearing, that Eriu turned back around at the same moment that Banbh raised her bloodied lips from Nemhain's throat. Macha had appeared suddenly beside the stone, her face contorted with anger.

"Get you gone from here!" she commanded. "Return to the rook and go nowhere else. You have not obeyed me; you will answer for this transgression."

In a flash the two sisters were gone. Eriu could hear a raven flapping and winging toward the sea at the same moment that a cold wind passed across her face.

She leaned back against the rock, her knees gone wobbly, trying hard not to let Macha see the weakness.

"They will be severely punished," said Macha.

"They will enjoy that, I am sure."

Macha tilted her head and a curious expression came into her eyes. "What do you mean?"

"When you punish Banbh, Nemhain will feed on her rage and indignity. When you punish Nemhain, Banbh will feed on her . . ." Eriu trailed away, her mind picturing the carrion sister at the neck of her own sister.

"Her blood," finished Macha. "Aren't you the wise one, Little Triad Sister? One would think you were as old as we. But you should know me better. I have found ways to punish that do not feed either of them, that leave them hungry and void. How do you punish your sisters?"

"Punish? I love my sisters; they love me. We care for each other and bear each other up."

Macha seemed completely taken aback by the admission. "You have never had to punish them? Not even once?"

"Of course not," Eriu said angrily. "They are not mine to punish. They are the Danu's children, as am I, as are . . ."

"Ah," said Macha. "Now you see. Whose children are we?"

The sea breeze wafted Macha's gown, and her scent drifted toward Eriu—musk and spices, exotic and dark. Quite beautiful really. Eriu closed her eyes, inhaled. When she opened her eyes, Macha was inches from her face, the dark inquisitive eyes taking her in, the long black hair drifting against Eriu's wrist and hand.

"But you have asked to meet with me. Privately. I too like you best of your threesome."

Eriu laughed. "Do not play your games with me, Ravener. You know why I have asked you to come."

Macha sighed. She folded down onto the ground in a sitting position and gestured to Eriu. Eriu slid down the rock, glad for its support for her quavering legs.

"I know why you have asked," said Macha. "You have asked because my sisters are beasts. They function on instinct alone, and all their instinct drives toward sating their endless desires for chaos and carrion. And you see in me something else."

"I see in you a tree that thrashes in the storm, throwing branches first this way, then that. I see lightning, jumping cloud to cloud, then striking at some poor soul skittering along the ground. I see a wind that can shift direction in a moment, here leave destruction, here spare another. You are the bringer of battle, Macha, but you fight a war within yourself, always. And yes, I see intelligence. And loneliness. Vast as these stars."

Macha's mouth had formed into a wide circle of surprise; her dark eyes had gone soft. "It is the loneliness, Eriu," she whispered. "The loneliness drives it all."

As if she had admitted too much, her whole face closed up.

"And the fact that I am tethered to those two fools for all of time. How would that do for you, Triad Leader? To be a woman of mind, linked forever to two giant, dark, hungry mouths? Never mind; time will come, I will find a way to destroy them . . . or to swallow them; I will find a way to move in the world alone."

"And when you do that, will you be worse or better for the action?"

Macha shrugged. "I neither know nor care."

"Do you not fear that they are listening, that they will hear you say these things to me?"

"It is a relief to say them to you. And no, I do not fear it. I have told them the selfsame thing many times. 'Beware of me. Obey me. I am coming for you and I will destroy you.' They fear me well."

"Ah," said Eriu, the dynamic becoming suddenly clear to her. "And this is how you feed. When you cannot feed your battle lust with Danu war or human war, you cause a war within your triad, and so you feed on Morrigu itself."

"Aren't you the clever girl," said Macha admiringly, "to see through us so clearly? You have a good mind, Eriu. But you did not call me here to unwarp and unweft Morrigu."

"You have the arms," said Eriu bluntly.

Macha nodded. "This time we have all three. In the war against the Fomor, we had but one."

"And it would do no good to ask you to return them to us?"

"None whatever."

"And you know how to use them?"

"We know enough. We used them once before. In human wars, it is enough to cause chaos. They do the rest themselves. But . . . you do not know their uses, do you? Would you like us to teach you? Morrigu will be happy to provide such a service to the Sisters."

Eriu felt her arms and neck prick up again at the very thought of spending time in the company of Macha's sisters. "I thank you, no," she said formally, as if she were declining an invitation to share a feast.

Macha chuckled. "Well, I cannot say I blame you. We are not a pleasant threesome. But you can trust us. What we want from those who come will not harm the Danu; that will not be necessary."

"I ask you not to harm these humans until we know their character. I think that they will be again unlike either Fir Bolg or Fomor."

"Why should I do this for you?"

Eriu took a deep breath. "I know uses for the arms that you cannot imagine."

Macha regarded her silently. "This is not possible," she said. "All those who knew the arms have passed."

Eriu said nothing. She had promised herself that she would make no one but herself vulnerable. Not her sisters, not Airmid. She waited quietly. Already she knew that Macha would ask for knowledge; already she knew which function of the arms she would trade. It was almost funny to imagine the Morrigu unleashing music against the coming invaders.

Macha closed her eyes as if she were thinking. At last she opened them. "Well, I will promise you this. If you give me just one gift, we will kill none of them unless they come for us in battle."

"What gift?" She prepared herself to explain the steps which would result in music.

"I ask you to take my hand again."

Surprise welled up in Eriu. This was not what she had expected. "I took your hand once before; your darkness poured into me like rain," she said.

Macha nodded. "That is why I ask. For that one moment, I will not be lonely."

"And for this you will kill none of them?"

"None until they come for us in battle."

"And if they do not?"

"They will, Eriu. They are human. Generation after generation, they make war on each other. Morrigu has depended upon it for thousands of years."

Eriu held her hand forward. She leaned back hard against the rocks. "Take it," she whispered.

"I will remember this," said Macha. "For you and for yours I will remember."

And she closed her hand around Eriu's own small hand.

25

"What did they do to her?"

"I know not. Her eyes are bruised and swollen and she cries out as though she is asleep."

"All our time in Lia Fail did not weaken her like this. Only Airmid looks closer to death!"

"Banba! Hold your tongue!"

"I am afraid, Fodla. What should we do without her?"

"I fear to wake her with the sorrowful news."

"We must."

Eriu opened her eyes to find her two sisters bent above her bed and whispering. She smiled softly. "I do love you both."

"We know that," said Fodla.

"It was awful, wasn't it?" asked Banba. "You should have let us go with you."

"She asked to hold my hand. For that she promised not to kill the Invaders unless they come against us in battle."

"For holding your hand?"

"That cannot be all; you look like a ship that has washed against the rocks."

"I tell you now that was all. But it was enough. What she contains is terrible beyond belief. All of the darkness, all of the evil of all of the worlds."

"You pity her?"

"No. And yes. She chooses for darkness. But I pity anyone who dwells in those choices. At the same time that they fill me with loathing."

"Are you well enough to rise, Sister? We bring news."

"Airmid has passed? Her work in the dolmen took too much of a toll upon her?"

"No, she is at the shore," said Banba.

"At the shore? When the Invaders are nearly upon us!" Eriu sat up. "Is she maintained in Metaphor?"

"Something has washed up on the beach," said Banba.

"Someone," said Fodla. "A woman and a little boy."

Eriu leaped to her feet.

"The Banbh said that there would be dead in the water."

"The Banbh?" asked Banba, her tone cross.

Eriu waved her hand. "They tried to join us. The Macha sent them away. Now come, we must go to the sea."

For a moment they stood silent at the headland. Below them Airmid worked feverishly, waving her arms at the Light Spear warriors who ran for the portal.

"At first the people thought a porpoise had beached," Fodla whispered softly. "Or perhaps one of the seal folk. When they realized what they were seeing, they posted a guard."

"Against the Banbh?"

Fodla nodded; she pointed skyward. Ravens and gulls swooped and circled.

Eriu moved to the shore with a heavy heart. She stepped to the first figure on the sand.

It was a woman, pale and heavy with child, her long hair matted against her head like seaweed. Airmid had lifted her gown to expose her pale skin. Over her swollen belly she had placed a long transparent strip. Near the woman on the beach was a small boy, now pale as the moon, his sightless eyes wide.

Eriu knelt beside Airmid. "Is there any hope for them, Ancient?"

"Not for the woman or the boy," she said, shaking her head sadly. "They were too long without breathsong." Suddenly she pointed, trembling, to the long clear strip, which had begun to pulse with faint red rhythms. "But look you now! The womb-child lives. It lives! Hurry, daughters. Send for bier bearers. We have much work to do."

"Surely the Danu watches over both of us with this blessing."

Airmid nodded. "Then pray that she continues to watch. She is not out of danger, this little one; look how tiny she is, nearly as small as a Danu babe. Too early; we have been forced to bring her into the world too early."

The baby was suspended in fluid in a tube which hung from the ceiling in Airmid's Healing Chambers. Lights of various warmth and colors shifted position on the infant.

"What is this chamber?" asked Eriu softly.

Airmid sighed. "It is my father's womb cradle; this is the way the Homeworld made him; remember that the Braided Ancients were not born of women, but of science." She shook her head. "You see now why such practices were banned, and yet, with this tiny child, my father's womb cradle will sustain her and allow her to grow. She dwells in her mother's own fluids. How sometimes we receive gifts from sorrows." She smiled. "The Mother never wearies of finding ways to care for us."

"Why did the child live?"

"Because her mother was so cold; because inside her mother she was so cold. Because she did not need breathsong to live. The boy and his mother were too long without breathsong under the cold sea. Had they been there less time they too might have survived. The cold slows all of the processes of the body, it . . . suspends. It holds functions in a kind of stasis."

"Imagine the joy of a man of the Invaders who finds that his child lives, that something of his love for his woman has survived," said Fodla.

"You cannot tell him!" Airmid shook her head. "No. You must not!"

"But, Ancient," said Eriu. "We must. She is not our child."

"Her survival is not yet guaranteed, Sisters. You look into the womb cradle and you see a little child. I see a child that has been too cold for too long. Will all of her functions return? And what of her mind? I see a child who cannot yet draw breathsong. She cannot be removed from this cradle."

"For how long?" asked Eriu.

"These humans carry their infants for nine full turnings of the moon. This wee one I judge to be at six turnings."

"We must keep her a secret for three months?" asked Fodla.

"Well, what else would you do? Would you bring him here to see her, this Invader father?"

"If we do, he will return to his people a withered Ancient," said Banba. "He is not one of us."

"No, nor Hybrid," said Eriu softly. She looked at the tiny child. "Nor is she."

"No," said Airmid. "We have brought her here among us and we can raise her here among us, but she is neither Danu nor Hybrid."

"So she cannot return to them. By Danu, what have we done?"

"Now you see our dilemma," said Airmid softly. "And why our ancestors so struggled with this knowledge. And why they outlawed Braid Creation. And why my father chose for Miach as he did. And why it took so long to change our laws even to allow ReBraiding. It slips away from us like water, the answer to this question; soon it becomes a raging cascade." Airmid sighed. "Should we have let her die, Eriu, her little heart beating away inside the womb cradle of her drowned mother?"

"No!" said Eriu in horror. "To abandon a child of the Mother that way! Never."

"And yet," said Airmid, "we must now answer a great question. If she were a child who could not breathe, or a child with a missing limb, or a child whose mind was trapped inside itself, I could alter her braiding, re-bind the sequence with our own braid, correct the problem. The laws that we have revised permit us to do that; to return a child to normalcy. Then, like Illyn and like we of the Danu, this little girl would be so long-lived that she could come and go in both worlds as she pleased; the added age for moving in their world would not even show upon her, as it does not show on Illyn.

"But she is a perfect human child. They age much more rapidly than ours. Their leaf of time progresses much more swiftly than ours. She will have to remain in the womb cradle for three more turnings of the moon. And then what do we do? Do we take her back among them, she appearing suddenly as a woman of bearing years, but with no speech and no experience of one that age? Would they believe she was one of them, or would they think her bewitched, a creature of their superstitions fit only for burning or drowning or exile? Or do we wait until she is of bearing years and then take her among them, a woman in her late years, past her bearing, a woman raised by Danu, speaking Danaan, possessed of Danaan knowledge, thrown suddenly among humans?"

"So we must raise her here," said Fodla quietly. "The only one of all of us who can never leave the confines of Tara."

"Or braid her," said Banba quietly. "This you could do, Ancient. A healthy human braids well with Danu. This we know from those who have been born of both. Lugh. Bres."

"But those were births of mating between a Danu and a human. The law does not permit me to alter that which the Braid has made whole. The law provides that I can repair and mend and heal. I cannot wholly alter that which is already whole."

"What should we do, Ancient?" asked Eriu softly.

Airmid walked over to the womb cradle where the infant was sucking on its thumb. "I don't know," she said softly. "I did what a healer does; I saved the life of a child of the Mother. Now I do not know what to do. My life seems to have been composed of these choices." She shook her head. "I will do the only thing I know to do. I will prepare her mother and her brother for burial with all the love and care of the Danu. I will hide the fact that the womb-child is no longer within the mother. I will bring this child healthy into the world. I will love her as if she were my own child, but I will give her no name until I know their tongue. The language of the Invaders. And then I will give her one of their names. That will be her braid. Beyond that, I cannot say. She is here among us; it is done."

For a long moment the Sisters stood in silence; then Eriu moved to Airmid and put her arm gently around the tiny woman's shoulders.

"Come," she said. "We will help you prepare their dead for the journey."

PART THREE

Á ILIU
ÍATH NÉIREANN

I CALL YOU FORTH,
O IRELAND

I SING THE LAND OF ERIU,
MUCH TRAVELED ON THE FERTILE SEA.
FERTILE THE FRUITED MOUNTAIN,
FERTILE THE ABUNDANT WOOD,
SHOWERED THE RIVER OF WATERFALLS,
WATERFALLS TO LAKE OF DEEP POOLS,
POOLING DEEP THE HILLTOP WELL.
A WELL OF TRIBES BE GATHERED,
A GATHERING OF KINGS AT TARA:
TARA BE THE HILL OF THE CLANS,
THE CLANS BE THE SONS OF MIL:
MIL OF THE SHIPS, OF THE GREAT BARKS.
THE HIGHEST BARK TO ERIU,
LOFTY ERIU, WIND-SUNG
A CHANT OF DEEP WISDOM ...
I SING THE LAND OF ERIU.

THE INVOCATION OF AMERGIN

26

I came to shore a broken man carrying a broken child on my shoulders. Skena and Ir were waiting for us.

The were laid out on a bier of some kind of transparent crystal, their heads raised as if they gazed out to the west.

I have seen the drowned before; many have perished in the Internum Mare. Someone had ministered to them with love and care. Skena's auburn hair had been washed and braided with flowers, and her face looked in repose as it had in life, gentle and full of love. She was dressed in a white gown of some iridescent material. Ir was curled into her arm, his little body seeming to sleep with his head on her shoulder. Someone had positioned their hands so that both the hand of Skena and the hand of Ir rested gently across our unborn child. Between her feet was the cup of Ith, the gift that he had carried with him across the water. It had been filled with iridescent stones of blue and gold.

Somehow the kindness of it, the beauty, opened the wide doors of my sorrow. I dropped to my knees on the sand and wept in great, gulping sobs, much to the embarrassment of my brothers, who made signs against the bier and would come nowhere near me or it. Though I knew that my behavior was unseemly for a warrior, I am not one of them. I could no more have stopped my tears than I could have stopped the wind. I could not even let Ceolas sing our gratitude for this kindness, so shaken with sobs was my body.

Bile, on seeing his two beloved ones so carefully adorned, could not stop vocalizing, circling the bier, throwing his one arm into the air over and over and crying out "Ah, ah, ah" like a wounded, lopsided seabird. Pity for him moved me to further weeping.

At last, my mother came up behind me and rested her hands on my shoulders. "See where they watch us," she whispered, inclining her chin toward the top of the cliffs. "Consider your duty to the tribe."

There on the headland were three women, dazzling, beautiful, obviously Greek from their white gowns to their elaborate cascades of curling hair. The wind caught at their gowns and swept them out to the side so that collectively they looked like a sail. It was that image which brought me from my sorrow; I looked back at our own ships, at our people unloading goods and gear. I sighed and stood.

I gathered Bile into my arms and half carried, half dragged him away from the bier. He leaned into me as he had when he was first injured, but his body, now at twelve years, was much larger and harder to carry.

It struck me that all the work that Skena had done, all the wonders that Ir had wrought, were lost to Bile now; he was as inarticulate and uncoordinated as he had been when he was first injured. In the short three days since Skena and Ir had disappeared into the sea, Bile had retreated into the body of that child who had been broken on the wagon wheel. I did not know if we would ever bring him back.

An Scail had been standing a little way behind me, silent and still, her white-clad body in an attitude of waiting. I came to stand beside her, deposited Bile on the sand. He curled into himself, shaking and vocalizing.

"Bile is most troubled," I said softly.

"Skena and Ir are here?" she asked quietly.

"They are, Wise One. I apologize for my grief; when I saw them I could not contain my sorrow."

"Never apologize for love or sorrow," she said softly. "Your weeping will help to cleanse your heart and make it ready for what must be done here. Describe to me what you see."

For a moment I felt startled—it was the first time that An Scail had ever asked me to describe our surroundings. And then the strangeness of all of it washed over me. She needed my descriptions because, for the first time in her life, she had departed from Galicia. No longer did the tower and the oaks, or even the roots of trees, dwell in her memory. I came out of myself then, forced myself up from my own sorrow.

"You would not have come if Ith had not died," I said to her softly.

"No. But I must now take on the burden that he would have carried. I must be eyes and ears and wise choices for you and for our people. That is what Ith would have wished of me; I give it gladly."

The greatness of her sacrifice strengthened me for my own; I bent myself to the task of describing for her what I saw. "Three women watch us from the headland."

"How do they appear?"

"As Greeks in both clothing and mien."

"Describe Skena and Ir to me."

"Skena and Ir have been cared for; they are washed and dressed and flowered, laid on a crystal bier."

"So they do not burn their dead."

I was startled at the conclusion, saw its correctness immediately. "On such a bier they could not. Their faces are raised as if they face the west."

"And in their care of our dead, they show themselves to be a civilized people. People who know that the soul continues."

"Yes, I can see that conclusion."

She nodded, gestured for me to continue.

"We have anchored in a great, round bay at the mouth of a wide river that winds in toward the land. Here, the hills slope upward toward the headland. The sea is richly blue, the land green and forested."

An Scail nodded. "That is all well. Describe for me the women on the headland."

I did so, observing their blowing white gowns, the long, ringleted hair.

"Red hair, black hair, and golden hair, you say?"

"Yes, all long and perfectly coiffed."

"Hmm. We will speak to these three, I think. Let me walk on your arm."

Bile, who had been sitting on the ground beside us vocalizing, suddenly stood and raced around to An Scail's other side, threading her hand through his one good arm.

"Bile," I said gently, but she raised her hand at me.

"I thank you, young man," she said in a dignified voice. "In this new country I am blind. You must be my eyes and ears."

He seemed to draw himself up, ceased vocalizing. Once again the wisdom of An Scail penetrated my grief.

I offered her my other arm, and together we made our way up toward the headland, surely the three most broken members of the Galaeci to make a first impression on those who dwelled here.

When we were halfway up, Airioch dashed up behind us, his heels kicking up sand.

"Wait until you see them," he said, excitement threading through his voice. "So beautiful. And the gold and jewels."

"You shall not accompany us," said An Scail. Her voice brooked no disagreement.

"But I have met them before. They are the Sisters, Banba, Fodla, Eriu."

"Yes, and you must tell us later of all that you learned of them, but for now we must form a new and first impression of our own. Return to the work of the ships."

I did not tell her that he had been doing none of that work; in truth I myself had been doing none myself, though not for lingering.

Airioch returned to the beach and began to give orders to Greeks and Galaeci alike.

When we reached the Sisters, I could see that in person they were more beautiful still, tiny women who just crested five feet, perfectly shaped in their billowing white gowns, their exquisite hair. Only their eyes seemed a little off, not quite the size or shape or color that I remembered the dancing eyes of the Greeks. They wore no jewels, no gold or silver, but for odd triangular shapes at their throat, crystalline, each incised with three spiraling and intertwined vines.

They were standing in a sort of triangular shape, the sister with the curling red hair at their head. I mimicked their formation, placing An Scail before me and stepping slightly back and to her left. Bile, in perfect silence, his eyes wide, did the same on the right.

I said nothing at all, assuming that there could be no way that any of their people could know the language of the Galaeci, so I was startled when the threesome inclined their heads toward An Scail and spoke in perfect Gaeilge.

"Elder woman, we welcome your wisdom among us. We are surprised at the return of the sons of Mil. Where is Ith among you?"

"Ith's spirit has departed from among us. I am An Scail, the Shadow. He sends me as his voice, his eyes and ears."

I was surprised again to see an expression of real sorrow shift over the faces of the Sisters.

"We sorrow to hear that he is not with you. We valued his wisdom. It was the decision of Ith that the sons of Mil would not return to this place. May we ask what it was that made him change that decision?"

I spoke for the first time. "Ith returned to us wounded and unable to speak. He was not able to tell us of a decision."

The lead sister turned her face up toward me; her eyes seemed to take me in and swallow me. "How was he wounded, Amergin?"

"How do you know my name?"

"You were beloved of Ith. He spoke of you often and in detail, as he did also of An Scail and Bile and of Mil, your father. We thought that the chief of the sons of Mil would attend this first meeting."

"Our father has also died," I said.

The little woman looked down at the bier on the stony beach below, looked back at me. "And these?"

"My wife, our unborn child, and my brother." I could feel my eyes filling again with tears. I blinked them back.

She sighed, a sound so reflective of our own sorrow that I nodded my head and raised a shoulder at the obvious overabundance of our sorrows. There was nothing more to say on the subject and I could not speak.

"What names do you bear?" I asked when I could speak, hoping to move away the awkwardness of the moment.

The lead sister looked flustered. "Forgive my rudeness," she said quietly. "We have forgotten the courtesies. It has been long since strangers came among us. I am Eriu. These are my sisters Banba and Fodla." She gestured first to one side and then the other. The sisters inclined their heads in acknowledgment, but still they said nothing. I began to wonder if, like Bile, they were mute.

"Is it you who have cared for . . . our dead?" I asked quietly.

"We have," she said softly.

"Then I thank you for your kindness." My voice broke on this last and I lowered my eyes from her gaze.

"Tell me their names that we may honor their journey with our chant."

"She was my wife, Skena. The boy is our brother, Ir."

Bile raised his eyes skyward but he made no sound.

"And you are his beloved brother?" Eriu said. She had turned her whole attention to Bile, her eyes fastened upon him. He nodded once. "And you loved Skena as though she were your mother?" He looked startled, vocalized once, a long "Ahhh." Eriu smiled gently. "I understand. I saw you weep them, child; your very bearing spoke of love."

She turned back to me. "She was bearing with you a child of the Braid?" she asked this softly.

"The Braid?" I shook my head. "I do not know the term; Skena was bearing our first child."

A look of such sadness passed over her face that for a moment I thought she might also weep.

"What does this mean? The Braid?"

"The cup," she said. She gestured with her slender hand. "The gift of Ith. It is chased and incised with braidwork. We assumed that it was important, thought perhaps that it might refer to your god."

"It is the pattern of life," said An Scail quietly. "Life is braided into life, ever and eternal."

"And there is no death," said the woman quietly.

"Ith has told you this?"

"It is what we believe, as well."

Eriu seemed to think for a moment, then raised her hands skyward. Without a word, her sisters stepped forward and caught at the upraised hands. A deep chanting sound began to issue from them that reminded me of the sound of our gaita.

"From this moment," said Eriu, "this place shall be known in your tongue and in ours as Inver Skena, the river of Skena."

Bile could not help himself after this pronouncement. He threw back his head and cried out, "Ah, ah, ah."

"It is our honor to do this," said Eriu, inclining her head toward Bile as though he had said something she understood perfectly.

He nodded and then suddenly stepped forward and extended his good hand toward her. She put hers into his instantly with no hesitation. He lifted it gently to his lips. It was an old Galaeci custom, courtly, an expression of appreciation, but I feared that she might not understand it that way. I stepped toward him; she turned her face toward me and shook her head once. Her eyes shimmered with water.

And that was the moment when I knew that at least she had not wounded Ith.

I interrupted them. "Speak to us of how Ith was wounded."

She looked perplexed. "This is what we asked of you, Amergin."

"We have been told that it occurred on the night before his return voyage, which he spent with you in his dwelling."

For the first time, the dark-haired sister spoke. "And was that piece of intelligence given to you by Airioch Feabhruadh?" Her voice was caustic, intelligent. I looked at her in surprise.

"It was," I said.

"He is your brother, is he not?"

"He is."

She said nothing more.

Now the golden-haired sister spoke.

"Know that Ith was safe among the Danu. He was an elder of great wisdom, and so we treated him."

"The Danu? That is the name of this place?"

"No . . . No . . . This place has no name." The tone of her voice was surprised, as if it were something she had not considered before. "We call it as we found it—the Green Isle."

I looked around and nodded; it was green in shades and gradations, richly emerald.

"We are the Danu," said Eriu. "That is what our . . . tribe . . . is called. The Children of the Danu."

"And you have come here from Greece?"

"A very long time ago, yes."

"I have traveled much in Greece."

She nodded and smiled. "Then we must speak of it further. We have not returned for many years. It has undoubtedly changed behind us."

"I knew of no Danu in Greece," I said softly. I changed my language to Greek, asked softly, "Where did you dwell in your time there?"

For a moment Eriu was quiet. She lowered her head, touched the triangular shape at her throat. I was reminded suddenly of the shape that had appeared in Uncle Ith's ogham curve.

In perfect Greek, Eriu answered me. "We lived on the isle of . . . Thrace."

"My mother gave birth to my brother—he that you have cared for—on Irena." I felt suddenly ashamed for the trick, remembering their gentle care of Ir and Skena.

Still in perfect Greek she continued. "And for that she named him Ir? Ah, our neighbor then. So you too have seen the exquisite blue of the waters?"

I could not fault her answers, yet all the while that we were conversing, the Sisters seemed to tighten their formation, to move closer to each other in their odd triangular shape.

Suddenly, An Scail spoke. "But surely these are all things of which we will speak further, Sisters, as time does not hurry us to know all things at once. Will you join us for the Feast and Spirit Fire tonight?"

"Spirit Fire?"

"We release the spirits of our dead in fire."

"Release them to where?"

"To the Western Isle of Feasting."

Suddenly Eriu smiled full on and her face lighted with the look. "We have much in common, An Scail," she said. "We would be honored to join you."

27

That did not go well at all," said Banba. She tapped her triangle, releasing Metaphor, and folded back into her tiny, wide-eyed self.

"Banba!" said Fodla. "The Ancients have asked us to remain in Metaphor at all times."

"I don't care; it wearies me. We are safe here in Tara."

"Remember the Fomor," said Fodla. "They penetrated the cities. These Galaeci strike me as very intelligent indeed; they do not miss much in conversation. What would happen if they saw us as we are?"

"Fodla speaks wisely," said Eriu. "They did seem especially skilled at nuances of conversation, winding back to the things they wished to know when we least expected it, picking up on every slip in our story. Always with great courtesy." She shook her head. "Of course there were no Danu among the Greeks. No city-state with such a name. What a fool I am. Amergin lulled me into a feeling that I was safe; how was this done?"

"Do not berate yourself overmuch, Sister. It is the same story we told to Fir Bolg and Fomor alike, and they never questioned our journey," said Fodla.

"But they had never been in Greece," said Banba. "These sons of Mil have journeyed there and farther. And Ith. Wanting to know how he was wounded and when and by whom. As if we, with our little hands, would knock an elder to the ground. And Ith one of their priests!"

"Evidently Airioch has hinted so," said Fodla.

"Oh, do you think so?"

"Banba!" said Eriu. "You take out your worry on our sister with your stinging tongue."

"I do," said Banba. "I am sorry. But Eriu is right; even the eyes of Amergin are intelligent . . . questing. We must be careful."

"We are all worried," said Fodla with a shrug.

Banba nodded. "He is beautiful though, is he not, their Amergin?"

Fodla shook her head. "Do you never stop?"

"Well, so tall. Taller than a Greek. And all that dark hair and those eyes. So large a man."

"He is a man in grief for his beloved and his child," said Eriu. "A child he believes that he has lost."

"That, in effect, he has lost," said Banba.

Eriu nodded. "These are the things that we must remember when we speak to him. His sorrow may make him overquick and oversensitive for quite some while. He may be too quick to draw conclusions; he will think with his anger and his loss. He may wish to place the blame for their loss on this journey, and hence on the Green Island or on us, who dwell here. Or his own grief may cause him to miss things among his own people, to make decisions based in haste and sorrow. Such a man is dangerous."

"Less dangerous, I think, than Airioch, who thinks with his greed and his lust, or Eber Donn, who thinks with his anger," said Fodla.

"Not so," said Eriu. "You are right, Banba. Amergin is intelligent. Dangerously, deeply intelligent. Know it, Sisters; I see it clearly in his eyes. He is a seeker of truth; he does not rest until he knows the truth. The Children of the Danu are in much danger there." She sighed. "Well, I am glad for our care of his lost ones. Such kindness will mean much to such a man. And he is, I think, a voice of wisdom for his tribe. I do so wish that we could tell him . . ."

"We cannot," said Banba. "And we must not speak of her except among ourselves. Ever."

"Come," said Fodla. "Think not on it. When the time comes for the child to be born we may all be surprised. The Mother works in the world in ways that none of us understands."

"True enough," said Eriu. She sighed. "We will prepare for their feast."

*   *   *

Sparks rose skyward at the edge of the water, in preparation for the funeral pyre. In the quiet bay, the Greek ships rode at anchor, their sails furled. The cargo ships, hired for the trip only and returning empty of plunder, had made for the sea at first light.

Already, the Galaeci had begun to make themselves a permanent place at the edge of the river. Dwellings had hastily been erected near elaborate tents of silk. Horses were penned at one edge of the beach, cattle at the other. Though there were not many, they looked like good breeding stock. With each group were giant dogs with curly hair. They seemed to patrol the stock both within and without; they were themselves the size of ponies.

At the very edge of the tide, the Galaeci had built a great bonfire. They had placed Skena and the child together on a wooden bier at the edge of the water. Beside the bier were two urns.

From the headland above, Banba whispered to her sisters. "These must be the vessels for their dead."

"There are so many of these Galaeci," said Fodla softly. "They number more than two hundred surely."

"And they have not even begun to reproduce," said Banba dryly. "From the look of them they can do that very well indeed."

"Banba!" said Eriu sharply. "And they do not know how few our numbers are." She sighed. "Let us go among them and try to behave as Greeks."

"How do Greeks behave at Galaeci funerals?" asked Banba.

"How should we know that?" asked Fodla, her tone exactly like that of her more caustic sister.

The funeral feast that followed the fire was held at hastily assembled trestle tables under the open sky. The Sisters were given a place of honor between Bile and An Scail although most of the Galaeci avoided them completely, not even meeting their eyes.

To the Sisters it seemed a raucous celebration for a funeral feast. The Galaeci danced wildly under the stars while they beat on drums and whistled on bone flutes. From time to time, their pipers would play haunting and eerie tunes on the pipes. At those times the Sisters saw several couples slip away into the darkness.

"I told you that they would mate well and often," hissed Banba to Eriu, who sat at the center.

"Hush," Eriu said softly.

Only Amergin and Bile sat silent at the table, eating nothing and speaking not at all.

In a lull in the merriment, An Scail leaned toward the Sisters. "You wonder why we celebrate with such gusto at such a time."

"It seems a most joyful occasion," said Eriu cautiously.

"We keep vigil with the dead. We wake with them and celebrate the journey they begin. Our couples mate that we celebrate the force of creation and life, which will eventually return them to us. There will be time for grief on the morrow."

"We too celebrate the passage of our Ancients, Wise One. We are only sorry that these two have left you so young."

"Three," said An Scail. "For among us, a child is a returning spirit."

Eriu drew in her breath, closed her eyes briefly.

An Scail continued. "Among you, few die young?"

"Few until this time," said Eriu. "We have lived without war for a very long time."

An Scail nodded. "We too. Galicia was far removed from Rome and Greece, from Carthage and Persia. We mined our metals and herded our cattle. We made our wines. We traded, but we had precious little contact with the outside world."

"And you were happy?"

"We were."

"So why did you come here? What impelled this journey?"

"Mil, the father of Amergin, was ever a wanderer. A restless warrior and a dreamer. Inisfail was his dream."

"Inisfail?"

"That was his name for this place. Isle of Destiny."

"And how did he hear of this place?"

An Scail closed the rheumy silver eyes. "I know not," she said softly. "Sailors speak of it; they say it is a place of magic. They have seen lights emanating from the place, even far out to sea. Perhaps Mil heard of it from them. Ith told me that Mil had dreamed of the place from childhood, saying that here the clan of Mil would meet its destiny."

"And you wish that he had not."

An Scail smiled, a small, sad smile. "In the pursuit of this place we have lost Ith and Mil, Skena and Ir, and Amergin's unborn child. Scota, the mother of Amergin, has lost her beloved husband and her child. She continues on fury. Eber Donn, eldest of Mil, vows revenge. I suspect that we are not yet done with losses."

"Why do you tell us this?" asked Eriu, astonished.

"We have come among you with our purposes and our sorrow. I hear in your voices that you are . . . older . . . than we, and perhaps wiser. I tell you so that perhaps wisdom will prevail."

"And Amergin?"

"He is our Bard; his word carries much weight with our people."

"And yet he does not seem to be of your people."

"A bard stands apart. He trains with druii. He captures the history of the tribe. He sings our history. He directs its behavior when it is most required."

"Druii?"

"What I am. Perhaps what you are to your people."

"His wife was also druii?

"Skena was that rarest of healers, a weaver."

"A weaver?" Eriu felt excitement coursing through her. "Speak to me of this."

"A weaver binds people together. Skena wove Amergin and Bile into the tribe. She wove the tribe together with her presence and her calm. She wove the sick into the care of the healthy. She saw us as one people, and so she behaved. Among us, as among all people, are those who weave and those who sunder. We will miss her great skills here in this new place."

"We have among us a healer of great wisdom. I should like for you to meet her."

Eriu turned toward Amergin, spoke softly. "When you were at sea, we thought that we heard the sounds of music. It was . . . most sorrowful. Was it you?"

"It was Ceolas."

"Ceolas? Who is he?"

Suddenly Bile stood and loped away from the table.

"Have I said something to trouble him?" Eriu half stood, as if she would follow the child.

Amergin halted her, his hand on her wrist. Eriu stared down. The great hand covered and encircled her slender bones, seemed to cover half her forearm. Would he feel the true bones beneath the skin of Metaphor?

Fear beat suddenly in her throat. Then just as suddenly he released his hold. "See where he returns bearing Ceolas."

Bile came loping across the beach, a small harp in his arms. It was shaped almost like a triangle, small enough to sit on the lap of the singer.

"Ceolas is a harp."

"She is a clarsach, a bardic harp for traveling. She is my singer."

"Will you sing for us?"

Amergin shook his head, but Bile thrust the harp at him repeatedly. "Ah, ah, ah!" he cried, pointing toward the wooden biers at the edge of the water.

Eriu spoke softly. "Bile says that they would wish to hear your song for their journey."

Amergin turned toward her. He looked directly into her eyes. The expression that moved across his face moved from anger through surprise and then to something else. He leaned in, as if he would regard her more closely. Eriu turned toward Bile, held out her hand. He took it immediately.

"What song would they hear?" she asked him, as if he could answer perfectly.

For answer Bile began to hum.

Amergin nodded. He ran his fingers gently along the strings and began to sing.

> *"Green is my longing, Inisfail,*
> *Isle of Destiny, northern diadem.*
> *Why do you call to me?*
> *How shall I sing them,*
> *sloe-eyed creatures at your shore?*
> *Do you await me, Inisfail?*
> *Country of my dreams;*
> *I am Amergin, son of Mil,*
> *warrior, wanderer.*
> *Dream of the father now become*
> *the harpsong of the son.*
> *Inisfail, land of mystery,*
> *Sing to me."*

"It is beautiful."

"It is the song which began our journey. Long long ago."

"And now you wish that it had not."

"I do."

"I cannot blame you, Amergin. You have sustained too many losses. The heart is hard-pressed to bear them."

He nodded, silently, his mouth working.

"What sloe-eyed creatures do you speak of? The deer of the Green Isle? They are large indeed."

He faced her directly, looked full at her eyes. "I speak of you. Of your people. Of your eyes. I think that I saw them once on the journey."

Eriu could think of nothing to say, found that she could not look away. Her heart thundered in fear. What did he see? Did Metaphor waver? O Mother, do not let him see us beneath this guise!

From across the beach Airioch danced with a woman of the tribe, moving through the elaborate squares, his handsome face lit with laughter. He leaned down over the woman, his golden hair falling across his face. He said something into her ear. She laughed and pushed him away. He turned away from her, began to weave his way toward their table, calling aloud, "Banba! Fodla! Eriu!"

"Trouble approaches," Banba said aloud.

The whole table burst into laughter, Amergin with them. He broke his gaze with Eriu.

Airioch stumbled toward them. When at last he reached the table, he bowed low before the Sisters. "I fear that we have not made you a part of our feasting," he said. "Allow me to correct that. Come and dance with me." He stared directly at Banba. Eriu turned toward her sister, her eyes dancing mischief. Banba raised a hand.

"I dare not," she said. "I do not know the dances of the Galaeci. I will damage your feet for trying."

He laughed aloud. "One so small and light as you? Come then, we will dance a Greek dance." He grabbed a square of linen, held it up from the table, shook it in the air.

An almost palpable stillness fell over the table. Banba gently fingered the triangular necklace that she wore around her throat. The Sisters turned and looked at each other as if they would ask or answer a question.

"He means no offense," said Amergin. "It is our custom to sing and dance for the dead."

"Well said, Brother," said Airioch. "Well?"

Banba stood suddenly and smiled. "Prepare yourself," she said. "I can dance forever, son of Mil."

28

"Who invited them?" Scota moved angrily across the tent, pacing before her assembled sons.

"This An Scail has done," I said quietly. "Will you question her druid wisdom, Maither?"

Scota was fairly spitting. "These who have wounded Ith? These who have killed your father? Why would she invite these among us?"

"Father died in Galicia, Maither; these three had naught to do with him. And as for Ith, I do not think that they are responsible for his death."

"How can you say that?" shouted Eber Donn. "Airioch has told us that he was wounded in their company."

I felt so weary that it was an effort even to speak in the company. I wanted to lie down and sleep. Perhaps forever. I sighed. "Airioch is at the mating," I said softly.

"With the Danu woman?" Scota sounded horrified.

"Of course not," I said. "He mates with one of our own and he is not here to defend his position. Only I tell you that I do not think these Sisters wounded Ith. They seem to me small and gentle."

"Do not equate gentle with small," said Scota, a warning in her voice.

"In your case, Mother, none would dare equate the two." I spoke wearily but I smiled nonetheless; it was hard not to smile at the power in her little frame.

"Good then," she said, rapping me on the forehead with a flick of her finger. "Now consider this, my sons. Are there more of them than these three? Surely there must be, but where are they? Have we seen any but the Sisters? Why do they hide their numbers from us? We must find their dwelling places. This is what your father taught us; know the enemy's position."

"Why must you think of them as the enemy?"

"Why do you not think of them so?"

"I would rather wait to know them. They have been most kind to Skena and Ir in preparing them for the crossing."

"They have killed Uncle Ith!"

"And Mil," said Eber Donn.

I sighed again. It was like reasoning in a circle; they came back to their original argument like dogs to bones. "Do you look for reasons to war?" I asked aloud.

"You reason with your grief," said Eber Donn. "You do not think like a warrior."

"Well, if it means thinking like you, then I am glad that I do not."

Before Eber Donn could turn his wrath upon me, our brother Eremon stood among the company. "We should begin investigating the land," he said. "There may be good cattle pasturage, good running land for the horses. We should decide how to divide up the land."

Eber Finn nodded. "Eremon speaks wisely," he said. "What do we care for these Danu? At dawn we should leave this beach to begin our mapping."

"It is not ours to map!" I snapped. "Has it escaped you that there are others living here?"

"Three Greek women," said Eber Donn, shrugging. "Between Airioch and me we can mate with those or marry them."

A burst of laughter spread throughout the tent.

"They are the representatives of their people," I said softly, trying hard to be reasonable. "Surely there are others. We are on the beachhead here; we have not yet seen the interior. There may be vast cities of the Danu."

"Danu?"

"This is what they call themselves."

"But you have just made my argument for me. And Scota's as well," said Eber Donn. "We must know what we face; we must be ready to work from a position of strength."

Scota nodded. "You speak well, eldest of Mil. You speak as your father would speak. We will go among them and investigate."

"This should be done in darkness," said Eber Donn. "And quickly, while they are still surprised by our arrival."

"They did not seem surprised," I said.

"What do you mean?" asked Scota.

"They seemed to be expecting us. Although they said that Uncle Ith had told them that he had decided to recommend to father that we not return." I sighed at the complexity of that chain of logic; my brothers would reject it, I knew.

"So you see?" said Eber Donn. "The very fact that they expected us puts what they say about Ith to the lie. They would not have been awaiting our arrival if Ith had not told them we would come. So much more does that put to the lie their claim that they did not wound him."

His argument was actually logical, and I nodded as I thought it over. "Only that they seemed to hold him in such respect."

"Seemed," said my mother. "I care not for seemed. I will avenge the deaths of Mil and Ith."

"Here, here, Scota," shouted Eber Donn. "Most worthy wife for Mil."

My mother basked for a moment in his admiration, then made a decision. "I claim the right of a chieftain's wife," she said. "We will go among them this night with a party of exploration. We will scout and we will map. We will search out their weaknesses."

She chose for the party Eber Donn, Eremon, Eber Finn, and, for balance, two warriors of the Galaeci who were not of our clan. They all scrambled for their shortswords and daggers, their cloaks and sandals. I removed to my tent and began to assemble my equipment. Bile was sleeping soundly on his little cot; I envied him the deep oblivion of sleep, but my preparations awoke him. He did not vocalize, but watched me with his huge dark eyes, now so full of sorrow.

"They go to explore the Danu territory," I whispered. "I must go with them."

Bile shook his head violently. He jumped from his cot and scrambled among his chalks and papers. From the pile he drew up a portrait. It was of the Three Sisters of the Danu, standing in perfect triangle. They were surrounded by a nimbus of warm light.

I nodded. "I see what you see, little brother. I will do my best to keep them from mischief. They think with their grief and their anger."

He came to me suddenly and wrapped his arm around my waist. This he had not done in more than a year, Skena being the recipient of all his hugs, his incipient manhood keeping him from such displays with his brother, but I could feel in this hug all his grief and loss, all his love for me.

"I will return to you," I whispered. "Then we will have time to mourn for Skena and Ir. All will be well."

His eyes met mine and I could see that it was too late for such a statement, that Bile would never fully believe such a thing again. Nor, I knew, would I.

CEOLAS CAUTIONS WISDOM
Do not think with your anger
Do not act on your grief
Do not reason with sorrow
Sorrow does not reason well.
Oh, think and be still, Mother,
Reason, Brothers, do not act in haste
Haste is the father of regret,
Haste will increase our sorrow.

"I did not choose you for this party, Amergin," said my mother.

I silenced Ceolas, set her beside me. "I am a poet," I said softly. "You know that we choose for ourselves. You know, too, that the clan should heed the wisdom of the poets, for we are the voice of the past, the whisper of caution, the hint of what will be."

My mother simply waved her hand at this, dismissive. "And what is your purpose here?"

"It is the same purpose as always with poets, Maither. Wisdom."

She tossed her head and set off toward the headland. I reflected that wisdom was in very small supply in this company, nor would any chant of mine increase its supply.

We moved through the dark forest at the crest of the hill. Here, the trees were towering and ancient, their trunks thicker than the arms of several druids linked. I reflected on how much Uncle Ith would have loved them, anticipated showing them to An Scail, letting her place her hands against their contained wisdom. We had gone less than an hour's time from the sea when we came upon a doorway of stone, two huge white pillars, carved entirely in braidwork and standing thirty feet tall. Stretched across them was a lintel of almost transparent crystal. All around this doorway the forest stretched in profusion; it was a doorway to nowhere.

Eber Donn signaled.

The company stopped. He circled around the structure, examining the pillars, peering up at the capstone. He did not walk through it as one might a door, nor lay his hands upon the intricate carvings. He circled back to us. For a time we stood silent in the forest. Eber Donn shrugged. "I know not," he whispered softly. "Perhaps it is the doorway of a fallen temple. I think we should continue on."

Suddenly, with no warning, our little mother simply stepped between the pillars.

Brave and foolish Scota.

"Mother," I hissed. "Come out from there."

She stood staring at us, then stepped through the other side. She looked at us through the portal and shrugged. She stepped back between the pillars again. Still nothing happened. She looked to either side. Something caught her eye; I saw her peer toward it, concentrating on something in the pattern of carvings on the pillar.

"Touch nothing, Maither," I whispered, but it was already too late.

She had pressed her hand to some shape in the pattern.

There was a sudden flash of light, white and pure. For a moment it seemed to me that I could see through my mother, could see her bones and her beating heart, could see her held in the white light like the rabbit who dwells in the moon.

Behind me I could feel the scouting party moving back away from Scota, and I knew that they too had seen the same thing.

And then just as suddenly the light went out.

My mother fell forward, crumpled to the forest floor.

I knelt over her, pulled her from between the pillars. I cradled her against me, my brave and foolish warrior mother.

"You were right, Amergin," she whispered. "Their city is vast. It is . . . I have seen it. Do not let them stay here; take them home." Her breathing stilled; she closed her eyes.

I closed mine with her. I knew it was too late for that. We might have learned the truth of Uncle Ith, given time. But now Scota was dead, mother of the clan. The sons of Mil had just declared war on the Danu, and there would be no going home.

29

Y ou gave me your word!" Eriu spat the accusation at Macha.

"Nor did I break it. I understand honor even if it is not our practice."

"They have laid out another of their dead, the little woman warrior."

"Really?" asked Macha. "Her death was not of our doing. But then why should this trouble you? If they lose enough of their company, surely they will return to their homeland with tales of the terrors of the place. That in turn will keep others from our shores. Is this not what you wish?"

Eriu was leaning back against the stone, its face warmed in the May sunshine.

Macha stretched out an arm, leaned it against the stone above Eriu's head.

For her aspect of Metaphor she had chosen a man, tall with thick golden hair and green eyes, his body rangy and muscular.

"Do you like him?"

"Who?"

"Him that I have adopted?"

"Did you wish to look like a Fomor?"

Macha laughed aloud. "You know as well as I that I imitate these new-comers with their height and their warrior bodies. I like them well; I would be just as happy if they did remain. My sisters enjoy the simple Fir Bolg, but these seem much more sophisticated folk. I like my . . . chal-lenges . . . sophisticated. I have begun to imagine all of the ways that I could . . . interact . . . with these Invaders. I could trouble them for years, for centuries."

Eriu shook her head. "You weary me."

Macha shrugged. "That's as may be, but I tell you this so that you will understand. I did not kill their woman. I would prefer for them to stay. Why do you not ask them how she died?"

Suddenly and without warning, Amergin appeared over the crest of the hill. He looked weary, old, his steps heavy, his head lowered. He did not raise his head until he was nearly upon them.

Eriu watched as he took in the huge man leaning over her, his arm on the rock, her back against the stones, her face tipped up toward Macha's Metaphor. Amergin's face changed like the sea: sorrow to anger, confusion to certainty. His pace changed, lengthened into long, deliberate strides.

Eriu had the sudden wild urge to duck from beneath the arm, to run, to press her triangle to the stone and vanish into the city below, to scream for her sisters. He must have read the emotions in her face; she saw him nod, as if he had reached a decision. He moved toward them.

Eriu lifted her chin, stepped forward. "We see that another of your company has died. We extend our sorrow."

"You see it? You did not cause it?" Amergin leaned toward her as he spoke.

Macha drew an arm around Eriu's shoulders, protectively. Eriu shot her a look of contempt. Amergin looked between them, confused.

"Your . . . mate . . . need not fear me, Eriu. I will not harm you. I seek to know what caused the harm to Scota."

Macha laughed aloud, a rich, masculine sound, ripe with promise. "You could not harm her as long as I am here. So this is the one you have spoken of, Eriu, sweet. Amergin, is it not?"

"It is." Eriu straightened, ducked out from beneath the arm.

"And you are?" Amergin addressed Macha directly, a challenge in his voice. Macha strode forward, clasped his arm at the elbow.

"Macha," she said. "I welcome you among us. You and all your clan." She bared her teeth in a blinding smile. "The Sisters speak well of you; Eriu knows how much I value her opinion."

Eriu wanted to slap the grinning face, to warn Macha not to toy with Amergin, to warn Amergin not to trust Macha, but she could say nothing.

"Have you come looking for us?" Eriu asked.

"I have," said Amergin. "It is my clan I come to speak of."

"Ah, certainly," said Macha. "Eriu has told me; one of your company has died. A pity. How did it occur?"

"It is Scota," he said. "My mother." He closed his eyes, inhaled a deep, shaking breath.

"Oh no!" Eriu pressed her hands over her mouth. "Your mother. Oh, Amergin, the weight of your sorrow."

He nodded, but before he could speak again, Macha broke in.

"How did it occur, for we do not know." She gave a strange sidelong smile to Eriu.

"We were hiking in the forest last night when we came upon a door."

"Why?" said Macha. Eriu saw with a start that even in Metaphor Macha was not as tall as Amergin.

"Why . . ." Amergin seemed confused by the question, but he did not retreat before Macha. He seemed untroubled by her approach, though he shook his head.

"Why were you hiking in the forest? The forests of the Green Island are most dangerous, especially in darkness." Macha turned toward Eriu. "Did you not tell him, sweeting?"

Eriu ignored the gambit, looked directly into Amergin's eyes. "She was struck by a bolt of white lightning?"

"More than struck," said Amergin. "She was immersed in it, bathed. She held her hand to the stone and seemed to be caught in the light. It killed her."

Eriu closed her eyes. She nodded. "These are ancient doorways, Amergin. They are . . . harnessed with lightning for the protection of my people. Had you asked me before you wandered, I would have warned you from them. No one has tried to enter them for . . . many years."

Amergin let out a long breath, shook his head as if he searched for something to say. A long silence prevailed.

"Doorways to where?" he asked at last.

It was not what Eriu had expected. She thought for a moment, then answered honestly. "Into our city."

"I saw no city, though Scota said that she had seen it."

"It is there; you will not see it. Nor can any of your people pass through the doorway into the city."

Amergin thought about this in silence.

"So much for Greece," he said at last, softly. He met Eriu's eyes.

"We came here from Thrace as we told you," she said. She could hear the defensiveness, the panic in her own voice.

Macha spoke. "Any who try to pass through the doorway will be wounded or die. We are quite skilled at weapons, Amergin. Would you like to see more?" She grinned, easy in her superiority and enjoying her masculine Metaphor.

"Do you threaten the sons of Mil?" Anger moved across Amergin as suddenly as a thundercloud and he stepped toward Macha. She actually stepped back, so sudden was his movement. It struck Eriu that it would be most unwise to underestimate these Galaeci. Both their intelligence and their anger seemed swift.

"She does not threaten," said Eriu, holding up her hands.

"She?"

"Macha. He. You frighten me! Both of you." She leaned against the rock and pressed her hands over her face, her knees weak with terror, with the certainty of trouble. Suddenly she heard familiar voices from the other side of the hill.

"She said that she would be here."

"Eriu, where are you, dear? We bring the morning repast."

Fodla and Banba came up over the hill. Each maintained her original Metaphor, but they were dressed as Greek peasants might be and swinging between them a woven basket full of bread and skins of wine.

Eriu nearly collapsed with relief. She ran to them, embracing them both. "I am glad to see you," she said loudly. "The men are threatening war."

"The men?" said Banba.

"Amergin and Macha. They posture with each other like stags."

She saw Banba's eyes widen, saw Fodla turn a white face in the direction of Macha. Suddenly, Banba ran toward Macha, raising up high on tiptoe to kiss his cheek.

"Macha," she said. "How wonderful you look; we haven't seen you looking this good for so long."

Macha burst into laughter, rich and masculine. "You Sisters never cease to surprise me," she said.

"Well good, for we bring the morning feast. Will you join us, Amergin?"

"I cannot." He shook his head. "My mother stepped into one of your doorways. She was . . . wounded unto death."

Banba ran to him and took both of his hands in hers. "No. Oh, the doorways. Your mother. Oh, Amergin, we should have warned you about the lightning. Sister, we must speak to the Ancients. Surely we must change the doorways. We would not wish for any more of the sons of Mil to be injured."

"I shall do that," said Eriu. She was working hard to keep a straight face, her true sorrow for Amergin's loss at war with her sister's overdone performance. Still, the arrival of Banba and Fodla had broken the tension of the moment.

"Can you change the doors?" asked Amergin.

"We can," said Eriu, "though we have not done it for many . . . years. There was no need until you came. Certainly we will try."

"Will you come before our Council? Will you say so?"

"Does their anger move them toward war?" Eriu asked. She met his eyes directly, saw the answering response. He nodded.

"Will they be in any danger if they come among you?" asked Macha. "I would not want the Sisters put at risk."

"Come with them then," said Amergin. "And bring as many warriors as you like. Come armed if you like."

Eriu understood. Amergin too was worried, thought that perhaps a show of strength might calm—or frighten—the warlike Galaeci. Before she could speak, Macha responded.

"So we shall," said Macha. "We will be among you at the noon hour."

Amergin turned and walked down the hill, his shoulders bowed.

Eriu turned angrily on Macha. "You make a mockery of his sorrow!"

"I care not for his sorrow. I am playing a game. I am sorry that you did not enjoy it. Banba did."

Banba shook her head. "One does not enjoy you, Dark One. One plays with you, like a fidchell board, moving the pieces, vying for position."

Macha inclined her head. "You play well. Next time you should kiss me here." She tapped her lips and grinned.

"There will be no next time."

"But there will. For we will accompany you at noon. My sisters and I. Warriors to protect the beloved Sisters from the sons of Mil. He's a thick one, this Amergin, though surely not as thick as the Fir Bolg. Although he saw through none of us, I did think the question about the city was well chosen and well timed. And he will not be accepting Greece as our origin place. He might prove an enjoyable player. Still, if he is the best of his lot, they are ripe for the picking."

Eriu closed her eyes. "This becomes too tangled," she said softly. "O Danu, if only they had not come."

30

I saw them assemble at the crest of the hill, a huge company of them this time.

I alone climbed the hill to meet them, our people gathered below on the beach in a tight semicircle, weapons at the ready.

The Sisters stood to the forefront; Eriu's eyes seemed overwide and fearful. With them was an ancient little woman with gray hair and gray eyes who looked remarkably like An Scail. Behind that quartet was a phalanx of warriors, among them the man Macha whom I had already met. Flanking him were two dark-haired warriors who looked as tall and fierce as any I had encountered in my travels and had in their bearing and their blank facial expressions the look of professional soldiers. Macha and his companions each wore on his arm an elaborate silver gauntlet, a mark, I supposed, of their military rank within the company.

To either side of that cluster were dozens of warriors, men and women, all surpassingly beautiful, all carrying slender spears which looked to be made of some kind of crystal. I wondered at the efficacy of such weapons.

I took in a deep breath and steadied my hand, then raised it to the company. "I am Amergin, poet of the Milesians. I give you greeting and guarantee of peace."

"How will you guarantee that, poet?" asked Macha.

"I will," I said simply. "I have spoken to my people. If any of them moves against you, you may have my life."

Behind Macha, the two dark soldiers exchanged a glance.

I heard Eriu inhale sharply.

"No such penalty will be necessary, poet," she said. "We will take our safety at your word."

"Nor are we without recourse of our own," said Macha.

"Hush!" said Eriu.

Macha shifted his stance, met my eyes. His eyes seemed to hold some dark amusement in their depths.

"Come among us and we will talk as civilized peoples do," I said.

Eriu nodded.

I moved to the head of this great parade and led the people of the Danu down among my own people, feeling somehow as though I were leading wolves into the fold, although my own people were larger and better armed than these.

When we had everyone seated on opposite sides of the circle, I stood. I drew my longsword from over my back and drove it upright into a bale of hay that Bile had covered with fabric for the occasion.

"Here I draw erbe ndruad," I intoned, "the fence of battle. None shall cross it."

My people raised their hands, palms out, to indicate their agreement. I saw Eriu watch the gesture, raise her own hand. Her people followed, though Macha and his warriors seemed reluctant and he looked at me with insolence as he complied.

"I invoke the right of Poet. All will hear!" I called out. The company came to immediate silence. "People of the Danu, people of the Galaeci." I nodded at the assembled tribes. "I will speak truth before you. Teangu do dhia, teanges mo thuath. This I swear by the god by whom my people swear. Hear me.

"We need not come together as enemies if we will reason with wisdom. The Galaeci have come here to Inisfail as journeyers. Yes, we have seen this place ever as our destiny, but we know now that these, the people of the Danu, have preceded us. Surely that gives them first rights on the land."

Eber Finn and Eremon bristled and twisted in their seats, but I raised my hand. They remained silent.

"Although we do not know your numbers, the land and sea seem vast to us. If there be an empty space upon this isle, send us there. There we will raise our cattle and ride our horses. There our women will give birth to our children. We have sustained many sorrows in recent days."

I drew in a deep breath to steady my voice; for a moment I felt over-whelmed by the thought of our dead—Skena and Ir, Ith, my father and mother. Surely this was a fool's journey, a journey of sorrows. But what should we do now; turn around and go back upon the sea from whence we came? I shook my head.

"We wish only for pasturage and a green hill on which to build our vil-lages. We wish to bind our wounds and increase our clans. We will not trouble the people of the Danu, nor will we attempt to enter your door-ways." Behind me Airioch cleared his throat. I gestured at the upraised sword; he remained silent. I continued.

"Eriu of the Danu, what response do you make?"

Eriu stood among the company. She closed her eyes and raised her hands. Her sisters stood suddenly and took them. They issued forth the deep, throaty chant that sounded so like the bass note of the pipes. Though I had heard it before, none of my people had heard it. I saw them move restlessly in their places; one or two made the signs against enchantment.

Eriu spoke. "People of the Galaeci. The Children of the Danu have lived here on the Green Isle for hundreds of years. When your heralds came among us, we explained our ways to Ith, your druid. Ith decided that it was best for the sons of Mil to remain in Galicia, where their ways were known and loved. Yet now you tell us Ith has died. Here you are among us with your goods and your gear, and on your first night among us one of your number is wounded unto death by the doorway to our city. This brings us great sorrow. It seems but a poor welcome to ask you to return to the sea, but this is what we ask."

A wave of angry murmuring swept over the Milesians.

Eber Donn jumped to his feet. "We will not return to the sea! Here we are and here we will remain!" Some of our people cheered him; I saw others turn and look longingly for the water.

Eriu raised her hand.

I put my hand on the hilt of my longsword. "She has not finished her argument!" I thundered it out. "I have commanded silence. Silence will prevail."

A complete silence fell over the company; Eber Donn dropped to his seat. Eriu met my eyes, and I saw something that resembled surprise move across her face. She nodded, continued.

"Sons of Mil. We do not ask you to return to the sea forever. Nor do we ask you to sail back from whence you came. We ask you for three days. Three little days. Retreat to the ninth wave of the sea; give us time. In those three days we will change our doorways that none will wound you anymore; this we have not done for many years, and it requires time. There will be some danger while we work.

"We will select from the great fields and forests of the Green Isle pasturage and fortified hills where you may build your cities."

"Our cargo ships have departed," shouted Eber Donn.

Eriu nodded. "Leave your cattle and your horses here on shore; none of the Danu will trouble them. We do not herd cattle, nor do we own horses. You need not reload your ships. Only take yourselves to sea that our . . . lightning . . . will not trouble you. When you return, we will retreat into our cities. Perhaps in time, our peoples can learn of each other's ways. Perhaps in time we will encounter each other without fear. But until that day comes, Danu will keep to Danu cities, Galaeci to Galaeci."

I looked at my brothers and at our assembled clan. Eber Donn was shaking his head. Eber Finn and Eremon, having heard of pasturage and hillsides, were debating with each other whether or not it was safe to leave the cattle and horses with the Danu. Airioch was doing his best to catch the eye of Banba, the dark-haired sister. I noted with surprise that our youngest brother, Colpa, was seated beside him, his hand clasped firmly in Airioch's. I felt a sudden wash of shame for not considering him, suddenly motherless and fatherless at not quite ten years. Too many sorrows.

I took a deep breath. I spoke for the company.

"It is decided. We will retreat to the ninth wave of the sea. At sunset, we will send Scota's spirit to join our father's. When we have waked the dead, we will depart. We will return at dawn in three days' time."

Across the circle, Eriu nodded at me, her face a mixture of relief and sorrow. Behind her, Macha was shaking his head.

CEOLAS SINGS FAREWELL
Proud spirit, Scota,
mother of many sons,
go into the West,
seek there our father, Mil;
say that his sons remember.

Seek there our uncle Ith;
say that we will try
to bear wisdom in a new place.
Seek out our brother Ir,
say that Bile misses his laughter.
Seek out Skena my beloved,
who will bear our child in the West;
say only that I love her,
say only that my song is for her.

From the darkness at the far edge of the beach, I watched quietly as the sparks carried the last of my mother's spirit skyward, as the drums began the waking that would last throughout the night. In the quiet bay, our Greek companions began the process that would allow us to go to sea on the remaining three biremes. They muttered among themselves, perhaps worried at being in the employ of the crazy Galaeci, who could not decide whether to go or stay. I sat down heavily against a sea rock. I dropped my head down on my knees and let the tears spill.

"Amergin?"

I leaped to my feet and wheeled around, the tears still making rivers on my cheeks. Eriu was standing right behind me, the sea wind moving her long gown. I could not imagine that I had not heard her approach. I realized suddenly that I towered over her, saw her sudden fear of my size flare up in her eyes. She waved me back to a sitting position; I dropped to the sand so as not to frighten her further. I motioned for her to sit beside me; to my surprise she did so unhesitatingly.

"I have heard your song. I grieve your many losses. We of the Danu are sorry for the loss of your mother," she said softly. "We did not anticipate the . . . curiosity . . . of your people. The Fir Bolg are not a curious folk."

I smiled sadly. "It is our strongest trait. We roam the world and we learn the world. We question and we voyage. It brings us always to trouble and to grief, but that is the way of the sons of Mil." I shrugged. "But speak to me of these Fir Bolg."

She smiled suddenly, and I knew that her smile made reference to my curiosity even in the midst of my grief. I smiled back through the glistening water in my eyes, nodded my head, shrugged.

"They are the others who dwell on this island, in the far, stony north. They are a simple people; they hunt and gather, farm a little. I would ask that you not mention them to your clan. They are under our protection and I would not want them harmed."

"And you trust me not to do this?"

She nodded. "You are a man of honor; this I know."

I met her eyes. "I have thought that same thing of you. Yesterday when you spoke to Bile. I do not know who injured our uncle Ith, but I know that it was not you or your sisters."

"I thank you for this trust. I will give you something in return. I also do not know who injured Ith, but I give you warning; do not trust the Macha in any of her guises."

"Her? This is the second time you have referred to this warrior as a woman."

She shrugged. "Like my sisters and me, Macha comes always in her . . . threesome. I tend to think of her . . . that way. As I think of my sisters," she amended.

"The threesome with the silver gauntlets! They are companions."

"They are . . . a warrior triad. Be wary."

"Macha seems to favor you. Is he your . . . beloved?"

"No! Never! Macha plays games with everyone; even I am not immune to them."

"Ah. I have a brother cut from that cloth."

"Yes, Airioch Feabhruadh. We see that as well."

"Do you think it was Macha who injured my uncle Ith?"

"I do not know. There are some among you who also move with dark, specific purpose."

I leaned back against the rock and sighed deeply.

"You are troubled, Amergin," she said. "You have good reason. Your griefs crowd around you like gulls, and your clan will be hard to control."

I nodded. "My clan is impossible to control as always. We should not have come. Ith had died and my father . . . So many of them wished to come, some for vengeance, some for gain."

"And you?"

"Where Skena was, I was home. It would not have mattered where. You must understand that, Eriu."

"No."

I turned to look at her, surprised by her answer. "You are beautiful, gentle, and wise. I cannot believe no man has spoken for you."

"We were bonded once, my sisters and I, but those to whom we were wed have died. They were good men and kind."

"It was arranged for you?"

"Yes."

"We do not arrange among the Galaeci. We choose, each for the other and both must agree."

"And the tribe as well?"

"Not so much agree as see what is before them and recognize it."

"And if they do not agree?"

I shrugged. "I have not seen it happen. We are . . . a strong-willed people."

"I envy you so great a love. Even in her leaving, your Skena remains with you in the chamber of your memory."

"Yes." I drew in a raggedy breath; Eriu touched my hand lightly with her own.

"Our ancient, Airmid, whom you saw tonight?"

I nodded. "She who resembles An Scail."

Eriu laughed aloud. "She does, doesn't she?"

"Your Ancient has told An Scail that she can restore her sight. Can you imagine?"

"If she says that she can do so, then it is so. Airmid is a healer of great skill."

"Why do you bring up her name?"

Eriu smiled. "Because once she had so great a love as yours." She was silent for a while, and then she spoke softly beside me. "So surely you are thinking that if you had not come here, you would still have your great love to you. And your uncle, your father, your brother."

"And my child."

She turned suddenly and looked up the hill toward the headland. Her face, which had been open, suddenly shuttered.

"Do they watch us?"

"No, we are alone."

"What do you fear?"

"Fear?"

"Something has made you suddenly afraid."

She shook her head and stood.

"Wait," I said.

She turned back toward me. I was struck again by the fact that her eyes did not quite fit her face, that even here in the shadows they looked overlarge. I found that I wanted her to remain, that the thought of being alone again with my sorrows gaped before me like the vast cold sea. I composed a hasty question.

"What will you do while we are at sea?"

"We will destroy all of the doors between our . . . cities and yours. They will vanish from this place; you will not see them again. We will depart and leave the land to you."

"Depart? Forever?" I felt suddenly bereft. "I shall miss you. And I am deeply sorry for the grief my clan has caused you with our arrival."

She looked surprised and then nodded. "I shall miss you too, Amergin. We are a strange pair, are we not, two outsiders who bear the weight of their peoples? Here in the shadows we have unburdened to each other. I thank you for bearing my troubles."

"And you for bearing mine."

"We shall try, Amergin, that our people do no more harm to each other, but I think that is a battle that we two will fight alone."

She turned and walked into the darkness.

31

b ow shall this be done?" Eriu spoke to the assembled company of the Danu.

"It should not be done at all! We have had the run of the Green Isle for nearly a thousand years. Ever since we vanquished those disgusting Fomor." Macha had resumed for the occasion her true aspect; the huge dark almonds of her eyes snapped, the cloudy nimbus of her darkness crackled with electricity. To either side, Banbh and Nemhain regarded the assemblage with their unblinking predatory eyes.

"This we know," said Eriu. "But change has come among us; they do not know that our numbers are barely double theirs, nor do they know that we are not a warlike people. They are; I see it clearly. We cannot vanquish them, so we must change to accommodate them. That is wisdom, Ravener."

"No! Wisdom says that we should go among them now, before they set foot on their ships. Of course we can vanquish them. We should use the arms, destroy them all, but for a few souls who can race back to Galicia with the terrible news and frighten the rest of their company away forever."

Eriu could hear some agreement among the Raveners, but most of her people would, she knew, seal up the cities and vanish like the mist before they would destroy the Invaders. She faced Macha.

"You have given me your word."

"I have. I wish that I had not. But I have said that I will not injure them until they come against us in battle. And they will, people of the Danu. Believe me on this; they will!"

She stormed from the chamber, Nemhain and Banbh hissing along in her wake.

Eriu sighed. "Can any speak to us of how we might seal our cities and hide our doorways?"

Airmid stood. "I can," she said softly. "But oh, my people, you will not like what I will say. The doorways must be destroyed. All the dolmens and the sarsen circles. All the passageways. They must be razed so that stone no longer stands on stone. All the triangle portals must be ground to dust, for it is in touching those that the woman was killed. Then we will dwell in complete safety here on our leaf of time. None will see us."

"Speak to us of the benefits and of the sacrifice," Eriu said quietly.

"None on the Green Isle dwell on our leaf of time; we will be able to frolic in the fields and the forests alone. None will molest us or trouble our children. These are the benefits. But we will be alone. We are fewer than a thousand people. We who are Ancients among you will die soon. We will have to abandon the Fir Bolg because to remove them with us would be too terrifying and too lonely for them. We will no longer be able to heal their children; those who are abandoned will die. Should the Invader come against them, we cannot defend them. We will also have to make a difficult decision for our own Hybrid children. Will they seal themselves into this time with us? If so, they will never see their parents again. Or will they go alone into their own time on the Green Island, a tribe at once neither Fir Bolg nor Milesian, brilliant and long-lived, but few in number and vulnerable, in danger from both their own clan and from the sons of Mil, fitting in nowhere." Airmid sighed.

"Speak the worst, Ancient."

Airmid nodded. "We were many, many more when first we came to this world. For our safety, our company divided. In our own part of the world, we have lost all who came here before us. Of our own number, we lost many when the volcano sent our island into the sea. We no longer have the numbers to rebuild great cities beneath the sea or elaborate cities in their world. Our race is depleted. The Danu create few children and those slowly. Our numbers will begin to diminish. Even when our numbers were larger, the Danu have depended, since we arrived on this world, on our contact with humans, on the blending of their Braid with ours and also on their knowledge and their need for our knowledge. Without them, our line will die out, little by little, but as surely as the trees grow ancient and then die. We will be alone, unheard of and unseen, a diminished race of people on an empty leaf of time. And then we will vanish entirely."

One of the historians stood. "Can we raise the Light Ships, go elsewhere?"

Airmid replied. "Surely we can go. The question is where would we go? We are familiar with the world of the Internum Mare, but it is too crowded for our return. When first we came to this world, we chose three directions. Some of our company traveled here before us; they are gone. Some traveled to the far west; are they also gone? Are there Danu elsewhere in this world? We know not."

Eriu held her hands out. "What say you, people of the Danu? I am but young in wisdom. Shall we journey? Shall we depart from the Green Isle? Or shall we seal our cities shut?"

"Perhaps a delegation," said the historian. "Those who have no children here, who are not healers for the Fir Bolg. We could take one or two of the small Light Ships, look for our lost brothers and sisters."

General agreement moved across the company. A dozen volunteers assembled themselves before the Danu.

"Go now," said Eriu. "While the sons of Mil put out to sea. While they stand no chance of seeing either our ships or their hiding places."

The group departed from the chamber.

Soft weeping moved across the room, and Eriu felt like joining them, like dropping into sorrow for their lost companions.

"How will they return to us if all the doorways are sealed?" Eriu asked softly, turning to Airmid.

Airmid just shook her head. "They will not," she said softly. "Once the doorways are destroyed, there can be no return. These twelve will be alone in the great world unless they find our lost companions."

"Perhaps Macha is right," said Eriu softly. "Perhaps the time has come to use Nuada's Silver Arms."

Airmid regarded her quietly. "Many will die, both Danu and Milesian."

Banba whispered softly. "It is our duty to protect the Danu, Ancient. Help us to choose."

Airmid smiled sadly. "I cannot. Only that I tell you that each choice has consequences; this I well know."

"Come, Sisters," said Fodla softly. "Together, we must decide."

Eriu stood before the company, raised her hands. Behind her, Banba and Fodla stepped up, linked with her arms.

"People of the Danu!" she said. "We have examined all of the choices. We have heard all of the arguments. Now, the Council Triad will decide the course of the Danu. Prepare yourselves to enter the Braid." Behind her, Banba and Fodla began the deep, nasal chant. In the room the people began to chant with them, to counterpoint the sound. They linked hands over and under, their eyes closed. In a high sweet voice, Eriu began Braidsong.

"Mother of the World,
All-Maker, hear us.
Bringer of Fire,
Singer of Song,
Keeper of Creation's Forge,
Womb Cradle of the World,
Cradle are you,
Comfort are you,
Hear our cry.
We call upon you,
Children of the Mother.
Sing wisdom to the Danu,
O Weaver of the Braid."

Eriu could feel her people entering the deep state of awe, the reverence in which they would wait upon the wisdom of the Braid. Eriu closed her eyes, tipped her head back. She felt herself begin to slip from her body, to enter the stream of the Braid, where wisdom dwelled.

Suddenly, the chamber door slid open.

Illyn rushed into the room. "People of the Danu," she cried. "Forgive me for interrupting Braidsong. We Hybrids have been watching from the headland; the Morrigu is there, pointing her Silver Arms at the water. There is a great storm at sea; the Milesian ships are in danger of the rocks; they will drown in the sea!"

32

You trusted them! See what a fool you are." Eber Donn shrieked it over the wind.

"It is a storm!" I cried. "Do you assume that these Danu control the wind and the sea?"

"Perhaps they do not control it, but perhaps they knew that it would come. Why else send us out to sea, vulnerable to wind and weather? It was a strange request, and you assented to it."

I could not deny his point, turned from him to hasten our company belowdecks, where at least they would not be washed overboard. I was glad that An Scail had refused to accompany us, had insisted that she would remain on shore. I looked out at the roiling water.

"I will prove it to you, Amergin!" shouted Eber Donn. "This is a Danu trick. And when I have shown you, we will attack them. We will kill every Danu on the island. That you will owe me, you great fool."

He began to clamber up the rigging toward the crow's nest.

"Eber Donn," I called into the wind. "The ship pitches. Do not go aloft."

But he scrambled higher. The fog was so thick that in a moment I could barely see him.

"Come down, Brother!" I called into the tearing wind. Suddenly and without warning, all went still. The ship ceased its pitching, the fog began to clear away from the rigging. I could see Eber Donn dangling high above me though I could not yet see our other two ships on the sea around us. Eber Donn looked down from his perch.

"Now do you see?" he called.

I nodded. How could I help but see? The very suddenness of the change was proof enough. No storm ceased in midrage, sudden as a cry. The Danu had sent us to the waters and they had stirred the waters, hoping that we would drown. Just as suddenly they had stopped them. We were nine waves from shore and completely at their mercy; at any moment they could stir the tempest again. And I had trusted them. I had led the whole of our tribe out to sea on that trust.

Rage coursed through me then, hot as fire. I felt it shake my very core.

"I see!" I called up to my brother. "We will kill them all! Come down, Brother. Before they set the sea to raging once again."

Eber Donn screamed in toward the shore, shaking his fist, clinging with one hand to the rigging. "We will destroy you, Children of the Danu. Prepare yourselves for the sons of Mil! Prepare yourselves for the thunder of battle!"

Airioch Feabhruadh came up from below, Colpa by his side, as he had been since the death of our mother. They stood looking up at Eber Donn.

"He believes that they brought the storm?" he asked softly.

I nodded. "What else could he believe?"

Suddenly and without warning, the storm came howling down upon us again, a huge wind catching at our sails. Our ship tilted on its keel.

Colpa was thrown to the deck, began to slide toward the water.

"No! No!"

I heard Airioch scream, saw him throw himself across the deck, reaching for Colpa. At the same time I saw Eber Donn, clinging with a single arm to the mast. I saw him swing out over the sea, hanging by a thread over the surging water. I saw precisely the moment when his great arm would no longer hold. He plunged into the sea, looking for all the world like a child's doll of rags.

"No!" Rage coursed through me, stronger than the storm.

"Beware, O Danu!" I cried. "Beware the vengeance of the sons of Mil."

As suddenly as it had begun, the storm ceased again. The sea was quiet. At first I could see nothing, but slowly the fog began to lift. Against the wall of the ship I saw Airioch, his body curled around a thick rope. I ran to where he lay. Curled in his arm was Colpa, coughing seawater and looking anxiously at Airioch. I knelt and held my hand to his neck.

"He lives," I said to Colpa; "he has banged his head."

Airioch moaned and opened his eyes.

"You'll be all right in a moment," I said softly. "But Eber Donn is gone from us."

Airioch dragged himself to his feet and stared up at the mast. "My brother," he whispered. "Oh, my brother. O you gods, what have I done?"

The wives of Eber Donn surged up from below the deck, looking around for his presence, their many children clinging to them.

I told them what had happened; the deck was filled with their high keening wails.

I stood; one of our ships, its sails broken, limped toward us across the water.

"Where is our third bireme?" I called across the water to the Greek captain.

"We do not know; we could see nothing."

"Make for shore!" I cried. "We will anchor in the bay."

An Scail came to meet us on the shore, her hand shading her eyes.

"You were wise to elect to remain on shore, Wise One. See what they have wrought with their false promises. We arm for war!"

"Are you certain they have done this?"

"Who else could raise a storm and make it cease, all in but three hours' time?"

"What of the three days the Danu requested?"

"It is they who began this storm," I said, my fists clenched in fury. "They no longer deserve our trust or our promise."

An Scail shook her head. She turned and walked toward the headland, her hand still shading her eyes.

"Do not go among them," I shouted, but she continued, raising the back of her hand against me.

"Someone must make wisdom if you will not," she called. Her voice carried out over the sea, above the watery grave of the Milesian dead.

By nightfall, our Greek sailors began to ready themselves for departure in the remaining two biremes. The sons of Mil would now be residents of Inisfail, like it or no.

33

On the headland, Eriu ran at Macha, pushed her hard from behind. Macha staggered under the blow, dropped to her knees. The Silver Arm pointed downward at the rocky beach and carved a long trench into the sand. For a moment Nemhain and Banbh ceased their work with the arms, turned in their sister's direction.

At sea, the storm suddenly abated.

"You gave me your word!" Eriu screamed. "What will you bring upon the people of the Danu?"

"I said that I would not harm them and I did not; I stirred the sea and that is all."

"What, will you dance words with me? Cease now!"

She screamed it at Nemhain and Banbh, who had begun to direct their streams of light at the sea once again, roiling the water and thickening the fog. Nemhain's lips curled in a smile. Suddenly a burst of light struck Nemhain's arm. Another grazed the shoulder of her sister Banbh. Banbh screamed. Simultaneously, the two sisters shook their arms free; the silver gauntlets crashed to the ground.

Banba and Fodla swept in from either side, Light Spears in their hands. Lightning swift, they gathered the abandoned Silver Arms into their hands and ran toward Airmid, who stood silhouetted in a doorway.

Airmid held out both arms; the Sisters slotted the gauntlets down over her hands.

"Go, Ancient!" screamed Banba. "Hide them where none will find them."

In a flash of blue light Airmid vanished.

With a scream of frustration, Nemhain and Banbh began to transform, Banbh's cloak spinning into iridescent black feathers, Nemhain's hair beginning to sweep outward in a wind of chaos.

"Cease!" cried Eriu. On Eriu's right arm gleamed Nuada's Silver Arm. Macha lay on the ground, a bolt of lightning seared onto her right shoulder. "Stand before me, Raveners, as you are, or before Danu I swear that Macha shall die."

Slowly, reluctantly, Nemhain and Banbh ceased transformation, stood beside Macha. Macha raised herself up on her elbow, used her good hand to feel at the scar on her shoulder. "It will be permanent," she said, her eyes flashing angrily at Eriu.

"Good, then all will know you at your coming and your going for what you are, a force of destruction, a faithless, lying . . ."

Macha stood. "Your decision for the Danu was unwise. You chose to close the doors. And that is wrong."

At that moment, three triangular Light Ships rose up into the sky, one from the sea, two from the deep interior. Like winged birds of light, they rose and hovered, then vanished toward the west.

"Do you see?" cried Macha. "You would divide the Danu, each from the other. And for what? A race of uninvited Invaders who would destroy us on a whim, were not the poet reining them in. How long do you think they will be controlled by a poet, a maker of words?"

Eriu shook her head.

"You would wall us up in isolation. The Morrigu cannot survive in isolation. We heard your arguments in Council; their conclusion would spell our death. How would we feed in a world that contained only our own kind? Or would we remain in this world forever isolated from our own kind? But did your conclusions take the Raveners into account? They did not; I have my own people to defend. How much better for us to destroy the Invaders, to drown them in the sea, to continue here as we have always done, Danu and Ravener, with the wide human world available for us to explore. We did what we always do—that which must be done. If you had not stopped us, your problem would now be solved." She faced Eriu. "See it, Sister, for it is true." She met Eriu's eyes, waited quietly.

"I cannot deny the truth of what you say," said Eriu. "But you have made the Three Sisters liars all; the sons of Mil will never again trust our word."

"As you should never trust theirs."

"There are other ways; yours is not the only way."

"It was the best way," said Macha. "The best and the most necessary. And now you have caused it to fail. We will pay a price for that failure."

She gestured toward the bay. Two Greek ships limped into harbor, their masts broken, their sails in tatters.

"Where is the third?" asked Eriu.

"Perhaps it was our only success," said Macha. "We shall see."

She made a flicking motion with her hand; suddenly Banbh was a raven. Just as suddenly, she dug her claws into Eriu's shoulder, twisted her beak to pluck at her eyes. Eriu raised her hands to defend her eyes. She felt Macha wrench the Silver Arm from her hand, saw her transform as swiftly as her sister.

An eagle lifted north, dangling a Silver Arm from its talons; a flock of ravens followed, borne on a sudden wind.

By afternoon, the third ship had still not returned to harbor. Eriu and her sisters stood at the headland, watching as the remaining Milesians moved from the ships to the shore, disappeared into their dwellings, some bearing wounded. Beside the Sisters now, a contingent of Danu Light Spear Warriors stood uneasily by, Light Spears at the ready.

Toward evening there was sudden movement in the tents below. Suddenly and without warning, the Milesians burst from their dwellings in full war garb. Beside them were the huge curly-haired dogs. The dogs bolted for the headland, moving faster than the Milesians on their long slender legs. They were howling in unearthly discord. Behind them, the sons of Mil let out a huge, visceral yell and ran straight for the headland, brandishing their shortswords high in the air as they ran. At the back of the company came Milesians on horseback, among them Amergin. Eriu could see his black hair streaming out over his cloak. Fear clutched at her heart.

"Mag Tuiread!" cried Eriu. "There at least we stand a chance. There at least there will be enough portals. And tell Airmid to have the physicians at the ready."

Some of the Danu made for the portals, for the swift transport to Mag Tuiread. But there were not enough portals to accommodate them all.

Eriu began to run beside the Light Spear carriers.

"No!" cried Banba. "You must transport to Mag Tuiread."

"And what of these?" Eriu screamed, gesturing to the runners.

"We run, Sister! We have trained for it well!" cried the chief of the spear carriers. "To the portals. Meet us at Mag Tuiread."

Swift as wind, the Danu veered into three columns, began the run toward the Plain of Mag Tuiread, the furious Milesian dogs hard upon their heels.

34

I watched as they ran from us, dividing at the headlands, their spear bearers seeming to vanish before us in the green forest. From beyond them, I saw the white flashes of light from their doorways.

"They vanish into their cities!" I called. "Avoid their doorways! They harness their lightning against us!"

I am not a man much given to anger, but it felt good, thrusting through me, hot as lightning, carrying my losses with it—all rising, raging, in my internal fire. Gone was all my wisdom, my knowledge of the Danu as dwellers here before us, my feeling that we should not have journeyed here at all.

And now we would be trapped here, for our Greek sailors would sail away from us, even while we were fighting these Danu. And some of our remaining number would surely be among them.

I could not blame them. We had returned from the sea with only two of our ships. A third of our company was gone into the sea. At our return, there was no sign of An Scail. Had they killed her as well?

Then consign her as well to the fires of my vengeance.

They had played us false, the Sisters. They had brought the sea against us. I did not stop to consider how they had done this deed. It did not matter now. I would avenge them all with the white-hot fire of my rage. Ith and Mil, Skena and Ir, Scota, An Scail. My child, my unborn child.

I ran in the forest, heedless of branches, heedless of direction, following the swift retreating forms of their Light Spear bearers, following the baying of our own great wolfhounds. My only prayer was that they would lead me to the Sisters. To Eriu. Let her feel the weight of all our losses. Most damnable of liars.

In a hot, white heat I ran.

It was not until I reached the forest at the base of the Plain of Many Towers that I thought I heard the voice of Skena, calling me.

"Amergin!" it cried. "Husband! Hear me!"

I stopped and drew in a ragged breath, my heart thundering against my chest wall. I looked around me. At the crest of this hill were stone doorways, a dozen of them in a great circle.

Skena's voice seemed to come from between the standing stones. I looked up the hill toward them.

"Amergin!"

Was there a figure there? Standing between the stones?

"Skena?" It came out as a half-strangled gasp.

I saw a shadowy form between the stones. This I swear. It spoke.

"Anger is a hot healer. This you know. Anger heals a wound with scars." I saw the form shift, begin to coalesce.

Eber Finn came up beside me then, Airioch behind him. He followed my eyes.

"What is it?"

"Who is there between the stones?"

"I see nothing. Wait . . . no. It is the shadow of a great tree."

I looked again. Eber Finn was right. A shadow moved between the stones. I closed my eyes, took in a deep breath.

Eber Finn clasped me hard at the elbow. "They have not reached the place. Victory is ours. We will avenge our dead."

Whatever I had seen or thought that I had heard was gone. I nodded, clasped him back in the warrior grip. Behind us Airioch Feabhruadh regarded us both in silence. He lowered his eyes, would not clasp arms with either of us.

Before I could address him, our warriors came into the forest behind us. They had some of the Danu spear bearers in their possession, wounded and struggling, their huge eyes shifting and widening.

Blue light snapped between the doorways.

"The Sisters come," I whispered to my brothers. "Gather the dogs. Vanish into the forest. I will circle behind the stones; await my command."

I slipped into the darkness, a man in whom the god of war was raging.

35

Dusk was falling on the Plain of Mag Tuiread.

In doorways between the standing stones, the Three Sisters waited. Opposite her, in separate doorways, Eriu could see Banba and Fodla. She had hoped to find Airmid in the city below, to supply each of her sisters with an arm, but the Ancient was nowhere to be found, applying herself to their own command to hide the arms, Eriu thought, securing them from Macha.

In each doorway of the circle, she could see Danu spear carriers, one facing inward toward the circle, two facing outward toward the forest at the base of the hill.

They scanned the forest anxiously for their companions.

Suddenly from a distance, Eriu heard the baying of the Milesian dogs. "They come," she whispered. "Danu, guide my hand."

No sooner had she spoken the words than the first dogs burst into the circle, running wildly in across the open space, crisscrossing each other. Eriu saw the outward-facing spear carriers turn inward toward the dogs momentarily, then return to their post.

The inward carriers pointed their spears; arcs of blue light flashed across the open space. There was a high squealing sound from some of the dogs.

Now Danu spear carriers began to run in among their companions; they were flanked by the horses of the Galaeci. Eriu did not see Amergin among them but she cringed as one of the horses trampled over one of the Danu spear carriers. She saw him tumble beneath the horse's hooves, saw Metaphor slip from him as he fell.

"Physicians!" she called into the gathering dusk.

A flash of blue light sparked in an empty doorway. Two physicians swept onto the field and spirited the little Danu back between the uprights, only to vanish below.

"By the gods!" cried the Milesian on horseback, the look on his face reflecting terror.

Then suddenly the whole company was upon them, scrambling up the hill, dogs and horses, spear carriers and riders, Milesian runners, their swords clanging metal on metal. Flashes of blue light echoed crazily around the circle. Eriu heard screams, but she could not tell if those screaming were Danu or Milesian. It crossed her mind that creatures in pain screamed alike regardless of their origins.

Now flash after flash began to appear between the doorways as physicians came and went with the wounded.

Eriu heard the sound of hooves behind her; a horseman swept past. She stayed still and silent in her doorway, waiting for the signal to use the portals, to unleash upon the Milesians the full fury of the time portals.

Suddenly, she felt a huge hand at her throat and the cold horror of a thin, metal blade against the soft flesh.

The voice of Amergin boomed out over the chaos. "I have as prisoner Eriu of the Danu. Cease or I will kill her as she stands."

Slowly and by degrees, the field died to silence.

"Assemble!" cried Amergin.

From behind the stone doorways, torches flared to light. Eriu saw Fodla held tight in the grip of two Milesians.

"Portals!" she called aloud, and she saw the flashes of blue as some of the spear bearers escaped below. She heaved a sigh of gratitude; at least the Danu would continue.

"Bring the prisoners to the center of the circle," called Amergin.

As the Milesians led the spear bearers into the circle, Eriu began to weep, the tears streaming silently down her cheeks. Some of her people were bleeding from the face and arms. At least two dangled limbs that would be difficult to save, even if she could get them to the physicians. A few of the wounded were slipping in and out of Metaphor. She could see their eyes go large and ovoid, their height drop and then return to human size as they struggled to hold to their human aspect. She could hear the

Milesians cursing as they held them, probably wishing that they could run away, held past their fear only by their military training.

In violation of everything the Council had decided, Eriu called aloud in Danaan. "Have we lost any of our company?"

"Five have fallen in the forest," one of the spear bearers answered. He received a cuff for his trouble, but Eriu knew that physicians would be running even now for the fallen. They would be taken below, restored to health. More of the Danu to safety.

"You will speak no more!" said Amergin low into the back of her head.

She nodded once. How had this happened? The Danu had the advantage of weapons, of age, of wisdom, of technology, of knowledge of the place. Even for all her saying, she had underestimated the sons of Mil.

As if he had read her thoughts, Amergin leaned close to her ear. "Did you think us fools?" he whispered. "We have fought with Greeks and Romans, Carthaginians and Egyptians. We know how to track and how to fight in darkness. We know how to circle the enemy and come in from behind. I should never have trusted you; I should have fought you and your sisters this way from the first."

So. The Danu had become the enemy. Eriu wished that she had destroyed the doorways, that she had let the Morrigu drown all of their ships in the sea.

"Take me before my people," she said softly, in defiance of his edict.

The circle was now lit by torchlight, the flames flickering eerily against the huge stone uprights, throwing the elaborate braided carvings into relief.

Eriu closed her eyes. Years from now, when the remainder of the Danu had died, humans would come here among the stones. They would stare at the carvings and wonder at those who carved them. They would never know of the little people of the Danu, the Children of the Braid. She stifled a sob.

Amergin led her into the center of the circle. He had lowered the knife from her throat, maneuvered her gently into the ring of flickering light.

Opposite her, Eriu could see Fodla, her eyes wide. Where was Banba? Eriu prayed that she had opened portal, vanished into the city below.

Amergin released her. Eriu started to turn, to face him, but he placed his hands on her shoulders.

"Face those you have betrayed," he said.

She looked at the assembled company. "Will you allow our physicians to care for the wounded?" she called to the assemblage. "We will care for yours as well."

"Why should we allow that?" called Eremon. "Today we have lost an entire ship of our comrades in the sea. We have lost our mother and our father, our beloved brothers Eber Donn and Ir, our uncle Ith, Skena our healer, wife of our bard. For these deaths you and yours must pay the price."

"I invoke the right of Poet!" Eriu called into their midst. "All will hear."

She heard Amergin's intake of breath. The Milesians began to call out in anger. Behind her, Amergin spoke.

"She invokes the right. She is their Poet. Even among these who have betrayed us, we can obey our own law."

The company fell to silence.

Eriu closed her eyes.

"It is true that those of our company have called up a storm at sea," she said. Even the Raveners were of the Danu; she would not give them away. "For the loss of your comrades we are most sorry. But hear me, sons of Mil. This island has been our place. We have lived here for a thousand years. We did not ask you to come among us. What would you do if your own country were invaded by such as you?"

"You gave us your word," said Amergin from behind her back. "We expected to battle you, but you promised our safety for three days' time. You broke your word."

"And the penalty for breaking such a vow is death!" called Eber Finn.

Eriu drew in a deep breath. "Then take my life. But spare my people. They will return to their cities. They will never trouble you again."

"We have lost fifty of our company on such a promise; even now their souls cry out from the sea," shouted Eremon. "Why should we believe a further promise from one who looks at us and lies?"

"She did not lie." The voice was nasal, soft. "She never lies."

In one of the empty doorways Macha stood, bathed in blue light. She was garbed in her male warrior Metaphor, wearing one of the Silver Arms. Eriu blinked and closed her eyes. What damage would Macha do among them now?

Slowly, Macha lowered the arm and pointed it directly at Amergin. Suddenly Eriu felt his body close around hers, felt his arms encircle her Metaphor.

Macha hesitated.

"Do what you must," Eriu cried. "Save the Danu."

"I will lose you," said Macha quietly. "You took my hand; I gave you my vow."

"Your beloved keeps his word," said Amergin, low against her ear.

"Where did you come from?" The voice belonged to Airioch Feabhruadh, who called from the crowd.

"From wherever I wish," Macha said softly. "Do you see this Silver Arm upon my own? With it I control the wind and sea. With it I have drowned your ships."

"That is not possible," called Eremon.

Macha flexed a finger of the arm and pointed it toward the canopy of trees. They began to whisper, then to thrash and sway, heaving above the forest floor. Branches crashed down into the center of the circle. Macha withdrew the arm; the forest quieted.

"It was I who brought the storm to your vessels. Eriu knew nothing of it; she and her sisters forced me to stop, else I would have rid our isle of all of you. When you experienced the lull in the storm, it was because this little one"—she gestured at Eriu—"had knocked me flat on the ground to stop me."

"Why?" asked Amergin quietly. "Why would you do these things in violation of the word of the Sisters?"

"Because Eriu and her sisters would have closed the doors to Tara. They would have sealed the Danu away from the sons of Mil. We Raveners cannot live apart from humans."

"Raveners?" asked Amergin.

"Will you see me as I am?" asked Macha. The voice was mocking, dangerous. The company shifted and murmured, obvious fear now threading through the Milesians.

"Sisters!" Macha called. A high wind sped over the tops of the sarsen circle; the flames danced and whirled. A huge flock of crows suddenly wheeled in the sky above the torchlight. One huge raven descended among them, landed on Macha's shoulders.

"We are Morrigu!" Macha cried. Suddenly the threesome began to shift and vary, now three women with dark hair and robes, then wolves and ravens, wind and fire, suddenly three small, pale creatures with dark ovoid eyes, surrounded by clouds of darkness, then just as swiftly the three warriors of the headland, then three beautiful women of Greek bearing. A few Milesians ran screaming in fear for the forest; the warriors stood their ground, their eyes wide, their hands making signs in the air.

"You should not be among us," said Macha, her tone offhand. "Now you see why."

"Return to the ships!" called one of the wives of Eber Donn.

"We will return to Galicia!" shouted several of the Milesians.

"Hear me!" cried Amergin. The crowd fell silent. "Our return is not possible. Even while we followed these Danu into the forest, the Greeks departed from us. We have no choice but to remain on Inisfail."

"Then we must exact a penalty from these Danu," cried Eremon, his voice echoing in the circle.

"Exile!" cried Eber Finn. "Exile. Make them pay the price that they would have exacted from us. Put them on rafts and set them adrift on the sea."

The murmur spread through the Milesians like a fire. "Exile," they cried. "Send the Danu away from the isle."

"If that is what you wish, we will go," said Eriu. "We will depart the isle tonight."

She did not say that they would depart in their own great Spear Ships.

"Morrigu will not depart," said Macha, her voice echoing from the doorway.

With a sudden snap of light, she and her sisters were gone.

Suddenly there was a thunder of hooves from the outside of the circle. Between the sarsen stones rode a great horse of the Milesians. Clinging to Banba front and back were two tiny white-haired women, An Scail and Airmid. Each wore a silver gauntlet on her arm.

"Cease!" the two ancient women cried at once. "Hear the wisdom of your elders."

Banba swung from the saddle, her diadem askew, her Greek gown twisted. "Bloody, vicious animals," she spat. She swatted at the flank of a great horse three times her size. "Stupider than the dirt." This brought a laugh from the company of Milesians. Some of the tension dissipated.

"However do you big fellows ride them?" Banba asked, straightening her gown and looking around the circle in admiration. "Really, one of you must teach me."

"I would be happy to . . . ride." The voice of Airioch Feabhruadh drifted from the darkness.

Again the company laughed.

The two Ancients stood side by side, their hands linked. As one, they pointed their weapons at the assembled companies.

"Will you use the arms, Ancient?" asked Eriu, her voice filled with terror.

"First we will call physicians," said An Scail.

Airmid nodded. She tapped her triangle; blue light snapped at the portal. Physicians appeared and began to minister to Danu and Galaeci alike.

"Now we will use the arms," said Airmid softly. A gasp arose from the assembled company, both Danu and Milesian. Airmid and An Scail pointed the arms skyward. Gently, each flexed a finger. Sweet music began to weave itself through the portals and around the company, joyful and light. Tiny firework stars arced over the assembly in blues and greens and reds, then fell upon them, cool as snowflakes.

"Like people, such weapons can be turned to good or ill," said Airmid.

"It is time that we both turn to the good," said An Scail.

"I call forth the Triad Sisters of the Danu," said Airmid. Eriu stepped next to Banba. Fodla's captor released her and she stepped into triangle.

"Sons of Mil." An Scail turned and pointed into the darkness. "Eremon, Eber Finn, Airioch, come forward." The three oldest sons of Mil stepped uneasily into the circle.

"Hear me, sons of Mil," said An Scail. "These, the people of the Danu, did not ask for us to come among them. We have. They defend themselves. That is their right."

"Hear me, Children of the Danu," said Airmid. "These sons of Mil are a learned and well-traveled race. They are deeply spiritual and their love of learning carries them around the world. The vision of their leader compelled them here and they cannot now return; we must accept them here among us."

"True enough," said Eber Finn. "Though we would not be here had the Danu not wounded Uncle Ith and rendered him unable to warn us from their shores. For that alone, the Danu must suffer exile. Or one of them must die."

He lunged forward suddenly and caught Banba by her hair, raising his shortsword as he did so. He hacked at the hair, then put the blade to the point of her throat.

"No!" Airioch stepped beside Eber Finn. He moved the blade gently so that it rested just beneath his own chin. "None should die for that transgression but I. The people of the Danu did not wound Ith. I was responsible for that."

A wild babble erupted on both sides.

Amergin drew his longsword from his back, stepped among them, and stabbed it into the dirt. "Silence."

The crowd grew silent.

"Speak, Airioch," Amergin commanded.

"It was our last night here. Ith had spent it in the company of the Sisters. He told me of his decision not to return. I had seen their jewels, their diadems. I had seen the rich fields and the deep forests. I wanted to return. I argued with Ith, but he would hear none. He insisted that the place belonged to the Danu. He said—I remember it well—'They dwell in beauty and in magic, Nephew. Our presence would take that from them.' I said that I would not leave without treasure. I had seen you come through one of your doorways in the forest." Here he pointed at the Sisters. "I thought that if I could cross that portal I could return with gold and silver. I knew then that I could convince my father and my brothers to return, even against Ith's wishes.

"Ith followed me. He knew me well, our uncle. I stepped into the portal. I began to feel along the wall. Suddenly a bolt of hot light seared me. And then there was Ith. He simply stepped between me and the lightning. It knocked him flat to the ground. I carried him back to the hut, left him there until morning. He returned with us to Galicia as you saw him, unable to speak. And I blamed the Sisters."

"How do we know that this is true?" asked Eber Finn. "You have the eye for this dark one." He gestured at Banba. "Perhaps she has promised you riches if you will speak this tale."

For answer, Airioch rolled back the sleeve of his tunic, pushed it up above his elbow. A puckered scar streaked all the way to his elbow.

"That night at the shore," said Amergin suddenly. "You tried to tell me."

Airioch nodded. "And I could not. I know how much you loved him."

"Why now?"

"Colpa. He has no one now. He deserves a man like Father, like Ith. A man who speaks the truth."

Airioch turned to face the Milesians. "I will take responsibility. I will pay the price. Exile or death."

"It is too heavy a price, Brother," said Amergin. "For any to pay, Danu or Milesian. An Scail is right; we came here with our vision and our greed. All of us bear responsibility. We owe you our apology, Sisters; we judged you unfairly. We were wrong."

"Hear our brother!" Eremon called out.

An Scail smiled suddenly. "Look at you, Eremon. How strongly you resemble your father. He would want you to learn to dwell with these of the Danu. Did he not dwell with Greeks and Egyptians, Scythians and Persians?"

Suddenly from behind Eriu, Amergin drew breath. "An Scail," he said softly. "Wise One. How do you know that Eremon resembles our father?"

"I can see him," she said. "As I can see you, dark Amergin. And you, beautiful Eriu. And these stars that fall upon us cool as snow. And the beach and the sea. This is the gift that Airmid has given me," said An Scail. "A gift that would bring joy to Ith. Return the gift, Amergin. As bard of the Milesians, rule on the fate of both of our peoples."

Amergin stepped forward. He looked long into her eyes.

"How handsome you are, my dark-eyed boy," she whispered.

He turned to Airmid. "For this I thank you, wise one of the Danu." He looked long at her eyes as well, but she met his with perfect Metaphor.

He closed his eyes, stood silent at the center of the circle. Both the Milesians and the people of the Danu were silent.

At last he spoke. "I will rule. I give to the people of the Danu their cities beneath the ground and sea. I give to them their doorways. We of the Milesians will not enter their cities or cross their doorways. We will take nothing that belongs to them and trouble none of their kind. We will build our own great rath on a hill." He paused. He looked at Eriu. "What do you call your city?"

"Tara," she answered.

"Just so we will call our rath. We have begun ill, all of us. We will require time to think things through. There will be no contact between our people for one year. We will each mourn our dead and consider these events. At the end of that time we will meet in Council. We will decide then whether we will seal the doorways between us forever or open them wide. For that year, the Silver Arms will be kept, one each by Airmid and An Scail. Hide them well, elders. Let none know of their whereabouts."

Eriu spoke. "We have no control of Morrigu, as you have seen. But with the exception of this last, we of the Danu will abide by your ruling. Remember that Morrigu too possesses one of the Silver Arms. She will not relinquish it to either side," said Eriu.

Amergin nodded. "Airioch Feabhruadh, in accordance with our law, you will be responsible for those to whom you have brought much sorrow for the period of one year. You are the companion of An Scail; you will do as she bids in all things. You are both husband and father to the wives of Eber Donn and to their children. Into your care we place also our brother Colpa, who has neither mother nor father. You are father to the children and grandchildren of Mil."

Airioch nodded solemnly, then suddenly broke into a huge smile.

"You punish him by making him part of the family," An Scail whispered softly. "This is wise, Poet."

Amergin looked now at the assembled company of the Danu, many still held at the swordpoints of the sons of Mil.

"Release them," he commanded.

The Danu moved silently and immediately between the stones. Flashes of blue light moved stone to stone around the circle, illuminating the circle with bright blue light, brighter than the light of day. In moments, all but the Sisters and Airmid were gone.

Airmid stepped into a portal, the Silver Arm gleaming on her hand.

"Good work this night, friend," she said to An Scail.

"How beautiful the torches are," said An Scail in return. "With each day of this year, I shall think of you. With each sight that I see." She raised the Silver Arm in salute.

"I will take this horse," she said to Amergin. "Lift me to his back."

Eremon and Airioch rushed to comply.

"You can ride, Ancient?" asked Eremon.

"I have lived long. I can do many things." She saluted them with the arm, which gleamed in the torchlight, turned the horse, and rode through the portal.

Eriu stepped into a portal with her sisters. She lifted her triangle.

"Eriu! Wait!" Amergin called. She hesitated.

"We owe you reparation and apology," said Amergin to Eriu.

"You owe us nothing but peace," said Eriu. "Please, I beg you to leave us alone."

In a snap of blue light she was gone.

36

CEOLAS SINGS OF PASSING TIME
A year of peace is like a thousand,
A year of peace is like a sea,
A year of peace unfolds slowly
like a blossom in the light,
like the promise of the spring.
Bloom and heal in a year of peace,
Bloom and heal, my people.

For me, it has been the most difficult year of my life." Airioch Fe-abhruadh leaned back against the rock, his golden hair ruffled by the wind. He grinned at me. "This child needs a new cloak and the cows are calving and this wife of Eber Donn wants mating. . . ."

"How sad for you, Brother," I said, grinning back at him. "Three wives requiring mating."

"Sometimes all at once!" said Airioch. "They wear me down to the bone. And Colpa! He grows taller than your Bile."

"So the punishment was too much."

"Too much, too much, too much entirely." He laughed aloud.

I looked at him and shook my head.

His face grew serious. "You are thinking that you would never have thought it possible that we could sit here side by side in friendship, as we do."

"I am thinking exactly that."

"I wish that Ith could see it," Airioch said softly. "And Mil."

"Ith knew that the heart could change, Brother. He knew."

Airioch nodded. "I think much on what my selfishness cost us."

"Do not carry all the burden, Brother. Scota was herself a force of nature, full of loss and determined to avenge it on someone, anyone. And Eber Donn was ever angry, always putting action before thought. And me. I am Poet of the clan and yet I did not trust their word. I nearly took us all to death."

"I think much on your losses, Brother."

I nodded. "I think on them too. Skena would have made me wise. I would not have gone to war against them had she been by my side. I know this now and I am ashamed."

"Well, shame sits upon us both then, Brother."

I nodded. "And I wish that I had known my child."

"I wish that for you," Airioch said solemnly. I shrugged, sighed. He punched me lightly on the shoulder. I smiled at him.

"Thank you, friend."

"Thank you for your gifts to me, Brother."

We sat side by side in companionable silence. I fingered Ceolas lightly, dreamed the poem that I had been composing, telling the tale of the Battle of Mag Tuiread. I sang a bar or two.

> *"They have vanished from among us*
> *In a sudden flash of light,*
> *The Danu with their large eyes;*
> *In my dreams I see them,*
> *Always I remember their eyes."*

Airioch turned toward me. "Do you think that they will ever emerge from the portals?"

I shrugged. "It has been three days more than a year and we have seen no signs. Bile stands vigil at the portal on the headland."

"Why?"

"I know not. He dresses himself each morning and rolls his pictures beneath his arms. He marches up the headland and stands at the portal in the forest. He has thirteen years upon him. Who knows what they think at that age? And Bile cannot tell us, but for drawings. Those we must puzzle at for meaning; when the meaning will not come, he grows angry and shouts aloud." I shrugged. "I trouble for him, but I know not what to do."

"What does An Scail say?"

"She says only that she and Airmid have discussed the problem."

"I thought that I had seen them together once near midwinter, the two of them seated side by side in the leafless forest. But when I approached, An Scail was there alone. So she admits freely that they have both broken the year of exile?"

"She does. She says that she and the ancient Danu have left to them but little time, and there is much that they must learn, each from the other. What should I do, Airioch? Call our most ancient druid before the Council for violating the ruling of her own pupil?"

He laughed. "She has you trapped there, does she not?"

"She does."

For a moment, he looked out to sea; then Airioch faced me. "What do you hope, Brother, that they do or do not return among us?"

"I do not know what to hope. Eber Finn has gone north and built his rath. Eremon constructs the rath of Tara on his hill. Those who have remained here in Inver Skena have made a quiet life, dwellings and cattle, mating and babies." He gestured at the village that straggled up the headland from the sea. "It is quiet; I like it quiet. And if I never saw their Morrigu again, never would be soon enough."

Airioch shivered. "True enough, though I would like to see that darkhaired Banba once more."

"Is Banba what you see when you see her?"

"That was far too druidic for me, Brother."

"It is just something that I wonder, something about Eriu's eyes."

"Well, never mind," said Airioch. "I do not know that I would have anything left to give her if she did arrive. Look where they come for the mating." Two of Eber Donn's wives approached, hand in hand, their hair coiffed, wrapped in their finest shawls.

"Airioch," they called, "we find ourselves with a free hour."

"Go have your sport," I said. "You and I both know that you enjoy it."

"They have offered to share with you, Brother. The wives of Eber Donn like you well; this you know. You need not remain without a woman forever. I know that you are lonely." Here he paused. "I have been lonely in the tribe, Amergin."

"Well, perhaps lonely is the proper way for the poet. We keep the history of the clan; should we prefer one over another? We rule for the clan; in any ruling, half are satisfied and half are not."

"I cannot solve those problems for you, but women, ah, women I know and love. I can solve that problem for you, Brother. I do not want your loneliness to dwell on you forever."

But I shook my head; Airioch's idea of the mating was as unlike mine as the moon is unlike the sun.

"Hurry, Airioch," called the wives of Eber Donn. "We have but little time."

Airioch groaned but he stood and dusted off his braichs.

I grinned up at him. "You know that you were released from your promise to Eber Donn's family three days ago. The period of punishment was one year. You need not oblige any longer."

Airioch grinned. "Well, I owe them at least this much, now don't I?" He rubbed his hands together. "Ladies, what is your wish today?" He wrapped an arm around each waist, looked back over his shoulder at me, and winked.

I shook my head. Still laughing, I stood and dusted off my braichs. I chose a flat stone from the beach and skipped it across the still bay. I could not fault Airioch his pleasures. For the past year, Airioch had been husband and father to a host of women and children, had built dwellings and walked his brother's children along the shore and discharged all of his responsibilities like a man on a mission.

I glanced up toward the headland. Perhaps Airioch would have done better with Bile this year. But I owed him at least my attempt to be a father.

In a little while I would climb to the headland and sit beside Bile, give him my brotherly duty. I leaned back against the rock and sighed. In just a little while.

CEOLAS DREAMS OF LONGING

What am I but a man?
A strange and lonely man,
a man composed of words and dreams.
What am I but a dreamer
in a world where no one dreams.
I am as lonely as the wind,

I am as vast as the sea.
Oh, my beloved,
sing to me as wind and sea,
say that I will not be lonely forever.

"Bile, I do not think that they will return among us. We frightened them terribly. As they did us. Perhaps we are better apart from each other."

He shook his head stubbornly.

He had grown tall, this baby brother. At thirteen years, he approached six feet tall. His hair was a sweep of thick darkness, his eyes an expressive gray. His one good arm was well muscled and strong and his legs were thick with muscle. His stump he hid well behind tunics and cloaks. When he did not vocalize, one might think him a strong and well-made man of the Galaeci.

We had long since run out of paper and chalks; Bile had exhausted what supply we had brought on our journey. Those that he carried so carefully rolled under his arm were the record of his life, the Internum Mare, the wild reaches of Spain, the towers of Galicia, our mother and father and Uncle Ith. Now he carved on rock and metal, imitating the spiraling patterns of the Danu, linking them with our own braidwork, incising ogham and spirals onto stones and cups and cauldrons. Our people much prized him for his craftsmanship.

Now I walked around the portal, stood at the opposite side, facing him through the uprights.

"Come back to the village, Brother. I do not think they will come."

He shook his head. He waved his arm at me and began to vocalize, "Ah, ah, ah." His roll of drawings dropped to the ground.

Suddenly there was a flash of blue light. Airmid stood in the doorway. Because I was behind the doorway, her back was to me.

Bile went silent; his face turned crimson that she had seen him vocalizing. He stooped and gathered up his drawings. He shot a baleful look in my direction.

Airmid followed the look, turned around to see me.

"Well hello, Amergin. Have I startled you?" She sounded as though she had seen me only yesterday and not a year ago.

"It is most difficult to accustom to the comings and goings of the Danu."

"I suppose that's true," she said brightly. "You have decided to accompany your brother, then? Are we ready?"

"Ready for what?"

An Scail appeared suddenly, moving through the forest, leaning hard on a beautifully carved cane covered with Danu braidwork. She was puffing with the effort.

"You should have waited for me," she said quietly to Bile when she reached us.

He lowered his gaze. "We are ready," she said to Airmid.

"For what?" I asked again.

"Bile has asked Airmid to evaluate his speech, to see if aught can be done. She has waited for three days past the year mark to accord you their respect of our law."

"It was nothing," said Airmid, waving her hand. "What is three days more or less? Or three years for that matter? Except to this young man."

Bile regarded her solemnly, held his drawings forward.

"I like it not," I said.

"It is not yours to like," said An Scail. "Come then, Bile. Airmid and I have prepared a place to work." And the twosome led Bile away through the woods. I made to follow, but An Scail held up her hand. "Bile will let you know when you may join us," she said.

I was dismissed.

I sat down heavily and leaned my back against the stone.

"Now I am the outsider with my tribe, my teacher, and my brother," I muttered.

Suddenly, there was a crack of blue and Eriu stepped forward into the forest. She was exactly as I remembered her, the long, curling red hair, the sweeping white dress. She looked away into the forest.

"Are you following them?"

She started back when I spoke, turned quickly to face me.

"I did not see you there," she said.

"Well, I never see you or yours coming or going," I replied.

"Where did they go?" she asked.

I gestured toward the forest. "Out there, and I was not invited to accompany them."

"Nor was I."

"I feel much better knowing that."

"A year has not improved your disposition," she said tartly.

"Nor yours it would seem," I said.

"I advised against this plan."

"I do not even know what this plan is."

"Our physicians have some skill with the . . . brain, with the . . . pathways of speech and movement."

"You need not speak as though you speak to a child. Mehmet explained all of this to me when both Bile and Ith became wounded. Pathways become blocked. Sometimes new pathways develop; sometimes they do not."

"Very well; we have techniques to allow new pathways to develop. Airmid told An Scail so and An Scail told Bile. Evidently Bile has petitioned An Scail, and An Scail and Airmid have decided that it would be a fine idea to see what they could do. These two Ancients are harder to control than . . . Morrigu!"

At this I laughed aloud. "I doubt that, but I will say that they are very . . . strong willed, the pair of them. And my little brother becomes just like them, silent and stubborn."

"Airmid came through the portals, in defiance of the ruling. I was so afraid for her."

"Afraid for her? What? Do you think us barbarians that we would molest an Ancient wisdom keeper, wandering in the woods, accompanied by one of our own druids?"

"I do not know," she said, waving her hands at me. "What I have seen of you is dangerous and . . . ill-disposed. Hard to predict. We love Airmid; we have a responsibility to protect her. And off she goes, wandering around your world."

"And what if they damage Bile?"

"They will not damage him! They are physicians of great skill! How could you think that of us?" Her eyes had actually begun to fill with tears.

I stared hard at them; they seemed to me once again overlarge.

"What do you stare at?"

"Your eyes; when you are frightened or sad, they seem to shift shape within their orbs, changeable as the sea and nearly as large."

Now her eyes grew measurably larger; terror flitted across her face.

"Do your people know?"

"Know . . . what?"

She glanced around at the forest as if she expected an answer suddenly to appear. "Do they know that Airmid has been on the Green Isle in defiance of the year ruling?"

"Only Airioch, and he will say nothing."

"Airioch will say nothing?"

"Human beings have immense capacity for change, Eriu. Do not underestimate that capacity; it is larger than any of our other traits."

"For good and for ill, I am supposing."

I inclined my head. "But if we speak of ill, surely we must speak of Morrigu. Does she bear that same capacity?"

"No. She is a constant, is Morrigu. Constant as darkness. Do your people . . . talk of her, talk of the Danu? What do they say in the year that has passed?"

"At first they spoke of nothing else. What they had seen at the Plain of Mag Tuiread terrified them. They wanted to swim after the ships. They wanted to leave the cattle and the horses and the dogs behind and return home on rafts with sails made of their tents. Some of them wanted to run into the sea, preferring drowning to remaining here where the portals could open at any moment."

"She terrifies us as well."

"They were afraid of more than Morrigu, Eriu."

"What do they think they saw?"

"Not think. Saw. I saw it too. Your wounded warriors, those golden-haired Greeks. Our people saw them grow small and tall again, saw their eyes shift shape and return, as yours have just done."

"O you gods!"

I stood, though that may not have improved anything, as I towered over her little frame. She cringed back into the doorway.

"I will not harm you, Eriu," I said softly. "Only tell me the truth. I do not fear the truth."

"The truth is that you very well might hurt me. When last we met, you held me as a shield."

"When last we met, I thought you responsible for all of our troubles on the sea. I was a fool."

"I was no wiser," she said, though she did not leave the doorway. "It might have ended badly were it not for these two Ancients who so frustrate us."

I laughed aloud. "When I think of those two heaving into the circle on that horse."

She began to laugh too; her laughter tinkled like the soft bells that Galaeci women braid into their hair. Our laughter together seemed to make her less fearful. She stepped back out from the doorway and tipped her head up; her eyes were laughing.

"And fearless Banba, asking someone to teach her to ride."

I shook my head. "And she got offers!"

"O Danu, what fools we are, Amergin."

"We were afraid. We did not trust each other. We were strangers. People who act on their fear and their lack of wisdom often make foolish choices."

"A year was wise."

"It was? What do they say of us in your cities?"

"That some of you are worthy of . . . consideration. Of course, Airmid has helped that opinion to prevail."

"What do you say, Eriu?"

"What I say does not matter. It matters what the Danu say."

"It matters to me." I actually put my hand up to my own lips, surprised. Having spoken the words, I knew them to be true.

"I . . . think our life was simpler before you came."

I shrugged. "True enough. Ours was certainly simpler before we came." I felt dismissed, turned to walk away.

"Amergin," she said quietly.

I turned back.

"Given time, I think that it might be more interesting now that you have come."

Her face was tipped up again.

"Your eyes," I said softly; "they are like the sea. They change color and mood and shape. They are . . . quite beautiful, Eriu. I do not fear them."

I watched as her face began to suffuse with color. She stepped back into the doorway.

"I did not mean to offend you. Did I frighten you? I simply spoke the truth. You need not fear the truth with me."

She lifted her triangle.

"Wait!" I commanded. She stopped, her hand held aloft.

"Will you return?" I asked. She stood as if frozen. "Please?" I said it softly, so as not to frighten her.

She smiled. "I will return, Amergin."

She nodded once, then slotted her triangle into the portal and was gone.

I took to waiting at the portal, dressed in my finest tunic. I felt stupid and hopeful all at once, like a boy new with sap. Oh, I made pretense that I was accompanying Bile and An Scail to the doorway, awaiting the arrival of Airmid, but they were not fooled.

Worse, Eriu did not come. For three days I stood there, dressed in my finery, Ceolas by my side, feeling like a great fool as Airmid came through the portal, as she and Bile and An Scail made their lopsided way through the forest, as content and as odd a threesome as ever had lived. On the third day Airmid took pity on me.

"You await Eriu."

"She . . . indicated . . . that she would accompany you. I thought it only . . . courteous . . . that the bard should be here to greet the chief of the Sisters."

"Courteous."

I nodded, but I could feel the hot blood moving under my cheeks. I longed suddenly for Skena, for the sweet familiarity of her touch, for our easy movements together, for the long life that we had planned.

What was I doing here?

"Well." I smiled brightly. "If she will not accompany you, then surely I am not obligated to appear. I have much work of the tribe to do."

"Obligated," said An Scail, nodding. She met the eyes of her Ancient friend. Some message seemed to pass between them.

"Eriu comes with me tomorrow," said An Scail. "For these past days, she has had much work of the Danu to do."

I knew that they were laughing at me, two Ancient women with all the experience of love and change in their past. I hung my head like a stripling boy. Bile slid his hand into mine. I looked down at his face. He smiled, radiant, encouraging. He nodded. Something in his eyes made me feel less stupid, brave.

"You are so brave," I said to him suddenly.

I saw the surprise flare up in his eyes, but I knew it to be the truth. He had moved through his life with determination, learning to walk, drawing with his weak hand. Now whatever work he did with An Scail and Airmid was brave as well. How could I do less than my broken brother? And suddenly I knew that Skena would want me to be here, would want me to heal, to change, to be brave in the world without her. I turned to Airmid.

"Tell her that I will await her tomorrow," I said. "Tell her that I request her presence."

A tiny smile played at the edges of An Scail's lips. Never mind, Skena would say.

Airmid met my eyes. "I will surely tell her, Amergin."

And so she came, her gown a soft sky blue, a vessel for the breeze, the spiraling red hair caught up at the sides, cascading down her back in glorious ringlets that lifted and curled in the wind, all of her seeming to me light as a breeze, vast as the sky. We sat by the portals when the Ancients had departed with Bile. I played Ceolas for her and she tilted her head back and regarded me as I sang. I swam into her eyes, into the secrets there, and I trusted that she would tell them to me when she knew that she could trust me as well. For the first time since Skena had died, I felt hope lift in me, a birdling, a breeze, but singing, singing.

37

CEOLAS SINGS OF AWAKENING DESIRE
I did not think I would love again.
Joy rises in me, trembling.
I am the green force in the leaves,
I am the turn of the tide.
I have been winter, cold and still.
My fires have been banked.
Today, the earth smells green;
the wind is full of promise and the sea.

From behind the portal, from behind the doorway of time that separated them, Eriu could hear the harpsong of Amergin. She sighed deeply. She was, she knew, the source of the song. Had she skill with the harp, she too would have been singing. She closed her eyes to the soft sound of the song, muffled by the temporal distance between them. She hummed softly in accompaniment. Her heart lifted. She would see him again! In a moment, in a little moment of time, her tiny hand would rest inside his, like a ship coming safe into port. Today, she would tell him the truth. All of the truth. Today he would know who she was, know that she kept his child safe and well. Today she would trust the great soul of Amergin with the complicated truth. He would understand it; she knew this now.

In that sudden knowledge another truth came suddenly to Eriu.

She loved him. Eriu of the Three Sisters, ancient herself and stranger to the place as well, loved Amergin, son of Mil, poet of the Milesians. What would come of that love she knew not, but it moved through her with certainty, with joy. Surely Danu herself rejoiced at this, at the love that bloomed between the people of Mil and the people of the Danu.

"Mother," Eriu whispered. "Make my voice fearless; bless the truth that I will tell."

She stepped toward the portal, raised her triangle toward the key.

"Eriu!" She turned. Banba stood behind her. "Where are you going?"

"I . . ."

Banba stepped up to the doorway, heard the harpsong on the other side of the portal. "Did you not hear it? He is there, the poet."

"Yes . . . I know."

Banba regarded her sister for a long moment. Eriu watched as disbelief flitted across her face, then knowledge, fear, disappointment.

"Were you going to tell us, your Triad Sisters?"

"You meet with him . . . every day?" Fodla's tone was disbelieving.

"For these past weeks, yes. I . . . escort Airmid to the portal, and he brings Bile and An Scail. And when they go off for their work, we sit at the portal and talk until they return."

"Every day? For weeks?"

"I have said so, Banba; why do you taunt me?"

"What do you talk of?" asked Fodla.

"We talk of everything. The world. He tells me of Greece and Egypt. He has told me how Bile was injured so long ago and of how his people traveled in their wagons. I have told him of the earthquake and of how it destroyed our ancient city."

"And did you tell him that you were alive when that happened? That you were a babe on that isle off the coast of Greece?" Banba's tone was caustic.

"No. Here, give me the baby."

Eriu lifted little nine-month-old Skena from Banba's arms and dandled her against her knee, bouncing her up and down. Skena giggled aloud and threw her chubby hands into the air.

"And did you tell him," asked Banba, "that you care for his nine-month-old daughter that he believes to be dead and gone?" Her voice was slow and soft, as though she spoke to a lunatic or an idiot.

"No."

"And do you remain in Metaphor all the while, or are you Danu and just so he thinks you beautiful, with your vast eyes and your fluted, feathered ears, your many long fingers twined in his, in your true form with a thousand years upon you?"

"Enough, Banba," said Fodla. "She talks with him; she does not Braid him or bond with him."

"Thank you, Fodla," said Eriu.

"Not yet," said Banba.

"It is just that you do not talk to him honestly," said Fodla.

"Sisters! Will you allow me no peace, no moment of joy in my existence? I do my duty by the Danu as I always have."

"No one faults your duty," said Fodla quietly. "We worry for your heart."

"My heart is fine."

"At least in those 'moments of joy' with Amergin," said Banba.

"Perhaps I should not say joy. Perhaps I should say pleasantry," said Eriu. She twirled little Skena around and laughed aloud as the baby giggled.

"Have you noticed how pleasantly this baby looks like its mother?" said Banba, her voice caustic.

Eriu dropped down onto a curved chair. She held the baby on her lap. Tears welled up in her eyes. "Oh, Sisters, what should I do? We cannot keep this child from him forever; he is so lonely. Nor can we forever hide our true selves from the Milesians."

"We must do both," said Fodla.

"Precisely," said Banba. "We have no choice. What good would it do him to know of his child? He cannot come into our world to see her; she cannot go into his. The knowledge would lodge in him like a seed; it would grow and give fruit to a bitter and frustrated tree. It would make his loneliness worse, and you would be its cause. His heart would turn against you and then against the Danu, and our tribe would be in danger. We have seen how quick these Milesians are to go to war."

"And as for our appearance," said Fodla. "We have seen that the Milesians are quick to act and slow to think. Already, there are rumors about us from the night of the Battle of Mag Tuiread. They call us 'little people' and 'shape-shifters,' and whisper about our eyes. Were they to see us as we are . . . I believe that they would kill us all simply from the fear of it."

"It would be better," said Banba, "if you did not see him anymore, unless we two are with you."

"But I—"

Banba held up her hand. "We speak from our love of you. You know this. But more, we speak from our love of the Danu. From our duty to our people."

The tears spilled freely from Eriu's eyes then. Banba lifted the baby from her. Fodla enfolded Eriu, holding, hushing. At last her weeping subsided. Eriu sighed, a great gusting of wind. Suddenly she looked old in her tiny body, a vessel for centuries of sorrow. She nodded.

"I have heard you, Sisters, and I know that you are right. I will do as you have said."

He was standing at the portal, on his face a look of anticipation, when the blue light snapped and all three sisters stepped into view.

"Banba," he said courteously, "Fodla. I am glad to see you again." But his eyes did not leave Eriu's face. "Eriu, I have been waiting. I feared that you might not come today. It is almost time for Airmid and An Scail to return with Bile."

"Amergin," she began. "My sisters and I . . ."

"Wait," he said, holding up his hand, his face all smiles. "It is good that you are all here! Today I bring an invitation. The festival of Lughnasa approaches, the feast of samhradh, the warm months. We will celebrate our first planting season here on the Green Isle. There will be a feast and dancing, Banba, just for you, and music and song, poetry, horse races. We will hold a naming ceremony for the Green Isle. We would like for the people of the Danu to be our guests. All who wish to come!"

Eriu stood quietly between her sisters. She shook her head.

Banba tilted her head sideways, regarding him. "Is this the Amergin that once we knew?"

He laughed aloud and shrugged. "I have reason for joy," he said softly, his eyes on Eriu.

"Human beings have a great capacity for change, Banba," said Eriu. She smiled at Amergin sadly. "But I am sorry to say that—"

"Hello, children!"

From the forest Airmid and An Scail came wandering along the path, deep in conversation. Behind them Bile walked side by side with a girl of his own age. Their two dark heads were bent together. The girl was chattering to him of something, and Bile nodded solemnly and then broke into a huge smile. He seemed unaware that anyone else moved in the forest at all. They joined the little group by the dolmen.

"How lovely," said Airmid, "for all of us to be together."

"Who is this?" asked Amergin, gesturing at the young woman.

"This is my . . . foster daughter, Illyn," said Eriu. "She was born of the Fir Bolg." She turned toward Banba and Fodla. "Sisters, did you know of this?"

Banba and Fodla shook their heads, eyes wide.

Illyn came forward and held out both of her hands to Amergin. Amergin extended his to her almost automatically.

"You are Amergin!" she said with delight. "I would know you anywhere. Bile speaks of you constantly."

"He . . . speaks . . . of me?"

"Oh yes," she said. She turned to Bile and in his finger language said rapidly, "He is very handsome, your brother the bard."

"And you are quite the charmer," said Amergin.

"Oh my," said Illyn. "I forgot that you also spoke the finger language."

"Of course you did," said Amergin, but he grinned nonetheless. "She has had some training from you, Banba, I see."

Banba laughed aloud, her tone surprised. Amergin turned to An Scail and Airmid.

"Ancients"—Amergin inclined his head—"I was just asking the Sisters to the Lughnasa Feis," said Amergin. "And all of the people of the Danu who wish to come."

"Of course we will come," said Airmid.

"Ancient," Banba began. "We of the Council Triad—"

"We will be there," said Airmid. "Give notice to the Danu."

*　　*　　*

"You come to me without your sisters, Eriu; you must be troubled."

Airmid was bent above her instruments, incising notes on leaves of silver.

"I am . . . I do not know . . . oh, Ancient, help me," she said. Tears began to stream from Eriu's eyes.

Airmid stood and regarded her quietly. "I will assume that this sudden shower has to do with Amergin."

"Only that we care for his child and cannot tell him."

"Only that? Then do not worry. Care for the child with all your love and let me worry. If that is all, I will return to work."

But she did not return to work and stood watching Eriu, her head tilted to the side.

"And he thinks me a tall Greek woman with copper hair."

"Why should it matter if he thinks you that? The Milesians seem to think our aspect pleasant enough."

"What does An Scail think of you? In your chosen Metaphor you look so much like her."

"An Scail has seen me as I am; she does not fear it. She came to know me when I was but a voice and she was sightless; she trusted that person in any aspect."

Eriu regarded the Ancient in stunned silence. "You have let her see you?"

"We have worked hard with Bile these past months. First medical work, then therapeutic work. There came a day when Metaphor slipped."

"And what did she say?"

"She said, 'I knew there could not be two in the world who looked as much alike as we.'"

"And that was all?"

"No. She said, 'Choose carefully among the Galaeci those who see you truly.'"

"Wise advice surely. Would you choose Amergin?"

"Ah, so we come to the heart of the matter. It does not matter if I would choose Amergin."

"My sisters say that I must not see him unless they accompany me."

"And what do you say?"

"I am one of the Council Triad."

"What does Eriu say?"

"Ancient, my hours with Amergin at the portal . . . they fill me with . . . joy. And when I am not there beside him, I anticipate the next time that I will be there. And yet, how could he feel that way for me? He knows me not at all. He sees a Greek woman; it is his visits with her that he anticipates."

"And you want him to anticipate his hours with Eriu?"

Eriu nodded. "But I fear that once he sees me as I am, he will not anticipate. He will feel . . . revulsion, fear. He will cease to come to the portal. And I fear that I will put the Danu in danger if he knows. Perhaps my sisters are right; perhaps I should not see him at all."

Airmid nodded. "You think through it well, Daughter. All of these things are possible. But something else is possible too."

"What have I overlooked?"

"It is possible that Amergin loves the soul of Eriu, that his soul is braided to her soul. And that spirit would be the same in any body, would it not?"

"O Danu," Eriu whispered. "I am afraid."

They attended Lughnasa Feis by the hundreds, the Danu garbed in their finest Greek raiment, their diadems and armlets. Banba wore deep red, Fodla soft gold, Eriu a shifted gown of beautiful emerald green, the color of the Green Isle.

For the Children of Mil, the Danu brought gifts, hammered gold torques for the men, spiraling armlets for the women. The Galaeci, who loved fine raiment, put their gifts on with delight and exclaimed their thanks again and again.

Eber Finn had returned from the north with his wife and his clan, Eremon from his rath, and the Milesians were joyful with reunion.

The feasting tables were prepared and spread with abundance; fish steamed in seaweed, deer and boar roasted in deep pits in the ground. For the occasion, a cow had been slaughtered and beef roasted over a turning spit. Honey cakes and loaves of bread, mead and precious wine still remaining from the journey burdened the trestles. While the people were preparing the food, the Galaeci raced horses up and down the beach. The Danu looked on in admiration.

"Come, Banba," cried Airioch. "Try it once again. We all saw you ride before; you were . . . most natural at the horses."

Banba laughed aloud. "Do not taunt me, Airioch Feabhruadh; as I recall I nearly wore you out with dancing!"

She approached a beautiful white horse with trepidation. She walked from one side to the other and stroked his neck gently. At last she placed her hands on either side of his face and blew gently into his nostrils.

She turned. "He has agreed to take me," she said. "But I will need a lift."

The Milesians burst into laughter and Airioch rushed forward to assist her onto his back.

"Use your legs," he whispered softly as he was boosting her up. "He will understand your directions that way."

Banba looked at him. "You do not toy with me?"

"You are far too beautiful for injury," said Airioch, and he grinned. "Now go!" and he smacked the rump of the horse.

At first Banba wobbled from side to side, clinging hard to the horse's mane.

"Hold on!" cried Fodla. "Oh, Eriu, I fear she will be injured!"

"She is Banba," said Eriu. "Watch her."

Halfway down the beach, suddenly Banba shifted position. She sat up straight and then released her arms from the mane. Then, in a single, graceful gesture, she lifted her arms up and out and backward, like the wings of a bird. Her red dress floated out behind her and her black hair streamed backward in the wind. She and the horse seemed to drift gently together, as the sea itself, as wind.

"Ohhhhh," said the people of the Galaeci and the Danu on one great sigh of admiration.

Before Banba had returned to them, Danu were standing in line for their turn to ride, and the Spear Carriers were already bargaining for breeding stock.

"How will we get those great beasts through the portals?" Fodla whispered to Eriu.

"I know not," Eriu replied, "but we will have to think of something. I doubt that the Danu will ever be without such creatures again."

"Call to feast!" shouted Amergin, and there was a rush to the tables followed by silence as the entire company fell to eating. When the tables had been cleared, Amergin stood before the company. He tuned Ceolas and began to sing. Colpa came to one side of him with his little bone whistle; the haunting notes floated out across the company; they were matched by Bile, humming the accompaniment, as always. Amergin drew a deep breath, looked toward Eriu where she sat between her sisters.

"This is our gift to the Danu," he called aloud. "You have let us share your Green Isle; we name her for one of your own: I invoke the land of Eriu," he sang.

> *"Much traveled the abundant sea,*
> *Eire of the wild fruited mountains*
> *Eire of the tumbling waterfalls,*
> *I invoke the land of Eriu."*

On and on he sang, weaving in the rivers and the green forests, the great trees and the fish who swam the waters, returning again and again to his verse, "I invoke the land of Eriu." On the fourth time that he sang the verse, he heard a voice accompany him, male, clear, though the words were slurred and slightly round.

"I . . . voke the wand of Airuu."

He turned. Over his shoulder Bile was singing, his eyes closed, his head tipped back, the speech childlike, but nonetheless speech.

Amergin stopped playing. He stared. Bile opened his eyes and smiled full into the eyes of his brother.

"I um 'ere, Broher," he whispered, "no diffent than fore, but now my voi can sing my 'eart."

Amergin handed Ceolas to Colpa. He stepped to Bile. He pressed his fingers against his brother's lips. He turned toward where An Scail and Airmid were sitting; suddenly he came at them at a run, dropping to his knees before them. Gently he lifted first one ancient hand and then the other, and pressed his lips to the withered fingers.

"This day," he whispered, "in Tir Nan Og, Skena herself is singing."

38

Why joy cannot remain joy always I do not know. Surely it is one of the most sorrowful mysteries.

Our feast was a moment of joy; it was a joy that was not to last.

Bile was the first to see them; he was walking by the sea with his enchanting Illyn when he pointed up toward the headland. I almost expected to hear him vocalize again, his "Ah, ah" sounds puncturing the evening, so unaccustomed was I to his speech.

"Bro'her," he cried. " 'Ere dey come!"

I looked up at the headland. Macha stood silhouetted in the torchlight, his handsome warrior face angry. He was flanked by his two dark warrior companions. Behind them was a company of some two dozen or so. They descended the headland in procession and chaos began again.

Our warriors ran for their weapons, swearing aloud as they strapped on broadswords and bucklers. Eriu and her sisters stood quietly and formed themselves into a triangle, facing the approaching Morrigu. That threesome stopped and did the same.

"We see that there has been a feast among the Danu and the Milesians and we were not invited. We and our companions are deeply offended."

Suddenly, among the Milesians, women began to scream and run for their children. One or two ran into the sea, their infants in their arms.

"Nemhain!" Eriu shouted. "Cease, or this day we will contend, Danu to Morrigu."

"Nemhain," said Macha quietly. "Now is not the time."

The screaming stopped. Women who stood in the sea looked around them, surprised to find themselves there, their babes in their arms.

"What is happening?" I asked softly.

"Her sister curses your women with fear; she has ceased now."

In the triad of Morrigu, one of the threesome turned his head to me and smiled. He tipped his head in a gentle, female gesture and put a slender finger to his lips.

"It was not the intention of the Children of Mil to offend you," I said to the threesome. "We have not seen you in more than a year; we did not know how to find you to invite you."

"Your attentions are for naught now. The feasting is over and my little company is hungry. How shall they feed?" Macha made a little sweeping motion with her arm.

She waved her hand, and those who had accompanied Macha and her sisters straggled into the firelight. They were as terrifying a lot of creatures as ever I have seen in all my travels. Some were ancient stick-men with long, bony arms and huge eyes, their mouths a round and toothless O. Others looked as though they had cobbled themselves of parts, horns of beasts and hooves of goats, their dark eyes flickering with firelight. Women with long, eerie faces of alabaster white were dressed in unrelenting black from their hair to their sweeping gowns.

Our warriors flanked me on all sides now, weapons at the ready, all of them making signs against the evil. My own hand itched to come up and do the same.

"People of the Galaeci, hear me," Eriu called into the darkness. "What you see is not the true appearance of these creatures. They . . . bewitch . . . your minds to see what is not there."

"Yes," said Macha softly. "Eriu knows well how we . . . bewitch . . . your minds."

Airmid stepped forward. "This will cease. You bait them with your repertoire. You delight in their fear. I command you to cease."

Macha tipped her head. "Very well, Ancient," she said. "We shall obey." She tapped the triangle at her neck; her company followed suit.

Suddenly the entire company shrank before our eyes. They appeared to us then as folk of half our size. The heads were huge, their dark hair crackling with some kind of electricity. Their eyes were black as night, huge and ovoid, devoid of any color or expression, their skin a pale and dusty gray. Their ears winged up and back in folded layers tipped with dark feathering. Their arms were extremely long and their hands possessed of long, slender fingers. Macha pointed one of these fingers at me.

"Is this better, Poet of the Milesians?"

I could say nothing. I stood riveted to the spot, speechless, our warriors around me, our women sobbing in the darkness. I have traveled the wide world, but never in my travels had I seen creatures such as these.

Macha tapped her triangle again and her sisters imitated the gesture. Now before us stood three women, all beautiful. Macha had long dark hair, and dark eyes. Her figure was slender and feminine. Her sisters too were dark and compelling. Behind me in the darkness, I heard my brother Eber Finn call out.

"By the gods, oh, by the gods." I heard him fall to the ground, his swords and armor clanging on the stones.

Macha turned toward Eriu. "How easy it is then, is it not, Little Sister? It requires so little to make such a change."

Suddenly Eremon ran forward, his sword outstretched. Macha simply gestured toward him. Lightning traveled up the sword and into his arm. He was lifted off his feet and landed hard on the ground near Eber Finn.

"Almost too easy," said Macha. She heaved a great sigh, then simply turned and walked toward the headland.

Eriu stepped into our silent midst. "Hear me, sons of Mil," she said. All of the faces of the crowd turned toward her, including those of her own people. Banba and Fodla stepped up behind her.

"Among you, have there been those who carried a darkness within them? Who worked not for the good of the tribe, but for other, darker purposes?"

No one made response. The dark power we had seen this night far surpassed anything our people had ever seen.

Suddenly from the crowd Airioch Feabhruadh called aloud. "We must admit to our own darkness. Though such dark creatures as we are look the same on every given day."

His caustic self-criticism broke the mood of terror.

A wave of uneasy laughter moved among us.

"These are our dark ones," said Eriu. "We call them the Raveners. They are ours; we claim them so. They journeyed here with us from . . . Greece. But we of the Danu bear no such dark magic. Our magic is of science, our portals and our spears. You have come here among us, unaware of what awaited you. We tell you this now. We, the Children of the Braid, do here declare that you are under our protection. Call upon us and we will come to your side. We will meet you at the doorways between our worlds. For all of time, I do declare that we will be your friends and your companions."

Behind her suddenly her warriors began to range up with their Light Spears; her physicians encircled her. I saw the look of gratitude flood across her face.

"We will defend you with our knowledge and presence, with our Light Spears and our Silver Arms. When you are ill, our physicians will heal you. We ask that we do not return to our ways of a year ago. Here at the feasting table, we have known joy together. We offer you our friendship; we ask you to return it in kind."

Some of our people backed away. I could see others shaking their heads in the negative. But Eremon and Airioch stepped forward.

"Eriu of the Danu, we have heard you," said Eremon. "I and my clan accept your offer of friendship."

"As do I and mine," said Airioch.

Eber Finn said nothing, but I felt gratitude for the courage of my brothers wash over me.

An Scail came up beside me. She whispered softly. "I think this night that our people begin what will be a long and troubled relationship with the Children of the Danu."

"Troubled defines it well," I whispered back.

Eriu spoke again. "We thank you for the hospitality of this wondrous night. Accept our apology that these of ours have sundered the celebration. We will depart from you to give you time to contemplate these things."

She met my eyes; hers were brimming with sadness, and as usual, they were overlarge.

When the Danu had left us, I helped Eber Finn to his feet. He lay where he had fallen, still as a log but for the look of terror on his face.

"We have seen these before," said Eremon. "At the Plain of Mag Tuiread. Granted not as horrible as what we have seen tonight. But, Brother, you are a warrior. You set a bad example for your clan."

Eber Finn hissed under his breath. "Brothers, I must speak with you." He glanced around, saw his wife with a group of women by the fire, their heads bent low in whispered conversation. "Alone," said Eber Finn.

We settled in my dwelling, Airioch, Eber Finn, Eremon, and I. At the last moment, Colpa and Bile ducked beneath the door of the dwelling.

"We are brothers too," said Colpa.

"You have but fourteen years upon you," Eremon began, but Airioch held up his hand.

"There is much wisdom in these little brothers. They should stay."

Eber Finn cleared his throat, looked at the assembled company.

"My wife does not like the north."

"Then return back to us here at Inver Skena," said Airioch. "We have missed you; how easy it is."

"It is not easy," said Eber Finn quietly. "It . . . there is a woman in the north. I have been . . . bedding her for quite some time. She . . . was most beautiful. And she knew . . ." He glanced at our two youngest brothers. "She knew of new and pleasurable ways to mate that my wife did not know."

Airioch shrugged. "So what of this? It is the way of the Galaeci to like the mating."

"The woman," said Eber Finn. "It is she that you saw tonight."

"Who?" said Eremon. "One of the sisters?"

"Not Banba I hope," said Airioch, grinning. "I would still have designs there had I not so many wives wearing me out."

But I was watching Eber Finn's face; it was white as the sea foam, his eyes large and unfocused.

"O you gods," I said softly. "You have been mating with Macha."

"I have," he said. "In this last visage you have seen. I had not seen her as a man. Nor had I seen her as . . . whatever those dark-eyed little folk were. I have all along been mating with . . . that . . . and I did not know. My wife." Here he looked again at our youngest brothers. He swallowed and closed his eyes. "She came upon us once in a wooded glade. She flew into a fury and cast herself upon us. She tried to scratch at the eyes of Macha—she did not call herself that, Brothers—and Macha simply stood, naked in the clearing, lifted her arm, and threw my wife to the ground."

He shook his head. "I scrambled to help my wife. I voiced my anger at . . . Macha, but my wife stopped speaking to me entirely. And when

Macha came again for me, with her raven hair and her pendulous breasts, I went."

Airioch put up his hand. "You will move back among us; you will never see her again. You will be an attentive husband and father. Your wife will come to forgive you."

"No," said Eber Finn. "There is more. My wife has made a friend among the people of the north. She is a woman, a warrior. She has taught my wife the ways of war, to swing a broadsword and wield a dagger, to move in the forest silent as the deer. She has whispered to her that Eremon got the better piece of land, that he builds a better rath, that he is safer and happier where he is. My wife stirs our people to come against Eremon."

Eremon shook his head. "But why should they do so? Clan is clan."

"Because the woman is Banbh," I said softly.

"Banbh?" said Eremon.

"Sister of Macha, Brothers. She is the bringer of war."

"Still," said Eremon, "your clan will not come against me. I am your brother."

"Our cattle fail, our crops wither in the ground. Our children are thin and the darkness around us moves with strange lights and odd noises."

"Because the Morrigu causes such things to happen; those sisters feed upon destruction and rage, confusion and greed," I said. "Think clearly, Eber Finn."

"I think that my clan will come against you, Eremon. And my wife will be at their head."

"And where will you be?" asked Eremon.

"They are my clan; I am their chief. I wish to remain as chief; I wish to return my wife to me."

"But you need not do that with war," said Airioch. "Hear me, Brother."

"You are not really my brother, are you?" said Eber Finn. He stood and left the dwelling.

"I am sorry for that last, Airioch," I said softly.

"My broher," said Bile. He held forth his good arm and Airioch clasped it.

Eremon followed suit.

Colpa looked thoughtful. He turned toward Airioch. "Each day before us there are choices. For good or evil. For strength or weakness. For care of the tribe or care of the self. Is this not what you have taught me, Brother?"

Airioch nodded.

"You have taught him this?" I regarded Airioch.

"I had to learn it the hard way," said Airioch.

"But that is what Eber Finn is doing," said Colpa. "Do you see? We cannot blame the Morrigu entirely. They put choices before Eber Finn, before his wife. They are choosing badly."

"Very wise indeed," I said.

"What shall we do?" asked Eremon.

"I do not know," I said. "We shall try to keep him here with us. We shall hope that his thinking clears. We shall pray that brother will not come against brother."

CEOLAS SINGS OF DARKNESS
Why must you move in the world,
Sower of evil, bringer of sorrows?
And why do we turn toward you,
Licking our lips for desire,
Losing ourselves to sate a hunger?
Who are you, darkness?
Why are you always among us?

39

"He has been waiting at the portal for more than a fortnight." Banba shook her head. "Ever since the night of the feast."

"He waits at the rising of the sun and he returns after sunset. It makes my heart ache to see it," said Fodla.

"What would you have me do? You were the two who told me not to see him. I have done as you asked."

"Well, we were wrong," said Banba. "It has been known to happen before. And we have made you both miserable."

"Well, I happen to think that you were right after all," said Eriu.

"If you let Morrigu change your mind," said Fodla, "then she has won."

"It is not Morrigu," said Eriu. "It is what they saw inside Morrigu. They saw Morrigu without her Metaphor and they were repulsed, terrified."

"But we look nothing like the Raveners."

"Of course not," said Banba. "Not to us. But Eriu fears that perhaps to them we would. Perhaps they would see us and see our common ancestry. Perhaps they would think that we are all evil, as Morrigu is. Perhaps this poet of Eriu's would take one look at her without her Greek Metaphor and run screaming for the sea, having lost his mind, a gibbering idiot, reduced to drooling in terror for all of time."

"Banba!" said Fodla. "You go too far."

"She does it to make me see my foolishness," said Eriu softly. "And she is right. But there is more than just my fear that a human man cannot love a Danu woman. We have his child and she is trapped with us and he is trapped in his world."

"But neither of them knows that," said Banba softly. "Skena is the happiest of babies, and Amergin has put aside his grief for his lost wife. He loves a woman of the Danu. It shines from his eyes. Did you hear his song? He calls the place Eire—the land of Eriu."

"And if he sees me as I am?"

"Why is that necessary? Let him see you as your Metaphor. If I were to succumb to Airioch's invitations, as I just might one of these days, I would surely encounter him as that Greek woman he seems so smitten by. Why not do the same?"

"Because I do not want Amergin to be smitten by a Greek woman. It will be more than just mating, Banba. I love him; I love his eyes and his hair and his big human frame and his soul and his song. I will not cease to love him. I will love him when we both have left these bodies and have gone into the Braid."

"And you want him to love you as you are," said Fodla softly.

"Is that too much to want?" asked Eriu.

"There is only one way to know that," said Banba.

Moonlight was streaming over the clearing when she came through the portal, the blue light snapping shut behind her.

He was seated with his back against the rock, Ceolas on his lap, but he leaped to his feet as she stepped into the clearing.

"I thought that you would never come again."

"I considered never coming again."

"But why?"

"We terrified your people and wreaked havoc on your Lughnasa feast. Is that not enough?"

"Eriu, we Galaeci can wreak havoc all by ourselves. Even now, my brother Eber Finn threatens to make war against my brother Eremon."

"Why?"

"Because his wife wants Eremon's land. Because Eber Finn has been mating with . . ." Amergin paused.

"Macha! In one of her guises." Eriu waited for his answering nod. "You see, it all comes back to her, doesn't it? She likes you; she finds the Galaeci complex and troublesome. You are her favorite new target. I am ashamed of that, ashamed that she is related to the Danu. And I fear all the trouble that she will cause you."

"As my brother Colpa says, Eber Finn had to choose for her as well. But that is not all, is it? I have waited for you for almost one full waxing of the moon."

Eriu sighed. "I know. I have stood on the other side of the portal and listened to Ceolas."

"Why did you not come to me?"

"Because you are right. Macha is not all that troubles me. Is there somewhere we can go, Amergin? Somewhere where your kinsmen cannot happen upon us."

"There is the dwelling where An Scail and Airmid taught Bile to speak. It is that way"—he pointed—"through the forest."

"Take me there," she said softly. "There is something I would show you."

He built up the fire, shook out the pelts and skins. When the little conical hut was warm and bright, he took her hands. "Show me," he said quietly.

She withdrew her hands, took a long, deep breath. "O Danu, I am afraid."

"Of me? I would never harm you, Eriu."

"This I know," she said softly. "I am afraid of me."

She raised a trembling hand to the triangle at her neck. She closed her eyes and tapped it once. She remained quite still, her eyes closed.

"Open your eyes, love," he whispered softly.

She opened them.

"Can I . . . touch you?" he asked softly.

"Yes," she said, her voice broken and small.

He ran his hands gently along her cheeks, then traced a finger gently along the multiple curves of the ear, threading up along the fine feathering there.

"Like shells of the sea," he whispered softly.

He slipped his fingers into her curls and watched as they slipped back into place with sparks of electricity. He leaned back.

"I remember these eyes," he said softly. "I have been watching for them ever since I first saw the magic of them hidden inside the . . . Other. How beautiful they are, how like a sea, turquoise and blue and gray. I feel as though I could drift away inside them."

She sat very still, her long fingers pressed together. He lifted them quietly, pressed his lips to each hand.

"You are not still afraid, are you?"

"I am," she said softly. "You can see that I am not . . . human."

"I have known that something else was underneath your guise from the night that I held you on the Plain of Mag Tuiread. I could feel the tiny fragility of your bones beneath my arms. And I have seen your eyes and the eyes of your companions."

"I do not repulse you?"

"You are like quicksilver, like moonlight on water, like the water itself. I would think that I might frighten you, all of us Galaeci, great hairy beasts that we are."

"You have never seen the Fomor," said Eriu. A small smile played at the edges of her lips.

"They must be hairy beasts indeed, then."

A little laugh escaped her; it sounded half like a sob. "Oh, they are." She shook her head. "I thought that you would find me . . . frightening, that you would see in me the Morrigu."

"How could I see her at all? She seemed to me a wizened lump of darkness, a void where there should be color and light. But you; you are all color and light. It is like looking at the sun upon the water. Oh, Eriu, for months we have sat side by side against the portals and we have talked of all the world. I hear the same voice that I heard beside me. It is the voice that I love. Beyond that . . . how magical you are, how delicate and beautiful to me. I am almost afraid to touch you."

"Touch me here," she said softly, putting her hand against his lips. "Touch your lips to my lips. I have been longing for it, Amergin."

"Ah, sweeting," he said softly. "So have I."

And the kiss, when it came, was like a feather, like a breeze, oh, like a promise.

CEOLAS SINGS OF LOVE REBORN
My heart, oh my resilient heart,
My joy, oh you my joy.

I am laughter once again
I am sweet desire
I am a man made whole in you.
How shall I bless you, love
For this gift of yourself
Perfect as you are?

40

I wo go 'mong them, Amer'in."

"But why, Bile? Are you not happy here among the clan?"

At fifteen he had become a giant of a boy, long and lean, with a quick smile. He turned to look at Illyn, and I saw the shining black braid that cascaded down his back. I knew that she must have braided it for him. His good hand held tight to Illyn's hand. He inhaled.

" 'Ear me, Amer'in," he said. "Once when I 'as 'oung," he struggled.

"Young," I said.

He nodded. "We 'ere live ina t . . . tower by the sea. I woke dark."

"You woke in the dark?"

He nodded. "You 'ere stand window, arms round Skena. I watch." He took a deep breath. It was still difficult for him to string together multiple sentences. I had to hold myself back from saying it for him.

He continued. "I 'oped one day I love someun 'ike 'at."

"And you have found that with Illyn?"

He nodded. "More. I wish two"—he held up his fingers, falling automatically into his old finger language—"arms, two wrap round Illyn I love."

"That is not possible," I said. "And surely that does not matter to Illyn; she loves you as you are."

"I do," she said softly, smiling up at Bile.

"Is," said Bile. "Possbe."

"What do you mean?" I looked at An Scail and Airmid.

Airmed took a deep breath. "You know that we have physicians of great skill among us."

I waved my hand. "I know who you are and where you are from. I know how old you are."

She smiled and her whole mien relaxed. "Good," she said. "She has told you everything." She nodded. "We can restore his arm," she said.

"With a Silver Arm?"

"No. A real arm with nerves and sinews and bones. It is a technique that my brother and I perfected . . . long, long ago."

"But we have been among you now for three years. Why did you not restore it before?"

"In the beginning, to have done so would have frightened your people too much. But they have grown . . . accustomed to our oddities now, although they still see us in Metaphor. A new arm, more or less, will no longer frighten them."

I thought about this for a while and realized that it was true. I smiled, and shook my head. "True enough," I said. "Will Bile be in danger or in pain?"

"No."

"Then I say that it should be done."

"There is one other thing," she said softly.

Bile spoke then. "Go 'mong."

"To go through the portal?"

He nodded.

I looked at Airmid. "Will he be able to return?"

"Yes."

"But I too have asked Eriu if I can travel through the portal; she has denied me."

Illyn smiled at me. "What do you see when you see me, Poet?"

"I see a bright and beautiful girl of the Fir Bolg. I see my brother's beloved. Why?"

"Would it surprise you to know that when the Danu took me in I had a harelip and a clubfoot?"

"They . . . repaired these, as they will Bile's arm?"

"They did."

"I am less fearful, then, seeing you here whole and well."

"Would it surprise you also to know that I was . . . slow and stunted, unable to speak?"

"That would surprise me greatly. I see no trace of that young woman before me now."

"To repair those damages, it was necessary for the Danu to blend some of their braid with mine. I am Fir Bolg and Danu. This is why I can come and go through the portals as the Danu do."

"You are . . . as old as the Danu?"

"No. Nor will I live to their age. But I will live much longer than you will live, Amergin. I am a Hybrid of the Braid."

I turned to Bile. "And this is what it will take to repair the arm? You too will be a Hybrid?"

Airmid answered. "We will repair the arm and the pathways in the brain to make it work and we will clear the pathways of his thought and speech. . . . And yes, he will be a Hybrid of the Braid. He will be as Illyn is. He will live as long as she lives. He will have two good arms and perfect speech and he and Illyn will be together for a long life."

"I fear this," I said softly. "And at the same time I wish it."

"Good," said Airmid. "Because I am very old and have little time."

"You have been saying that for as long as I have known you," said An Scail.

"It has been true for at least that long. You are no blushing maiden yourself, Ancient." The two burst into laughter.

"For myself," I said softly. The idea formed completely as soon as I spoke it. "I wish it for myself as well."

Airmid shook her head. "I cannot give you that gift," she said softly. "We cannot tamper with what the Braid has made whole. You are well and strong. Our law permits us to repair that which is damaged; we do that in the name of the Braid, that all of her children be made whole. But I cannot tamper with what is not damaged. It is Danu law."

"What would happen if I went through the portal with Bile?"

"You would never be able to come back again," she said softly. "If you did, all that you knew and loved would be gone. You would instantly age into a withered and ancient old man and you would die among strangers. That is why Eriu denies you; it is her love for you that makes her say you nay."

"Then it must be my love for Bile that lets him go," I said softly.

The light in his face tore at my heart as he threw his arms around me.

CEOLAS SINGS OF BELONGING
When you go among them, Brother,
Take my soul for keeping
For I cannot go with you,
I cannot be of them.
Journey with my spirit
To the children of the Light,
Carry me into belonging.

"Brother, awaken." It was Colpa, his frame bending low to move through the doorway.

"I am awake," I said softly into the darkness. I had been lying awake for hours staring at the ceiling of my dwelling, my heart hammering with fear for Bile. I had stood with him as he stepped into the portal, lifted his good hand to me. Then he had raised the triangle that the Danu had given him, pressed it into the slot in the portal, and disappeared into an eclipse of blue light.

Eriu had stood beside me, silent, her hand on my arm.

"I am afraid," I said softly. "And I am . . . envious. He goes where you go. And if all goes well he will be able to come and go, while I wait here, forever at a portal, waiting for your return, stealing little moments with you until I die."

"I will always come to you, love. Forever."

I bent my frame and closed my arms gently around her; even in Metaphor I was always aware of her delicate fragility. It was one, only one, of the reasons I loved her.

"And all will go well. Bile will be back among you soon, with two good arms and a tongue as glib as that of his brother."

But it had been six weeks and Bile had not yet returned. Each time Eriu came through the portal I looked anxiously for Bile, for Airmid, but they did not accompany her. Though she protested that all was well, I wished to see my brother with my own eyes.

"Amergin!"

I bolted upright. "I am sorry, Colpa. I worry for our brother. Why do you keep such late hours?"

"Eremon approaches at the headland. He is gravely wounded. He brings with him the wounded of his tribe and those of Eber Finn's who have survived. He needs you to send for the Danu physicians."

"Oh no. O you gods! Eber Finn has gone against Eremon then. I will punish him dearly for this."

"I think not," said Colpa quietly. "Eber Finn is dead."

"No. Oh no."

I threw on my braichs and ran from the dwelling. My bare feet drove against the stones as I ran. Eremon was staggering down the hillside, leading a horse on which one of his own warriors was draped. Blood ran down Eremon's face and leg, down the side of the great beast.

"He came in darkness," he said softly. "Against his brother he came in darkness."

"Where is he?"

He gestured back. I ran along the line of horses, of men supporting their wounded brothers. Eber Finn was dangling over the back of a great black horse. His eyes were wide and white, his mouth surprised. His head was nearly severed from his neck. Perched on the flank of the horse was a large black raven.

"Get you gone!" I screamed. I swatted at the bird, which rose into the darkness, cawing out.

"Keep away from us, bringers of darkness," I cried.

"Amergin." Colpa was beside me, Airioch straggling up the headland behind him. "You must find the Danu physicians or we will lose many more."

I turned. I began to run toward the portal, my bare feet cut and bleeding now with trampling over stones.

I saw a figure running toward me in the darkness. I reached for my sword and remembered that I had come away swordless.

"Halt!" I cried. "Or I will cut you where you run."

The voice that came from the darkness was familiar, strong and whole.

"It is I, Brother. Bile. We have heard of this tragedy. I bring the Danu physicians."

He emerged from the shadows and embraced me, his two strong arms closing around me.

"Light!" he cried, and the Danu physicians lit their ice-blue torches as they followed us down the path.

Bile was gathering his drawings and some of the tools that he used to etch in metal and stone. We had sent Eremon, healed and much saddened, back to his rath, which he had called Tara. The wounded of Eber Finn's tribe had remained here among us at Inver Skena. Now that several days had passed, they seemed to be shaking off some horrible malaise, to be themselves shocked that the sons of Mil had turned against each other. I had seen great warriors standing by the sea, their arms around each other's shoulders locked in shame and weeping. I shook my head.

"It will be well," said Bile.

"Will it? Sometimes I think it will never be well, that the smallest time of joy will always be followed by sorrow or crisis."

He smiled at me. "This is not the Amergin who raised me," he said softly.

"I know," I said. "I suppose that I am lonely."

He knelt before me and clasped my upper arms.

"Do you think I would ever abandon you, Brother? You who have loved me from the start, and in all my imperfections?"

I shook my head at the beauty of him, at the completeness of his arms and his speech. "I cannot believe it is you," I said softly.

"Nor I," he replied. "I dwell in this body with such joy and gratitude." He jammed a few more tools into his leather pack.

"You will dwell among them now?"

Bile smiled. "No, Brother. Do not fear. I will go back and forth with my goods and my gear. The portal will be snapping so often that you will forget that there is any other kind of doorway."

"What are their cities like?" I asked. I knew I sounded like a lost and plaintive child, but Bile seemed to understand.

"How you would love it," he said softly. "This world is . . . the same world, but . . . different. It is so hard to explain. The cities are beautiful, Brother, crystal and soft fabrics billowing and music as soft as wind and chambers where memory is stored like the stories of Ceolas." He shook his head. "I cannot describe it; I will bring you a sketch when next I come."

"I will miss you," I said softly. It was not that he seemed different, so much, but that he seemed so much himself, so much the young man that I had thought he would grow to be before we left Egypt, before the wagon. And that he would now become different. And that the new man would come to prefer the country of the Danu. How strange and simplistic our journey must seem to him now, our wagons and our ships. He had gone beyond us, beyond our knowledge.

"How Skena would delight for you. For your recovery. How she would love to see you this way, restored."

"She would delight for you too, Brother. For your love for Eriu."

"It seems a long, long time ago, does it not?"

"To you too?" Bile said softly. "How often I wished to talk to you about it, Amergin. All of it. Egypt and the isles. Uncle Ith. Our tower by the sea. And Skena . . . oh, I . . . brought you something, Brother, while I remember." He rummaged around in his bag and brought up a roll of fresh parchment. "They have supplies for me to draw again. Although I'm still drawing with my left hand, that being the hand I'm accustomed to. Maybe soon I'll draw with both hands," he said, grinning.

He spread out his roll of sketches and began to page through them. "There is a child among them. Perhaps two years old or a little more . . . Ah, here she is."

He drew forth a sketch and laid it before me.

I stared at the little face, the thick, curling hair. "O you gods!"

"So you do see what I see? Does she not look like Skena?"

"She is the portrait of Skena. Who is she?"

"Illyn did not know. She said she thought she was a Fir Bolg child, a new Hybrid of the Braid. She said the Three Sisters themselves care for the child as they did for Illyn. I would have asked Airmid, but then Eber Finn went against our brother." He shrugged. "Illyn and I will ask her when I return."

I looked long at the little sketch.

"May I keep it?" I asked quietly. "Perhaps Eriu will know."

41

Eriu came through the portal in Metaphor. She looked around her, as she always did, for any of the sons of Mil who might have accompanied Amergin. When she saw none, she tapped her triangle and folded down into herself, the tiny wide-eyed woman of the Danu.

Amergin looked into her eyes. "You are troubled, love."

"Have I become that easy to read?"

"Yes; your eyes are their own story. Is Bile unwell?"

"No. Bile is well and happy and sends you greetings. He and Illyn will come through the portal at the new moon."

"Then what? Speak quickly or my mind will anticipate the worst."

"It is Airmid. She has taken to her chamber. She says that soon she will return to the Braid. She wishes to see An Scail."

"I will tell our An Scail."

"No! You cannot! Airmid is not well enough to come through the portal, and if An Scail were to go to her . . ."

"She too would die?"

"She would, Amergin. She could never return through the portal. The minute she returned, she would die."

"Then Airmid will die without her. They are as twin daughters of two different worlds. An Scail will never forgive me if Airmid departs this world without her, and yet, I cannot put An Scail in danger. I don't know what to do. What is the right thing to do?" He stood and began to pace around the tiny hut, rapping a rolled scroll of papers on his hand.

"What do you carry, love?"

He looked down, surprised. "Oh, I forgot that I carried it. It is some sketches that Bile made for me among your people."

"Let me see."

Amergin opened the sketches out onto the little table in the hut. The first was of a city, all spires and intricate scrollwork, all crystalline light and color.

"Tara," said Eriu softly. "How beautifully he captures its magic. But you must hide these, Amergin. Your people would be frightened to see so vast and complex a city in a place where they could not 'see' it at all."

He folded out the next one.

"O Danu," said Eriu softly.

"Who is she?"

Eriu drew a deep breath. She closed her eyes. "I have feared this day for so long, and now that it has come, I find that I am glad."

"Speak clearly; you frighten me."

"Clearly then. She is Skena's child. We call her Skena. Skena's child and yours."

"This is not possible. I saw Skena and Ir. I burned their bodies on the seashore. What have you done? Have your people worked some dark magic?"

"No magic, love. Their bodies washed up on the shore. Skena and Ir were gone; their bodies had been too long without breathsong. But the child in the womb; she lived, Amergin! Her heart beat. But she was too small to yet live outside the womb, so . . . Airmid took her from the womb and took her into our cities and kept her alive there until she was ready to come into the world."

"Kept her alive?"

"Yes, love, in a Danu womb cradle."

"She was born of a Danu woman?"

"No. No. It is a womb cradle, a cradle of life fluid. Airmid used Skena's life fluid. She is a beautiful child, Amergin. Happy and sweet and loving. She is as Skena must have been."

He stood staring down at her, his expression horrified. Suddenly, he leaned forward and lifted her into the air with his great hands, until her eyes were level with his.

"Are you telling me that I have a child of almost three years? That she lives and is well? And that you never told me?"

Eriu spoke very softly. "Yes," she said. "That is what I am telling you."

"O you gods!" He released her, staggered backward, away from her. "I see now that you are like Morrigu after all. All deception. All subterfuge. All this time that you have proclaimed your love for me. And instead you have been keeping this secret. This terrible secret. You have been keeping me from my child. You knew how much I loved Skena. You knew. Oh, my child!"

The sound wrenched from him like a cry thrown to the heavens.

Eriu began to weep, the huge tears falling from her eyes. She tapped her triangle and folded into Metaphor, the tall red-haired woman of old.

"I am sorry, Amergin," she whispered. "Please forgive me."

"How can I forgive this? Oh, my child. I would see my child."

Suddenly his hand flashed forward; he closed it around Eriu's triangle and yanked with all his might. Her head jerked forward, but the pendant did not come loose.

"Please, love," she whispered. "Please do not make me hurt you further. You cannot go into our world."

Amergin yanked again hard, the triangle in his palm.

Eriu reached into his palm. She touched the triangle once. A bolt of lightning shot up Amergin's arm. He was knocked back onto the ground; the cloth of his tunic smelled of burning.

Eriu was weeping, her tiny body shaken with sobs. She stepped into the portal, leaned against it weeping.

"Think, love," she whispered. "Please. I know that you will understand."

He gathered himself to his feet and launched toward her with a roar, his face a mask of rage. She pressed her triangle into the portal. In a flash of blue light, she was gone.

42

I ran. Away from the portal. Away from the hut in the forest where I had loved her. Away from the village of our people. I ran like a man possessed by demons. It seemed to me that I ran forever. At last I came to the shores of a small lake, and there I collapsed onto the shore. I wept for a while, like a child. Then, for a time, I raged, heaving rocks into the water, screaming my rage at the sky.

When I had exhausted myself at last, I leaned against some boulders there by the water and closed my eyes. I must have slept. When I awoke, a soft dusk was beginning to fall over the water. I saw a woman walking toward me along the shore of the lake.

She was a woman of the Galaeci, tall with dark auburn hair, her plaid cloak undulating with her as she walked. She moved closer and I was able to see her clearly.

It was Skena.

I stood, unthinking, and ran to her, drew her into my embrace.

I ran my hands through the thickness of her hair, lifted her face to mine. She returned my ardor, lifted on tiptoe and pressed her lips against mine.

"Oh, love," I whispered. "Oh, how I have missed you."

I unpinned the cloak and watched it drop to the beach. Underneath she wore her finest silk tunic, and I watched as she shrugged it from her and stood before me. Her belly was flat and white. I ran my hand over it.

"They took our child," I whispered. "They took her from us."

She said nothing at all, just lifted her arms around my shoulders and pressed into me, her long white nakedness gleaming in the evening light. She smiled. "Come," she said softly, seductively. "Remove your cloak."

I tilted my head sideways. It was not Skena's voice. Not the voice that I remembered.

"How is it that you have come to me?" I said.

"That was easy, love. Now come to me." The voice was throaty, deep, seductive.

"Macha!" I pushed her from me. "What have you done? Where is my Skena?"

Macha laughed aloud; she folded down into the male warrior form that I knew best, stood before me naked on the beach.

"Your Skena is dead, of course."

"This is cruel."

She shrugged, nodded. "Well, cruel, I suppose, from your point of view. From mine, it is a game."

She shifted again. Before me on the beach was a black wolf with gleaming yellow eyes. It bared its fangs at me and growled.

I arched my head backward and exposed my neck.

"Here," I said, "I offer it to you."

She folded back up again, a tiny gray Danu with dark ovoid eyes.

"You do not find it cruel that the great poet of the Galaeci would be found dead by the shores of a lake, his throat torn out by a wolf, all his golden words ripped away from him?"

"More ironic than cruel, Macha."

She burst into laughter. "Very good, Poet. This parsing of the language, the subtle shades of meaning."

I shrugged. "Is this what you did to my brother?"

"Eber Finn? There was almost no challenge there. It wasn't quite as easy as terrifying the Fir Bolg in the forest, but it came close." She shifted again, a beautiful woman with large breasts and long hair. She lifted the breasts in her hands, ran her tongue over her lips. "As easy as this. Eber Finn was captivated by human breasts and a human tongue. His wife was captivated by her own rage; my sisters and I do no more than feed what is there."

"What did you hope to feed in me?"

"Betrayal. Betrayal is always a good doorway," she said.

"Why?"

"Why do we do it?"

I nodded.

"It is . . . what we do. What we are. Always. Many forms. Many worlds." She smiled, shifted again as Skena. "Some find us . . . comforting."

"I do not," I said. "Skena was real and I loved her. We had a child."

She shifted, the tall woman with dark flowing hair. "Well, that is a child that you will never see."

"No," I said softly.

"But I can help you there," she said softly. She reached behind her neck and withdrew the triangular pendant. She put it into my hand. "Now go and get her," she said softly. "Just press the triangle into the recess in the portal. Go and get her and bring her back into your world where she belongs, among your people."

I looked down at the pendant in my hand. "Why would you do this for me?" I asked softly.

"She is your child. You deserve to have her. The Sisters should never have kept her from you." She pointed at the far side of the lake. "Do you see the dolmen?"

I nodded.

"It is a doorway, just as the portals are. You may enter there."

I turned toward the dolmen, the triangle in my hand. I thought of my child, Skena's and mine. Something that Eriu had said stopped me in my tracks. I turned back toward the Macha.

"And if I find my child and I bring her among our people . . . she will die. Of course. That is why you have offered me this key. My child will die. She has lived among the Danu for many years."

"Not right away," said Macha with a shrug. "For a time she would look like this." She folded back into her metaphor of Skena again. "That would be a comfort to you, would it not?"

"Yes," I said softly.

"Well, there you are." She pointed again at the dolmen. "Go and get her."

"But my comfort would cost her life. Oh, Eriu. Oh, love. Now I see. My comfort would cost my child her life."

I looked up at Macha, where she stood before me. "Dark one," I said. "You have helped me to see Light."

"I have?" She looked nonplussed, angry. She folded out of Skena and into the form of a Ravener, the dark-eyed Danu.

"Skena would be very proud of you," I said. "And Eriu."

I held the pendant with its triangle out to her.

"Keep it!" she snapped. "I do not enjoy you, Amergin. I do not like the way you play the game."

"Thank you," I said. "I am gratified to hear it."

CEOLAS SINGS OF SACRIFICE
I will keep you safe,
Child of my heart,
Child of my first love,
As Eriu has kept you safe
Within the walls of Tara.
Now do I see clearly;
More worlds than ours,
More loves than one,
More sacrifices asked of us
that love must give.

I knelt before An Scail and put the pendant gently into her hand. "Airmid is dying," I said softly. "This pendant will take you to her. But if you use it, know that you will not be able to return to us. To return would be death."

"Why do you give me this?"

"Airmid is your friend. And they have my child among them."

"Eriu bore you a child?" She shook her head, confused.

"Skena bore me a child. They have kept that child alive. She dwells among the Danu. She cannot come into this world or she will die. I cannot go into that world, for if I do I can never return."

"And yet you give me this knowing that I would have to remain with them or return and die."

"All of our life you have given to our tribe. You endured years of separation from Ith and came here with us when I knew that you would rather have remained among the Wise Ones in Galaeci. You trained me in the druid ways and now you train Colpa. Yet I know well enough that Airmid is your sister in spirit. The choice should be yours."

"And why do you not use the triangle to go among them? Bile is there and Eriu and now your child."

"I am Poet of the tribe; I cannot leave the tribe."

She regarded me for a long time, then placed an ancient hand against my face. "I love you my sweet, sad boy."

I nodded my head. I could say nothing.

"Take me to the portal," she said softly.

At the doorway, I raised my hand to her.

"Live well among them, Ancient," I said.

She smiled. "I have lived well, Amergin. I have lived well indeed." And then she was gone.

I do not know how long I sat in that forest. Day passed into night and then into day again. Eriu did not come to the portal. I knew that she would never come again. I had seen to that with my anger and my lack of understanding. Beyond that door were those I loved. Eriu and Bile. An Scail and my child, unknown to me. And I would never see them again. And I would never be able to go among them.

At last I stood and dusted off my braichs. I turned back toward our village. I had moved only a few steps toward the path when I heard the distinctive crack of the portal. I turned, expecting to see Eriu, hope rising in my heart. An Scail stood in the doorway.

"No!" I screamed. "No! Why did you return?"

I could see that she was folding down into herself; her ancient face looked withered, her body frail and brittle. I rushed to the portal and gathered her into my arms.

"Why, An Scail? Why?"

She smiled softly. "Airmid has passed," she said. "Wake us together; that is our wish." She pressed the pendant with its shimmering triangle into my hand.

"Oh, why?" I said. The tears streamed down my face.

"Because the choice should also be yours," she said softly.

43

The door slid back on its silent track and Illyn entered. It was clear she had been weeping. Eriu held out her arms.

"Do not weep for the Ancient, sweeting. She goes into the West."

Illyn nodded, gulping. "An Scail returned through the portal."

Eriu jumped to her feet. "Why? O Danu, she went to her death."

"For Amergin," Illyn said softly. "She and Airmid . . . They wish to be woken together. In the world of the Galaeci."

At dusk the Danu emerged from their doorways, shimmer after shimmer of blue light. Down to the sea they moved, hundreds of them, devoid of Metaphor, the small bodies and long limbs like so many wide-eyed children on the sea paths.

Airmid was borne on a bier of light, moving through the air with a soft humming sound. At her head and feet and at her sides, the bearers were chanting, the sound like whalesong, asking and answering, calling the name of the Braid again and yet again.

At the shore, the Galaeci were ranged up around the bier of An Scail with its attendant fire. The Danu moved beside them.

When they came among the Galaeci of Inver Skena, the people did not shy away. They simply bowed to the Danu.

"They knew!" whispered Eriu to Banba.

"Maybe it's just that we are so much an improvement over Morrigu," Banba whispered back.

Together they placed the two Ancients side by side facing away over the water.

"By the wish of Airmid," Eriu called, "Illyn, Hybrid of the Braid, is called to the foot of the bier."

Illyn moved into place.

Amergin stepped forward. "At the wish of An Scail, Bile, Hybrid of the Braid, is called to the foot of the bier."

Bile stepped to the foot.

Eriu and Amergin each moved to the head of the bier. Amergin turned his head toward Eriu, but she looked far out over the sea and did not meet his eyes.

Now Banba and Fodla and the Spear Bearers of the Danu moved to each of the platforms. Into the sand, they staked spiraling, twisting, braided poles of light in blue and gold, streaming arcs of electricity around them in winding spirals that looked like strips of sparkling cloth.

In ancient Danaan Eriu chanted, "Comes our beloved to the shore; oh, bear her into the West."

In Gaeilge, Amergin followed suit: "Comes our beloved to the shore; oh, bear her into the West."

The Danu and the Galaeci ranged around the biers, still chanting, Danaan in counterpoint to Gaeilge.

The tall Galaeci in their plaid cloaks flanked the tiny Danu, their iridescent garments blowing and shifting in the sea wind, their collective presence giving off such a nimbus of blue and gold light that the beach seemed to contain its own crescent moon.

From within the bier of Airmid, Eriu lifted a long braided rope of diaphanous fabric. In its depths tiny lights sparked and glittered. Carefully, she placed Airmid's arms together before her and then gently tied one end of the rope around Airmid's wrists in a braided knot. She passed the rope to Banba, who looped it around one of her wrists and turned to Airioch, who wound the braided rope around his own right wrist.

Danu by Milesian, Milesian by Danu, the braided rope made its way among the people, knotting and twisting, weaving itself throughout all of the company.

At last it made its way back to Eriu. She looped it around the wrists of An Scail and wove it into a gentle, braided knot.

She returned to the base of the bier and nodded at Illyn and Bile. Together they reached for the torches that stood at either end of the bier. Together they locked them together high above the reclining figures of Airmid and An Scail so that they were overarched by a braid of pulsing, streaming knotwork.

"Lift our sisters into the Braid," called Eriu. "Oh, bear them into the West, Danu, Weaver of Worlds."

As one the people of the Danu and the people of the Galaeci lifted their braided arms. The looped and braided fabric that moved among them began to pulse and spin, to discharge streams of light into the air.

The Danu began to sing and the song was wondrous with joy. It wove itself again and again into the night sky, a canticle of joy, arcing out over the waves and up toward the stars.

Suddenly Banba gave out a cry. "See where they come, the messengers of the Danu!"

From far to the west in the water, lights began to stream toward shore, triangular phalanxes of light in blue and gold that broke above the Danu and the Galaeci and showered down upon them, raining light over the braidwork on the beach.

Now Eriu called aloud in prayer. "Danu, our mother, Weaver of Worlds, we return to you two of your children. The Children of the Braid and the sons of Mil have borne them to you with joy. We thank you for sharing them with us. We will embrace them again in the Braid."

Amergin lifted Ceolas. He began to sing.

"I am the wind on the Water
I am the wave of the Sea
I am the light of the Sun
I am the hawk on the Cliff
I am the fire in the Mind
I am the salmon of Wisdom
I am the hill of the Poem
I am the noise of the Wind
I am the wave of the Sea.
Who sets fire to the Mind?
Who throws light onto the Mountain?
Who sings the ages of the Moon?
Who teaches the pathway of the Sun?

Who carves the pathways on the Sea?
It is I.
It is I."

Silence and darkness fell over the beach.

The people began to disperse, to return to the village for the Feast of Waking. Eriu turned toward Amergin, her eyes full of sorrow.

"I am sorry that An Scail came back through the portal," she said softly. She turned to go.

"This is why she came," he said to her retreating back.

She turned. He had lifted the triangular pendant from beneath his tunic. It glistened against the rough wool of his cloak.

Eriu's eyes grew wide.

"You understand? Why we have kept her from you?"

"I understand. Forgive me, love. Is she beautiful?"

"Beautiful and good and kind. As her mother must have been. As her father is." Eriu held out her hand. "Give me the pendant. You must not come among us. You would never be able to return."

"An Scail said that the choice should be mine."

Eriu shook her head. "You belong to your people."

"Are you not now my people as well? For among you are those I love—Eriu of the Danu; Bile, Hybrid of the Braid; and my child, whom I love sight unseen."

Eriu shook her head. "You must think upon this carefully, for what is done cannot be undone."

She turned and walked into the darkness, Bile and Illyn beside her.

He sat for a long time on the beach, watching the stars throw their gauzy veil across the sky, watching the sky lighten toward dawn.

Airioch appeared suddenly beside him, Colpa by his side.

"Why did you not come to the feast?" Airioch asked. He saw the triangle at Amergin's neck. His eyes widened. "She returned to give you this?"

Amergin nodded.

"You will go among them then?"

Amergin smiled sadly. "Skena's child lives. My child. My little girl. There among the Danu."

Tears welled up in Airioch's eyes. "She lives? And you cannot see her?"

"Do not weep for me, Brother," said Amergin.

"I do not weep for you," Airioch said softly. "As always, I weep for myself. I shall miss you. Remember always, Amergin, that I am a man because of you. Because you remained my brother. Because you knew what to do that I would become a true son of Mil."

"I have not said that I would go."

"Your heart has said so. Your child has said so. You have given your life to the clan. Now go to them. Be joyful."

"What of my duties to the tribe?"

Gently, Airioch lifted Ceolas from Amergin's lap; gently he placed it in Colpa's hands. Colpa strummed the strings softly.

"I invoke the land of Eire," he sang,

"Much traveled the abundant sea."

Amergin laughed aloud. "You know them?"

Colpa nodded. "All of them, Brother. I will sing them just as you wrote them. I will pass them down from bard to bard."

Dawn light was pearling up in the sky.

"Come," said Airioch. "We will walk you to the portal."

In the doorway, Amergin raised his hand to them, his heart thundering in his chest. "I am afraid and I am joyful!" he called.

"Send word with Bile!" Airioch cried. "And tell Banba to come and see me!"

Amergin laughed aloud. "Remember me!" he called.

"Ceolas will remember," said Colpa, lifting the harp into his arms.

With a shaking hand, Amergin pressed his triangle to the depression in the stone. There was a flash of blue light and he felt himself shrink and expand suddenly.

Then he was standing in the archway, exactly where he had been a moment before. Airioch and Colpa were nowhere to be seen.

He stepped from beneath the portal. The forest was the same forest. He ran down the path to the headland. Below him, the hills stretched gently to the sea. No village of Inver Skena scattered itself along the river and down toward the waiting sea. Amergin turned around, confused. He walked back to the portal, walked through it, walked around.

A soft pathway seemed to weave itself away from the portal toward the forest, and he began to follow it. He came through a patch of trees; glistening in the distance was a city of crystal towers and buildings of rich turquoise and coral hue. He began to run.

And then he saw them.

Bile and Illyn were coming over the hill on horseback, their white garments shimmering in the light. Behind them were Banba, Fodla, Eriu; before Eriu on the saddle was a tiny child with curling auburn hair. And behind her, hundreds of the Danu.

They were singing. The Children of the Danu were singing him home.

Amergin ran then. He ran toward his child. He ran toward his beloved. He ran toward the people of the Danu. He ran, at last, toward belonging.

epilogue

CEOLAS REMEMBERS
Among us once was a Poet
Beloved of his people
Bard of the Galaeci
Amergin the Voyager
Who has gone among the Other.
In Harpsong we remember,
Poet of the Braid.

Tell us again, Skena," said the three boys.

The beautiful woman with the flowing auburn hair laughed aloud. "They are Da's people and they are your people. And when you go among them for the first time, you must say, 'We are the children of Amergin, Poet of the Galaeci, and of Eriu, mother of the land of Eire.'"

"And they will know us?"

The door slid back softly and a tiny woman entered.

"They will know of you, Airioch," Eriu said softly. "All who knew your father in that time are gone now. But those who dwell beyond the portals are their children. And their children's children. They will know of you. They will remember your father in their stories and their songs."

"So some of them are older than Skena?" asked the dark-haired boy called Airioch. He blinked his huge grey eyes at his sister Skena.

"Oh, ancient. Older than I if that is possible," said Skena. She ruffled his hair. "Now listen, you three."

The three boys looked up attentively.

"Airioch, Ith, Colpa."

"No," said Ith. "I am Ith and he is Colpa. You would think that you could tell us apart; you are our sister, after all."

"It's not so easy," said Skena to the three dark-haired boys. "Even for your mother." She pointed at Eriu. "And she gave birth to your triad!"

"Aither could tell us apart," said Colpa.

"Aither could do everything well," said Skena softly. "And besides, you look like Amergin, except that your eyes are Eriu's."

Eriu crossed to the woman; although Skena was almost double her height, Eriu hugged her hard at the waist. "I miss him too," she whispered.

"I know, Little Mother," Skena said softly.

The door slid open again.

"Uncle Bile!"

The tall dark-haired man swung into the room. "Are we ready for our first visit then? Illyn awaits us at the portal. You are seven years of age; you are to be on your best behavior."

"That is what we say? That we are seven?"

"That is how you will look to the villagers of Inver Skena."

"And how do we call ourselves?" asked Airioch. "Do we say that we are the people of the Danu? Or do we say that we are the sons of Mil?"

Eriu blinked. "You are neither. You are both. You go into the land of Eire, the land your father named."

Skena smiled. "You are the Eireann," she said softly. "That is what you say. Wherever you go in the world. Wherever you carry Amergin's songs. Wherever you carry Eriu's magic. You are the people of song and magic. You are the Children of the Braid.

"You are Eireann."

HISTORICAL AND
MYTHOLOGICAL BACKGROUND

The next time you are at the movies, munching on a huge tub of buttery popcorn, consider myths, legends, folklore. Why? Because mythology is popcorn; inside each fluffy, buttery, rich, and multifaceted puff of corn is a hard kernel. You know this; you have bitten down on those hard nuggets, and you know that they do not yield. The puffs are stories, i.e., myth and legend; the kernels are history, i.e., verifiable truth.

An incident in history becomes a myth or a legend because something happened, something awesome, something memorable, something which carried deep significance for those people in that time, deep significance on the journey toward understanding. That incident is captured in story, elaborated and decorated, passed down through generations.

Myth and legend embellish upon history because human beings seem to need patterns—archetypes, if you will. The archetype of the wisdom keepers, the archetype of the hero, the archetype of the villain, the archetype of the journey, the archetype of the grailquest. Story seems to be one of the essential, even necessary, ways for human beings to learn the world and our purpose in it. You might say that we come "hardwired" for story.

This book weaves together a complex myth and an ancient legend over a repeating thread of real history.

The myth of the Tuatha de Danaan, the tribe of the Danu, is, as all myths should be, large and metaphysical, incomprehensible and strange. It is one of the oldest and most pervasive of the Irish myths, so much so that the perception of the "little people" or "An Sidhe"—the Other—of Ireland continues even in our day. What is its kernel? We do not know, but we have numerous clues.

Let us begin, however, in "real" history. The legend of the sons of Mil and their journey to Ireland comes to us from an ancient Irish text, the *Lebhor Gabhala*, the *Book of Invasions*.

Written by the early Christian monks, possibly in the eleventh century, the *Lebhor Gabhala* posits five "races" of creatures—not all human—who inhabited Ireland: the Partholon, the Nemedians, the Fir Bolg, the Fomorians, and the Tuatha de Danaan. By the time of our story, the Partholon and Nemedians had vanished from the Irish landscape and the Tuatha de Danaan had negotiated a peace with the Fir Bolg and banished the Fomor. Sometime around 500 BC, this chain of residence was capped by the arrival of a huge (more than sixty-five ships and forty chieftains, according to the legend) invasion force of ships from Spain bearing the Celts of the sons of Mil (descendants, according to the *Book of Invasions,* of Japheth, the son of Noah of flood fame; this is most likely an attempt by the monks to give Mil and his lineage a Judeo-Christian ancestry). This force landed in Kerry on Beltaine, the first of May, in the Bay of Kenmare, at the place called Inber Scene, named after the drowned wife of Amergin the bard.

However, the *Lebhor Gabhala* is currently the source of major controversy in the archaeological branch of Celtic studies (the other branches being anthropology and mythology, anthropology containing language and culture, mythology containing folklore, legends, myths, stories, and songs). So in those fields of study, how can we "know" exactly what happened in or around 500 BC in a culture that kept no written records? Evidence. Thus, archaeology. Currently, the archaeological evidence does not fit the legend. At least not precisely.

Archaeology deals with artifacts, the sifted detritus of a past culture. And nowhere in Ireland can anyone find evidence of a massive invasion from Spain. There is, however, evidence of a rather advanced culture moving into Ireland at this time and taking up residence next to an already existing group. At the Hill of Tara, the seat of Ireland's high kings, archaeologists have found Roman artifacts such as wine goblets, lead seals, and glass vessels. This would indicate a well-traveled trading culture.

Anthropologically speaking, there is no question that the Celtic language and culture came to dominate Ireland. Linguists tell us that a language can come to dominate only if large groups of people predominate in a certain area over a long period of time.

While archaeologists are the "crime scene investigators" of historical study, folklorists and mythologists work from a basic premise: that inside each story is a core element of the "real"—real people, real events, real history.

For the storyteller, finding that "core" in the Milesian "invasion" becomes one of degree. All stories are embellished. Scale back the embellishment; remove the embroidery. What if the original "invasion" force was basically a single clan and its circle? Their language and culture would come to dominate as the clan grew, if the clan was sophisticated, if the news of the new location filtered throughout the Celtic world. Successive waves of immigrants would further increase that cultural dominance.

So who were these Milesians of legend? Well, we know that Goidelic-speaking Celts began to migrate and settle across the Iberian Peninsula of Spain during the Bronze Age. (Goidelic is the form of Gaelic which includes the Irish, Scots, and Manx languages.) By the seventh century BC, Greek mariners had established numerous trading harbors with these Celtiberians, and these Spanish Celts also traded with Phoenicians and Etruscans. There was, for example, a thriving silver trade among the Greeks and the Celtic tribes of a king named Arganthonios and his tribe of silver miners near the Tartessus River in southern Iberia.

Near the Douro River in Spain, Celts of the Arevaci tribe built the city of Numantia, which covered twenty hectares and boasted houses of stone, huge multistory stone *brochs* or towers, and a planned city street system. Evidently the prosperity of these people arose from their mining of copper, tin, gold, and silver and their production and trade of fine jewelry and weaponry throughout the civilized world.

Nowhere was the Celtic influence more predominant than in the northwest corner of Spain. According to Galician travel guides, the first city founded by the Celts in this region was Saefes in the tenth century BC. In the region that is today called Galicia, an ancient Celt named Breogan or Breogam built a lighthouse tower by the sea and founded the ancient Celtic city of Brigantia. The weather and topography of Galicia are much like those of Ireland, and even today that region of the world retains its Celtic identity.

These Celts spread their culture throughout the region, building *castroes* or circular stone hill fortifications with multiple ditches (similar *raths* or ring-forts were built for hundreds of years afterward in Ireland). Likewise dolmens, two upright stones with a slanted capstone, or lintel, are similar in both Spain and Ireland. The Galaeci worshipped creation in forest cathedrals with their druids; had a fluid but general concept of numerous tripartite gods throughout the Celtic world; understood the idea of an eternal soul; cremated their dead; played a special bagpipe called the *gaita* (listen to Carlos Nunez—his music is so eerie and beautiful that it will raise the hairs on your arms); rode domesticated horses; herded cattle; made rye bread; and were generally known for their unique combination of delicate artistry and advanced warrior skills (as were all the Celts on the European continent). In fact, the Celtiberians were so renowned for their warrior skills that they served as mercenaries in the Carthaginian army and as cavalry in the Roman army.

Eventually their settlements were abandoned around 400 BC. This may have been because of war, or it may have been because of a plague that traveled through Greece in 430 BC. Even if the plague had not reached Galicia, it would surely have curtailed or ruined the trade lanes. Perhaps more Galicians traveled to Ireland on the heels of these catastrophes; we do not know.

In Irish history, the most famous son of the Spanish Celts was Milesius or Mil (whose original Celtic name was Golamh). According to the legends, he served as a mercenary chieftain for the king of Scythia and married his daughter. One theory says that the Milesians were originally Scythians, whose tribes stretched from the Carpathian Mountains to the Don River. The Scythians were known as stunning horsemen and nomadic wagon travelers. Scythians and Celts may indeed be ancestrally related.

Later, Milesius served the pharaoh of Egypt (who at this time was actually Cambysis of Persia, this worthy having overthrown the last native Egyptian pharaoh, Psamtek III); married the pharaoh's daughter Scota; and by his two wives fathered numerous sons, some versions of the legend saying seven, some nine.

This period in history was a sophisticated one in the countries surrounding the Mediterranean Sea (the Romans' Internum Mare, later Mare Nostrum, "Our Sea"). The democratic Greek city-states were well known for their learning, advanced philosophies, and high culture, for their ships and trade, complex architecture, beautiful physical adornment, and sexual sophistication (or decadence, depending upon the period and your particular cultural viewpoint).

Nearby Rome had declared itself a republic in 509 BC and continued to practice that form of government until 44 BC, when the age of emperors (and Rome's eventual decline) began.

The clan of Mil, then, would have been very sophisticated indeed, well traveled, probably fairly fluent in four or five languages, accustomed to sophisticated thought and government patterns, and certainly familiar with advanced fashion and architecture—full dwellers in the highly civilized Aegean culture of the time.

Why then did the Milesians decide to return to wild Galicia? Did Mil tire of war? Did he run into trouble in Egypt? And when they had returned to Spain, why journey from there to even more remote and less civilized Ireland, at that time an unnamed dot in the Atlantic Ocean? There, of course, lies mystery, for we can know the food and clothing and vessels of the ancients, we can know their wars and migrations, but their "quest" motivations, the reasoning of their hearts and minds, was known only to them and is lost to us forever. There, of course, is the doorway for the storyteller.

Practically speaking, although the Celtiberians themselves possessed boats, both coracles (round wickerwork vessels covered with hide and often navigated with a pole) and curraghs (longer and wider fishing vessels), it is unlikely that they would have used either of these vessels to travel the open sea to Ireland, or even to hug the coasts. We are told that the Veneti of western France were actually Celtic sailors who manned very large boats, but the Galicians did not. Such boats as theirs were not equipped for sea travel and would have had to hug the coastline and try to cross the channel with the weather. Too, their little vessels could never have carried the Galaeci horses, which were precious. It is much more likely that the sons of Mil would have used the services of people who regularly plied the sea and knew its vagaries, hence the Greeks.

It is when the Milesians reached Ireland that legend begins to intersect with myth. For there, in Ireland, the Milesians would first encounter the Tuatha de Danaan, the Children of Danu, whose mythical leaders would become the adopted gods of the early Irish Celts and whose tribe would dwell with the Irish, even unto this day, as their "little people" or "other people."

Who were they?

All cultures have myths of the little people. For the Welsh they were the Fair Folk; to my Seneca Indian friends, the *jo-ge-oh;* to the Ojibwe friends of my childhood, the *manitou;* to the Hawaiians, the *menahune.* In

most cultures these little people share some traits. Sometimes they function as "tricksters," causing travelers to become lost, stealing items or
even babies, rearranging households. Oftentimes, they are agents of great
good, repaying kindness with good luck, by doing household chores, or
even by bestowing wealth. In many of the myths, time does not pass normally among these others; Americans will recognize that concept in the
Rip Van Winkle tale of little men who dwell in the Catskill Mountains of
New York.

This timeshift is, in fact, one of the most difficult aspects in the myths
of the Irish little people, the De Danaan, because we are told that some
humans could pass back and forth between the real world and the "time-
stretched" world of the Danaans and return unscathed, while others
would return to real time only to age suddenly, turning from youth to old
age in a matter of moments. How to solve or explain this timeshift in the
myth and its uneven application to travelers in that realm?

How also to explain that the ancient myths abound with stories of
"fairy children," humans who are stolen from their own families to be
raised among the little people, sometimes replaced in their cradles by
fairy babies or "changelings"? Why would the little people do such a thing,
and what purpose would it serve?

It is important to realize that "little people" need not literally mean
little. "Other" people can range in size from the diminutive through human size to giants. We are probably more accurate to call them "other" as
opposed to "little" because whatever their size or appearance, they are
other than human. Very few cultures exist that do not have some sense of
the presence—and interference—of the "other." At the most basic psychological level, such stories indicate the deep-seated human need for the
"other," the wish to not be alone in the world. Such a need might serve to
explain the bug-eyed alien abduction stories that abound in modern times.

Or are they just stories?

The myth of the Irish Danu is a complex and multifaceted story. They
came to Ireland: (1) perhaps from Greece, (2) perhaps from a city beneath the sea, (3) on cloud ships that simply appeared over Ireland, much
to the consternation of the hunter-gatherer people who dwelled there.

One permutation of the myth indicates that they were an ancient race
who settled at various places around the world, serving as architects and
designers, inspiring or assisting with the construction of pyramids and

sarsen circles, palaces and temples, and serving as wisdom-keeper figures in various religious myths. One group (our own for the purposes of this story) first settled on an island off the coast of Greece, but when that island sank into the sea, these people migrated to Ireland. Historically, a volcanic eruption and earthquake of massive proportions did occur around 1500 BC in the Mediterranean Sea in the vicinity of Thrace and the island of Santorini, taking a large portion of the latter to the bottom of the sea. This may be the Atlantis of legend. In mythological time, it caused the Danu to flee north.

We do know that the pyramids of Egypt and Stonehenge are actually contemporaneous, both being under construction around 3000 BC. This is actually one of the interesting sources of controversy in the current debates. For many years, scholars claimed that the stone circles of Ireland and the British Isles could not have been erected by the Celts, who came to those areas later. Previous scholars had claimed that they were Celtic structures serving druidic religious and calendrical purposes. Current scholarly argument goes back and forth between claims for the people who dwelled in those areas prior to Celtic arrival and the Celts themselves, the idea being that their arrival was not much later after all.

Then who did erect them? It was great fun to speculate on an entirely new set of architects for all ancient structures, though such speculation falls, of course, into the realm of fantasy.

The obvious complexity of such structures has also led both scholars and mythologists to contemplate their possible metaphysical significance. Certainly such structures do possess a sense of transition, of cathedral, of gathered awe. We may never know their specific original purposes.

However, the Danaans themselves were deeply metaphysical according to the mythology. They considered themselves Children of Danu, a mother goddess who presided over all of the creative forces of life—childbirth, fire, poetry, spring lambs, song, women, language. Danu had a tripartite aspect: she is referred to in the myths as Brid/Anu/Dana and is beautiful, loving, protective of her children. So powerful and enduring a figure is she that in later times in Ireland she was permuted into Brigid and then in Christian times into Saint Brigid, known in Ireland as the Mary of the Gaels and reputed to have been the midwife at the birth of Christ.

Evidently the Milesians of Spain arrived in Ireland without knowledge of her and later adopted her as their primary female deity. They also adopted as deities characters in the Danaan pantheon who were chieftains or skilled warriors: Dagda, a provider who became known as the "good god"; Ogma, an orator who became known as the "honey-mouthed god"; Lugh, the all-craftsman who came to be known as the son of the Sun; and so on.

Perhaps it was the attributes of these De Danaan that caused the Milesians to elevate them to godly status, for the Danu themselves seemed to hold their mother creator in her three aspects as the only god of the universe.

However, like human beings, the Danu were not immune to either evil or bad behavior. According to the myths, Dian Cecht the physician did have his son executed for re-creating the arm of Nuada, though some of the versions say that it was jealousy that caused his anger, that he killed his son with four blows to the head and subsequently destroyed his daughter's pharmaceutical gardens.

More terrifying than bad "human" behavior is the presence among the Danu of a tripartite goddess called Morrigu. Her three aspects—Macha, Banbh, and Nemhain—live for the purposes of bringing hatred and war, death and carnage, panic and chaos into the world. Morrigu is pervasive and long-lived in Irish mythology, a shape-shifter who appears variously as a wolf, a raven, a fog, a heifer, an eel, an old hag, and a beautiful woman. She shows up in the first myths, is still wreaking havoc in the Cuchulainn legends in the first century AD, and is still sowing chaos in the Fionn legends of the third century AD. So powerful is Morrigu that by the time of the Arthurian legends she has conflated into a single person—Morgan le Fay, the dark sorceress who is responsible for the downfall of Camelot.

Other than Morrigu, however, the Danu are reputed to have been quite beautiful. In physical appearance, they are described as being slender and tall, with golden or strawberry hair and compelling eyes. They are almost always surrounded by a nimbus of eerie blue or white light. They never grow old or sick, and although they can die, it is usually through warfare or attack, not sickness, and not until extreme old age.

They dwell in huge cities below the ground and the sea, and their culture is reputed to be highly sophisticated. Moreover, the ancient story of Nuada indicates that these were people who not only knew how to create sophisticated and terrifying weapons, but had also mastered the art of

limb regeneration, indicating at least a mastery of the processes of cell regeneration, DNA, etc.

The legends tell us of three battles on the Plain of Mag Tuiread. The
exact location of these battles is unclear, and several places in Ireland lay
claim to the distinction. Some say that Cong in county Mayo is the proper
location; it is a place riddled with dolmens, sarsen stones, and circles.
Others claim that the battles took place in Sligo. Whatever the location,
the Danu seemed to find it the only "safe" place for their battles, as they
were not a warlike race, but rather a race who relied on subterfuge and illusion as the strongest weapons in their arsenal. There are, of course,
hundreds of dolmens, passage graves, sarsen circles, and standing stones
throughout Ireland. The pre-Christian people of Ireland believed that
these were entrances to the otherworld, the country of the Danu. What
would cause such a legend to arise? Even today in Ireland, numerous of
these locations are reputed to be haunted; there are reports of fires and
strange lights on the hillsides.

The legends also speak widely of the fact that these people were often
led by tripartite sister and brother groups. Mac Cuill, Mac Cecht, and
Mac Grene as well as Banba, Fodla, and Eriu are specifically named in the
tales. Ireland is named, of course, for Eriu.

Eventually in Ireland, these "others" became an accepted presence,
from the banshee (from *bain sidhe* or "woman of the other") who attaches
herself to human families and sings the impending death of a family member, to the widespread idea that eventually there were generations of intermarriage between the Irish and the Danu, creating a race of people
who could travel in and out of their world and our world and who possessed, at the very least, some special psychic or healing abilities.

Certainly the Danu's truce with, care for, and adoption of the Fir
Bolg has some historical status; the people of Connacht claimed to trace
their history to the Fir Bolg all the way up until the eighteenth century.
Too, the story of years without summer is also historically accurate. Beginning around 1159 BC there was no summer growth of trees for a period
of eighteen years; a long cold nuclear winter may have been caused by a
volcanic eruption in Iceland, or by comet debris. Modern movies which
posit such a catastrophe do not seem to be far off the mark. People and animals starved; crops would not grow. In mythological time, this is when

the Danu began rescuing and rebraiding the Hybrid Fir Bolg children of our story.

Of course, the Tuatha de Danaan, the tribe of the Danu, dwell in Ireland still.

The Milesians were, in all likelihood, a real and historical clan; much specific detail accrues to their travels. We also have three poems that are purportedly by Amergin, generally called the "Invocation," the "Song," and the "Challenge." The "Song" and the "Challenge" contain many similar lines, so the two may actually be one poem that has been separated for content or theme. The "Invocation" is a celebration of Ireland. There are literally dozens of translations of these three poems. However, all three poems meditate on the interconnectedness of all life, on joy and sorrow. All three are written in a first-person voice in broken lines characteristic of ancient verse. Are they really Amergin's words? Conventional wisdom would have it that they were written down by monks sometime after the eighth century, largely because the Celtic world did not permit writing. However, the Milesians were members of Aegean civilization, which highly valued written records and kept vast libraries of history and literature. Perhaps Amergin himself wrote the poems; perhaps not. If they are Amergin's poems, they indicate a large soul, a man aware of the Braid that binds the universe. I would like to have known him.

Can we also believe in the Danu—the Tuatha de Danaan—as a "real" people? Some say impossible; others hope that they did—or do—indeed exist. And you? More things under heaven and earth, friends.

As for me, I have loved my time with all of them, braided as I have been into the fictional complexities of both worlds. I hope that this story affords you the same journey.

Bail O Dhia ar an obair
Bless, O God, the work

Juilene Osborne-McKnight

kick the
clutter

CLEAR OUT EXCESS STUFF
WITHOUT LOSING WHAT YOU LOVE

ellen phillips

RODALE

*To everyone who struggles to fit too much stuff into too little space
(no matter how much space that is).
And to my mother, who taught me the secret of gracious living.*

Direct edition first published in 2007. Trade edition published in 2008.

Rodale books may be purchased for business or promotional use or for special sales. For information, please write to: Special Markets Department, Rodale Inc., 733 Third Avenue, New York, NY 10017

Printed in the United States of America
Rodale Inc. makes every effort to use acid-free ♾, recycled paper ♻.

Illustrations by Michael Gellatly
Interior design by Patricia Field

Library of Congress Cataloging-in-Publication Data

Phillips, Ellen.
    Kick the clutter : clear out excess stuff without losing what you love / Ellen Phillips.
        p.   cm.
    Includes index.
    ISBN-13 978–1–59486–717–0   hardcover
    ISBN-10 1–59486–717–8   hardcover
    ISBN-13 978–1–59486–718–7   paperback
    ISBN-10 1–59486–718–6   paperback
    1. Storage in the home.   2. Orderliness.   I. Title.
TX309.P56 2007
648'.8—dc22   2007018711

Distributed to the trade by Macmillan

2   4   6   8   10   9   7   5   3   1   hardcover

2   4   6   8   10   9   7   5   3   1   paperback

LIVE YOUR WHOLE LIFE™

We inspire and enable people to improve their lives and the world around them

For more of our products visit **rodalestore.com** or call 800-848-4735

CONTENTS

Part Four: Trash (Yours) to Treasure (Theirs)

Part Five: Controlling Clutter Creep

ACKNOWLEDGMENTS

If you enjoy this book and find it helpful, it's because of the many friends and family members who have so generously shared their tips, their clutter woes and triumphs, and their expertise with me—and now, with you. Special thanks to my wonderful editors, Anne Halpin White and Karen Bolesta; project editor Hope Clarke; copy editors Erana Bumbardatore and Amy Kovalski; designers Susan Eugster and Patricia Field; and illustrator Michael Gellatly, all of whose enthusiastic participation in this project has been invaluable; and to the professionals who generously gave of their time and expertise to make this a better book, especially Diane Albright, Janet Brito, Patrick McWilliams, Karen Moyer, Pat Robertson, Jaap van Liere, Brendan Strasser, and Jackie Tepper. Many thanks to the many friends who contributed their first-person experience to help augment mine, especially Jennifer Bright Reich and Christine Bucks. And my most sincere thanks to the members of the Kutztown Curves, who got almost as excited about the book as I was; to my boyfriend, Rob Hays, who kept his sense of humor throughout the project and helped me keep my sense of perspective, and to his father, George Hays, who is eagerly awaiting his copy; to my own father, who graciously put up with my taking over his office and working 'til all hours to get the book finished when I was supposed to be visiting him; and to Pat Brown, who invented the word "dustables." Finally, special thanks to Janine, Katrina, and Karen for believing.

INTRODUCTION

Are you ready to stop stumbling over your clutter and start kicking it out of your house and your life? If you are, this book is for you. You may be a first-time clutter fighter: Clutter may have crept into your home gradually, and you've just recently realized that you have a problem. Or you may be a seasoned veteran: You've been trying to shovel out for years and have either given up after a struggle or have finally cleared out all the clutter, only to watch with dismay as it piled back in. Whether you fall at either end of this spectrum or somewhere in the middle, these pages contain tips and tools to help you. And I think you'll have fun as you go!

That's because *Kick the Clutter* goes where other clutter books fear to tread—to the heart of controlling clutter once and for all. The chapters in Part One: Clutter-Kicking Basics (beginning on page 1) give you the basic tools you need, from the real secret of lasting clutter control to a five-step clutter-kicking program, an overview of organizing and storage aids, and lots of 5-minute fixes that let you jump-start the clutter-kicking process.

In Part Two: Clutter-Kicking Room by Room (beginning on page 69) and Part Three: Clutter-Kicking Outside the House (beginning on page 289), you'll find hundreds of tips to help you conquer your particular clutter issues, whether you're trying to make more room in an apartment or RV, combine two households in marriage or partnership, or deal with an avalanche of inherited clutter (from parents or kids or both). Each chapter will show you how to prioritize your clutter-kicking strategy for that room or space and give you a unique tool to inspire you to clear out the clutter *and* help you keep it from coming back.

What happens when you've amassed a pile of stuff to get rid of? That depends on the stuff—and on you. You can have a lot of fun with this part of clutter-kicking, as you'll see in Part Four: Trash (Yours) to Treasure (Theirs), beginning on page 349. You can help people in need, swap stuff you don't need for things you do, or even make some money from your clutter. The choice is yours!

The High Cost of Clutter

Clutter costs us. Clutter is not just an inconvenience or an eyesore—it's an industry. Several, actually. Consider some of the hidden costs of clutter:

❊   The sadly ironic name "self-storage facility" is only too accurate. We'd rather pay a hefty monthly charge to store our stuff than just get rid of it. Since the first self-storage facility appeared in 1966, their numbers have increased to a whopping 55,000 US facilities today. That's 6.68 square feet of storage space for every US resident—for a total of 72 square miles of American land not just storing clutter but also covered up by the clutter of these metal structures.

❊   One in 11 US households rents a self-storage unit, for a total cost of almost $20 billion a year.

❊   Despite the fact that household size continues to dwindle (2.57 people per household in 2004), the houses themselves just keep getting bigger. The average home size has been supersized, French-fry fashion, from 1,500 square feet in 1970 to 2,400 square feet today. With the fastest-growing housing segment being singles and couples, what's occupying all that space? You guessed it: stuff.

❊   Top 10 self-storage states (accounting for almost half of all self-storage facilities): California, Florida, Georgia, Illinois, Michigan, New York, North Carolina, Ohio, Pennsylvania, and Texas.

❊   Another outgrowth of our increasing clutter and its related chaos is the professional organizer, who charges an hourly fee to help get your clutter (and life) back under control. The National Association of Professional Organizers has more than 3,900 members.

❊   Believe it or not, there are 12-step programs (like Alcoholics Anonymous) for clutterers, including Clutterers Anonymous and Messies Anonymous.

❊   Randy Frost, PhD, professor of psychology at Smith College and an expert in obsessive-compulsive disorder, studied compulsive hoarders, the most extreme form of clutterer, in the 1990s. He estimates that there are as many as four million hoarders in the United States alone.

❊   A Google search for "Clutter" brings up 37,600,000 results. If you search on Amazon, you'll get 45,793 results for "clutter"; add "organizing," and you'll get 158,983 more, for a grand total of 204,776. Yikes!

What's the Deal with Dustables?

You'll find a lot about dustables in *Kick the Clutter*. What are they? Those knick-knacks, collectibles, art objects, or what have you that just sit around collecting dust. My friend Pat Brown coined this delightful word, and now it's become so much a part of my thought process that the "dustables light" will often go on when I'm out shopping and see a particularly intriguing kitchen gadget, antique, or craft item. Hard as they are to resist, unless I know I have the perfect place for them, I leave them on the shelf. After all, who likes dusting?

Finally, there's that little issue of keeping your clutter from creeping back into the house, like those unwanted pounds that always seem to make their way to your midsection minutes before swimsuit season begins. You'll learn the tricks to keeping clutter at bay in Part Five: Controlling Clutter Creep, beginning on page 439.

Throughout *Kick the Clutter,* I've only included tips that I know will work. And I've also been up front about what *won't* work and what happens when real life intrudes on your clutter-kicking plans. I'll be speaking directly to you on every page because I want you to not just succeed at kicking your clutter, but to have a good time while you're doing it. (And yes, of course you can!)

There's one more thing about *Kick the Clutter* that I want you to know: It's not just about me talking to you. This is an interactive experience, and I want you to be a very big part of it because unless you are, you won't get the most out of it. Throughout the book I've included formats for various worksheets and exercises for you to do because I want it to be *your* book, and only you can make it your book. If you do, you'll do more than kick your clutter. You'll finally know exactly what you need to make the home you have into the home you love. And that's a promise.

Ellen Phillips

PART ONE

Clutter-Kicking Basics

Chapter 1

Get a Clutter-Clearing Mind-Set

It's safe to say that, if you actually live in your home, you live with clutter. And that's true whether you live in an eight-bedroom mansion or a one-room apartment with a sofa bed. Those photos in design magazines of immaculate rooms with empty shelves and one perfectly placed *objet d'art* on the coffee table are essentially sets, unlived in and unloved. You may have a little clutter, you may have a lot of clutter, but you *do* have clutter.

Why is that? It's because—and we should face this up front—clutter is simply part of the human condition. But that doesn't mean we're stuck with the messy, stacked-up status quo. You *can* kick the clutter, as you'll see throughout this book. And the best—really, the only effective—way to start is by figuring out how bad your "clutter condition" is and how it happened. So let's begin at the beginning: How bad *is* it?

THE CLUTTER SCALE

There's clutter, and then there's clutter. Before you get rid of it, you have to understand what your clutter is, so take a deep breath, take a good look around your

The Clutter-Hoarding Scale

You may think you have it bad—or just wonder how bad you have it. Find out by seeing where you—or someone you live with or care about—fall on the National Study Group on Chronic Disorganization's Clutter-Hoarding Scale (at www.nsgcd.org).

Yikes! This is very serious stuff. The organization categorizes clutter levels in four different areas—structure and zoning issues, pets and rodents, household functions, and sanitation and cleanliness—and then rates you on a scale depending on how you score in each area. The scale rates you from Level I (all doors and stairways accessible, clutter not excessive, no odors, and so on) to Level V (rodents—and they don't mean pets!—evident and in sight, kitchen and bathroom unusable due to clutter, client sleeping elsewhere as house is not livable, and so on). If you or someone you know scores above Level I, you can find referrals and assistance on the organization's Web site.

house, and then ask yourself what you mean when you say that it's cluttered or messy. Do you mean that there's a pile of magazines, catalogs, papers, and assorted bric-a-brac all over the coffee table and you have to shove it all out of the way (often accidentally spilling it in a heap on the floor) in order to set a cup down? Or do you mean that there are so many boxes, piles, and heaps of stuff in the room that you've given up on spending time there and instead navigate from the front door to the kitchen through a narrow path you've left between piles?

How did you—or more accurately, your home—get into this mess?

YOUR CLUTTER, YOURSELF

There are lots of ways to end up with a cluttered home, and the best way to start dealing with your own clutter is to see why you have it to begin with. The categories below describe several clutter-attracting "types," and as you read through them you may find one that seems to have been written just for you. Of course, you may also find that several of these categories apply to you—you might be a Collector and a Compulsive Shopper, for example—but that just means that you'll need to fight clutter on two (or more) fronts instead of just one. And the same holds true if you're a

Compulsive Shopper and your spouse or partner is a Collector. But don't panic! Knowledge is power here, so let's take a look at the causes of clutter—*your* clutter.

The Collector

I'm starting with this category because I'm in it. You name it—kaleidoscopes, fossils, shells, books, guitars, Pueblo pottery, beads, vintage Christmas ornaments, Audubon prints, yarn—I collect it. Hopefully, if you fall into this category, you collect only one or two things. But even so, it's all too easy for a collection to take over every available shelf and display area, then start taking over actual living

Clutter and Capitalism

You may be thinking that your clutter really isn't your fault—and of course you're at least partially right. We live in a capitalist society; the production and consumption of goods are the foundation of our economy. So the goal of our economy is to persuade us all to keep buying . . . and buying. And buying. Clutter is one of capitalism's unwanted side effects. After all, when you buy more than you need without tossing what you already have, things start to pile up!

I once read that if no more shirts were ever made, there would still be enough shirts in existence to clothe all of humanity for all time. Talk about a sobering thought! So if there are already enough shirts out there for the duration, why do we keep making—and buying—more? Because our society tells us that it's not fashionable to wear the same style or color season after season or year after year. Because it's socially unacceptable to wear the same shirt to work more than once a week, even if it's washed between wearings. Because, because. I'm sure you can think of plenty of other reasons—and so can the advertisers who spend billions of dollars to persuade us that we need this exclusive designer top or that fantastic bargain blouse.

What does this mean for you? Should you stop buying new shirts? Not much chance of that, right? (And of course I don't mean to pick on shirts here—I'm really talking about all nonperishable items.) But it does help to be aware that you're being bombarded with messages to buy, so that next time you head off to the store, pick up a catalog, or shop online, you can at least make it a two-step process. Before you buy the next new thing, ask yourself: What old thing will I get rid of to make space for this?

The Accidental Collector

Sometimes, becoming a collector is an accident. As people's gift lists become longer and time to buy presents seems to always grow shorter, everyone's tempted to take the easy way out. So if they think a friend, family member, or co-worker collects something affordable, they'll keep an eye out for the collectible objects and add them to their gift stash. A sure hit, and one more thing off the list, right? Not necessarily, as these stories show.

Miss Piggy

I'll never forget the first time I went to see the office manager of sales at the company I worked for at the time. Patsy's cubicle was literally crammed with pigs. Pig statuettes of every conceivable material and style leered down at me from every surface. There were hundreds of them. I was so appalled I almost forgot why I'd come up to see Patsy.

Someone else in sales explained that Patsy adored pigs. The whole sales department made a point of bringing Patsy, a delightful person, pig collectibles of every conceivable kind back from their (frequent) travels. Patsy's pig collection grew exponentially as the years went by.

Eventually, Patsy retired. As I passed her abandoned cubicle, I noticed that every single pig was still there! Astounded, I asked another co-worker about this. Can you guess her answer? Patsy never really liked pigs at all. That poor woman. Surrounded all those years by a horde of unwanted "dustables," all because she was too sweet, too polite, to say no.

How had this false notion of Patsy's love for pigs gotten started in the first place? I can only guess. Maybe a grandchild had gotten her a little china pig for some occasion, and Patsy, the proud grandma, had brought it into the office to display. Whatever the case, I'm sure she never foresaw the result of her modest display. I still think of her working among all those pigs for decades, loathing them all the while.

spaces by cluttering up tables and counters. Take it from one who knows: It doesn't have to be that way. There are two ways to escape from the Collector trap—without giving up your beloved collections.

Review. Tastes change—even yours. Trust me. As you learn more and your collection evolves, you'll find that some of your early treasures begin to lose their appeal. In fact, you may be humiliated to recall that you once thought that garish

If you can relate to Patsy's story, let me just say that it doesn't have to be that way. Here's how another friend escaped from a similar situation.

Just Say No

My friend Sandy loves Majolica ware, including colorful statues of hens and roosters. She also loves ceramic representations of fruits and vegetables, and she both gardens and raises chickens. What could be easier than getting her ceramic chickens and ceramic fruits and veggies for every occasion? They sound like the perfect gifts, right?

Wrong. After a few years of being barraged with hens, roosters, and a cornucopia of ceramic produce, Sandy stared at her shrinking counter and storage space and took action. She began telling all her friends and relatives about how Majolica was a very special kind of ceramic and that, in general, she really despised crockery, stoneware, and country ceramics of all kinds. Because she was so particular, she explained, she felt that it would be best if people let her choose her own ornaments rather than trying to guess her taste. Then, Sandy packed up all the gift chickens and veggies and traded them at a favorite antique store for something she really wanted.

This may sound harsh, but it saved Sandy from Patsy's fate. You can bet that, after one of these "talks," no one ever gave Sandy a chicken—or any other decorative "dustable"—again! But at least a few of the well-intentioned gift-givers may have been taken aback by her directness. In my view, it would have been even better for Sandy to have told people what she'd appreciate instead—a fruit basket, locally made jams and jellies, a gift certificate to her favorite book or clothing store. If you find yourself in this position—the recipient of collectibles you don't want—I suggest that you let the gift-givers off the hook by giving them an easy gift option that you'd really appreciate.

mass-produced vase was a priceless Native American collectible. Rather than mindlessly amassing more and more, make a point of reviewing your holdings monthly, twice yearly, or whenever you add a new piece to your collection. See if there isn't something you could dispose of now without feeling deprived. Remember that there are probably collectors out there for your former treasures—*you* bought it at one point, after all—and selling it now will free up more money for your current collection. Don't be ashamed of your early purchases—collecting is educational, if nothing else. Pack up the pieces you've decided you can live without, say good-bye, and turn your attention to streamlining your collection.

Rotate. Here in America, we like to display *all* our treasures. One of my (as yet unrealized) dreams is to have all of my books out on shelves where I can see them at a glance. We like to have all our Hummel figurines or Hallmark ornaments or first editions or Colonial textiles on display. And what do we get? Dustables. Unless you're lucky enough to have glass-fronted display cases or shelves, every object you choose to display will have to be dusted, again and again and again. Instead, let me suggest a brilliant alternative from the Far East.

One of the things I collect is shells, and of course I have books about shells, as well. In one of them, one of the great American shell collectors recounted his surprise when he went to visit a Japanese counterpart. The Japanese collector was reputed to hold one of the greatest collections of shells in the world. The American shell collector was practically drooling when he arrived at his host's residence for a rare viewing. But to the American's dismay, instead of being shown room after room and case after case of beautiful shells, he was taken to the living room and decorously seated. Then, a servant brought out . . . *one* shell. After a half hour, the servant removed the shell and returned with . . . another shell. In the course of the visit, the astounded American was shown perhaps five shells. To the Japanese collector, appreciating the rarity and beauty of a single shell was more important than displaying the entire collection.

The lesson here is that you really don't have to set out every last bear carving or Roman coin you own at the same time. Instead, rotate your collection, choosing a few choice specimens to display at any given time. This will keep your collection fresh to viewers as well as to you. And if you happen to collect paintings or first-edition prints or photographs, this tactic is especially useful. You can enjoy open wall space and still display your collection of original Julia Longacre barn paintings. Just make sure you have proper storage for the pieces that are not on display.

The Inheritor

A variant of the Collector is the Inheritor, the person who's inherited his or her parents' stuff, in-laws' stuff, great-aunt's stuff, or even grown kids' stuff. This is worse than being a Collector—unless you're an Accidental Collector—because you never asked for or would have chosen this stuff, but now there it is in your house, jostling with all your own stuff and filling up every available nook and cranny. People who haven't experienced this (yet) may wonder what the big deal is—why don't you just get rid of it? But if you're in this place, you *know*.

Sentiment can play a big role in turning you into an Inheritor. That was Great-Aunt Ethel's giant armoire! Those were Grandma Jones's second-best breakfast dishes! But there can be more to it than that.

For example, my sister's small, super-cluttered house includes a Victorian sofa, coffee table, and two chairs that she inherited from our grandmother. She doesn't like them and has no space for them—and to top it all off, she could use the money she'd get from selling them to a local antique store. But she doesn't dare sell them because she knows our father would be horrified if she tried to unload his mother's precious stuff, even though he himself has no room for it. And my sister is quite right—I've heard him rave about it myself. In fact, I have another Victorian sofa set from the same grandmother. It's taking up an entire room in my tiny cottage, and I don't sell it for the same reason: What if my father came to visit and saw that it was gone?

Being the recipient of unwanted or unneeded wedding presents may inadvertently turn you into an Inheritor, as well. You may have an atticful of bulky boxes you haven't opened in 25 years. And what if you're in an apartment? I recently saw a home show on HGTV where the cabinets of the newlyweds' apartment kitchen were all filled to bursting, not with dishes and pantry staples, but with boxes of wedding presents. Yikes! But, of course, Aunt Peggy would never forgive you if she came over and saw that her gilded epergne had vanished from your dining room table, right?

If you're thinking of marrying (or remarrying), it's not too late to preempt the gift debacle. (See "Beat the Wedding Blues" on page 10.) But if you're thinking about all the drawers and closets and attic space you've filled with wedding presents as you read this, all is not lost.

The trick is to be bold but tactful. If you never liked the crystal Aunt Martha gave you but your cousin chose it as her own pattern, give it to your cousin. Explain that it doesn't really go with your china and it would make you very happy to think of her using it—plus it's great insurance against breakage!—and

Beat the Wedding Blues

Engagement presents. Shower presents. Wedding presents. I'll bet if you had it to do over again—or ever found yourself actually doing it over again—you'd ask for cash, checks, and gift certificates, right? In the past, people thought it was crass to ask for or give money or gift certificates instead of actual gifts, so a pileup of wedding presents was virtually inevitable (unless you eloped). But these days, when many marriages involve combining two households (or apartments), even Miss Manners couldn't object to a couple's asking for what they actually want rather than just sitting back and waiting for the gift avalanche.

So don't be shy! If you're getting married, ask for what you want, and simply explain that you already have all the possessions you could possibly use and would rather remember the gift-givers by treating yourself to Italian or horseback riding lessons, going on a romantic getaway, indulging in a spa day, or enjoying a delightful dinner at the best new restaurant in town. And if you really, really don't need or want a thing, either say so nicely and insist on "no gifts" early on and again in the invitations, or ask that donations be made in your names to your favorite charity or charities, instead. No fuss, no muss, no clutter!

steel yourself to tell Aunt Martha the same thing if it ever comes up. (Believe it or not, chances are it won't.) Or donate the crystal to a charity auction or consignment shop whose proceeds are given to Aunt Martha's favorite charity or cause. Or sell the crystal on eBay, to an antiques store, or at auction.

The Parent

Your kids are grown and gone. But somehow, they've left all their stuff behind. "Don't throw it out—we might need it!" "We'll be back for it . . . someday." "We don't have room for it right now . . . we can't afford a mover . . . we're too busy . . . we live too far away . . ." The excuses are endless, but they all boil down to the same thing: We love our childhood stuff, but we don't want to deal with it, so *you* keep it. And don't you dare throw it out!

I've met lots of moms who have fallen for this and who have told me over and over that they don't have room for the kids' stuff anymore—especially if they've become Inheritors and are also trying to find space for their parents' or in-laws' stuff. But of course they feel trapped, since they're afraid the kids will think they don't love them anymore if they get rid of their things. Luckily, I also met one mom who had come up with a no-fail solution.

Diane, one of the members at my local Curves fitness center and also one of the most practical people I've ever met, told me this story: "One year, I went upstairs to the attic to get the Christmas ornaments, and I realized I couldn't even get *into* the attic, much less find the ornaments, because of all the stuff my kids had left behind. So I brought down every single thing that belonged to my kids and put it all in the guest room. Then I told them that they had 2 weeks to come and pick up their stuff, and whatever was left after 2 weeks was going. Sure enough, every kid appeared like magic. And now I can find everything in my attic!"

Not only did Diane get rid of the next generation's junk, she did it without the sky falling. Each and every child still calls and visits as much as ever. So don't despair. Use Diane's technique, explain firmly but gently that it all must go, and then sit back and bask in your own happy ending!

The Compulsive Shopper

Okay, no one likes to think of herself as a Compulsive Shopper, so if you'd rather call yourself a Bargain Hunter, Smart Shopper, or anything else that lets you see yourself here, go right ahead. But whether you can't resist a great deal—whether you need the stuff or not—or you find yourself shopping for entertainment and then buying (and buying), you have come to the right category.

Sometimes, the Compulsive Shopper merges with the Scout (see page 13), justifying extreme purchasing on the grounds that now he or she is prepared for an emergency or breakdown. Here's one chilling example.

When my friend Carolyn heard that I was writing this book, she asked if I had seen her down-the-street neighbor's yard. Apparently this guy had bought so many lawn mowers, snow blowers, lawn tractors, and every other kind of equipment at auctions and yard sales that the stuff now spilled out of his overflowing garage and covered the entire lawn. (Hey, they were great deals! And what if he needed a replacement part?) Carolyn even suggested that a photo of his "private junkyard" would make a great cover for this book. Yuck! The scariest part to me is that the

Free Stuff!

Ever fallen into the "free stuff" trap?

I was about to throw out the ticket stub from a movie I saw last weekend when I noticed that the back of it proclaimed, "Join Brand X MovieWatcher and start getting FREE stuff!"

Yikes. Free stuff. Like the ads that announce how much you'll "save" by buying their products (just think about how much you'd save by *not* buying them!), this approach is irresistible to pretty much everyone.

guy has a wife and a daughter, who of course are forbidden to touch his precious junk. I hate to think of them living up there, creeping like rats among all those piles of future scrap.

Thank goodness, most Shoppers are compulsive about smaller and nicer things. But they can still add up. And when your great buys start spilling out of drawers and off surfaces, they no longer look so nice. In fact, they look just like junk.

Fortunately, there are two ways you can still enjoy your shopping habit without letting it take over the house (or your credit cards). The first way works best if you have lots of so-so stuff you really ought to get rid of, be it dishware, clothes, jewelry, or CDs. The other works well to keep you from refilling the house with more.

Trade up. The first way is to trade in all that okay stuff for a few pieces of really good stuff. Sell your masses of so-so jewelry on eBay or through a consignment shop, yard sale, or flea market stand. (You don't have to have one of your own—see if a seasoned yard-saler or flea-marketer will buy the stuff from you.) Then take the proceeds (and yes, you'll end up with a lot less than you thought; this isn't *Antiques Roadshow,* but it will still be good money) and buy something really nice for yourself, a piece or two you'll love and be proud of. See Part Four: Trash (Yours) to Treasure (Theirs), beginning on page 349, for a wide range of ways to sell your stuff.

Specialize. The second way is to narrow your hunt. Rather than heading down to the antiques mall with your checkbook blazing, prepared to get whatever strikes you (and it's amazing how striking all that stuff always is), set a goal and stick to it. Here's how this works: You adore Christmas ornaments. But when you head to the store, you are *not* looking for Christmas ornaments. Instead, you are looking for a heavy green German-made kugel Christmas ornament from the 1920s. Or maybe you love cookware. But when you head to the store, you are *not* looking for cookware. You are looking for a 4-quart Le Creuset Dutch oven in Lemongrass. This way, you still get to go shop and enjoy yourself, but your money usually stays in your billfold and your house stays clutter-free. You can still enjoy the thrill of the chase—now more than ever, since you're chasing something specific. And just think how delighted you'll be if you happen to stumble on that kugel ornament or Dutch oven!

The Scout

I really wanted to call this one the Survivalist, but I didn't, since I want you all to read it. Instead, I settled on the Scout because it's all about that famous Boy and Girl Scout motto, "Be Prepared." If you still have boxes of canned food under the bed from the Y2K scare, or you can't throw out an empty mayonnaise jar because you might need it for canning someday, or your fridge is full of bottles and jars with a half-spoonful of whatever was in it because "it's still good" or "it's a sin to waste it," you are definitely a Scout. (So am I, by the way. Not because of mostly empty bottles and bags, but because I find things like wind-up radios and battery-operated lanterns absolutely irresistible. After all, what if there was a power outage?)

The Great Depression in the 1930s created an entire generation of Scouts, people who were so poor as children—and for whom so many goods were so unavailable—that they had to use foil gum wrappers to make Christmas ornaments. Saving rubber bands, string, bits of soap, clean foil, and jars was serious business—it could be the difference between comfort and want. (I still remember seeing a book about this sort of "Yankee frugality" called *String Too Short to Be Saved*.)

Fortunately, most of us in America aren't faced with these shortages today. But we *are* faced with such hazards as power outages, climbing gas prices, technological breakdowns, downsizing and layoffs, and terrorist threats. Some of you may have stocked up on duct tape and plastic sheeting a few years ago at the government's urging, in case the country faced a terrorist attack.

Being prepared can seem like plain old common sense, and it is . . . to a point.

But if it means turning your home into a garrison, with emergency supplies and "extras" taking up so much space in the basement, attic, garage, closets, and under the beds—everywhere!—that you have no space for "normal" stuff, it's out of control. It's clutter. You don't really need an entire bathroom full of 24-packs of toilet paper, unless you're running a summer camp out of your home.

Use common sense—and use your available space in the ways that make the most sense. (And that includes *open* space for people to move and breathe and relax in.) A kitchen drawer full of rubber bands, bottle caps, and twist-ties could hold a lot of utensils or silverware or teas or spices, instead. And know what? You can buy a whole pack of rubber bands if you really need them. So don't be penny-wise and pound-foolish. Buy what you need, buy what you can use, buy what you have room for. And buy no more!

The Host(ess)

Another friend, Margaret, loves to entertain. She has two kitchens inside and one outside, all loaded with appliances, dishes, cookware, and cooking staples. Oh, and did I mention the bar? But because she and her partner, Frank, who loves cooking and entertaining as much as she does, planned the house around this, there's plenty of room for all their paraphernalia.

If you love to entertain but are trying to do it from the family kitchen, where space is almost always at a premium, repeat after me: You are not, you don't have to be, Martha Stewart (or even Margaret). You can enjoy having people over just as much as Martha and Margaret do, as long as you keep the entertainments in scale with your home's physical limitations—not to mention your own.

My mother was the perfect hostess. Every formal dinner, every party, was just *perfect*. Mama would spend days, sometimes weeks, cooking. We'd all spend days polishing silver, hand-washing fragile china and crystal, laundering linens, cleaning, and decorating. By the time of the big event, everything looked stunning. The food was phenomenal. And my mother, a frail person, was completely wiped out.

After years of watching this cycle repeat itself, I've developed my own rule of entertaining: If the food is good, the hosts are happy, and the company is congenial, everybody's going to have a great time. I really enjoy decorating and cooking, but I make sure I keep my goals realistic and don't attempt more than I can fit into my schedule—and kitchen. As a result, my guests are happy; my boyfriend, Rob, and I are happy; and everybody has a good time.

Scaling back the scope of your entertaining may simply mean keeping less entertainment-specific stuff around taking up space. Sure, the Christmas plates and Santa mugs are cheerful, the snowman placemats are adorable, the snowman salt and pepper shakers are cute, the Christmas tree dishtowels are . . . well, you can see what I'm getting at. One of the smartest tips I've ever heard is this: Resist buying holiday-specific tableware because you use it once a year but have to store it *all* year. It makes a lot more sense to buy seasonal accessories—placemats and napkins in fall colors, for example—that you can use for many months each year and for all the holidays that fall in that season. The same goes for party napkins and the like. Trust me, your guests will *not* miss them!

From Weakness to Strength

Once you know your susceptibilities, you can fight them. And you can win! You just have to make sure they don't creep back in and bite you from behind. If you're a Parent or Scout, for example, buying ingenious clutter-control tools might really help you keep stuff contained and free up space. But I'm a Collector. If I start buying clutter-control containers, racks, and the like, before I know it, I'll have a new collection—of them.

For many of these categories, avoiding temptation is the best policy. If you're trying to lose 5 pounds and you absolutely adore the cannoli at Louie's Italian Bakery, it's not rocket science to keep out of Louie's until the weight is off. If you're a Compulsive Shopper and you know there are certain stores you can't resist, consider them off-limits until you've kicked your clutter. Then see if you can handle limited exposure—but watch the number of times you find yourself there and the number of bags you bring home! If you're starting to see a pattern re-forming, kick the habit so you don't have to start kicking clutter all over again.

Laissez-faire is also a good way to handle some kinds of temptation. For example, I love catalogs. I read catalogs to relax when I'm too wiped out for a magazine, much less a book. And of course, when I get my favorite catalogs, I want lots of the goodies shown and described so alluringly inside. But instead of rushing to the phone—unless I actually need something, like a replacement for a worn-out skirt—I tell myself, "I'll get that tomorrow." You won't be surprised to hear that tomorrow pretty much never comes.

So keep your weak spots in mind as you read through the rest of this book, because not all of the ideas in here will work for you. (What a relief that there are so many to choose from!) Pick the ones that you *can* work with, and you, too, will be a clutter-kicking success story.

CLUTTER-KICKING STRATEGIES

Right about now, you're probably itching to embark on your new clutter-free life. Try these tactics to get started. There's a clutter-control program in Chapter 4—Five Simple Steps to Kick Your Clutter, beginning on page 54. In addition, the room-by-room chapters in Part Two contain some "5-Minute Fixes" that will let you start to make a difference in your clutter in a hurry. But whatever else you do to control clutter, keep the simple strategies below in mind and you'll have some great can't-fail backup plans.

Clutter Mythbusters: One In, One (or Two) Out

I was talking about clutter control with a group of women at my local Curves in Kutztown, Pennsylvania. One of them, Sylvia—not surprisingly, an interior decorator—said that she kept clutter out by a strict policy: If something came in, something had to go out. That makes sense, I thought. And in fact it's a classic approach to keeping clutter-free. But the one in, one out rule just helps you maintain the status quo, so as far as getting *rid* of clutter, it's a myth. Here's a way to beat it. Another Curves member, Diane, says that *her* policy is that when one thing comes in, *two* have to go out. Yes! If you can do that, your clutter will melt away. Try it—aim for at least one thing, a one-for-one exchange. If you can think of—and bear to sacrifice—two things (or three, or four . . .), do it. Your clutter will head out the door even faster.

When in Doubt . . .

My dear friend Cole is an inveterate Collector like me, though his partner, Bruce, is anything but. Bruce's idea of clutter is an extra napkin in the drawer. When I

SANITY SAVERS

When dealing with clutter, most of us need all the help we can get. And that includes what I call "borrowing"—taking clutter-kicking inspiration not just from books, articles, or Web sites about clutter control, but from all sorts of areas that have nothing to do with clutter. You'll be reading about specific examples of borrowing as they apply to other chapters, but here, let's talk about one source that always applies: spiritual advice.

Whatever your faith or spiritual leanings, you can find a lot of support for your clutter-control efforts in the writings and sayings of many great spiritual teachers. Whether you turn to Jesus's straightforward comments about having too many possessions—as relevant today as when they were spoken 2,000 years ago—or to a modern spiritual teacher like Eckhart Tolle and his wise discussion of amassing material goods in his book *A New Earth,* or to the Buddha's fleeing his princely palace to sit under a tree with a rice bowl and the clothes on his back, or to St. Francis's rejection of his father's wealth and possessions, it can really help to think that there are higher reasons to kick your clutter than to avoid living in a crowded or messy house. After all, the lighter the weight of the material stuff you carry, the higher your soul can fly!

asked him about his philosophy of clutter control, he replied, "When in doubt, throw it out!" (Can't you just picture me and Cole wincing?) If you can achieve Bruce's take-no-prisoners mind-set, clutter won't stand a chance. But don't try it on your family's precious stuff without their permission, or you may find yourself on *Family Feud!* Stick to your own stuff and generic stuff that other family members won't miss, like the seven extra Pyrex pie plates you have in the cupboard "just in case," or that stack of plastic bags under the sink.

Throw the Guilt Out First

In both of these cases (the "one, two, or more" switch and the "when in doubt" approach), I'm saying, "throw it out." But that's not necessarily what I mean. Bruce, a committed environmentalist, would never really throw anything out. But he *would* recycle, compost, donate, or give it away. If trashing stuff makes you feel guilty, or if you can't bear the thought of losing money on something you paid for, turn to Part Four: Trash (Yours) to Treasure (Theirs), for a wealth of guilt-free suggestions for disposing of your clutter without throwing it out.

Set Priorities

When clutter confronts you everywhere you look, it's easy to be so overwhelmed that you become paralyzed. Your good intentions give way to procrastination—you'll deal with it tomorrow. And of course, that particular tomorrow never comes. Instead, try this: Go into all your downstairs (or public, if you live in a one-story house) rooms and decide on the worst clutter problem you have in each room. Don't dither—just look around and see what hits you in the face first. Then deal with that one thing in each room.

After that, set the next level of priorities: Do you want to do the same for the upstairs (or private) rooms? Or should you choose the second-worst clutter problem in each downstairs room and tackle each of those? Or maybe you'll focus on one room (see Part Two: Clutter-Kicking Room by Room, beginning on page 69) and keep tackling the clutter issues there in order from worst to least bad until the job is completely done?

It's a lot easier when you have a plan of action—and follow it!

Take Small Bites

Related to setting priorities is keeping your clutter-kicking goals manageable. There's nothing as horrible as pulling everything out of a closet (or cabinet, dresser, pantry—you know what I mean), then realizing you don't have time to deal with it right now and shoving it all back in. Ouch! Instead, tackle just your shoes. Or just *some* shoes. Purses. Sweaters. Underwear. Whatever.

Budget your time realistically. Every morning, after I finish my household chores and before I start working, I try to accomplish one clutter-kicking task, whether it's tossing outdated coupons, packing up plastic bags to drop off at the grocery or magazines to take to the library "free" boxes, or cleaning out a drawer and bagging the discards for Goodwill, the Salvation Army, or the Society of St. Vincent de Paul. I always feel great starting my day with a small accomplishment, but I make sure I don't launch into a big, distracting project that I can't finish—or that will eat up the whole morning at the expense of work.

Jobs, families, friends, a household to manage, pets to play with, errands to run . . . unless huge piles of clutter are threatening to topple over and kill somebody, clearing out just isn't going to be your top priority. But that's no excuse for embracing the status quo. I say, break it up and get it done. Book by book, bra by bra, paper clip by paper clip. If you keep at it, one day you're going to look around and realize that the clutter that comes into the house today (and don't kid yourself, it *will* come—in the mail, with the kids, in a shopping bag, and so forth) is the only clutter you have to deal with. Aaaah, what a feeling!

To get started, I recommend trying the "5-Minute Fixes" in the chapters in Part Two. You'll find fast ideas for accomplishing some clutter-kicking. And when you see how much difference even 5 minutes can make—both in a room's appearance and in how good you feel—I think you'll be hooked.

Be Entertaining

There's a story I've always appreciated about a slovenly woman whose house was dirty and cluttered—which is to say, a real mess. One day, someone gave the woman some beautiful roses. Thrilled, she dug out a vase, washed it off, and put the roses in it. Then she set the gleaming vase with its beautiful flowers on her cluttered, dusty table. Immediately, she saw that it looked terrible, so she cleared off the table and dusted it, then set the vase back in its place. But as she looked at her now-shining table with its beautiful vase of flowers, the woman realized that the area around it looked terrible with all the chaos, mess, and dirt. So she began cleaning it up so her flowers would look nice. Of course, you can see where this is going. Before she knew it, our heroine had cleaned the entire room—and all because of a vase of flowers!

For most of us, it's not a vase of flowers but the impending arrival of guests that triggers our long-dormant desire to de-clutter and clean our houses—or at least our "public rooms." I say, make the most of this: Have people over as often as you can manage, and see what a transformation it makes in your home! You don't need to engage in grand-scale entertaining to make this work for you. An informal dinner with friends; an afternoon get-together to cook, knit, or chat; a monthly book club meeting—whatever you'd actually enjoy works fine, as long as it's on a regular and fairly frequent schedule. My friend Carolyn and her husband, Gary, host a weekly "Friday Night Supper Club" for a group of friends at their house. You can bet it's always spotless when we arrive!

Get Help

I'm not referring to professional help here, though a team of in-shape guys to haul off heavy stuff or move things around can sure come in handy. Instead, I'm talking about asking your family to pitch in and help you kick your collective clutter.

To use another example from the world of dieting, professionals always tell you to get your family, friends, and co-workers on board before you try to lose weight. If you explain to them that you're counting on them to help you stay motivated, praise your progress, and keep you away from temptation (for example, by going with you on a walk or to a show as a social outing rather than to the ice-cream

The Unwilling Accomplice

What if your spouse or partner *won't* help? What if he or she is the root cause of your clutter problem? If you or the kids are the main culprits, though your spouse or partner may not lift a finger to help you, he or she will probably be relieved to get rid of the mess. It's not ideal, but you'll still end up with a clean, de-cluttered house.

If you're in it together, you can start small and make it a contest—sort of like *The Biggest Loser*. Then, rather than a threat, he or she may see it as a fun competition and get into the spirit. You'll get help—*and* a de-cluttered house.

If he or she is the real clutterer in your home, though, it's super-important to be reassuring: Tell your spouse that you'll work with them to take it in easy stages, and promise not to ever get rid of anything they love. Assure them that they'll be consulted at every stage. (This is important no matter what your situation is—even if you have the world's most enthusiastic clutter-kicker for a spouse or partner. And remind them that they need to consult *you*, too.) If you think they might go for it, share some of the "5-Minute Fixes" in Part Two to see if you can get them interested.

But what if you've tried everything and you can't get your significant other to budge at all? He or she announces, in effect, and despite all your efforts, "It's my stuff and it's staying. Got that?" I'm no psychiatrist, but I'd say that's a control issue. If you're in this situation—and I hope nobody reading this is!—you're not really dealing with clutter; you're dealing with a basic couples problem. I'd say it's time to call in the professionals for a consultation—and I don't mean professional organizers!

stand or coffee shop), you're much more likely to succeed. This is even more true when we're talking about clutter. After all, your family can't literally put food in your mouth, but they can put stuff in your house!

So shamelessly steal this tip from successful dieters and put it to work for you. Get your spouse on board first, then hold a family meeting. Tell the kids what you're doing, why you're doing it, and how everyone can help. (See page 216 for more on getting everyone from toddlers to teens in on the act.) Suit the tasks you want your kids to do to their ages, and for goodness' sake, don't make them overwhelming! After all, *you* haven't been able to cope with the clutter, so you can't expect your kids (or spouse, partner, roommate, or live-in parents) to do any better.

Keep it fun, upbeat, and manageable, but most of all, keep at it. And don't forget to praise everyone for his or her progress.

What about nonfamily members? Tell friends, co-workers, and anyone else who might give you things that your house is bursting at the seams and you can't accept another *anything*. Ask them for clutter tips and favorite clutter-control and organizing tools. (They might have great ideas!) And let it be known that you want gifts like food, flowers, donations made in your name, memberships, or gift certificates rather than things, however lovely, that will pile up.

ONWARD!

I hope that, after reading this chapter, you've found the reasons why you have clutter that needs kicking, you've evaluated how bad your clutter problems really are, and you've already started to think of ways you can get to work to get rid of unwanted and unneeded stuff.

But please, before you begin kicking your clutter, bear in mind that "unwanted" and "unneeded" aren't the same thing. Before you toss the first rubber band, make sure you know the difference between simple clutter and something—however useless—that you really love. Chapter 2—Sorting It All Out, or How Much Do You Love It?, is all about thinking through your stuff and pinpointing where it falls in your affections (or dislikes). Making sure you keep all of your most-loved things—be they cracked, moth-eaten, ugly, or even unrecognizable to anyone else—is the key to successfully kicking your clutter once and for all.

Now, let's get started!

Sorting It All Out,

OR HOW MUCH DO YOU LOVE IT?

This chapter is going to be short but sweet because its focus is narrow but totally essential. It's about recognizing and keeping what you love, no matter what anybody else says. If you don't do that, you'll never be able to kick your clutter. Why? Because if you toss or give away what actually matters to you—from a chipped mug your first love gave you to the stuffed animal you carried around obsessively when you were 2 years old—you will not only regret it for the rest of your life, you will also become angry with clutter control and you'll retaliate by trying to compensate for the loss with more stuff.

Now, what does all that mean? Let's look again at dieting; it's closely related to de-cluttering, because when you diet, you're trying to change your eating and exercise habits to de-clutter your body of excess pounds. Okay, if you love low-fat, low-carb eating and strenuous daily exercise, you probably don't need to diet, now do you? But if you hate exercise and love carbs and fat—and have packed on the pounds as a result—to get and keep them off, you have to make a deal with yourself. Draconian diets that make you eat salads with no dressing, skinless chicken, and steamed veggies with no butter will *not* work—at least not for long—unless you're in prison and have no other choice. If you have to give up every single thing you love, you will fail, because really—who can do that for the rest of his life?

The diets that work are the ones that let you indulge in your favorite foods, but only occasionally and only in moderation. That way, you don't feel deprived. You feel like you can keep going if you know that you can have a Krispy Kreme doughnut once a week—but only one Krispy Kreme, and only once a week. If you felt that you could *never* eat another Krispy Kreme, guess what? One day, you'd find yourself eating a whole box of Krispy Kremes and hating yourself. Or a whole bag of M&Ms. Or a big plate of French fries. Or whatever.

Just as people throughout human history have prized fat, salt, and sugar because they make us feel good, at least for a little while, people prize objects that trigger positive associations for them—happy childhood memories, things that create a sense of connection (such as a family heirloom), things that mark important occasions, things that commemorate personal milestones and achievements, and things that remind us of people, pets, or places we love. These objects become symbols of who we are, and their loss is devastating.

I still remember an adult friend's inconsolable grief when her favorite stuffed animal was stolen, along with a gym bag, from her car. The surprised thieves probably tossed the stuffed toy in the nearest dumpster, but my bereft friend put up "missing person" posters—complete with a photo of her stolen hedgehog—all over town. And in case you're wondering, my friend never found her beloved toy, but her story *does* have a happy ending: Years later, she saw another one in the window of a secondhand store in the town where she was living. Though the original was lost, she now has Hedgehog II to fill its place.

THE FIRST ESSENTIAL CLUTTER RULE

This is *so* important that I'm going to put it in big letters so you can find it easily whenever you feel pressure from friends or family members to throw out something you cherish. I call it the First Essential Clutter Rule, and you should remind yourself of it often. Here it is:

$$\left[\begin{array}{c} \text{If you love it or you use it,} \\ \text{it's not clutter.} \end{array} \right]$$

Dear Claire,

When I married, my great-aunt Violet gave me her mother's antique cherub bowl. This heirloom is made of pink bisque with gold dots all over it and has a cluster of cherubs hovering around the rim. It's huge and fragile, and my whole family hates it. I could use the attic space taken up by the big box I have to keep it in. My husband thinks I should take it to an antiques dealer or an eBay store, but it's been in my family for more than 100 years and I feel like a traitor when I think about getting rid of it. What should I do?

—Cherubic

Dear Cherubic,

Is dear Great-Aunt Violet still extant? If not, you might present it to one of her offspring—or their offspring—as a touching memento of their mother or grandmother. If she had no offspring, take your husband's advice—it's excellent. Unless, of course, one of your other relatives is always commenting on the bowl when she visits you. In that case, you should give it to her at the next opportunity (even if the relative is your mother). And if she suddenly has some reason why she couldn't possibly take it, tell her you understand, but you wanted to make sure she had the opportunity before you sold it. If Great-Aunt Violet is still alive, you could always return the bowl to her, telling her how much you've appreciated her gift over the years but that you couldn't possibly keep it with rambunctious children in the house—you'd never forgive yourself if it got broken. When she eventually leaves it to you in her will—and steel yourself, she will—take your husband's great advice and sell it. Perhaps you'll be pleasantly surprised at its value!

Good luck,
Claire

The key to successful clutter control is really that simple. I don't care what it is, and I don't care what shape it's in, if you love it, or if you use it, it's not clutter—no matter what anybody says. As I write this, I have in my attic the stuffed lion that, though it was bigger than I was, I carried with me everywhere when I was 2 years old. (Thank goodness the pacifier and baby blanket I also carried everywhere are long lost.) My boyfriend, Rob, has the antique model of a Chinese junk (a kind of

Love It–Lose It Spectrum

Lose it	Don't like it	Don't especially like it	Don't like it much but have a sentimental attachment	It's okay	Like it	Like it a lot	Love it!
			grandma's rocking chair				
silver plate							
				floor lamp			
	coffee maker						
		plaid bathrobe					
							Pendleton blanket
							paper shredder
				fireplace screen			
		blue martini glasses					
						hot pink raincoat & umbrella	
					ceramic toothbrush holder		

Your first step is to evaluate each of your possessions on this Love It–Lose It Spectrum. Here's my version and how I rated some of my things. Create your own spectrum and rate your personal items, then move on to the Useful–Useless Spectrum on page 28. Make it easy on yourself and use a separate spectrum for each room!

boat) that his father bought him when Rob was a child living in Hong Kong. Its sails are too tattered to actually attach to the model, but they're lovingly stored away, and someday Rob hopes to have new ones made that he can attach to his model junk, based on the antique prototypes.

The same rule holds true if you use something. If you till your garden with an old wheel-hoe every spring, it's not clutter. If you knit gift scarves and mittens every year with some of your massive yarn collection, it's not clutter. If you make homemade sauerkraut with your antique mandoline, it's not clutter.

True, in both cases—love and use—other people might call any and all of these objects clutter, or even junk (so to speak). But they're *not*. You know it, and by God, you owe it to yourself to defend your well-loved and well-used possessions against the forces that want them out.

However.

If you find yourself clinging to *everything* on the basis that you love or use it, you're probably deceiving yourself. Rather than being defensive to the point of coming to a clutter-kicking standstill, look at your possessions as falling on a scale—the Love It–Lose It Spectrum. You can create your own scale based on your feelings about things, or you can rate your stuff on mine. I'm reproducing it on the opposite page so you can use it.

When you're thinking about getting rid of any given object, do a quick mental check to see where it falls on the Love It–Lose It Spectrum. Even if it's as battered as the sails on my boyfriend's boat, if you love it, keep it. (But keep it out of sight—see "The Second Essential Clutter Rule" on page 32.) You should probably keep anything that winds up in the "Like it a lot" range, too, and should consider the merits of keeping versus tossing anything in the "Like it" range. Don't like Aunt Adele's Victorian china but have a sentimental attachment? Keep a piece or a photo and sell the rest. Anything scoring below "Like it" that's not an heirloom should go in the get-it-out pile, unless it belongs to someone else in the family. Ask everyone to rate their stuff on the Love It–Lose It Spectrum as well, so you don't inadvertently toss something another family member treasures. (Check out Chapter 11—Clutter-Free Kids' Rooms, beginning on page 207, for advice on how to kick your kids' clutter.)

I Don't Like It, but I Use It

What if you couldn't care less about it as an object, but you think it's useful? This can apply to everything from a leaf-eater to a deicer, from Great-Grandma's potato masher to the only vacuum cleaner that actually sucks up pet hair. Here's another case where you may not love it, but if you really use it, it's not clutter. Before you throw out a tool or kitchen utensil, ask yourself (and your family, if it's someone

Useful-Useless Spectrum

Don't know what it is	Don't use it, don't like it	Don't use it	Don't use it, but keep it because it might come in handy	Use it seasonally	Use it once a month	Use it at least once a week	Use it at least once a day
	grandma's rocking chair						
	silver plate						
							floor lamp
							coffee maker
			plaid bathrobe				
				Pendleton blanket			
						paper shredder	
				fireplace screen			
	blue martini glasses				hot pink raincoat & umbrella		
							ceramic toothbrush holder

Once you've placed your items on the Love It–Lose It Spectrum, it's time to rate each of your possessions in terms of its usefulness. This chart shows how I evaluated some of my possessions. Once you create your own charts, move on to the Item Action Plan on page 30.

else's) to rate it on the Useful–Useless Spectrum. As with the Love It–Lose It Spectrum, I'm reproducing mine for ready reference, but feel free to create something that works better for you and your family.

You may not "like" your slow cooker or air popper, but if you use them regularly, they're not clutter. The same is true of your silver-polishing cloths, even if you use them only before Christmas. But if you have duplicates of useful things—several electric razors, in case something happens to the one you use, or, God forbid,

How Much Do I Need?

If you found that you fall into the Scout category in Chapter 1 (see page 13), you've probably stocked up on staples of all kinds, from toilet paper to batteries, first-aid kits to bottled water, reflective blankets to flashlights. After all, you might need them someday!

And yes, if there's an emergency, you really might need extras of basic necessities. If your area is prone to ice storms in winter, it's smart to keep extra staples on hand *in winter*—toilet paper, milk, butter, eggs, tissues, bread, and anything else you and your family might use up in less than a week. The same holds true if your area is prone to power outages. In my case, if the power goes off, so does my septic system, so I keep jugs of water on hand for manual flushing, just in case. But how much is enough?

Certain faiths believe in "preparedness," the stocking up of staples so that families could survive a disaster of considerable magnitude, one serious enough to interrupt supply lines for anywhere from 6 months to 2 years. Survivalists and some Libertarians also believe that this is smart practice. And once again, if you're concerned about the stability of our supply system *and* you have the space for storage, go for it.

The keys here are to stock only what your family will actually consume—it won't help you to stock up on split peas if your family won't eat them—and then to rotate your stored goods. You want to use the oldest stores first. If you don't cook from your home storage, there's no point in keeping it. Fortunately, there are books, magazines, and online guides to help you. Three that leap to mind are *Backwoods Home* magazine, their book *Backwoods Home Cooking*, and *Cookin' with Home Storage*.

If your "preparedness" is more a matter of compulsion than a religious tenet or a carefully planned life strategy, you can probably put your shelf space to better use. After all, those unused batteries get old, and who needs a fossilized box (or 10) of laundry detergent? Instead, for frequently used items, use the one-plus rule: What you're using currently and a spare. Then make sure you use the spare next and replace it with the new spare, and you'll be sure to keep things current and fresh. As always, use your good sense: If your kids drink three bottles of fruit juice a day, you'll need more than three extras unless you go to the grocery every day. (Or you could switch to space-saving concentrate!) Balance your needs with your storage space, though—more frequent shopping trips make more sense, clutter-wise, than pantry items stacked all over the house and spilling out of closets and entryways.

Item Action Plan

Item	How I listed it on the Love It-Lose It Spectrum	How I listed it on the Useful-Useless Spectrum	Action(s) I will take
grandma's rocking chair	Don't like it too much but have a sentimental attachment	Don't use it	See if any relative wants it; if not, take it to local antiques store or consignment shop
silver plate	Hate it	Don't use it/ Don't like it	Take it to antiques auction
floor lamp	It's okay	Use it at least once a day	Keep an eye out for one I like better & replace when I find one
coffee maker	Don't like it	Use it at least once a day	Replace now. Donate old coffee maker & get receipt for taxes
plaid bathrobe	Don't especially like it	Don't use it but keep it because it might come in handy	Never worn designer robe; sell through upscale consignment shop or eBay drop-off store
Pendleton blanket	Love it♭	Use it seasonally	Keep it
paper shredder	Love it♭	Use it at least once a week	Keep it
fireplace screen	It's okay	Use it seasonally	Replace when I have the money & see one I really like
blue martini glasses	Don't especially like them	Don't use it/ Don't like it	Sell through an eBay drop-off store or an antiques store or secondhand shop
hot pink raincoat & umbrella	Like them a lot	Use it once a month	Keep them
ceramic toothbrush holder	Like it	Use it at least once a day	Keep it

After listing your possessions and evaluating them on the Love It-Lose It and Useful-Useless Spectrums (pages 26 and 28), it's time to decide what you'll do with each item. Keep it, give it away, toss it, donate it, sell it, or replace it—the choice is up to you. Here's how I'll be handling some of the clutter in my life. Create an Item Action Plan for your possessions, then get started on de-cluttering!

multiple lawn mowers and large appliances (because you just might need that black-and-white television set one day)—it's time to reevaluate. Think of the space saved (and potential money earned) by clearing out those "extras."

If you inherited Grandpa's antique hand tools and you don't know what they are, much less how to use them, you can either sell them or keep them and display them. (We'll get to both options later.) In either case, there's no reason to feel guilty. Just be honest with yourself and your family as to what you really want to do with them, and then do it. Maybe your favorite nephew has decided to become a house carpenter. Voilà! You've given him the gift of a lifetime and cleared out your garage at the same time.

In my opinion, anything that falls within the "Use it at least once a day" through "Use it seasonally" categories is worth keeping, though if you're really short on space, I could make a strong argument for renting the seasonal stuff rather than owning it. Unless you live in a mansion and have space for a museum's worth of stuff—in which case, why are you reading this?—everything else falls into the sell it/donate it/give it away/trash or recycle it category. To borrow a phrase from Dr. Phil, let's get real. If you're not using it, you *don't* need it. It's just taking up space. So get it out!

PUTTING IT ALL TOGETHER

To get the truest picture of where your possessions fall in the scale of trash or treasure, you need to put together your Love It–Lose It Spectrum and your Useful–Useless Spectrum for any given item. Let's combine them into an Item Action Plan.

Use your Item Action Plan as a guide to show you what to do with your stuff. As you list each item and see how it lines up on the Love It–Lose It Spectrum and the Useful–Useless Spectrum that you created earlier, you'll be able to see clearly what you should do with it. If you love it and use it daily, it's a clear keeper. If you hate it but use it daily or weekly, it's a good candidate for replacement. (After all, if you hate your coffeepot but use it constantly, wouldn't it be a good idea to replace it with one you love? And the same is true of your everyday dishware and the clothes you wear to work.) If you hate it and never use it, for goodness' sake, toss, sell, donate, or give it away. Ask yourself why you're letting it take up space to begin with!

Obviously, it makes no sense (unless you've just won the lottery) to replace every single object you're not wild about but use, so prioritize: Try to replace the ones you use or look at most often (the ones, for example, that live on your kitchen counter) when the opportunity presents itself. If you really hate your blow-dryer and you use it every day, it makes more sense to replace it than to replace the clunky leaf shredder you use for 2 weeks every fall. It may take a while, but if you make it a priority, a year or so from now, you'll be delighted to find that you really like the equipment or utensils you actually use. And isn't that worth it?

THE SECOND ESSENTIAL CLUTTER RULE

Before we leave this chapter and dig into kicking our clutter, I want to share with you my Second Essential Clutter Rule. Here it is:

[If you can't see it, it's not clutter.]

If my boyfriend's, Rob's, beloved model trains (tracks, buildings, accessories . . .) are piled in and out of boxes that are spilling out all over the floor and stacked all over the tables and chairs, they're clutter. If they're neatly boxed and shelved or displayed attractively on their own table, they're not. If my cats' toys are thrown all over the floor, they're clutter—potentially hazardous clutter, at that!— but if they're kept in a toy box on a closet shelf and brought out for playtime only, they're not. If your houseplants, watering can, extra pots, fertilizers, and the like are mixed in with everything else on the kitchen counter, they're clutter; if the plants are displayed on an attractive stand with a storage cabinet for their accessories, they're not.

The same holds true for big and infrequently used objects. If your pressure canner is out on the counter all year, it's about the only thing that will fit on there because it's so huge. And unless you can all year, you'll want it out for only a few weeks in late summer. But if you can fit it under the sink, it's there when you want it—convenient but out of sight. It may be big and ugly, but it's not clutter. (Unless you never use it!) The same is true of power tools, the chipper-shredder, and the

The Artful Dodger

One very clever, very creative way to deal with potential clutter is to turn it into a decorative display. Remember my Collector friend Cole and his minimalist partner, Bruce, from Chapter 1? Cole has accumulated and inherited a wonderful collection of handmade and antique baskets, wooden bowls, and other rustic kitchen-related implements. But instead of trying to set them around the house or put them out on the kitchen counters, both of which would have aggravated Bruce and caused his clutter-kicking to really go into overdrive, Cole did something brilliant: He created a decorative tableau.

Cole and Bruce live in a wonderful and largely handmade house, and the kitchen has a fine set of rustic handmade wooden cabinets. Because the roof slants upward, there's quite a bit of room above one wall of cabinets. Cole created a montage of his rustic kitchen baskets and bowls, even including an old rocking chair at the high end of the ceiling. The result is a beautiful display that's totally in keeping with the look of the kitchen—and also out of everybody's way. It was the perfect solution for both Bruce and Cole. And, of course, their guests enjoy it, too.

So don't overlook seemingly "dead" space when you're thinking about what to do with beloved possessions, and don't forget the power of an effective combination. (For tons of ideas on creative ways to combine things, pick up a stack of back issues of *Martha Stewart Living* and *Mary Engelbreit's Home Companion* at your library. Then return them so *they* don't become clutter!) Just remember, setting out everything you own in a cheek-by-jowl fashion is *not* creating a display, attractive or otherwise; instead, you're just making more dustables. Using some restraint, mixing and matching different things, and varying the scale and texture will give you the most pleasing results. (For example, Cole's baskets and wooden bowls look better together than either group would have looked alone.)

chainsaw. If they're out rusting on the lawn or waiting to break someone's neck on the garage or mudroom floor, they're clutter. But if they're put neatly in the tool shed or on a shelf or wall peg in the garage, they're useful tools.

Mind you, there are limits. If your massive collection of LPs or antique pitchers is out of sight because they're stored in pieces of furniture bought expressly to hold them and then crammed all over the living room, you still have clutter. But now it's a clutter of furniture! I'm convinced that there are appropriate, attractive ways to store just about anything, as long as you're not trying to store too many of too many different things. (See Chapter 3—Tooling Up for some great storage options.) Choose either the LPs or the pitchers. Or some LPs and some pitchers. Unless, of course, you have the room but just don't know how to do it. In either case, read on! And make sure you didn't skip "The Artful Dodger," on page 33.

ONWARD!

Now that you feel confident that the things you really love will be safe from your clutter-kicking work and you've confessed that, yes, you *do* own things that you don't really love, it's time to get to work. And as with all work, the right tools can make a huge difference in the ease of and pleasure you'll take in the job. So let's head to Chapter 3—Tooling Up, and take a look at what's out there to help you turn the things you choose to keep into objects that are orderly, easy to find, and attractively displayed—rather than just a bunch of clutter.

Tooling Up

Sometimes kicking your clutter is as simple as finding the right place to put it. In this chapter, you'll discover where to get the best organizational tools, from ingenious storage systems and professional shelving systems to simple containers and functional furniture. The right tools can make the job of clutter control so much simpler, and that will save time—and your sanity, too!

But tooling up isn't just about actual tools like buckets and files. It's also about finding the right help for your clutter-kicking needs, whether it's a great book, magazine, or Web site; a professional organization; or a support group. You'll find those here, too.

Most books bury their resources lists in the back, as if they were afterthoughts. But as you'll see, not just in this chapter but throughout this book, I think being able to find and use the right tools and resources can make all the difference in whether your clutter-kicking efforts succeed or fail.

In fact, if you've tried to get your clutter under control in the past and it hasn't worked, this list may be the missing link. So not only am I putting this chapter right up front, but I've also included appropriate tools and resources in every chapter in Parts Two, Three, and Four. That way, you'll have the resources you need where you need them, and you'll be able to act on a great tip immediately, while you're feeling inspired! Tools and other resources are recommended throughout the tips, but look for the specially marked sidebars "Tools of the Trade" and "Love

It or Lose It?" to find some of my favorites—plus tools that are often recommended but are, in my opinion, overrated.

MY TOP 11 CLUTTER-KICKING TOOLS

Let me start by recommending the clutter-kicking tools I can't live without. These certainly aren't the only ones that work. (See "The Pros Know" on page 40 for some excellent suggestions from Diane Albright, a professional organizer.) But these tools are the ones I use every single day to keep my own home (and life) in order. Some are old favorites, dating back to my first dorm room and even before, while others are essentials I've discovered over the past 5 years. Some are free, most are inexpensive, and a couple cost a bit more (though you can often find them for much less if you buy them used).

Because your house is different from mine and your needs are probably different, too, please don't consider this the end-all and be-all list. I don't: My list is always growing as I add new finds! And the list doesn't even include two things that are absolutely essential for me—adequate bookshelf space to have all my books easily accessible and enough CD display and storage space to house my collection—since they're about me, but maybe not you. What I *have* included here are things I think everyone could use. See if you agree!

1. **Plastic storage boxes.** These inexpensive storage containers can be found everywhere, from supermarkets and pharmacies to home improvement stores. They come in all sizes, from tiny (great for pins, staples, and other office and crafts accessories) to huge (such as under-bed storage containers for clothes and bins for basement and garage storage). I like the ones with handles and side clamps best, since they're easiest to move. One definite advantage of these containers is that they're clear or translucent, so you can see what's inside!

2. **ClickClacks.** These rectangular and square plastic storage containers have lock-down lids to keep all sorts of food safe and fresh. I love them because they stack very nicely, saving you valuable storage space; you can see what's inside, so you can tell at a glance if you need more rice, cereal, dried fruit, or what have you; and they keep food pest-free. For more on ClickClacks, see "Tools of the Trade" on page 92.

3. **Copy-paper boxes.** I couldn't manage without copy-paper boxes, those sturdy, heavy-duty lidded cardboard boxes that are the perfect size for lifting—not too heavy!—and will hold a lot. I keep tax records, yarn, collectibles not currently on display, Christmas ornaments, and many, many other things stored in these boxes. I keep my "wrapping station" in two boxes, with wrapping paper, tissue paper, and gift bags in one box and ribbon, bows, and other adornments in the other. And I find that these boxes are perfect for storing framed (and unframed) artworks upright and safe, with paper or bubble wrap between them, when it's not their turn for wall display. I always label the top and all sides of the boxes so I can tell what's inside no matter what part of the box I can see. And of course, I wouldn't store cardboard boxes anywhere damp, such as in a basement or garage. (See "Plastic storage boxes," above—they're great for damp storage.) I used to get empty copy-paper boxes at the corporation where I worked. Now that I work from home, I ask my boyfriend, Rob, to collect them for me at the college where he teaches, and I also beg them from my local office-supply store.

4. **Shower and bath storage.** I absolutely love the wire baskets that you hang over the showerhead or suction to the walls of the bath or shower stall. They hold all your bath and shower essentials high and dry, so they're not sitting at the corners of the tub, collecting grunge and falling into the tub or shower. (See "Stash the shampoo" on page 132 for more on these bathroom lifesavers.)

5. **Under-sink shelves.** Unlike many organizing devices that end up taking up so much space that you actually lose storage space when you install them, the plastic shelving systems that snap together under the kitchen or bathroom sink are fantastic. (See "Tools of the Trade" on page 112.) They instantly double your storage space, are supereasy to install (even for a klutz like me), and let you actually see what you have stored in there. I have one in the bathroom and one in the kitchen, and I'm grateful for them every single day!

6. **Rolling carts.** I suppose you could call me a cart junkie. I have four of them in my house and use them constantly. In my opinion, they're clutter-kicking lifesavers. I have one in the kitchen with a butcher-block top that serves as a mobile island and storage unit; one in the living room with the TV,

DVD/VCR combo, remotes, and other accessories, so we can roll it out when someone's watching TV but keep it out of the middle of the floor the rest of the time; one in my office, holding projects I'm currently working on conveniently next to the computer; and one in my plant room, with houseplants and supplies conveniently corralled in one attractive display. (That one has glass surfaces to contain spills.) I bought mine new at various times, but I often see them selling for almost nothing at thrift shops and secondhand furniture stores.

7. **Metal storage tins.** These convenient cylindrical tins come in any number of attractive colors and designs (some of mine have beautiful songbirds on them, while others have whimsical pet art and still others have Colonial toile fabric designs), so you can display them wherever you need pest- (or possibly pet-) proof storage. They're capacious and easy to stack and access. I keep seed for my outdoor birdfeeders; dry dog and cat food; parrot toys; and kitchen staples like chocolate and butterscotch chips, dried fruit, beans, and pasta in mine. (Not together, please!)

8. **Plastic buckets.** Like metal bins, plastic buckets make great clutter-containers. I use heavy plastic buckets with lock-on lids to hold my bunny and chicken feed, potting soil, and other gardening supplies like orchid bark. Smaller buckets keep my cleaning supplies and small gardening tools like trowels, pruners, and weeders contained in one easy-to-find place. I also keep a small covered bucket to hold kitchen scraps for the compost heap. Handles make plastic buckets and bins easy to pick up and carry to where they're needed, and they stack easily, too, for the most efficient use of space. Unlike decorative metal tins, plastic buckets aren't attractive enough to display in plain sight. I keep mine in the mudroom, laundry room, greenhouse, and under the kitchen sink.

9. **File cabinets.** I love my two-drawer file cabinets! I bought them used at a secondhand office supply store in an assortment of cheerful colors, getting them over time as I needed them. I keep hanging folders in them with work-related files, topical files that are relevant to me (such as a home-repair file) or simply of interest (a backyard chicken file), a bills file, and even files of garden catalogs. (For more on my bill-filing system, see "Bite the bill bullet"

on page 242.) They keep information organized and easy to find. I keep my work files in a separate cabinet from my personal files, and I keep all file folders labeled and alphabetized by topic. A file cabinet can be an organizational lifesaver—no more time wasted looking for a paper or article that "you know you have somewhere." Everything's right there when you need it. But any filing system is useful only if it's maintained. If you have drawers of outdated stuff or papers packed in so tightly that you're afraid to pull out a file lest a volcano of papers erupts from the drawer, or if nothing's in a recognizable order, so you might as well have shoved it all in a box in the attic, then file cabinets won't help you. The trick is to buy them, keep them clean, keep them organized, keep them current—and they'll keep *you* happy!

10. **Desk planner.** My yearly desk planner is my lifesaver. Every December, I pick up one of these compact books (the size of a small notebook) at a local bookstore, and I'm set for the year. I like the ones that show a week on each two-page spread, since they have plenty of room to write but aren't too bulky. I write in appointments, upcoming events, work-related things like meetings and deadlines, vacations, birthdays, payment-due dates—anything that's time-sensitive. If a time is involved, I'll include that ("supper Carolyn's 7 p.m."); if it's an appointment, I'll include the phone number so it's right there if I need to call for any reason. I check the planner every evening to make sure I'm on top of upcoming obligations, and I check it again the next day as I progress through the day's events. (As you can probably guess, I keep my planner on the rolling cart next to my computer desk!) This does away with the clutter of sticky notes all over the fridge, computer, bathroom mirror, desktop, and other places I've seen people post notes in usually futile attempts to remind themselves of upcoming events. (After all, once the surface is bristling with notes, who even reads them anymore?) And it keeps track of all your engagements and obligations in one place, so you don't waste time looking through computer and print calendars trying to remember if some appointment has slipped your mind.

11. **Your eyes.** They're your best clutter-kicking tool, so keep them open. Familiarity breeds oblivion. When you see the same clutter all the time, you just stop seeing it. Make sure you look at your rooms, yard, car, closets,

(continued on page 43)

the Pros Know

In the realm of clutter-kicking tools, I know what works for me (see "My Top 11 Clutter-Kicking Tools" on page 36). But I wanted to know what a professional organizer—someone who's helped at least hundreds of people choose the best tools to de-clutter their homes and get their stuff orga-nized and contained—would recommend. Fortunately, Diane Albright, organizing expert and owner of All Bright Ideas (see page 48) in nearby Emmaus, Pennsylva-nia, agreed to share her expertise with all of us. Diane not only sells wonderful tools and organizing systems through her store and Web site (www.allbrightideas.com), she also consults with residential and business clients and teaches seminars on organizing and clutter control. I have been consistently impressed with Diane's tool selection over the years and originally discovered some of my own favorites, including ClickClacks and the showerhead organizer, in the All Bright Ideas store, so she was the first person I thought of when I started writing this chapter. I think you'll find her advice as useful and down-to-earth as I did!

Q: If someone's working their way into de-cluttering or getting organized and can't afford to do it all at once, how (or where) would you suggest that they start?

A: Getting organized does not necessarily mean that you'll need to spend money hiring a professional to work on the project—that is, if you are capable of doing it on your own. Nor does it mean buying containers or totes. As a matter of fact, getting organized should save you money because you will see what you already have and won't be buying duplicates or replacements when you can't find what you need.

The first step to getting organized is de-cluttering, so you can see what you have left to organize and store. After you have thoroughly de-cluttered, you may be surprised at how much you have pared down your belongings. If you find yourself in need of containers or totes to organize your belongings more efficiently, try reusing something you already have.

I recommend keeping a stash of containers or baskets that you no longer need. Keep this stash on a shelf in your basement or attic. Every time you need a storage container, browse your stash.

However, there are times that it is better to buy an organizing product than to try to use a makeshift one. If you aren't finding a container that suits your needs in your own stash, consider purchasing an item that is specifically made for that purpose.

Q: What do you consider the one essential big-ticket organizing tool, and why?

A: The most worthwhile item to invest in is a closet system. A closet typically has an enormous amount of wasted space. If designed correctly, a closet can easily double your storage space and save you significant time when you're searching for a particular item. Your redesigned closet does not need to be elaborate. If you shop around for a good-quality closet system that is designed for homeowner installation, you should be able to find one for under $300. You *do* need to make sure you are purchasing a quality system.

A standard closet in most homes is a 6-foot reach-in closet with one single rod and one shelf above it, providing 6 feet of long hanging space and 6 feet of shelf storage. Unfortunately, this type of closet does not maximize your storage space. With a good closet system, you can easily increase your storage space to 8 feet of hanging space for short items like shirts and skirts, 2 feet of hanging space for long items like dresses and bathrobes, and 14 feet of shelf storage space. To do it, remove the old system and install two 4-foot rods, one at 84 inches from the floor and the other at 42 inches from the floor. Also include a 2-foot rod for hanging long clothes, with two 2-foot shelves above it; an upper 6-foot shelf spanning the width of the closet at the top, and a 4-foot shelf above the bottom double hanging rod.

Q: What would you consider the most essential small organizing tools, and why?

A: I'd recommend these six small organizing tools for every home.

1. Every house should have a junk-drawer organizer (even though most houses have five junk drawers in the kitchen alone). By using a junk-drawer organizer, you have a place to toss paper clips, rubber bands, scissors, pens, pencils, erasers, and other small items. The ultimate junk-drawer organizer has a sliding top tray, giving you two tiers of compartments.

2. Always have a place to put your keys. It can be a wall plaque with hooks or a box you keep in a drawer or set out on a piece of furniture. You need somewhere to habitually put your keys so they're always in the same place.

3. If you have a family, a sales receipt storage box is a must. The ideal size is 4 by 6 by 6 inches deep. The box can be plastic or, if storage space is at a premium, you can use a decorative box that can be left out as part of your decor. Put index cards labeled from A to Z in the box so you can sort your receipts alphabetically. Just toss your receipt behind the alphabetical letter of the store name.

(continued)

the **Pros Know**

(cont.)

4. Use two coupon organizers—one for grocery store coupons and a separate one for restaurant and retail store coupons. The organizer for the restaurants and retail stores will need to accommodate a larger coupon. I recommend keeping both coupon organizers in your car—this way you won't forget them. If you walk into a store or restaurant without your coupon organizer, it is very easy to go out to the parking lot to retrieve the coupon rather than driving all the way home.

5. No tools required for this one: Put your spices in alphabetical order. The order doesn't have to be exact; instead, it can be a grouping of spices under each letter or group of letters ("A,B,C," and so on).

6. Buy a desktop file box, typically 12 inches wide by 10 inches high by 7 inches deep, to hold file folders for the papers you most frequently refer to throughout the week. You may have files such as "bills," "to do," and "to read," or special projects such as "house hunting" or "college search."

Q: **Do you have any tips you'd like to share with our readers on how to kick clutter or get more organized?**

A: The key to being organized is having a designated place for everything. So first designate "homes" for all your belongings, even socks with missing mates and mystery keys that unlock who-knows-what.

Next, institute "Clutter Patrol" in your household. "Clutter Patrol" is a daily designated time when your entire family puts away their belongings. Now you may laugh and say that the first patrol would take a few days. That may be true, but instead, start out with 20 minutes a night until it is down to 10 minutes or less. If you have five family members and each of you goes on "Clutter Patrol" for 10 minutes a day, that adds up to 50 minutes a day putting away clutter. You may need to motivate your family to go on "Clutter Patrol." Do what works best in your household: Postpone a privilege or add a privilege to inspire your family to get it done.

Q: **Finally, do you have any advice on how people can keep clutter from coming back?**

A: Once you have your home organized, you shouldn't need to have a big de-cluttering project ever again. Instead, keep a give-away box or bag in a convenient location like your garage or coat closet. Every time you discover something that doesn't fit or that you don't want, put it in the bag or box. Donate the contents to charity.

and other spaces with "fresh eyes"—a realtor's eyes, a guest's eyes, your boss's eyes, Martha Stewart's eyes, whatever works for you—and see what they'd see. It will help keep you sensitized, not just to the clutter that's there now, but to that insidious phenomenon, clutter creep.

[
Familiarity breeds oblivion.
Just because the clutter's been there
so long you don't even see it anymore
doesn't mean it's not still clutter.
]

CLUTTER-KICKING RESOURCES

Beyond individual tools, consider this section your clutter-kicking toolkit. You'll find links to clutter-fighting organizations; professional organizers; Web sites, stores, and catalogs full of great clutter-beating products; plus organizations and links that can help you offload clutter once you've isolated it from the rest of your stuff. If you have a computer with an Internet connection, you can go online and check out any of these resources that interest you right away. (Ah, the joys of instant gratification!) In case you don't, I've tried to provide a phone number and address (where possible) so you can still contact the ones you want to know more about. Bear in mind that most libraries provide Internet access, and the librarians would be happy to help you get online and explore Web sites if you feel uncomfortable venturing into computerland by yourself. Read on and see what's out there!

Organizations and Programs

If you do better when you have a support group or you're in a structured program, one of these organizations may be for you. Check them all out and see which one is most appealing—and most affordable. (Many are online groups, so it helps to have computer access.) Then try the one you like best and see if it works for you. If not, keep in mind that as with diets, you may have to try several before you hit on the right one. In any case, good luck!

The Clutter Diet
LivingOrder, Inc.
PO Box 40460
Austin, TX 78704
866-915-3438
www.clutterdiet.com
program works like a diet

Clutterers Anonymous
PO Box 91413
Los Angeles, CA 90009-1413
310-281-6064
www.clutterersanonymous.net
12-step support group

Clutterless Recovery Groups,
Inc.
5413 N. 32nd Street
McAllen, TX 78504-1560
512-351-4058
www.clutterless.org

FlyLady and Company, Inc.
www.flylady.net
*FlyLady Marla Cilley's
Web site; see also* Sink
Reflections, *page 52,
and "Tools of the Trade,"
page 237*

Messies Anonymous
5025 SW 114th Avenue
Miami, FL 33165
800-637-7292
www.messies.com
12-step support group

The National Study Group
on Chronic Disorganization
(NSGCD)
4728 Hedgemont Drive
St. Louis, MO 63128
314-416-2236
www.nsgcd.org
Clutter-Hoarding Scale

Organize Yourself Online
www.organizeyourself
online.com

Professional Organizers

These aren't individual organizers; they're organizations and groups of organizers who can refer you to an organizer in your area. Their sites often provide organizing tips, as well.

National Association of
Professional Organizers
(NAPO)
4700 West Lake Avenue
Glenview, IL 60025
847-375-4746
www.napo.net

The National Study Group
on Chronic Disorganization
(NSGCD)
4728 Hedgemont Drive
St. Louis, MO 63128
314-416-2236
www.nsgcd.org
*gives referrals to local
professional organizers*

www.OnlineOrganizing.com
PO Box 1942
Clinton, MD 20735
301-659-2203
www.onlineorganizing.com

Professional Organizers Web
Ring (POWR)
PO Box 298
Mt. Ephraim, NJ 08059
www.organizerswebring.com

Catalogs and Web Sites

You'll notice that I recommend many catalogs in this book. I'll confess that I'm a catalog junkie. I enjoy the adventure of browsing through catalogs, never knowing what I'll find on the next page. And the same is true of product-oriented Web sites, with their virtual catalogs. But the catalogs and Web sites I'm recommending here really do have wonderful furniture, tools, products, and organizing systems of all kinds that make it easier on you when you're trying to kick your clutter. If you have Internet access, you can go to the Web sites and browse, and then either buy if you find something you like (or want to get something I've recommended) or ask them to send you a catalog. Most of these companies also have stores in various locations. If you're lucky enough to live near one, you can go check out their wares in person. Store locations are listed in their catalogs and on their Web sites. If no street address is given here, it's a Web site– or catalog-only company.

As with everything else in this chapter, I'm sure there are many fantastic stores, catalogs, and Web sites I don't know about. If you don't see some of your favorites here, write them in the margins under the appropriate category so you'll have them right where you need them.

Closets

If you're trying to get your closets under control, look no further—these companies specialize in closet organization. Many offer free consultations, and many also have franchises or sell through other retailers across the country, so call or check the Web sites rather than going by the parent office's address. They may be closer than you think!

California Closets
1000 4th Street, Suite 800
San Rafael, CA 94901
800-274-6754
www.calclosets.com

Closet Factory
12800 S. Broadway
Los Angeles, CA 90061
800-634-9000
www.closetfactory.com

ClosetMaid
650 SW 27th Avenue
PO Box 4400
Ocala, FL 34474
800-227-8319
www.closetmaid.com

Closet Masters, Inc.
9515 Deerico Road, Suite 1012
Timonium, MD 21093
800-548-1868
www.closet-masters.com

Closets By Design
13151 South Western Avenue
Gardena, CA 90249
800-293-3744
www.closets-by-design.com

Contemporary Closets
19 Chapin Road, Building D
Pine Brook, NJ 07058
877-647-7331
www.contemporaryclosets.com

Easy Closets
19 Chapin Road, Building D
Pine Brook, NJ 07058
800-910-0129
www.easyclosets.com

Containers

We can all use some good containers, right? Check out these companies and see what they have to offer. You'll be amazed at the variety of containers that are available! Choose the ones that work for you.

Clares Closet
58 Noble Street
Kutztown, PA 19530
610-683-8112
www.shopatclares.com
eBay store: clares_closet

The Container Store
500 Freeport Parkway
Coppell, TX 75019
888-266-8246
www.containerstore.com

Organize.com
PO Box 2348
Riverside, CA 92516
800-600-9817
www.organize.com

Stacks & Stacks
1045 Hensley Street
Richmond, CA 94801
800-761-5222
www.stacksandstacks.com

Furnishings and Accessories

These companies also have containers but don't specialize in them like the companies listed in the "Containers" section. Look here for furniture designed specially for storage and all sorts of other intriguing and effective innovations. Don't forget to check their Web sites or catalogs for store locations near you.

Ballard Designs
5568 West Chester Road
West Chester, OH 45069
800-536-7551
www.ballarddesigns.com

Bed Bath & Beyond
650 Liberty Avenue
Union, NJ 07083
800-462-3966
www.bedbathandbeyond.com

Crate & Barrel
PO Box 3210
Naperville, IL 60566-7210
800-967-6696
www.crateandbarrel.com

Exposures
1 Memory Lane
PO Box 3615
Oshkosh, WI 54903-3615
800-222-4947
www.exposuresonline.com
  *albums and archival
  materials*

Frontgate
5666 West Chester Road
West Chester, OH 45069
888-263-9850
www.frontgate.com

Gaiam Living/Harmony
Gaiam, Inc.
360 Interlocken Boulevard,
  Suite 300
Broomfield, CO 80021
877-989-6321
www.gaiamliving.com

Home Decorators Collection
8920 Pershall Road
Hazelwood, MO 63042
877-537-8539
www.homedecorators.com

The Home Depot
8920 Paces Ferry Road NW
Atlanta, GA 30339
800-533-3199
www.homedepot.com

IKEA
498 W. Germantown Pike
Plymouth Meeting, PA 19462
www.ikea.com

Kitchen Accessories Unlimited
1136-1146 Stratford Avenue
Stratford, CT 06615
800-667-8721
www.kitchensource.com

L.L. Bean Home
Casco Street
Freeport, ME 04033
800-411-5713
www.llbean.com

The Lane Co., Inc.
Altavista, VA 24517
800-750-5263
  cedar chests

Lillian Vernon
100 Lillian Vernon Drive
Virginia Beach, VA 23479-
  0002
800-901-9291
www.lillianvernon.com

Linens 'n Things
6 Brighton Road
Clifton, NJ 07012
866-568-7578
www.lnt.com

Lowe's
1000 Lowe's Boulevard
Mooresville, NC 28117
www.lowes.com

Michaels, The Arts and Crafts
  Store
8000 Bent Branch Drive
Irving, TX 75063
800-642-4235
www.michaels.com

Moss
150 Greene Street
New York, NY 10012
866-888-6677
www.mossonline.com
  *individual pieces of china,
  flatware, and crystal*

NapaStyle
574 Gateway Drive
Napa, CA 94558
866-776-6272
www.napastyle.com

OXO International
C/O Helen of Troy
1 Helen of Troy Plaza
El Paso, TX 79912
800-545-4411
www.oxo.com
  kitchen organizers and tools

Pier 1 Imports
100 Pier 1 Place
Fort Worth, TX 76102
800-245-4595
www.pier1.com

Plow & Hearth
PO Box 6000
Madison, VA 22727-1600
800-494-7544
www.plowandhearth.com

Pottery Barn
3250 Van Ness Avenue
San Francisco, CA 94109
888-779-5176
www.potterybarn.com

Pottery Barn Kids
3250 Van Ness Avenue
San Francisco, CA 94109
800-993-4923
www.potterybarnkids.com

Shaker Workshops
PO Box 8001
Ashburnham, MA 01430-
  8001
800-840-9121
www.shakerworkshops.com

Sturbridge Yankee Workshop
90 Blueberry Road
Portland, ME 04102
800-343-1144
www.sturbridgeyankee.com

Target
1000 Nicollet Mall
Minneapolis, MN 55403
800-440-0680
www.target.com

Through the Country Door
1112 7th Avenue
Monroe, WI 53566-1364
800-341-9477
www.countrydoor.com

The Vermont Country Store
PO Box 6999
Rutland, VT 05702-6999
802-362-8460
www.vermontcountrystore.com

West Elm
3250 Van Ness Avenue
San Francisco, CA 94109
888-922-4119
www.westelm.com

Williams-Sonoma
Mail Order Department
PO Box 7456
San Francisco, CA 94120-7456
877-812-6235
www.williams-sonoma.com

Home Office

Try these companies first when you're looking for equipment and tools to organize your home office.

FileSolutions Filing Systems
PO Box 671295
Dallas, TX 75367
800-336-2046
www.filesolutions.com

FlyLady and Company, Inc.
Mail Order
703 N. Broad Street
Brevard, NC 28712
www.flylady.net
  "Office in a Bag" and "The Office Pack"

Kiplinger's Taming the Paper Tiger
The Monticello Corporation
4060 Peachtree Road, Suite D-339
Atlanta, GA 30319-3020
800-430-0794
www.thepapertiger.com
  software system

Office Depot
Corporate Support Center
2200 Old Germantown Road
Delray Beach, FL 33445
800-463-3768
www.officedepot.com

OfficeMax
3605 Warrensville Center Road
Shaker Heights, OH 44122
800-283-7674
www.officemax.com

OnlineOrganizing.com
PO Box 1942
Clinton, MD 20735
301-659-2203
www.onlineorganizing.com
  "Office-on-the-Go" System, a traveling "office" that fits in your car's trunk

Staples
500 Staples Drive
Framingham, MA 01702
800-378-2753
www.staples.com

Tax Tabs
PO Box 54513
Atlanta, GA 30308
www.onlineorganizing.com

Problem Solvers

These catalogs seem especially designed to solve homeowners' problems, including clutter, storage, and organizational issues. They're amazing!

Hammacher Schlemmer
147 E. 57th Street
New York, NY 10022
800-321-1484
www.hammacher.com

Herrington
3 Symmes Drive
Londonderry, NH 03053
800-903-2878
www.herringtoncatalog.com

Improvements
5566 West Chester Road
West Chester, OH 45069
800-634-9484
www.improvementscatalog.com

The Sharper Image
350 The Embarcadero, 6th
  Floor
San Francisco, CA 94105-1218
800-344-4444
www.sharperimage.com

Solutions
PO Box 6878
Portland, OR 97228
800-821-1282
www.solutions.com

Storage Systems

I discuss these storage systems, most of which are designed to cover entire walls and offer a range of customized storage options, in more detail in Chapter 15—Cleaning Out the Garage, beginning on page 311.

The Accessories Group (TAG)
1123 Delaware Street
Salem, VA 24153
866-404-8570
www.theaccessoriesgroup.com
  garage storage systems

All Bright Ideas
217 Main Street
Emmaus, PA 18049
866-632-8911
www.allbrightideas.com

Gladiator GarageWorks
Whirlpool Corporation
Benton Harbor, MI 49022
866-342-4089
www.gladiatorgw.com
  GearWall systems

Grid Iron
222 S. Promenade Avenue
Corona, CA 92879
800-486-4932
www.gridironusa.com

ONRAX
815 Houser Way N.,
  Suite C
Renton, WA 98055
866-637-8828
www.onrax.com
  overhead storage racks

ORG
Windquest Companies Inc.
3311 Windquest Drive
Holland, MI 49424
800-562-4257
www.home-org.com

Organize.com
PO Box 2348
Riverside, CA 92516
800-600-9817
www.organize.com

Racor Home Storage Products
102 S. 1st Avenue
Sandpoint, ID 83864
800-783-7725
www.racorinc.com

Rubbermaid Inc.
Attn: Consumer Service
3320 W. Market Street
Fairlawn, OH 44333-3306
888-895-2110
www.rubbermaid.com
  FastTrack system

SCHULTE Corporation
12115 Ellington Court
Cincinnati, OH 45249
800-669-3225
www.schultestorage.com

storeWALL
4119 W. Green Tree Road
Milwaukee, WI 53209
866-889-2502
www.storewall.com

Yard and Garden

I'm a *real* sucker when it comes to gardening catalogs! Here are some of my favorites for yard and garden clutter control and useful gadgets. (Just be glad I'm not listing all my favorite nursery and seed catalogs! That would be a book in itself.)

Cabela's
One Cabela Drive
Sidney, NE 69160
800-243-6626
www.cabelas.com

Charley's Greenhouse &
  Garden
17979 State Route 536
Mt. Vernon, WA 98273
800-322-4707
www.charleysgreenhouse.com

Gardener's Supply Company
128 Intervale Road
Burlington, VT 05401
800-876-5520
www.gardeners.com

Gardens Alive!
5100 Schenley Place
Lawrenceburg, IN 47025
513-354-1482
www.gardensalive.com

Growers Supply
1440 Field of Dreams Way
Dyersville, IA 52040
800-476-9715
www.growerssupply.com

Kinsman Company
PO Box 428
Pipersville, PA 18947
800-733-4146
www.kinsmangarden.com

Orvis
178 Conservation Way
Sunderland, VT 05250
888-235-9763
www.orvis.com

Smith & Hawken
PO Box 8690
Pueblo, CO 81008-9998
800-940-1170
www.smithandhawken.com

Worm's Way
7850 N. State Road 37
Bloomington, IN 47404
800-274-9676
www.wormsway.com

Donations, Barter, Junk Removal, Free Stuff, and Yard Sales

Do you have something to give away, sell, or trade? Or some stuff that's in such bad shape you'd just like someone to come haul it off? Not sure where to donate something? Start with these organizations. Some of them, like Earth 911, Just-Give, and Excess Access, specialize in matching donors with nonprofit organizations. Others accept specific types of donations. A few, including Craigslist, Freecycle, and Trashbank, encourage various sorts of barter, giveaways, and (in the case of Craigslist and Trashbank) sales. Got Junk and TrashBusters have hauling franchises across the country. And Winning Edge has resources for yard sales. Please don't assume that just because the organizations' headquarters are in particular places, the programs and services they offer aren't national in scope—they are! Check out their Web sites to see the extent of their outreach.

America's Second Harvest
35 E. Wacker Drive, #2000
Chicago, IL 60601
800-771-2303
www.secondharvest.org
  *the national food bank and
  food-rescue network*

BookEnds
6520 Platt Avenue #331
West Hills, CA 91307
818-716-1198
www.bookends.org
  children's books

Books for America
1417 22nd Street NW
Washington, DC 20037
202-835-2665
www.booksforamerica.org
  books

Career Gear
120 Broadway, 36th Floor
New York, NY 10271
212-577-6190
www.careergear.org
men's work clothes

Computers & Education
  Computer Recycling Center
1275 4th Street
Lockbox 200 PMB
Santa Rosa, CA 95404
888-887-3372
www.crc.org

Computers for Schools
  Program
3350 N. Kedzie Avenue
Chicago, IL 60618
800-939-6000
www.pcsforschools.org

Craigslist
60 Spear Street, 9th Floor
San Francisco, CA 94105
415-566-6394
www.craigslist.org
classified ads, barter, and
free stuff

Dress for Success
32 E. 31st Street, 7th Floor
New York, NY 10016
212-532-1922
www.dressforsuccess.org
women's work clothes

Earth 911
14646 N. Kierland Boulevard,
  Suite 100
Scottsdale, AZ 85254
480-889-2650
www.earth911.org

Excess Access
5813 Geary Boulevard, Box 111
San Francisco, CA 94121
415-242-6041
www.excessaccess.org

The Freecycle Network
PO Box 294
Tucson, AZ 85702
www.freecycle.org

Goodwill Industries
15810 Indianola Drive
Rockville, MD 20855
800-741-0186
www.goodwill.org

Got Junk
8th Floor, 1055 W. Hastings
  Street
Vancouver, BC V6E 2E9
Canada
800-468-5865
www.1800gotjunk.com
hauling service, franchises
across the United States

Habitat for Humanity
121 Habitat Street
Americus, GA 31709
229-924-6935, ext. 2551
www.habitat.org

Hear Now
The Starkey Hearing
  Foundation
6700 Washington Avenue S
Eden Prairie, MN 55344
800-648-2327
www.sotheworldmayhear.org/
  hearnow/
hearing aids

JustGive
312 Sutter Street, Suite 410
San Francisco, CA 94108
866-587-8448
www.justgive.org

Lion's Clubs International
  Headquarters
300 W. 22nd Street
Oak Brook, IL 60523-8842
630-571-5466
www.lionsclubs.org
eyeglasses

Pets 911
14646 N. Kierland Boulevard,
  Suite 100
Scottsdale, AZ 85254
480-889-2640
www.pets911.com
pet-related donations

Play It Again Sports
Winmark Corporation
4200 Dahlberg Drive, Suite 100
Minneapolis, MN 55422
800-567-6600
www.playitagainsports.com
used and new sporting
equipment

The Salvation Army National
  Headquarters
615 Slaters Lane
PO Box 269
Alexandria, VA 22313
800-958-7825
www.salvationarmyusa.org

Share the Technology
www.sharetechnology.org
online computer donation
service

TechSoup
435 Brannan Street, Suite 100
San Francisco, CA 94107
415-633-9300
www.techsoup.org/recycle
computers

Trashbank
www.trashbank.com
barter, sell, trade, or swap
online

TrashBusters Garbage and
  Trash Removal Service
PO Box 2530
Blaine, WA 98231-2530
800-743-6348
www.trashbusters.com
hauling service

Winning Edge
2440 Willow Glen Drive
Colorado Springs, CO 80920-
  1200
800-841-4248
www.win-edge.com/
  GarageSale.shtml
online garage sales expertise

The Women's Alliance
3745 NE 171st Street, Suite 62
Miami, FL 33160
305-762-6400
www.thewomensalliance.org
women's work clothes

eBay

Start with eBay's official site, then explore the other Web sites listed here to check out eBay drop-off stores, insider eBay selling tools, and eBay's official payment service, PayPal. (See Chapter 19—eBay and Other Online Auction Sites, beginning on page 372, for more links to online auction venues and drop-off stores.)

AuctionDrop
1355-B Adams Court
Menlo Park, CA 94055
650-470-6920
www.auctiondrop.com
eBay drop-off stores

Cool eBay Tools
www.coolebaytools.com
Web site of Marsha Collier,
author of eBay for Dummies
and many other eBay books

eBay Inc.
2145 Hamilton Avenue
San Jose, CA 95125
866-696-3229
www.ebay.com

iSold It
155 S. Highway 101 #7
Solana Beach, CA 92075
858-436-2800
www.i-soldit.com
eBay drop-off stores

PayPal
2211 N. 1st Street
San Jose, CA 95131
402-935-2050
www.paypal.com

QuikDrop International
3151 Airway Avenue, Suite M-3
Costa Mesa, CA 92626
714-429-1040
www.quikdrop.com
eBay drop-off stores

Antiques

If you have antiques and think they may be worth more than you could get from a consignment shop, an eBay auction, or even a local antiques store, check out these resources. Appraisers evaluate your antiques and estimate their worth. Christie's, Skinner, and Sotheby's are three of the premiere auction houses worldwide.

American Society of
Appraisers
555 Herndon Parkway,
Suite 125
Herndon, VA 20170
703-478-2228
www.appraisers.org

Antiques Roadshow Online
www.pbs.org/roadshow
antiques and show infor-
mation; links to appraisers

Appraisers Association of
America
386 Park Avenue S, Suite 2000
New York, NY 10016
212-889-5404, ext. 11
www.appraisersassoc.org

Auction Guide
www.auctionguide.com
online live auction locator

AuctionZip
www.auctionzip.com
online live auction locator

Christie's
20 Rockefeller Plaza
New York, NY 10020
212-636-2000
www.christies.com
antiques auctions

Guide to Auctions
www.guidetoauctions.com
links to auctions and auction
sites

Internet Auction List
www.internetauctionlist.com
list of online auction sites

New England Appraisers
Association
5 Gill Terrace
Ludlow, VT 05149
802-228-7444
www.newenglandappraisers.
net

Skinner, Inc.
63 Park Plaza
Boston, MA 02116
617-350-5400
www.skinnerinc.com
antiques auctions

Sotheby's
1334 York Avenue
New York, NY 10021
541-312-5682
www.sothebys.com
antiques auctions

GREAT CLUTTER-RELATED BOOKS

I love books. They're incredibly handy, useful references, and I turn to them first when I'm facing an especially challenging clutter problem. Here are some of my favorites. Once again, this list isn't meant to be comprehensive by any means—I'm sure there are plenty of great books out there that I'm not familiar with. And as you'll discover, I've recommended many topic-specific books, such as *eBay for Dummies,* in the chapters where they're relevant. The books listed here are the broad-based clutter-control books I own and use—my personal clutter library. Check them out and see if you want a few for your permanent collection!

Alexander, Skye. *10-Minute Clutter Control Room by Room.* Gloucester, MA: Fair Winds Press, 2005.

———. *10-Minute Clutter Control.* Gloucester, MA: Fair Winds Press, 2004.
> Skye is a feng shui master and brings her feng shui sensibility to clutter control—a great combination. Try Skye's quick tips, and see if they bring you feng shui benefits such as prosperity and good fortune as well as clutter control!

Aronson, Tara. *Mrs. Clean Jeans' Housekeeping with Kids.* Emmaus, PA: Rodale Books, 2004.
> When Tara, aka Mrs. Clean Jeans, wrote this book, she had a toddler, a preteen, and a teenager in the house. Lucky for her, she knew how to get them all (even 2-year-old Payne) to pitch in with the household chores. And lucky for us, she's shared her tips, rules, and chore lists (divided by age) with us. If you have kids (or grandkids), you need this book!

Aslett, Don. *Clutter's Last Stand,* 2nd ed. Avon, MA: Adams Media, 2005.
> Don Aslett has written an armful of cleaning and clutter-control books over the years, and I own several of them, but I've chosen to list this one as a great starting place mostly because I love the title so much. Don is the Dr. Phil of clutter control—he steps right up and tells you to get real about your mess and its cost to you in terms of time, money, and quality of life.

Baird, Lori, ed. *Cut the Clutter and Stow the Stuff.* Emmaus, PA: Rodale Books, 2002.
> This clutter classic is packed with tips. Lori and her team interviewed dozens of "everyday experts"—folks who use their hard-won wisdom every day—to come up with a wealth of practical information.

Cilley, Marla. *Sink Reflections.* New York: Bantam Books, 2002.
> Marla, aka FlyLady, sets forth her principles for changing your life and conquering clutter by learning her system for overcoming clutter and CHAOS (Can't Have Anyone Over Syndrome), starting with cleaning your sink (hence the book's title). For more on Marla, see "Organizations and Programs" on page 43 and "Tools of the Trade" on page 237.

Cobb, Linda. *The Queen of Clean Conquers Clutter.* New York: Pocket Books, 2002.
> Linda Cobb, the Queen of Clean, is one of my personal heroes. When it comes

to cleaning and laundry, she's been there, done that—*all* of that. So when Linda says something works—or doesn't work—I listen. In this book, the Queen turns her attention to clutter control, but you'll still find tons of great cleaning tips thrown into the mix. Enjoy!

Culbertson, Judi, and Marj Decker. *Scaling Down*. Emmaus, PA: Rodale Books, 2005.

Though aimed at people who are moving to smaller homes or retirement homes or who are helping their parents do so, this book offers wise, compassionate advice to anyone who's trying to kick their clutter. If you're having trouble letting go of your stuff—or need some help persuading your parents that it's time to release the death grip on their clutter—Judi and Marj will come to your rescue.

Koopersmith, Linda. *The Beverly Hills Organizer's Home Organizing Bible*. Gloucester, MA: Fair Winds Press, 2005.

Linda's approach to clutter control is unique, and it makes a ton of sense. Her book is organized like a cookbook, with step-by-step directions and photos, a list of essential tools, the degree of difficulty, and how long it takes for every organizing "recipe," so nothing is left to chance. The recipes break organizing down into manageable bites, so you won't be overwhelmed by the scope of the task. And after helping thousands of clients organize their homes, Linda knows all the best tools and shares them in her book.

Stewart, Martha. *Martha Stewart's Homekeeping Handbook*. New York: Clarkson Potter, 2006.

Leave it to Martha to produce the *Joy of Cooking* for the home. In addition to providing great organizing tips, she covers cleaning and maintaining every room in the house, with weekly, monthly, and seasonal checklists, as well as how to perform household repairs. While I'm talking about Martha, please check out *Martha Stewart Living* magazine's Web site, www.marthastewart.com, for tons of ingenious organizing tips.

ONWARD!

I hope you feel as if, at this point, you have all the resources you could possibly need to corral your clutter and organize every part of your house and yard. You may not be ready to use them yet, but it never hurts to order some catalogs (I'd start with the "Problem Solvers" on page 48) and start seeing what's out there. As you read the room-by-room tips in Part Two and yard and garden tips in Part Three, you can return to this chapter to get things you've decided you need. And all the resources I mention in Part Four, on how to unload your clutter, are here in one convenient place. But first, let's take in the big picture—a five-step plan to kick your clutter. Turn the page and start bringing your clutter under control right now!

Chapter 4

Five Simple Steps to Kick Your Clutter

Now that you know what's causing the clutter, how to evaluate your clutter, and what clutter-clearing tools are available, it's time to dig in! Follow these five simple steps, and you're on the way to a clutter-free life.

WHY STEPS?

Multistep programs aren't for everyone, and if you don't think they're for you, you can skip this chapter and move on to Part Two: Clutter-Kicking Room by Room. I'd suggest that you at least read through the chapter first, though, because it might give you some useful ideas as you tackle your own clutter problems.

For those who are open to them, step programs offer some real advantages: First, they give you a clear, straightforward plan of attack, so you know what you'll be doing every step of the way. (As one of my fellow fitness-club members remarked, "I just want to know that I'm doing it right!") Second, they break the plan into distinct phases, so you're not overwhelmed. And third, they pace the steps so that you move through the plan in logical order, from a motivating beginning to a triumphant end. You can review the plan anytime you need an overview, and if you faithfully stick to the program, you *will* get results. So look this one over, and if it makes sense to you, give it a try. You won't be sorry!

FIVE STEPS TO A CLUTTER-FREE LIFE

That's a big promise from just a few steps. But if you try them, you'll find that I'm not exaggerating. Let them help you break the bonds of clutter and start living clutter-free right now!

What are these miracle steps? We'll discuss each one in detail, but basically, they are:

1. **Get a contract**. Motivate yourself to kick the clutter out of your home and your life. Make a commitment to yourself to tackle your clutter problem once and for all—and stick to it!

2. **Get prioritized**. Decide which areas to tackle first, next, and so on, and make a priority list so you can check off each area as you move along, until you've finished the whole list.

5-Minute Fixes

In later chapters, you'll find "5-Minute Fixes" with quick fixes for different rooms. But this time, I'm talking about taking 5 minutes, or 10, or 15, instead of tackling an entire room at once. It's a lot easier to tackle your clutter if you break down each task into manageable chunks. After all, who has hours to spend sorting through stuff? And even if you did, who'd *want* to spend hours that way?

For example, think about taking down your Christmas ornaments. If you decorate the way I do, it seems to take as long to get those ornaments down and packed up as to perform all the other tasks of the Christmas season combined! Instead of working 'til you drop (and breaking a few heirloom ornaments in the process), you'll have a much easier time if you divide the chores over an entire week. One day, tidy away the things under the tree. Another day, take down the outside display. Then put away the ornaments on the tree. Then the lights. Then the other ornaments in the house. Then take out or put away the tree. And so on. Not only does this make the job more manageable, it also gives everyone a chance to say good-bye to the tree and ornaments for another year.

So pick a time limit based on your time constraints and the task at hand, and get going. Make sure you don't overshoot—if you can't keep up with the time commitments you make to yourself, you will get discouraged and won't stick with it. To keep track, you can set an alarm clock or kitchen timer. When you hear the ding, you know it's time to stop.

This is a good way to motivate your kids to pitch in, too. You can make it a game and see who gets the most done before the timer goes off. It's fun!

Remember how the exercise gurus say that working out in 10-minute increments spread throughout the day is just as effective as doing the entire workout at once? The same is true of a clutter-kicking "workout." And in both cases, if you stick to your workout because you're doing it bit by bit, it will be a lot more effective than if you try to do it all at once and then give up because it's too hard.

3. **Get started**. It's easy to get so caught up in planning the details that you never get around to actually de-cluttering. Instead, plunge in right away while your resolve is still strong. Once you start seeing how much better things look, how quickly you can make a difference, and how much better and more in control you feel, you'll keep on going!

4. **Get organized**. As you clear out each area, organize what's left so it looks great and it's easy to find everything. You'll get rid of the frustration and wasted time you experience every time you try to find stuff you know is in there (somewhere), only to give up and buy it again and again.
5. **Get rid of it**. Toss it, sell it, give it away—but get it out of there! Otherwise, it will just pile up somewhere else, and your sense of accomplishment will evaporate. Kick it out once and for all.

Let's look at the steps one by one and see how to go about them.

Get a Contract

By drawing up a clutter-kicking contract, you make a concrete commitment to getting out from under your clutter. A contract also helps you visualize the scope of your clutter-control needs. It also lets you set a time frame that will be there, staring you in the face in black and white (or blue and white) every day, reminding you that you need to get going—and keep going until the job's done.

What should your contract contain? A good contract should include these features:

❑ **The date.** You need to be able to see when you started kicking your clutter.

❑ **The agreement.** State clearly exactly what you intend to do and the date when you will finish.

❑ **The terms.** Break the process into manageable chunks, and set goal dates for those chunks. This gives you checkpoints to measure your progress and keeps you from waiting 'til the last minute to start.

❑ **The payoff.** Here's where you can assign yourself rewards to mark your progress. List the reward you'll give yourself for a job well done after each chunk is finished. And make sure you think of something really special to do for yourself when it's *all* done!

❑ **The sign-off.** Your signature and date make the contract official. You're making an important agreement with yourself here, so don't skip this step. It's a strong psychological reminder that you've literally signed on for the long haul.

— SAMPLE CLUTTER-KICKING CONTRACT —

Clutter-Kicking Contract

January 1, 2____

    I, _____, do hereby agree to go through every room in my house and systematically get rid of the clutter in each room, permanently removing any object that is not useful or valued and organizing the rest in an attractive, easy-to-find, easy-to-use manner on or before July 1, 2____.

    I will proceed in the following manner:

- By January 31, 2___, I will have reviewed each and every room in my house and made notes of the clutter in each room and what needs to be removed, as well as noting messiness that needs to be cleaned up and organized and potential furniture or equipment needed to control or contain the items I want to keep.
- By March 1, 2___, I will have de-cluttered and organized every room on the first floor of my house.
- By April 1, 2___, I will have de-cluttered and organized every room on the second floor of my house.
- By June 1, 2___, I will have de-cluttered and organized the attic and garage of my house.
- By July 1, 2___, I will have de-cluttered and organized the basement of my house.

In return for faithfully meeting these deadlines, I will reward myself as follows:

- On January 31, 2___, or within the following week, I will treat myself to a spa day.
- On March 1, 2___, or within the following week, my husband has agreed to take me to dinner at the restaurant of my choice, followed by the entertainment of my choice. This agreement is here signed and dated by him: _____
- On April 1, 2___, or within the following week, I will treat myself and two friends to a shopping day in New York.
- On June 1, 2___, or within the following week, my husband has agreed to treat the family to a week at the shore. This agreement is here signed and dated by him:

    _____

- On July 1, 2___, or within the following week, I will treat myself to the new appliance of my choice.

This agreement is hereby signed and witnessed by me:

_____ <Signature> _____ <Date>

─── MY CLUTTER-KICKING CONTRACT ───

Clutter-Kicking Contract

_____ <Date>

I, _____, do hereby agree to _____ on or before _____.

I will proceed in the following manner:

- By _____, I will have _____
_____.

- By _____, I will have _____
_____.

- By _____, I will have _____
_____.

- By _____, I will have _____
_____.

- By _____, I will have _____
_____.

In return for faithfully meeting these deadlines, I will reward myself as follows:

- On _____, or within _____, I will _____
_____.

- On _____, or within _____, I will _____
_____.

- On _____, or within _____, I will _____
_____.

- On _____, or within _____, I will _____
_____.

- On _____, or within _____, I will _____
_____.

This agreement is hereby signed and witnessed by me:

_____ <Signature> _____<Date>

A Quick Note on Worksheets

This book has been designed as an interactive workbook, so that it can help you work through your clutter. In addition to the contract on page 59, I've included sample worksheets in all the room-by-room and outdoor chapters so you can target each area where clutter has a foothold. I encourage you to make a clutter-kicking notebook with your own worksheets, so you'll have one easy-to-find reference for your clutter record and clutter-kicking strategies. But if you'd rather not write in the book, you can make photocopies of the workbook pages in each chapter. If you do use photocopies of sheets of paper for these exercises, I'd recommend that you create a "Clutter-Kicking Notebook" or folder where you can keep them together so they're easy to find when you need to refer to them. Otherwise, they may get scattered everywhere and simply create more clutter!

Check out the sample contract on page 58. Then photocopy the contract form on page 59 and write your own contract—or, if you'd like, write it right in the book! If you want your family to pitch in, discuss the idea of a contract with them and get them on board. Then you can have each person create his or her own clutter-kicking contract. Just make sure you read it closely before signing off, especially in regard to the tasks, deadlines, and, of course, rewards!

Get Prioritized

In clutter-kicking as in life, your priorities should reflect what really matters to you. And you absolutely *must* set them. Otherwise, if you're dealing with clutter in more than one room, you'll bog down and give up—guaranteed. But if you set your priorities based on what matters most to you—or what bothers you the most—and then follow them, you'll end up getting the job done. And you'll have the satisfaction of eliminating the most aggravating annoyances first!

You'll find a form on page 63 to use in setting down your priorities (you can make photocopies or work right in the book, if you prefer). But first, let's take a look at some typical priorities to jump-start your thinking:

- ❑ Clear out and straighten up the main entrance to the house.
- ❑ De-clutter the rooms visitors see most.
- ❑ Clear off the kitchen counters.
- ❑ Empty out the bedroom closet.
- ❑ Empty out and organize the hall closet.
- ❑ Pick up anything on the floor that's not supposed to be on the floor.
- ❑ Clean the clutter out of the car.
- ❑ Clear out the fridge.
- ❑ Take any outgrown clothes to Goodwill/the consignment shop/your cousin.
- ❑ De-clutter the main/kids'/guest bathroom.
- ❑ Make the guest bedroom look like a guest room, not a storage room.
- ❑ De-clutter your bedroom and make it look nice and inviting.
- ❑ Clean out the garage so there's actually room for cars.
- ❑ Tackle the piles of newspapers, magazines, and catalogs.
- ❑ Haul the expired/"we're never gonna eat this" food out of the pantry.
- ❑ Finish the first floor before starting on the rest of the house.

I'm sure you can think of plenty more. Obviously, in this case, we're talking about big priorities, the large-scale projects that will get you to your contract goals. There are also plenty of helpful small priorities, such as "Every day, I'll put three more things in the Salvation Army bag" or "Every day, I'll go through and recycle or give away one magazine or catalog." These small priorities will encourage you to keep kicking your clutter because you really will see the little things add up, and faster than you think. Even something like "Every day, I'll make sure there's no clutter on the stairs" or "Every day, I'll make sure the waste baskets are emptied" will make a big difference in how the house looks and how you feel about it.

Big or small, your priorities should reflect both your feelings and your situation. If paper pileup has reached mountainous proportions, dealing with it should go on your priority list. If cans and boxes fall on you every time you open the kitchen cabinets, dealing with that should be a priority. If you cringe at the thought of inviting friends over because of the state of your living room, put de-cluttering that on your priority list. If you're sick to death of shoveling through toothbrushes,

Make It Rewarding

I'm a big believer in rewards as motivation. It goes without saying that seeing an attractive, clutter-free drawer, room, or home is a reward in itself. But when you are faced with a dusty, dirty mess or feel like you should start kicking some clutter but really aren't in the mood, sometimes you just need something more.

Now, I'm not advocating a massive expenditure every time you toss a plastic bag or clean the refrigerator. I think the best rewards are in scale with the task accomplished. I also am not suggesting that you buy more stuff to re-clutter your newly cleared space! Instead, think of all those pleasures you enjoy but don't usually make time for, and pick one each time you need a reward. Here are a few examples to get you started:

❋ Light the candles and have wine with dinner.

❋ Get out a pretty vase and buy some fresh flowers to put on that newly cleared-off table.

❋ Before bed, take the time to actually *use* that luxurious foot cream you bought months ago or got as a gift.

❋ Treat yourself to the latest issue of a magazine you love but don't often indulge in. (But make a vow to pass it on after you've read it.)

❋ Get some great DVDs and popcorn and invite some friends over for a "girls' (or guys') night in."

❋ Get your car washed, waxed, and vacuumed.

❋ Make the time to go to a concert or a game.

❋ Have your favorite jewelry cleaned.

You can bet I use this tactic on myself when I want to get going! As you might guess, I love to write. But to make sure I keep going, I choose a little reward for myself at the end of every chapter. When I've finished, I "collect" my reward for what I hope is a job well done!

toothpaste tubes, and other bathroom detritus to clear off enough counter space to set down a hairbrush, put the counter on your list. Make it work with your needs.

Thinking about what areas to tackle first also helps put your overall clutter situation in clear focus. You may be so inspired that you'll make lists of second- and third-tier priorities, and once you do, you'll have your clutter-kicking checklist set and ready to go!

My Clutter-Kicking Priority List

❏ _____
❏ _____
❏ _____
❏ _____
❏ _____
❏ _____
❏ _____
❏ _____
❏ _____
❏ _____
❏ _____
❏ _____
❏ _____
❏ _____
❏ _____
❏ _____
❏ _____
❏ _____

Get Started

You'll never finish kicking your clutter if you never get started. And as we all know, it's easy to procrastinate, fixating on something or other and telling ourselves that "we'll start de-cluttering as soon as . . . ." Uh-huh.

Rather than waiting, start doing something, anything, to clear out some of your clutter *now*. (Well, when you finish reading this chapter, anyway.) The "5-Minute Fixes" you will find will help you jump-start the process. Look there to find suggestions for fast things you can do to start getting your clutter under control room by room. Just tossing a few almost-empty shampoo bottles into the recycling can give you the lift you need to keep going—because you'll see the difference even something that small can make.

Get Organized

Okay, I know it's not as easy to get organized as it is to get started, or even to write your Clutter-Kicking Contract or your Clutter-Kicking Priority List. But take heart: You don't have to organize until you've kicked the clutter.

That's the plus side. The minus side is that you *do* have to organize every single time you kick some clutter—or you'll just end up in a hopeless mess again.

The secret is to organize as you go along. That's what keeps the task manageable. Once you've cleared out a drawer in the bathroom, organize what you've kept so you know what's in there and can find it easily. Same for your underwear drawer, pantry shelf, and shoe rack.

Shoe rack, you say? Ha! You think you had one of those at one point, but you haven't seen it in years. In fact, you haven't seen the closet floor in years. Well, don't despair. Once you've gotten rid of old, damaged, and beat-up shoes, not to mention shoes you never actually wear, shoes that don't fit, and shoes you don't like, you'll find that there are a whole lot fewer to organize. And if, as it happens, you *don't* have a shoe rack—or a shampoo holder, or some other gadget that will make organizing your stuff a whole lot simpler—turn back to Chapter 3—Tooling Up (beginning on page 35) and remind yourself what's out there. Check the "Tools of the Trade" features in upcoming chapters, too. Remember, the right tools can be better—and cheaper!—than a good professional organizer.

5-Minute Fixes

Here are five things you can get rid of right now to put yourself on the fast track to a clutter-free life. They may not seem like much—which is the point—but they will make a difference. Every little bit helps!

1 Toss out every pair of snagged, run, or otherwise beat-up pantyhose you own.

2 Toss out every stubby pencil and dried-up pen you can get your hands on.

3 Toss that broken umbrella you've been keeping "just in case."

4 Empty and recycle those dusty, musty old spice bottles that have been hanging around for the past decade.

5 Recycle all the duplicate catalogs that have gotten buried in piles of mail, magazines, and other "someday" reading.

Think of how good it will feel to actually know what you have and where it is. Instead of spending precious time looking for things, you could spend it on something you enjoy—or actually need to do. You'll be able to see right away if you need to replace something. (If all your umbrellas are broken or none of your dress shoes fit comfortably, it's time to buy that one new umbrella or one new pair of heels that works for you.) Have you ever been in the position of buying something you think you already have—you're *sure* you already have, and you actually have a suspicion you have several of—but you can't find it anywhere? Well, once you get organized, you'll never have to go through that embarrassment, frustration, and waste of time and money again. So, make a vow to yourself right now:

> The Organizing Vow: Every single time I clear out any clutter, I will not consider the job done until I've organized the things that are left so they're easy to find and use.

Every time, every single time you clear out any clutter, be it just recycling those duplicate catalogs or tossing outdated coupons, you will not consider the task finished until you've put what's left in good and logical order. And remind yourself of your vow as you go through all the chapters in Part Two: Clutter-Kicking Room by Room (beginning on page 69). If it will help you stay focused, write your vow on a few sticky notes and put one on the refrigerator, one on the bathroom mirror, one on your closet door, one on the dashboard of your car, and anywhere else you see often.

Don't overlook the organizing step. It's every bit as important as getting rid of the clutter. Because, after all, anything that's messy and disorganized is, by its very nature, clutter!

Get Rid of It

You've dutifully cleared out the kids' closets and drawers and amassed three big garbage bags of beat-up, despised, and outgrown stuff for Goodwill. Good for you! But there's a problem: Those big bags are still sitting by the front door 3 weeks later.

[Collected clutter is still clutter as long as it's still sitting around.]

It may seem obvious, but it bears repeating: Collected clutter is still clutter as long as it's still sitting around.

I'm a huge fan of reuse, and I've devoted an entire section of this book—Part Four: Trash (Yours) to Treasure (Theirs), beginning on page 349—to telling you all the ways you can donate, recycle, and sell your former clutter. But I will say this loud and clear: If you know for a fact that, with the best intentions or otherwise, you will not get that collected clutter out the door if it means taking it someplace farther than the trash can, *throw it out.*

It may seem like a shame, or even a crime, when the Salvation Army is 10 miles down the road or you think your cousin John could use that trench coat or clunky old grill. But if you've tried to take stuff away before and found that final step overwhelming, and if you can't think of a zealous friend or sibling who'd actually enjoy doing it for you, it's better to put it out for the trash than not to put it out at

Dear Claire,

What about regifting? Isn't that a good way to get rid of stuff you don't like (not to mention the money you'll save on gift purchases)?

—Thrifty Giver

Dear Thrifty,

Regifting is fine as long as you know that the person you're giving the item to would *really* like it. Be honest about this: If you're not absolutely sure they'd want it, "regift" it to Goodwill instead. And remember the two drawbacks of regifting: First, you'll need to keep track so you don't inadvertently regift something to its original giver or anyone he or she knows. And second, if the gift is not your taste and you pass it on to someone else, don't be surprised if you start getting things like it from that person in the future. After all, you must have loved it or you wouldn't have given it to them!

My own favorite form of regifting is to have a gag gift that circulates among family and friends year after year. In my case, a dear friend had come upon—in a junk shop, appropriately enough—a large, hideous bird ornament with gaudily dyed real feathers. That Christmas, the bird materialized in another friend's pile of packages; the following year, it returned to its original purchaser; the next year, his sister was the lucky recipient; and so it went. Of course, he made sure the joke was obvious and got real presents for the recipients, as well. It was fun to speculate about who'd be getting "the bird" for Christmas!

Good luck,
Claire

all. (And who knows? Maybe somebody will be passing by and decide to "collect" it for themselves!)

Of course, I'd feel a lot better—and I think you would, too—if you recycled, gave away, donated, or sold your excess stuff. Think how great it would be to get that check from the eBay store or the consignment shop, hand over your donations list to your accountant to reduce that tax bite, or see your sister's face light up when you give her the sweater she's always admired and you haven't (ahem) been able to squeeze into for years.

the **Pros Know**

Every now and then, you need a good talking to. Psychologists, motivational speakers, and life coaches all know that the way you think about and talk about a challenge influences the outcome. As they say, if you think you can't do it, you're probably right. You'll find yourself getting a lot more from your clutter-kicking efforts—maybe even enjoying them!—and you'll find it easier to keep going if you can catch negative-speak in the act and replace it with something positive.

For example, let's say you're confronting a chaotic, cluttered closet with the attitude of, "I'll never get this mess cleaned out!" After working in there 'til you're exhausted, you look at the stuff still to be dealt with and you think, "See? I *knew* I could never do it!" What will you be most likely to do next—keep at it or shut the door on the problem and eat a bag of potato chips?

Now suppose you confronted that same chaotic, cluttered closet and said to yourself, "Let's see what I can do here in 10 minutes." At the end of 10 minutes, you'd say to yourself, "I've found six pieces of clothing and a pair of shoes that I can bag for the Salvation Army. That's made some space in here. I'll do another 10 minutes this afternoon and see if I can add to the bag or find some better clothes for the consignment shop."

Who's more likely to end up kicking their clutter, the can't-do you or the will-do you?

ONWARD!

Now that you know the Five Steps to a Clutter-Free Life, it's time to really get your feet wet. In the next section, Clutter-Kicking Room by Room, you'll find hundreds of ways to conquer and contain clutter in every part of the house. So pick a room, any room . . . and let's go!

PART TWO

Clutter-Kicking Room by Room

Chapter 5

Incoming Clutter

HALLS, STAIRS, MUDROOMS, AND DOORWAYS

It's all too easy for stuff to stop coming into the house as soon as it starts. And when your entryways turn into drop-off sites, the result is a pileup of bags, backpacks, shoes, umbrellas, gear, coats, and other paraphernalia just inside every door and spilling down every hall (not to mention up the steps). Eventually you're picking (or tripping) your way among piles of clutter, trying to find enough bare space to set down your keys, never mind your purse or coat. What a way to say "Welcome home!" Use the tips in this chapter to get the clutter up and out (of sight, anyway).

PRIORITIES FOR ENTRYWAYS

Unless you have so little stuff cluttering your entryways that 10 minutes of straightening will tidy it all away, you should begin clearing the entries to your home by setting some clutter-kicking priorities. Set your priorities by first focusing on what matters most to you about how the entryway looks. Then keep moving along to what matters least. The best way to do this is to take a good, hard look at the "before" state of the room and then visualize the "after."

An Entryway Visualization

To get to the "after" of your entry, you need to start with the "before"—the way things look right now. So get out some paper or use the "My Entryway—Before" form (or make a photocopy of it and write on that). Write down every place around the entrances to your home where there's clutter, and note what that clutter is. It might help to remember the Love It–Lose It Spectrum (see page 26) as you consider what needs to go. Go on—you can do it!

Once you've jotted down an inventory of the clutter in your entryway, it's time to move on to the "after"—what you want to happen and in what order. To get there, describe how you want the room or area to look when you've kicked the clutter. As a reality check, make sure you look at the room every few minutes while you're doing this.

Your description can be short and to the point: I don't want to see coats piled on all the chairs; piles of keys, change, and other stuff spilling over the hall table and onto the floor; and kids' toys, dogs' toys, and shoes scattered all over the floor. I'd like an entry that looks clean and welcoming. I'd like a place to put my keys and I'd like to easily find the day's mail. I want a place to showcase my antique table (or bench, or a painting or vase). I need an easy-to-see place for boots and umbrellas.

If you want, you can make a detailed picture of exactly how you'd like your room to look if it were perfect (for you). You can picture the colors of the walls and what would be on them, the rugs, furniture, flooring—everything. Write it all down on a piece of paper or on the "My Entryway—After" form—or on as many photocopies of it as you need to do it justice. (If you use photocopies, keep them all together in a "clutter" file so you can refer back when you need them.)

Getting There

Now that you've captured your entryway's "before" condition (including all the specifics) and you've imagined its "after" appearance, you can finally set priorities that will let you get there from here. Again, bearing both "before" and "after" in mind, I'd recommend starting with what bothers you most about the "before" condition and working down from there to make a list of what needs to be done.

My Entryway—Before

_____
_____
_____
_____
_____
_____
_____
_____
_____
_____
_____

My Entryway—After

_____
_____
_____
_____
_____
_____
_____
_____
_____
_____
_____

My Entryway Priority List

_____

_____

_____

_____

_____

_____

_____

_____

Maybe you're concerned that toys, bags, and other stuff on the stairway poses a tripping hazard and you want it cleared up first. Or you're sick of having your floors ruined by wet, dripping shoes. Or you want to scream every time you even think about cleaning up those muddy shoe and paw prints. Or you'd really like to be able to sit down on a chair—without having to shovel coats and backpacks off it first—to take off your boots on a rainy day.

Get your priorities straight by writing down whatever's driving you to distraction on the "My Entryway Priority List" (or photocopy it, if you'd prefer). Work in descending order from most to least maddening. Once you've finished, you can turn to the tips below to find ingenious ways of dealing with each problem.

THE ENTRYWAY TIPS

Now it's time to get your hands dirty. Dig into whichever tips appeal to you or suit your circumstances, and bid hallway and mudroom clutter good-bye.

Table it. When you come in the door, you pile all the loose stuff on the nearest surface: keys, cell phone, sunglasses, purse or billfold, cigarettes, chewing gum, mail, gloves, dog treats, change—whatever it is, down it goes. And it may keep going down, all over the floor or under furniture, never to be seen again, as each member of the family dumps their stuff on top of yours when *they* come in. You'll have a better chance of keeping everything together if you put a table near the door where everybody has room to dump their stuff. If it's a butler's table with a raised edge around the outside, so much the better—nothing can slide or roll off.

Add a basket. Better yet, add several low, open, square or rectangular baskets to your hall table. Label or color-code one basket for each family member so they can put their own change, sunglasses, mail, and the like in it. The table will look a lot neater, and you'll cut down on fighting. ("That's *my* quarter!")

Don't forget Fideaux. If you have a canine companion, you know that there's little chance of getting in or out the door without an enthusiastic greeting. You'll probably have a package of mini-treats, maybe a clicker (a popular obedience tool), and a toy or two adding to the hallway clutter. If it's also the door he uses to go in and out, there'll be at least one leash and possibly an electric-fence collar and "zapper" as well. So why not give him his own labeled or color-coded basket? Then everyone will know where to find his stuff. Just make sure it's out of his reach!

Box it up. An assortment of attractive wooden, lacquer, or toile boxes can also contain the tabletop clutter. If they have tops, everybody's stuff will be both contained and out of sight.

Take a tip from the kitchen. Rather than a box or basket, use a decorative utensil organizer to hold tabletop clutter. I've seen some really attractive wicker and cane versions. The dividers are just the thing for containing wallets, cell phones, sunglasses, and mail.

👍 Love It *or* Lose It? 👎

What about hat racks, coat trees, hall trees—whatever you prefer to call those Victorian footed stands with branched arms at the top to hold outerwear? At first glance, they may seem like a space-saving solution for corralling coats, scarves, hats, raingear, umbrellas, and other outerwear. But I'd think twice before you rush out to buy one. Instead, picture what that rack will look like laden down with, most likely, several layers of everybody's stuff. It may look like an organizing solution to some, but it just looks like more clutter to me.

Verdict: Lose it!

5-Minute Fixes for Entries and Exits

Here are five fast ways to jump into controlling clutter in entryways. Once you see how much you can accomplish in 5 minutes, you'll be energized and confident enough to tackle some bigger projects.

Start with a stand. An umbrella stand, that is. These old-fashioned ceramic, metal, wooden, or bamboo cylinders once stood in every home's entryway, and they're still available for very reasonable prices at flea markets and antique stores across the country. I recommend a ceramic stand, since wet umbrellas won't rot or rust them. You'll be surprised by how many umbrellas they hold—all upright for easy grabbing. They also work to neatly contain other upright objects like baseball bats and brooms.

Take a tip from the Shakers. The ever-practical Shakers installed strips of wooden pegs in their halls for hanging their coats, capes, and hats. If you do the same, your family and guests can hang up coats, backpacks, purses, and the like when they come in the door, and everything will be easy to see and grab when it's time to go back out. Pegs make hanging almost two-dimensional, unlike a space-eating coat rack. (Not to mention that coat racks look hideous once you hang coats on them.) You can order peg racks by mail from Shaker Workshops (see page 47) or buy them from your local home store.

Box your boots. Nothing says clutter—or maybe that's "squalor"—like a pile of wet, muddy, or otherwise grungy footwear by the door. Not to mention all the mud, melting snow, grass stains, and other tracked-in stuff all over the floor. But

Hang your keys. I know—in "5-Minute Fixes for Entries and Exits" I said that hanging keys look unsightly, but there are ways to make it work and preserve the aesthetics of your entryway. Keep keys from becoming clutter by putting a small bulletin board, corkboard, pegboard, or square of wood on your wall and attaching hooks for the household and car keys. You can also buy key holders ready-made from accessories shops. Keep everybody's straight by using the color-coders or personalizers you can slip over the backs of keys (you can find them at any hardware store), by making sure everybody has distinctive key chains (mine is hot pink and has a compass and mini-flashlight attached), or by putting labels under each hook. Make sure the key board is out of reach of small hands. And needless fortunately, some ingenious companies have come up with wonderful rectangular shoe-and-boot organizers that will keep that footwear in line (literally). They are durable, come in several sizes, and even feature optional rubber inserts so water can drain right through and your boots and shoes can dry faster. You can find them in mail-order catalogs like Smith & Hawken, Plow & Hearth, and Gardener's Supply Company (see pages 47 and 49). Your entryway or mudroom will look much neater (and stay much cleaner) if you get a boot box and insist that your family use it.

Buy a hall bench. These are available with a seat that lifts up to reveal a storage compartment underneath, or with rectangular storage baskets that fit neatly in place under the seat. You can stash mittens, gloves, scarves, and other outdoor essentials within easy reach but out of sight—and create welcome seating in your hall or mudroom. And they're so much neater and more attractive than a mass of knitwear all over the place. I see these offered in mail-order catalogs all the time. These convenient benches serve double duty as seating and storage—a good idea!

Try a silver salver. Or something similar that suits your taste or matches your decor. Why? To hold keys and other car-related clutter that often gets spilled out all over the closest surface to the door. Yuck! Hanging keys up on a rack is just as unsightly, unless it's in the garage, so make sure you keep a covered container on the hall table that's big enough to hold keys, sunglasses, and the occasional wallet.

to say, don't put your keys where they can be seen from outside! Make sure your curtains or blinds hide the key board from view from the door and windows, or put it where a cabinet, clock, mirror, or picture blocks it from view. Better safe than sorry!

Get a key cabinet. A small wall cabinet is a decorative way to keep keys within easy reach and organized but out of sight. Attach hooks to the inside back for the keys.

Clock it. A grandfather clock can add elegance to an entrance, but working grandfather clocks—whether new or antique—are pricey. Instead, look for a "gutted" one at a flea market, junk shop, or secondhand store, and use it to control

SANITY SAVERS

The entryway your family uses most is the best place to locate essential things that everyone uses. The problem is, you want them to be easily accessible, but you *don't* want them to turn into yet more clutter. The solution is to give each item its own attractive, easy-access place. Then, as each family member passes through, they can check to see if there's anything for them. Here are some ideas:

✳ A "Lost and Found" bin, box, or basket. Whether it's a misplaced button or sock, a CD case, reading glasses, a homework assignment, or a toy, if everyone knows to put straying items in the Lost and Found and everyone knows to look for them there, you will cut down on a lot of wasted time and annoying whining.

✳ A "Post Office." This should have separate sections for incoming and outgoing mail and be placed where the family has easy access but addresses can't be seen from the door or windows. If you have a space for stamps and self-sticking address labels, it will be easy for everyone to make sure the outgoing mail is ready to go (or for you to do it if they forget). It'll be easy to see when it's time to buy stamps, too.

✳ A "Happy Returns" bin, basket, or shelf for library books, DVDs, borrowed toys, magazines, and anything else that needs to go back whence it came. Say good-bye to late fees!

Success with the Lost and Found bin, the Post Office, and Happy Returns depends on everyone knowing where they are and what they're for, and agreeing to use them. Make it happen!

hallway clutter. The clock will be as handsome as a functioning model, and you can put hooks in the empty case for scarves, purses, leashes, and the like. You can also use the tall, narrow space inside the case for baseball bats, hockey sticks, golf clubs, or fishing rods.

Get the skinny. Sometimes the only storage space available is beside the door—and since hallways are often narrow, there's not a lot of width to work with. In this case, a tall, narrow cabinet—known as a chimney cupboard because it's shaped like a chimney—can be a clutter-kicker's best friend. Tuck it beside the door (or place one on each side of the door), and you'll have shelf space for mittens, scarves, earmuffs, sweaters, purses, travel umbrellas, hats, a box of tissues, and the like. There will even be space for a basket or box for keys, cell phones, change, mints, hand sanitizers, hand lotion, and other items that always seem to escape as soon as they're put down. And the bottom's big enough for attaché and computer cases.

Borrow a bookcase. Another tall, skinny option is a narrow bookcase. On the plus side, you can see at a glance what's on the shelves. On the minus side, you can see at a glance what's on the shelves. It will be off the floor, but if it's not attractively organized, it can still look like clutter. Assigning shelves for like items—all hats on one shelf, a to-be-returned shelf for library books and DVDs—is one way to make your stuff look orderly.

Add a shelf. Instead of simply installing a plain strip of pegs—which is actually pretty decorative in its own right—you might consider a peg shelf, which is exactly what it sounds like: a strip of pegs with a shelf on top to display ornaments or hold boxes, baskets, and so on. Shaker Workshops (see page 47) makes these in a range of lengths, and they're as beautiful as they are functional. You can also get more contemporary-looking versions from L.L. Bean (see page 46) with a shelf, hooks, and cubbies, and from Sturbridge Yankee Workshop (see page 47), with pegs, two shelves, and rectangular baskets to hold bills, keys, and the like. I'm sure there are many more.

Walk up to a wine rack. Wooden wine racks can make great, attractive, off-the-floor shoe storage, with a shoe in each bottle opening. I've found used wine racks in perfect shape many a time at Goodwill, the Salvation Army, and the Society of St. Vincent de Paul—usually for less than $4!

KID-FRIENDLY CLUTTER CONTROL

It's not rocket science to realize that kids won't hang up their stuff if they can't reach the hangers. Just as you want to put adults-only stuff like keys up high out of little ones' reach, if you want your kids to be responsible for putting up and taking down their outerwear and gear, make sure it's easy for them to do. Get a second strip of Shaker pegboard and put it at chair-rail height, or attach a strip of wood with decorative but durable blunt-ended hooks (brass hooks work well).

Dress it up. If you have room, a dresser is a great place for out-of-sight hall storage. (I have one in my mudroom that I found beside the dumpster at a long-ago apartment. I dressed it up with paint, and now I use it to hold tools and supplies.) If you put a dresser in your hallway, make sure its style suits your decor. Dressers are, of course, ideal for sweaters, scarves, mittens, hats, and the like—as long as they're dry—but can also be used to hold briefcases and computer cases, paper, and backpacks, too.

Wash it up. My editor Anne recommends putting an old-fashioned washstand in the hall. They're great for smaller halls because they take up so little space, and they add a stylish touch, too. "I had one in my house in Allentown that I wish I still had!" Anne says.

Screen it. What could be more attractive than a decorative folding screen in a corner at the end of your hall? And no one needs to know that it's literally screening anything from storage shelves and sports equipment to your recycling. As before, use a decorator's eye when choosing the screen—try a light color like natural wicker or rattan if the hallway's dark, or perhaps a Japanese lacquer screen in an art nouveau house. You can often find screen frames that have lost some or all of their screening. If you are handy or know an upholsterer or someone who's good at alterations, look for these screenless screens at bargain prices at flea markets, yard sales, and junk shops. You can put curtains or upholstery fabric on them, and voilà! No one outside the family needs to know what's behind curtain number three.

Use some kitchen leftovers. If you're remodeling your kitchen, hang one or more of the old cabinets in your mudroom for storage. They're roomy and useful. Obviously, you wouldn't want to put kitchen cabinets in an entrance hall, but a mudroom or other informal entrance is the perfect place for this sturdy, roomy, *free* storage unit. No remodeling plans? See if any of your friends or co-workers are remodeling, and offer to pick up and haul the cabinets away. Or check flea markets and secondhand home shops, or place an ad on www.craigslist.com or another local service for bargains.

Try the medicine cabinet. If you happen to be redoing the bathroom instead of the kitchen, consider using your old medicine cabinet in an informal family entryway. Not only will it have a mirror so people can check themselves out on the way out the door, but the handy shelves inside will hold tissues, gum, cough drops, breath mints, bandages, hand lotion, hand sanitizers, and anything else that's likely to be in demand on the way in or out.

Hope for a hope chest. A blanket chest makes a wonderful storage bin for sweaters, coats, hats, scarves, and mittens. It's decorative, so it will look good in your entryway. If you don't have a door at the end of the hall, you can set it against the wall there as a focal point. You could even place decorative cushions on top so people can use it as a bench if they need to sit down to remove outerwear or shoes (but try it first—very carefully!—to make sure the chest will take the added weight). Or try a trunk for storage in your entryway.

👍 Love It *or* Lose It? 👎

A hall wastebasket seems so obvious, but I can't say I've ever seen one in anybody's entrance hall. But think about it. A hall wastebasket. People are coming into your house. They have wrappers, empty bottles, tissues, bags, receipts, who knows what. What could be more logical than putting a wastebasket in your entryway so family and guests can toss their trash as they come in? It's the perfect place to unload unwanted mail, too—as soon as you get it inside. Of course, you don't want the wastebasket to look like another piece of unsightly clutter, so get one that matches your decor, and empty it regularly. Tuck it under a hall table to make it more inconspicuous. If everyone enters your house on all but formal occasions through a mudroom, the garage, or the deck door, you can set up a three-bin system for trash, recycling, and shredding. But if you do, think about color-coding the bins as well as using readable labels.

Verdict: Love it!

Add an armoire. If you have a spacious entryway but no hall closet for your family's and guests' outerwear, take a tip from our ancestors and use an armoire. These large, spacious freestanding clothes closets were in vogue in the days before houses had built-in closets. They're roomy enough for outerwear and decorative enough for display.

Aim for the moon. A demilune ("half-moon") table, that is. These rectangular tables fit flat against the wall but are rounded in front, making them perfect for entry halls because no one will get hooked by a corner as they pass by.

Go back to school. They were ugly, all right, but those school lockers sure held a lot of gear. You can put up your own metal lockers in a mudroom or secondary entry if you want to, but fortunately, you also have more attractive alternatives. For example, L.L. Bean (see page 46) now offers a wooden "Mudroom Locker" in a variety of bright colors. It comes with adjustable shelves, jacket hooks, behind-closed-door storage cabinets, and containers to collect loose odds and ends.

Set out a secretary. Not a live one, of course. (You wish.) You can now find small secretaries, aka drop-front desks, in home stores and catalogs. They are small enough to tuck against the back wall of the hallway and will hide mail, rubber bands, keys, and all the other doodads of coming and going behind the raised front, which turns into a writing desktop or organizing station when it folds down. There's a drawer, too, for even more storage options. L.L. Bean (see page 46) even offers one with a book rack at the bottom. A great place for those borrowed library books and DVDs!

Watch those cords. Lamp cords are the worst kind of clutter in an entryway

👍 Love It *or* Lose It? 👎

What about plant stands? They're attractive, affordable, and they certainly don't take up much space. My feelings about them are split: If you want to display a vase or other decorative object or add some life to your entryway with live plants, I think they're great. (Just keep them out of the line of traffic.) But as clutter-controllers, their surfaces are too small to do much more than hold one purse—precariously, at that.

Verdict: Love it for plants; lose it for clutter control.

because they're tripping hazards and can cause lamp breakage as well as bone breakage. Floor lamps pose a double hazard, since, even without the cord issue, they're easy to knock over as people go in and out with parcels or pets and kids race heedlessly through the hall. So skip the floor lamps in your entryways—unless you have a live butler to preside over comings and goings. Instead, opt for ceiling or wall lighting. If you want to put a lamp on your table or on another piece of furniture, make sure the piece of furniture is securely against the wall and the cord runs down behind it, where it's out of tripping (and chewing) reach.

Keep steps clear. Cat toys, cups and saucers, dirty clothes, games, shoes, grocery bags, mail—all sorts of stuff can end up on the stairs. And that's not just unsightly, it's also dangerous. Make keeping all your stairways clutter-free a priority, and make sure it's a priority for everybody else in the household, too (except, of course, the cats). See "Tools of the Trade" for a handy gadget that can help you.

Go belowstairs. If your staircase has either open space below it or a door under it, you can use the space for storage. If it has a door, it's as good as a mini-attic— and a great place for storing holiday ornaments and other things that are used seasonally and then stored. If it's open space, you'll need to put attractive storage containers under it, since people will be able to see inside. Low shelves with decorative rectangular baskets are one option; wicker hampers are another; decorative

the *Pros* **Know**

Linda Cobb, the wonderfully practical and entertaining Queen of Clean, has a great idea for keeping clutter from creeping back into your entryways once you've succeeded in kicking it out. In her book *The Queen of Clean Conquers Clutter*, she recommends a practice she calls "Toss-Out Tuesday." Once a week, Linda takes a few minutes to sort through the stuff on her hall table and look for junk, broken things, and other unneeded items. As a result, clutter doesn't have a chance to sneak in.

trunks and bandboxes stacked with the largest at the bottom are yet another. If you have a solid wood wall under your staircase, you might consider asking a carpenter to see if he or she could cut a door and create a storage space for you.

ONWARD!

You've gotten your feet wet—probably literally!—in your hall, mudroom, and other entrances. Now it's time to tackle a real challenge. Are you with me? In Chapter 6 we'll take a look at one of the most cluttered rooms in the house—the kitchen.

Kitchen Clutter Control

Food. Dishes. Homework. Bills. Art supplies. Knickknacks. Junk. Clutter accumulates in kitchens faster than anywhere else—sometimes it seems impossible to find enough counter or table space to set down a mug, much less make a meal. Some kitchen clutter can create safety issues. Papers piled too close to the stove could start a fire. Appliances can clog counters, and their cords can become a tangled mess. Drawers and cabinets overflow with years' worth of pie pans, canning jars, cookie sheets, dishes, and glassware—way more than you use or need. This chapter helps you sort through the stuff, kick the hoarding habit, "find" more storage space, and create displays that are as practical as they are attractive.

PRIORITIES FOR KITCHENS

Start your kitchen de-cluttering process by setting some clutter-kicking priorities. To do that, focus first on what matters most to you about the way your kitchen looks. That will be your first clutter-kicking priority. Then you'll work your way through the clutter problems until you get to what matters least. The best way to do this is to take a good, hard look at the "before" state of the room and then visualize the "after"—how you want the kitchen to look when all the clutter's gone.

A Kitchen Visualization

To get to your "after," you need to start with the "before"—the way things look right now. Maybe your countertops are buried under mounds of mail and coupons and grocery bags. Or you have the food processor, blender, mixer, toaster, toaster oven, microwave, popcorn popper, and milkshake maker all sitting there. Open some drawers and cabinet doors—what do you see? Open the refrigerator, too—how's *that* look? Get out some paper or use the "My Kitchen—Before" form (or make a photocopy of it and write on that). Write down every place there's clutter and note what that clutter is. Don't let yourself be overwhelmed or discouraged, even if every drawer and surface looks like complete chaos. Instead, keep the list simple and remember that you'll be breaking the actual work down into manageable bites.

Once you've jotted down a quick clutter inventory of your kitchen's "before" state, it's time to move on to the "after"—how you want the room to look when you've kicked the clutter. Write it all down on a piece of paper or on the "My Kitchen—After" form (or on as many photocopies of it as you need to do it justice). To make sure you're being realistic, look at the room every few minutes while you're doing this.

Your description can be short and to the point: "I want a clear counter space where I can actually work without having to shove things out of the way. I want to open the cabinet without a mug or glass falling out. I want to be able to see—and reach—everything in the refrigerator." Or it can be a detailed picture of exactly how you'd like your room to look if it were perfect (for you). You can picture the colors of the walls, cabinets, and appliances; what the cabinets and countertops would be made of; your dream appliances; whether there would be an island, a wine rack, or a gorgeous set of copper pots and pans hanging from the ceiling; what the lighting would look like; if there would be an eating area—everything.

Getting There

Now that you've captured your kitchen's "before" condition, listing all the specifics, and you've imagined its "after" appearance, you can finally prioritize the steps you need to take to get there from here. Again, bearing both "before" and "after"

My Kitchen—Before

_____
_____
_____
_____
_____
_____
_____
_____
_____
_____
_____

My Kitchen—After

_____
_____
_____
_____
_____
_____
_____
_____
_____
_____
_____

My Kitchen Priority List

_____

_____

_____

_____

_____

_____

_____

_____

_____

in mind, I'd recommend starting with what bothers you most about the "before" condition and working down from there.

Maybe you're concerned that the drawers stick because they're jammed too full to open, and that when you do pry them open, you can't find what you need because of all the junk inside. Or you want to have all your spices in one place. Or you never get to the older cans and boxes of food because of the mass of new ones piled in front of them.

Write down whatever's driving you to distraction on the "My Kitchen Priority List" (or on a photocopy of it, if you'd prefer) in descending order from most to least maddening. Now you have your priorities straight! Once you've finished, you can turn to the tips below to find ingenious ways of dealing with each problem.

THE KITCHEN TIPS

Because so much goes on in the kitchen, I've divided the tips in this chapter into sections and grouped them by topic so it will be easier for you to find what you're looking for. Dig in!

Cabinets, Shelves, and Pantries

Say adieu to ancient spices. If your herbs and spices have become bleach-blondes because you've had them for so long, or if their labels have faded beyond recognition, or if they no longer taste or smell distinctive and fresh, dump them. If you're reluctant to just throw them out, you can add them to the compost pile or, if they still have *some* fragrance, add them to potpourris. This time, replace only the ones you really use—and keep them in a dark, *cool* place, not on a spice rack over the stove like, ahem, I used to do.

Clear out empty cartons. There's always someone who leaves a carton in the cabinet with just one cracker, half a cookie, or a disintegrated pile of cereal in the bottom. (You know who you are.) Make it your mission to find these and toss them. You may find that you don't even need to replace half of them, creating instant shelf space.

Bag the empty bags. Now it's time to tackle the bags—those same one-cracker culprits tend to leave bags on the shelf with a few broken pretzels or crumbling chips. Toss the almost-empties (give the dog the broken pretzels) and see if you need to replace all of them or if there were really four half-empty Doritos bags and you can replace them with just one.

Toss stale stuff. While we're talking about crackers and chips, throw out the

👍 Love It *or* Lose It? 👎

Lazy Susans are another organizer favorite. Go to any kitchen design store and you'll see them as practically standard equipment. The theory is that they help you get to all your stuff in deep cabinets, especially corner cabinets, since instead of having to root around in there you can just give Miss Susan a turn and see all your stuff circle within easy reach. This makes sense if you don't need a lot of space or have a lot of stuff—because sure enough, lazy Susans are huge space-wasters. My friend Rudy got them when he had his kitchen redone, and I was appalled at how little he could get into those beautiful new cherry cabinets. There are better ways to get to your stuff; you'll find many right here.

Verdict: Lose it!

5-Minute Fixes for the Kitchen

Here are eight fast fixes to get your clutter-kicking started in the kitchen.

Trash the trash bags. If you—yes, you—have an accumulation of paper or plastic grocery bags lying around, pull them out and throw them out. You say you use them to pick up after the dog or to line your trash cans? Okay. Do a quick calculation: How many do you use each week? How many do you usually bring into the house each week? Keep enough for one week and toss the rest, or take them to the supermarket's recycling bin—you'll replenish your stash fast enough.

Raid the fridge. Throw out five old, mostly empty bottles or jars right now. It's that easy! Make a note of anything you need to replace.

Try a fridge facelift. Take down five things from the front of the fridge—outdated notes, old menus, tattered artworks, faded photos.

Toss the take-out junk. If you save the stuff that comes with take-out food—little plastic bags of sauce, packets of plastic utensils and paper napkins, salt and pepper packets, and the like—round them up, put them in a bag, and throw them out. Come on, buy a bottle of soy sauce, for goodness' sake! You'll always be able to find it and use it—and you can get the brand you like. No more horrible little squishy bags littering your drawers!

stale stuff. Okay, so you set out only 10 of those crackers at your dinner party. That was 3 months ago. Who's going to eat them now? Check your boxes and bags and toss anything you wouldn't eat—with pleasure—right now.

Try the cookie-sheet solution. I read this wonderful reader tip in an issue of *Cook's Country* magazine. The reader wanted an inexpensive but effective way to reach the stuff at the back of her cabinets. Instead of buying expensive organizing supplies, she bought used cookie sheets (the kind with shallow edges) and put them on the cabinet shelves, then put her supplies on top. When she needed something from the shelf, she simply pulled the cookie sheet forward until she could reach what she wanted. Great idea! No more groping around. Two caveats if you try this, though: Make sure you don't pull the sheet too far forward, or you'll have an instant avalanche. And you have to play fair and store stuff one layer deep!

Round up the rubber bands. And the twist-ties, paper clips, and similar stuff that's found its way all over your kitchen drawers. (Start with one drawer, then move on to others as you find time.) If you want to save these little items, sort through them, toss any that are dried out, bent, shredded, or otherwise useless, and put the rest in a zipper-lock bag so they're all together and easy to find. They'll take up a lot less space, and the next time you bring some into the house you'll be able to toss them because you'll see how many you already have—or to add them to the bag if you feel you need more.

Cut the coupons. Throw out as many expired coupons as you can in 5 minutes. Bet you'll find you've done them all!

Sort your coupons. Go through your coupons regularly to get rid of any that have expired. Once you've thrown out the expired coupons, you can put the remaining coupons in order by expiration date. That way, you can just check the front of the pile to see what's coming up and make sure you use them before they expire. Now you won't have wasted time cutting them out for nothing!

Clean a cabinet. Not the *whole* cabinet—if you can do that in 5 minutes, either you don't cook or you don't need this book. Instead, find five cans that are outdated or that contain food that you and your family will never eat. Toss them! It's a start.

Put in pull-outs. Home improvement stores and organizing stores, catalogs, and Web sites have wire pull-out shelves on rollers that you can install in cabinets to create more efficient storage space. Because they're rectangular, they make the best use of the space, and their wire-mesh sides keep the contents from spilling out. When you need something from the middle or back, pull out the shelf until it's easy to reach the jar, box, or bottle in question.

Add more shelves. Kitchen cabinets tend to have a set number and arrangement of shelves, which can leave a lot of unused space above the items you store on them. Rather than stacking mugs or cans, you can make better use of the space by adding more shelves. But there's a trade-off: You get more (stable, as opposed to stacked-up) storage space, but the less space there is between shelves, the harder it is to reach the back of the shelf. If you do decide to add shelves, consider the cookie-sheet idea above—unless you seldom or never use the things you put at the backs of your shelves. (And if you don't use them, why are they there?)

Stack 'em up. Buy some wire stacking shelves to put in your cabinets. (Again, they're available from home and organizing stores, catalogs, and Web sites.) These cabinet stackers create a shelf-on-shelf effect to hold additional plates, bowls, and other things so you don't have a single giant stack piled to the top of the next shelf. If you put dinner plates on the bottom and lunch or salad plates on the stacking shelf, you won't have to lift off the salad plates every time you want to set the table for dinner. Ditto for bowls. Using stackers cuts down on the chances of a china avalanche and the resulting broken china.

Use your cabinet tops. There's usually a good bit of space between the tops of your cabinets and the kitchen ceiling. Don't let it go to waste! Store seldom-used items in attractive, lightweight covered baskets that are easy to take down when you need them. This is a great place to put linens, seasonal items (if you can't bring yourself to sell or donate them), decorative cookie tins, party goods, even your sterling silver service (neatly wrapped in tarnish-proof cloth, of course). Label the baskets if you don't think you'll remember what's in them.

Use the cabinet sides, too. Your cabinets probably have exposed sides that

$$\left[\ \textbf{Tools of the Trade}\ \right]$$

Honestly, I try to resist either buying or recommending a lot of organizing gizmos. (I have enough stuff already, and more than enough claims on my checkbook.) But I have to put in a good word for ClickClack food storage containers (available through cooking and organizing stores and Web sites). These square and rectangular clear plastic containers are rigid, well-made, and durable—we're not talking about flexible opaque plastic containers—and they have lock-down lids that easily snap on and off (thus, "ClickClack"). They are just the best for storing perishable stuff that comes in bags and boxes, from flour, sugar, and popcorn to pasta, cereal, and lentils. (You can, of course, store anything in them, including craft and office supplies, but they're pricey, so I'd at least start with the basics and add on as your budget allows.) They come in numerous sizes and stack to make the most of cabinet space. They will keep your food fresh and pest-proof, won't spill if they're knocked over, and let you see what and how much is in them at a glance. Bravo!

aren't doing too much besides holding them up. Add hooks and hang potholders or trivets, cutting boards, or anything else that's useful and flat (and not too ugly to have out in plain sight). Remember that anything you can see can quickly contribute to visual (and actual) clutter if it isn't attractively organized, so don't litter your cabinet sides with stuff.

Use the cabinet bottoms. You can buy and install wire under-cabinet glass racks from home stores like Pier 1. They're inexpensive and can be great space-savers for wine glasses, martini glasses, and any other stemmed glassware that hangs upside-down from the rack. But! Don't hang glasses you don't use at least weekly, or they'll just become dustables. And don't hang them where someone is likely to smash them while doing something on the counter below.

Hook your mugs. You can also attach hooks under a cabinet to hang your mugs. The same caveats apply here as for the under-cabinet glass racks: Hang the mugs you actually use, and hang them out of harm's way.

Hang your paper-towel holder. Why waste counter space with an upright paper-towel holder when you can hang one horizontally under a cabinet? The towels will be easier to pull off the roll, too.

Don't forget the cabinet doors. You can also hook things to the insides of your cabinet doors—as long as they're flat and lightweight but unlikely to come loose and go flying everywhere when you open the door. Pot holders are a good choice. Or you can tack a calendar flat (if it will stay flat) against the inside of the door, where you can consult it easily but it isn't adding visual clutter to the room.

Turn your doors into towel racks. Thanks to stainless steel hangers that fit right over the door (and install without tools!), you can turn a lower cabinet door into an instant towel bar for dish towels. Or add a convenient double-hook hanger for pot holders. Look for them in catalogs like Solutions (see page 48) and at housewares stores.

Magnetize your cabinet doors. Attach a magnetic board inside a cabinet door and put important (but unsightly) refrigerator magnets there—the ones with addresses and contact data for the doctor, dentist, vet, ambulance, fire company, furnace company, auto dealer, and take-out pizza place. Make sure everyone knows where they are, and if you have smaller kids who can't reach an upper cabinet, either put the board on a lower cabinet door or install a duplicate down where they can get to it if they have to.

Recognize your pantry. Think you don't have a pantry? If your concept of a pantry is like mine—my grandmother's fabulous, roomy, walk-in area with a window (she always had plants on the sill) and tons of storage space—you may think you don't have one. But think again: The tall cabinet that's at the end of the counter in most kitchens is the modern equivalent. Treat it like a pantry and use it to store your staples. True, you may not be able to hang brooms and mops on the back of the door, but your "pantry" can hold a surprising amount of stuff—once you kick out the clutter. Which brings me to . . .

Make a date with your pantry. Painful as it is, you really need to pull the stuff out of your pantry and put it back in reverse order. I know—how I know!—it's easier to just put the newly bought stuff in the front and let the older stuff age to greatness in the dark at the back of the shelves, but really, what's the point? Get a notepad and pen and a garbage bag and settle in. (Remember, you can do this a shelf at a time if you can't face tackling the whole pantry at once.) Pull everything off the shelf and put anything that's outdated in the trash bag. If you actually use whatever it is, make a note on the pad that you need more of it. But be realistic. If you've never used it, let it go, even if your mother insisted that every well-stocked pantry had to have it. If you use it once a year, buy it when you're ready to use it. (If some national crisis keeps you from buying the cranberry sauce, I think you'll have other things to think about!) If you don't use it but it hasn't expired, set it aside for the local food bank. Give the now-empty shelf a quick swipe with a dust cloth. Then put everything back with the oldest stuff in the front, where you'll use it first, and the newer replacements in the back. Make sure the stuff you use most often is on the shelves that are easiest to reach. Think of the satisfaction of knowing that from now on you won't be wasting food because you've forgotten it was in there or you just didn't feel like digging for it.

Light your pantry. If your pantry is a walk-in or closet rather than a cabinet, add lighting so it's easy to find what you need and see what's there. Have an electrician install ceiling lights or buy cordless, battery-powered lights and install a row of them. They are inexpensive; use long-lasting LED bulbs; are easy to install with adhesive, nails, or screws; and are readily available from home catalogs, home improvements stores, and hardware stores.

Add more shelves. If your pantry shelves are so deep that you're stacking things in dangerous towers or wasting space, add more shelves to suit your needs. Use metal strips and brackets or other attachments for wooden shelves, insert free-standing wire shelves that fit on top of existing shelves, or add under-shelf wire or plastic shelving that simply slides in.

Put the snacks up front. Save time for everyone by putting cookies, corn chips, granola bars, and other snacks within easy reach (and sight). Save the upper and lower shelves for less frequently eaten (or needed) items. For example, you can store canning supplies and seldom-used appliances or dishes on the top shelf.

Use the pantry floor. Use the pantry floor under the lower shelf (or use the lower shelf, if it's a long cabinet) to store cleaning supplies, buckets, dishpans, paper garbage bags, and other necessary cleaning supplies. If you have young children or pets with free access to the pantry, make sure you keep any potentially harmful cleaning supplies under the kitchen sink with a childproof lock on the cabinet doors.

Use your pantry door. Pantries, including those tall cabinets, have long doors that are great for stashing necessary stuff out of sight. If your pantry is a closet and there's room between the door and the shelves, you can use clasping hooks to securely hang up brooms, mops, dustpans, and other cleaning necessities. If it's a long cabinet, there's still space to tack or hang up memos, add a magnetic board (see page 93) or a chalkboard, and keep your take-out and local restaurant menus where they're easy to find (more on this in the next tip). You can even use special chalkboard paint (available from home improvement centers) to create a chalkboard inside the door for everybody's messages, doodles, and so on. Just make sure you attach a little wire or plastic storage rack for chalk, pens, and other supplies.

Hang your take-out menus. Ever notice those hanging files in your doctor's office? They're on the doors of all the examining rooms so the doctor can quickly check a patient's chart and history. Put these hanging files to good use holding take-out and local restaurant menus inside the pantry door. They're available from office-supply stores.

Put your wraps on the door. You can also get special racks just for aluminum foil, plastic wrap, parchment, and wax paper. Check out organizing stores, catalogs, and Web sites for lots of options. These racks attach to the inside of the door and are a very convenient way to store wraps within easy reach.

Put up a pegboard. The pantry door (or inside wall, if you have a walk-in pantry) is also a great place to put a pegboard. Use it to hang up cleaning tools or small utensils that you don't use often but can never find when you need them, and you'll free up space in your drawers and under the sink.

Hang up a bag holder. The pantry door is also a great place to hang up one of those cloth tubes for holding plastic grocery bags. My friend Edith gave me one of these "bag sausages" for Christmas years ago, and it's a great invention. Just shove the bags into it the way you'd stuff a sausage, and pull one out when you need it. (Yes, we all do use them, for storing onions, picking up after the dog, and other necessities.) My rule is that once the bag holder is full, you take the rest of the bags back to the supermarket and recycle them in the bin outside the door. No more plastic bags spilling out from under the sink!

Contain the kid stuff. If you have kids—or grandkids who visit frequently—and they make the kitchen table command central for projects and homework, stash their supplies on your pantry shelves where they're easy for the kids to reach. Use the lightweight and inexpensive (but sturdy) plastic storage containers with handles and lock-down lids—they're easy to lift and carry, even for small kids, and you can quickly see what's inside. They're available at every pharmacy, department store, grocery store, and housewares store, in a huge assortment of sizes. (Keep them on the small side for small hands.) Perfect for art supplies, school supplies, or toys!

Collect the pet treats and toys. Plastic storage containers (see the previous tip) are also perfect for storing pet toys and treats, not to mention things like fish food and aquarium supplies. Instead of a gadzillion toys and little bags and containers of treats all over the place, you'll have them all rounded up in your pantry in one easy-to-find location.

Corral craft supplies. If you enjoy working on scrapbooking, knitting, beading, or other crafts in your kitchen, you can use lightweight plastic storage containers with lock-down lids and handles to hold your own supplies, too. There's bound to be a size that works for your stuff. You can see what's in the container and fit it neatly on a pantry shelf, where it's ready when you are.

Don't forget first aid. People are more likely to get cut, burned, scraped, or stung in the kitchen or outside than anywhere else, so it makes sense to keep a first-aid kit in the pantry rather than letting it languish somewhere it's unlikely to be found (or used).

Pet Alert!

If you have pets, chances are they share the kitchen with you. There are a few tricks you can use to contain their clutter (and chaos) so you can all just enjoy being together. I use a (waterproof) doormat under my golden retriever's, Molly's, food and water bowls—no fuss, no muss. My friend Anne uses vinyl placemats under her dog's dishes and they work fine, too. I also have Molly's feeding area tucked against the wall on the side of one set of cabinets, so nobody's tripping over it.

If you have cats but no dogs, you can put their bowls on a mat like Molly's. But I have cats *and* the dog, so I had to convert my shorter countertop to a cat-feeding station or the poor cats would never get a mouthful. (They take the high road and Molly takes the low road.) I keep their food and treats in attractive but vermin-proof canisters on "their" counter, so I don't have bags of cat food lying around. Molly's food and treats go into large Molly-proof canisters by her feeding station. I keep the food scoops in the canisters so they're with the food and not adding visual clutter. If you have room, you can store your pet food under the sink (in vermin-proof containers, please).

Those Dreaded Drawers

Cut back to one junk drawer. One day when I was working out at my local Curves, I was told this classic anecdote by Sherry, another member. "A friend was in my kitchen when I opened a drawer to get something and a lot of stuff burst out. 'That's all right, Sherry,' she told me. 'Everyone has a junk drawer.' I couldn't bring myself to tell her that that wasn't my junk drawer!"

If your kitchen drawers are in this shape, get a big trash bag. Then open your drawers and pull out everything that isn't a kitchen implement. Put stuff that should really be in a different room in one pile, stuff that you need in the kitchen (like a flashlight) in a second pile, and stuff you don't really need at all in the trash bag. Your goal is to get the "stuff you need in the kitchen" pile so small that you can fit it all in a single drawer, so be ruthless. Imagine all the drawer space you're freeing up for your utensils and small-but-essential kitchen gadgets! Finish what you start, though: Put the stuff that stays in the kitchen in its drawer, take the stuff that should be elsewhere to wherever it belongs, and throw that trash bag out.

Divide and conquer. Use an old utensil or silverware organizer to corral the jumble in your junk drawer. Put like with like so it's easy to see what—and how much—you have. The organizer will help keep sharp objects like scissors and utility knives away from vulnerable fingers; keep the flashlight and batteries from rolling around; and keep tape, correction fluid, and other seeming necessities upright. If you don't have an ugly organizer you'd like to upgrade for your utensils, thrift stores are full of them.

Keep just one tool. Maybe you're using your junk drawer as a second tool chest—after all, you might need a hammer, pliers, two kinds of screwdrivers. . . . Yes, you *might* need them, but why take up all your junk-drawer space with them when you can buy a multitool that combines 12 or so common tools in one? Whether you get a classic Swiss Army Knife, a Leatherman multitool, or anything in between, you'll save oodles of space by stashing a multitool in the junk drawer and keeping your "real" tools in the tool chest. These tools are built to last and are available from home improvement centers, home catalogs, and camping suppliers like Cabela's and L.L. Bean. If the multitool doesn't handle whatever you need to do, you can always get the single-purpose tool for a given job. (But please put it back in the toolbox afterwards!)

Monitor the junk drawer. After all, it's not called the junk drawer for nothing. Junk has a way of creeping in there, seemingly from nowhere. Once a month, take 5 minutes and give the drawer a good going-over, tossing what you can, putting anything that's strayed in there by accident where it belongs, and neatening up what's left so it's easy to see and reach. Small plastic storage containers and glass spice jars both make good holders for little stuff like twist-ties, paper clips, tacks, magnets, and rubber bands. So do baby-food jars. They all fit nicely in the drawer. Just make sure you buy colorful sticky dots at a stationery or office-supply store and label the containers' lids so you can tell what's inside at a glance.

Store spices heads-up. Now that you've freed up all that drawer space, you can devote one to herb and spice storage. You know that herbs and spices should be stored in a dark, dry, cool place, so choose a drawer that isn't near the stove.

I saw the neatest drawer spice display in, where else, *Martha Stewart Living*. Martha had her spices neatly lined up in a kitchen drawer. She had dealt with the problem of how to know which spice is which when all you can see are the caps by making beautiful vanilla-and-robin's-egg-blue round labels for all the tops, with the name of each herb or spice elegantly printed on the label. Pull out the drawer and you could see every herb and spice at a glance! Being Martha, she had put all the spices into matching glass spice jars (available from housewares stores), a nice "extra" if you want to go to the trouble.

I don't know if they'll still be there by the time this book comes out, but you could find Martha's gorgeous labels online and download them yourself from her Web site. (Go to www.marthastewart.com and search for "spice jar labels.") If they're not still available, you could always e-mail the site and see if someone could locate them for you. Of course, you can also create homemade versions by writing the names of your herbs and spices on those colorful round sticky dots you can buy at office-supply stores.

They'll stay fresh and keep their color longer—and it's amazing how many spice jars you can fit in a drawer when you stand them upright!

Centralize your cookie cutters. If you love making and decorating cookies, designate another of those freed-up drawers for cookie-making supplies. Stash your cookie cutters and containers of colored sugars, jimmies, cinnamon dots, and all those other cookie-making essentials in the drawer. No more time wasted trying to find it all! And you can admire all those wonderful cookie-cutter shapes every time you open the drawer.

Appliances and Gadgets

Don't keep duplicate appliances. How many homes have you been in where multiple coffeemakers, microwaves, and other appliances and gadgets were taking up valuable storage space, "just in case" the one in use broke? Guess what: They're not planning to stop making them anytime soon. And meanwhile, you could use that space. So give the extras to friends and family who don't have one, sell them at a yard sale, or donate them to Goodwill, the Salvation Army, or the Society of St. Vincent de Paul.

[Don't hoard what's easily replaceable.]

If it's broken, toss it. Or fix it—unless you've already bought a replacement. If you're not ready to take it to the repair shop right now, get rid of it. And bear in mind that a replacement is probably cheaper than a repair.

If it malfunctions, toss it. Okay, it's not *really* broken—the lights just go on and off sporadically when you're using it, it sometimes shuts off halfway through, or it works only half the time. As Dr. Phil says, get real! Get it fixed (and see the previous tip on this), or get rid of it and buy a fully functioning model.

If it's missing parts, toss it. Again, why use up valuable space storing that lidless blender, that pot with the broken handle, the serving fork you used to use all the time before a tine broke? If you can repair it or replace what's broken (and haven't already bought a replacement), go for it. But frankly, if you were going to do that, wouldn't you have done it by now? Be honest with yourself and throw it out or donate it.

If you don't use it, don't keep it. If you've bought every gadget on late-night TV but find that you've never used any of them, or you decided to invest in the latest hot appliance only to realize that your family didn't really like fresh spinach-beet juice no matter how healthful it was, it's time for deaccessioning. Sell those unused gadgets on eBay. Donate them. Give them away or—if they've never been used and are still in their "As Seen on TV!" boxes—give them as gifts. Yes, that appliance or gizmo cost money—sometimes, lots of it. And maybe you can make some (or even all) of it back if you sell it. But one thing is sure: It's making you no money sitting on or under your counter, and it's taking up valuable space.

If it does the same thing, don't keep it. If you use your food processor as a blender, you probably don't need your blender. But if you find that you *only* use your food processor as a blender, maybe you should give *it* away and keep your blender. Don't keep multiple appliances that do the same thing—keep the one you like and find yourself using and get rid of the rest.

SANITY SAVERS

If you're crafty, there's no end to the creative ways you can reuse beloved kitchen objects. Except for Native American baskets, the most wonderful basket I ever saw was made of grapevines twined around and through red plastic heart-shaped cookie cutters. It was in a fine crafts shop in Virginia, and I fell in love with it at once. (But no, I didn't buy it. I'm trying to abide by the "if you can't picture a place for it, don't get it" rule.) What a fantastic idea! It transformed those cookie cutters into a work of art. Think of how you can incorporate objects you love but don't use into something you can display proudly.

If you haven't used it in a while, don't keep it. This one is harder. Give yourself a bearable deadline—have you used it in a year, 2 years, 5 years?—and look at your tools and appliances with that in mind. If you haven't used that aspic ring in 20 years, you're not likely to use it now. If you've long since abandoned your food mill for a food processor, it's time to send the mill packing. If your bread machine, yogurt maker, or sprouter have seen no use since the Stone Age (or ever), find better homes for them. Mind you, sometimes what goes around does come (back) around—you could have used that Crock-Pot from the seventies when slow cookers came back big-time in the nineties. But you could also just go out and buy another Crock-Pot if you want to give slow cooking another try. And there are plenty still out there at secondhand shops if you don't want to spring for a new one!

If you can't bear to lose it, reuse it. What if you simply love the look of that old butter mold or whisk or copper chocolate-melter, even though you know you'll never use it? Or you have such a strong sentimental attachment to Grandma's antique wooden spoon or potato masher that you can't bear to part with it? Give them a new life as kitchen wall art. My father's girlfriend has a huge brick wall in her kitchen, and she's hung dozens of antique cooking implements on it. If you enjoy cooking, as I do, it's a fascinating display—like a culinary museum. Most of us may not have that kind of display area, but there's probably some wall space where you could hang one or two implements. I once found a very old handmade wooden washboard at an antiques store. When I turned it on its side, it looked just like a fish. My unique "fish" has been hanging on the kitchen wall ever since. Bear in mind that unless you have a huge display space, it's better to showcase like items together for the most attractive, coherent presentation—a group of cookie cutters, some antique silver spoons. You can even frame them or put them in a shadowbox.

Ditch the hanging baskets. Not plant baskets—those three-tiered wire baskets for fruit, onions, and so on. It may look like Old World charm to you, but it looks like visual clutter to me. Any time you have a bunch of different stuff hanging down, it looks messy and cluttered. So store your produce in bowls or baskets on the counter (or under the counter or on a table or in the fridge) instead. Take the hanging baskets to Goodwill, give them away, or turn them into plant baskets— fill them with flowering vines, and hang them from a tree.

Where to Put the Pots and Pans

Make your stove a storage center. When you're not using your oven to cook, use it to store pots, pans, baking sheets, cookie tins, and the like. Yes, you'll have to take them out to use the oven, so be realistic about how much you're prepared to haul around. (I think of it as doing arm-toning exercises.) If you're not the only one who's likely to turn on the oven, make sure everything you store in there is ovenproof!

Make the most of your stovetop. Keep the teakettle and the pots and pans you use every day right on the stove. I keep mine on the burners I use them on, with a smaller pan in the center front that I switch off with my teakettle. Everything else is shelved or in drawers where it won't collect dust between uses. Admittedly, my used-every-day cookware is beautiful Le Creuset enameled cast iron (worth every penny, if you can lift it), so it gives me joy to see it out and waiting. But even if yours isn't quite so attractive, I'd think it would be cheering to see these faithful kitchen helpers waiting to greet you as you begin preparing each meal. And it certainly saves time and effort getting them out and putting them up every time!

Use stoveside storage. My beloved old Caloric (!) gas stove came with my house. It has a tall, narrow storage drawer on the left side that's as deep as the stove itself and another storage drawer below that's as wide as the stove. I store baking pans, racks, spatter screens, and cutting boards in the tall, narrow drawer, and I keep the broiler and assorted pan lids in the under-stove drawer.

Double up your pots. Use your big pots to store smaller ones. If you have Dutch ovens, deep steamer pans, or any capacious cookware, it makes sense to keep

Dustables

Home-decorating magazines are full of great-looking ceiling hangers for pots and pans. You probably know at least one person who has one. People who have beautiful pots and pans like to keep them in sight, and at first blush it may seem like a brilliant storage solution, freeing up cabinets and counters. But unless you own a restaurant and use all those pots every day, they're dustables. Do you really want to spend your free time risking a broken neck as you clamber up there and dust all those pots and pans? I didn't think so.

smaller pots and other cookware items like soufflé ramekins tucked inside. Again, make sure the doubled-up pots aren't too heavy for you to lift comfortably.

Make a wall hanging. If it will look good with your decor, you can hang a few pans on the wall beside the stove. But hang only the ones you use (and wash) regularly, or you're just creating dustables. And remember that anything hung near the stove is going to get gummy and spattered. Pans hung like this will be very eye-catching, so you (and everyone else) will be spending more time than usual staring at their undersides, which translates into more time scrubbing them. Why do I say it's all right to do this and all wrong to hang them from the ceiling? (See "Dustables.") Pans hung flat on a wall—as long as there are just a few and they're decoratively spaced—are flat, so they reduce visual clutter. Pans hanging in midair create a "flying clutter" effect.

Put up a pegboard. My editor, Anne, says the best thing she did in her small kitchen was to put up a pegboard in an alcove near (but not too near) the stove. She hangs pots, lids, strainers and colanders, potholders, oven mitts, and dish towels—all things she uses regularly, so dust and grime aren't problems.

Rack it up. Do you have wire cooling racks for cookies, cakes, bread, and other baked goods? If so—and if they have no plastic parts—you can store them in the bottom of the oven, below the lowest oven rack. They fit neatly and don't have to be removed when you use the oven, unless you're cooking something really messy.

Utensils and Dishware

Group the utensils you use most often. At the back of my stove, I keep the gorgeous handmade ceramic crock that holds the utensils I really use—wooden and bamboo spoons, pasta tongs, spatulas, potato masher, soup ladle. (The less-often-used utensils are in the drawers on either side of the stove so they're easy to reach as needed.) You can use a jar, a sturdy vase, a *big* coffee mug—anything that will hold all your most-used utensils. Keep them on the stove or nearby on the counter. They'll be tidy, upright, and in easy reach. Note: Make sure the mouth of the container is as wide as its body. I started out using a lovely handmade bowl with a narrow mouth but switched to my current crock after having too many utensil avalanches.

Minimize mugs. End mug madness by sorting through the mug shelf, tossing battered or broken mugs, and putting every too-big, too-small, too-ugly, and even too-boring mug in the Goodwill box. In 5 minutes, you can cut your mug collection in half (or more, if you're really ruthless).

If it's chipped or cracked, throw it out. This is a *really* hard one. You have a matched set of glasses, dishes, or crystal. And one or more pieces are chipped or cracked. But hey, it's part of the set, right? So back on the shelf it goes. Now, it's true that every time I attend the local antiques extravaganza, I see a booth where someone is smoothing the chips on crystal and glassware. But tell me three things: (1) Are you really going to take your stuff to get it smoothed out? (2) If you do, would you give a guest a glass with a dip in the rim? (3) Would you want to drink out of it? Same with cracked plates. Unless you're talking about a priceless antique, why look at those ugly cracks a minute longer? Sure, it hurts to throw them out. (If you have a friend who makes mosaics out of broken china, you can see if he or she wants them. But don't *you* hold onto them in case some day you might decide to make mosaics!) And yes, it leaves you with fewer pieces in your set. But please don't tell me you actually use those cracked and chipped pieces now, anyway! Throw . . . them . . . out. You can use the space. And you can find intact replacements if you really want to via specialty services like Replacements, Ltd. (Find them on the Web at www.replacements.com.)

Buy just one. (Or two.) We're so conditioned to buy whole sets of china and glassware that it's almost an automatic response—yet most of us have neither the space nor the budget to indulge ourselves this way. Instead, indulge yourself by buying one or two pieces of china, mugs, or glassware you really love—or just enough for the immediate family. I was thrilled to see that Moss in New York had set up a registry that does just that—lets you get as few pieces as you want. (See www.mossonline.com's Me, Us, and Them Registry.) Or just tell yourself that it's really okay to buy just two glasses next time you see them at a store and fall in love.

Double up your bowls. I'll bet you're all already doing this, but just in case you've somehow overlooked this basic tip, stack 'em up, with the largest on the bottom and the smallest on top. Colanders usually fit nicely in a stack of bowls, too.

Remember to display and use. One great way to make the most of your kitchen display space without sacrificing storage is to choose "collectible" kitchenware that you can also actually use. Wonderful old (or new) crockery bowls, redware, yellowware, and many other kitchen items can either be bought new or still be used even if they're antiques. (Though I for one wouldn't want to use an old wooden spoon or wooden cookie mold unless it had come down in my own family and I could remember someone using it.) These evocative collectibles can be displayed to add a vintage or homespun look to your kitchen, but you can use them as you would any modern piece, so they do double duty.

Hide the big stuff in plain sight. My mother kept her gigantic silver and fine-china turkey serving platters—with their still more gigantic domed lids—and covered soup tureens on display in the dining room all year. The silver turkey platter and tureens were displayed on a sideboard with silver candlesticks, while the lovely white-and-gold china platter sat proudly in the center of the dining-room table, flanked by silver candlesticks and soup tureens at either end. The display looked great, and it freed up a world of storage space for other things. Remember, it's not clutter if it looks intentional!

[**It's not clutter if it looks intentional.**]

Hang your cutting boards, part one. Wooden cutting boards can make a really attractive wall display—as long as they actually look good and you hang only a few of them. Hang them over the counter where you'll be using them.

Hang your cutting boards, part two. You can hang more weather-beaten wooden cutting boards and plastic cutting boards from the insides of your lower cabinet doors. Again, hang them in the cabinets that are closest to where you'll use them.

File the plastic cutting boards. Buy one of those office organizer racks that have wire rungs to hold files upright (think of the reception desk at the doctor's office). Put your plastic cutting boards in one of these to hold them upright and ready to use. If you use plastic cutting boards, remember that old trick of using one color cutting board for meat, a second color for aromatic veggies like onions and garlic, a third color for fruits and veggies, and a fourth color for bread.

Minimize the plastic storage containers. I've seen whole cabinets in friends' houses devoted to plastic-container storage. In addition to containers that are intended for food storage, some friends who shall remain nameless even store empty yogurt, cottage cheese, and margarine containers. Yuck! Surely you can find better things to do with your space. I certainly agree that plastic containers are useful for storing leftover refrigerated food compactly and for packing lunchboxes. High-quality plastic containers can be relied on not to leak or break and are less likely than glass containers to slip out of your hands. The problem is not the containers themselves, but that people seem to hoard them like priceless collectibles.

So with that in mind, here are my six steps to a manageable plastic pile:

1. Throw out or recycle any plastic stuff not meant for storage.
2. Determine about how many containers you usually have in the fridge and send out in lunch bags at any given time.
3. Collect your best storage containers and set them aside, together, so you can see what you have once you've gotten rid of the rest.
4. Recycle any cheap storage containers, as well as any that are discolored, stained, smelly, bent, or broken, as well as any that have lost their tops (or bottoms).
5. See if you have enough left to meet your needs, and if not, write down how many replacements you'll need and in what sizes and shapes. (Don't exceed your limit! You can buy more later if you find that you really need them.)
6. Buy high-quality containers to fill your quota if you no longer have enough. Hopefully, you'll now have most of your plastic storage containers in use rather than taking up space in your cabinets!

Match up your plastic storage containers. If it's not obvious at a glance which tops go with which bottoms, there are several ways to avoid confusion. By now you should have a manageable number of plastic storage containers to work with (see the previous tip). So get them out and group all of the same-size tops and bottoms together. Then get an indelible marker and number the tops and bottoms. Start with a 1 on all the tops and bottoms of one size and shape, a 2 on the next group of matching tops and bottoms, and so on until you've numbered them all. Stack all of your 1s and store them together, and do the same for the rest. Now if the tops and bottoms get separated, you can match them up at a glance.

Store your picnic supplies in the hamper. Stash all the plastic or paper plates, utensils, straws, and cups—as well as napkins and picnic cloth—right in your picnic basket or hamper. You'll be putting that empty hamper to good use, and your supplies will be ready when you are!

Put your dish rack in the sink. If you depend on a stainless, wood, or plastic dish rack to hold washed dishes, glasses, mugs, and utensils, you probably keep it on the counter on one side of the sink (as I do). But if you have a double sink, you can buy specially sized stainless dish racks that will fit right in the sink. This frees up extra counter space and lowers the dishes' profile, reducing the visual clutter of a tangle of dishware at counter height.

Make sure you have this magnet. If you have a dishwasher, here's one magnet you can't do without: One of the ones that has "Clean" on one end and "Dirty" on the other. I, of course, hope that you put away your clean dishes as soon as they've cooled down, but even if you do, this magnet will prevent dirty dishes from being shoved in among the clean ones—or someone grabbing a dirty glass or mug and drinking out of it. (Ee-eewww!)

Sharp Advice for Knife Storage

Put your knives on the block. A wooden knife block keeps knives (and a sharpening file) upright, safe, and in easy reach. I put mine at the back of the counter under a cabinet and beside the stove, where it can't be tipped over. It's amazing how little space a knife holder takes up, and it will keep you and your family from cutting yourselves while rooting around in the utensil drawers. This is a must-have! (Too many knives for one block? Buy another one—it still won't take up much space and will be worth every inch that it does.)

Dispose of dull knives. People seem to have an awful time getting rid of knives—even wealthy people who could buy a knife company with pocket change and those of us with three generations' worth of hard-used knives spilling out of our drawers. Now, I certainly don't mean that you should toss perfectly good knives that just need to be honed. (Unless, of course, you know you'll never sharpen them.) But a dull knife is a bad knife. Not only is it dangerous, it also makes you work much harder for worse results. If you got a cheap set of knives when you started cooking and have since upgraded, keep that original wooden knife holder but give the knives it held to the local thrift store. Now you have a free knife holder for your new knives!

Store knives flat. If your counter cabinet has a shallow drawer, devote it to knives and store them side by side. They'll stay sharper if they aren't jumbled up with other utensils, and they'll be within easy reach.

Store knives in a tray. If you're afraid to just lay naked knives in a drawer, try an in-drawer knife tray. I saw a beautiful wooden one at Crate & Barrel that held steak and kitchen knives securely.

Kitchen Furniture and Furnishings

Match your space. When I bought my cottage home, I was lucky enough to acquire a recently renovated kitchen with a hanging bookcase that exactly fitted the wall between the refrigerator and the laundry-room door. I was thrilled—a place to put my, ahem, cookbook collection! But of course there was that open space between the bookcase and the floor. One day, I was driving past an antique store when I saw an oak dry sink (a sort of large hutch) in the display window. A bell went off in my head. The bookcase and my kitchen cabinets and woodwork were also oak. I pulled over, went in, eyeballed the dry sink, and decided it would exactly fit the available wall space. (I'm guilty of eyeballing rather than measuring things all the time, and for me, it seems to always work out. But as they say, don't try this at home.) I won't go into what it took to get that heavy old dry sink into my tiny Volkswagen Golf, or to get it out again and down to the house, but sure enough, once I'd wrestled it into place, it was a perfect fit. Whew! Now I had a place to put my good china, crystal, and silver where no one could disturb it, and I could use the top of the dry sink to hold my handmade ceramic canisters. If you need more storage and have an odd corner or space, keep alert. You never know when (or where) the perfect piece will turn up!

Shelve it. Bookcases aren't just for books. You can store plates, cups, bowls, and glasses in full view and easy reach in a bookcase—and the narrow shelves don't take up much precious floor space. Two things, though: Unless your shelves have glass doors, put only what you use every day on the shelves, or you're just creating dustables. And remember that it's easy to knock things off of open shelves—something to bear in mind if you have little ones. Lining the shelves with thin white rubber matting (it's easy to cut it to fit) will help keep the china in place. (You can put it between plates, bowls, and other pieces as well, if you're stacking them. But I think a better idea is to put cloth napkins between them—you'll be protecting your china *and* storing the napkins at the same time!)

Make your door work harder. Often, the space around the kitchen door is just that—space. But if you add tall, narrow shelving on either side and a connecting shelf over the door, you suddenly have a fantastic storage space for cookbooks, china, or cooking gadgets. Turn the space into an instant pantry by putting doors on the narrow shelves.

Go to Fantasy Island. If your kitchen is wide enough, an island in the middle of the floor is a real blessing. You can use the top as extra counter space when it's time to prepare food, and the shelves or cabinets below will hold appliances, pots and pans, bowls, a wine rack—whatever you need to keep within reach. Islands are especially great when you have several people cooking at one time—one can work on the island while others work at the stove and counters. Make sure there's good light over your island so it's a pleasure to work there, and make sure the top of the island is at countertop height so it's comfortable to work on it. Two things I don't like: Bar seating at an island, and pots and pans hung overhead (for some reason, designers tend to hang them over islands). Bar seating is always uncomfortable—the height is awkward, and the overhang is never deep enough to be really usable. If you want to eat in the kitchen and the only space you have is where you might put an island, go with a table instead. You can still prep food on it!

Make your island ambidextrous. While shopping at their local farmers' market, my friends Carolyn and Gary bought a kitchen island with cabinets that had doors on both sides and drawers that you could pull open from either side. I love this idea—you have total access to the drawers' and cabinets' contents from either side!

Block it out. A butcher-block top is a real luxury on an island, since it converts the entire island top into a cutting board. But if that's outside your budget, you can always get a nice freestanding butcher-block cutting board to set on top.

Cart it around. No room for a permanent island in the middle of your kitchen floor? Get a kitchen cart. These wonderful mobile furnishings come in all styles and price ranges and are readily available at DIY and housewares stores like Target. You'll probably have to assemble them yourself, but the tools and hardware are usually included and it doesn't take more than half an hour, even for the least experienced DIY-er. A butcher-block top is certainly a nice feature, and some come with hooks on the sides so you can hang utensils (nothing sharp, please), aprons, and pot holders. Just roll the cart to where you need it when it's time to make a meal, and store it out of the way when you're not cooking.

Be a basket case. If your island or cart has open sides, you can add handsome rectangular storage baskets to give it an uncluttered, attractive look while still providing plenty of storage.

Tuck in the trash. I saw a wonderful mobile kitchen island in the Improvements catalog (see page 48 or www.improvementscatalog.com) that took up only 18 square inches of floor space but had a granite top for cutting and food prep, three drawers, and a tilt-out compartment to hold a 13-gallon garbage can. It's really nice-looking, too!

Take your medicine. An attractive medicine cabinet that goes well with your kitchen's decor (say, an oak one in my oak kitchen) makes a good storage place for spices, herbs, and flavorings—it is dark and won't be located over the stove, where the heat would shorten the cooking life of your spices and herbs. The cabinet can also be a good place to stash keys, cell phones, sunglasses, and other stuff you might need to grab on your way out of the kitchen—and if it has a mirror on the front, you can even give yourself a quick check as you go by!

Add an armoire. If you can't afford a Hoosier cabinet or an expensive built-in storage system but you have the space for one, see if you can find an armoire at a flea market (or in your attic). These big old freestanding closets were all the rage before built-in closets became the norm. You can add hooks, shelves, drawers—whatever you need—inside, and store table linens, pots and pans, cleaning supplies (including tall tools like mops and brooms), or staples. You can paint or finish the armoire to match your kitchen's decor. Close the massive doors, and the content's secrets are safe with you!

Dress it up. If you don't have room for an armoire (or can't find an affordable one), consider using a dresser. These are readily available pretty much everywhere, from flea markets and yard sales to thrift and secondhand stores, and they come in all styles and sizes. (And again, you can always paint yours to match your other kitchen furnishings.) They're great for storing table linens; paper towels, napkins, and other paper goods; trivets; dish towels; cleaning supplies; pots and pans; and even cookbooks.

Try a wine tower. If you enjoy wine but don't have the space for a bulky wine rack, consider a wine tower. I saw a great one in the Crate & Barrel catalog; it took up only 16 square inches of floor space but stored 18 bottles of wine, had a drawer and two shelves, and had a top hanging rack that would hold 12 wineglasses.

Hang your wine on the wall. If you lack the room for a wine rack or like to keep only a few bottles on hand at a time, try this wonderful space-saving idea: Buy a hanging wine rack that attaches to the wall and holds four wine bottles securely on their sides in no more space than a cutting board. (The one I admired is from Ikea and costs less than a bottle of wine.)

Ditch the dish towels. If people know you cook, they'll often give you dish towels. And they're *so* pretty. You might need them. So into the drawers and under the sink they go . . . and go. Find them, drag them all out, and pick two (or four, or six). Put the chosen ones away, toss the worn-out rags, and put the new or good-as-new towels in the Goodwill bag.

Under the (Gulp) Sink

Unstuff the sink. Look around and under your sink and throw out any worn-out scouring pads, sponges, and dish brushes—and let's not forget that browning bar of French kitchen soap. Collect the remaining brushes (bristles up, please) in one of those mugs you just couldn't bear to throw out, and see if you can survive with a single sponge and scrubbing pad. Doesn't that look better?

Make the most of under-sink doors. Don't waste this valuable space. Attach hooks for dust cloths, dishcloths (not the one you're currently using, please), brushes, and other small cleaning tools. Screw on short, narrow wire bins to hold sponges, soaps, steel-wool pads, and other small supplies. You'll be surprised how easily this door storage can organize your under-sink area, making it a snap to find those small cleaning items when you need them. Now you can quit rooting around in the dark under there or digging through drawers!

Keep a flashlight on your under-sink door. Whether you hang it or put it in a hanging wire bin, make sure you have a small flashlight on the inside of the door.

$$\left[\text{ Tools of the Trade }\right]$$

I think under-sink organizers are one of the greatest things around. Unlike some organizing tools that take up more space than they create, under-sink organizers instantly add two or three times the space of an "unimproved" under-sink area. That's because when you have just the open space beneath the sink, you can put in only one layer of cleaning supplies—all those spray bottles and cans of cleaning powder—or face a pile of unrecognizable junk in there if you toss in more stuff than will fit in a single layer. (And then you just buy new stuff because it's easier than trying to dig the old stuff out, right?) But an under-sink organizer gives you two, three, or even more deep shelves, and thus three layers, to keep everything upright and easy to find.

The organizers I use are made of sturdy plastic and snap together without tools. They're specially built to fit around sink pipes, and the shelves are adjustable, so you can space them just as you like and use as many or as few as you need. You can buy them from organizing catalogs and Web sites like www.allbrightideas.com, or look for them in your local home store. Highly recommended!

When you need to find something in the murky darkness under the sink, the flashlight is conveniently at hand.

Put what you use in front. You know how deep and dark it is down there under the sink. So make it easy on yourself. Organize the area so the supplies you use most often are in front and the ones you seldom use are in back. (And while you're at it, ask yourself if you really need those, anyway.) You'll save time and effort, and you'll also cut down on your bending, crawling, and cursing.

Junk the gunk. Gross, rusting cans of solidified abrasive cleansers. Spray bottles with a teaspoon of solution in the bottom. Jars with crusty gunk oozing out from under the lids. We've *all* (ahem) reached under the sink and grabbed hold of something we'd rather not see, much less touch. Since you're working down there now anyway, get rid of all that stuff. Once you've kicked out the clutter and put your small flashlight down there, you can easily see if something's getting into "it came from outer space" mode and pitch it ASAP.

Put in some plastic. Organize your under-sink cleaning supplies in plastic buckets, plastic pans, a plastic laundry bin, or a colorful plastic crate. (The plastic pans will fit neatly on under-sink shelves, if you opt to install them.) They'll make it easy to haul out the supplies when you need to use them, and if anything spills, well, it's a lot easier to clean a plastic container than your sink cabinet!

Recycle those sponges. Like toothbrushes, kitchen sponges should be given limited working lives—certainly no more than 3 months between replacements. But that doesn't mean you have to toss those "perfectly good" sponges right away. Instead, take a tip from my friend Chris and give old kitchen sponges a second career by using them to clean the bathroom before they're permanently "retired."

Corral compostables. I keep my compost bucket under the sink, where it's easy to grab when I'm preparing a meal or cleaning up afterward. I use a plastic bucket with a plastic lidded container inside—it's not fancy, but it's functional. I have seen many gorgeous ceramic and stainless compost buckets in garden- and home-supply catalogs. They've been designed to sit out on the counter, but ugh! I just can't stand the thought of that. To me, given what's going inside it, even the most elegant compost container should live under the sink.

Skip the poisons. Don't store poison baits, insecticides, flea sprays, or any other toxic pest controls in the kitchen. Period. Keep them locked in a cabinet in the garage or tool shed.

Lock it up. By the same token, if you store caustic chemicals like bleach and drain de-cloggers under your sink and you have small children, make sure you keep the cabinet locked. If you set a mousetrap under the sink, lock the cabinet to keep the unwary of all ages from sticking a hand in there in search of something. Put a big, scary-looking note on the inside of the door where it will get someone's attention (not outside, where it could scare off visitors). And don't forget to check the trap at least once a day!

The Fearsome Fridge

Manage the magnets. If you have more magnets, coupons, calendars, photos, take-out menus, kids' artwork, lists, and schedules on the fridge than the bulletin board at your favorite supermarket, it's time to take charge. A messy refrigerator door broadcasts visual (and actual) clutter into your kitchen, and with it a feeling of restlessness and loss of control—clutter chaos. But it's simple to fix. Put the need-to-know magnets on a magnetic board inside a kitchen-cabinet door (see the tip on page 93 for details) and keep the fun, decorative magnets everyone loves on display. (But not too many. If you have more than enough to make an artistic display, put the "extras" in your junk drawer and rotate them with the ones that are currently on display.) File the take-out menus in a hanging file on the pantry door (see the tip on page 95 for more on this). Frame the kids' art in the kind of clear plastic frames that allow you to simply slide the art in and out, so you can hang one frame for each kid and make a wall display. Change the art when new masterpieces come home. Keep your grocery lists inside a cabinet or pantry door. But do by all means keep one of those tiny magnetic calendars that show a month at a glance. Talk about a helpful at-a-glance tool!

Put up a memo pad or board. They now make magnetic memo boards and pads just for the fridge. Rather than covering the doors with sticky notes and layers of lists, memos, and other papers held precariously with magnets, try one of these and get rid of the mess. Everyone can leave messages where the whole family will know to look for them, and if it's a memo board, you can just erase or wipe it clean at the end of the day.

Print your grocery list. My friend Delilah has a checklist of the groceries and other supermarket items her household eats and uses most often. She keeps a set of printouts of the list on the refrigerator door. Before she goes shopping, she checks off the items on the list that need replacing and adds new items in the blank spaces at the end of the sheet. What a time-saver!

Hang a flashlight. If at least one side of your fridge is exposed, you can put it to good use by hanging a flashlight with a magnetic attachment on it. Make sure the batteries are always fresh, and everyone in the family will be able to find at least *one* working flashlight if the power goes off!

Don't waste the fridge top. The top of the fridge can provide valuable real estate for large pots and appliances. I keep my enormous pressure-canner, bread kneader, and heavy-duty nutcracker on mine—appliances I don't use every day and that would be a huge pain to try to store in my cabinets. Because this space is on view, you don't want to put anything unsightly (or unstable!) up there. You may also, like me, have a shallow cabinet over the fridge that only a contortionist could easily reach. This is a great place to store things that you seldom need but have to keep on hand in case your mom drops in and asks to see them.

Make your fridge top work harder. Because the top of the fridge stays warm—it has to do with the cooling process—you can use it to do quite a few ingenious things. Start seedlings, culture yogurt, set bread to rise—things that would ordinarily take up counter or oven space.

Clean out the fridge before you shop. My friend Chris suggested this great idea. She cleans out the fridge and disposes of any lingering leftovers the day before she goes grocery shopping. Not only does this give you a first-hand look at what you need to get, it also, as Chris points out, means you're cleaning an emptier fridge, so there's less to clean up!

Organize what's in there. There are several ways to organize the contents of the fridge, but whichever you choose, the goal should be convenience and easy access. I try to put the stuff I use most often closer to the front, with the tallest bottles, cartons, and containers behind the shorter ones. My own goal is to be able to see everything that's in the refrigerator when I open the door—and as my boyfriend, Rob, could tell you, there's a *lot* of stuff in there!

Check your stuff weekly. Perishables can go bad faster than you can say, "Eeewww! What's that?" Make sure you check the contents of your fridge—including the crisper drawer—at least once a week and discard anything that's less than fresh. (My chickens love fridge-check time.) Force yourself to peek into those opened cartons of sour cream, cottage cheese, and yogurt. Smell the milk and half-and-half. Look inside the mystery containers. It may be only slightly less entertaining than cleaning the cat's litter box, but it won't take 5 minutes and it's for a great cause. Think how great it would be to know that literally everything in the fridge was fit to eat!

Don't keep your eggs in the egg rack. If you have an older fridge, it may have one of those open-air egg racks in the door. You're supposed to take the eggs out of the carton and pop them into the egg-shaped depressions so they're on full display. The problem with that—besides the fact that it's easier for them to get knocked off and break—is that the air around them will dry them out faster. Your eggs will last longest in a plastic egg carton like the ones sold in stores that carry camping supplies (check out Cabela's, Coleman, and L.L. Bean). But if you don't have one of those, store them in the carton in which you bought them.

Group perishables by type. My father's girlfriend, Alice, has three crisper drawers in her fridge. (Boy, am I jealous.) She keeps her cheeses in the shallow drawer on top, her veggies in the middle drawer, and her fruits in the bottom drawer. It's easy to see what's there and what needs to be replenished just by pulling open a drawer!

Put onions in produce bags. Onions won't make you cry when you cut them if you refrigerate them and cut them cold. But onionskin all over the crisper drawer, or worse, glued to the bottom of the crisper drawer, is just plain yucky. Avoid this mess by storing your onions in one of the clear or opaque plastic bags from the supermarket's produce section. (I keep the bulk of my onions in a dark lower cabinet with the potatoes and refrigerate just a few at a time to conserve precious crisper-drawer space. But even in the cabinet, I store them in plastic grocery bags to avoid footloose onionskins.)

Don't buy the big jars. Unless you go grocery shopping only once a month, you don't really need those giant bottles of ketchup and salad dressing, the huge jars of mayo, or the monster-size vat of pickles or jalapeños. Buy the small size and replenish them as needed.

Don't keep what you don't use, part one. The diet parmesan-peppercorn dressing seemed like a great idea. Trouble was, nobody liked it. But there's still half a bottle left! Wake up. Throw . . . it . . . out. Nobody's going to use it, and it's sitting there taking up space, along with the exotic shredded ginger–garlic sauce, the antibiotics you got for your cat 2 years ago, and the bottle of lemon juice you forgot was in the door (but suspect dates from your daughter's third birthday). Free up the space for stuff you really do use, or just free up some space so you can actually see (and reach) what's left.

Don't keep what you don't use, part two. This goes double for the freezer, whether it's part of the fridge or a freestanding model. Check the contents every month. Pitch any food that's iced over, is unrecognizable, is over 6 months old, or is unlikely to ever be eaten. If you bought three boxes of frozen lasagna on sale and the family hated the first box, I have a feeling they're not going to suddenly love the other two. Take them to work, give them to a neighbor, see if the local homeless shelter wants them, nuke them for the dog, or throw them out! Make room for the things you really eat.

Don't keep what you don't use, part three. If you have a hard time throwing out "perfectly good" food that just isn't very good, you'll probably have a *really* hard time with this: Your freezer is stocked with healthy veggies like spinach, green beans, and Chinese stir-fry mix. You feel virtuous because you've bought all these healthy foods for your family. But . . . you can't get anyone to eat them, including yourself. This goes for the fruits and veggies in the crisper drawer, too. Don't feel guilty. You really were trying. Instead, take them to work, give them to friends, or

Dear Claire,

Help! My wife insists on storing every dab and drop of leftover food in our refrigerator. But once they go in, these leftovers never come out. Our fridge is so crammed with plastic storage containers that there's no room for my beer! What can I do?

—Fed Up and Left Over

Dear Fed Up,

It sounds like your wife has a classic case of "waste not, want not" guilt. You need to recommend my "3-Day Rule for Leftovers." First, tell her that all the leftovers are taking up space that could be used for food the family really wants to eat. (I wouldn't mention the beer, if I were you.) Then, ask her if you can clear out all the leftovers for her. (Make sure you toss them!) Next, tell her that if leftovers haven't been eaten in 3 days, they probably will never be eaten, and that from now on she should throw out any leftovers that have taken up residence in the fridge for more than 3 days. (This is the 3-Day Rule.) Reassure her that it's okay to throw them out. Hopefully, one of two things will happen: Either she'll start using those leftovers and moving them out of the fridge on a timely basis, or she'll cook less food so she won't have to deal with leftovers anymore. Either way, there'll be no more guilt!

Good luck,
Claire

compost those babies and replace them with the healthy fruits and veggies your family actually enjoys. Who cares if they hate kiwifruit and papayas? Stock up on apples, grapes, strawberries, and oranges—they'll still get real health benefits.

Put up bamboo shelves. Shallow magnetic shelves and deeper magnetic bamboo file boxes attach directly to the doors or sides of your refrigerator. You can store spices or sticky notes, pens, grocery lists, and other small stuff in the shallow shelves. The deep file boxes can hold telephone books, catalogs, and magazines. They really stay put without scratching surfaces, and they're shallow—less than 4 inches deep—so they don't take up valuable room space. Check home improvement stores, housewares stores and catalogs, and online at ingenious-products sites like www.solutions.com (see page 48).

Eating In

Minimize your table. If your kitchen is small but it doubles as your dining room or your family just has breakfast and snacks there, you can save space by downsizing the table. Use a drop-leaf table and keep the leaves down when the family's not using it—it's amazing how a standard-size round table can suddenly turn into a tiny rectangle that fits snugly against the wall! Add candles and a bowl of fruit and you have an instant sideboard. Or get a table with removable leaves and add them when you need to (as long as you have a place to store the leaves when they're not in use).

Use a folding table. The ultimate space-saver is a folding card table (or two put together, if there are more than two of you). Keep it folded away when it's not needed, and put a tablecloth on it when you use it to dress it up. This option works best when the kitchen adjoins a garage or basement where you can stash one or more folded tables. Two pluses: Without the tablecloth, the kids can use the table for homework or projects, and you can use it as an extra work space, without any fear that it will get messed up!

Ditto for the chairs. You can now buy padded wooden folding chairs that are attractive (and comfortable) enough to use as everyday chairs. Or go for the metal standards. If you can't stand the look of them or want something fancier for company, dress them up with slipcovers that are made just for folding chairs, available from home stores and catalogs.

Nix the diner decor. Many older homes have a breakfast nook with wooden booths and a bolted-down wooden table. It's just like a diner, but not nearly as comfortable. The family is crammed together, which can lead to trouble, and the rigid seating can't be made comfortable no matter how many cushions you use. Plus, the booth benches tend to have high backs, blocking both the view of the diners and the view from the rest of the kitchen. Bad idea! Yes, it saves space, but at the price of comfort and attractiveness. There are better options. Tear it out and install a pantry, shelving, a second fridge or a freezer, or a kitchen island in its place.

Don't forget lighting. If your kitchen table is an afterthought, there may be no overhead lighting for it. Don't make your family eat in the dark! Food looks more appetizing when it's attractively lit (and you all will look and feel better, too). And good lighting is a must for the homework and projects that invariably get done at the kitchen table. No matter how bright the rest of the kitchen is or how many windows you have, it's worth hiring an electrician to hang a light fixture that matches your decor or install recessed lighting. Whatever you do, don't succumb to the temptation to just put a floor lamp or two by the table. The last thing you need in a place where people are constantly walking, standing, sitting, and moving chairs in and out is a clutter of cords!

Make the condiments convenient. Keep the napkins, salt, pepper, and other condiments you use regularly (that don't need refrigeration) on a tray or in a basket on or near the table. That way, they can be carried easily when it's time to eat or time to clear the table for homework or other activities.

Create a coffee corner. You can minimize morning chaos by dedicating a part of the countertop nearest to the table as your morning coffee station. Put the coffee machine, grinder, filters, and any other equipment you use to prepare your coffee together on the counter with a tray of mugs, sweeteners, spoons, and napkins. If you have tea-drinkers in the family, set out their tea as well, and position the kettle on the nearest burner. Now it's all ready when you are!

Reining in the Recipes

Clip 'n' save. My boyfriend's father was in the Foreign Service, so he knows a thing or two about staying organized. He also enjoys cooking and trying new recipes, so he subscribes to all the cooking magazines. But he doesn't just let them stack up. Each month, he goes through the magazines, chooses recipes he wants to try, and cuts them out. Then he can recycle the magazines and get all that paper out of the house. But he doesn't stop there. Once the recipes are clipped, they go into a special recipe notebook that has dividers separating types of recipes. The new recipes go in the front of each section, so that they can be saved or discarded once they've been tried. Can't face setting up your own notebook, or want something prettier than the classroom standard? Bookstores now sell attractive notebooks just for recipes, and you can get self-stick notebooks just for clipped recipes at sites like www.solutions.com (see page 48).

Read at the library. Save money and space by reading cooking magazines at your local library instead of subscribing to them. If you see a recipe or article you just have to have, make a photocopy while you're there.

Hang a magazine rack. The kitchen is a great place for a magazine rack because it lets you keep your favorite cooking magazines in easy reach. If you don't have room for a floor rack—or are afraid that you, your pets, or your family will crash into it—there are specialty wall-mounted magazine racks that are very attractive. Check home improvement stores, home decorating stores like Pier 1, and catalogs like Improvements (order online at www.improvementscatalog.com)—they're really easy to install with the special grippers provided.

Get a magazine butler. If you can't bear to toss, recycle, or give away your favorite cooking magazines (shame on you!), at least keep them upright, compact, and easy to find and use. Clear acrylic holders store a year's worth of magazines and are available from home centers, organizing stores, and catalogs.

Limit cookbooks in the kitchen. After spending what seems like a lifetime trying to get all my cookbooks *into* the kitchen, it hurts to recommend this. But frankly, it makes too much sense to pass up. Think about how many cookbooks you have. And then think about how many you actually use. If you have the space to shelve all your cookbooks in the kitchen, great! But if you don't, make space for the few that you use most often and shelve the rest in the bookcase that's closest to the kitchen. They'll still be nearby when you need them, but they won't be taking up precious kitchen space.

Cull your cookbooks, part one. Ouch! Ouch! This one's probably harder for me than it is for you. While you're sorting through your cookbooks, see if you can donate some to the library book sale or the local thrift store, or pass them down to the kids (if and *only* if they want them!). You may have some that you were given as wedding presents and never liked, some that sounded great but proved disappointing, some that you bought when they were the rage or when you got a new appliance, some that you got while traveling, or some that no longer reflect the way you eat. If you can get them out, do it.

Cull your cookbooks, part two. What if you have a cookbook you never use—except for that one special holiday recipe or favorite cake? If you use just a few recipes from a cookbook, it makes sense to photocopy those recipes and give the book itself away. (Make sure you note on the photocopy what book you took it from; that way, you'll be able to find it again if the photocopy gets torn or stained.)

Keep the one you love. Here's where I'll give you a break. The kitchen is rightly called the heart of the home, and there's a lot of sentiment attached to it. If you

Tight-Space Solutions

My friend Delilah loves to cook, and she loves to watch cooking shows. She hit on the ingenious idea of putting a TV in the kitchen so she can watch the shows while she's puttering around in there. But she and her boyfriend, Chaz, didn't want to take up valuable kitchen space by putting the TV on a counter or even mounting one on a wall. Instead, they bought a small set that is specially adapted to mount under a kitchen cabinet. Some of these even include CD and DVD players! (Delilah put hers under the tall cabinet over the refrigerator, where it's out of harm's way and easy to watch.) Now she can watch her favorite cooking shows and learn new recipes and techniques while she works!

never, ever use—but really, really love—an old cookbook (perhaps your first-ever Betty Crocker kids' cookbook or your grandma's battered, splattered first-edition copy of *The Joy of Cooking*), keep it. Display it with pride. You might want to hang it in a shadowbox on the kitchen wall. But I have to say it again: Make sure you're not using sentiment to justify keeping *all* your cookbooks.

Check out the library's collection. Let the library come to your rescue again by looking over their cookbook selection. You can check out the ones that interest you (one at a time, please), and put sticky tags on any recipes you think you'd like to try. Photocopy the tagged pages at home or when you return the book to the library. If you really fall in love with a library cookbook, you can buy it for your own collection next time you go online or to the bookstore. Meanwhile, think of all the so-so cookbooks you'll get to test drive without buying!

Get your recipes online. Lots of online sites offer extensive collections of free recipes. Try www.epicurious.com and www.recipes.com to start. Your favorite cooking products will often feature recipes on their Web sites, too, so use a search engine to find one—say, King Arthur Flour—and check it out. Enjoy comparing recipes online, then print out the one you want to try. If you like it, save the printout for the next time you want to make that dish.

Save your recipes on your computer. You can also keep recipes you enjoy or plan to try in a file on your computer (or on a disk) and print them out or refer to them as needed. If you have Martha Stewart- or Mary Engelbreit-like tendencies, the Internet has many sites that let you create beautiful recipes to print out with gorgeous borders and charming typefaces. (A quick Google search for recipe cards yields www.razzledazzlerecipes.com, www.graphicgarden.com, www.nextag.com, www.recipecards.net, www.countryclipart.com, and www.freeprintablerecipe cards.net, to name just a few.) Otherwise, just head for the copy paper.

Don't forget the faithful recipe file. It's not so great for clip 'n' save recipes, but if you write down your own, that old card file with the 3- by 5-inch (or 6- by 8-inch) cards is still a workhorse, holding a lot in a small space. You can find attractive wooden card files (or decoupage a metal card file, if you're handy). And you can get colored file cards, so you can use different colors for different types of recipes. And of course, you can keep them in alphabetical order with those handy dividers. Just be sure you write new cards to replace the ones that are wearing out (keeping a computer backup is a good idea), and go through the file at least once a year to clear out recipes you've never used or no longer use.

Go back to school. My friend Anne uses a three-ring loose-leaf binder for recipes. Recipes she clips from cooking magazines can be glued to the pages, and she can also write down her own. It's easy to get rid of recipes she doesn't use, too. She uses colored index tabs, just like kids use in school, to divide the notebook into sections.

Set up a cooking station. If you love cooking and spending time in your kitchen, it's a great place for a specialized mini-office. I call it a "cooking station." Rather than setting up your laptop on the kitchen table or counter, dedicate a space in the kitchen to this mini-office so you can have it set up all the time (and will therefore actually use it). Create an "office nook" with a computer desk and comfortable chair. Not enough space? You can find "roll-around microstations" at home centers and catalogs like Improvements (online at www.improvementscatalog.com), with an adjustable top, drawer, and two adjustable shelves for your printer and other essentials. It's on casters, so it rolls easily to where you want it or out of the way, and it comes in attractive wood finishes so it's as handsome as it is functional. Add a chair and a basket for necessities like your cell phone, pens, and paper, and you're in business! Now you can search for recipes online, exchange recipes with friends and family via e-mail, input your favorite recipes—and print out what you need, where you need it. If you have room for a permanent

Pet Alert!

My back door opens out of the kitchen, so I keep my golden retriever's, Molly's, leash hung on a hook on the wall beside the door. (You could also hang a leash on a hook on the side of a kitchen cabinet, if that side of the cabinet is near the door.) I have doormats both inside and outside the door, to give muddy paws maximum wiping time. And I keep a "Molly towel" neatly folded on a stool just inside the door if more paw-drying (or coat-drying, if it's raining and she gets drenched) is needed.

cooking station, you can hang bookshelves over it for your cookbooks, add a hanging magazine rack for your cooking magazines, and hang a TV under the shelves so you can watch favorite cooking shows (see "Tight-Space Solutions" on page 122).

The Door to the Great Outdoors

Use two mats. If, like me, your door to the great outdoors is in your kitchen, you already know that lots of the outdoors seems to get tracked in. (My house's previous owners, who in general did a great job decorating, put white tiles in the kitchen. Consequently, I can see every dab of mud. Ugh!) Fight the mess by using two doormats—a heavy-duty one outside the door and a decorative (but still functional) one indoors.

Get a second stand. You may recall that I recommended that you put an umbrella stand by the front door. Get a second one of these super-helpful stands for near the kitchen door. They take up a tiny amount of room but will keep everyone from dumping dripping umbrellas on the floor. I recommend a ceramic stand, since wet umbrellas won't rot or rust them. You'll be surprised by how many umbrellas they hold—all upright for easy grabbing. They also neatly contain other upright objects like baseball bats and brooms.

Box up your boots. With everyone tramping in and out through the back door, your kitchen is likely to accumulate a pile of wet, muddy, or otherwise grungy footwear. Not to mention all the mud, melting snow, grass, and other tracked-in stuff all over the floor. Fortunately, some ingenious companies have come up with wonderful rectangular shoe-and-boot organizers that will keep that footwear in line (literally). They are durable, come in several sizes, and even feature optional rubber inserts so water can drain right through and your boots and shoes can dry faster. Some of them even have two levels. You can find them in mail-order home catalogs and stores.

Add a bench. If you have room, put one of those ubiquitous benches that have storage under the seat by your back door. Whether they're the kind with a seat that lifts up to reveal a storage compartment or the type with rectangular storage baskets that fit neatly in place under the seat, these convenient benches serve double-duty as seating and storage. And they make it easy for everyone to pull off their shoes before they track gunk from outside all over the kitchen floor.

ONWARD!

Whew! You've conquered the kitchen and kicked the clutter out of every drawer, cabinet, and even the fridge. Now it's time to take on that other clutter-sink (so to speak)—the bathroom. Take a deep breath, turn the page, and plunge (those puns just keep coming) in!

Chapter 7

Bathroom De-Cluttering Basics

Bathrooms are usually small. Everybody uses them. And everybody's shampoos, cosmetics, lotions and potions, towels, dirty clothes, hair dryers, razors, medicines, toothbrushes, and you-name-it end up falling off every available surface. Then there's the issue of people slipping, tripping, and otherwise injuring themselves on the clutter. Try the tips in this chapter to kick out that clutter and organize what's left without causing a palace revolt.

PRIORITIES FOR BATHROOMS

Start the de-cluttering process in the bathroom by setting some clutter-kicking priorities. First, focus on what matters most to you about the way each bathroom (if you have more than one) looks. Next, consider your other concerns about the bathroom's appearance and make a list of everything that bothers you. Eventually you will rank your clutter concerns in order until you get to what matters least. The first step in setting clutter-kicking priorities for the bathroom is to take a good, hard look at the "before" state of the room, and then to visualize the "after."

A Bathroom Visualization

To get to your "after," you need to start with the "before"—the way things look right now. So get out some paper, or use the "My Bathroom—Before" form on page 128 (or make a photocopy of it) and write on that. Write down every place there's clutter in the bathroom, and note what that clutter is. Are there piles of unread magazines and newspapers? Towels tossed in a corner and getting smelly from dampness? Uncapped toothpaste tubes leaking on the counter? Scuzzy soap dishes? Maybe there are trailing toilet paper rolls and wadded-up tissues escaping from the trash. If there are, write 'em down.

Remember, the bathroom may be cluttered, but it's probably a small room. It won't take but a few minutes to finish your list!

Once you've jotted down a quick description of your bathroom's "before" state, it's time to move on to the "after"—how you want the room to look when you've kicked the clutter. Write it all down on a piece of paper, or in the "My Bathroom—After" form on page 128 (or on as many photocopies of it as you need to do it justice). To make sure you're being realistic, look at the room every few minutes while you're doing this.

Your description can be short and to the point: "I don't want to see tubes, bottles, hair and makeup accessories, nail polish, and spilled gunk from all of the above on the vanity top. I don't want to slip on one of the 17 bottles of shampoo and other hair and body products on the bathtub floor. I'd like to be able to organize the space under the sink, so I can see and reach everything. I'd like to see all the towels hanging up neatly instead of falling off the towel rack and onto the floor." Or you can create a detailed portrait of exactly how you'd like the room to look if it were perfect (for you). You can picture the colors of the walls, towels, and shower curtain; whether there would be tile, and if so, what it would look like; describe your ideal sink, vanity, and mirror—everything.

Getting There

Now that you have captured your bathroom's "before" condition, listing all the specifics, and you've imagined its "after" appearance, you can finally prioritize the

My Bathroom—Before

_____
_____
_____
_____
_____
_____
_____
_____
_____
_____
_____

My Bathroom—After

_____
_____
_____
_____
_____
_____
_____
_____
_____
_____
_____
_____

My Bathroom Priority List

_____

_____

_____

_____

_____

_____

_____

_____

steps you'll need to take to get there from here. Again, bearing both "before" and "after" in mind, I'd recommend starting with what bothers you most about the "before" condition and working down the list from there.

Maybe you're concerned that soggy towels and washcloths on the bathroom floor are not just unsightly, they're also mildew and tripping hazards, and you want them picked up and hung up where they are easy to reach and will dry out quickly. Make that your top priority. Or perhaps you think you'll scream if you see another uncapped tube of toothpaste or all-but-empty shampoo bottle. Put that high on the priority list, too.

Write down whatever's driving you to distraction on the "My Bathroom Priority List" (or photocopy it, if you'd prefer), in descending order from most to least maddening. Now you have your priorities straight! Once you've finished, you can turn to the tips below to find ingenious ways of dealing with each problem.

THE BATHROOM TIPS

Take care of the towels. One great "Tool of the Trade" for towels is a towel rack that fits over the shower curtain rod, giving you a towel rack that extends the entire length of the tub. This is a great way to create space for everyone's towels if all you have now is the typical one-towel rack that several family members have to share. Get one of these, and keep those towels dry and off the floor.

Tone down the towels. For a guest bath, or if you have your own bathroom, keep the bath towels, hand towels, and washcloths all the same color. (If it's your bathroom, you can obviously have several sets in different colors and rotate them when you need a new look.) It will make things look less busy, and thus, less cluttered. Plain towels without patterns or contrasting colors will also give the room a cleaner, less cluttered look.

Give each his (or her) own. Then again, if several people share a bathroom, giving each person his or her own color of towels, washcloths, and the like will simplify things. In this case, a plain bath mat is a necessity. But you can liven things up by getting bath mats that match everyone's towel colors and rotating them.

Throw in the towel. Take the towels off the shelf and sort through them. You love that shade of peach, but there's a worn patch on the front and . . . yes, that *is* a little hole. Throw . . . it . . . out. Do you ever really set out those snowman guest towels? Has your child stopped using the Scooby-Doo beach towel? The "his and her butt" towels that seemed so funny at the time? What about those horrible velour towels that looked so gorgeous but don't absorb any water? Put all the worn-out towels in one pile, the "don't like 'em, don't use 'em" towels in a second pile, and the "still-good, still-used" towels in a third. Toss the worn-out pile; pack up the don't-use pile for Goodwill, the Salvation Army, or the Society of St. Vincent de Paul; and put the rest back. Whew! Look how much more room there is in your linen closet now! And maybe you can find a new peach towel on sale.

Stick with one mat. I've been in bathrooms where there was a bath mat or rug in front of the tub and another one in front of the sink. Even the toilet had its own fitted rug—and there was a fuzzy covering on the toilet lid, too. This polka-dot rug approach adds visual clutter—not to mention actual clutter! It creates tripping hazards, provides plenty of places for germs to collect and hide, and adds to your mountain of laundry. If you have multiple mats, clear them out! One per bathroom is plenty—surely people can move the mat to the sink if they need to. Or you could compromise: Splurge and buy a bigger mat that covers more of the floor.

Keep the mat on the floor. I see a lot of bath mats hanging over the sides of tubs. This looks messy and adds to the visual clutter. Make sure your bath mat or rug looks clean and presentable; keep a backup to rotate in so you won't have to do without when you're washing one; and keep that mat on the floor, where it belongs.

Simplify the shower curtain, part one. A child's bathroom with zebra, moose, or seashell shower-curtain hooks is cool. In an adult's bathroom, they just add to the visual clutter. Don't draw attention to your shower-curtain rod with elaborate hooks. Do you *really* want people looking up there?

Simplify the shower curtain, part two. You can guess what's coming next: Donate your busily patterned shower curtain to Goodwill and replace it with a plain one. A plain shower curtain in a pale or neutral color will make your bathroom look bigger and less visually cluttered. Save the fun shower curtains for the kids' bathrooms.

Simplify the curtains, period. What goes for the shower curtains goes for your window treatments, too. Curtains with busy patterns close in a room visually—especially when it's a small room like a bathroom. And all those little design elements just add to the visual clutter. You'll notice the same effect if you look at wooden or bamboo blinds that are a single pale color versus the ones that have darker spots and splashes patterning them. Whatever window treatment you choose for your bathroom, keep it light, bright, and simple.

Nix the naked shower-curtain liner. By this, I don't mean that you shouldn't use a liner without a shower curtain. If that's your choice, that's fine. Just don't use a *clear* shower-curtain liner. After all, you can see things through a clear liner. Things that look like clutter. Instead, opt for a solid liner and keep what's in the tub your secret.

Say "it's curtains" for the shower. This goes for the tub, too. Keep your shower curtain and liner fully drawn across the tub or shower stall at all times. It will look so much neater than a full view of the tub—even if it's the cleanest, least-cluttered tub in creation. The blank canvas of the curtain reads like a clean, spacious, uncluttered wall. And there's an added bonus—an extended curtain and liner will dry out faster, which really helps to keep germs and mildew at bay.

Hang it up. If you need a mirror in the shower, buy one of the fog-free versions (available in home catalogs and home improvement stores) that you can attach to the wall.

Add a shelf. I think a shelf in the shower stall or tub looks neater and less cluttered than razors and the like hanging on the walls. A mirror is one thing—people

5-Minute Fixes for Bathrooms

Here are six quick fixes for the bathroom. See what a difference you can make in just 5 minutes?

Stash the shampoo. Buy a shampoo holder rack that fits over your showerhead and put your shampoos, conditioners, detanglers, and other hair-care products on its shelves. You'll get rid of all those bottles lining the sides of the tub (or sitting in the tub, for that matter). Put the almost-empties in the front and tell everybody to use those first. Or, if you don't think they will, bag the full bottles and stash them out of sight until the others are used up.

Switch to liquid soap. This one's easy! No more dirty bars, slimy soap dishes, or slippery showers. (Confess: How many times have you dropped a bar while showering and then had to grope around trying to find it? Ugh!) You'll save space on your vanity, and you can put the tub bottle in your new shower-head rack with the shampoos.

Do one drawer. Pick any drawer in your vanity, then sort through it and toss anything you don't use—no matter how "good" it is or if it has never been opened!—and anything that's broken (including worn-out ponytail holders and broken barrettes). Wipe down the drawer, replace the in-use items, make a note of any broken stuff that you want to replace, and you're done. There! Doesn't that feel better?

Chuck old cosmetics. Yes, you loved Raven Red lipstick in high school, but that was 20 years ago. Yes, there's still a smear of blush in the case. And yes, that glitter nail polish was a lot of fun to wear three Christmases ago, but now it's separated into six sticky layers. Some people may not believe it, but many of us

expect to see mirrors on walls, after all, and a hanging one frees your hands. But a bunch of little stuff hanging all over sure says clutter to me. If you have more bits and pieces than a single shelf will hold, put up several, or put attractive waterproof containers on the shelf and group the objects in each container by type so you can quickly find what you need. (Of course, the shelf should be waterproof, too.) Don't put it any higher than you can comfortably reach.

Add a bookcase. One great way to add narrow bathroom storage, if you have the space, is to put a bookcase in the bathroom. You can run one from the floor to have sentimental attachments to our old cosmetics because of the memories they inspire—of a special date; of our mom (isn't that her French Blue eyeshadow?); or just of a time when we were young, thin, and carefree. And some of us can't stop trying the latest and greatest that we read about in a women's magazine—while, of course, not throwing out any of our other makeup. But please. The bathroom isn't a cosmetic museum or The Body Shop. If you must keep Mom's French Blue shadow or your Twiggy nail polish, tuck them into a keepsake box. Then toss your old makeup and any new makeup that doesn't look or feel good on you—unless the kids want it and will really wear it. (I don't care how much it cost or how new it is, if it doesn't look and feel good, you know you're never going to wear it.)

Pitch the perfume. Perfumes go bad. You know that, right? So why is that stinky old bottle of Love Potion Number Nine still taking up shelf space? Collect all those bottles and smell them right now. Toss any that smell "off," making a note to replace any you really love. Next, toss any perfumes you've never liked and never wear. (The sales clerk probably made him buy you that bottle of Shalimar, anyway.) If anyone asks what happened to the Evening in Paris, just inform them that hey, perfumes go bad!

Make sure your meds are current. You knew I'd get to this one, didn't you? Just do it. Open the medicine cabinet and check those expiration dates. Toss the old stuff in the toilet and flush. (Not the bottles, though, please.) Make a note of anything you need to replace. And don't self-medicate—if there's a prescription medicine in the cabinet for an old illness, even if the medicine hasn't expired, throw it out (unless it's for a recurring illness).

the ceiling, or you could use a two-shelf model and use the top for storage or display. Make sure the color suits the room—paint it to match or buy a neutral color or natural-wood case. Voilà—you've just doubled or tripled your storage space while taking up only a foot of floor space!

Buy some baskets, part one. A bookcase is a great bathroom storage solution. But because bookshelves are open, it's easy for them to look like a chaotic jumble of clutter once you start storing things on them. One way to avoid that is to buy a set of square or rectangular wicker, grass, or other woven baskets that are the

Dear Claire,

My mom is trying to de-clutter our bathroom. She's told me and my sister that we have to share the same shampoo, detangler, conditioner, gel, mousse, body wash—everything! And she says *she* wants to use the same ones, too! Eeeewwww! How gross is that? How can we tell her that we each want to use our own without getting in trouble?

—My Shampoo

Dear My Shampoo,

I suggest a compromise. What if you and your sister could agree to choose just one of each product to use at a time? You can keep the rest in a plastic bin in your drawer or closet and rotate or alternate as you please. And maybe in return for being allowed to use your own stuff, you could also agree to cut down on the number of cosmetics, curlers, ponytail holders, brushes, combs, perfumes, nail polish bottles, and all the other indispensable stuff you keep in the bathroom? (The rest of it can go in another plastic bin, if there's no room left in the first one.) Out of sight, out of (your mom's) mind, right? Show her that now there's plenty of room for *her* shampoo and conditioner, too.

Good luck,
Claire

right size to fit your shelves. You can stash your stuff in them and still have a beautifully neat, uncluttered look. Baskets are great holders for extra toilet paper rolls, feminine hygiene products, bars of soap, guest or hand towels, and washcloths—you name it. Out of sight but not out of mind!

Buy some baskets, part two. Large round wicker, grass, or other woven hamper-style baskets are beautiful storage solutions, too. You can put one at either end of your bathroom bookcase, cluster a trio of different sizes in a decorative grouping, or situate one as a focal point. Use them as traditional laundry hampers, roll towels and stash them inside, or use one to keep a plentiful supply of toilet paper or diapers at hand.

Table it. Need some counter space in the bathroom? Try a nightstand or bedside table. These are readily available at flea markets and secondhand shops—and probably in your or a relative's attic, too. Paint one to match the bathroom's decor and you'll not only gain a space-saving dressing table, you'll get a storage drawer, too!

Don't forget the trash. Talking about a bedside table reminds me that the area underneath it is the perfect size for a wastebasket. And we all know how important it is to have a wastebasket in the bathroom, right? I'm always dismayed to walk into someone's bathroom and see no wastebasket and no facial tissues. To me, these are every bit as vital as toilet paper. What are they thinking?! So please, make sure you have a wastebasket in every bathroom. No reason to buy revolting plastic or industrial models, either (unless your bathroom has an intentionally industrial look). Mine is a cranberry red tin bucket. A basket or hamper makes a great trash can, too—just tuck that ugly plastic one inside to keep the basket fibers from getting yucky. It goes without saying that, if your wastebasket isn't covered, you need to keep it extra-tidy and empty it regularly.

Keep it clean. Some of the most necessary things in your bathroom are also the ugliest: the cleaning supplies. You've got to have cleansers, brushes, sponges, a plunger, drain openers, squeegees, and all that other fun stuff accessible and at hand. But talk about something that needs to be out of sight! Now, please don't buy a cutesy doll or other plunger cover, I beg you. That just adds more clutter while still reminding everyone of what's under there. If you add a bookcase or other storage solution, you can free up the under-sink area and use it exclusively for cleanup items. Buy a colorful bucket for brushes, scrubbers, and sponges and tuck it inside; put hooks inside the door and hang cleaning rags on them. Don't store cleaners in the same space with shampoos, cosmetics, and other family items—the cleaners will get lost, spilled, or worse. Give them their own space. And keep them behind a childproof latch or lock if you have young kids.

Tools of the Trade

I told you about how great under-sink organizers are in Chapter 6, and the bathroom's another place where they're superhelpful. These organizers make it easy to store cleaning supplies or other things under the bathroom sink. I highly recommend them. See page 112 for the lowdown.

Make a cleaning basket. Yes, one of those tall, round hampers will work beautifully to hold the plunger and two buckets of cleaning supplies, too. Stack the buckets beside the plunger, put the lid on the hamper, and voilà!

Dress it up. Mix your furniture to suit your needs. If you have an outgrown child's dresser (or have or can find a suitable used dresser at a flea market or secondhand shop), see if it's a good size for your bathroom. If so, transform it with an appropriate coat of paint and move it right in. Drawers can hold tons of towels, toilet paper, and toiletries. If the dresser has two small drawers on the top, they're a great size for holding bandages and other first-aid supplies.

Put a skirt on it. We didn't have vanities in the Colonial home I grew up in. In fact, we were lucky to have bathrooms, which generations of former owners had to do without. With tiny add-on bathrooms and storage at a premium, my mother had to get creative. Using elastic and curtain fabric, she created "sink skirts" to go around the bathroom sinks, each skirt matching the curtains in that particular bathroom.

Skirt the dressing table. If you're short on bathroom storage, you can create additional storage space if you have room for a narrow dressing table. My mother had taken a marble-topped hallway table and turned it into a dressing table in my childhood bathroom by putting a "skirt" on it in a fabric that matched the sink skirt and curtains. (See the previous tip for details on these.) She hung a mirror over it, and voilà! Suddenly there was a pretty, useful dressing table that took up only a foot of valuable floor space (of course it was longer—probably 3 or 4 feet). And there was that long, high space beneath for much-needed storage.

File it away. Still on the lookout for tall, narrow bathroom storage? Try a file cabinet. A four-drawer file, or four-high, has nice, deep shelves for towels, linens, and cleaning supplies. If you have oak accessories in your bathroom, try to find an old oak file cabinet at a flea market or secondhand store. Otherwise, get a modern white one that looks less like office-supply stock than the typical heavy-metal versions, or paint one to match your decor.

Peg it. What to do with all those bathrobes? Remember those Shaker peg strips we talked about in Chapter 5? They're perfect for hanging bathrobes, too. Buy a short peg strip and paint it to match your bathroom woodwork or the color of the wall.

Hook it up. For a two-for-one punch, use decorative metal hooks—they have a

Pet Alert!

Aren't cats great? There's just one bad thing about cats (not counting hairballs, of course)—the litter box. If you don't have a basement or porch where you can stash the litter box, you may end up—like me—sharing your bathroom with the family cats. In this case, it's essential that you keep the litter box presentable—clean, odor-free, and preferably out of sight but not out of the cats' reach. If your bathroom is big enough, you can screen off a corner of the room and hide the litter box behind the screen. If it's small like mine, you may end up stashing the litter box in the only available space—the bathtub.

Wherever you put the litter box, keep it cleaned up, swept up, and covered up. I use clumping litter and add both an enzymatic deodorizer and a product called Ammo Cat that removes ammonia odors—and I clean the box every morning! Here's a hint, though: You may like the way scented litter smells, but cats don't. They may boycott a scented litter box. So stick with unscented litter and your cats will thank you!

One more thing while we're on the subject of pets: If you have pets, make sure everyone in the family and all guests know to keep toilet lids down at *all* times. Dogs like to drink toilet water and cats have been known to jump or fall in when the lid is left up. If you use toilet fresheners with bleach and other additives, be aware that they are toxic to pets. Your beloved furry friends could die from drinking toilet water or licking themselves after landing in it. Don't let this happen to your pets!

---

larger hook for your bathrobe, and a smaller hook at the bottom for your pajamas or nightgown. If you have little ones, put their hooks where they can reach them easily, and make sure those hooks have ceramic knobs on the ends. Wooden hooks are also a good option.

Don't forget the door. Make the most of bathroom door space by hanging a full-length mirror, available at home and DIY stores, on the back of it so that it faces you when the door is closed. These mirrors are inexpensive and supereasy to attach—you just hook them over the top of the door. Before I got one for my bathroom, I had to wait until I got to work to see what I looked like from the waist down. Yikes! Mirrors make rooms look bigger, too—a definite plus. If you don't like the color of the frame (mine is white), paint it to match your decor.

Don't forget the toilet. You're bound to have some space over the back of your toilet, so don't let it go to waste. If there's a window behind your toilet, put a small cabinet (like a jewelry cabinet) on top of the tank to hold hair accessories, odds and ends, and even jewelry. (Not your good jewelry, though—what if somebody tipped it over?) I prefer a closed cabinet to a wicker or openwork stand, even though the shape of the wicker toiletries stand is perfect for the toilet back. But wicker collects dust, which tends to gum down in a humid bathroom, and the open style lets you (and everyone else) see all the stuff on the shelves, which then looks like . . . clutter. If you have a solid wall behind the toilet, you can install a cabinet or étagère specifically designed to fit around and over the toilet. They're available from home centers. Or you can hang a second medicine cabinet, perhaps with a decorative framed mirror on the door, or a set of shelves. Just remember: If it sits on the toilet tank, it has to be easy to lift off without creating an object avalanche. And if it sits over the tank, the bottom has to be high enough so you can lift off the top of the tank and get in there easily.

Don't read in the bathroom. This one seems like a no-brainer to me. There's enough stuff in the bathroom without bringing in a bunch of magazines, books, catalogs, and newspapers. Besides, unless you live alone, other people are probably waiting to use the bathroom. And even if they're not, there are better places to read!

Keep appliance cords out of sight. Reserve one drawer, cabinet shelf, or covered basket for blow-dryers, curlers, electric razors, electric toothbrush chargers, and other electrical equipment. Cords are unsightly and hazardous. Use the appliances when they're needed and keep them out of sight when they're not.

Store toothbrushes upright. I have an ingenious handmade ceramic toothbrush holder with semicircular holders for four toothbrushes and a cup in the center that will hold two or three tubes of toothpaste upright. An ordinary glass or cup would work fine, too, as would a short vase or (new, please) flowerpot. Just make sure everyone's brushes are different colors!

Put it under glass. Funny how clutter doesn't look like clutter when it's cleverly contained. If you store your cotton balls, swabs, emery boards, bath salts, little soaps, and bath oil beads in matching glass apothecary jars, they suddenly look not only organized, but also pretty enough to display on open shelves. Can't face the expense? Try canning jars. But if you have little ones who might tip a jar over, opt for unbreakable plastic and file the jar idea for a future bathroom makeover.

Magnetize your medicine cabinet. Steal this great tip from Martha Stewart: Have a sheet of galvanized steel cut to fit the back of the medicine-cabinet door and caulk it in place. Attach a magnetic notepad holder (available at office-supply stores) to hold combs and brushes and magnetized hooks for lightweight tools like eyelash curlers.

Add more cabinet space. Make the most of tall medicine-cabinet shelves by adding acrylic risers to double the shelf space.

the **Pros Know**

My friend Skye Alexander, feng shui master and author of several great feng shui–flavored clutter-control books (including *10-Minute Clutter Control* and *10-Minute Clutter Control Room by Room*), has a bathroom tip I really like. Skye suggests creating guest bath baskets with decorative soaps and personal-size toiletries like shampoo, conditioner, lotion, bath oil, toothpaste, and the like. Add a nicely rolled washcloth and hand towel. Skye points out that if you keep a couple of these baskets on hand, you'll always be ready when guests arrive.

Dustables

I know you see them in every magazine—certainly I do—those fascinating bathrooms with shelves or cabinets of decorative objects adding interest and beauty to the room. They look great—in the magazines. But in reality, they collect gummy dust and dirt faster than the dog. The heat, dampness, and humidity make bathrooms a bad place to display dustables—especially ones with porous surfaces like crystals and shells. If you want to feature a natural theme in your bathroom, add some plants, which will love the humidity and oxygenate the air. Then hang photos of seashells, rocks, a woodland scene, or whatever you find delightful—in waterproof, easy-to-clean frames.

Choose your cabinet carefully. If you're shopping for a new medicine cabinet, make sure it works as well as it looks. I saw a wonderful one just today that had a divided shelf under the cabinet. It was beautiful and provided extra storage or display space!

Stash the scale. What's most likely to trip you up when you stagger groggily toward the bathroom in the dead of night or rush in, thinking of something else? The scale. It lies there, low to the ground and usually in bathroom-ready camouflage, like a coiled reptile ready to strike. (This is also true if you're trying to weigh yourself.) If you have a bathroom closet, put the scale in there. Otherwise, keep it out of harm's way—under the lowest shelf or under a piece of bathroom furniture. It's easy to pull it out when you want to check your weight, and keeping it under there will be added incentive to vacuum frequently.

Beautify the facial tissues. I don't know which is worse—a naked cardboard tissue box (no matter how colorful the design is) or a frilly tissue holder that looks like a dust storm waiting to happen. A box of tissues is a bathroom essential, but it can also be an eyesore. Make your tissue box work for your bathroom rather than against it by matching it to the bathroom decor. If you store your bathroom staples in decorative baskets, buy a tissue box–cover in a matching basket style. Oak bathroom? Get an oak tissue box to match. (I did.) Lots of chrome? Get a chrome box. Unique bathroom style? Buy a standard plastic box and cover it to match your decor.

Watch for rust and rot. There are lots of gorgeous styles of modern and antique metal and paper canisters, and also canisters of all kinds with decorative paper labels. I see them featured in lush magazine shots of bathrooms all the time, and they're supposed to be for storing cotton balls, cotton swabs, makeup squares, soap balls, and the like. But unless you have a guest bathroom that's used infrequently or a half-bath without a tub or shower, I'd advise saving these containers for a drier room. Glass, stainless steel, ceramic, wood, breathable basketry, plastic—there are lots of bathroom options that can stand up to the splashing and humidity better than metal and paper.

Add a little vanity. My bathroom's barely big enough to turn around in—and that's the *big* bathroom, not the half-bath in the laundry room. But I still needed more space—basically, space to set down clothes or put down small stuff on the way in the door. A dressing table or any other sizable surface was out of the question, so I stopped at a local antiques store that had an assortment of tiny children's vanity tables out front. These tables had three legs and were flat in back so they could butt up against a wall. The smallest was about 2 feet long and 1 foot wide at its widest—perfect! And it was already white, so it would blend into the bathroom wall. Best of all, it was on sale for $15!

Let there be light. In no room is a nightlight more essential than the bathroom. People need to be able to find the door and the light switch quickly and easily. Choose one that's attractive but not fussy, and put it where it will be out of reach of water.

Keep lamp cords off the floor. Yes, it's important to have lots of good light in a bathroom. But floor and table lamps, with their hazardous cords, are especially out of place here. Instead, use wall sconces, ceiling fixtures, and light strips to provide enough light.

ONWARD!

These tips will help you kick your bathroom clutter. But *keeping* the bathroom de-cluttered requires a combination of cunning, incentives, discipline, and threats. You're on your own with those! (But I know you can do it.)

Meanwhile, let's turn to some rooms that are easier to keep organized once you've cleared them out—the living and family rooms.

Chapter 8

Livable Living Rooms, Functional Family Rooms

Can't find any of the remotes under all the bags and magazines? Did Grandma sit on Jen's iPod last time she came over, buried as it was under the cushions? Wonder where your favorite mugs wandered off to, not to mention the cat? Formal living rooms that aren't used can become storage rooms when a family's accumulated clutter creeps into them. And any room with an entertainment center can become not a rec room but a *wreck* room as everybody's snacks, papers, and assorted projects pile up. But never fear—in this chapter, you'll learn how to clear out these rooms without making them into sterile showpieces.

PRIORITIES FOR LIVING AND FAMILY ROOMS

The first thing to do is to determine whether your living room *is* your family room (in which case you have only one room to worry about), or if you have a formal living room (it used to be called a parlor) where you would entertain guests, as well as a family room where your family actually "lives." In this case, decide which room needs your attention first, and then focus on it.

There's a third possibility, too—that you have only a formal living room that's supposed to be the "good room" for guests, but it either never gets used at all because you want to keep the furniture looking new (or protect your priceless antiques), or it's turned into a clutter repository, an upscale storage room, because it was never really used for anything else.

In this last case, the family has no relaxing place to get together and play, talk, read, watch TV, and entertain friends, so everybody probably either holes up in their bedrooms or piles into the kitchen. I'd like to suggest that, while a formal room like this works fine in a large, spacious house with plenty of other rooms for the family, or for households where formal entertaining is a frequent occurrence, if neither of these is the case, it's a waste of valuable living space. Who are you preserving it for?

Your family would be happier with a cheerful, comfortable gathering place. Or you could turn the living room into a home office, library, or craft room. Just because your parents, in-laws, and grandparents all had these formal rooms is no reason to continue the tradition if your lifestyle doesn't require it and the room isn't giving you and your family pleasure.

I have two friends whose cheerful, sunny front room is actually sealed off from the rest of the house in winter to conserve heat, since no one ever goes in there. Its many windows, hardwood floors, and serene views are completely wasted, a museum for unused furniture. Meanwhile, this couple spent quite a lot of money retrofitting a windowless basement that floods in very rainy periods to turn it into a family room. That's where they (literally) hole up, watching TV in the semidarkness while the sun streams in upstairs. And it's where they entertain their guests!

Mind you, this is not a tirade against antique furniture or beautifully crafted modern pieces. I love both and have both in my own home. But I *use* them—they're my everyday furniture. As a result, I get pleasure from them each and every day. In the case of the antiques, I can picture past generations lovingly using each piece just as I do, and in the case of the modern pieces, I enjoy thinking about the artisans crafting them. I refuse to live in a museum! Museums are beautiful, but they're not livable.

Hopefully, your family also lives in its space. Now you just have to make the most of it!

What Do You Use Your Room For?

Because a lived-in living or family room gets such a lot of use and foot traffic, before you do more than pick up the floor or straighten the cushions, you should give some thought to your layout. After all, the living/family room is the ultimate multitasker, performing some of the functions that go on in almost every other room in the house (except, hopefully, the bathroom!).

The first thing to do is to take this book into your living or family room. Look around and ask yourself what usually goes on in there. Does the family watch TV and movies, play video games, listen to music? Do the kids do their homework in there? Do people eat in there? What about reading, knitting, and other activities? Does the family play board games or work on crosswords, sudoku, or jigsaw puzzles? Do you or the kids entertain friends in this room? Do your kids and pets play on the floor? Is this where you pay your bills? Does it double as a music room, with guitars, keyboards, and a piano? Do you have a minibar in one part of the room? Do overnight guests sleep there?

Once you've thought about what you do in the room, think about exactly where you do it. Where is the activity taking place? What furniture is used for each activity? Is it convenient, comfortable, and well lit for its purpose? Is there enough or too much of it? Is it appropriate for the activity? What about walk-through space? Is it easy to move through the room, or are people always crashing into things? Try to look at the room as though you were an efficiency expert seeing it for the first time. What "works" in the room? What needs to be changed?

Make some notes about what's working and what's not as you look things over. It might help to sketch out the room as it looks now, just roughly blocking out and labeling furniture, and then sketch some alternative arrangements that might work better. If you'd enjoy using something more attractive than a rough sketch, there are plenty of room-design kits available in bookstores and online from sources like Amazon, including the *Home Quick Planner,* with reusable, peel-and-stick furniture, the *Room and Furniture Layout Kit,* and the *3D Virtual Reality Room Planner* CD-ROM.

Your goal is to make this room really work well for everyone who uses it (including your pets). Note what furniture needs to go into other rooms or out the

My Living Room—Before

This living room is so cluttered that it isn't welcoming. There are no clear paths through the room. The furniture faces away from the fireplace. Furniture is in here that belongs in other rooms, and the furniture that does belong here isn't placed well.

My Living Room—After

Same living room, different plan. This time, the furniture is arranged for comfort and use, the "stray" furniture has been relocated to rooms where it's more appropriate, and all piles have been picked up. Areas for reading and talking, watching movies or television, and relaxing in front of the fire have been created. An aquarium adds interest and helps family members relax. The room is easy to navigate without crashing into randomly placed furniture or clutter.

SANITY SAVERS

If your living or family room just doesn't meet your family's needs, it's time to get creative. Designing the space *you* want is a great sanity saver—and as my friends have found, everyone else will probably love it, too! Here's how some of my friends created the perfect space for their needs.

Let the light shine in. After flirting for years with the idea of a possible move to Maine, my friends Carolyn and Gary decided to remain in their Pennsylvania home. But rather than settling for less, they decided to reward themselves by adding on their perfect living/family room where they'd had a deck off the side of the house. Their new family or great room is wonderful—it has floor-to-ceiling windows that let in tons of light, ceiling fans to keep the air moving, and a propane "wood stove" that adds warmth and a romantic glow to the room. They also added floor-to-ceiling shelves on the wall that adjoined their existing home, so there's now plenty of room for beloved books, CDs, DVDs, and the occasional object or picture. Their new room is so welcoming that it's hard to get friends and family to abandon it, even for dinner! And it freed up space for them to create a real dining room in their home for the first time.

Indulge yourself. My friend Rudy inherited his present home, and its living room was small and dark. Rudy, who loves plants and birds, decided to add on a sunroom and make that his new living room. The result is a marvelous, light-filled space that lets him display his indoor plants and enjoy the colorful birds that flit around outside the windows. It's not a conventional living or family room, true, but it suits him and his needs, and it's so inviting visitors can't stay away.

Choose your own space. My friends Delilah and Chaz bought a house with a conventional living room—and they hated it. Instead, they converted a space they loved—their screen porch, with a fabulous view across their property to the mountains—into their living room. They sealed the screen windows and door with custom-made acrylic panels to keep the cold out, added a propane wood stove for warmth and atmosphere, set up a music system, hung gorgeous plants from Delilah's greenhouse, put down colorful Southwestern rugs, and added a comfy sofa and cushy armchairs around their wood stove. Given a choice of where to be in their beautiful home, I—and pretty much everybody else, including their Boston terrier, Duke—would opt for the porch-cum-living room. It's perfect!

door, what furniture you should move in from other rooms or buy, and how to group the furniture to make the best use of your space.

Many designers recommend clustering furniture by use—around the entertainment center, for example. I can't say I agree with this approach, though it's certainly practical. To me, clusters of furniture bunched around a room add up to clutter. I'd rather create a restful, open, multipurpose space, even if it means rearranging a chair to watch TV. But if the activity-based approach appeals to you, go for it! It may be the perfect solution for your family. And even I will admit that this design approach works well in a huge, cavernous room like some of today's great rooms, where furniture around the walls would get lost.

Once you feel comfortable with the big picture, it's time to take on the clutter. As you did in the previous chapters, start your de-cluttering process by setting some clutter-kicking priorities. The best way to begin is to take a good, hard look at the "before" state of the room, and then to visualize the "after."

A Living Room/Family Room Visualization

To get to your "after," you need to start with the "before"—the way things look right now. So get out some paper, or use the "My Living Room/Family Room—Before" form on page 148 (or make a photocopy of it and write on that). Write down every place there's clutter, and note what that clutter is. Things may look like a mess, but the clutter in these rooms is usually superficial, as you'll see when you start working on your list. It's not like dealing with the kitchen! Check each area of the room. Are there piles by the doors? Can you see the cushions on the sofa, much less sit on them? What about the coffee table?

Once you've jotted down a quick description of your living or family room's "before" state, it's time to move on to the "after"—how you want the room to look when you've kicked the clutter. Write it all down on a piece of paper, or in the "My Living Room/Family Room—After" form on page 148 or on as many photocopies of it as you need to do it justice. To make sure you're being realistic, look at the room every few minutes while you're doing this.

Your description can be short and to the point: "I don't want to see stacks of newspapers, catalogs, magazines, and mail all over the tables, floor, sofa, and chairs. I don't want dirty dishes, bags, crumbs, and drink rings all over the place.

My Living Room/Family Room—Before

_____
_____
_____
_____
_____
_____
_____
_____
_____
_____
_____
_____

My Living Room/Family Room—After

_____
_____
_____
_____
_____
_____
_____
_____
_____
_____
_____
_____

My Living Room/Family Room Priority List

_____

_____

_____

_____

_____

_____

_____

_____

_____

_____

I don't want to hear one more person whine that they've lost one of the several dozen remotes, their phone, their MP3 player, or anything else. And I don't want to break my neck on one of the kid's (or cat's) toys. I'd like to see all the CDs and DVDs in their cases and shelved in the entertainment center."

You can even create a detailed picture of exactly how you'd like your room to look if it were perfect (for you). You can picture the colors of the walls, woodwork, and window treatments; what the floor would look like; what furniture would be in the room, and how it would be arranged; whether there would be a fireplace; what art would be on the walls—everything.

Getting There

Now that you have captured your living or family room's "before" condition, listing all the specifics, and you've imagined its "after" appearance, you can finally prioritize the steps you'll need to take to get there from here. Again, bearing both "before" and "after" in mind, I'd recommend starting with what bothers you most about the "before" condition and working down from there. Focus on what matters most to you about the way your living room or family room looks, and make that your top priority. Then work your way down your list of concerns until you get to what's least important.

For example, you hate the big, ugly television and desperately want either one that hangs on the wall or an attractive entertainment center you can hide it in. If you want the sofa to be clutter-free so you and others can actually sit on it but right now it's piled high with magazines, empty potato chip bags, and other junk, one of your priorities will be to clean off the couch. Choose the most important thing you need to do, then make it Priority #1. Take your Before list and spell out what you need to do to arrive at the After state you want. Rank all the items on your list in order of importance and you're ready to get started.

Write down whatever's driving you to distraction on the "My Living Room/Family Room Priority List" on page 149 (or photocopy it, if you'd prefer), in descending order from most to least maddening. Now you have your priorities straight! Once you've finished, you can turn to the tips below to find ingenious ways of dealing with each problem.

THE LIVING ROOM/FAMILY ROOM TIPS

Just as in the kitchen, because so much goes on in the living or family room, I've divided the tips in this chapter into sections and grouped them by topic so it will be easier for you to find what you're looking for. Skim through the pages until you find where you want to start, and then get going!

Get the Big Picture

See what can go. Do you have furniture in the living or family room that's just taking up space? Maybe you have pieces nobody actually uses but that have somehow found their way in by default or because you felt at one point that you "needed" something there, but never thought about getting a more suitable piece once something was occupying the space. By now, you may have amassed a lot more furniture than you need—or you may need furniture you don't have room for because of all the "wrong" furniture that's in place. Take a hard look at each piece and see if it really belongs—if it's really serving a purpose now, if it's loved and used. Maybe it's a great piece but would work better someplace else in the house. Or maybe it's just time to send it to another home. (See Part Four: Trash [Yours] to Treasure [Theirs], beginning on page 349, for lots of ways to do that.)

A Cautionary Tale

One of my relatives was notorious in our family for the inhospitable nature of her home. Guests entered the house through a narrow corridor with boxes of unidentified stuff piled high on either side, slipping and sliding on a plastic sheet laid over the carpeting between the box barricades. It was like negotiating a landing strip. This hallway opened into the living room, which also had plastic not only on the carpet but also encasing every piece of furniture so guests couldn't somehow damage the upholstery by actually sitting on it. Trying to stay upright on any piece of furniture without sliding off on the slippery plastic was a feat few yoga masters could manage. (And mind you, this was department-store furniture, not priceless one-of-a-kind museum-quality stuff.) As a result, family visits were few and far between!

The moral of this story is: If your furniture and rugs are *that* valuable, auction them off at Christie's or Sotheby's, donate them to a museum, or lock them away in a room guests never see. Do your entertaining in an inviting room that everyone can enjoy. And get rid of those boxes!

Fill in the blanks. Now that you've evaluated what you have, you may realize that you're missing a few key pieces. Before you head to the store, think about the other rooms in your house and take a quick house tour with a notepad in hand. On the pad, write down what you need for the family or living room, then, as you take your house tour, see if a piece that's currently in another room would be a perfect fit for one of the items on your list. Be open-minded: Furniture doesn't have to serve the use it was made for (see the other tips in this chapter for more on that). As you're taking stock, think about furniture from the family room that might be better off in the room you're in now and if it would make sense to swap. Only when you've examined the options that are free and at your disposal should you consider heading off to the store or consulting a catalog.

Grow up. Does your living or family room look exactly like it did 20 years ago, when the kids were toddlers? Is it still displaying the furniture you moved in from your first apartment? Do you have very formal furnishings because you used to do a lot of entertaining for work, but now you're semiretired and would rather just kick back? Your life and needs may have changed while your furnishings stayed

5-Minute Fixes for Living Areas

Sometimes a list of clutter-cleaning priorities can seem so long and overwhelming that you wonder how you'll ever get through it. If that's how you feel, or if you're itching to get started but don't have much time, try one or two of these 5-Minute Fixes to get your feet wet. They're some of the easiest ways to start de-cluttering your living or family room. You'll be surprised by what you can accomplish in just 5 quick minutes, so get going!

Find the food. Nothing makes a room look messier, dirtier, or more cluttered than glasses and plates of forgotten food. Empty or otherwise, if the dishes are in the room and the diners aren't (unless, of course, they're in the bathroom), take those dishes to the kitchen and find a home for them in the dishwasher. Then tell the perpetrators you'll be finding a home for *them* if they don't start picking up after themselves!

Pack up the paper. Go into your family room, den, or living room—the place where you all actually sit and spend time when you're relaxing—and take a good look. See a bunch of magazines, newspapers, mail, and catalogs lying all over the place, spilling off tables, stacked on the sofa? Right. Get an empty copier-paper box from an office supply store, or a grocery bag, and stuff it all in there. Then tell everyone they have 24 hours to collect their stuff and put it in their respective rooms or where it actually belongs, or else it will go out with the recycling. This goes for your stuff, too.

Unstuff a shelf. If you're a bookaholic like me, your shelves are probably overflowing with books behind books and on top of books. Pick a shelf, any shelf, and try to find a few books to donate, consign, or give away. See if you can't get five books off the shelf (though even two would be a lot, in my experience). As you

the same. Think about what you and your family need *now*, and make sure your furnishings are supporting your needs.

Create a wall storage system. If you cover an entire wall with cabinets and shelving, all designed as a unit, you'll gain maximum storage space while keeping a uniform, uncluttered look. Put the most dominant element—usually your entertainment center—in the middle, with a row of cabinets below and shelves all around and over it.

sort, picture me jumping up and down while waving shredded-paper pom-poms and screaming, "Rah! Rah! Hurrah!"

Deck the dustables. If your shelves look like mine, they display a glorious array of little dustables in a neat line in front of the books. Yes, of course you love them. But remind yourself of the magic word: rotation. Put them in a shoe box or plastic storage bin (labeled with the contents, naturally), and choose one or two (okay, three) objects from the hordes within to actually display. Don't worry, they're still in there! Promise yourself you'll change the display every month.

Rein in the remotes. Sheesh! No wonder obesity is such a problem in America, with clutter hard on its heels. I'm always stupefied by the number of remote controls in any given household, and even more stupefied by the reluctance of pretty much everybody to drag themselves over to the actual appliance to push a few buttons. But then, I feel that way about drive-thrus at banks, fast-food chains, and pharmacies, too. Get out and walk, people! But I know I don't stand a huge chance of getting you all to give up your remotes, so here's an alternative suggestion: Get a box, tray, basket, or other container to put all of your remotes in. Mail-order catalogs carry tidy stand-up containers, but anything that corrals them so they're not spilling over every available surface works for me. What about labeling them while you're at it, so you know at a glance which appliance goes with which remote? Or get one universal remote and put the rest away.

Change your coffee table. This is an oldie but a goodie: Use a blanket chest as a coffee table so it can double as storage space. Chests are an especially convenient place to store afghans and lap robes so everyone can grab one if they get cold while sitting—but only if you don't pile so much stuff on top of the "coffee table" that no one ever opens it to get them!

Make sure you can move. Being able to move comfortably through the room—whether you're just passing through with a big box or basket of stuff or you're moving from the sofa to the bookcase or entertainment center—is essential, both to create a feeling of uncluttered openness in the room and to enhance your family's and guests' pleasure in being in it. If you have an open floor plan, with furniture spread around the walls and a rug in the center, make sure you don't block the doors by placing jutting furniture too close to them. If you cluster your furniture to create different sections within the room, leave plenty of space for navigation around each cluster. Picture two kids running through the room. Could they do it without hitting anything?

Let there be light. In a room that's used as much as your living or family room, lighting is at least as important as room to move, comfortable furniture, and ample storage. I actually decided to buy my cottage home based on the marvelous amount of natural light that streams through the living room and kitchen (and this despite the deep yellow of the living-room walls). This was especially important to me because where I live, there are seldom overhead lights. I've never understood why this was—where I grew up in the South, every room in every house had a ceiling light. But the lack of a ceiling light can make rooms really dark and shadowy, so make sure your room has enough usable, pleasing light to be inviting and to make it easy to actually use every part of the room for its intended purpose. A ceiling fan with lights can add welcome air circulation, as well. And wall sconces add light without taking up floor or table space.

But not too much light. Or I should say, not too many lights. Lots of little lamps all over the place look junky and become dustables, not to mention adding endless cords that can become tripping hazards. Choose a few good floor or table lamps that suit your decor and give off good light, and pack the rest up for Goodwill, a consignment shop, or the antiques store. (Or maybe you could use one in another room.) If you have a lamp you can't bear to get rid of but have no place for, remember that you can rotate lamps just like you do collectibles. If you have floor lamps that aim up rather than down, I'd get rid of those first. Yes, they're trendy, but they're also useless. Why would you want to spotlight your wall and ceiling? Good grief. Make all your lamps work as hard as you do. Keep the ones that light the space where you are!

Watch your head. If you have a chandelier, make sure it's high enough so it's not a head-hitting hazard for you or the tallest person in your family. Ouch! If a fixture hangs down low enough to hit someone, it's hanging in your eye space and creating visual clutter, too. Raise it or get a different fixture.

Keep it clean. Speaking of chandeliers, avoid those with zillions of multicolored fruits, flowers, or other assorted whatsits. More visual clutter! Clear crystals in a simple pattern are best.

Add life and light. I can't resist putting this in because it's so dear to my heart. Few things add as much quiet, fascinating entertainment to a home as a large, diverse aquarium, with colorful fish, plants, frogs, snails, shrimp, rocks, and branches. (Note that word "large"—a small aquarium is more clutter, unless it's in a kid's room.) The family and pets will watch for hours—but only if the aquarium is placed where it can be seen. And the bright, filtered aquarium light adds enormous ambiance. I love creating gorgeous naturalistic aquascapes, then sitting back and enjoying "fish TV" with my cats. But location is everything—if you can't find a place to display your aquarium where everyone can see it but no one can knock it over, it's just another maintenance chore.

Pick Up the Pieces

Keep a carry-all handy. Keep a decorative basket in the living or family room so it's easy to centralize things that have strayed in by mistake. You can take the basket with you as you go from room to room, replacing things in their rightful places. Or designate the basket as the family "Lost and Found" and make it a rule that everyone must collect his or her own stuff from the basket before bed (or before guests arrive) and take it away with them—or else! Let them know that anything that's not claimed will be tossed or given away.

Keep it moving. My friend Chris has a clutter philosophy we could all use. "Never walk empty-handed into another room in your home," Chris says. "Chances are, there's something you can take along to put away." This is especially true of the living or family room, and it's also true in reverse: Try to never walk *out* of the family room without taking something with you to put away.

Straighten your stacks. Neaten up those piles of magazines and catalogs on the coffee and side tables as you pass through the room and before bed. Not only will this simple act make the room look cleaner and less cluttered, it will also help you avoid the hateful paper avalanches that pitch magazines, catalogs, and the like all over your floor and tables in slippery slides.

Rack it up. Okay, a magazine rack is a more organized-looking way to store magazines and catalogs. But outdated magazines are not just going to vaporize on their own as new issues arrive. To mangle a phrase from the real-estate industry: rotation, rotation, rotation. Recycle old catalogs and put old magazines in the local library's giveaway pile (after cutting off the mailing labels). If you really, *really* want to keep something in either one, cut it out and toss the rest of the catalog or magazine.

Put up your puzzles. Cabinets with shelves and doors are the perfect storage places for board games and jigsaw puzzles. They're out of sight but within reach of even the smallest hands.

Tin your toys. Toys like Lincoln Logs, Tinkertoys, and Legos can have a billion little pieces. Corral them in decorative tins—you probably have some left over from candy, cookies, fruitcake (yikes), or popcorn that you received as Christmas gifts. If not, thrift stores and yard sales are always good sources. Needless to say, store just one kind of game per tin!

Be a mad hatter. Decorative hatboxes have made a comeback—but for storage, not hats. They're not as durable as tins, but on the plus side, they're quieter. If you need to store multipiece games on open shelves, hatboxes are an attractive solution.

Get a game center. No, I don't mean a PlayStation or an Xbox! In this case, I'm talking about an attractive wooden end table that has drawers that double as game boards and, of course, hold all the various game pieces. (Find them in catalogs like Solutions; see page 48.) If your family's wild for games like dominos, Chinese checkers, backgammon, chess, and the like, this is a great way to keep them at hand but out of sight.

Show it off if you can't hide it. My boyfriend, Rob, is a chess fanatic, always poring over the board (and trying to trick me into playing—and losing). Rather than pull the chess board out and set it up every night, we've made it a design feature by using a table with a built-in chess board inset in the top (also good for checkers) and a decorative chess set (Rob favors "Pirates versus the British Navy") on display.

Tote your yarn. If you enjoy working on knitting, crochet, quilting, or other yarn- or fabric-related projects while relaxing in the family room, tuck your supplies into a tote. You can find beautiful padded totes at yarn stores and quilt shops, but any sturdy, roomy tote, including the canvas boat-and-tote ones made famous by L.L. Bean, will work fine. I keep the yarn, needles, and other necessities for my current project in the tote and store my other yarns and supplies in boxes on a closet shelf, where they peacefully wait their turn. Bring your tote out while you're working on the project, and tuck it away out of sight in a cabinet or closet when you're not.

Take your plants to new heights. I love houseplants, but it takes only a few cat-induced disasters or guests reaching for a cactus to make you think twice about keeping them in easy reach. Instead, install hooks in your ceiling and hang plants in view but out of reach. You'll add life, interest, and more oxygen to the room. But again, don't block your light, don't dot the ceiling with a clutter of plants, don't hang them where they'll become head-banging hazards, and do rotate them when they're no longer looking their best.

Don't pile on the pillows. If you can't see your sofa and chairs because of all the throw pillows, you have too many pillows. Follow the three-pile rule to sort them out: Put the ones you love in the keepers pile; put the torn, stained, beat-up ones in the trash pile; and put the ones you don't like, need, or want anymore in the donation pile. If your favorite comfy pillow is battered but you can't bear to part with it, give it a facelift with a new cover. And what about the handmade pillow from Grandma Rose, the moose pillow from your spouse's co-worker Bob, the designer plaid pillow from your best friend—those sacred cows that no one likes or uses but that you're afraid to throw away? First, make *sure* no one likes them— if your son turns out to love the moose pillow, he can take it to his room, after all. Otherwise, take them to Goodwill, the Salvation Army, or the Society of St. Vincent de Paul. (Note: If you're really afraid that some day you'll wake up hating yourself for tossing out Granny's handiwork, you can always take it off the pillow and store it flat—maybe in your new blanket-chest coffee table. (See "Change your coffee table" on page 153.)

What about the Walls?

Don't clutter up the walls. I often see groups of a dozen or so paintings hung from ribbons over a mantel in design magazines. My own parents devoted a wall in their library to a museum-style display of art. But if you think back to your experiences in museums, or antiques shows, or galleries—anywhere a lot of art is displayed cheek-by-jowl on a wall—you may recall becoming exhausted. That's because seeing such a visual barrage tires the eyes, and that tires us. It's also why savvy museum-goers focus on a room or display per visit, savoring the experience and then getting out before they're worn out. And bear in mind that in a museum, there's nothing competing with the art for our attention—unlike a home full of furniture and other distractions! Avoid visual clutter. If you have more art than you can display in a spacious, focused manner, rotate your pieces. Don't show them all at once!

Hang pictures at eye level. Put your art where you can appreciate it. If you're very short and your spouse is very tall, or vice-versa, you have two choices: Hang the art midway between your eye levels, or hang each person's favorites at his or her eye level.

Showcase unusual art. If you have a striking quilt, a fantastic dream catcher, or a woven masterpiece, remember that you can display it as wall art. As long as the object is fairly flat—you don't want anyone to crash into it!—it can make a striking centerpiece or unusual accent. And if it's on the wall, you'll not only get to enjoy it, you won't have to find a place to store it!

Put up a mirror. A mirror can make your room look more spacious, and it can increase the amount of light. But note that little word "a." Multiple mirrors create a funhouse effect, as people moving through the room catch fragmented glimpses of themselves (or others) and flashes of passing objects. Instead, use one large mirror and position it carefully. If it faces windows it will bring in natural light and make it seem that both sides of the room open into the great outdoors. But if it faces a messy, cluttered view (say, a chaotic bookcase), it will double the clutter a viewer sees!

Hang the television. Even your TV can function as wall art if it's a flat-screen, wall-mounted unit. Not only does this save floor space, it also looks much better than a bulky television, and it makes the room more open and easier to navigate.

Show off with shelves. Wooden display shelves are small, ornamental, individually mounted shelves that will hold a single vase, potted plant, or three-dimensional piece of artwork or collectible. Attached with molly bolts (had to mention this because of my dog, Molly), they're a sturdy way to get breakables off tables and shelves and up to eye level. But use them sparingly to avoid a cluttered look.

Branch out. I had to mention this one because it's so unusual and interesting. My friend Edith, one of the most creative people I know, collects ornaments. But she also collects cats. To avoid the inevitable breakage, she displays her ornament collection by hanging groups of ornaments from branches, then mounting the branches on her wall so the ornaments hang at eye level.

Don't trash the mantelpiece. If you're lucky enough to have a fireplace, don't junk up the mantel with unsightly, distracting, and potentially flammable clutter. Except at Christmas, candlesticks are probably enough, especially if you have an impressive painting over the mantel. You can always add interest by creating unusual groupings of candlesticks. And you can add a bowl, vase, basket, or sculpture if you don't have a strong painting to hold the space.

Books and Bookcases

Think of books as art. If you have a bookcase full of colorful books, it has the same visual effect as a major piece of wall art. That's why white or neutral-colored walls are a smart choice if you have a lot of books. And no patterned wallpaper, please!

Take your books to new heights. For the same reason, give your books maximum space and visual impact by choosing a floor-to-ceiling bookcase. Put the books you read or refer to most often where they're easiest to reach, placing less-used books on higher shelves. Put the kids' books within their reach on the lower shelves.

Add built-in bookcases. Nothing adds class to a room like an entire wall of built-in bookcases. And they hold so much! Match their style to your room's decor. Make them deep enough to hold big books and LPs, but not so deep that they waste space (18 inches is about right). Fixed shelves that are the same height across the width of the bookcases add a unifying quality and aren't as chaotic-looking as randomly spaced shelves. But some of the shelves can be taller than others, as long as all the shelves across that row are tall.

Shelve books upright. Books shelved horizontally look messy, like they've fallen over. And it's harder to extract a book from a horizontal pile than to simply pull one from the shelf.

If you want to display some of your beautiful possessions but are short on table-top or bookshelf space (or worry that kids or pets will send your priceless treasures crashing to the ground), try lighted display shelves. These wonderful inventions, available from home catalogs like Solutions (see page 48), are made of wood and look almost like mini-mantelpieces. They range from a wall sconce (just over 10 inches long) to a "ledge" (just over 2 feet long), and are as easy to hang as a picture frame. The top of each display shelf is an acrylic panel that's lit from below by battery-operated LEDs. Because the light comes up from below, these shelves are especially good for showcasing colored glass or crystal. I wish I had one for my Vaseline glass! Now your goodies are high on the wall and out of harm's way, and they look more beautiful than ever.

Use bookends. Speaking of books that have fallen over, keep that from happening to your books by inserting bookends every couple of feet. The flat metal ones available from office-supply stores are thin enough to be almost undetectable.

Shelve magazines in acrylic cases. These durable cases, available from housewares stores and catalogs, hold a year's worth of magazines organized, upright, and together, making them fit on a shelf like a dictionary. You can read the spines at a glance through the clear plastic. Remember to go through your shelved magazines at least annually to see if you can finally bear to part with them.

Show off your bookshelves. You don't have to just store books, magazines, DVDs, videos, video games, and records on your shelves, either! Save some shelves to showcase favorite crafts or collectibles. But remember, less is more here. One piece of beautiful pottery or a striking basket or sculpture is a lot more dramatic than a clutter of dustables. (And remember, you can rotate them.)

Glass-in the good stuff. If you want to showcase a collection of valuable breakables, such as pottery or glass, put it in a glass-fronted bookcase. Choose the most impressive pieces to display, and arrange them in the most attractive manner. No overcrowding! You can dress up a shelved collection with complementary staging—for example, displaying Southwestern Pueblo pottery on hand-woven Navajo horse blankets, which are small enough to fit on the shelves. Remember: If it looks intentional, it's not clutter. And if it's safe behind glass doors, there's no dusting, either. If you have kids, lock the case—just in case.

Light up your treasures. Install under-shelf lighting over the shelves you plan to use to display collectibles. They'll look gorgeous!

Make beautiful music. CD players are now made to attach under shelves. Choose a shelf, attach the CD player, and add the small speakers to other shelves to create gorgeous stereo sound. What a space-saver! You can store CDs on the shelf below the CD player.

That's Entertainment!

Entertain in an armoire. Use an armoire—those huge, antique, freestanding closets, also called wardrobes—to house your entertainment center. They're readily available at antiques stores and flea markets. Add extra shelves for DVDs, CDs, video games, and videos, and you're ready to go!

Downsize the TV. I know this is blasphemy in these days of room-size televisions that turn your living or family room into a home theater, but you'll save space if you get a smaller TV. It can fit more unobtrusively into a cabinet or on a shelf. And you have to admit, TVs are ugly! Your room will look a lot better—and bigger—without that monster machine squatting in the middle of it. But make sure the smaller, sleeker model is big enough for everyone to watch comfortably and that it has a high-quality picture.

Make it mobile, part one. No room for an entertainment center? Get a rolling cart, available from any home store or housewares catalog. At my house, the TV, DVD/VCR, remotes, and to-be-watched DVDs (or videos) are all on a small rolling cart. When Rob and I want to watch a movie or program, we roll the cart over and plug everything in; when the show's over, the cart rolls back against the wall, out of the way until it's needed again.

Make it mobile, part two. Make it easy to watch TV wherever you are with a swivel turntable. These handsome stands or unobtrusive flat turntables are sized to fit your TV and let you turn it 360 degrees for easy viewing wherever you are—without having to move furniture. Great idea!

Stash the CDs. CDs need to be upright and easily accessible, not piled horizontally in an avalanche-prone skyscraper or spawning orphan jewel cases. Buy a CD

Dear Claire,

My family room is like a minefield because of the CDs and DVDs that are all over the floor. I've tried picking them up and nagging everybody else to pick them up, but to no avail. They seem to multiply faster than dust bunnies. Yesterday, I stepped on a jewel case and skidded clear across the floor! This has to stop before someone gets hurt. How can I get my floor back?

—Musically Challenged

Dear Musically Challenged,

Gather your family. Explain that *their* cluttering almost broke *your* neck and that you can't enjoy your family room with trash all over the floor. Both conditions are unacceptable. Then announce that everyone has exactly half an hour to put all their CDs and DVDs in their designated places, and after that time, any and all CDs, DVDs, and cases found on the floor will be taken to Goodwill. Three "make sures" here: 1. Make sure they know you mean it. 2. Make sure your spouse is apprised and on board before you hold your meeting. 3. Make sure there *is* a designated place for CD and DVD storage. Then stick to your guns! After the kids have to buy a replacement CD or DVD with their own money, they'll be less likely to play fast and loose with your floor.

Good luck,
Claire

rack and use it. You can get handsome wooden models that store 1,000 CDs (in their cases) from mail-order catalogs, CD "bookcases" in numerous styles, a CD pedestal, wire and plastic towers, CD-holding apothecary cabinets, and CD holders made to look like pretty much anything else you can think of, so get something that appeals to you and matches the rest of your furnishings. You can also find some very interesting CD racks for a few dollars at thrift stores. I'm very proud of the ultra-modern one I found at Goodwill! Don't want the CD racks on view? Buy shorter ones and hide them in the cabinet that houses your entertainment center or stereo.

Book your CDs and DVDs. Want to ditch those jewel cases once and for all? Store CDs and DVDs and their booklets or artwork in specially made notebooks with sleeves. The Herrington catalog (see page 48) has leather-bound CD and

DVD notebooks that look just like high-end books. They even feature labels for the spines, so you can group all your rock, country, comedy, or action discs together. Set them on your bookshelves with pride!

Consolidate your stereo equipment. Still clinging to your clunky, battered, space-eating stereo from the seventies? Give it up. Play your LPs on one of the many styles of Crosley turntables, widely available through mail-order catalogs. They're like a boom box for records—the speakers and player are all contained in an attractive retro wooden box not much bigger than a hatbox. The sound is good, and what a space-saver! You can buy models with CD and cassette players, a CD burner, and a radio, too, if you like an all-in-one. And you can buy a matching stand to hold the player and your records, CDs, and cassettes. It's an attractive, affordable, space-saving solution!

Make your furniture work harder. Choose furniture for your family room based on how hard it will work for you and how well it fits in with the room's decor. You don't need high-tech furniture to store high-tech stuff. If your family room has a country theme, look beyond the purpose the furniture was intended for and see what it can actually do for you. Can that quaint little drop-front cabinet hold the family's collection of videos and DVDs? Will the country pine cupboard double as a place to hold Dad's vintage collection of LPs?

Make Room for Guests

Get a sofa bed. Sofa beds can be lifesavers if you have frequent sleepovers or, like me, you don't have a designated guest room. Try it before you buy it—get a comfortable one you wouldn't mind sleeping on yourself. Of course, if you already have a less-than-comfy model, you can always add a featherbed or even an air mattress on top. But even without the added softness, it's still bound to be more comfortable than a futon!

Take to the air. Inflatable air mattresses are wonderful ways to add extra sleeping space. The thick ones available now are incredibly comfortable, and with plug-in pumps, it's a minute's work to set one up (and to deflate it, too, if your pump is reversible). Some of the beds have fold-out legs to accommodate those who'd rather not sleep on the floor. You can also use an air bed, as noted in the previous tip, like a second mattress on top of a sofa bed; that will make it really cushy.

Quick Fixes

Guests arriving on short notice? Grab a box, a hamper—even a trash bag!—and quickly toss in everything that's cluttering the floor, chairs, sofa, and coffee table. Stash the bag in a closet or room your guests won't go in. Your living room will look guest-ready in a flash! (Just don't forget to sort through that bag once they're gone.)

Try a fold-out. Some sofas and chairs are made of connected cushions that unfold to create a single (chair) or double (sofa) bed. They're available from home catalogs like Plow & Hearth (see page 47).

A Place for Everything

Add an ottoman. Ottomans, those big square cushioned footstools, can turn practically any chair into the equivalent of a recliner. But they have other uses, too. Not only can one function as additional seating, but many catalogs and stores now carry hollow ottomans with tops that lift up to reveal hidden storage. It's the perfect size to hide an afghan and pillow for an afternoon snooze on the sofa, knitting and crocheting supplies (safe from the cats), or linens for the sofa bed.

Get a sofa table. Sofa tables are high, narrow tables made especially to stand behind a sofa, basically creating a full-length "sofa shelf." This is a useful place to stash reading materials, reading glasses, and other supplies, as well as a plate and glass or cup, all within easy reach. (Just make sure you take dishes to where they belong when you leave the room, or you'll leave clutter behind.) If your sofa doesn't back up against a wall but the back is out of sight (say, angled against a corner), the sofa table can also be a good place to stash toys in baskets or colorful plastic tubs (sold in garden catalogs for carrying weeds, soil, and plants, and in housewares catalogs for a multitude of uses). Just make sure there's easy access to the back of the sofa for both you and the kids.

Work your windows, part one. Don't let the space beneath your windows go to waste. It's the perfect place to put an organizer bench with a cushioned seat and storage cubbies or a lift-up seat with storage beneath. If you can see the storage area, as is the case with cubbies, use attractive square wicker or rattan baskets to contain and conceal what you're storing.

Work your windows, part two. The space beneath windows is also perfect for a low bookcase or bookcase table.

Work your windows, part three. Don't limit yourself to the obvious! I have a roomy hanging sideboard under one of my living-room windows.

Don't forget your doors. Put the space above and around your doors to work with an above-door shelf and narrow shelves or cabinets on either side.

Screen it out. A decorative screen can hide a multitude of sins (from the TV to a folded card table) when they're not in use. A screen can even hide a workstation when you want it out of sight for more formal entertaining. Find one to suit your decor, either new from a housewares store or catalog or from a flea market, thrift store, consignment shop, or antiques store. (Thrift shops often have screen frames with damaged or missing covers available for practically nothing. If you're handy, you can cover them with cloth or heavy ornamental handmade paper to match your room's look.)

Use your fireplace year-round, part one. If you have a fireplace, it's unlikely that you use it in the warm months. This is the perfect time to turn it into "found" storage space! Put whatever you need to keep out of view in the (cleaned and swept, please) fireplace, then conceal it behind one of those decorative fire screens or chimney boards until it's needed.

Use your fireplace year-round, part two. You can also turn an unused fireplace into a display area. Besides the massive dried flower arrangements you often see in fireplaces in design magazines, I've seen awesome candle groupings, ornaments piled high in glass vases and hurricanes, even a gorgeous poinsettia or striking houseplant (these will need lighting or frequent rotation to better-lit areas).

Put your tables to work. The coffee table and sofa table aren't the only things you can use for storage. Instead of simple end tables, use nightstands or small chests with lots of drawers. Bedside tables have drawers with plenty of room for reading glasses, coasters, remote controls, pens, and other necessities, and antique versions are handsome enough to display in the living or family room without apology.

Choose bookcase tables. Mail-order catalogs carry handsome end tables called bookcase tables because they're skinny (just 12 inches deep) like bookcases and have shelves for books, magazines, tissues, and other chair-side necessities. If your family loves to read, these are the perfect end tables for you. They're sized so the top comes just to sofa-arm height. Nestle one against each side of the sofa, set a coaster and glass or mug on top, and you're good to go!

Table your collection. You can display a prized collection without worrying about it becoming a bunch of dustables if you house it in your coffee table. Mine **is** a rectangular cherry table with a type drawer (from the days when printers set type by hand and stored it in shallow drawers) on top and a cherry-framed glass top over that. The type drawer displays prized fossils, seashells, and buttons, safely shown off under glass where everyone can admire them. It's quite a conversation piece! Mine was custom-made by my great-uncle Max, but I have seen gorgeous coffee (or "cocktail") tables available commercially with glass tops and drawers that combine display, style, *and* storage.

ONWARD!

Are you excited about your living or family room now? I hope so! It's the most fun room to transform. And how satisfying it is to watch a chaotic, cluttered, uncomfortable mess turn into the most delightful and best-loved room in the whole house. It warms my heart to think of you sitting in your clutter-free family room, relaxing and enjoying yourself.

But now it's time to travel to one of the most neglected and least-loved rooms in most homes: the dining room. In the next chapter, you'll find tons of tips on transforming your dining room from wasteland to wonderland. Let's eat!

Chapter 9

De-Cluttering the Dining Room

So *that's* where the table went! Like a formal living room, the dining room can become a storage center, especially if the family eats in the kitchen, in their rooms, or in front of the TV. And there's that nice big work space just begging to be used for homework or bill-paying. In this chapter, you'll find solutions aplenty for restoring order to dining-room chaos, and you'll learn how to make the most of the space when you're not using it for meals.

PRIORITIES FOR DINING ROOMS

As in the living room/family room chapter, the first and most important step here is evaluating what you actually use your dining room for. Does your family eat there? My mother served us three meals a day at the dining room table. But your family might eat at the kitchen table or in the family room, instead. Do you entertain in your dining room? My friends Delilah and Chaz love to have guests in their dining room, and they pull out all the stops to make the meal unforgettable. And my friends Carolyn and Gary are kind enough to host a group of us every week for the "Friday Night Supper Club" I organized (I cook, they host, another friend brings wine, another dessert, everybody enjoys themselves). But you may find that you really only use that big, imposing table to serve meals at Thanksgiving and Christmas.

So what's the room doing the rest of the year? Do the kids do homework at the table? Do you pay bills? Is it your default craft room? Has it become a museum room, sealed off and unused? Is it a storage room, full of boxes and bags? Does anybody ever really go in there?

If your family still eats their meals in the dining room, congratulations! But if they don't, it's no cause for shame. Instead, look at it as an opportunity—a "free" room waiting to be reclaimed. You can use that space. This chapter will help you see your dining room with new eyes and make the most of it no matter what you use it for.

As I suggested in earlier chapters on other rooms, start your dining room de-cluttering process by setting some clutter-kicking priorities. You can do that by focusing on what matters most to you about the way your dining room looks and then working your way through a list of clutter issues until you get to what matters least. Then you're done! But before you can set priorities, you first need to assess the current state of the dining room and see what needs to be done. Take a good, hard look at the "before" state of the room, and then visualize the "after."

A Dining Room Visualization

To get to your "after," you need to start with the "before"—the way things look right now. So get out some paper or use the "My Dining Room—Before" form (or make a photocopy of it and write on that). Write down every place there's clutter in the room, and note what that clutter is. In the dining room, one of two things is usually going on: Either things that don't belong are crammed in there, so it's a cluttered mess, or it's a sterile, underused, and obviously unloved space. In either case, you can fix the problem and transform the room into one that works for you and your family.

So take a minute now to write down your "before" so you can get to your "after." Is the table piled with mail or catalogs? Are craft or school projects spread over the table? Are there coats and hats plopped on chairs? Are the houseplants dead from lack of attention? Is that wheeled serving cart or silver chest creating an obstacle course rather than serving a useful purpose? Write it all down.

My Dining Room—Before

My Dining Room—After

Once you've taken a quick inventory of your dining room's "before" state—its existing clutter problems—it's time to move on to the "after"—how you want the room to look when you've kicked the clutter. Write it all down on a piece of paper or on the "My Dining Room—After" form on page 169 (or on as many photocopies of it as you need to do it justice). To make sure you're being realistic, look at the room every few minutes while you're doing this.

Your description can be short and to the point: "I'd like to actually see the surface of the dining room table! I'd like to open up the room and put it to use. I'd like to be able to open the doors of the china cabinet without unleashing an avalanche. I'd like a room that's open and bright, with white walls, lots of wicker, and plants—almost a sunroom—rather than the dark paneling and big, heavy old mahogany dining room set that's in there now."

Or you can create a detailed picture of exactly how you'd like your room to look if it were perfect (for you). You can picture the colors of the walls, woodwork, and window treatments; what the floor would look like; what furniture would be in the room and how it would be arranged; how the room would be lit; what art would be on the walls—everything.

Getting There

Now that you have captured your dining room's "before" condition, listing all the specifics, and you've imagined its "after" appearance, you can finally prioritize the steps you'll need to take to get there from here. Maybe you really want to clear out the antiquated furniture you inherited from Aunt Ethel and have always hated and put in pieces that are more functional and that suit your family better. Or perhaps you want to create a space where it's easy to transition from eating to homework or crafts. Or you'd like to add a china cabinet on the back wall for much-needed storage.

Write down whatever's driving you to distraction on the "My Dining Room Priority List" (or photocopy it, if you'd prefer), in descending order from most to least maddening. Now you have your priorities straight! Once you've finished, you can turn to the tips on the next page to find ingenious ways of dealing with each problem.

My Dining Room Priority List

_____

_____

_____

_____

_____

_____

_____

_____

_____

_____

THE DINING ROOM TIPS

Add a centerpiece. Set out some candles and flowers or a beautiful bowl. People will be less likely to trash the table if it's decorated. And a clean, uncluttered table says, "Welcome!"

Store your dishes in the dining room. If you eat in the dining room, that's where you should put your china, glasses, cups, silverware—whatever you use every day. If you keep your dishes in the kitchen cabinets, someone will just have to carry them into the dining room two or three times a day. Instead, keep them where you use them.

Corner your china. A corner cupboard is a great piece for the dining room. It's space-saving and handsome, with closed cabinets below and shelves on top. You can use the shelves to display prized dishes or bigger or awkwardly shaped pieces—pitchers, the teapot, the turkey platter—and keep your plates, cups, and saucers dust-free down below.

Try the pie. A pie chest—one of those old-time cupboards with patterned tin fronts—makes a wonderful dish cabinet if it suits your dining room's decor.

Go for the buffet. A buffet or sideboard not only holds dishes, but also provides a long, showy surface for candlesticks, silver, and bigger pieces that would be awkward to fit into cabinets.

5-Minute Fixes for Dining Rooms

Jump-start your clutter-kicking process with these fast, easy tips.

Table the trash. Dining rooms tend to be trash magnets, especially if they're used for things besides eating—like doing homework and crafts projects. Crumpled papers, yarn ends, broken beads, napkins, a half-eaten cookie (she doesn't really like that kind), an empty pen, peeled-off crayon paper . . . they all end up scattered all over the table. Ugh. Rather than trying to stop the trash flow, contain it. Make sure you keep an attractive but functional wastebasket in the room, encourage everyone to use it, and empty it often. Don't forget to check the floor and chairs daily to make sure that none of these objects—especially round ones like beads and crumbs—have escaped captivity. Unsightly problem solved!

Clean your plates. Get the plates off the table unless it's set for a meal or you keep fine china out as a display. (My mother kept her gold-rimmed serving platters on our large antique dining table, with candelabra on each side—but that was all she had on the table so it looked impressive, not cluttered.) Don't let dishes—even clean dishes—pile up on the table between meals. Besides inviting breakage, it looks cluttered.

Check the chairs. It's amazing what can end up on dining-room chairs, from the dog's leash to that bill you couldn't find last week, spare change to a stack of CDs. Don't use your dining-room chairs for storage. Clean them off and then

Add an armoire. Need lots of storage space? An armoire or wardrobe fits the bill nicely. And if the dining-room table's your main crafting area, an armoire is an ideal place to store your craft supplies. There's plenty of room for tons of supplies for beading, knitting, quilting, egg-painting, scrapbooking—you name it!

Dress it up. A handsome dresser can be a perfect piece for the dining room, holding plenty of linens, everyday tablecloths, table runners, napkins, placemats, trivets, and napkin rings. Just make sure it's a good fit with the rest of your furnishings.

Box it up. Seasonal dishes, like a set of Christmas china or Valentine mugs, take up a lot of cabinet space. If you really can't bear to sell them or give them away, store them in labeled boxes in the attic or an out-of-the-way nook until it's time to set them out. Use your dining-room storage for dishes and glasses you use more often.

check them daily. You'll feel better every time you sit down on a clean chair for a meal—or a visitor pulls out a chair and doesn't find a surprise on the seat!

Watch the rug. If you have a patterned rug in your dining room, it can amass camouflaged clutter—clutter that's easy to step on or trip over but that remains almost invisible against the pattern. Kids' toys, cat toys, coins, food, pens, paper clips . . . find it before it finds you.

Ditch the dishes. Are you holding on to chipped, cracked, or broken china and crystal? Have you gotten tired of some of your dishes but haven't gotten around to getting rid of them? Toss the broken stuff and box the rest for the thrift store. If your cracked or broken pieces come from your good set or just a set you love, check Replacements, Ltd. (www.replacements.com) to see if you can find replacements in good shape. They carry more than 200,000 china, crystal, and silver patterns, some of them more than 100 years old.

Clear the sideboard. Has your sideboard turned into a drop-off zone for keys, glasses, backpacks, and papers? If the answer is yes, take a wastebasket in one hand and a decorative basket in the other and make a clean sweep. Trash in the wastebasket, stuff that belongs in the hall (or in someone's room) in the other. Set the decorative basket in the hall with a "Lost and Found" sign, and tell the family to leave your sideboard alone!

Wrap it up. If you have a full set of sterling silverware, tuck it on a shelf in the cabinet in its own tarnish-resistant box. No box? Buy tarnish-resistant cloth silverware holders. They're sized to hold each type of silverware, from dainty shrimp forks to large knives. Each cloth has slots to hold individual forks, spoons, or knives. When you've inserted all your pieces, you simply roll up the cloth and tie it into a bundle. Put the bundles in a drawer and they'll be ready to wash and use. No more tedious polishing!

Divide it up. Store your everyday silverware, or flatware, in a utensil organizer or in one of your dining-room storage pieces. There are some really attractive ones out there these days, so get a nice one—don't use a kitschy molded plastic model in the dining room. (Unless, of course, you have a fifties retro dining-room theme!)

Shelve it. Built-in shelving can create a gorgeous wall perfect for dining-room dish storage. If this look works for your room, go for it! I suggest that you put the shelves against one of the end walls, though—preferably the one at the "back" of the room, away from the windows. This will maximize the wall space without the shelves seeming obtrusive or overwhelming the room. A reminder: Glass doors keep dishes clean and dust-free.

Add music to your meals. Specially designed CD players fit under a shelf, taking up no valuable storage space. Tuck one into your dining-room shelves, and enjoy romantic or relaxing music while you dine.

Don't forget the door. If you need extra space for display or storage, don't overlook the option of a shelf over the door. This kind of shelf looks best when it's attached to narrow sets of shelves or bookcases that run down one or both sides of the door, but it can be as effective as a wall unit, especially where space is at a premium. Just don't overload it with dustables!

Hide it in a hutch. Antique hutches and dry sinks are also great places to store dishes. They're usually deep, so they can hold two layers of china and half a dozen goblets or glasses from front to back. As always when stashing dishes, put the ones you're most likely to use in front and the ones you're least likely to use (those finger bowls, for example) in back.

Get crafty. Don't think for a minute that a hutch, dry sink, buffet cabinet, cupboard, or any other storage piece has to be used for dishes or table linens just because it's in the dining room. If you already have enough storage for your dishware and your dining room doubles as your "crafts studio," any of these pieces will hold an absolute ton of crafting supplies. The only caveat is that the piece has to have doors. Looking at myriad craft supplies is looking at visual clutter, and that can be disturbing when you're trying to eat.

Put it in plastic—or a basket. Sherry, one of the most creative people at my local Curves, is a highly skilled basket maker. She's so good, she teaches basket making in her home. And, you guessed it, her studio is her dining room. Since Sherry's always working on at least one project and needs to prepare for classes, the dining room table is buried under basket-making supplies. This makes eating there a nonoption for her and her husband and causes panic when she has to clear the table to entertain. I say, enjoy the crafting space but keep your supplies contained. If you keep them in the sturdy plastic carriers available in any home improvement center, drugstore, or grocery, it's a snap (literally, if you get the ones with lock-on lids) to put your supplies back in the containers and put them away in your armoire, hutch, or wherever you stash your stuff. These plastic storage containers come in all different sizes and are very affordable. I like the ones with locking lids and handles that lift up for carrying but flatten for stacking. And you can just look through the side to see what's in each one. Another option is to store your supplies in baskets. Just make sure they have handles so they're easy to carry when it's time to clear the table!

Skirt the issue. Do you remember the "sink skirts" I told you about? (See page 136 for details.) You can also use the skirt idea to create an instant sideboard from a low bookcase or even a pair of wall-mounted shelves. Cover them with a slipcover that opens down the center, in a fabric that matches your dining-room curtains or table treatment, and you can store dishes inside, convenient but out of sight. Attach the skirt around the top of the shelves with Velcro, elastic, or discreet staples (if the fabric pattern will conceal them).

Skip the mirrors. Mirrors are great for making rooms look bigger and more open. But in the dining room, they're great for giving the family members sitting opposite them a clear view of themselves eating. Talk about visual clutter! Choose a picture for the wall, instead. (This is the right room for a still life of fruits and vegetables, after all!) But whatever you display, make sure it's tranquil. This is *not* the room for disturbing or distracting art.

Ban the busy wallpaper. A busy little (or big) wallpaper pattern can create a cluttered feeling in any room, but in the dining room it can have an especially bad effect. After all, you want to create a soothing, relaxing atmosphere at mealtimes. And of course, dark or brilliantly colored walls, even if they're a single color, are anything but appetizing. Choose soothing, warm-toned pastels, such as a very pale peach or bisque (cool shades like blue and green have been shown to be unappetizing), or go with a classic warm white or cream. (A rosy cream is especially inviting, and it's pale enough so the "rosy" part is almost subliminal.) If you want to dress it up, add a simple stencil pattern around the top of the wall.

Clear the decks. People are constantly coming and going through the dining room with food, dishes, drinks, and other stuff that can be dropped, spilled, or broken. Make sure there's plenty of room to move around between the furniture around the walls and the table and chairs. Don't put furniture, art objects, or anything else out in the middle of the floor. Make sure toys and other items are picked up off the floor before mealtimes. And while you're at it, make sure your table isn't too big for the room—people need to be able not just to walk around it, but also to sit around it comfortably.

Don't recreate Camelot. If there are just two or three of you, a small round table can be a nice, cozy place to eat. But the bigger the round table, the farther apart diners are. The center of a large round table is wasted space, since no one can reach it, and a table that large makes you feel like you're continents away from the people sitting across the table from you. Instead, choose a rectangular or oval table—it makes for better conversation and makes much better use of tabletop space.

Spread your wings. Crate & Barrel (see page 46) is a great source for furniture and furnishings for the dining room, but they've outdone themselves in the ingenuity department with their Pivot Table. Not only does it open out from the center to double in size when you need extra room for guests, but if you turn the top, it reveals a hidden storage compartment for linens!

Check the height. Spilled food is the worst kind of clutter, and when it comes to spills, kids are often the culprits. But if the table's not the right height, *it* may be the culprit instead of the kids. Imagine having to reach up over a table that's too high while trying to navigate food and utensils you can barely see! You already know how important it is to have your computer table at the right height to prevent wrist strain. To make sure even the smallest family members are comfortable when they're eating, look everyone over when they're at the table and adjust their chairs with comfy cushions if you need to. (That goes for your chair, too.) If the table's too low or too high for *anyone* in the family to eat at comfortably, I don't care what you paid for it, get rid of it and sit down as if you're going to eat at the next one before you buy it.

Take two. What if there are only one or two of you at the table most of the time? Rather than sit in regal isolation at a giant table, why not place two small, intimate tables in the room? If you have guests or kids (or grandkids) visiting, you can put the tables together if they're square and cover them with a single tablecloth or, if they're round, simply cover them in matching tablecloths and serve at both tables.

Fold it up, part one. Folding chairs can be lifesavers when you need extra seating. Some stores and catalogs now carry wooden folding chairs with padded seats;

these are attractive enough to display without hiding them under slipcovers. If you already have metal folding chairs, you can dress them up with slipcovers specially designed for folding chairs, available from housewares stores and catalogs.

Fold it up, part two. What if your dining room's full of big, awkward furniture—inherited or purchased when you married because, well, you had a dining room, after all—but your family always eats at the kitchen table? Rather than leave the dining room to languish for the rest of your days, why not sell that furniture, donate it, or pass it along to a relative who could really use it? Then get furniture that will give the room a much-needed makeover. Need a home office, a craft or sewing room, a game room, a music room? Presto—now you have one. But what if guests are coming or the extended family's descending for the holidays? A drop-leaf table is a handsome, space-saving solution. Fold the leaves down and it takes up almost no floor space as a side table against the wall. Move it to the center of the room and open it up, pull out the folding chairs, and you're ready to entertain. (Of course, it helps if your office furniture or sewing machine will roll out of the way!)

Pull up the covers. I remember my mother putting protective panels, or pads, on our dining-room table to save the surface from spills, stains, and scratches. She'd cover these panels with a decorative tablecloth. You may not want to go this route today, but the panels can still protect your table from craft-related accidents. (Think mashed crayons, overturned bottles of paint, or even hot wax that splashed when you were designing a Ukrainian egg.) Protective panels will also save your table surface if you need to use it to make a big, messy cooking project like a gingerbread house or (shriek) fruitcake, or if you need an extra surface so you can set down hot canning jars to cool.

Go for broke (or Baroque). Nobody's head will be in the middle of your dining room table, unless your cat gets up there or you're serving a roast suckling pig. So above that table is the perfect place to put a chandelier. No cracked skulls! Pick a fixture that fits the room's look—brass for a classic Colonial style, wood and wrought iron for a country room, crystal for an elegant feel, funky and floral if you want to add a whimsical note.

Light it right. Okay, this isn't about clutter, but because I feel so strongly about it, I just had to add it in this chapter. If you're like me, you love reading cookbooks and cooking magazines. But isn't it amazing how food can look so appetizing in one book or magazine and so cold, lifeless, or downright revolting in another? Here's the scoop: It's probably not the food, it's the photography. Good food photography depends on good, warm lighting. Take this to heart when you plan the lighting for your dining room. Candles (dripless, of course) are wonderful in the dining room because they're not just romantic, they also make food look great. You can mimic candlelight by installing "warm" (pinkish or purplish) light bulbs in your fixtures, not "cold" clear or blue-white bulbs. The dining room is not the place for glare! If you need brighter light for homework or projects, get an Ott-Lite or other bright, focused table light developed specifically for detail work. (I use mine for beading and it's fabulous.) When not in use, stash it in the cabinet with your other project supplies.

Sell the silver plate. Silver plate doesn't just refer to plates. Instead, it's a technique in which a thin coating of silver is applied over a baser metal. It's cheaper than sterling and worth a lot less. And the cheaper it is, the faster the silver wears

When professionals stack dishes, they don't just pile them up or separate them with paper towels or paper napkins. Instead, they baby the china by layering it with cut-to-fit pieces of soft flannel, fleece, or nonslip rubber matting. (For all of these cut-to-fit options, there's no need to cut round pieces to match the plates; square pieces are much easier to cut, and they work just as well.)

Pet Alert!

Pets plus food (yours). Not a good combination! Even if your pets go with you into every other room of the house, exile them from the dining room when you're eating there. (You can always give them a treat for "being good" or share the leftovers later—in their bowl, please, not from your plate!) Your guests will thank you. There's nothing more disturbing than a dog prowling around the table in search of a handout or a cat trying to jump up while you're eating. Every moving animal seems like 10 of them at mealtimes. Talk about clutter!

off, revealing the unsightly metal below. As if that weren't enough, silver plate requires as much maintenance as sterling. All that polishing! Unless you have a very special piece that's come down in your family, take it to an antiques store and unload it. You can probably buy at least one piece of sterling with the proceeds. It'll be a better investment and less to store!

Make it a piece of cake. You don't have a centerpiece for your dining-room table, but you do have a tiered set of cake stands? No worries. One hot trend is to set a two- or three-tiered stand in the center of the table and fill it with something decorative—fresh flowers, fruit, Christmas ornaments (in season), gourds and bittersweet (for autumn or Thanksgiving), collectibles (like colorful tiny teacups), a collection of African violets, petite party favors—or, of course, muffins, cup-cakes, petits fours, or other treats. By collecting the items on the cake stands, you're not cluttering the table with them—and by displaying the cake stands, you're saving your storage space for other pieces.

ONWARD!

Whew! You've made it through the first floor of your house—or most of it. Con-gratulations! Now it's time to tackle the bedrooms. Turn the page to find out how to reclaim your bedroom, make the most of a guest room, and confront your closets.

Chapter 10

Bedrooms, Guest Rooms, and (Shudder) Closets

Think about it: Could you really show your guest rooms to a guest? Or are they auxiliary attics? Can you find your clothes in the morning, or are you fighting with the not-so-mythical monster that lives in your closet? And would you really call your bedroom restful, or is refuse-full more like it? The tips in this chapter will help you restore order to chaos; clear out your closets without causing yourself pain; and create beautiful, uncluttered bedrooms for yourself and your guests—without "wasting" any precious space!

Because bedrooms, guest rooms, and closets each have their own distinct clutter issues, let's take them one at a time.

PRIORITIES FOR BEDROOMS

Once again, start your de-cluttering process in the bedroom by setting some clutter-kicking priorities. The first step is to focus on what matters most to you about the way your bedroom looks. One way to focus is to decide what bothers you more—the exposed areas of the bedroom (like the bed, floor, chairs, and dresser tops), or the hidden areas (like the closet and dresser drawers). Once you start thinking about the kinds of clutter that really drive you crazy, you'll be able to rank your bedroom's clutter problems from most to least aggravating. The best way to do this is by taking a good, hard look at the "before" state of the room and then visualizing the "after."

A Bedroom Visualization

To get to your "after," you need to start with the "before"—the way things look right now. So get out some paper, or use the "My Bedroom—Before" form on page 182 (or make a photocopy of it and write on that). Write down every place in the bedroom that there's clutter, and note what that clutter is. Are there volcanic piles on the bed? On the floor? Do you have a feeling that something's living under the bed . . . and it's not the dog? Are you afraid to open the bottom dresser drawer? Write it all down. After all, no one will see this list but you!

Once you've taken an inventory of your bedroom's "before" state, it's time to move on to the "after"—how you want the room to look when you've kicked the clutter. Use the "My Bedroom—After" form on page 182 (or make a photocopy of it and write on that) to describe the room's "after" state. To make sure you're being realistic, look at the room every few minutes while you're doing this.

Your "After" description can be short and to the point: "I'd like more dresser space. I'd like attractive bedside tables with room for books and magazines and a great reading light. I'd like less fussy curtains that don't collect dust. I'd like more hidden storage space so the bedroom looks less messy and more romantic. I want soft lighting to give the room a romantic glow. I'd like to add some mirrors to open up the room and bring in more light without sacrificing privacy."

Or you can create a detailed picture of exactly how you'd like your bedroom to look if it were perfect (for you). You can imagine the feel you want the room to have (restful? romantic? playful?). Think about the wall treatments—paint, wallpaper, stenciling, texturing, paneling—and colors; the woodwork and window treatments. What would the floor look like—plush carpet, gleaming wood, handmade rugs, rush matting? What style furniture would you prefer, and how would it be arranged? Would there be a fireplace, and if so, would it be real or a gas or electric model? What would be on the bed; what art and mirrors would be on the walls—everything.

My Bedroom—Before

My Bedroom—After

My Bedroom Priority List

_____

_____

_____

_____

_____

_____

_____

_____

Getting There

Now that you have captured your bedroom's "before" condition, listing all the specifics, and you've imagined its "after" appearance, you can finally prioritize the steps you'll need to take to get there from here. Again, bearing both "before" and "after" in mind, I'd recommend starting with what bothers you most about the "before" condition and working down your list of clutter issues until you reach what's least important to you.

Maybe your bedside is piled with books and magazines and you're lusting after a floor-to-ceiling bookcase to stash lots of bedtime reading in. Or you'd love an elegant armoire to hide the TV, DVD player, stereo, and all the movies and music that are covering every flat surface. Or you have clothes piled everywhere and you're wondering about options for under-bed storage.

Write down whatever's driving you to distraction on the "My Bedroom Priority List" (or photocopy it, if you'd prefer), in descending order from most to least maddening. This is the order in which you'll tackle your bedroom clutter problems. Now you have your priorities straight! Once you've finished, you can turn to the tips beginning on page 184 to find ingenious ways of dealing with each problem.

5-Minute Fixes for the Bedroom

If you are intimidated by the prospect of transforming your bedroom into a clutter-free zone or just want to get your feet wet, try these quick fixes. They're some of the easiest ways to start de-cluttering your bedroom.

Pick up your clothes. Or his clothes. Nothing makes a room look messier than clothes on the floor, draped across the bed, tossed on a chair, flung across the top of the door . . . you get the picture. But fortunately, nothing's easier to fix!

Make the bed. Rumpled bedclothes and tossed-around pillows create a chaotic, cluttered look. But it takes only 5 minutes to put things right. You'll thank yourself every time you walk into the room for the rest of the day!

Take out the trash. Sometimes weeks can go by before that bedroom wastebasket gets emptied, and an overflowing wastebasket really adds to a room's cluttered look. Just emptying it will make the room look better—and make you feel better! Don't have a wastebasket in your bedroom? Unless you're compulsive about carrying every Kleenex, renewal card, and clothing price tag to the kitchen trash can, invest in one next time you're out. That's 5 minutes well spent!

Nix the night-table pileup. Bedside tables are a huge convenience—I wish I had one!—but they can also become clutter magnets. Shovel off the magazines, catalogs, bills, mugs, jewelry, and everything else that's accumulated on there. Now that you can see the surface, dust it. Then put back one book, one magazine, and

THE BEDROOM TIPS

Look under the bed. Send the dust bunnies packing and put that big space under the bed to good use as free storage space. I use those big, flat plastic storage containers, available pretty much everywhere, because they hold a lot and slide easily under the bed. Because I have an antique bed that sits high off the floor, I can stack the containers two deep or use taller ones to make sure I fit as much as possible in the space. I recommend storing bedroom-related stuff under the bed—bed linens, sweaters, out-of-season clothes—rather than stuff like Christmas ornaments and canned goods. But if you have enough closet and dresser space (don't tell me—I'm already jealous!), you can put whatever else needs storing under the one catalog for nighttime reading (remember, you can rotate them as you finish), the box of tissues (if you must), a coaster for your mug or glass, and the alarm clock (if that's where it lives), and you are done. Your reading glasses, diary and pen, pills, and cell phone can go in the drawer; put everything else back where it belongs. Ahhhh . . . that's better!

Don't wait for laundry day. Unless you can fit a laundry basket in your bedroom closet (is that laughter I hear?), make a point of taking the dirty clothes to the laundry room every night before bed. (I'd say, "as soon as you take them off," but let's just say that all family members may not be too cooperative about that.) Just as in the case of picking up flung or fallen clothes and putting them away, you'll feel much better about going to bed in a dirty-clothes-free room. It may even put more romance into bedtime!

Do one dresser drawer. Pick a drawer, any drawer—pull hard now, you can get it open!—and sort through the overflowing contents. Make one pile for stained, holey, stretched-out, and "what *is* this?" items—that's the trash pile, of course; one pile for way too small or way too big (lucky you), I hate that color/pattern, and I never wear that—that's the donation pile; and one pile for still fits, still looks good, and still wearing it. That pile goes back in the (now much roomier) drawer. You can finally see what you have in there, so you can get to it that much faster and easier. And you have room to treat yourself to a new piece or two!

bed. And I confess, this is a "do as I say, not as I do" recommendation—I also have my guitar cases under my bed!

Roll it out. I have seen designs for wonderful homemade under-bed storage contraptions. Basically rolling wooden storage trays, they're shallow boxes on casters that either were sized for the bed or—much easier to maneuver, in my opinion—sized to fit under half the bed and used in pairs. If you or your spouse is handy, measure the space under your bed (leaving plenty of headroom, several inches to clear the bed's legs, and several more between boxes), and build a set of shallow storage boxes (to me, three would be easier to deal with than two). You can paint them to match the woodwork if you don't enjoy the sight of bare ply-wood, even under wraps. Or cover the boxes with old sheets—you can buy some fun, colorful ones at thrift stores if you don't have extras. Cut or fold the sheets to fit and staple or tack them down on one long side. And don't forget to add sturdy handles so you can pull the boxes out!

Skirt the issue. Under-bed storage is great, but *looking* at under-bed storage is another matter. If you use the space under your bed for storage, make sure you conceal it with a bed skirt or dust ruffle.

Invest in a chest. A blanket or "hope" chest is the perfect place to store, well, blankets. (Hope is another matter.) Quilts, sheets, extra pillows—they all tuck right into the chest. Put it at the foot of your bed, or put it under a window and add some flat pillows on top for an instant window seat.

Buy a bench. Speaking of window seats, those benches with lift-up tops for storage are perfect for blankets and bed linens and usually come with a comfy cushion on top.

Build it in. I love window seats—they're so romantic. One of the most ingenious ones I ever saw had been custom-built with a lift-up seat and a built-in storage bin underneath. Somebody was thinking!

Try a table. A long, narrow table can create additional storage at the foot of your bed. Get one that's the right length and height for your bed—you don't want it to be taller than the mattress! The Shakers designed a variety of tables that are perfect for this. Their Sabbathday Lake tailoring counter (available from Shaker Workshops; see page 47) is just 21 inches deep and has four drawers that are ample enough to act as a second dresser. Two-drawer worktables, serving tables, and Shaker sideboards are other options. Check local flea markets to see what you can find. Add attractive baskets under the table to create even more storage.

Don't treat your bed like a table. Maybe your problem is that you make the bed, but no one could tell under the mound of stuff that you/he/they have thrown on top of it. Under-bed storage is a great idea, but the same can't be said of *on*-bed storage! Clear that stuff off and put it where it belongs.

Don't pay bills in bed. My friend and feng shui guru Skye Alexander would say that using your bedroom as an office is very bad feng shui. It's also a fast way to clutter the bedroom with envelopes, receipts, and other easy-to-lose odds and ends. We'll talk about how to corral bills in Chapter 12—The Home Office (see page 242); for now, just collect any finance-related material, rubber-band it together, and take it downstairs.

Add an armoire. Before there were built-in closets, freestanding closets that were massive pieces of furniture were the norm. Called armoires, wardrobes, garderobes, or chifforobes, these capacious "closets" held the household's clothing. They still can. If you need extra space for clothes and have enough wall space for an armoire, look for one at a flea market or antiques store. There are modern versions, too, in furniture stores. Try to find one that fits with your bedroom decor, bearing in mind that you can always paint it. Add hooks for clothes, a rack for coat hangers, or shelves for sweaters, jeans, tee-shirts, and the like. Or use your armoire as a giant entertainment center and stash all that equipment in there, along with the videos, DVDs, CDs—even cassettes and albums—that you enjoy.

Capture a corner. When space is tight, a corner cupboard can be a lifesaver in the bedroom. Just as you can use an armoire or dresser in the dining room, a corner cupboard will give you handsome "found" storage space in your bedroom. If yours has open shelving or glass doors on top, use those shelves for your brightest, most ornamental quilts and coverlets. Stash the extra pillows, jeans, sweaters, and tee-shirts down below, where solid doors can hide a multitude of less-attractive sins.

Choose a quilt rack. Display your fine quilts and coverlets year-round on a quilt rack, which will show off three to six bed coverings (depending on how you fold them). You can find a rack to match just about any decor.

Put up a ladder. My friend and editor Karen has a great idea for storing afghans, lap rugs, and throws without wasting drawer or closet space. "Find a new or antique ladder and lean it against the wall as a decorator piece," says Karen. "Fold throws in thirds or quarters and hang them over the ladder rungs. I painted my ladder to match my country decor, and it's as decorative as it is useful."

Make a statement. The bedroom is a great place to display your fabric art. Use a quilt hanger to hang a quilt, coverlet, or weaving on the wall. Even full-size quilts make great bedroom art—and save storage space by hiding in plain sight!— but smaller wall quilts look wonderful, too, if you don't have space to hang a bed quilt. Make sure your display is out of direct sunlight to avoid fading your textile treasure.

Belt it out, part one. If your dresser has two shallow drawers on top like mine does, dedicate one to belt storage. Roll up the belts individually and tuck them beside each other in the drawer. This will keep them safe; make them easy to find, see, and reach; and keep them out of the way.

Belt it out, part two. The Shakers have contributed so many ingenious ideas to our culture, but I think my favorite is the oval Shaker wooden box. A shallow Shaker box is a great place to store belts. Roll them up and tuck them into the box side by side. Display the box on top of your dresser or on a side table.

Tackle those ties. If the man in your life has a collection of ties, you can store them in exactly the same way as you would belts: Roll them up and tuck them in a shallow dresser drawer or a Shaker box. If your guy loves gadgets, he might go for the clear plastic cylindrical "tie caddies" that each hold a tie and come with their own tie-winding mechanism. They're available from mail-order catalogs like Herrington and Solutions (see page 48). If your guy's on the go, he can just grab the ties he needs and toss them in his suitcase—no wrinkling, no worries.

Add a jewelry box. Whether it's a beautiful handmade walnut or bird's-eye maple chest; a Shaker oval box; or a jewelry chest that stands on the floor, has eight drawers, and doubles as a night table, if you have jewelry, you can find a beautiful way to store it. Choose a storage piece that matches your taste and budget (and, of course, the size of your jewelry collection).

Tray your treasures. Turn that shallow dresser drawer into a jewelry box with stackable, sliding jewelry trays, available from organizing catalogs, stores, and Web sites like Solutions and All Bright Ideas (see page 48). You can buy specially designed velvet-lined trays with compartments for necklaces, bracelets, earrings, rings, and brooches, then combine them into a compact, easy-to-use jewelry box in a drawer.

Get a jewelry mirror. Don't scoff—here's a brilliant idea for making the most of your bedroom space. Catalogs such as Improvements (see page 48) sell wall mirrors that open to reveal a long, capacious, two-sided jewelry cabinet. Wow! You can choose your jewelry for the day (or night), then use the mirror to put it on and see how it looks.

Don't forget the guys. What about *his* jewelry, watch, and cufflinks? Leather and guys—they seem to go together. As a child, I was fascinated by the small leather box my father kept his cufflinks and watch in. Now you can buy a leather organizer for your man with room for his wallet and cell phone as well as his watches and other accessories. Display it proudly on the dresser with your jewelry box, or tuck it discreetly into one of those shallow dresser drawers. But a guy's treasure chest doesn't have to be leather. I have a beautiful, ornately carved wooden box with velvet-lined compartments on my dresser just for Rob's things. (He picked it out himself.) And I've seen gorgeous wood dresser-top "valets" in catalogs like Solutions (see page 48).

Table it. Bedside tables, or nightstands, are infinitely useful, and not just by the bed. They come in myriad styles, so you can match your decor with new tables or find old ones at antiques stores and flea markets. They're just the right size for a lamp, mug, book, magazine, newspaper, and tissue holder. Choose a style with a drawer (or two) for storing reading glasses, coasters, pens, remotes, cell phones, sticky tags, hand cream, and anything else you find essential. Put a matching one on each side of the bed, with a decorative wastebasket tucked discreetly underneath. (Remember those tissues!) I don't have room for a bedside table beside my bed, but I do use one on the wall across from the bed; I piled beautiful wooden boxes on top to create a focal point, so it's functional as well as attractive.

Dress it up. Dressers are essential bedroom furniture for good reason—they can hold a lot of clothes. Get one or two you like, new or used, and divide the drawers according to use—nightgowns and PJs, underwear, jeans, tee-shirts, socks. Put the stuff you use most often in the highest drawers, the less-often-used items in the lowest drawers. If you must share your dresser drawers, give the highest to the tallest of you, then alternate on down. Make sure at least one of your dressers has a mirror so you can check hair, clothes, and jewelry before heading out. (Besides, the cat will love it.)

Deal with the drawers. Linda Koopersmith, the Beverly Hills Organizer and organizational expert and co-host of Style Network's series *Clean House* (see

"The Pros Know" on page 204) is a big believer in folding clothes and setting them end-up in drawers rather than laying them down horizontally. She points out that folding clothes and stacking them upright, with the smooth, rounded sides facing up, not only lets you pack more clothes into each drawer, it lets you have a "bird's-eye view" of everything in the drawer. No more lost or forgotten clothes! Need help keeping those rows upright? Linda recommends spring-loaded partitions called tension dividers to divide a drawer into sections and sock, bra, and brief boxes to keep your underthings in place.

Cache it in a cupboard. At a flea market many years ago, I found some cheap, colorfully painted old cupboards with doors that had once been glass-fronted but now were simply framed, and I brought them home to house my textile collection. The brilliant colors of the cupboards and textiles look smashing, and I thought I was being really creative and clever—until I saw the same idea in a home decorating magazine about 10 years later. Yikes! How humiliating that anyone else had my brilliant idea. But it's still a great idea!

Pack up the papers. I know one dad (who shall remain nameless) who is so sure he's going to get around to reading the entire *New York Times, Wall Street Journal,* and local papers that he saves them . . . and saves them . . . until he "can get to them." As if! The result is a mountain of papers under his bed. If you or your spouse falls into this category, even if you're not *that* extreme, make sure that all papers are recycled weekly. That gives everyone a full week to read the papers— and if they haven't read them by then, they're not gonna.

Hide it in a hatbox. Attractively covered hatboxes (or "nesting hatbox organizers" as I've seen them called) have been a design trend for more than 10 years. They're ornamental enough to display on shelves or on top of a dresser or table, and they're spacious enough to hold pretty much whatever you want to stash in them, up to blankets and clothes. I confess, I actually use mine for hats, which I stack on top of each other to maximize hatbox space, and costume-party wigs (Sweet Potato Queens, anyone?). Fun!

Find a folding screen. Create a dressing nook behind a folding screen in a corner of the bedroom. Add hooks and a full-length mirror on the wall, tuck a little bench back there, and you're good to go!

Add a low bookcase. A low bookcase along one wall not only gives you storage and display space, the top also acts as a table for a vase of flowers, candles (how romantic!), a bowl of potpourri, a lamp, an incense burner, or anything else you'd like to put in the bedroom to add beauty and atmosphere.

Or hang it high. A hanging bookcase or cabinet is also a wonderful way to add storage or display space in the bedroom. If you opt for a dresser without a mirror or a low bookcase, add a hanging cabinet or bookcase above and double your space.

Frame the door. Put narrow bookshelves around the door and a connecting shelf over the door to create a space-saving place for books, magazines, and treasures.

Don't junk up the walls. Your bedroom should be the most restful, soothing, romantic room in your home—a room that's just begging you to come in and kick back, park your cares by the door, and relax. Don't spoil the mood by jamming photos, paintings, and knickknacks on the walls. A few restful paintings, family photos, or nature scenes, plus a large mirror that captures a lovely outdoor scene, are plenty. In this room, excess quickly becomes wretched excess. Choose your artwork with care, leave lots of wall space, and remember that you can rotate your art and photos—you don't have to display them all at once.

Add some life. Plants not only add beauty to a room, they also remove pollutants from the air. But as always, your goal is to add beauty, not clutter. Choose single plants as accents or focal points, and then take good care of them so they look good—not dead. (Tip: Overwatering is as likely to brown up a plant as underwatering. Feel the soil before you water!) If you hang a plant near the window, it won't take up table space but will add beauty. Just don't hang it in front of the window and block your light—slightly to the side is fine. If you have a deep windowsill, a trailing or blooming plant in a lovely pot can add a burst of color and life. (But don't put a trailing plant over a heat source, and do keep after shedding leaves.) Choose a natural or single-color pot, not one with a busily colored pattern, so it accents the plant rather than fighting with it for attention and creating visual clutter. Finally, steal this great trick from my friend Delilah: She keeps plants in her greenhouse until they reach the peak of blooming perfection, then brings them inside to display, rotating out the ones that are past peak. You don't need a greenhouse to do this—just keep plants in a bright, sunny area where they're not in the spotlight when they aren't on display. Finally, do *not* keep more plants than you'll take care of! If one's your limit, better to have one beautiful plant than a dozen half-dead sufferers.

Light your fire. If you've always dreamed of a romantic firelit bedroom, there's no better time to get one than the present. I grew up in a Colonial home with a working fireplace in every room, including my bedroom. I can tell you straight out that there is *nothing* more romantic than a fire flickering away as you're falling asleep. But if you're not that lucky, that no longer means that you have to invest in major masonry to add a bedroom fireplace. Thanks to the wonders of modern technology, you can buy a plug-in electric fireplace with an attractive mantel or a gas fireplace or "woodstove" with wonderful warming flames. (I have two sets of friends who've opted for these pseudo-woodstoves, one in their family room and one on their porch, and I can attest to how warm and wonderful they are.) Many of the new models require no venting to the outside, so they can fit wherever you want to put them. All I can say is, "Wow!"

Add a mantel shelf. Gorgeous freestanding mantel shelves are available from home stores and catalogs like Plow & Hearth (see page 47). Dress up a fireplace or create the illusion of one with these easy-to-hang wooden mantels.

Feel the glow. Wall sconces are a great choice for the bedroom. They give the room a muted, romantic glow, and they don't occupy precious surface space!

Add display shelves. Rather than cover the surfaces of your dressers and bedside tables with your collection of crystals, shells, or other collectibles, show them off on a lighted wall shelf. These wonderful inventions, available from home catalogs like Solutions (see page 48), are made of wood and look almost like miniature mantelpieces. They range from a wall "sconce" (just over 10 inches long) to a "ledge" (just over 2 feet long), and are as easy to hang as a picture frame. The top of each display shelf is an acrylic panel that's lit from below by battery-operated LEDs. Because the light comes up from below, these shelves are especially good for showcasing transparent and translucent objects.

GUEST ROOMS

Okay, let's talk about guest rooms for a minute. In my view, unless there's a really good reason for setting aside an entire room for guests, you're wasting valuable space. Here are four good reasons for having a designated guest room that serves no other function:

1. You have partial custody of one or more kids. (In which case, hopefully, it's

Pet Alert!

If you have pets, chances are that they share your bedroom with you. If you give them their own space to relax in, chances are better that they won't try to take over yours. My golden retriever, Molly, has her own plush plaid dog bed at the foot of my bed. It's one of those cushy foam-filled dog beds from L.L. Bean or Orvis (see pages 46 and 49), and she sleeps on it every night (unless the cats push her off). My cats enjoy spending time on the tall "cat castle" that's tucked into a corner of the room and has three tiers of lushly carpeted sleep stations, as well as a sisal rope scratching post. I've added a variety of toys, and the cats alternate between spending time on the cat castle, curling up with Molly, and sunning in the picture window. Tripping over cat or dog toys en route to the bathroom at night is no fun, so I'd recommend that you keep an attractive basket or hamper in the bedroom to stash their toys in, too.

What about other kinds of pets? I think a bedroom aquarium is about the most relaxing, romantic accessory of all—the soft light, the soothing sounds of water cascading over the filter, the brilliantly lit fish swimming peacefully among the plants. But if you have parrots, parakeets, or any bird that can speak, keep them in another room! Birds tend to quickly pick up on any unusual or emotional words or noises, and you don't want your private affairs broadcast to the UPS man or your in-laws!

not a "guest" room, but your kid's room! See Chapter 11—Clutter-Free Kids' Rooms, for more on this.)

2. Your grown kids or grandkids come to stay almost every weekend.

3. Your house is a "vacation destination" for your friends and family because of its location near the ocean, lake, mountains, or Disney World, or just because of your famous hospitality.

4. You have more than one magnificent set of bedroom furniture and it's worth the space to display it. (If I'm lucky enough to inherit the fabulous Colonial cherry furniture in my childhood bedroom, I'll consider converting my music room back into a bedroom!)

Otherwise, sell or donate your guest room furniture and turn that space into something you want and need! Crafts room, exercise room/home gym, music room, home office, playroom . . . you can probably picture the room of your dreams right now. But what if you need the space for the occasional overnight guest? Here are some tips to help you be prepared to make guests feel welcome without sacrificing your precious square footage.

Set up a sofa bed. No matter what you decide to use your erstwhile guest room for, you're probably going to need some seating in there. Home catalogs like Plow & Hearth (see page 47) feature tons of options for seating that pulls out to convert into bedding. You can get a sofa, loveseat, chair, or ottoman, and some of them are quite lightweight—a real boon if you have to move them around to set them up.

Blow up the bed. As I've mentioned before, air mattresses are my all-time favorite guest bedding; they are supercomfortable. Some even feature double-depth mattresses, and others have foldout legs and frames, so guests don't feel like they are sleeping on the floor. But even standard on-floor air mattresses are more comfortable than most beds, and you can adjust the level of inflation to exactly match a guest's firmness requirements. With today's electric pumps, it takes less than 5 minutes to inflate or (if the pump is reversible) deflate the mattress, and the whole thing tucks away in a storage bag that's half the size of a sleeping bag. It doesn't

Love It *or* Lose It?

In the interest of saving space, you may be tempted to get a hat rack for your guest room, with the thought that guests can hang their clothes on the rack and you won't have to provide closet space. I've even encountered this arrangement in expensive inns. Ugh! Who wants to look at their clothes heaped on hat-rack hooks or coat hangers slung haphazardly on the hat rack? I travel light—I never take more than will fit in a small carry-on bag—but even I have more clothes than a hat rack can accommodate. Resist this temptation! Give your guests dedicated closet or armoire space, even if you have to temporarily move some of your own clothes to provide it. And make sure they have an ample supply of sturdy, presentable coat hangers—not twisted, wimpy dry-cleaner leftovers.

Verdict: Lose it!

get better than this! Incidentally, a full- or queen-size air mattress is the most versatile, since it can accommodate one or two guests.

Keep it close to the chest. A blanket chest isn't just attractive; placed in a guest room, it can hold the blankets, pillows, and bed linens for the guest bed. If you use an air mattress, the chest can hold the bed itself, as well. Add a flat cushion on top and you have seating, too.

Provide lots of pillows. Nothing says "welcome" like a whole pile of soft, cushy pillows for the guest bed—and nothing says "afterthought" like one pathetic, flat pillow. Keep plenty of extra pillows on hand for your guests and provide enough blankets so they can have all they want (which may be more than you'd use). Store pillows on the bed itself, so guests can use as few or as many as they like without feeling that they have to ask for extras. (And that way, the pillows don't use up extra storage space.) Same for the blankets—just fold them and pile them at the foot of the bed. Both pillows and blankets could also go in a blanket chest or trunk at the foot of the bed. That's hospitality!

Take a tip from hotels. My father's girlfriend, Alice, has fold-out luggage stands in all her guest rooms, just like hotels do. I love this—I can set my suitcase on the stand and have easy access to the contents whenever I want, without having to drag the suitcase in and out of the closet. You can get the stands from home stores and catalogs like Improvements (see page 48).

Make a guest kit. Another wonderful thing my father's girlfriend, Alice, does is to create a toiletries kit for every guest. You can do this by setting out a basket in the guest bathroom (or, if you don't have a separate guest bathroom, on a dresser in the guest room). Put a travel-size soap, shampoo, conditioner, lotion, toothbrush, toothpaste, emery board, razor, and talcum powder in the basket, along with anything else you think would give your guests a luxurious treat (bath oil balls or bubble bath, for instance). In these days of restricted carry-on toiletries, your guests will be especially grateful!

Bring out the rack. No closet space for guests? Instead of resorting to a hat rack (see "Love It or Lose It?"), get a rolling clothes rack. Yes, it will be right there in the room, but it will provide plenty of room for all your guests' clothes. And if you provide plenty of sturdy, attractive hangers, rather than a few bent, inadequate orphans, your guests will really appreciate it. Trust me on that! You can roll the rack back out of sight in the basement, garage, or other storage space when it's not in use, or make it part of the room when guests aren't there. (For example, it can hold quilts in a quilting studio, knitwear or crocheted sweaters in a yarn studio, or exercise clothes in a home gym.)

Make sure there's light. Guests need to be able to see to navigate in the dark, so put a nightlight in the guest room and make sure it's on when you have visitors. And don't skimp on the guest-room lighting—a dark room looks soulless and unwelcoming. Again, it's important here to keep lamps and cords where they won't become tripping hazards for unsuspecting guests. Ceiling fixtures and wall sconces are great options.

PRIORITIES FOR CLOSETS

I'm going to ask you to do a quick closet visualization exercise, too. "What?" you say, "Visualize a closet?" But think about it: Have you ever actually looked at your closet in an analytical way, at what the space might offer and how you're using it? Or have you, like most of us, been far too busy trying to cram things into it and pull things out of it (if you can find them) to really see the space itself? Bear with me here. It's just a closet—it won't take but a minute or two to look at the way it is now and then think about how it *could* look, probably with just a few quick changes.

As usual, start your de-cluttering process by taking a good, hard look at the "before" state of your closet, and then visualize the "after."

A Closet Visualization

Before you can visualize the closet you want to have after the clutter is gone, you have to start with the "before"—the way things look right now. So get out some paper, or use the "My Closet—Before" form (or make a photocopy of it and write on that). Write down the location of every bit of clutter in that closet, and note what that clutter is. Are there things in the closet that don't belong there? Is there enough rack space, or is everything crammed in so tightly that extracting a piece of clothing feels like a wrestling match? Do you have enough shelf space? Are shoes spilling out in an avalanche every time you open the door, or does it take so long to find a matching pair that you've started leaving the pair you actually wear

My Closet—Before

_____
_____
_____
_____
_____
_____
_____
_____
_____
_____

My Closet—After

_____
_____
_____
_____
_____
_____
_____
_____
_____
_____

My Closet Priority List

_____

_____

_____

_____

_____

_____

_____

_____

_____

_____

by the front door? Take a minute now to write down your "before" so you can get to your "after"!

Once you've jotted down a quick description of your closet's "before" state, it's time to move on to the "after." On a piece of paper or the "My Closet—After" form on page 197 (or a photocopy of it), describe how you want the closet to look when you've kicked the clutter. If you have any home magazines or catalogs that show fabulous closets, look through them now to get ideas. Make sure you look at your closet while you're doing this, too, as a reality check. There's no point in mentally creating the walk-in closet of your dreams when your real-life closet has barely enough room for the cat to walk in!

Your description can be short and to the point: "I'd like for all the shoes to be on a rack where they're easy to see and reach. I'd like plenty of light so I can see what's in there. I'd like floor-to-ceiling shelves on each side."

If you're lucky enough to have a walk-in closet, you can create a detailed image of exactly how you'd like your closet to look if it were perfect (for you). You can picture the colors of the walls and woodwork, what the floor would look like, whether there would be room for a chair and vanity, what the storage areas would look like, how it would be lit—everything.

Getting There

Now that you have captured your closet's "before" condition, listing all the specifics, and you've imagined its "after" appearance, you can finally prioritize the steps you'll need to take to get there from here. Again, bearing both "before" and "after" in mind, I'd recommend starting with what bothers you most about the "before" condition and working down from there.

Write down whatever's driving you to distraction on the "My Closet Priority List" (or photocopy it, if you'd prefer), working in descending order from most to least maddening. Now you have your priorities straight! Once you've finished your priority list, you can turn to the tips below to find ingenious ways of dealing with each problem.

THE CLOSET TIPS

Kick out the old clothes. Nobody wants to, but if you're looking at a closet revamp, you might as well start by de-cluttering your wardrobe. You'll have to take the clothes out anyway before you can do anything else. Here's how to pare down your wardrobe in seven stages:

1. Start with the stuff that's obviously beat—hopelessly stained, torn, shrunken, burned, and so on. Put it in a trash bag and get it outta there! If one or more of the damaged goods is a key wardrobe piece—something you actually need to have and wear often—write down what it is so you can shop for a replacement. (Assuming you don't find another one hidden in the closet somewhere.)

2. Tackle the clothes that no longer fit. Can I hear you screaming "But they're almost new!" or "Really—I'm going to lose the weight!"? Not to worry. If you can't bear to donate them or take them to a consignment shop, pack them up in a suitcase (see page 205) or plastic storage box, label it, and tuck it under the bed or in the guest-room closet. Maybe you *will* be able to wear them one day, or maybe you'll be able to part with them when you haven't seen them for a while and realize that you haven't missed them. (And might I gently suggest that styles do change!) In any case, at least you'll have

removed the clothes and freed up much-needed space for clothes that you *can* wear.

3. Now it's time to get tough with the clothes you don't like. Maybe that blouse cost a fortune, your mom or your husband gave that sweater to you, or that dress was the most gorgeous one you'd ever seen (just not on you). Whatever the case, whatever the reason—it's uncomfortable, it never fit right, you think it's ugly, it's last year's color or style—get it out of the closet and out of your life. Goodwill (or that high-end consignment shop) is waiting! If you're afraid your spouse will suddenly wonder where that gorgeous purple leopard sweater he gave you last Valentine's Day has gone, tuck it in the storage container with the clothes that don't fit. You'll have it within reach just in case. But don't be surprised if it doesn't come up! And now you have even more closet space.

4. What about clothes you love but no longer wear—your prom dress, wedding dress, first-date outfit, hand-embroidered hippie jeans? I have one question: What are those doing in your closet, anyway? Pack them away tenderly and put them where you can get them out and look at them when you're feeling nostalgic, but they're not taking up closet space you need now. Or, if you're a quilter or sewer, you can always photograph each garment, then cut it up and use the pieces to make memory quilts for yourself and the kids, make patchwork skirts or jackets for your kids, or add patches to their jeans. Keep the photos in a memory album, and put that quilt out on display where you can enjoy it!

5. While you're going through your clothes, see if any pieces need to be cleaned or repaired. Don't put them back until they're fixed and clean.

6. If you share the closet with your spouse or partner, you can go through this with his clothes, too. Just don't actually get rid of anything without his consent! I'll bet he'll be more willing to part with his ratty clothes when he sees how much of your stuff is going.

7. Repeat the process with your shoes, purses, hats, and other accessories.

Finally, you can see in there! Now it's time to start on the closet itself.

Let in the light. It's essential to have enough light in your closet to see what you're doing. My all-time favorite closet lighting is in my father's girlfriend's house: When you turn on the lights in a bedroom, the recessed lighting in the bedroom

the Pros Know

There are more specialty closet companies than you can shake a stick at. California Closets, EasyClosets.com, All Bright Ideas, Contemporary Closets, Closet Factory—the list is endless! If you want to go with the pros—many of which offer complementary consultations—turn to page 45 for contact data, or look in the local Yellow Pages for closet consultants in your area. Check out their offerings and pricing online, order a few catalogs, then give them a call. Decide on your needs and your budget beforehand, then find the best fit.

closet goes on automatically. Great idea! But whatever lighting system you opt for, make sure it's bright enough and is easy to turn on.

Color me beautiful. Too often, we view closets as afterthoughts—plain storage spaces that are painted white or another unremarkable color. But some of the most wonderful closets I've ever seen were painted vibrant colors or papered in fabulous prints. Use some imagination and spice up your space.

Use your door. Don't waste the inside of your closet door! Hang a shoe rack or a full-length mirror, both of which will hook over the top of the door comparatively unobtrusively. Some of the more heavy-duty over-door shoe racks can hold up to 36 pairs of shoes! Companies also make purse hangers for closet doors. And of course you can get those accordion racks with pegs to hang lightweight things like jewelry, scarves, and handbags, or a Shaker-style peg rack or decorative hooks for heavier items like purses, tote bags, or bathrobes.

Double up. You'll have a lot more space to hang clothes if you add a second clothes rod in part of your closet. (You'll want to leave part of the closet with a single rod for dresses, bathrobes, long coats, and other full-length garments.) But be prepared to raise up the top rod: A single clothes rod is usually attached at 66 to 72 inches, but double-hung rods should be spaced at 42 inches for the lower rod and 82 for the higher one. Hang blouses and shirts on the top rod and skirts and pants on the bottom one.

Add more shelves. Shelving can really add storage space to a closet. You can install standard wood shelves, painted to match your closet, or use plastic-coated wire shelf units (such as those sold by Closet Maid). Both ready-to-use wood and

5-Minute Fix for the Closet

Here's one of the easiest ways to start de-cluttering your closet!

Shed some shoes. Okay, it's not fun. But if you can't see your closet floor because of all the shoes—or you have a hard time finding a match for any shoe in the Mt. Everest of other shoes on the floor—it is time to unload. Just dive in there and pick two pairs of battered, stained, stretched-out, broken, you-name-it shoes and trash them. (Or donate them, if you think someone might be able to wear them.) You can do it! If you loved them back in the day, you can always take a photo of them in their current condition and write on the back what they meant to you. Hopefully, after a few viewings of the photo, you'll wonder why you took it and toss that, too—but if not, at least a photo takes up zero room in your clothes closet.

wire shelves are available in most home centers. (California Closets has an entire line at Target.) The wire shelving comes in all lengths and is designed specifically for closets, so it's sized to fit a standard-size closet. And it's durable, attractive, and easy to install.

Save the high shelf. Unless you're tall enough to reach that long, over-the-clothes-rod shelf, use it to store plastic containers with clothes that are out of season. You can see what's in them, but you'll have to take them down only a couple of times a year!

Use multihangers. Skirt hangers that have four or five cascading hangers can save a lot of space on the closet hanger bar. But now catalogs like Improvements (see page 48) also have ingenious hangers that allow you to hang five hangers for shirts, sweaters, or whatever you'd like from a supercompact "hanger holder." Instead of groping around for the one you want, you can simply reach in and remove the appropriate hanger. No fuss, no muss!

Hang clothes by color. If you hang all of your black skirts, gray skirts, khaki pants, and white blouses together, it's easy to see what's in the closet and what's in the laundry or at the dry cleaner's. It's also easy to see if you have wardrobe gaps! And it might be a bit easier to part with those ancient black slacks if you can see that you have five other pairs that still look good.

Sort through each season. I keep the current season's clothes in my bedroom closet and the off-season's in my office closet. When it's time to switch, I always take a critical look at both sets of clothes to see if some have finished their useful lives and others are out of style or out of shape (mine). Since I have to move them all anyway, it's the perfect time to review them.

Rack 'em up. Shoe racks—available in cedar, chrome, and any number of other materials—let you stack shoes vertically rather than leaving them piled at random on the floor or stashed in shoeboxes where you can't even see what you have. If you don't use your closet door for shoe storage or you have more shoes than an over-the-door rack can accommodate, shoe racks are the greatest thing going.

Hop on the carousel. An alternative to a shoe rack is a revolving shoe carousel, which holds two or three tiers (up to 18 pairs) in the floor space of two pairs of shoes. Give the carousel a spin and select your day's pair.

Corral some cubbies. Shoe cubbies are an attractive and durable way to keep shoes neat and accessible. Put them against the back of the closet wall for easiest access.

Dig out a dresser. Take this piece of good advice from Linda Cobb, the Queen of Clean: If you have space for a small dresser in your closet, you can store sweaters, tee-shirts, jeans, and other clothes that would just take up rack room (or, as is the case with sweaters, that keep their shape best if folded rather than hung). Get one at a thrift store, flea market, or yard sale. I'd suggest a child's dresser, since they're smaller and would fit more easily but are still big enough to hold lots of clothes. Paint it to match your closet and you're good to go!

Hang a medicine cabinet. If you have extra wall space in your closet and need shelves for purses, gloves and mittens, ties, hair accessories, and other small items, consider a medicine cabinet or other hanging wall cabinet. If it has a mirrored door, you have an instant closet mirror, too!

Hang up your ties. My boyfriend, Rob, has a tie hanger that looks like a short coat hanger with lots of stubby little arms. The hanger keeps his ties tidy and accessible—he can see them all at a glance—in an incredibly small amount of space.

Buy a belt ring. Another ingenious device in Rob's closet is a belt ring. It's like a giant circular key ring—the sort that latches open and closed—with a coat-hanger hook at the top. Rob flips open the latch, slides his belts on the ring (where they hang by their buckles), and hangs the whole thing on the clothes rack. He never has to wonder where his belts are!

Try a trouser rack. Compact wooden trouser racks can hold 10 to 20 pairs of trousers in an 18-inch space. The rack mounts to a closet door or wall and has swing-out wooden dowels to hold the trousers. Available from housewares stores and catalogs like Hammacher Schlemmer (see page 48).

Stop hanger hanky-panky. Have you noticed how those coat hangers seem to multiply every time your back is turned? Take a tip from my friend Chris and put an end to the population explosion. Chris has a designated spot to store hangers from the dry cleaner's, and she makes a point of returning them when the bag or box starts to fill up.

Use plastic hangers. Not the gross, brittle plastic hangers of old that would shatter as soon as you looked at them, but the smooth, sleek, colorful hangers available today in department and housewares stores. They're thicker than wire so they hold slippery and open-necked clothes better, and they don't bend. Don't want to pay full price? Thrift stores often sell them for pennies a bunch.

Book 'em. Add a bookcase to your closet (flea markets, thrift stores, yard sales, and secondhand furniture stores are all good sources). A low bookcase can add two or three shelves of storage for shoes, purses, sweaters, and so on, while not taking up more than a foot or so of precious floor space. Find one that's a good fit—again, a child's bookcase might be the best size because it's smaller—and paint it to match your closet. Put it against the back wall and fill it up!

Or bag 'em. I see a lot of really attractive square and rectangular fabric bags that are designed for storage. Some of them look fragile—the most beautiful ones I've seen are translucent and come in jewel colors—but they're up to the challenge when what you're storing in them is clothes. Because they're lightweight, they're good choices for that high closet shelf, and they have handles so they're easy to lift down.

Put your suitcases to work. Why let your suitcases take up precious closet space when you use them only a few times a year? Instead, make them earn their keep by using them to store out-of-season clothes like sweaters and flannel nightgowns or shirts in warm weather or tee-shirts and shorts in winter. Don't forget that you don't have to keep your suitcases in a closet at all—you can store them flat under the bed, instead.

Bring out the baskets. Those ever-useful square or rectangular woven baskets are great for closet storage, too. Put them on the floor or on shelves for a clean, tidy look. (Make sure they have lids to keep dust off your scarves, sweaters, purses, gloves, hats, or whatever you've stashed inside.) Print up attractive labels for them, since you can't see what's inside.

Hang up your hats, part one. Hanging shelves are suspended from coat-hanger hooks, so you just hang them on your clothes rod. Tuck hats, gloves, scarves, and handbags (not the heavy ones, please) into the shelf cubbies, where you can see them at a glance and keep them in easy reach.

Hang up your hats, part two. Hooks along one wall of the closet are perfect for hanging hats and purses. Put the hats on the high hooks and the purses on a second, lower row.

Get some wheels. If your closet is long but isn't a walk-in, getting to the far sides can be a challenge. A rolling cart makes it easy to store items like shoes and purses and to pull them within easy reach. Mine has three deep hanging baskets as well as a tabletop, so it holds a lot!

Use the one-for-one rule. Once you've gotten everything you don't wear and can't wear out of your closet and replaced the discarded pieces with clothes, shoes, and purses you really need, keep your closet in the clear with the one-for-one rule: When a new item goes in, an old one comes out.

Dear Claire,

My husband and I share a closet, and our clothes and shoes are so jumbled together we can't ever find anything. There must be a better way!

—Closet-trophobic

Dear Closet-trophobic,

Divide and conquer! I'm assuming separate closets are out of the question, so split your shared closet down the middle. Add shelving and double clothes rods on each side, as well as a section of single rod for long dresses and coats. Get yourselves two shoe racks and place one on each side. Buy some plastic storage boxes and divvy them up. Then pull out the clothes and shoes and divide them into yours and his. (I hope you can both dispose of some clothing and shoes at this point.) Put yours on your side and have your husband put his on his side. Problem solved!

Good luck,
Claire

ONWARD!

All right! You've conquered the clutter in your bedroom, given your guest room a makeover, and transformed your closet. Now it's time to tackle the kids' rooms. Read on to see how you can work with your kids to make their rooms clutter-free and fabulous!

Chapter 11

Clutter-Free Kids' Rooms

De-cluttering a kid's room presents its own challenges, since kids have their own ideas about how to use their rooms and all the stuff in them. Does this description sound familiar? Every available surface—beds, desk, dressers, the floor—is covered with a complete jumble of stuff: clothes, music, stuffed animals, chips and little cartridges for portable game players, toys, old gum wrappers, markers, crayons, toy figures—you name it. You may already have designated storage places for each kind of thing—clothes in the closet or dresser, books on the bookshelf, art supplies in one of the desk drawers, little toys in cubbies—but your kid simply doesn't put the things in them. In this case, you can still do a clutter-kicking visualization, to give yourself a clear picture of what you're trying to achieve. But then you'll still have to get your child to buy into your vision. (For help with that, see "The Pros Know" on page 216.)

PRIORITIES FOR KIDS' ROOMS

Start your de-cluttering process by setting some clutter-kicking priorities. First focus on what matters most to you about the way each child's room looks, then work your way through the clutter problems until you get to what matters least. The best way to do this is by taking a good, hard look at the "before" state of the room and then visualizing the "after." In the case of kids' rooms, the "after" part can really be a lot of fun, so go to it!

A Kid's Room Visualization

To get to your "after," you need to start with the "before"—the way things look right now. So get out some paper, or use the "My Kid's Room—Before" form (or make a photocopy of it and write on that). Write down every place there's clutter, and note what that clutter is. You'll be sharing the "after" visualization with your child (if he or she is old enough), but I'd recommend doing the "before" on your own—and when you can have the room to yourself so you can take a really good look.

Once you've jotted down a quick description of your child's room's "before" state, it's time to move on to the "after"—what you want the room to look like when you've cleared the clutter. In this case, if your child is old enough to have some concept of his or her own space, work with him or her to learn what they envision as their "perfect" room. (Make sure this is presented as imagining or "let's pretend," so they don't think you're making any promises!) Do the visualization with each child whose room you want to de-clutter. I promise, you'll learn a lot! If two kids share a room, get them both involved. Catalogs and magazines are great ways to jump-start everyone's imagination. Don't forget to take notes.

Next, keeping one eye on your child's vision and another on the actual room you're working with, describe how you want the room to look when you've kicked the clutter. Write it all down on a piece of paper or on the "My Kid's Room—After" form (or on as many photocopies of it as you need to do it justice). Your description can be short and to the point: "I want all the toys picked up off the floor and put away every day before school/every night before bed. Jamie wants a pink toy chest. I want the bed made neatly every morning. I don't want to see broken toys or bits and pieces of puzzles, Power Rangers, or anything else. I'd like a place to display some of Sam's drawings. He says he'd like to have a bulletin board." Or you can create a detailed picture of exactly how you'd recreate the room so it both meets your clutter-kicking needs and is perfect for your kid.

My Kid's Room—Before

_____
_____
_____
_____
_____
_____
_____
_____
_____
_____
_____

My Kid's Room—After

_____
_____
_____
_____
_____
_____
_____
_____
_____
_____
_____
_____
_____

Getting There

Now that you have captured your kid's room's "before" condition, listing all the specifics, and you and your child have imagined its "after" appearance, you can finally prioritize how to get there from here. Bearing both "before" and "after" in mind, I'd recommend starting with what bothers you most about the "before" condition and working down the list of clutter issues from there.

Maybe you can't deal with the CDs and video games strewn all over the place. Or you're sick of tripping over clothes on the floor. Or you wish there were more space for books and toys. Or you want furniture that works harder and better for the space.

Write down whatever's driving you to distraction on the "My Kid's Room Priority List" (or photocopy it if you'd prefer), in descending order from most to least maddening. Now you have your priorities straight! Once you've finished your priority list, you can turn to the tips below to find ingenious ways of dealing with each problem.

THE KIDS' ROOMS TIPS

Chalk it up. If your child loves to draw, consider creating a chalkboard wall in his or her room. You can paint a wall (or section of wall) with chalkboard paint,

---

My Kid's Room Priority List

_____

_____

_____

_____

_____

_____

_____

---

available from home improvement centers, and provide a giant canvas for your kid's creativity while keeping the mess confined and paper from proliferating. Bear in mind, though, that this paint is chalkboard black, and choose a wall area where it won't darken your child's room.

Lighten up. Kids need lots of light. But their rooms also need to be safe—no cords to trip over, lamps to knock over, shades to crash into. Ceiling fixtures and built-in lights over desks, on walls, over the bed, and under tall shelves are all good options.

Choose furniture that works. My friend Karen has this to say about furniture for kids' rooms: "Give up traditional thoughts about children's furniture and go for the most storage possible in anything you buy, inherit, or refurbish. If it doesn't work for your situation or it's a space-eater, don't feel bad about passing it by. A feminine vanity would be nice, but most styles take up 4 feet of floor space and feature only a few drawers. A grand dollhouse is a beloved possession, but it's better placed in a room that has plenty of space—usually not a child's bedroom. The dollhouse furnishings inevitably spill onto the floor and gobble up even more space. A desk in a child's bedroom sounds like a great idea, but most children do their homework at the kitchen table, on their bed, or on the carpet. The desk becomes a space-waster and a catchall for clutter that could be tossed or given away."

On the other hand. Then again, says my friend Anne, older kids need a computer for homework (not necessarily one with Internet access, though, so you don't have that whole set of safety issues—computers with Web access should ideally be in a public part of the house for better monitoring). Since laptops aren't really

5-Minute Fix for Kids' Rooms

Here's one of the easiest ways to start de-cluttering your kids' bedrooms:

Don't overdo the animals. If your kids cover the bed—made or otherwise—with dolls, stuffed animals, or other toys, you have instant clutter. So ask each kid to pick one, two, or three toys to display on the (made-up, please) bed, and have them put the rest in the toy box, on the shelves, or in another designated location. (See page 215 for toy-storage tips.) Make it fun for them to choose each day's "bed toys" after they make their beds.

sturdy enough for kids, an older child might well need a desk and computer in his or her room.

Choose furniture that's stable. I guess it should go without saying, but before you put it in a child's room, rock and pull on all furniture to make sure your child can't climb on it and pull it over, with or without anything in it. If there's any doubt, as is the case with some freestanding bookcases, secure it to the wall. Better safe than sorry!

Head under the bed. Send the dust bunnies packing and put that big space under your kid's bed to good use as free storage space. Use those big, flat plastic storage containers, available pretty much everywhere, because they hold a lot, are lightweight, and slide easily under the bed. I'd suggest using the space for things that don't have to be pulled out too often, like out-of-season clothes and bedding. But as previously noted, I also use this space for my guitar cases. Your kid might want to do likewise!

Cover it up. Under-bed storage is great, but *looking* at under-bed storage is another matter. If you use the space under your kid's bed for storage, make sure you conceal it with a bed skirt. Try to find one that matches the rest of the bedding or the color of the room.

Check out a chest. A blanket or hope chest is a great place to store stuffed animals as well as blankets, quilts, sheets, extra pillows—they all tuck right into the chest. Put it at the foot of your child's bed, or put it under a window and add some flat pillows on top for an instant window seat. But remember that those wooden lids are heavy! Don't get one for your child until she's old enough to raise the lid with ease. Plow & Hearth (see page 47) has one just for children that you can have personalized with your child's name.

Add a low bookcase, plus. Putting a low bookcase along one wall of your kid's bedroom gives him tons of storage for books and toys—at his height. Add wooden storage cubbies and cabinets to match and create an entire wall of usable, kid-friendly storage and display space. You can even add a desk to this wall array if you use a board the same width as the other elements and attach it to the wall at the same height. Tuck a kid-size rolling chair under it and your child is set!

Make your own bookcase. No, I don't mean block-and-board bookcases, though I happen to love them and still have them out in my studio. Instead, you can make an appealing and interesting bookcase by stacking two wooden benches and bolting them together with a drill and wood screws. They're still low enough to be at the kids' level, and they're supersturdy. Paint them to match your child's room or taste.

Try shallow shelves. One of the most innovative room designs I've ever seen featured an entire wall covered with lengths of shallow shelving. The shelving, painted a color that contrasted with the wall behind it, was a design element itself, and the clever creator hadn't overburdened it with stuff, but merely accented it with the occasional starfish or bouquet. I immediately thought that this shallow shelving would be perfect for displaying small dolls and other toys, collectibles, and treasures in a child's room. But to keep from creating an entire wall of dust-ables, I'd suggest limiting it to the wall behind the bed. This will eliminate the

👍 Love It *or* Lose It? 👎

Armoires. Those big, tall, freestanding "closets" of old. Should you get one to add storage space for a child's room? I'd say that depends on the child's age. For a young child, opening the giant armoire doors is a real challenge, and it's impossible to reach the higher levels inside. (Trust me on this—I grew up with them.) But for a teen, it's a wonderful solution, especially if you add enough shelves and hooks to really maximize the space.

Verdict: Lose it for young kids. Love it for teens!

need for a night table, too—your child can put an alarm clock and a glass of water right on the lowest shelf.

Mix and match storage options. Look around for storage systems that allow you to mix and match different components. One of my friends swears by a storage unit with lots of little cubbies for her son's little cars, windup toys, card collections, sunglasses, swim goggles, and other disparate stuff. Another unit with a couple of dresser drawers fits on top, and there are several other mix and match pieces also available.

A tisket, a tasket, put stuff in plastic baskets. Kids—and those of us who remain kids at heart—love color. And parents love indestructible, convenient storage options. Put the two together and you have the big, colorful plastic tubs that garden catalogs like Gardener's Supply Company (see page 49) offer for hauling compost, weeds, produce, and the like around gardens. Capacious and inexpensive, these flexible tubs make perfect storage bins for toys, stuffed animals, and anything else you need to keep neat and off the floor, bed, and other surfaces—but in easy reach of small hands.

Or use bins. Plastic storage bins with snap-on lids are good storage options, too. You can stack them. You can sit on them when they're closed. Stuff doesn't spill out of them. And they are easy to wash out or wipe down when something leaks or spills in them.

Supply a stool. Remember what it's like to be too short. (Some of us still are, so we remember all too well.) Help your kids reach everything easily with a sturdy four-legged stool. Catalogs like Solutions (see page 48) carry sturdy, colorful plastic models that lock open for use, then fold up flat so they'll easily fit in a closet or under a bed.

Take time for trash. Kids generate trash, too (have you noticed?), and they need a place to put it. Make sure they each have a wastebasket (plastic ones that are scrubbable are good) in their rooms, and make sure they empty them weekly, or as often as is needed.

Box it up, part one. My friend Karen has her own way of handling her adorable daughter, Audrey's, art supplies. "The problem is too many tattered boxes of crayons, markers, glue sticks, and so on that kids stop using," Karen says. "The solution is to buy stackable plastic shoeboxes. They allow for the collection to grow as relatives bestow even more art supplies on the household."

Box it up, part two. Karen also has a way of dealing with what she describes as "the big shoe-toss on the bedroom floor." Her solution was to buy a large, unpainted wooden box at a craft store and paint it a bright color. She says, "You'll still have a jumble of sneakers, shoes, slippers, and flip-flops, but at least it's contained in the box (most of the time!)."

Get a rolling desk. If your kid has a laptop, consider getting a rolling laptop desk. I have a handmade one that lets me use a real keyboard and mouse and hook my laptop to a docking station (more on this in Chapter 12—The Home Office, beginning on page 227). But Improvements (see page 48) also carries one that is very attractive, comes in a variety of finishes, and takes up very little space—it's just 20 inches wide and 15 inches deep. The height is adjustable, and it has a drawer for screen cloths, sticky tags, and the like, as well as two shelves for textbooks, notebooks, and supplies.

Post a bulletin. Kids' rooms practically scream for bulletin boards; they let kids tack up anything from blue ribbons to art, homework assignments to photos. I think a wood-framed corkboard looks just fine. But if you want to dress it up, make your own by having a piece of Homasote board cut to fit a wooden frame, covering it with the fabric of your kid's choice (using your trusty staple gun), and securing the board to the frame.

Get a good hamper. One of my friends has a great place to put all the stuffed animals you're not displaying on the bed. "Buy a nice wicker hamper with a lift-top lid for your child's bedroom," she advises. "They come in lots of great colors now. Stash all the stuffed animals, dolls, and throw pillows in it every night. The clutter comes off the floor but is easily accessible when they wake up in the morning and want their favorite huggie bear or doll."

Then get another one. Get a second hamper for your kid's dirty clothes. Make sure it has a lightweight lid and is easy for small hands to open, so kids can corral their own clothes. And make it a different color from the stuffed-animal hamper, so there's no confusion.

Try tubular art storage. My friend and clutter expert Skye Alexander suggests storing kids' art rolled up in cardboard tubes. Use recycled tubes from wrapping paper, aluminum foil, and so on, matching the size of the tube to the size of the art. Roll up the drawing or painting and pop it in the tube (you can usually store quite a few in each tube). Put the child's name on the outside to avoid confusion.

The tubes keep the art safe and contained, and they're easy to store in a drawer, plastic storage container, or basket.

Check it out. Give children's books a trial run before you buy them by checking them out of the library. Once you see which ones are hits, you can buy just those and save some shelf space. That goes for DVDs, too!

Trap the trains. My friend Holly's son, Caleb, is crazy for Thomas the Tank Engine and his (seemingly) 500,000 friends. So her husband, Mike, built a train table for Caleb that's just the right height for him to play at. He sets up the tracks, equipment, and favorite train cars and engines on the table's ample top and stores the rest in drawers Mike built into the sides. No more trains on the floor! Your family might not boast a member with Mike's woodworking skills, but you can check around at thrift stores, flea markets, yard sales, and second-hand shops for tables that could fit the bill. (Don't forget about those drawers! You could also slide a plastic storage box or two under the table for easy train storage.)

Raise the stakes. Or tracks, in this case. Once your kids reach school age, their dad might want to start getting them model trains, especially if he himself is a train fanatic from way back. If this is the case in your household, try this space-saving tip, courtesy of my friends Carolyn and Gary. Gary has set up his model train track on narrow shelving that goes around the wall of his workshop. It takes up no floor or storage space, and his trains run happily around their elevated

the **Pros Know**

If you want to not just kick kids' clutter but teach them effective ways of kicking it themselves, the best resource I know of for getting your kids to pitch in is a book called *Mrs. Clean Jeans' Housekeeping with Kids* (Rodale, 2004, $14.95). The author, Tara Aronson (aka Mrs. Clean Jeans), really knows how to get kids of all ages motivated to help with the housework and object control. Every chapter divides chores by age, so you can see exactly what you should expect your kids to be able to do. (Her own kids ranged in age from 2 to 13 when she wrote the book, and yes, there were chores for the 2-year-old!) Tara gives a lot of pointers on how to make chores more fun—more like family games. You may read this for help corralling your kids' clutter and end up getting them to help clean the house, too!

Dear Claire,

I have a baby and a toddler. But that's not all I have. I also have about 3,000 stuffed animals, all gifts from well-meaning friends and relatives. I don't want them, the kids don't want them, and I sure don't have any place to put them. But I don't want to hurt anybody's feelings! What can I do?

—Overstuffed

Dear Overstuffed,

I suggest that you take photos of your children with each adorable toy. On the back of each photo, note the date the photo was taken and who gave the animal to your child (or label the photos on the disk so you know what's what). Then donate everything you don't want to Goodwill or the Salvation Army, give it to a children's consignment shop, or send it to a home for unwed mothers, a shelter for abused families, or another suitable charity. If Aunt Martha asks about that fabulous stuffed rhino she gave baby Billy, show her the photo and tell her how much he loves it. Or loved it, before that unfortunate accident. I'm sure she'll understand.

While we're talking about stuffed animals, let me mention a lifesaver that's worth planning for. We all know how kids can latch onto certain stuffed animals and literally love them to death—until they're ripped, dirty, and generally abused beyond repair. If one of your children develops an obsession for an animal, rush out while they're still available and buy a duplicate. Then hide it. You can either alternate them while you're washing one or save the "twin" to use as a replacement when the original finally falls apart.

Good luck,
Claire

track, making all the train noises that enthusiasts find so endearing. His grandson, Jeremiah, and my boyfriend, Rob, can hole up in there with him for hours, watching the trains go round and round. Try it in your kids' rooms. Whoo-whoo!

Try hardware for hair accessories. Sick of picking (or sweeping, or vacuuming) up all the hair clips, bands, barrettes, scrunchies, and endless other little hair-related accessories your girls find indispensable? Head for the hardware store. Plastic tool trays and drawer sets are inexpensive and come with partitions or drawers in all sorts of sizes and combinations, so your daughter can pick just the right one to hold all her stuff. And since they're clear, she can see the contents without having to pull out the drawers or open the lid.

Ditto for doodads. Plastic tool trays and drawer sets are also great for holding beading supplies, puzzle pieces, marbles, tiny model cars, plastic animals, cosmetics, jewelry—you name it. If it's small and has lots of pieces, it's a match made in heaven. If your kid wants to carry his or her stuff around, choose a small plastic tool or tackle box with a handle.

Use pretzel logic. My friend Robin has a great solution for all those arts and crafts supplies. "In grocery stores, look for food containers that can have a second life after the treats are gone," she says. "Our family's particular favorites are those sturdy plastic bins of pretzel rods. Once the pretzels are gone, we recycle the containers to hold beads, foam pieces, chalk, and pom-poms. They're free, and since they're clear, it's easy to see what's inside."

Pull out the plastic. Donate some of those Tupperware and other plastic containers from your kitchen to your kids so they can easily store and find small toys, puzzles, Lincoln Logs, marbles, and other stuff with lots of bits and pieces. If you number the matching tops and bottoms with indelible markers—a trick I learned from Kathy, one of the members of my local Curves (see page 107)—the kids will be able to match them up quickly. Don't forget zipper-lock bags, either! They're great for containing little pieces and are ideal if kids want to store more than one batch of gizmos in one box.

Don't lose it. Give each kid a little cardboard or plastic "Lost and Found" box in his or her room. Then they'll have somewhere to store the odds and ends that inevitably turn up on the floor or in the bottoms of drawers until they eventually realize that they have the missing jigsaw piece (or their friend Mary's barrette) in their box.

Make a memory. Instead of preserving all your kids' bulky school projects for posterity, photograph them and keep them on a disk or in an album, one for each kid. Your kids may still want to save a few of the best, but the rest of the 3-D versions can be tossed, while the memories are there to look at anytime.

Box up outgrown clothes. My friend Jennifer tells me, "When my son outgrows a clothing size, I place the clothes into a labeled plastic tote. That way it's ready for the next child or to give away."

Rose Kennedy knows a thing or two about kids and clutter. She's written a whole book on the subject—*10-Minute Kid Clutter Control.* Rose recommends cardboard "dressers" for preschoolers and kindergartners. You can buy them in cheerful patterns or cover them yourself. They're shorter than "real" dressers, and the lightweight drawers are much easier for small hands to pull open and push shut, so your children will be more likely to put stuff away themselves. Rose also recommends putting comforters on children's beds. Not only are they supercomfy, she notes that they're much easier for a child to pull up over the bed than a bedspread, which will help encourage them to make their own beds. Great ideas!

Don't sweat school art. My friend Chris has a super-sensible method for dealing with her son's artwork: "Prior to the beginning of the school year, purchase a sweater box or other large storage container for storing your child's papers and artwork that you want to save for the year," Chris says. "Each day, cull through your child's folder or backpack. Toss what you don't want and put what you want to keep in the box."

Send school art to boot camp. Lillian, another enthusiastic member of my local Curves, had another great way of dealing with her children's art, projects, and other beloved toys and possessions. As a young mom without a big budget, Lillian bought each of her children a metal trunk at the Army-Navy store. She painted each trunk that child's favorite color, then painted their name on top. Over the years, she stored their best or favorite artwork and projects, as well as photos, letters, stuffed animals, favorite outfits—anything that really meant a lot to them. She went through their trunks with them often, switching out anything that no longer had a lot of meaning and exchanging it with other things they valued. When the kids left home and set up their own places, Lillian sent their trunks along with them—treasured keepsakes that captured the best of their entire childhoods. Great idea!

Get stuff out of sight. My editor Anne has a time-tested tactic for cleaning out clutter from her son's room. "I sneak stuff that he doesn't play with anymore into a bin in the attic that he doesn't know about," Anne confesses. "If he doesn't miss it after a while, I can get rid of it. When I put junk in his wastebasket, he just pulls

Pet Alert!

Do your kids keep pets in their bedrooms? A parakeet, a hamster cage, maybe a little aquarium or terrarium for the lizard or hermit crabs? It's amazing how much clutter pets can introduce to a kid's (or anybody else's) room. There's the pet food, litter, toys, and dishes—not to mention the feathers, litter, fur, and unmentionables that are constantly being tossed out of cages. And then there are the free-roaming pets. One adorable little puppy or kitten can pull out every toy, book, and doodad in a child's room faster than you can get in there to see what they're up to. (And your furry friends will chew them up, too, if you're not fast enough.)

I admit, I think pets in kids' rooms are a great idea. They're fun, they're fascinating, they're friends. I'm sure growing up with pets made me a better and more caring person. But this is one case where the house rules must apply. If your child doesn't keep her pet's cage, tank, or aquarium clean, she loses her pet-keeping privileges.

Of course, you need to help her keep the area tidy by getting an aquarium/terrarium stand with a cabinet to hold the supplies, a sturdy little table with shelves and a waterproof surface (even if you have to staple plastic cloth over it), or another sturdy piece of furniture with kid-friendly storage (drawers or shelves with doors—pet supplies are *not* attractive!). Help your child keep all the pieces in place with plastic shoeboxes or other plastic storage containers. And make sure you have a sturdy plastic trash can (with plastic trash-bag liners) either stashed inside the cabinet or right beside the pet's stand. You can't expect your kid to clean a cage or tank if there's no place to put the old litter or filter! A roll of paper towels in the cabinet is essential for spills and cleanup time, too.

it out again, so that doesn't work. I think he inherited his grandmother's pack rat gene!"

Scout for suitcases. Here's another unique tip from my friend Robin. "Scout for tiny suitcases (toiletry or carry-on size) to hold doll clothes and teeny, tiny, troublesome doll shoes," she says. "When you find a great sale, buy a few matching suitcases in the same size to make stacking and storing easier. It's great for kids

What about that kitten or puppy? Make it a rule that they can be in your kid's room only when he's there (and awake) to supervise. And make sure there's a basket or box of cat (or dog) toys in each child's room so the pup or kitten has something appropriate to play with—not your kids' stuffed animals and other stuff! At nighttime and nap time, put the little furballs where *you* can keep an eye on them.

Give adult dogs and cats cozy beds of their own if you let them sleep in your child's room. Catalogs like L.L. Bean, Plow & Hearth, and Orvis (see pages 46, 47, and 49) offer plush dog and cat "nests" in every conceivable size and a wonderful selection of colors and patterns. (Let your child choose the color or pattern for the one in her room.) Many have removable covers for easy washing.

One last thing: Resist any and all pleas, tantrums, and other attempts on your kids' parts to let them have age-inappropriate pets. If the family is sharing a pet and you're willing to be the primary caregiver, that's fine. But no matter how badly your 3-year-old wants a kitten of her own or your 5-year-old begs for a parrot, do not give in. Give her a stuffed kitten and have her care for it as a "trainer" until she's old enough for the real thing (or try a stuffed mechanical kitty that meows and purrs). Give him a parakeet—those colorful little birds have big parrot personalities without the complex requirements of parrot care (including the space requirements). Goldfish make great first-aquarium fish and require only a fraction of the care that a tropical aquarium does. (But they still need a bright, roomy tank with a filter!) Any reptile can escape from its tank, and so can those crickets (or, yikes, mice) you have to feed them. Ease your child into pet ownership and he or she will have a delightful—rather than dirty and overwhelming—experience. And so will you!

who are on the go: Now there's no need to gather up a tote bag of toys each time there's a play date or a visit to relatives."

Save your surfaces. Want to put a table, desk, or other crafts/eating/play surface in your kid's room? Of course you do. But look out! Spills and stains are a fact of life when you have kids (or, ahem, even when you don't). The solution is to cover that surface with an elasticized pad. You can get these in innumerable patterns and shapes (including one that adjusts to any shape) from housewares stores and catalogs like Improvements (see page 48).

Buy some sleeping bags. Once your kid's old enough to have friends come for sleepovers, get a couple of sleeping bags and stash them in his closet. You can store them on a high shelf where they're out of his way but easy for you to bring down when his friends are due over.

Or blow up the bed. Air mattresses are great fun for kids. They can jump, roll around, and wrestle all over them, and if they roll off, it's not far to the floor! A full- or queen-size air mattress can transform your kid's floor into a super sleepover space. With an electric pump, it takes less than 5 minutes to inflate or (if the pump is reversible) deflate the mattress, and the whole thing tucks away in a storage bag that's half the size of a sleeping bag. Stash it on a high shelf in your child's closet between overnights.

Camp out. Make that underused tent do double-duty when your child has overnight guests. Set it up in his bedroom and put his friends' sleeping bags inside for a fun "camp-over." Don't forget the marshmallows! The high shelf of a kid's closet is also a good place to store the tent once it's folded up.

Go back to school. A metal locker is a great storage accessory for a kid's room. Get one in your kid's favorite color, or paint it to match his room. Hooks hold jackets and caps, and kids can keep sports equipment in the bottom of the locker. And because lockers are metal, you can hang magnetic hooks, a magnetic mirror, and a magnetic memo board inside.

Get a rolling cart. A great storage option for kids' rooms is a rolling storage cart, such as the GuideCraft Moon and Stars See, Store, and Take Along. These carts are designed especially for kids' toys, books, art supplies, and other treasures, and are widely available from stores and Web sites like www.amazon.com and www.babyage.com.

Bring out the big guns. I think this tip from my friend Karen is one of the all-time most ingenious! "Our old house without closets couldn't corral the coloring books, workbooks, packs of colored paper, lined handwriting paper, and craft kits our daughter, Audrey, uses," Karen confesses. "Then we happened upon an old gun cabinet in a secondhand shop. It was 5 feet tall but only about 10 inches deep, perfect for our small space. We gutted the inside, added fresh paint inside and out, installed new hardware, added a few shelves, and hung a pretty lace curtain on the glass door. Now we have a wonderful kiddy storage cabinet that's fancy enough to fit right in with our decor."

KICK THE KIDS' CLOSET CLUTTER

Closets can be scary for kids. (Isn't a monster hiding in there?) But even when no terrors lurk behind the door, a closet can be an awkward, hard-to-use, hard-to-reach space for kids. In this section, let's look at ways to make your child's closet both kid-friendly and less cluttered.

If you'd like, you can use the same before-and-after visualization exercise for each child's closet that you did for your own closet. (See page 196 for directions and worksheets.) Or you can skim through these tips and just plunge in!

Let in lots of light. A dark closet not only makes it hard to see and find things— it makes it even scarier for kids. Make sure your child's closet is brightly lit, and put the switch low enough for them to reach it easily. (A pull-on light in a child's closet is *not* a good idea.) If you can't wire in a new fixture, you can use a battery-operated push light.

Add color and fun. Your child's closet should be an extension of their room. Add paint, wallpaper, stencils, stickers, and other design elements from their bedroom, or treat it like a separate room and brighten it up with whatever colors, patterns, or decorations your kid wants. Multicolored stripes? Big, goofy flowers right out of the sixties? A beautiful nature poster (or NASCAR or movie poster)? Get your kid in on the act and enjoy yourselves! But remember that a lot of the wall surface will be covered with clothes and storage units, so don't get *too* carried away or you'll be disappointed when that glorious decor isn't on view.

Make it easy to get dressed. Here's a great tip from my friend Betsy. (I've got to pass this one along to my brother and sister-in-law!) "It's important for kids to plan out clothing ahead of time to avoid the morning rush and frantic search for matching socks or gym sneakers," Betsy says. "Buy a weekly clothes organizer that hangs over the closet rod. It usually features sturdy fabric shelves with five to seven slots (in boy and girl colors). It's ideal for planning out a week's worth of school clothes, undergarments, shoes, socks, and baseball caps or hair accessories. And it keeps the daily clutter off the dresser top, off chairs, and off the end of the bed." Betsy got her daughter's from Lillian Vernon (www.lillianvernon.com; see page 46).

Use the door. Don't waste the inside of your kid's closet door! Hang a shoe rack or a full-length mirror, both of which will hook over the top of the door comparatively unobtrusively. Bear in mind that you don't have to use the shoe rack for shoes. Plastic shoe racks with pouches for the shoes will hold toys, socks, mittens, hats, and accessories just as easily.

Hook it up. Another alternative is to add big hooks on the back of the closet door for backpacks, bathrobes, and purses. Again, put them low enough for kids to reach easily, and make sure they have big knobs on the ends so nobody gets hurt!

Clip it on. For some reason, sports equipment is hard to store in a closet. It seems to immediately work its way to the very back of the space or to just disappear entirely, which doesn't make it easy or fun to play with! Keep it where it's easy to see and reach with the sort of door clips that housewares stores and catalogs sell to clip brooms, mops, and other cleaning implements to the pantry or basement door. When it's time to practice or play, your kids can grab what they need off the backs of their closet doors.

Stand 'em up. Another way to keep baseball bats, hockey sticks, and other sports equipment together is to tuck an umbrella stand inside the closet door. (Unlike the one in your hallway, though, you want this one to be wood, metal, plastic, or another unbreakable material—not ceramic. And make sure it's sturdy enough not to topple over when it's full of bats and sticks or when somebody's trying to pull one out.) Or use one of the metal umbrella racks you often see in offices and restaurants, with a grid of square openings on top to hold the umbrellas—or, in your case, sports equipment—upright.

Lower your sights. Make it easy for your kids to reach their own clothes by installing a clothes rod at their level. Then do as you should in your own closet and hang similar clothes (jackets, dresses, pants, skirts, tops) together so they're easy to find.

Put a case in the closet. Help bring your child's closet down to a more comfortable size by putting a kid-size low bookcase in there. Set it against the back wall and your child can walk right up to it—something her own height—to put things in or take them out. Pick up one at a thrift or secondhand store or a yard sale, paint it a cheerful color, and put it to work!

Move in a module. Customized closet modules, available at home improvement stores, let you get great use from your kid's closet space. You can get a module with dresser drawers under open shelves, attach two levels of clothes rods from either side, and add open shelving at the top, then paint it all whatever color your child desires.

Add more shelves. Shelving can really add storage space to a child's closet. You can install standard wood shelves, painted to match the closet, or use plastic-coated wire shelf units (such as those sold by Closet Maid). Both ready-to-use wooden and wire shelves are available in most home centers. (California Closets has an entire line at Target.) The wire shelving comes in all lengths and is designed specifically for closets, so it fits standard-size closets. And it's durable, attractive, and easy to install.

Save the high shelf. Store stuff that kids need but won't be tempted to try to get down themselves on that long, over-the-clothes-rod shelf. Blankets and other off-season bed linens, plastic containers with clothes that are out of season, sleeping bags, and other "occasional" items are the best choices for this shelf. You can also display beloved but no-longer-played-with stuffed animals and toys up there so the kids can visit with them when they open the closet door but they aren't taking up bedroom space that's needed for the "now" toys.

Corral some cubbies. Shoe cubbies are an attractive and durable way to keep shoes, purses, scarves, hats, caps, mittens, sweaters, umbrellas, and baseball gloves neat and accessible. And they sit on the floor, where even the smallest child can get to them without asking for help. Put them against the back of the closet wall for easiest access.

Use plastic hangers. Avoid the old, brittle plastic hangers that can snap and break. Instead, choose the smooth, sleek, colorful hangers available today in department and housewares stores. They're thicker than wire so they're easier for little hands to hold—and not nearly as tempting to use as weapons (and not as harmful if they are)! Don't want to pay full price? Thrift stores often sell them for pennies a bunch.

Clear out old clothes. Use the same techniques to sort through your kids' clothes that you use for your own (see page 199). If your child hangs on to favorite outfits like grim death, no matter how beat they are, suggest that you turn them into doll clothes (or bear clothes). Or save the best patches to use on their skirts, jeans, or jackets. If you're crafty, make them into a quilt for the kid's bed. Or put them in a plastic storage container and move them to a high shelf. (You can always move them to the attic or basement later, and eventually out the door once your child's wardrobe interests have moved on. But meanwhile, he or she will know they're there.) If you're dealing with a teen who refuses to relinquish any of her outfits, no matter how many there are and how squashed into the closet, the best approach is to divide them up by season and pack up the out-of-season clothes in plastic storage boxes to stash under her bed. When the next season rolls around, pull out the appropriate box and switch. Once she takes the clothes out and really looks at them, she may decide they're so out of style she'd be happy for you to take them to Goodwill. The exception is too-small clothes: If they're outgrown, unless it's a favorite outfit or two she wants to save, they go *now*.

ONWARD!

Okay, we've tackled all the bedrooms and all the (gasp) closets. Now it's time to move on to one of the scariest rooms in the house—the one you use as a home office. (And you thought the kids' rooms would be bad!) But it's not going to be as awful as you fear. Believe me, a home office can be organized, efficient, and functional—even all those files and bills—and once you've set it up right, it's easy to keep it that way. Mine is, and yours will be too. Promise! So read on and let's start shuffling papers.

Chapter 12

The Home Office

Bills. Files. Records. Research materials. Can you say "clutter"? In this chapter, you'll find tips that show you how to set up your home office most efficiently and make it a space where you truly want to spend time. Whether you just use it to pay bills and check e-mail or you actually work from home full- or part-time, and whether you have a whole room to yourself or just a computer desk tucked in a corner, kicking office clutter will make your office work harder. These tips will "work" just as hard at any other type of office, as well!

PRIORITIES FOR OFFICES

As I've recommended for all the other rooms in your home, start your office de-cluttering process by setting some clutter-kicking priorities. Do it by focusing on what matters most to you about the way your home office looks and functions, and then following the chain along to what matters least. The best way to do this is by taking a good, hard look at the "before" state of the room and then visualizing the "after." Once you've finished your visualization, you're ready to start tackling the clutter. Start with the most bothersome clutter problems, and work down your list of priorities until you get to the minor irritations. Then you're done!

Paper Escapers

When it comes to bills and the mounds of mail that pour into our homes every day, there seem to be two kinds of people—the ones who deal with it and the ones who don't. You'll find tips from the ones who deal with it throughout this chapter. But right now, let's focus on the ones who don't. Hopefully, they'll both reassure you that you're not as bad about dealing with the mail as you think and also inspire you to keep it under control.

I have a dear friend who, to hear her talk, spends every spare moment of her life "doing her paperwork." It's what she does every day after work and every weekend, or so she says. (Perhaps her husband and kids would tell a different story.) She pulls out the boxes of bills and other paper, pours them onto the dining room table, and . . . fade to black. I honestly can't say what happens then, because I have a terrible feeling that they're always the *same* papers. When Rob and I went to my friend's house for a cookout this past summer, she was frantically shoveling papers off the table while her husband fired up the grill. Six months later, she e-mailed to say that she was about to sit down once again with the same paperwork she'd been doing when Rob and I came over that long-ago summer day! She calls it "avoiditis." She e-mailed me today to say that she was still working on the pile and had just unearthed an unopened birthday card (to her) from last May and a wallet she'd bought a couple of years ago! Mind you, this is not someone who works from home. Presumably, she has no more paperwork to do than anyone else with a spouse and two kids. I don't know about you, but having the same bills, tax forms, and so on looming over me month after month would drive me insane.

Speaking of which, if you think my friend's story is scary, listen to this one: Years ago, I knew a woman who had a very responsible corporate job, where she managed a staff and a deadline-laden schedule and made quite a good salary. You'd have thought that if anyone could stay on top of bills and other paperwork, she'd be the one. But one night, I went over to her house for supper and saw the entire dining room filled with large cardboard boxes and bags. She'd been living there for 9 months at that point, so I was surprised that she hadn't gotten the boxes unpacked or at least stowed out of sight. But it turned out they weren't moving boxes. Instead, the boxes and bags contained all the mail she'd received for the past 9 months, unopened, unread. I frankly don't know why she still had heat, running water, and phone service when I arrived. I do know that, eventually, she hired someone to get it all sorted out. She has since married, and all I can say is, I hope her husband takes care of the mail!

An Office Visualization

To get to your "after," you need to start with the "before"—the way things look right now. So get out some paper, or use the "My Home Office—Before" form on page 230 (or make a photocopy of it and write on that). Write down every place there's clutter, and note what that clutter is. Are your files exploding? Has your desk disappeared under a pile of stuff that really belongs in other rooms? Is your computer comfortable to use, or is it perched precariously on a heap of telephone books? Try to think about where you get hung up when you're trying to get things done, where you lose things, and what distracts or irritates you. Take a good look. Take your time. Because the home office is usually a small room or part of a room, it won't take as long as you think to finish your list.

Once you've jotted down a quick description of the "before" state of your home office, it's time to move on to the "after"—how you want the room to look when you've kicked the clutter. Write it all down on a piece of paper, or in the "My Home Office—After" form on page 230 (or on as many photocopies of it as you need to do it justice). To make sure you're being realistic, look at the room every few minutes while you're writing your description.

Your description can be short and to the point: "I don't want light from the windows blinding me while I try to work on the computer. I want a better organizing system for my files. I want to get on top of my appointments, bill-paying, and birthday cards. I want a better-looking file cabinet and a comfortable office chair."

Or you can create a detailed picture of exactly how you'd like your office to look if it were perfect (for you). You can picture the colors of the walls, floor and floor coverings, and window treatments; imagine every piece of furniture, including where it would be, what it would do, and what it would look like; and try to see where the books, files, paperwork, equipment, and supplies would go. Think about what you don't have now but need in order to work well. Lots of magazines feature home-office makeovers, and catalogs such as Solutions and Improvements (see page 48) are full of furniture and accessories for the office. Look some over for inspiration. Visit your local Staples, Office Depot, or Office-Max store.

My Home Office—Before

_____
_____
_____
_____
_____
_____
_____
_____
_____
_____
_____
_____

My Home Office—After

_____
_____
_____
_____
_____
_____
_____
_____
_____
_____
_____
_____
_____
_____

Getting There

Now that you've captured your home office's "before" condition, listing all the specifics, and you've imagined its "after" appearance, you can finally prioritize the steps you'll need to take to get there from here. Again, bearing both "before" and "after" in mind, I'd recommend starting with what bothers you most about the "before" condition and making that your first de-cluttering priority. Then organize the rest of your "to do" list in descending order of importance.

Maybe you're sick of losing bills and getting overdue notices. Or you can't ever find your clients' addresses, no matter how many times you write them down. Or you've stopped even looking in your file folders because you're too scared to go into the file cabinet. Or your computer desk puts the keyboard and mouse at the wrong height and it makes your wrists, shoulders, neck, and back hurt to work there. Or you can't even find your computer among all the accessories that have colonized the desk.

Write down whatever's driving you to distraction on the "My Home Office Priority List" (or photocopy it, if you'd prefer) in descending order from most to least maddening. Now you have your priorities straight! Once you've finished, you can turn to the tips beginning on page 232 to find ingenious ways of dealing with each problem.

My Home Office Priority List

_____

_____

_____

_____

_____

_____

_____

_____

_____

THE OFFICE TIPS

Since there are so many aspects to home offices, I'm going to divide up these tips by topic to make them easier to find and use. Whether you're trying to improve your home office setup, figure out a better way to pay bills, or determine how long to keep those #@!%$** records, scan the pages that follow and you'll find what you need.

Office Furniture, Files, and Other Necessities

Get a shredder. And use it. Not just to cut down on paper clutter—though it does a good job at that—but also to protect yourself from identity theft. The finely shredded paper is great for your compost pile, or you can use it in shipping boxes, or you can recycle it.

Build in portability. I love my home computer setup so much that I'm going to share it with you. Rather than having a desktop computer with a huge hard drive, I have a laptop with a "docking port." The docking port lets me hook up everything I need to operate comfortably—Internet hookup, printer, speakers, keyboard, and mouse. (When you work with words all day, as I do, that laptop keyboard and mouse just don't cut it.) When I travel and need to take my computer, I simply detach the laptop from its docking port and depart. It couldn't be easier, and it takes up so much less space. I don't know why anyone would want a clunky desktop computer!

Rack it up. Okay, I know this tip isn't clutter-related, but I want to share it anyway because it works! If you already use a laptop in your home office or I've convinced you to get one, you'll want to keep it from overheating. Despite the fact that it's vented, it can get quite hot after a while (ever heard that ominous buzzing when the fan kicks on?). To help my laptop keep its cool, I set it on a cooling rack—the kind you'd cool cookies, cakes, or bread on. Mine is coated wire with legs that hold it about an inch off the desk and allow air to circulate beneath the laptop while I work. It's just big enough to let me put my speakers on either side of the laptop. It brings the screen up to a better viewing height, too. Try it!

Go wireless. As the name implies, you'll avoid the clutter of wires, modem, and cables if a wireless network (wi-fi) is available in your area or you are technically savvy enough to install your own. But make sure the one you choose is protected from freeloaders (usually with a password), since the more people are using it, the slower it is. And if it's your own network that's wireless, be sure that the router you have purchased includes a firewall.

Get rid of old computers. If your home office is really more of a graveyard for your family's old computers—or it's simply time to upgrade to a laptop or better model—it's time to recycle the old ones. Have you been holding onto them because you don't want to throw them out and don't know what else to do with them? Go to www.earth911.org to find out how to recycle them.

Cart your work around. I find a rolling cart—the kind home stores like Target and Home Depot sell for kitchens—to be invaluable for my home office. I put my inbox, calendar, and address boxes on top and my projects in progress in each of the slide-out baskets. (Once the projects are finished, I go through the baskets and discard or shred anything I can, then put the rest in a labeled file in my file cabinet.) I can pull the cart up next to my computer workstation while I'm working, then stash it out of the way when it's not needed. It's a lifesaver!

Get a file cabinet. Whether you opt for a luxurious oak file cabinet or a metal version (they don't have to be ugly—I have turquoise and red file cabinets as well as the typical gray and beige), treat yourself to this essential office organizer. Then get hanging folders for bills (see page 242), projects, warranties (see below), health-related papers, tax forms and records, house-related information and services, school-related materials (one folder for each child), wills, living wills, powers of attorney, car-related papers (insurance, titles, manuals, repair and maintenance records), pets, take-out menus . . . the list is endless! Label each file with its contents so it's easy to find, and organize them in a way that makes sense to you. (Most people opt for alphabetical organization, but do what works for you.) To me, file cabinets are as essential as my computer, phone, and calendar—a vital piece of home-office equipment. I even keep my gardening catalogs in file folders in one of my file cabinets!

Make your desk do double-duty. No room for a file cabinet *and* a desk, you say? Consider turning your desk space into storage. Buy a flat door or a thick plywood sheet and put it across two file cabinets to make a roomy desk.

Cart your files around. You can also get rolling carts specifically designed for offices. These are designed for hanging file folders, so you can roll your files over to your desk and then stow them away in a closet when you're not using them. They're a great alternative when a permanent file cabinet's not an option.

Organize your files. File cabinets and carts are not, repeat, *not* museum vaults. If they're not working for you, they're just clutter. Keep your files current. Shred or recycle material you no longer need. If you have files you aren't using but may want to refer to again at some point, store them in labeled printer-paper boxes in the office closet or a dry basement or attic. Make sure the files you keep in your file cabinet are clearly labeled and organized chronologically, with the most recent additions in the front of the file. If your projects are complex, divide the contents of your files into labeled folders and tuck them back in the file. Again, organize each folder chronologically. And make sure your file drawers aren't so overstuffed that you can't even remove the files! When you have to pull to get a file out, it's a sure sign that your drawer is overdue for cleaning.

Stand them up. My editor Anne keeps paperwork for active and ongoing projects in folders in a standup file rack where she can instantly put her hands on them. She reports that this method works for kids' school projects and reports, too.

Clear your desk. My friend and feng shui guru Skye Alexander says that, according to feng shui, an uncluttered office can increase prosperity. In her book *10-Minute Clutter Control Room by Room*, Skye says, "By putting your office in order, you demonstrate a willingness to deal with problems involving your finances and to increase prosperity."

Corner it. No good place to put your desk? Get a desk that's designed to fit in a corner, like Ballard Design's Winston Desk (see page 46).

Add an armoire. By now you're probably sick of hearing me recommend armoires—those freestanding closets so beloved of the Victorians. But they can really hold a lot of office supplies, especially if you add extra shelves. You can tuck in file and document boxes, too, creating a file cabinet that looks like furniture. Open the doors, and there's everything you need to work efficiently; close them, and it's all out of sight.

Or add an entertainment center. If you don't have room for an armoire but would still like to close up your files and supplies in a conventional piece of furniture, an entertainment center might be the perfect thing.

Get the right chair. You're probably either using a leftover chair from someplace in the house or a really cheap office chair in your home office. Stop! It's worth every penny to get a padded, supportive, adjustable office chair. Sell or donate the old one and treat yourself to a chair that will make it a pleasure to get to work. You may find that you're using your home office much more often—and no more aching back!

Make it like Martha. Leave it to Martha Stewart to create the perfectly organized, perfectly civilized office. Her perfect tone-on-tone files, boxes, and accessories are all decorated with ornamental floral moldings! This may seem like a bit much for us mere mortals, but her office did offer some other excellent take-away ideas. First, it was painted and accessorized in restful but attractive colors. Next, she'd installed a wall of shelves with a full row of storage cabinets at the bottom. But instead of filling the shelves with books (as in my office), she'd used rows of magazine boxes to neatly contain files in an accessible, easy-to-find manner. Because the spines of the folders face the office, the files are hidden from view but immediately at hand. No file cabinets for Martha! Finally, I was pleased to see that Martha had a laptop on her desk rather than a clunky desktop computer. Sleek and savvy!

Case the books. A small bookcase in the office is a handy place to keep phone books, a dictionary, home maintenance guides, and a family medical encyclopedia.

Hang your shelves. No room for an office bookcase? Hang a set of shelves or a hanging bookcase over your desk.

Don't forget the trash. (And recycling.) Because a home office generates so much paper, a wastebasket is as essential as a shredder. My corporate office had dual bins in each office—one for trash and one for recycling. Great idea!

Put your printer to work. Why have a printer, a fax machine, a scanner, and a copier cluttering up your office when you can buy a compact, inexpensive machine that does it all? Make your printer earn its office space.

Ditch the desk phone. Use your cell phone in the office instead. If you must have a regular office phone, get a wall phone that won't eat up precious desktop space.

Have one drawer for office supplies. Unless you use them constantly, there's no reason to clutter your desk with all the little office supplies that are essential when you finally do need them. Designate a drawer for sticky notes, paper clips, scissors, rubber bands, clips in various sizes, stamps and stamp pads, colored tabs, tape, and anything else you need.

Get yourself a tray. You can stash office supplies—pens, pencils, erasers, a calculator, glue sticks, a stapler, staples, liquid paper, map pins and tacks, magnets, and tape—in a utensil tray. Keep the tray in a drawer in your home office or out on the desk within easy reach. My boyfriend, Rob, has his office essentials in a desk organizer (a plastic tray with compartments for office supplies). He got his at OfficeMax but says they're available at all office-supply stores.

Hang an office medicine cabinet. Another good place to stash office supplies is in a medicine cabinet, where they're out of sight but within easy reach. When you upgrade your bathroom, donate your old cabinet to your office!

File your warranties. My editor Karen has some useful advice for the rest of us: "I keep a file folder of receipts, warranties, and instructions for appliances, electronics, and toys, roughly in alphabetical order," she says. "I go through the file once or twice a year to get rid of the information for things we no longer have or use."

Keep a file for the kids. Karen prefers to keep daughter Audrey's papers in an accordion folder with dividers. She puts Audrey's long-term school assignment instructions, absentee blanks, Scout handbooks, classroom lists, and other paperwork in the folder, so it's all together and easy to find. Karen recommends one accordion folder for every child in the family.

File your family papers. My friend Chris has a filing system worked out for all her household papers. She keeps separate file folders for receipts, tax information, warranties, car-related material, school papers, and insurance policies.

Bank on it. Unless you happen to have an indestructible, fire- and flood-proof safe at home, keep your important documents—birth certificates, Social Security cards, passports, wills, marriage and divorce papers, insurance documents, titles to vehicles, medical records, and the like—in a safe-deposit box at the bank. For your own use, keep photocopies in a labeled file folder in your file cabinet. Add a sheet with important addresses—your family doctors, accountant, attorney, and the like.

Put it on the board, part one. At the corporation where I worked, bulletin boards were standard issue for every office. There's no reason not to have one in your home office, as well. Keep only current materials on your bulletin board— business cards, your daily to-do list, outlines, appointment reminders, and so on. At the beginning of your workday, update the board and toss, shred, or file anything that you're not working on right now.

Put it on the board, part two. I love the way my friend Skye deals with her to-do list: She writes it on a blackboard! She uses different-colored chalks for different tasks and degrees of importance (red chalk for urgent projects, for example). At the end of the day, she can simply erase the list and start over.

Put it on the board, part three. A magnetic memo board may be more your style than a bulletin board. If you get one, though, the rules are the same: Don't overload it, keep only current items on it, and update it daily.

Do like the doctors. Those over-the-door plastic file organizers and hanging plastic magazine bins make great "in-and-out" boxes. You can find them at office supply stores. Rather than taking up desk space for your in- and out-bins, you can use the pockets in the organizer for incoming and outgoing mail, memos, and projects. Just make sure you check them daily and keep their contents moving in and out!

Hold pens up. Keep a stash of pens contained and upright on your desk. Here's the place for that beloved but no longer usable mug (or one that's gorgeous but really isn't big enough—or is too big—to use for coffee or tea). Years ago, a friend who knew how much I love gardening gave me a little vase shaped like a pair of green Wellington gardening boots. I couldn't imagine putting flowers in these Wellies, but I could instantly see their utility—and appropriateness!—as pen-holders. I don't know about you, but I've found that even new pens won't write if I wait too long before I use them, so I think the number of pens a mug, tumbler, or vase will hold is perfect. When they're gone, it's time to buy new ones! And meanwhile, pen-makers, could you *please* work on making a pen that will keep forever? Thanks.

Dare to duplicate, part one. Back up your files! Keep backup CDs and zip disks in a disk holder (available from any office supply store) so if your computer crashes, *you* don't crash with it. Don't want to keep track of a bunch of disks? Then do what I do—e-mail them to your spouse or partner. As I finish writing a chapter or other important document, I send a copy off to Rob to store on his computer. If mine crashes, I'm still covered.

Dare to duplicate, part two. Try this tip from my super-organized freelancer friend Jennifer. What a time-saver! "I keep duplicates of often-used items in the locations where I use them," Jennifer says. "For example, I have scissors in the office, kitchen, and laundry room; nail files in the bathroom, kitchen, and car; and diaper-changing supplies in the nursery, living room, and office." No more time wasted looking for something, or losing it, or leaving it out (and creating clutter) so you can return it "later."

Reuse your paper. "I have a basket in my office to store paper that has printing

SANITY SAVERS

A lot goes on in offices, even in home offices, and it's hard to keep things spic-and-span. Rather than hold yourself to an impossible standard—that horrid old ideal of the spotless desk and bare walls with nothing but schedules, forecasts, and other business-only papers tacked at eye level on a bulletin board—take comfort from two books that take the opposite approach.

In the first, with the great title *A Perfect Mess* (Little, Brown and Co., 2007, $25.99), authors Eric Abrahamson and David H. Freedman contend that in business, "moderately messy systems can be more profitable and creative than their organized counterparts." They point out that working in disorganized, messy environments never slowed down the likes of highly successful folks like Einstein, Bill Gates, and Arnold Schwarzenegger.

Then there's *Yearnings: Embracing the Sacred Messiness of Life* (Hyperion, 2006, $23.95). In it, author Irwin Kula talks about how office mess is "never about the desk." "We have this dance between messiness and order, messiness and order," he says. "When it feels messy, that is the moment when there will always be some discovery. Even in the clutter of a messy desk, when you're looking for that one thing, you find something else."

I once saw a sign that said, "If a cluttered desk is a sign of a cluttered mind, what is an empty desk a sign of?" Good point. I despise sterility in any home or office surroundings and am a big believer in surrounding yourself with what pleases you wherever you are. My offices, at home and in the workplace, have always been full of color and life—books, plants, stones, art, even an aquarium. But the thing is, in less than a minute I could put my hand on anything I or anyone else wanted or needed because my actual work was well organized.

And that's my point: Having a rich, stimulating work environment is ideal, and yes, it does boost creativity. But having a cluttered, chaotic work environment simply means that you waste a lot of time trying to find things, duplicating work because you can't find what you're looking for, even avoiding certain kinds of tasks because you're not prepared for them. In your home office, strive to create a work environment that enhances your creativity and well-being without compromising your efficiency—an environment that "works" for you.

on one side," Jennifer says. "My son can draw on the other side, or I can print out nonwork things on the other side."

Save on ink. You might guess that Jennifer does a fair amount of printing (see the previous tip), so she's come up with ways to save on ink. "I always print on 'fast' and 'grayscale' to save on ink," she says. "This saves money and time on trips to the store, and reduces the need to store lots of extra ink cartridges."

Add a little life. An office shouldn't be a dull, lifeless space. Instead, brighten it with a hanging plant or two and some inspiring nature photos. Just make sure they're not *so* inspiring that looking at them makes you want to forget about work and head outside!

Keeping Up with the Calendar and Addresses

Put it in plain sight. If you don't see your calendar, you won't use it. I use one that has a two-page spread for every week—plenty of room to write down appointments, engagements, birthdays, and so on—and I keep it on my rolling cart beside my computer desk and telephone. It makes it easy to check, and I can write down appointments as soon as I make them via phone or e-mail.

Keep track online. If you have a program like Microsoft Outlook, which has a built-in calendar, use it! I used my Outlook calendar faithfully when I worked for a corporation, and it was great. But I'll admit, I always had a print calendar as well as a backup so I wouldn't miss any meetings if the computers were down. My Yahoo! calendar is versatile. If you use a different e-mail service, see if it has a calendar feature as well.

Get a perpetual calendar. I found this great device at a store that specialized in French housewares. A Victorian staple, the perpetual calendar is a small, circular device that lets you manually rotate the day of the week, date, and month. I change the date on mine every morning when I turn on my computer (and check my lottery tickets!). Mine is in French, so I can practice my French while I see what day it is. I love it!

Keep addresses up to date. Most of my colleagues keep their addresses in their computer's address system. (Microsoft Outlook has a good one, and my Yahoo! address book is excellent.) Some people use Rolodexes (see below). I keep my addresses on good old 3- by 5-inch index cards in a recipe file with alphabetical dividers. Use the system that works for you. But whatever system you use, keep it current. Go through your addresses at least every 6 months, culling any that are no longer relevant. If you receive a new address from someone in your address system, update the address immediately and delete the old one to prevent confusion. I like my cards because they give me room for each person's name, address, phone numbers, cell phone number, e-mail address(es), and spouse's name—plus their children's and parents' names, nicknames, e-mails, addresses, and birthdays. Follow my system and you won't lose anyone's address if your computer crashes. But you could put all that in your electronic address book, too.

Don't use an address book. The one kind of address system I wouldn't recommend is an old-fashioned address book. People—at least the ones I know—seem to move, change jobs, change phone numbers, and change e-mails constantly. I like to write addresses in ink so they're easy to read, and obviously, keeping an address book would involve a lot of crossing out. It's a lot easier (and less messy) to simply write out a new card or update your electronic address book. Besides, you can lose an address book if you take it on trips. (A friend lost hers when a thief stole her purse.)

File business cards. Tape the business cards you need to keep on hand to your 3- by 5-inch cards or Rolodex cards and alphabetize them. Make sure you remove and replace them when someone leaves a company or changes their address! If someone's name isn't pronounced the way it's spelled, I always make a note on the card of how it's actually pronounced so I can remind myself before I speak to them.

Work your Rolodex. My friend Jennifer has some fabulous ideas for keeping track of family and friends' data. "I keep a Rolodex in an office-supplies drawer," she says. "On each friend or family member's card, I write their name, address, and phone number. On the back I write directions to their home and the amount of time it takes to get there. Down one side I keep track of whether or not I sent them a Christmas card each year, and if I received one back."

Put it in your planner. "I keep a list of each family member's clothing sizes and doctor's names and phone numbers in my planner," Jennifer says.

Buy your birthday cards, part one. I write upcoming birthdays on my calendar so I don't forget them, but Jennifer takes her birthday record-keeping to a higher level. "I write friends' and family members' birthdays on my calendar," she says. "I go to the card store only a few times a year and buy as many birthday and anniversary cards as possible. Then I label them with the appropriate person's name and, in the space where the stamp will go, I write the date that I need to mail the card. Once I buy the card, I place a check mark next to their names on my calendar so I don't accidentally buy another one."

Buy your birthday cards, part two. While we're on the subject of birthday cards, my friend Chris has a different system. "At the end of each month, buy all the greeting cards you'll need for the next month," she says.

Cross-check your calendars. Jennifer also has a system in place to make sure family obligations and occasions aren't forgotten. "When an event includes both my husband and me—such as dinner at my parents'—I write it on my calendar and put a check mark next to it on my calendar after I've made sure it's on his calendar, too," she says.

Get a PDA. Palm is probably the best known of these electronic "personal digital assistants," but there are plenty of others out there, including Nokia, HP, and BlackBerry. (A quick Google search will give you a ton of info on the latest, greatest models by these and other makers. Do your homework before you go shopping.) Basically hand-held computers, PDAs allow you to connect with the Internet, check e-mail, check appointments and addresses, make phone calls, navigate, do math calculations, and much more. They are pricey—$200 to $400 or so, depending on the model—but if you need access to your home office's computer or to the Internet while you're on the road, they're certainly handy.

Bills, Bills, Bills

Bite the bill bullet. I hate paying bills as much as anyone. There's nothing like that sinking, pit-of-the-stomach feeling of watching your money drain away! But I make it as painless as possible by organizing the bills so at least I can pay them quickly and not have to worry about late fees. Here's my system:

❑ I have a file folder in my file cabinet labeled "Bills."

❑ In this folder, I keep the previous month's paid bills banded together with a rubber band. I also keep stamps, return-address labels, and a few envelopes in the folder.

An Ounce of Prevention

Starting out with a sensible approach to home office management can save you a lot of grief. Use these tips from Jaap van Liere, an art curator who works from his home in Berks County, Pennsylvania. He's renowned for having a home office that "never shows signs of clutter."

"The key is always order," says Jaap. "Deal with stuff as it comes in and file it or get rid of it." Here's what Jaap has to say about his approach to managing his paper piles:

❋ Adequately sized work surfaces allow you to see what has to be done next and allow you to spread papers out so you can actually see them.

❋ Important information and resources can disappear if your focus on keeping it orderly means that piles of paperwork are hidden on shelves and in filing cabinets.

❋ Anything that hasn't been looked at or worked on in the past 18 months can probably be thrown away.

❋ A lot of what you have to deal with probably comes in .pdf form, so even if it is absolutely necessary to print it out to have on hand so you can read it and have it in front of you for a meeting, that certainly doesn't mean that it has to be stored. The electronic version is already on a hard drive somewhere.

❋ Three-ring binders and legal-size file sleeves, paper or plastic, are great for keeping things organized.

❋ Filing boxes are really useful. The smaller vertical size can go onto a bookshelf for short-term stuff, and the bigger boxes with lids can go into storage in the closet or basement.

❋ Lastly, small office equipment helps. Laptops and little printers or all-in-one printer/scanner/fax/copier units are a big help. And wi-fi connectivity helps get rid of a lot of wires.

❏ When a new bill arrives, I open it and note the due date. I write the due date on the outside of the envelope and circle it.

❏ I also note if my previous payment was received, and if so, I take the previous month's bill out of the rubber-banded batch and shred it.

- ❏ Then I file the new bill with the other unpaid bills, putting them in order of soonest to be paid to latest. (Occasionally—but never often enough!—bills won't come due for 2 or even 3 months after they're sent.)
- ❏ I check the file weekly and pay any bills that are coming due.
- ❏ When I've paid a bill, I write "paid" and the date under the due date on the front of the envelope and circle it. Then I put the paid bill in the rubber-banded stack.
- ❏ I keep my credit-card receipts in the envelope with the credit-card bill.
- ❏ I'm a stickler for writing down everything I pay for in my checkbook as well, and I do that as soon as I write each check.

Because bills tend to dribble in one at a time, it takes only about a minute a day to keep up with this system. And when it's time to sit down and pay up, you'll be so grateful everything's in order and ready to go. No more lost bills and wasted time!

Pay upfront. My boyfriend, Rob, is the original absent-minded professor. To make sure he doesn't miss a payment, he pays his bills the day they come in. That way, he never has to worry about where they've gotten to or think twice about whether he's remembered to pay them.

Pay online. Sign up for online bill payment and avoid the paper problem, or use online banking software to schedule transfers.

Pay automatically. Many bills can be paid automatically each month through your bank. Sign up for these services and the bank will pay your bills for you!

Get a bill organizer. My friend Jennifer has a different version of my bill-paying system. "Whenever I receive a bill, I toss the extra paperwork and flyers and place the bill in the envelope," she says. "Then I write the date the bill is due where the stamp will go and put the bill inside a bill-paying organizer on my desk."

Pay and toss. My friend Chris also has a simple system for dealing with the clutter bills create. "Throw away phone, electric, cable, and similar invoices after you've paid them," she advises.

Consolidate your credit cards. The more credit cards you have, the more bills, clutter, and stress you have with them. Yes, store clerks are trained to try to talk you into getting a store card every time you check out, but don't let them! The "great deals" you'll get with the card aren't worth the bills that come later. Try to

👍 Love It *or* Lose It? 👎

Don't you just love cubicles?

I didn't think so. So why should you be expected to love having a home office in a closet? I'm amazed by how often I see gushing articles in glossy magazines extolling the joys of converting a closet into your home office. Somehow I doubt that the authors of these articles have their own offices in closets!

But what if you don't have an extra room to devote to a home office and can't even really spare the space to turn a corner of the kitchen or family room into your home office space, but you *do* happen to have a closet you could convert? Here's what I'd suggest: Add as many shelves to the closet as you can, to hold office supplies. Tuck a file cabinet—preferably on rollers—into one side. And get the smallest computer desk on rollers you can find, like the laptop desk Improvements offers called "the roll-around Microstation" (see page 48). No room in your closet even for that? Get a full-height, telescoping laptop worktable (also available from Improvements) that folds up when not in use and tuck it into any closet. Then you can roll (or carry) your desk out into the natural light, rather than shoving yourself into a closet.

Verdict on closet offices: Lose 'em!

cut down to one general credit card per person and a gas card if you find it convenient. In addition to having fewer bills to deal with, you'll be able to see what you're actually spending.

Checkbooks and Bank Statements

Write it down and add it up. I write down every check I write or deposit and every ATM transaction I make in my checkbook's record section as soon as I've finished the transaction. Then I add or subtract the amount and balance my checkbook. When I'm using the ATM, I also compare the balance they show with the balance I've recorded. (Of course they don't always match up, since things clear at different times, but this gives me a way to see if I'm on track.) I know that some people have *never* balanced their checkbooks (think of that old joke about how there must still be money in the account, since there are still blank checks in the book). But unless you really enjoy getting overdraft notices (and charges), I don't understand this. It takes only a minute to bring the checkbook up to date. This is simple addition and subtraction, not rocket science! If you don't trust your math, use a calculator.

Do it online. My friend Jennifer swears by online banking. "I balance my checking account using the online statement, so I can just shred the statements when they arrive," she says.

Shred your ATM receipts. I used to hold on to all my ATM receipts—what if I was audited and the IRS needed them? But gee, they certainly piled up. Now I check my bank statement every month and shred the receipts as soon as I'm sure they're on there.

The Taxman Cometh

All those forms, receipts, and other tax-related documents may seem like the worst kind of clutter. But this is one type of clutter you'd better hang onto, and even accumulate before you need it. Here's how to get ready for Uncle Sam so you're not panic-stricken when mid-April rolls around.

Get it together. Keep each year's tax materials together in a file, accordion folder, or large envelope. I like to keep mine in one of those giant manila envelopes that offices use to route things in. They have ties at the top that hold the envelope closed securely. I write the year on the front, then include smaller envelopes to hold receipts for donations, tax receipts, W-2 forms, and other relevant data. When my federal, state, and local tax forms arrive, they go in the big envelope, too. When it's time to do my taxes, everything's right there. I keep the envelopes from previous years in a labeled printer-paper box, with the most recent on the top and the oldest on the bottom, so if I need to check my records, they're all in the box.

Keep your stuff for 7 years. You need to keep your tax records and supporting material for 7 years because the IRS has 6 years to audit your return. (You may have heard that it has 3 years, but that's true only if it thinks you made a good-faith error on the return! If it thinks you underreported your income, it has 6 years to go after you.)

Check your forms. Don't wait 'til the last minute to make sure you have all the forms you need to file your taxes. A lot of forms aren't included in the standard

Pet Alert!

Pets in the office? It certainly doesn't sound like a good idea. When I started telecommuting a couple of years ago and began using my home office full time, I was worried about what my pets would do. Would the cats jump up on the keyboard or onto my lap, yowling for attention? Would my golden retriever, Molly, make a nuisance of herself? I was prepared to shut the door and lock them all out, but I decided to give them a chance first.

To my surprise and delight, what happens is this: In the morning, when I settle down at the computer, the cats and dog follow me into the office. My kitten Layla curls up in the rocking chair and goes to sleep. My Maine coon cat, Athena, settles on the nearby desk and goes to sleep. My kitten Linus crawls under a chair and falls asleep. And Molly lies down behind my chair and goes to sleep! I was so relieved—companionship without chaos. They really just wanted to be in the same room. Admittedly, I keep the parrots and parakeet in the kitchen, where we can spend quality time together but they won't take it upon themselves to add raucous commentary to my phone conversations.

Come to think of it, though, perhaps I shouldn't have been surprised. One of my publishing friends, John Smallwood, and his colleague, Emma Stewart, both took their dogs to their New York offices at Smallwood & Stewart every day. The dogs were always well behaved (at least, after the scruffy Walter, John's junkyard rescue dog, leaped from the open window shortly after his arrival), and I'm sure their staff enjoyed the stress relief that pets can bring to a busy workplace.

If you have pets, I suggest that you give them a chance and see how they behave. They may turn out to be first-class office animals!

federal booklet they send you. If you need a form that's not there, check at the post office or download it from the IRS Web site's forms and publications page (www.IRS.gov).

Avoid the midnight rush. File electronically and avoid those long tax lines at the post office. Print out copies of the forms for your tax file or folder.

Be a copycat. If you mail in your tax forms, make sure you photocopy them (front and back) for your records before you send them off. My father the accountant always made me send mine in by certified mail, so I would have a record both that I sent them off in time and that the government received them.

Get help online. My friends who do their own taxes swear by programs like TurboTax (www.turbotax.com) and H&R Block's TaxCut Online (www.HRBlock. com). These programs are inexpensive ($14.95 to $29.95, depending on what you order) and include their own e-file, so you can mail your returns in electronically when you're done.

ONWARD!

You've chased down the last paper, finished organizing the last file, and gotten your bill-paying system in gear. Take a deep breath, and get ready to tackle those legendary clutter repositories: the laundry room, basement, and attic. But don't worry—you don't have to do them all at once! As you read through the next chapter, pick just one tip that appeals to you and start with that. You'll be on your way!

Chapter 13

De-Junking the "Junk Rooms"

LAUNDRY ROOM, BASEMENT, AND ATTIC

Maybe there are rooms in your house you don't even want to go into because of all the creepy piles of stuff; the basement and attic are often the prime suspects. But what a waste of potentially useful space! Then there's the laundry room, the last refuge of dirty clothes, ancient, half-empty containers of cleaning supplies, and heaven alone knows what else. In this chapter, you'll find out how to reform and reclaim these dreaded clutter-catchers.

PRIORITIES FOR LAUNDRY ROOMS

Let's start with the smallest of these problems—the laundry room. Since most laundry rooms are either very small rooms, are combined with a bathroom, or are part of the basement, I'm of two minds about including a visualization exercise for them. But I want this book to be a complete record for you of your clutter issues and control solutions, so I've included one. If, like me, you can take in your laundry room's current situation and potential solutions at a glance, you can skip directly to the laundry room tips on page 253. But if you'd like to take a good, hard look at the laundry room and see what's there and what needs to be done, here are the forms. Fortunately, this is one visualization exercise that should take less than 5 minutes!

Start your laundry room de-cluttering process by setting some clutter-kicking priorities. Begin by first focusing on what matters most to you about the way your laundry room looks and functions. That will become your top de-cluttering priority. Then you'll work your way through the clutter problems until you get to what matters least. The best way to do this is to take a good, hard look at the "before" state of the room and then to visualize the "after"—how you want the room to look when the clutter's all gone.

A Laundry Room Visualization

To get to your "after," you need to start by assessing the "before"—the way things look right now. So get out some paper or use the "My Laundry Room—Before" form (or make a photocopy of it and write on that). Write down every place there's clutter and note what that clutter is. Is dirty laundry heaped on the floor and spilling out of the laundry basket? Are there detergent boxes and bottles, some without caps, haphazardly sitting on top of the dryer or on the floor? Maybe you can't find the bleach, or there are used fabric softener sheets all over the place. Try to think about where you get hung up when you're trying to get things done, where you lose things, what distracts or irritates you. Take a good look. Take your time. Because the laundry room is usually a small room or part of a room, it won't take as long as you think to finish your list!

Once you've taken an inventory of your laundry room's "before" state, it's time to move on to the "after"—how you want the room to look when you've kicked the clutter. To make sure you're being realistic, look at the room every few minutes while you're doing this.

Your description of your de-cluttering goals can be short and to the point: "I want to be able to get to the machines. I want enough space to stash the dirty laundry and plenty of room to fold the clean laundry. I want a system that makes it easy for everybody to put their dirty laundry in the laundry-room hamper and put away their own clean clothes."

My Laundry Room—Before

_____
_____
_____
_____
_____
_____
_____
_____
_____
_____
_____
_____

My Laundry Room—After

_____
_____
_____
_____
_____
_____
_____
_____
_____
_____
_____
_____

Or you can create a detailed image of exactly how you'd like your laundry room to look if it were perfect (for you). You can picture the style of washer and dryer, the equipment in the room, any other furnishings, and what the room itself looks like. What sorts of storage, equipment, and furniture that you don't have now do you need to make the room more functional? What would make the laundry room a more pleasant space that you'd enjoy spending time in? Curtains, a mirror, a cheerful shade of paint on the walls, a comfortable chair or stool—once you know what you want, write it all down on a piece of paper or on the "My Laundry Room—After" form on page 251 (or on a photocopy of it).

Getting There

Now that you've captured your laundry room's "before" condition, listing all the specific problems, and you've imagined its "after" appearance, you can finally prioritize the steps you'll need to take to get that room cleaned up and functioning better. Again, bearing both "before" and "after" in mind, I'd recommend starting with what bothers you most about the "before" condition and making that your top priority. Work down your list from there and put it in descending order of importance.

Maybe you feel—especially if it's in the basement—that your laundry room is

My Laundry Room Priority List

just a dark, dank hole, and you hate going down there. Or maybe it's not designed efficiently, so you have to take the clothes to a different room to iron them. Or you're just sick of fighting stains and static—not to mention those mysterious disappearing socks.

Write down whatever's driving you to distraction on the "My Laundry Room Priority List" (or photocopy it, if you'd prefer) in descending order from most to least maddening. Now you have your priorities straight! Once you've finished, you can turn to the tips below to find ingenious ways of dealing with each problem.

THE LAUNDRY ROOM TIPS

Stack 'em up. You can save a lot of space with a dryer-over-washer arrangement. I have a tiny laundry room/bathroom, so mine's apartment-size, but I've seen some really attractive full-size models recently. Check them out!

Add some shelves. Shelves next to your washer and dryer add much-needed storage for detergents and other laundry supplies. My laundry room is also my "bathroom pantry," so I keep soap, sponges, tissues, toilet paper, and cleaning supplies—including those venerable standbys, vinegar and baking soda—on the shelves. I stash wash buckets with brushes and bottles of detergent under the lowest shelf. And to make sure they're there when I need them, I keep my household cleaning books on one of the shelves, too. If I need to handle a spill, stain, or other household crisis, I turn to the Queen of Clean, Heloise, Vicki Lansky, or another household diva for a fast solution.

Opt for utility. A set of those metal storage shelves that are more commonly found in basements and garages are perfectly fine for laundry-room storage. They're spacious and stable. If you can't find a color you like, buy some metal paint and get creative!

Get a rack. Drying racks are great—they expand when you need to air-dry clothes, then fold up accordion-style to tuck beside your dryer or into any tight space in your laundry room. I have an old-style wooden rack, the kind you hang the clothes right on, but I've seen sleek metal racks that let you air-dry clothes on hangers and that fold to just 2 inches wide! Look for them in housewares and hardware stores and catalogs.

5-Minute Fixes for Laundry Rooms

Want to jump-start your laundry-room clutter-kicking? Try these fast tips first!

Ditch dried-up detergent. If you have boxes of powdered detergent, borax, and bleach that have hardened to concretelike consistency, stop deluding yourself that they're still usable and throw them out. Make a note to replace the ones you actually use.

Let go of lost socks. If you have a collection of partnerless socks and gloves, now's the time to bid them adieu. (And no, I don't know what happens to the missing ones, either.)

Pitch yellowed paper products. If you're like me, you have a stash of "emergency" paper towels, toilet paper, napkins, and tissues in the laundry room, but somehow, you never get around to using them. If they still look good, vow to rotate them into use and buy fresh replacements as soon as you use them. But if they're warped, yellowed, water-stained, or otherwise unusable, throw them out.

If you can't get it out, throw it out. If you have a pile of stained clothing waiting to be cleaned—but you *have* cleaned it, tried spot-remover, bleach, and everything else you can think of, and the stains are still there—bundle it up and give it to Goodwill, the Salvation Army, the Society of St. Vincent de Paul, or a shelter. (Don't worry, these won't be sold to shelter residents as clothes. Shelters often sell these beat-up clothes as rags and get some money for them.) Those stains are there to stay! Then pick up a good spot-removal guide (see "The Pros Know" on page 257).

Circular-file the fabric softener sheets. I don't care how many times you've heard that there are 150 ingenious uses for used fabric softener sheets. If you're hoarding used fabric softener sheets, throw them out. If you use fabric softener sheets, trust me—you'll have one on hand when you need to soften the burnt-on food in that casserole dish.

String 'em up. You can still find outdoor laundry lines in houseware and hardware stores and catalogs. Look for the kind with a reel for the line so you can pull out the line, hook it to a wall or tree, then unhook it so it can automatically retract. And there's no reason you can't attach one inside the laundry room! Hook up the line to air-dry your clothes, then retract it when they're dry and swivel the case flat against the wall.

Cart it around. A great option for storing all your laundry supplies is a rolling laundry cart. Improvements has one with three sturdy shelves, and it's just 8¼ inches wide, so you can roll it between the washer and the wall when you're not using it. (See page 48.)

Put up a pole, part one. Housewares and home improvement stores sell tension poles for tubs and showers. You install the pole in a corner of the shower and adjust a group of organizer baskets to hold shampoos and other supplies. This kind of pole is a good idea for the bathroom, but it's also a great idea for the laundry room, where space is always at a premium. The poles will extend to 8 feet tall. Tuck one into a corner and put your laundry supplies in the baskets.

Put up a pole, part two. Hang a shower-curtain tension rod over the washer and dryer and use it to hang up clean clothes as you take them out of the dryer or off the ironing board. This will give you a place to hang all your clothes without wasting floor space. And it's great for wrinkle prevention!

Set it on the side. If you have the space, set a sideboard or hallway table against one wall of your laundry room. You can put baskets for darks, lights, and delicates on top, then stash the empty baskets under the table when the laundry's done—and you can use the tabletop for sorting and folding. These narrow tables are ideal for a narrow space like a hallway or laundry room.

Buy a bench. Again, if you have the space, a hallway bench is another good option for the laundry room. The kind with three square wicker baskets for storage underneath and cushions on top is ideal. You can use the baskets to sort darks, lights, and delicates for laundering and sit down when you need to repair a piece of clothing or just need a break! Look in home stores and catalogs like Plow & Hearth (see page 47).

Keep a sewing kit. You'll often first notice clothes that need repair—loose buttons, ripped hems, or the like—as you're getting ready to put clothing in the washer. A small, basic sewing kit can be a lifesaver here, since you can stick it on a shelf and grab it to make a fast repair when you see a problem. I keep mine in a plastic food-storage container—just a small pair of scissors, needles and a needle threader, a thimble, some extra buttons, spools of black and white thread, and one of those tiny sewing kits you can buy in the grocery or pharmacy with lots of colors of thread. Instead of putting all those clothes to be mended in a pile (clutter), fix them on the spot.

Brighten it up. It's hard to see stains, tears, loose buttons, and the like if your laundry room is dark and dingy. When a friend broke her leg, I did her laundry in her cavernous basement, and it was enough to make anyone swear off laundry for life! Get some bright lights for your laundry room. Use cheerful, colorful wallpaper or stencils to liven up the area. If you're dealing with a concrete basement floor, put a cheerful throw rug (or at least a big bath mat) in front of the machines. Your feet will thank you!

Throw it out. Keep a wastebasket in your laundry room for stray threads, dryer sheets, and—of course—dryer lint. Yes, I'm sure someone's written a book on knitting with dryer lint, and I don't care. Clean your lint trap *every single time* you use the dryer, and throw that darned lint out.

Get a sink. I've always envied people who have those old-fashioned galvanized wash sinks—the huge, square tubs on legs with a drainage hole in the bottom. I myself have a teeny, tiny sink in my laundry room, barely a foot wide. But whether you have a spacious stainless sink or a plastic bucket, you need someplace to pretreat stained and soiled clothing. Make sure you have one on hand, and if it's not attached to the wall or held up on legs, get a stool or bedside table to set it on. If there's no water source, keeping big filled bottles of water by the bucket or washbasin is a convenient solution.

Dry sweaters on a rack. Housewares and home stores and catalogs sell nylon-mesh racks that let you dry sweaters flat so you don't stretch them out of shape.

$$\left[\text{ Tools of the Trade }\right]$$

One of the most ingenious laundry room gizmos I've come across is a handsome oak wall cabinet that opens to reveal a fold-down ironing board. It's just 4½ inches deep when it's closed, so it takes up hardly any space in the room. And the door can be attached to open to the left or right to suit your space. You could even attach a mirror or artwork to the door if you wanted to. It sure looks a lot better than an ironing board! Look for this dandy invention in home improvement stores and catalogs like Improvements (see page 48).

When I have a laundry problem, I turn to Linda Cobb, the Queen of Clean. Her book *Talking Dirty Laundry with the Queen of Clean* is my laundry-room bible. (I see that it's out of print—sob!—but you can buy it used on www.amazon.com or buy a spiral-bound edition of both her bestsellers, *Talking Dirty with the Queen of Clean and Talking Dirty Laundry with the Queen of Clean* (Pocket Books, 2001, $24.95). Or you can go right to the heart of the matter with *The Royal Guide to Spot and Stain Removal* (Pocket Books, 2001, $5.99).

The Queen likes to use a host of quirky but effective spot removers, including rust remover, meat tenderizer, paste-style (nongel) toothpaste, shaving cream, salt, vinegar, baking soda, club soda, and denture-cleaning tablets (and that's just a start!). She keeps them in a shoebox-size plastic storage container on her laundry-room shelf, so they're at hand the second she needs them. Great idea!

The racks are stackable, so you can dry multiple sweaters at a time, and they fold up and have a coat-hanger hook at the top, so you can hang them up when they're not in use.

Use a rolling rack. Use a rolling clothes rack in the laundry room to hang clothes fresh from the dryer or iron. Improvements (see page 48) sells one that folds up to just 5 inches deep for storage when it's not in use.

Put it in the pantry. Do you like to store a lot of staples like toilet paper, paper towels, paper napkins, tissues, soap, and, of course, laundry products in your laundry room? Well, if you do and you have the space, consider getting one of those tall kitchen cabinets that serve as in-kitchen pantries for your laundry room. They hold a ton—and there's room to stash the laundry basket, too!

Go over the appliances. Lots of organizers recommend putting a storage shelf over your side-by-side washer and dryer to make the best use of the space. That's a start, certainly, but I've seen whole wire organizing systems that surround the washer and dryer and create a wealth of useful storage space for all your essentials. Like most of these systems, they have a white plastic coating over the wires or are gleaming stainless steel and are very attractive. If I had side-by-sides, I'd be getting one!

Put it in a basket. No room for a pantry—or even a shelf? Store all of your laundry staples in a bucket or laundry basket where they're easy to find and use.

Put it in a bin. Housewares and home stores and catalogs like Solutions (see page 48) sell magnetic storage bins. They're advertised as an accessory that you attach to the refrigerator, but these shelf- and file-size bins work just as well on the washer and dryer. They're a great place to stash a stain-removal guide; laundry checklist; those small, easy-to-lose bottles of sweater washing fluid; and the like.

Put it in pull-outs. If you have a deep storage space beside your washer or dryer, install wire pull-out baskets on rollers so you don't have to grope around the backs of deep shelves to find what you're looking for.

Spring for some steel. You don't really know the meaning of the word "mess"—not to mention sodden, disintegrating clutter—until your washer hose bursts at 9:30 p.m. on a Sunday night, spewing scalding water all over the laundry room and its contents. (Take this from one who knows.) So do as I say—and as I (subsequently) did—and replace those old hoses with flexible steel-wrapped safety hoses that are guaranteed never to burst.

Put laundry on a pedestal. If you have a front-loading washer and dryer, you can buy pedestals for them with drawers for storage. Great idea!

Crown it with a countertop. Front-loading appliances also give you the option of adding a countertop (many colors and kinds are available at home improvement stores) over them to create a stable, attractive work space.

Use the door, part one. Hang or attach towel racks to the back of the laundry-room door. You can put clean clothes on the racks as you fold them, or hang clothes on hangers hooked over the towel racks.

Use the door, part two. Home improvement centers and organizing stores sell wire racks for pantry doors. Find the sizes and widths that work for you, and store your laundry products on your door.

Use the door, part three. Attach a fold-down ironing board to the back of the door for a space-saving ironing solution.

See? That wasn't so hard. Let's hope it's inspired you to go on to greater things, because now it's time to tackle the dark, the dank . . . the basement.

PRIORITIES FOR BASEMENTS

I remember the basement of my family home as a dark, dank space. There were jumping spiders leaping around when someone turned on the single bare lightbulb, boxes of ancient family photos, and papers that had warped, cracked, and moldered. That fifties-era bomb shelter became a playhouse for those of us brave enough to venture down there. But despite the dankness and creepy-crawlies, I always loved exploring the basement as a place of mystery and surprise. One of my great regrets about my cottage home is that it has no basement—it's beside a stream (which is otherwise a wonderful thing). But fortunately, I have lots of friends with basements that aren't dark and dank, and they've passed along some great tips to share with you all.

In this section, I'll talk about storage, crafts rooms, and other basement options. (There are so many great things you can do with a basement that it makes me jealous just thinking about it!) I won't talk about using your basement or part of it as a den or family room, though, since you can turn to Chapter 8 (beginning on page 142) to find tons of tips about that. I won't talk about using part of it as a laundry room, since we talked about that earlier in this chapter. And guys, I also won't talk about turning your basement into a workshop or "man cave"—you can read all about that in the garage chapter (Chapter 15, beginning on page 311). But that doesn't mean I think these options are bad ideas! For goodness' sake, go for it, if that's the space you want to use for any of these options.

But before you can use your basement for anything, you've got to get it cleaned up. First, let's begin by thinking about exactly what you want to use your basement space for. You're going to start your basement de-cluttering process by setting some clutter-kicking priorities. To do that, first focus on what matters most to you about the way your basement looks and functions—that will become your top de-cluttering priority. The goal at this stage is to list the basement clutter issues from most to least bothersome. The best way to bring your priorities into focus is to take a good, hard look at the "before" state of the room, and then visualize the "after."

A Basement Visualization

Start with the "before" of your basement—the way things look right now. Get out some paper, or use the "My Basement—Before" form on page 260 (or make a photocopy of it and write on that). Write down every place in the basement there's clutter, and note what that clutter is. Try to think about what you could be doing

My Basement—Before

My Basement—After

with your basement space and what you're using (or not using) it for now. Really *look* at your basement, as if you were the design team from *Extreme Makeover: Home Edition* or, say, Martha Stewart, and you just happened to wander down there. What do you see? (Assuming you can see through all the gloom.) Cobwebs? Shelves of dust-covered whatsits? Disintegrating cardboard boxes slumped haphazardly on the floor?

Once you've taken an inventory of your basement's "before" state, it's time to move on to the "after"—how you want the room to look when you've kicked the clutter. Write it all down on a piece of paper or on the "My Basement—After" form (or on as many photocopies of it as you need to do it justice). To make sure you're being realistic, look at the room every few minutes while you're creating your "after" description. Bear in mind that there are actually lots of things you can do with the space once you've shoveled it out. You may want to read through the tips in the section called "Options for Basements," beginning on page 274, before you complete your "after" description. I feel certain you'll be inspired!

Your description can be short and to the point: "I don't want to fight water in the basement. I want better lighting. I want lots of shelves. I want to turn the space into a cozy family room."

My Basement Priority List

_____

_____

_____

_____

_____

_____

_____

_____

_____

Or you can create a detailed picture of exactly how you'd like your basement to look if it were perfect (for you). Think about how you'd divide up the space. What sorts of rooms do you need that you don't have space for in the rest of the house? Then picture the colors of the walls, floors and floor coverings, and window treatments. Imagine every piece of furniture—where it would be, what it would do, what it would look like. Write it all down!

Getting There

Now that you have captured your basement's "before" condition, listing all the specifics, and you've imagined its "after" appearance, you can finally prioritize the steps you'll need to take to get there from here. Bearing both "before" and "after" in mind, start with what bothers you most about the "before" condition and work down your list of clutter problems and wishes for the de-cluttered basement.

Maybe you'd love to have a home gym. Or you'd like more storage space. Or you've been wondering if you could turn the basement into an in-law apartment and make it really inviting. Or you'd just like to think you could store things down there without worrying about whether they would rust, rot, or be eaten by mice.

Write down whatever's driving you to distraction on the "My Basement Priority List" on page 261 (or photocopy it, if you'd prefer) in descending order from most to least maddening. Now you have your priorities straight! Once you've finished, you can turn to the tips below to find ingenious ways of dealing with each problem.

THE BASEMENT TIPS

Let's talk about storage first—and protection from the elements. If you need a sump pump (or several) in the basement, there's not much I can tell you that you don't already know: Before you do anything, hire a professional to dry the place out! And seal any cracks and leaks while you're at it. *Then* turn to the storage tips. After those, we'll talk about all the things you can use your basement for. That's the fun part! I think you're going to see your basement space in a whole new (good) way.

Safe Storage

Solve the water problems. My friend Delilah's house is on the side of a mountain, and when it rains really hard for a long time, sometimes the water comes down the mountainside and heads through her basement on the way to a stream far below. While waiting to have her yard bermed to reroute the water, she hit on a great idea. Heading to her local Tractor Supply store, Delilah bought heavy-duty rubber mats—the kind sold for horse stalls—and covered her basement floor with them. They're, of course, waterproof, and they raised the functional floor surface about an inch, so nothing would get wet even if water came in. The water runs under the mats and ultimately out through the floor drain. The mats added great insulation and softness to the hard concrete floor, making it much more pleasant (and warmer) to walk around on. Delilah put rugs over the rubber mats, and voilà! Her basement was transformed into a welcoming living space.

Go for the high ground. Store stuff on shelves, not on the floor. That way, if the basement *does* flood, there's less chance that your things will be ruined.

Clear the stairs. If you have steep stairs going down to your basement, don't make them even more hazardous by leaving stuff on them—not even along the sides. Get a basket or hamper to carry things that need to go from the main floor down to the basement, but keep it on the house side of the door, not the basement side. A lot of people hang stuff on the wall alongside the stairs, but this can also be hazardous, since you or a box or laundry basket that you're carrying could

Tools of the Trade

If you think there's the least chance that water might pool on your basement floor, it's safest to store everything at a higher level. Fortunately, some inventive soul created rust-proof, rot-proof plastic Hi & Dri Storage Pallets to raise basement storage out of harm's way. They come in two sizes, can support 1,000 pounds, and lift your boxes 3½ inches off the floor. If water seeps in, it will just flow underneath the pallets while your stuff stays, well, high and dry. Look for them at home improvement centers and in catalogs like Improvements (see page 48).

crash into them and dislodge them. I feel this way about hanging things on the basement door, too. You don't want something swinging into or falling onto you as you're going down the stairs. Secure a flashlight to the wall by the door and leave it at that. You can always display the kids' art on the wall to brighten the space, but tack it up; don't put it in frames that could be dislodged. While I'm at it, make sure the stairwell is well lit and there's a strong, well-secured banister that will take someone's weight if they lose their footing. Better safe than sorry!

Park the paint. Keep paint cans together in a plastic storage bin on the floor or the bottom shelf of a storage unit. They'll be less likely to spill or get knocked over.

Park the paint permanently. One of the best clutter-control tips I've learned (from Martha Stewart, of course) is to create a decorator's folder. Get a small clear or translucent plastic accordion file from an office supply store. Mark each sectional divider with the name of a room in the house, then put paint chips, carpet samples, and fabric swatches from the curtains and upholstery in that section, with a card that gives the name of each, the date you bought it, and where you got it, as well as the dimensions of the room and the room's door. No need to keep paint cans lying around now—if anything needs refurbishing, the data is at your fingertips and the folder is small enough to take to the store with you! Stash it where you're sure you can find it—in your home office, on a shelf in the basement, or in a drawer in your craft room.

Pint-size the paint. One cool gadget I've found is a paint bottle with a sponge applicator top. If you need to touch up a surface, you just pour leftover latex paint into the 4-ounce bottle, press the sponge applicator against the surface, and dab on the paint. Wash the sponge applicator in hot water between uses and cap the bottle. (Label the bottle with the paint color and the room and surface you used it on.) Look for them in home improvement centers and catalogs like Improvements (see page 48).

Pitch the paint. Latex paint spoils after 2 or 3 years, or if it's exposed to freezing temperatures (32°F or below). Dispose of any latex paint in your basement that's old or cold!

Work your walls. Maximize your basement storage with wall-to-wall shelving. Be creative—if you've upgraded your bookcases or a wall unit in the living room, move the old one to the basement. Don't be shy about using metal storage units, either. You can paint them more inviting colors than the usual black or gunmetal gray! And you can choose from a plethora of wire storage units from home improvement centers and organizing stores like All Bright Ideas (see page 48). I will say that using all one type of shelving looks a lot better than a hodgepodge of different sizes and materials—your basement will have a tidy, intentional look that will be much more pleasing.

Say "curtains" to pipes. If you have a wall of exposed pipes, you can cover them by putting open storage shelves in front of them, but that makes it a bit challenging to get to them if you need to make repairs. An alternative is to hang floor-length curtains in front of them to cover the entire wall. Choose a color that complements or matches the wall paint. (You *did* paint the walls an inviting color, right?) Turn that part of the room into an entertainment center with a TV and DVD or video game player, some comfy chairs or a loveseat, and a bright rug, and suddenly your hideous wall becomes the attractive backdrop to a cozy retreat.

Hang some cabinets. If you have old kitchen cabinets left over from a renovation or can find some at a flea market or yard sale, put them to work in your basement. (Remember, if they're dark or ugly, you can paint them to match or complement the walls.) They'll look best if you have a set of them, so they look intentional, and they'll look even better if you install the matching counter and storage cabinets below them. As in the kitchen, you'll gain a wall of storage space and a big surface for projects.

Add a door. Another way to add useful work and storage space under hanging shelves or cabinets is to get a flat door or thick piece of plywood and use it as a table or work surface. Put it on two two-drawer file cabinets (you can find these in neutral or cheerful colors or paint them to suit), paint it if you like, and you're ready to go.

Get your freezer in gear. If you're lucky enough to have a chest freezer in the basement (can you tell I'm jealous?), don't let it become the final resting place for a bunch of frost-coated body bags. (*How* long has that been in there?) Date your food, eat your food, and replace it regularly. If someone gives you something you don't think your family will eat, don't throw it in the freezer, throw it out. (The same holds true for unpopular leftovers. If they didn't like it the first time. . . .) How to tell what you have in there? Use this technique from my friend Jennifer. "I always keep food in my freezer in roughly the same location so I can see at a glance what I have and don't waste time, money, and space buying extra things," she says. Super-organized Jennifer puts the same technique to use in her refrigerator, pantry, bathroom, and office.

Dress it up. An old dresser or two can add much-needed storage in a basement and can look especially good grouped with chairs and a sofa in a seating area. If you don't have any extras hanging around, keep your eyes open; sometimes you can find perfectly good old dressers set out at the curb for the trash, or you can pick one up at a thrift store, flea market, or yard or estate sale. And—let me say it one more time—if you don't like their color, you can always paint them! As with any furniture, if you use more than one, they'll look best if they match.

Make a wall for wire. I don't think pegboard is great for basement walls—hanging stuff all over it creates visual clutter, unless you're using the space as a workshop or crafts room. But you can make an attractive wall display with wire shelving (the kind sold for pantry and cabinet doors in home improvement and organizing stores and catalogs). If you can't mount shelves directly to your wall because it's concrete block, mount a large plywood sheet, paint it to match or complement the wall color, and mount the white-coated wire shelving to the plywood in a pleasing and functional pattern.

Minimize cord clutter. Anywhere you use a lot of electrical devices, including the basement, you can accumulate a lot of cord clutter. Confine it to one place with a Squid Power-Outlet Multiplier, which lets you run five electrical devices off one grounded outlet, even if each device has a large transformer plug or timer. This ingenious contraption (which does look rather squidlike) is available from home improvement stores and catalogs like Improvements and Herrington (see page 48).

Put it in plastic, part one. My boyfriend, Rob, absolutely swears by those plastic storage units, such as the ones made by Rubbermaid. He points out that they're waterproof and indestructible—both advantages in a room that can take a lot of abuse. And they have doors, so you can hide your boxes out of sight.

Put it in plastic, part two. Speaking of Rubbermaid, if your basement is home to an ever-expanding collection of sports gear, contain it in the Rubbermaid Sports Station Organizer, which has compartments and hooks for racquets, bats, and hockey sticks, as well as storage space for balls and helmets and a mesh bag for storage or carting off to the game.

Put it in plastic, part three. Plastic storage containers, available from groceries, pharmacies, hardware stores, home improvement stores—pretty much anywhere!—in a wide range of shapes and sizes, are ideal for basement storage. You can see what's inside so it's easy to find things, and you can buy whatever size you need to fit your shelves or your stuff. No more bits and pieces raining down when you're trying to find something! And, of course, they provide great protection from water and dust.

Get a folding stool. Use a step stool to stay safe while reaching for stuff on high basement shelves. If you get one that folds, you can tuck it almost anywhere when you're not using it—you'll just need a 2- or 3-inch-wide space.

Raise your water level. If you store 5-gallon water bottles in your basement, you can stack them for easy retrieval and get them up off the floor with a three-tier water-bottle rack, available from housewares stores and catalogs like Improvements (see page 48).

Store your wine. One thing the cool, dank conditions of a basement favor is wine storage. (They don't call wine cellars "caves" for nothing!) Set up your wine rack where no one will crash into it, and enjoy!

Store your cleaning supplies. My friend Jennifer wanted to free up her kitchen storage space. "We built a huge storage closet in our basement in which we store the vacuum, rug scrubber, and all of the cleaning supplies," she says. "The only cleaning product we keep under the sink is the dishwashing detergent. This frees up the cabinet so we can keep the trash and recycling containers under there, safe from the baby, behind cabinet locks."

Use common sense. Basement conditions are tough on fragile things. Whether it's mildew and damp or just wear and tear, life in the basement makes the Damage Rule a necessity:

> # Damage Rule: If you can't stand the thought of it getting damaged, don't put it in the basement.

This goes for everything from antiques and supersensitive electronics to photos and books, and, of course, art and clothes, quilts, and other fragile textiles. (If your quilting studio or sewing room is in the basement, it should be climate controlled.)

Lighten and Brighten

Add some flash. A basement's a bad place to be if the lights go out. Hang a flashlight on the wall by the basement door and put another on a shelf where you can reach it easily if you're working down there when the power fails. Check both regularly to make sure the batteries are working.

Brighten it up. A dark, dingy basement can look even smaller and more cramped and cluttered than it really is. And yet many older basements are painted horrific colors like brown or dark green. Time to lighten up! Give the basement a facelift with white paint (on the ceiling, too) or a soft primrose yellow, cream, or other pleasing color. Add plenty of bright light (preferably ceiling lights or wall sconces, to keep cords off of the floor) and put a durable rug, grass matting, or laminate flooring on the floor. Make your basement a place you want to be!

Fire it up. If your basement has a family room, den, or entertainment area with a big, blank wall, make it warm and welcoming with a fireplace. You can now buy a fireplace—complete with a mantel in any number of styles—or a faux wood-stove and install them anywhere. It's amazing! They're available at hardware and home improvement stores and catalogs like Plow & Hearth (see page 47) and Improvements (see page 48). Whether you're burning fuel-gel cells or just plugging in, the soothing flames will cheer and relax the whole family and bring warmth and life to the room. Put bookshelves on either side of the fireplace for storage (some fireplace models even have bookshelves built in), add a wall-mounted TV screen over the fireplace, and cuddle up.

Craft or Hobby Rooms

Dedicate the space. Whether you have a corner of the basement for your quilting, sewing, scrapbooking, dried flower crafting, beading, basket-making, knitting, painting, or pottery, or you have the luxury of an enclosed basement room, dedicate the space to your craft. In this space, functionality should reign supreme. The worktable, chairs, wall space, lighting—*everything* should contribute to your comfort and convenience as you work. And you shouldn't have to be distracted by toys, bills, home storage, and other clutter intruding on your space. Banish everything else to other parts of the basement.

But make it appealing. There's no reason your craft room should look like a workshop—unless you just happen to like that bare, functional look. Brighten your work space with color and art. Add a music system—even if it's just a boom box—so you can relax as you work.

Make your walls work. In this room, inspiration should edge out my usual injunctions against visual clutter. You need open, uncluttered work space, but your walls can be a rich collage of ideas. Put up bulletin boards, magnetic boards, pegboards—whatever works best for you. On them, display photos, fabric scraps, yarn, patterns, works-in-progress—whatever will boost your creativity. Don't overlook the value of synergy—sometimes something totally unrelated can spark your best work. A pattern in an oriental carpet or a close-up of a bird feather could turn into

(continued on page 272)

Tools of the Trade

"If you haven't seen a Big Board yet, you're in for a treat," says my friend (and avid quilter) Karen. "It's a huge rectangular ironing board that sits atop drawer towers. You get a great ironing surface (without the pointy end) and loads of storage space underneath, rather than the space-wasting X design of a traditional ironing board." Visit www.bigboardenterprises.com and see for yourself!

Pet Alert!

If you have both a basement and cats, chances are that you keep at least one litter box down there. You may have a cat door cut into the basement door or just leave the door ajar so they can come and go. (Hopefully you don't choose the latter option if you have little kids!) But just because the litter box is out of sight doesn't mean it should be out of mind. Nobody's going to want to go down to the basement if they'll be confronting a reeking, overfilled litter box—and that includes your cats! Here are some tips to keep the litter box bearable:

❉ **Put up a screen.** A decorative screen will keep the litter box out of sight, but you and the cats will still have easy access.

❉ **Make sure the box is big.** Make sure the box is big enough to accommodate your cats.

❉ **Have enough boxes.** Ideally, you should have one box for each cat.

❉ **Use the right litter.** Besides preferring a clean, fresh litter box, cats also have different litter preferences than their owners do. For example, many people use scented litter in their cats' boxes. But cats can't stand those perfumy smells and may boycott the box as a result. Some people line their cats' litter boxes with plastic liners to make them easier to clean. But if you don't clean the box and change the plastic liner every day—thoroughly drying the bottom of the box—urine can build up under the plastic and smell to high heaven. Finally, not all litters are created equal. Clumping litter is by far the best option—it won't get smelly, and you can simply sift out the used clumps and leave the rest. So skip the plastic liner and put that money toward better litter. (I'm a big fan of EverClean, which was recommended to me years ago by the cattery owner where I got my Maine Coon cats. Trust me, it works!)

❉ **Add some deodorizers.** Not perfumes, remember! But there are some highly effective additives you can sprinkle on your litter to help it stay fresh-smelling. The ones I use are Ammo Cat, which removes ammonia from the litter, and Nature's Miracle Litter Treatment enzymatic powder, a powerful odor-eater. Since I don't have a basement, my cats' litter box shares the bathroom with me, and I'm not about to tolerate even the faintest smell!

❈ **Clean every day.** Make it a point to clean your litter boxes at the same time every day—first thing in the morning's my time. It will be a lot easier to remember (and do) if you make it part of your routine.

If your family has dogs, cats, parrots, bunnies, or any number of other pets, you may store their food in the basement. Ditto if you set out birdfeeders. Keep it safe from insect pests and rodents by storing it in decorative tins. You can sometimes find them at pet stores for free—pet food manufacturers use them as giveaways—and stores that cater to wild birds often have gorgeous ones for sale. These are not only pest-proof and stackable, they look a lot better than most storage options—certainly better than opened sacks of feed!

I see wooden barrels and bins offered for pet-food storage, but I don't trust them to keep out insects or mice. And I see recommendations to store large amounts of feed in metal garbage cans, but I wonder about how pest-proof they are, as well. And of course, you do have to look at them! I'd rather look at a decorative tin than a plastic container, too. To me, metal tins are the gold standard. I just tuck a scoop inside, and I'm ready to dish out everybody's dinner.

Finally, if you and your pets spend family time in your basement, remember that the floor gets awfully cold for your furry friends. Whether you put down a braided rug in front of the sofa or add a dog or cat "nest" (available from catalogs like L.L. Bean, Plow & Hearth, and Orvis; see pages 46, 47, and 49), make sure your pets have someplace warm and comfortable to lie.

a beaded masterpiece; a leaf or machine part could become the basis for a pair of earrings. Let your mind fly!

Find functional furniture. Open your eyes to the possibilities around you. Besides the obvious shelves, cabinets, and filing cabinets, consider a hutch, dry sink, buffet cabinet, cupboard, dresser, or armoire. Any of these pieces will hold an absolute ton of crafting supplies.

Put it in plastic—or a basket. If you keep your craft supplies in the sturdy plastic carriers available in any home improvement center, drugstore, or grocery, it's a snap (literally, for the ones with lock-on lids) to put your supplies back in the containers and put them away on your shelves or in your armoire, hutch, or wherever you stash your stuff. These plastic storage containers come in a myriad of sizes and are very affordable. I like the ones with locking lids and handles that lift up to carry but flatten for stacking. And you can just look through the side to see what's in each one. Another option is to store your supplies in baskets. Just make sure they have handles so it's easy to carry them when it's time to clear the work table.

Tackle the small stuff. I like to store small supplies like beads in compartmentalized plastic cases, which you can find in any hardware or craft store. But I know plenty of people who store small supplies in tackle boxes!

Shelve the small stuff. My friend Karen has her own smart system for craft-supply storage. "Make or hang shelves over doors and windows in your hobby room," she says. "Plan ahead and find storage containers that can be stacked two or three deep between shelf and ceiling. Use them to organize all your notions (elastic, zippers, ribbon, variegated thread, needles, knitting and crochet supplies) in a dust-free environment."

Don't forget totes. I love roomy totes for carrying my in-progress projects. I have padded totes specifically designed for crafts projects, with lots of inside pockets and attractive patterns; I have woven African basket totes with handles and bright designs; I even have a tall rectangular Shaker basket with leather handles. And I admit, I love them all. Whether I'm working on my knitting, quilting, or beading, I have my supplies in the appropriate tote and can "tote" it along with me from room to room. If you're working on a lap project in the family room, you can take it upstairs in your tote, then stash it back on its shelf in your craft room until you have another chance to work on it.

Share your supplies. If you share your craft room with a child, take a tip from one of my friends. "I finally merged my collection of fancy craft scissors, decorative hole punches, and fancy scrapbook papers with my daughter's," she says. "She constantly borrowed them, and I constantly gathered them up and stored them safely away after she was done. Once I realized that she wasn't damaging the 'good' stuff, I gave up the ghost on 'hers' and 'mine.' A few quick lessons on caring for things, and she's benefiting creatively from access to the higher-end art supplies."

Put patterns in plastic. Here's another great tip from Karen, who's also an accomplished sewer. "Instead of stuffing pattern pieces back into the envelope, get plastic sleeve pockets for a 3-ring binder," she says. "Store the pattern envelope, tissue patterns, and any special notions that you purchased for the project in the sleeve pocket." Then put the sleeves into a labeled binder and it will be right there on your shelf when you need it.

Get a grip on gift wrap, part one. If you spend a lot of time wrapping presents, cut down on the clutter of wrapping paper and ribbons with a gift-wrap organizer. Get a big plastic under-bed storage box that is long enough to hold long rolls of wrapping paper but shallow enough to fit on a shelf in your craft room, and tuck smaller plastic boxes inside to hold ribbons, tape, gift tags, and scissors. Or buy the "official" version, a gift wrap case that has flip-down legs to turn it into a wrapping station, clips to hold wrapping paper in place while you work, a lift-out organizer bin, a lid compartment for flat sheets, and special sections for ribbons and bows. (You can find this marvel at Solutions; see page 48.) You can get portable plastic carriers that organize and dispense up to 16 spools of ribbon and padded, heavy-duty polyester gift wrap and bow organizers and gift bag organizers that are as well built as suitcases and have carry handles and hooks for wall mounting (from Improvements; see page 48).

Get a grip on gift wrap, part two. Don't feel like buying a gift-wrap holder? Do as my friend Chris does and store your wrapping-paper rolls upright in a clean trash can. (Crafty Chris also saves the Christmas cards she receives each year, then cuts them out and uses them as gift tags the following year.) I keep my tall wrapping-paper rolls upright in a tall tin flower bucket like the ones vendors use in French open-air markets, and I stash my flat wrap and gift bags in a labeled printer-paper box, both tucked away in my crafts closet where they're easy to reach.

Options for Basements

Go for a gym. My friend Delilah has set up a home gym in part of her basement. She's made sure the space is bright and inviting, and for inspiration, she put up posters of Marilyn Monroe working out with barbells. Make sure you have a good selection of music or a TV on hand to make the time go by faster. Delilah has a rack on her stationary bike that lets her read magazines while she cycles.

Build a plant paradise. My ex-husband is an orchid enthusiast. He created a fabulous basement setup with rows of plant-laden tables (actually called "benches," but trust me, they're steel-and-wire tables), fluorescent lights, and a type of aerial sprinkler system that misted, watered, and fed his plants on a regular basis. Going into the basement and seeing the exotic orchid blooms—and the sea of green leaves—as you descended the steps was incredible, especially in winter when the garden was buried in snow.

Start some seeds. Creating a plant room in the basement may be too ambitious for you, but if you enjoy gardening, you can easily set up a seed-starting area. Garden catalogs sell "light gardens," tiers of shelves with fluorescent lights suspended over them, that are ideal for starting seeds. You can buy special seed-starting setups and heat mats that will give your seedlings the best possible growing environment. Check out the Gardener's Supply Company catalog (see page 49) for an introduction to all the possibilities. If you don't want to invest in a light garden, you can always buy a table at a yard sale or thrift store and string up a couple of shop lights.

Spruce up houseplants. Light gardens are also good "sanatoriums" for exhausted or past-peak houseplants. Give them light and TLC while they revive, then bring them back up to show off in other rooms of the house while you move other tired houseplants from upstairs back under the lights to recover.

Add a potting shed. My friend Delilah uses part of her basement as a potting shed. Again, you can buy a potting bench (really a table) setup from garden catalogs like Gardener's Supply Company and Charley's Greenhouse & Garden (see page 49). These benches are made of wood or metal with shelf space below for pots and potting soil, racks to hang tools, and lots of other neat features. Or you can head to a thrift store or flea market and buy a table you wouldn't mind spilling dirt and water on, then set up shop with a plastic tub to hold the soil, a trowel, and some pots.

Make some music. My friend Tom and his sons have turned their basement into a music room, complete with guitars (electric, acoustic, and bass), drum sets, a piano, keyboards, and recording equipment. They all compose, play, and record together, just for the fun of it.

Play Ping-Pong. I love Ping-Pong (aka table tennis), and the basement's a perfect place to set up a table, because Ping-Pong takes up a lot of floor space. Also, unlike when you play Ping-Pong outside, the balls won't get lost, and unlike upstairs, they won't hit anything they shouldn't (except maybe your opponent).

Set up a snack center. If you have a den, family room, or TV room in the basement and your family spends a lot of time there, it makes sense to set up a basic snack center. Get a cabinet, table, or kitchen island and place it against the wall of your entertainment area. Put a microwave or an electric popcorn popper, a hot plate, and a blender on top, tuck a mini-refrigerator inside or underneath, and stash some small pans, bowls, mugs, glasses, straws, napkins, paper towels, and utensils inside. Stock popcorn, pretzels, chips, crackers, cookies, candy, and other family favorites in glass jars or ClickClacks (see page 92), and put drinks, fruit, cheese sticks, yogurt snacks, and butter in the fridge. Add a slow cooker to keep soup and hot drinks like cider and hot chocolate warm. If you don't have a sink in the basement or if it's across the room, make sure you have a plastic dishpan so you can carry the dirty dishes to a sink or dishwasher and bring them back clean.

Add another bathroom. A feature of older basements in the area where I live is a basement bathroom. These older houses often had only one bathroom, so they took advantage of the plumbing to create a second bathroom underneath it. Some of these are no more than a toilet on a pedestal with a sink nearby—not good for your decor or your privacy!—but it's certainly a good idea to add a little basement bathroom, especially if your family spends much time down there. But wall it off, please!

Add a retro rec room. It's your basement—why not have some fun there? If you have an enclosed room in part of the basement and you have a favorite decade, make a retro hideout for yourself. An Elvis lounge? Seventies love nest? Hippie hideaway? Flapper speakeasy? Eighties disco? Shop flea markets for retro fabrics, fixtures, and furnishings for your chosen era. Look for accessories in your parents' attic (or your own) and at yard sales. Make it fabulous! My friend Candyce even painted her formerly dingy basement stairs in a beautiful spatter pattern of purple, black, gold, and red—positively psychedelic!

Put in a playroom. If part of your basement is enclosed, you can create a play-room for your children. My brother, Ben, and his wife, Julie, created a wonderful play space for my nephew and niece, with twirling swings anchored securely to the ceiling, a trampoline, a bookcase full of games and children's books, and lots of beanbags and other kid-size cushioning. It instantly became their favorite place to be—you were sure to find them down there the minute they got out of bed. Kids too big for a playroom? What about a clubhouse or pirate's lair?

Put in a pantry. My friend Rudy's house was built in the forties, when victory gardens were the norm in backyards across America. His home has a wonderful setup of open wooden shelves that his grandmother kept filled with jars of glisten-ing jams and jellies and home-canned fruits and vegetables, as well as bottles of his grandfather's home-brewed beer. If you enjoy preserving your own food, a cool, dry basement is a great place to store it.

Add a root cellar. Another old-fashioned essential for food preservation was a root cellar—a cool, moist area of the basement where folks stored bins of home-grown apples, onions, potatoes, carrots, cabbages, and other long-keeping staples. If your basement has a damp corner, you might want to try this yourself. (I've always fantasized about having a root cellar, so you can imagine how jealous I was when my friend Delilah bought her house and there was a big one in a separate room in the basement!) If the idea appeals to you, the classic book on root cellar-ing is Mike and Nancy Bubel's *Root Cellaring*. It's no longer in print, but you can look for it used on www.amazon.com, www.barnesandnoble.com, and other bookselling Web sites.

Build a bomb shelter. Duct tape and plastic, anyone? Those Cold War–era basement bomb shelters don't seem so farfetched in today's post-9/11 world. They don't take up much space, and you can always use them to store staples. But if you do, remember the three rules of long-term food storage: 1. Make sure what you buy will keep. 2. Don't buy what your family won't eat. 3. Rotate your stored food (which means, go down there, bring it up to the kitchen, cook it, and replace what you took out of the basement on a regular basis). And don't forget to store water!

Can you believe you've made it out of the basement alive? Congratulations! Now it's time to take on the biggest clutter-catcher of all (except, possibly, the garage)—the attic.

5-Minute Fixes for Attics and Basements

Save the art and photos. Art and photos don't belong in attics and basements, where they'll be exposed to temperature swings, dampness, and possible pest problems. Get them out of there! And once you've gotten them out, go through the art and see what you really want to keep. As for dealing with photos, turn to Photo Finish on page 450 for tips on conquering photo clutter.

Kick the cobwebs. Wrap an old rag around the head of your broom and make a clean sweep of the cobwebs cluttering your basement and attic. You'll start to feel better the minute they're gone, and the room will look bigger and brighter, too.

Throw out the trash. Take a quick survey of your attic or basement and see what's in there that's obviously trash. Pitch the rusty nails, the moldering box of wrapping paper, the moth- or mouse-eaten blanket, and the stack of decomposing newspaper someone forgot to put out for recycling.

Clear the walks. If there are no clear paths through the basement or attic, or the stairs and the area around the stairs are blocked, clear them first for safety's sake. Even if you have to temporarily put stuff down in another part of the room, you really *must* make the area navigable or you'll never succeed in clearing the clutter. After all, you can't clean it if you can't reach it!

Take five. Fast, grab five things in your attic or basement that you can take to the thrift store. Duplicates, old toys, an appliance or piece of furniture that's past its prime—take them to the car right now. It's a start!

PRIORITIES FOR ATTICS

I think attics can be the most eccentric, individualistic areas in the whole house. They can be wonderful or just bizarre. (In my house, the previous owners built their addition over the roof of the original summer cottage, so the original roof comes up through the attic floor!) But attics can also be repositories for generations of castoffs and other clutter that's exiled there to die slowly in obscurity, like Mrs. Rochester in *Jane Eyre*.

If you have structural problems in your attic such as leaks or a lack of insulation, deal with them first. If your attic overheats, add vents and an automatic fan that comes on (and opens the vents) when the thermostat directs it to. If you have exposed ceiling joists instead of a safe, solid floor, install flooring or at least put down heavy plywood sheets (and insulate under them). Make sure your stair or pull-down ladder is secure and will take not just your weight, but your weight hauling up heavy stuff, and make sure it has a secure, weight-bearing railing or banister so you can steady yourself while climbing it. Install plenty of lights so you can see into every corner, and keep a flashlight handy on a wall or shelf where you can reach it fast if the power fails.

Get an exterminator or wildlife specialist to come and remove any lurking critters, be they squirrels, bats, pigeons, mice, snakes, or ominous spiders. (My friend Edith had a raccoon—a very large, very angry raccoon—trapped in her attic at one point, and my sister Liz had a very large, very stinky opossum crawl into her attic and die. Don't let this happen to you!) You want your attic to be a safe, dry, well-lit place in which to store your stuff.

Once you have dealt with any basic problems, you can start your attic de-cluttering process by setting some clutter-kicking priorities. To do that, focus first on what matters most to you about the way your attic looks and functions and take a good, hard look at the "before" state of the room. Then you'll go on to visualize the "after"—how you want the attic to look when all the clutter's gone. Then you can set your priorities.

An Attic Visualization

To get to your "after," you need to start with the "before"—the way things look right now. So get out some paper, or use the "My Attic—Before" form (or make a photocopy of it and write on that). Write down every place in the attic where there's clutter, and note what that clutter is. Be frank here—you may have no idea what's in some or even most of the boxes up there. Note those areas for special attention later. Can you see where you're going? Is the roof cracking you in the skull unless you stand right in the center of the attic? Can you get to everything— or anything? Put it all down.

Once you've taken an inventory of your attic's cluttered "before" state, it's time to move on to the "after"—how you want the room to look when you've kicked the clutter. Write it all down on a piece of paper, or in the "My Attic—After" form

My Attic—Before

_____
_____
_____
_____
_____
_____
_____
_____
_____
_____

My Attic—After

_____
_____
_____
_____
_____
_____
_____
_____
_____
_____

(or on as many photocopies of it as you need to do it justice). To make sure you're being realistic, look at the room every few minutes while you're doing this.

Your description can be short and to the point: "I want to be able to see where I'm going. I don't want to run into cobwebs. I want to have clear paths so I can actually get to everything. I want sturdier storage boxes. I want to be able to find the Christmas ornaments without looking for an hour. I want to use the space under the eaves."

Or you can create a detailed picture of exactly how you'd like your attic to look if it were perfect (for you). You can picture the lighting, types of storage containers, built-in shelves and cabinets—everything.

Getting There

Now that you've captured your attic's "before" condition, listing all the specific clutter issues, and you've imagined its "after" appearance, you can finally prioritize the steps you'll need to take to get there from here. Again, bearing both "before" and "after" in mind, start with what bothers you most about the "before" condition and make that your top priority. Then order the other items on your list.

If it's the clog of clutter—no clear path through the piles—that's driving you

My Attic Priority List

_____

_____

_____

_____

_____

_____

_____

_____

crazy, list that first. Or maybe it's the dust that's coating all the broken-down furniture and giving it a ghostly (or just ghastly) air. Or maybe it's the disintegrating boxes and trunks of old clothes. Or your grown kids' "priceless" possessions that they don't want but don't want you to toss.

Write down whatever's driving you to distraction on the "My Attic Priority List" (or photocopy it, if you'd prefer) in descending order from most to least maddening. Now you have your priorities straight! Once you've finished, you can turn to the tips below to find ingenious ways of dealing with your attic's clutter problems.

THE ATTIC TIPS

Come back from Neverland. First, look at what you can actually see and identify—the stuff like furniture that's *not* in boxes. Then ask yourself what it's doing there. Did you save all your kids' baby furniture, strollers, bassinettes, and so on for *their* kids? Well, get a grip. A lot of that stuff's no longer considered safe, and a lot of parents have objections to using grimy attic relics in their babies' rooms. If you have a real heirloom—say, a baby rocker that's been used by six generations of your family or a Victorian wicker stroller—see who wants it. They can display it even if they don't actually use it and so, for that matter, can you. Ask around and see if any of the kids want any of the rest of the stuff—with the stipulation that if they want it, they have to come get it *now*. Otherwise, donate it, take it to a kids' consignment shop, or trash it.

Fix it or toss it. Still checking out the furniture, see if you have any broken (or just broken-down) chairs, lamps, and other furnishings lying around up there. If you do and you want them *and can use them,* get them repaired now. Otherwise, toss them.

Just say no to other people's boxes, part one. If you have boxes of your grown kids' clothes, toys, sports equipment, or high school yearbooks taking up space in the attic, invite each child to come over and sort through his or her stuff. (Remember how I told you about Diane (see page 11), who hauled all her kids' boxes and other clutter down from the attic to the guest bedroom and gave them 2 weeks to come and get it? Great idea!) Have a plan in place to donate, sell, or trash what they don't want, and make sure some or all of those things happen before they leave. Naturally, they can take their stuff and sell it themselves if they want. The point is to get it out of *your* house.

Just say no to other people's boxes, part two. Are Great-Aunt Ethel's alligator suitcases moldering in your attic? Do you still have a pile of unwanted wedding presents up there in their original boxes? Did you inherit Grandma's hideous china, and is it tucked away in yet another box in the attic? When you helped your parents move to a retirement home, did all of their stuff also move—right into your attic? It's time to say good-bye. It's your house, and it's your space. It's time to keep what *you* want. Here's how:

- ❏ Go through the stuff, and make "Keep It," "Shop It," "Sell It," "Donate It," and "Toss It" piles.
- ❏ If you put something in the "Keep It" pile, make sure you have a good reason. Is there someplace in your house you could use it? Can it replace a less-good appliance or piece of furniture you're using now? (And no, you should not then turn around and put *your* stuff in the attic!)
- ❏ The "Shop It" pile is for stuff you think other family members and friends might be interested in. Ask them, and if you don't find a taker, move that piece into the sell, donate, or toss pile.
- ❏ And then do it! Get that stuff out. Put it out for the trash. Call a hauler to take it away. Make a trip (or several) to Goodwill or the Salvation Army or the Society of St. Vincent de Paul. Drop by an eBay store, consignment shop, or antiques store. (They'd probably love Aunt Ethel's suitcases.)
- ❏ You don't have to do it all at once—this is potentially a Herculean task! But do a little each day or each weekend. Keep at it until it's all gone. If the job starts to seem overwhelming, stop, take a break, and focus on what you'll be able to do with all that space. Then go back in an hour or a day or a week and pick up where you left off.

Just say no to unfinished projects. Recently, my father presented me (with great ceremony, I might add) with a large box. Inside was an unfinished cross-stitch quilt that my grandmother had worked on perhaps 40 years ago. Now, my grandmother made a number of lovely cross-stitch quilts in her day, but I think she gave up on this one because it was so ugly. And it was also stained from its long life in storage. Perhaps you have a few projects of your own that fall into this category, all sitting in the attic waiting for that mythical rainy day. Or half a wall is taken up with your kids' ancient science projects. Or your Uncle Max's attempts at woodworking, or the model car kits your spouse collected when he was 12 but somehow never managed to put together (or throw out). You know how it goes. Now it's time for that stuff to go. If somebody wants one of the projects, they have to take it. Away. (Preferably far, far away.) And if it's a project you or said spouse really want to take up again, take it up—somewhere out of the attic. If you take it to your work-room or garage and it just sits there, you'll know it really is time to say good-bye.

Consolidate the kid stuff. This time I'm not talking about the stuff your kids dumped on you—I'm talking about the boxes of baby clothes, stuffed animals, school art, and the like that you kept because you couldn't bear to throw it out. Sweet memories are made of this! But you can keep the memories without keeping all the stuff. Make a video for each kid, showing each item and recording your memories of the happy times they bring to mind. Or photograph them and make a scrapbook for each child, including swatches of clothes and samples of art, school papers, and so on. Or make baby quilts for the grandchildren out of scraps of beloved baby outfits, blankets, and so forth. Get out the digital camera and record it all on a CD for each kid. Or pick a piece or two of each child's art that you'd like to frame and display somewhere in the house, then ask them to sort through the rest and choose what they want to take. Don't feel guilty! It's theirs, after all. And you'll still have the memories!

Stash what you can't trash. When you're de-cluttering the lower floors, you may find things you just can't bring yourself to part with, even though you can't find a place or think of a good use for them. Hey, that was Aunt Tillie's cameo! Put them in a "Review" box, label and date it, and tuck it in the attic. Then review it—check out what's in there once a year. If several years go by and nothing's migrated from the box back into the house, it's time for it to go. This is also a good way to wean kids (including rather large kids) from toys and other things they've outgrown. Move the stuff into the attic in a labeled box, either with their cooperation if they're eager for more space in their rooms or clandestinely if they're still clinging like grim death to toys or accessories they haven't actually played with in 6 months. If you don't hear any kicking and screaming for a year, get rid of it.

Clear out the clothes. A warm, dry attic is a fine place to store clothes, as long as they're well protected from moths and other hazards. But what if your attic is packed with boxes of moldering clothes—Grandpa's fine wool suits that were "too good to throw out," your college jeans and bikinis that you're sure you'll wear again, Tammy's high school outfits, your too big/too small clothes? Wake up and smell the mildew! Storing off-season clothes in the attic is one thing. Storing really sentimental clothes—your wedding dress (or your mother's), a Flapper outfit that belonged to your great-grandmother, your husband's uniform from his glory days as a high school quarterback, your daughter's christening gown, your mom's coolest tie-dyed shirt and hand-embroidered hippie jeans—is fine, as long as they're properly stored and there aren't dozens of them. But take stock of all the too big/too small/too torn/too stained/whose was this?/out of style clothes, and chuck them. If they're still wearable, donate them. If they're classics, like Gunne Saxe dresses from the seventies or original Diane von Furstenberg wrap dresses, take them to an eBay store or vintage clothing store. (As long as they're in good shape.) You'll finally have room for the clothes you need to put up there!

Store clothes with care. Let's assume that you have kicked all the old, moldy, unsuitable clothes out of the attic and are ready to put the still-good, still-in-style, still-the-right-size clothes back in. If you have lots of clothes and other hangables, you can put up a clothes rod in the attic (where it's accessible but no one will crack their head on it); otherwise, choose a rolling clothes rack (or two). Put clothes in heavy-duty plastic zipper bags with cedar inserts and hang them up.

Box your clothes. You can also box up out-of-season clothes like corduroy pants, sweaters, turtlenecks, hats, gloves, and so on—things that will still look good and keep their shape after being folded for a whole season—and store them in plastic storage boxes with tight-fitting tops. No toxic mothballs, please! Store them with cedar or lavender sachets to keep them smelling fresh. Label each box and stash them on sturdy shelves or under the eaves (as long as you can get to them easily and it doesn't get damp and humid under there).

Box the kids' clothes. If you have growing kids and want to keep their best clothes around to hand down to the younger ones, box those items the same way you'd box your own out-of-season stuff, but sort it by age or size. Label each box with the contents and appropriate age or size, and store it securely away.

Watch out for mice! If you have problems with mice and squirrels getting into your attic, be extra-careful about storing clothes up there. Mice in particular can get into the smallest opening, and squirrels are ferocious chewers. You don't want

My friend Skye Alexander is a wonderful artist, as well as a mystery writer, feng shui master, interior designer, and clutter-control expert. (And I'm sure she can do lots of other things I don't even know about!) So you can trust her when she says that the attic is no place to store photos, paintings, and other artwork. Anywhere it's damp or there are temperature swings can be very bad news for paper and canvas—not to mention what's on it. So keep your art, including art photos, in a climate-controlled closet when you're not displaying it in the house. (We'll talk more about family photos on page 450.) And take Skye's advice to store artwork upright rather than stacked flat. She recommends putting each piece between sheets of acid-free paper and then taping foam boards on each side to prevent damage and breakage. But then how do you know what's in there? Skye takes a photo of each piece and tapes it to the foam board.

to go up in the fall and find that your lovely sweaters have been making a family of baby mice or squirrels very comfortable all summer! If your attic has pest issues, heavy-duty hanging plastic zipper bags are probably a better choice than plastic boxes. Better yet, store your clothes, paperwork, and other temptations downstairs and put less-perishable items in the attic.

Add some storage. Too often, attics are nothing more than open rooms piled with boxes. Putting in wall-to-wall shelving, old dressers, and other storage options will really help you make the most of your space.

Don't let yourself be limited. I actually have recurring dreams about exploring wonderful, endless attics full of hidden treasures. An attic can be a wonderful space! When my friend Fern bought a twin home in Emmaus, Pennsylvania, she found that the previous owners had converted the attic into a fabulous bedroom and playroom for their two sons. I saw this transformed space—with lots of built-ins, good lighting, and color—and was incredibly inspired. If you buy an old home, you may find that the attic was divided into rooms for maids or a nursery for the children of the family. Individual rooms are always full of possibilities! I'm reminded of Jo March, the heroine of the children's classic *Little Women*, who turned her family's attic into her secret retreat and writing studio. Look at your attic space with fresh eyes, and you may be amazed by what you can do with it!

Don't overfill the attic. This is probably the most important tip in the whole chapter: Do *not* overstuff your attic! Make sure there are roomy corridors running both the length and, periodically, the width of your attic so you can not only see what's in there, but you can also get to it easily. The whole point of kicking out your clutter is to make it easy to get the most from your space.

The Ornament Issue

One thing that usually finds it way into (and, hopefully, back out of) the attic is the avalanche of holiday ornaments and paraphernalia that's become an intrinsic part of the season. With the ever-increasing popularity of faux Christmas trees, wreaths, and swags, there's a lot more to store than the ornaments and stockings. And that's just the indoor decorations!

Where I live, every year brings more elaborate displays to neighborhood yards. Outdoor lights, net lights, rope lights, and icicles; illuminated reindeer, giant candles, candies, elves, Santas, Rudolphs, and crèches; entire sleds, complete with a full team of reindeer and Santa in the driver's seat, perched on top of roofs; and now, those gigantic inflatable snow globes, Grinches, snowmen, polar bears . . . yikes!

Fortunately, along with all the stuff has come a range of sensible storage options. You're no longer limited to wrapping up ornaments and putting them in cardboard boxes or storing the tree in a big plastic garbage bag. (Though both of these options still work.) Read on for better storage solutions.

Decorate it once. My friend Delilah gets a real tree for Christmas, but she has the most gorgeous faux swagging for her fireplace and banister I've ever seen, with beautiful tiny amber lights and red, gold, and silver ornaments that exactly match the decorations and lights on her live tree. How do they look so perfect? Ever-ingenious, Delilah and her boyfriend, Chaz, decorated the swags and railing greenery *once*. Since then, they've carefully wrapped each piece—lights, ornaments, and all—and tucked it away in the attic at the end of each season. And there it sits, perfectly decorated, until the following season. All they have to do is unwrap the swags, attach them to the mantel and railing, and voilà!

Store extra bulbs in a box. Keep a collection of replacement bulbs for all those light strings and ornaments in a labeled plastic box with the rest of the Christmas ornaments, so they're at hand when you need them.

Ditto for hooks. Give ornament hooks their own labeled, lidded box. When you bring everything down from the attic, you'll be able to see at a glance if you have enough or need more.

Roll up the lights. You're probably familiar with those garden hose rollers that keep hoses wound neatly around a cylinder and prevent kinking. But did you know they're available for holiday lights, too? Each compact (just 8½- to 10½-inch) Wrap-N-Roll reel holds two or three 100-bulb minilight strands, two 150-bulb icicle light strings, or one 50-foot extension cord. They're sold in sets of four, and you can buy a convenient nylon storage bag to keep your rolled-up lights safe and dust-free in the attic when they're not in use. Say good-bye to tangled lights! Look for them at Christmas shops and catalogs like Solutions and Improvements (see page 48).

Bag the tree. No, I don't mean a body bag like the kind sold for disposing of poor live trees. (It still practically makes me cry to see once-beloved real trees tossed out for the trash.) Instead, buy a suitcase-quality padded poly bag to hold your faux tree from year to year. It's water- and stain-resistant, with plenty of carrying handles to make the trip to the attic easier. Some of them are like long duffel bags and others have wheels to help you roll them to their final resting place. They also have wall hooks, so you can use your attic floor space for other things. They're designed to hold trees up to 7½ feet tall. Look for them in Christmas shops or catalogs like Improvements (see page 48).

Bag the wreath. If you have a faux wreath, you can buy a cylindrical padded bag for it to match the one for your tree and lights, from the same source. A convenient feature of these storage bags is that—in addition to protecting your Christmas adornments from dust and damage—they all match, so you can find all your decorations in seconds.

Bag the big stuff. Sure enough, there are even padded poly holders for all those outdoor ornaments like the inflatable snowmen and the lit-up wire-and-twig ornaments, giant candy canes, and reindeer. Look at your local Christmas store or a catalog like Improvements (see page 48) for a variety of sizes and shapes.

Buy an ornament box (or two). I still store my Christmas ornaments—and trust me, I have zillions, including fragile breakables and heirlooms—in tissue or their original boxes inside labeled copy-paper boxes. Shame on me! There's no excuse now not to buy plastic or padded storage containers designed expressly to protect

Christmas ornaments. They have individual compartments for up to 60 ornaments, or partitions for big ornaments like those Santa and moose statuettes you just had to buy. The rigid plastic boxes are stackable, with handles for easy storage; the cushioned boxes store ornaments just as you would fine china. If, like my mother, you have several themed trees, you can label each box with the kind of ornaments and which tree they are for. And, of course, you can store them with their hooks still attached, since they'll be safe from entanglement with other ornaments. What a time-saver! Look for ornament cases at your local Christmas shop or in catalogs like Solutions or Improvements (see page 48).

Or put them in cardboard. Linda Cobb, the Queen of Clean, advises against storing ornaments in plastic and comes down squarely in the cardboard-box camp. She's concerned about moisture buildup ruining ornaments, not to mention mold and mildew. Gee! Maybe I'm not as big a slacker as I thought.

Store stuff by season. If you love decorating for every holiday, as everyone does in my part of Pennsylvania, you'll appreciate this tip from clutter-control expert Skye Alexander: Store all your decorations by season. Keep separate labeled boxes for Valentine's Day, St. Patrick's Day, Easter, the Fourth of July, Halloween, Thanksgiving, Christmas or Hanukkah, and so on. Skye recommends storing the boxes chronologically in the attic so they're supereasy to find.

Store eggs in the carton. I had to mention this because I collect Easter eggs—everything from traditional Ukrainian pysanky (wax-resist eggs) and Colonial-era dyed-onionskin eggs with pin-scratched designs to my Araucana hen's naturally robin's-egg-blue eggs and eggs I've watercolored myself. If you keep Easter eggs—mind you, not the hard-boiled kind!—keep them safe in egg cartons stored in a labeled cardboard box. If the cartons don't fit tightly, pad them with tissue, crumpled newspaper, or bubble wrap for a snug fit, and tape the lid.

ONWARD!

Whew! We've tackled the whole house now. Congratulations! Take a break, and reward yourself with something wonderful. Now . . . are you ready to take on the great outdoors? In the next section, you'll find clutter-kicking tips for decks, porches, patios, the garage, and, of course, the yard and garden. Let's take a walk outside.

PART THREE

Clutter-Kicking Outside the House

Chapter 14

Clear the Decks!

(AND THE PORCHES, PATIOS, AND DOORSTEPS)

That outdoor kitchen seemed like a great idea. But now there's no room for anyone to walk out there, much less sit on the deck or patio and enjoy a meal. Pots of plants are all over the place; decaying furniture and boots, volleyballs, and other outdoor gear have taken over the porch. And the pileup of umbrellas, backpacks, roller blades, and racquets has made doorsteps walks of shame. Save these great outdoor living spaces with the wealth of clutter-kicking tips and techniques in this chapter.

PRIORITIES FOR DECKS, PORCHES, PATIOS, AND DOORSTEPS

Decks, porches, and patios are wonderful "outdoor rooms"—extensions of your living space into the outdoors. Few things are as enjoyable as sitting in a porch swing, enjoying a meal hot off the grill on the deck, or sitting around the patio fire pit on a crisp night with friends. But unfortunately, these are all spaces that lend themselves to clutter accumulation. And few things are as trashy looking as a porch crammed with so much battered furniture and other family detritus that it looks like it's ready for an estate sale, or a deck or patio littered with tricycles, playground balls, baseball bats, toy trucks, rusting or collapsing lawn furniture, half-dead plants, and overturned pet food bowls. Then there are the doorsteps—the entries to your home. Do they say "welcome" or "watch your step"? (Or even, "abandon all hope, ye who enter here"?)

As you did inside the house, start your de-cluttering process by setting some clutter-kicking priorities. Before you can establish your priorities, you need to focus on what matters most to you about the way your deck, porch, patio, and doorsteps look. The best way to do this is to take a good, hard look at the "before" state of the space. Then you can go on to visualize its "after" condition.

A Deck/Porch/Patio/Doorstep Visualization

To get to your "after," you need to start with the "before"—the way things look right now. So get out some paper, or use the "My Deck/Porch/Patio/Doorstep—Before" form (or make a photocopy of it and write on that). Write down every place there's clutter, and note what that clutter is—a sagging lounge chair, a rusted wrought-iron table, a broken planter. I'm giving you only one form here, but it has enough space for you to note down the current state of the deck, porch, patio, and doorsteps. Mercifully, it shouldn't take but a minute or two to size up the present state of any of them.

Once you've taken an inventory of your deck, porch, patio, or doorstep's "before" state, it's time to move on to the "after"—how you want the space to look when you've kicked the clutter. Write it all down on a piece of paper, or in the "My Deck/Porch/Patio/Doorstep—After" form, or on as many photocopies of it as you need to do it justice. To make sure you're being realistic, look at the area every few minutes while you're creating your description.

Your description can be short and to the point: "I'd like to have a place to put the grill when we're not using it. I'd like to be able to walk easily across the porch. I'd like to be able to use the deck year-round. I'd like to make the front doorsteps look welcoming, not junky."

If you're more ambitious, you can envision a more detailed picture of exactly how you'd like your deck, porch, patio, and doorsteps to look if they were perfect (for you). Picture the layout of the space. If it's a patio, what would the surface be?

My Deck/Porch/Patio/Doorstep—Before

_____

_____

_____

_____

_____

_____

_____

My Deck/Porch/Patio/Doorstep—After

_____

_____

_____

_____

_____

_____

_____

_____

```
╔══════════════════════════════════════════════╗
║                                                ║
║   My Deck/Porch/Patio/Doorstep Priority List   ║
║   _____  ║
║   _____  ║
║   _____  ║
║   _____  ║
║   _____  ║
║   _____  ║
║   _____  ║
║   _____  ║
║   _____  ║
║   _____  ║
║   _____  ║
║                                                ║
╚══════════════════════════════════════════════╝
```

Does the deck have railings, multiple levels, a built-in hot tub? Is the porch screened in or enclosed? What furniture and accessories are in the space? What are the doorsteps made of, and what is the color and design of the door? Is there a lighted path leading to it? Are there plants? Write down everything.

Getting There

Now that you have captured your deck, porch, patio, and doorstep's "before" condition, listing all the specifics, and you've imagined their "after" appearance, you can finally prioritize the steps you'll need to take to get there from here. Again, bearing both "before" and "after" in mind, start with what bothers you most about the "before" condition—that will become your top clutter-kicking priority. Then rank the clutter issues in descending order of importance.

Maybe you have been using the same battered hand-me-down porch furniture since you got married and would like to graduate to a lovely matched wicker set. Or the cracked, stained, too-small surface of your patio makes you ashamed to

5-Minute Fixes for Decks, Porches, Patios, and Doorsteps

Bring on the blooms. Few things make a better impression than a couple of large pots of blooming plants. Set them on either side of the front door (after clearing off any toys, dog bones, and newspapers) or the deck door, at the entrance to the patio or on the patio tables, or on either side of the porch door or in front of the porch windows.

But clean up the pots. If you have broken pots, spilled potting soil, dying plants, or dropped leaves or flowers on your deck, patio, or porch, clean up the mess for an instant improvement.

Clean off one table. Pick one table on the porch, deck, or patio, and clear off the clutter. Then give the surface a quick wipe-down and put a centerpiece on the table—fresh flowers, an attractive bowl, some candles. See how much better the area looks already!

Put out a magazine rack. Corral magazines, catalogs, and papers in an attractive magazine rack by the seating area on your porch, patio, or deck. (Just remember to move it to safety when it rains!)

Pick up sticks. One fast way to kick the clutter and improve your outdoor living spaces is to pick up any fallen branches, twigs, and leaves on or around your doorsteps, deck, patio, or porch. While you're out there, deal with fallen nuts, fruits or berries, and flowers, too.

---

invite guests out there. Or you'd like some plants on the deck and need a safe place to display them where the dog and kids can't knock them over. Or you'd like to finally do something about your overgrown foundation shrubs so the family can use the front door again.

Note down whatever's driving you to distraction on the "My Deck/Porch/Patio/Doorstep Priority List" (or photocopy it, if you'd prefer) in descending order from most to least maddening. Now you have your priorities straight! Once you've finished your priority list, you can turn to the tips beginning on page 296 to find ingenious ways of dealing with each problem.

THE DECK, PORCH, PATIO, AND DOORSTEP TIPS

Because decks and patios, porches, and doorsteps each have their own challenges, I'm going to group the tips for each one so you can find the one that interests you without having to look through every tip in the chapter. But because decks and patios share so many functions, I'm going to combine their tips together. And I'm going to give you the doorstep tips first because that's usually the first close-up view people have of your house. Let's get started!

Doorsteps

Like the front yard (and I will have plenty to say about that in Chapter 16), the door where guests arrive—usually but not always the front door—sets their expectations for what they'll find inside your home. It also gives them a few impressions about you! Make sure they're good impressions by creating an attractive, inviting doorstep. Some of these tips may not seem at first glance to be about clutter, but I believe that the approach to the front door, if it's well maintained, clutter free, and attractively lit and planted, practically screams, "This is an organized, on-top-of-things household!"

Make it easy to arrive. Is there a clear (and cleared) path to your door? Does it have in-ground lighting so people can navigate at night? Is it paved, and if so, is the surface even, or are bricks or concrete edges sticking up? Are the bricks or concrete chipped or cracked? Are stepping stones smooth and secure in the ground? If it's a mulch path, is the mulch clean and thick, or weedy and uneven? If it's a grass path, is it neatly mowed and raked? Help people reach your door easily and safely with a smooth, uncluttered path.

Put out the welcome mat. Okay, you loved the "Warning: Dog Can't Hold Its Licker" mat when you saw it in the catalog. But now it's faded and dilapidated, creating visual clutter. And it never looked quite right with your Colonial home, anyway. Make sure your doormat is clean, new, and functional (especially if you want your floor to be clean once people walk in!). Replace it regularly. A simple doormat will go with any style of home and will encourage people to look at your house, not at the ground. If you just love a doormat with a funny message, why not put it by the back door? Or do what I do when I'm tempted by one of those humorous sayings catalogs offer on doormats, pillows, and plaques: Tear the page out of the catalog and keep it in a "Humor" file. Flipping through the file will always cheer you up without cluttering your home. (I keep favorite funny greeting cards and cartoons in the file, as well. It's so much fun to pull it out and page through it when I need to laugh out loud!)

Watch the steps. There's nothing like stained, cracked, sagging, or broken steps to give people that Bates Motel feeling as they approach your home. Why not just hang a big "Condemned" sign on the door and get it over with? Of course replacing steps or a stoop is a huge pain. But it's nothing compared to the cost of a lawsuit if someone falls and gets hurt on the way to your door. And just think of how much better it will feel to arrive at a welcoming entrance when you get home! It's too easy to stop seeing things when you see them all the time (just ask your spouse what outfit you were wearing yesterday). Get a fresh perspective by approaching your door as if you were a realtor planning to sell the house. *Now* what do you see?

Paint the door. If your door is falling apart or the paint is peeling off, that's the first impression people will have of you and your home. And some doors are just plain ugly. You may have disliked your door from the moment you bought the house but just never got around to doing anything about it. Get a door you love, paint it a color you love, and suddenly coming home will feel better than ever!

Clean the door. My friend Anne points out that a dirty front door—especially one painted a light color—looks messy. Clean the doors, and the windows in them, when they look dirty—screen doors and storm doors included.

Light the door. In addition to lighting the way to the door, make sure the door itself is well but not blindingly lit at night. Not only will this make guests feel welcome and get them safely down the path, it will save you time and aggravation groping for your keys (and then the lock) in the dark!

Ring a bell. Help people alert you to their arrival by making sure you have some sort of bell, knocker, or other device in place; that it's easy to see and use; that it's attractive (if it's a knocker); and that you can actually hear it throughout the house and out in the backyard.

Clear the way. Trikes on the path. Sports equipment at the door. Umbrellas. Shoes. Trash bags (God forbid). All kinds of stuff can materialize in front of doors, on the path to the door, and on the doorsteps. After a while, nobody even sees it—except people who are tripping over it on their way to see you. Get everything out of the way and contained somewhere else—boots and shoes on a shoe mat, umbrellas in a stand, sports equipment in the garage or hall closet, and so on—and make sure they're inside, not outside, the door.

Fix the foundation. A cracked, stained, grimy foundation is every bit as repulsive—though not as dangerous—as cracked, stained, and grimy steps. Seal it and paint it or cover it with low trellising or fencing, but make it look neat and tidy.

Prune the plants. Overgrown foundation plantings are unwelcoming. In fact, they're just plain creepy. Too many homes have contractor-selected plantings that looked good when the house was new but should never have been planted anywhere near a house. Why? Because they get too big, obscuring the windows, crowding the doors, and making the house look dank and neglected. And I don't know which looks worse, foundation plantings that have swallowed the house or sheared-off plantings with rigid rectangular shapes and bare branches exposed everywhere. Ugh! If you don't already have a foundation planting (they were originally created to cover up ugly concrete foundations), think about what your foundation looks like. Is it ugly? If so, select a low-growing evergreen shrub or a mass planting of evergreen ferns, hellebores, and other perennials to conceal it without consuming the house itself. If your foundation is not an eyesore, choose a low bed of evergreen perennials like vinca (periwinkle) and a changing display of flowers—daffodils and tulips in spring, bleeding-hearts and peonies in late spring, daisies and salvias in summer, mums and asters in fall, and so on—will create a lovely display without taking over. The key is to keep the plantings simple and symmetrical. This is *not* the place for a busy mixed garden!

Add a decorative element. Yes, you want to keep the entry to your home clutter free. But that doesn't mean it has to be bare or boring (unless "bare" in your home's case translates as "stately"). I have a pair of handmade wrought-iron "shepherd's crooks" in front of my house, one on either side of the entryway. During the growing season, I hang trailing plants from the hooks; in winter, I set out lanterns and light the candles when I'm expecting guests. A pair of planters, one on each side of the door, would look great as long as they're well composed *and* well maintained. What about statuary? I'd keep that pair of dogs with the baskets in their mouths for the front entry gate. If it suits your home's style and the size of the doorstep, try a single statue at one side.

Give guests the boot. The boot scraper, that is. You can find boot scrapers in hardware and home improvement stores and catalogs like Plow & Hearth (see page 47). Setting or installing one outside the door will not only be a courtesy to your guests, it will help keep mud and snow out of your house.

Decks and Patios

Time spent on the deck or patio should be the most pleasurable, relaxing part of your day. But for too many of us, decks and patios are more like obstacles to be crossed on the way out to the yard—one more unpleasing, unmanageable space. And cluttered decks and patios invite tripping, especially when wet. If you're lucky enough to have a deck or patio, it's time to claim (or reclaim) that space.

Know what you want. Hopefully, if you did the "after" visualization on page 292, you'll have a clear idea of what you really want to do on your deck or patio. Having a plan in mind is the key to a restful, uncluttered deck or patio. Do you want a serene transition between yard and house, with flowering plants, a mini-water garden, and a seating area where you and friends can relax and enjoy your colorful, fragrant surroundings? Do you want an outdoor entertainment center, with a grill and dining area? Or a hot tub and lounge chairs for sunning? Or a place to set up the Ping-Pong table, card table, or puzzle boards? You can achieve any of these goals and a dozen others. But unless you have a really huge space, if you try to achieve more than one of them, you'll probably end up with a cluttered, overwhelming mess. There are ways around this—my friends Delilah and Chaz have a patio for grilling and entertaining that's surrounded by beautifully land-scaped gardens, for example. And my friends Barbara and Peter had a massive wraparound deck that had a seating area with plants on one side of the house and a hot tub on another side of the house. Each area was out of sight of the other and both had plenty of room. But for the most part, the simpler your plan, the less cluttered and more satisfying the results.

Unify the furniture. Your deck or patio will look planned, cared for, and cared about if the furniture matches. You can buy incredible teak, metal, or wicker sets with loveseats, chairs, dining and side tables, huge umbrellas, and more from home stores and catalogs (L.L. Bean, Plow & Hearth, Smith & Hawken, and Orvis are just a few companies with good selections; see pages 46, 47, and 49). But you don't have to go that route to get a unified look. When the wonderful folding wooden rocking chairs I received as a housewarming gift finally bit the dust, I decided to buy those heavy, super-comfortable vintage metal chairs for my deck—the ones with a curved tubular support that, thanks to their ingenious design, rock ever so slightly while you sit in them. I found two at an antiques store and a third at a flea market, and a friend gave me the gift of a round woven-metal table to put with them. So I had three colors and styles of metal furniture. I chose a soft moss-green metal paint and spray-painted them all. That's all it took to bring the group together. Another possibility is to buy matching cushions for your furniture—though if the furniture is made of different materials, this won't be as effective as if the pieces are all, say, wood or wicker.

Don't overdo the cushion patterns. Speaking of cushions, if you choose to put them on your deck or patio furniture, keep them simple. A single color for the cushions with a contrasting color for the throw pillows is pleasing without being busy. Cushions with busy, multicolor floral patterns can quickly become overwhelming, especially if there are lots of them and your deck or patio gets a lot of sun. If you add flowering plants as well as floral cushions, you'll create a whirlwind of visual clutter! Instead, if you'd like to use a floral pattern, use it on the throw pillows and choose a pattern that includes the color of your cushions. There are exceptions: If your deck or patio happens to be very shaded, a floral pattern might help brighten it, and if you have a huge space, patterned cushions will make it seem smaller and more intimate. Stripes are also popular on outdoor cushions, and they form something of a middle ground: You can use striped throw pillows, or have a couple of chairs with striped cushions and solid throw pillows in a group of furniture with solid cushions and striped throw pillows. In either case, the stripes should echo the solid color of the other cushions to unify the grouping and minimize visual clutter. But generally, solid colors work best in modest spaces.

Get some backup. If your deck or patio is a modest size, don't overdo the furniture. Set out as much as you and your family normally use, then get some comfortable folding chairs and tables that you can set out if you have a deck or patio party. Stash the extras in the basement or garage until they're needed. Here's a case where getting extra cushions that match the ones on your permanent deck or patio furniture would really pay off in terms of helping blend the temporary furniture in with the rest.

Organize with accessories. Judiciously placed small tables or cup holders can prevent the clutter of a sea of glasses sitting next to all the chairs on a deck or patio, according to my editor Anne. Just make sure they don't become tripping hazards.

Direct deck traffic. Make sure it's easy to get across your deck or patio and around the various groups of furniture and plants. Guests, kids, and dogs should all be able to move freely around the deck or patio without knocking anything over, hurting themselves, or going up in flames from a too-close encounter with the grill or fire pit.

Don't get busy. Patio surfaces composed of a mosaic of different-colored tiles, busy brick or stone patterns, or combination materials (like brick and stone) create

[Tools of the Trade]

Fire pits—those wonderful metal "bowls" on legs that hold wood for fires—are the greatest outdoor accessory since the grill and the half-barrel water garden. If you have a patio, you can put a fire pit on it and sit around it. Even if you have a deck, you can put the fire pit in the yard where you can watch the flames from the comfort of your deck chairs. (If it's in the yard, make sure you wait for wet grass—like the day after a rain—to light it.) Setting it on a stone slab or fireproof mat like the ones made to go under grills on decks can also help prevent runaway fires. Fire pits come in a wide variety of styles and sizes, from gorgeous hammered copper to basic black, and most have protective screens and grilling racks, too. They're available at home improvement stores and catalogs like Cabela's (see page 49), Improvements (see page 48), and Plow & Hearth (see page 47). (Plow & Hearth even has a propane-fired model that they recommend for safe on-deck use.) Or you might like to have a chiminea instead of a fire pit—they look like ceramic potbellied stoves on short legs, with a tall chimney to vent the smoke. They're widely available at garden centers and home stores.

But I'm not just recommending fire pits because they look wonderful and it's fun to sit around a fire. They are phenomenal outdoor clutter-controllers. I don't know about you, but my worst yard clutter issue (besides weeds!) is falling twigs and branches. Every wind, every storm, every *day* I'm out there playing pickup sticks. With the fire pit, I can toss them in until it's full, then enjoy a lovely fire and start again. Paper grocery bags, crumpled newspapers, and other uncoated trash paper make ideal fire-starters, so the fire pit helps control that clutter pileup, too. Try one—you'll love it!

visual clutter. They aren't restful. The same could be said of decks that are made of crosshatched wood patterns like a parquet floor. Keep the surface simple, and make the focus of attention what you put on it (or can see from it), rather than making it compete for attention.

Watch the weeds. My mother had a thing for brick patios, and we had one at both my childhood homes. A brick patio is beautiful to look at, but she favored the kind where the bricks were tamped into sand rather than mortared, and as a result, I spent my childhood summers pulling weeds. If you've ever tried to pull a billion tiny but obstinate weeds out of hard-packed sand, I'll bet *you* don't have a sand-based patio! I know I wouldn't. This doesn't mean that you should dump toxic chemicals on your patio to kill the weeds (God forbid—think of your poor kids and pets, if not yourself, your spouse, and guests!), but it does mean that you should consider your patio surface carefully. A weed-covered patio looks cluttered and chaotic. Whether you're laying brick or stone, when it comes to patios, concrete is your friend. And well-maintained concrete (which can now be stained, painted, and even stamped to look like stone) is a low-maintenance, weed-free option. If you do want bricks or pavers in sand, install a weed barrier fabric first. It won't last forever, but it will help.

Unify your plants. A billion little pots of individual plants crammed around your deck or patio is a study in visual clutter—take it from one who knows. But it's great to have the color, fragrance, and softening effect that plants can bring to a deck or patio. To have your plants without the clutter, use the same style of container and plant large pots or planters with multiple plants, or buy them already planted from your local nursery or garden center. (As with the furniture, the pots don't have to be identical; you can have some plain and some patterned, for example, as long as they are all terra cotta, or different colors and even shapes if they are all from the same pottery and the glaze is the same type.) And limit the number of pots you set out—a group of three or one large pot in two corners and one as a centerpiece on the table is probably plenty for a small deck or patio.

Group pots together. If you're a plant collector or you just want to have lots of individual pots, group them on tiered shelves or other multilevel stands to keep them all together. Not only does this look less cluttered, you also get better visual impact that way.

Raise up the plants. If you have kids or pets crashing around your deck or patio, or you need all the "floor" space you can get, you can still enjoy beautiful plants. Just grow them off the ground. Hanging baskets with beautiful trailing plants, window boxes, or baskets or planters that are designed to sit on or hang over the deck railing (Kinsman Company, page 49, specializes in English-style moss-lined wire baskets) are all great options.

Protect your deck. If you have plants on your deck, make sure you have sturdy plastic or glazed ceramic saucers under them to prevent water leaks and the hideous rings they make on deck surfaces. (Check any garden center to find strong terra-cotta-colored plastic saucers with nice high sides to go with your real terra-cotta pots.)

Care for your plants. While few things are as lovely as well-grown plants, practically nothing's as unattractive as brown, dying plants or an overgrown jungle of neglected plants. If you choose to grow plants on your deck or patio, make a commitment to groom, water, and feed them as needed to keep them looking and blooming their best. Cut off dead flowers and any dead leaves and stems regularly. Let your plants be a feature, not an eyesore.

Keep your eye on the ball. This seems like simple common sense, but I've seen enough disasters in this area that I'll mention it anyway, so bear with me. Do not site a basketball hoop, volleyball net, driving range, or anything else involving projectiles where they could crash into the stuff (or people) on your deck or patio. If you already have a sports area that's too close for comfort, it's easier to move the hoop or net than the deck or patio, so do it before you're sorry you didn't!

Add a privacy screen. Sometimes you buy a house with a deck or patio looking right out on the road, into the neighbor's yard, or—gasp—at the McDonald's and gas station on the corner. (What *were* the former owners thinking?) Or the only place you can put one is where you look out at something you wish you didn't have to see. Your own clutter isn't the only kind around—there's also borrowed clutter, when a busy scene or a bunch of somebody else's stuff intrudes on your visual space. If this is the case at your house, screen out that unsightly view. A tall, dense evergreen hedge makes a great screen, since it also filters out some of the noise and pollution that may drift over from outside. But I suspect that you don't want to wait a few years until the hedge grows up—and hedges tend to be pricey and labor-intensive, to boot. Alternatives include attractive wooden privacy screens (Improvements sells a lovely one; see page 48) and, of course, fencing. One advantage of a screen over fencing is that you can arrange it just around the deck or patio rather than having to fence in the whole yard (or one side of it). Fencing works best when it's used as fencing, not screening, as I know firsthand. One of my neighbors tried to block his view of a busy corner by putting up a small angled section of palisade fence, but rather than looking planned, it just looks like some-one walked off with the rest of it!

Aim for outdoor storage. Wouldn't it be convenient to store your outdoor fur-niture cushions right on your deck or patio? Well, you can, even in the worst winter conditions. But there's a trade-off: You have to store them in plastic. Home improvement stores and catalogs like Improvements (see page 48) sell heavy plastic resin benches with lift-up seats and hefty wheeled "deck boxes" with room to store your cushions, umbrellas, toys, and summer sports equipment. Can't face plastic furniture on your deck or patio? They also sell an attractive cushion storage bag that you can stash in the garage or basement in the off-season. Other good sources for outdoor storage are Frontgate and Plow & Hearth (see pages 46 and 47).

Store your stuff under the big top. Once it's too miserable outside to enjoy your deck or patio, if your furniture and furnishings aren't weatherproof and you don't have room for them in the basement, garage, or tool shed, you can put them in a storage tent. The tents are an unobtrusive gray and are made of weatherproof, triple-layer ripstop polyethylene, just like a real tent. Unlike a camping tent, however, they're made to stay up all season, with ground augers for anchoring, a tubular steel frame, and zippered doors at each end. Set up your tent in a part of the backyard where it will be at least partially hidden from view, and stash your deck or patio furniture, grill, equipment, and even the lawn mower inside. Unlike using individual furniture covers (see "Love It or Lose It?"), consolidating everything under a single cover that's away from the house reduces visual clutter rather than contributing to it. Look for storage tents at home improvement stores, stores that sell lawn furniture, and catalogs like Improvements (see page 48).

Thrill to an uncluttered grill. My friends Delilah and Chaz have the most wonderful outdoor kitchen on their patio, with a huge grill and an elaborate sink, fridge, and counter setup. It would be easy for a kitchen this size to overwhelm the rest of the patio, which they use for entertaining much of the year (at least until freezing weather finally drives them indoors). But they kept that from happening by careful planning—siting the kitchen setup against the wall of the house, where it would be least intrusive, and making all the elements match (the grill, fridge, and sink are all burnished steel). Because they put in lots of counter space, they have big under-counter cabinets where they can store all their outdoor dishes, condiments, and grilling supplies, all out of sight but in easy reach. And the refrigerator also tucks in under the counter so it fits seamlessly with the visual line— grill, sink, counter, and fridge are all the same height.

Put up the grill. It's no thrill to see a grill sitting abandoned through the winter. Around here, I can't get in the car in the winter without seeing grills half-buried under snow. This is *not* good for your grill, and it creates a junkyard effect in your yard. Please, when its season is over, put it away!

Go below deck. If your deck is off the ground and people can see under it, things can get ugly fast. A great-looking deck can be ruined by a bunch of unkempt weeds, half-eaten dog bones, or castoff junk lying under it. Conceal the space with lattice fencing, trellising, or shrubs that will not grow tall, and make sure what can be seen is clean and tidy.

Pet Alert!

If you put food, water, or toys for your pets on the deck or patio, make sure you use sturdy, attractive bowls, since they'll draw the eye, and have a basket or attractive box to stash the toys in when Maggie isn't playing with them. Most important: Do *not* leave food out overnight—at least, not unless you want a clutter of skunks, opossums, raccoons, and rats enjoying the all-you-can-eat buffet outside your door!

Out On the Porch

One of my all-time-favorite memories is of sitting with my grandparents in the porch swing on their open porch. Good times! And I love to see exquisitely designed and furnished porches in decorator magazines and catalogs. Unfortunately, people's porch reality is often more like a clutter nightmare: The porch has sunk out of sight under a mountain of discarded toys, junk furniture, whatsits, dust, and cobwebs. It's become the refuge of stray cats. (I've now known two people whose porches became stray-cat havens.) Between the mice and the spiders, you're afraid to go out on that porch. Reclaiming your porch may require a boot-camp mentality, but it's worth it. Read on to restore your porch from catchall to class act.

Take out the trash. Depending on what's on your porch, gather some trash bags and boxes and clear out everything that doesn't belong there. If it belongs somewhere else in the house, put it aside in a marked box or labeled bag (but in the house, not on the porch), and take it to its rightful home once you've finished with the porch patrol. Put anything you want to donate in a second labeled box or bag, and put everything else in the trash. Now, look at what's left (if you can see it under its shroud of dirt and dust). Ask yourself four questions: Do you like it? Do you want it? Do you need it? Can you replace it? If the answer to the first three is no, and the last one is yes, put it in the appropriate pile. That goes for ugly, battered porch furniture, too. Hose it off and take it to Goodwill or post it on Freecycle (www.freecycle.org) or craigslist (www.craigslist.org). By now, you should have a much smaller pile of porch-related items that will go back out there once they're cleaned up and refurbished.

Clean it up. Once you've emptied out the porch, it's time to clean it up. You can't really see your porch's potential until it's sparkling clean. So bribe the kids, hire a maid service, or just get out the mop and bucket and have at it. When it's empty and clean, take a good look at the space. What does it need? A new coat of bright, light-enhancing white or a soft cream or very pale pastel paint? (Wallpaper is a bad idea on a screen porch!) New screens or windows? A new floor? Better doors? Any TLC you can give your porch now that it's finally shoveled out will enhance your enjoyment every time you're out there from now on. And living space gained is worth some trouble and expense—it's still a lot cheaper than building a new room!

Choose furniture that fits your dreams (and needs). Whether you picture a row of white rockers on the veranda of a great Victorian resort hotel; a cozy, cottage-style arrangement of wicker furniture with chintz cushions and monster Boston ferns; or a porch swing tucked on one side, give yourself a reality check before you start rummaging around through catalogs and at flea markets. Don't forget the "needs" part. If you have kids, that row of white rockers isn't going to do them much good. You can still get a classic white rocker (or two), but make sure you also have kid-friendly furniture and activities planned into your porch's makeover. Try Ikea, L. L. Bean, and Pottery Barn Kids (see pages 46 and 47) for kids' furniture in a variety of styles.

Theme your furniture. As in the case of the deck or patio, your porch will look best if the furniture matches. This doesn't have to be true for all the furniture on the porch—your antique rocker or the kids' play table should absolutely have their place. But a room full of random furniture looks more cluttered than it is, while coordinated furniture makes a room look bigger. Again, it doesn't have to be an exact match—you can have a variety of wicker pieces, for example. But they'll work better if you paint them all the same color or the same intensity of color (all white; or all pale green; or one pale green, one pale blue, and one pale peach, for example) and give them matching cushions. You may recall that I railed against using floral cushions out on the deck or patio, but because of the subdued light and quiet colors of the porch, chintz cushions are not just appropriate, they're also traditional.

Warm it up with rugs. Whether you'd like to cover the entire floor with grass matting or toss some cheerful braided rugs (with nonslip backing, please!) around to contrast with the painted wood floor, your porch will be warmer (both in look and in fact) and more comfortable if you add some floor coverings. But keep them quiet—you want people to look out, not down, when they're on a porch.

Add some acrylic (and light a fire). My friends Delilah and Chaz turned their screen porch into a year-round retreat, thanks to acrylic window panels and a gas fireplace. They had a local window and door shop cut acrylic panels to fit the porch windows, and they had them framed in aluminum. Now when cold weather arrives, they screw the panels on; once it's balmy again, they unscrew them and enjoy the cooling breezes through the porch screens. It's their favorite place to enjoy steaming mugs of coffee or cocoa, curled up on the sofa in front of the comfy blaze of their propane "wood" stove.

Remember that less is more. Don't re-clutter your porch with furniture, games, and other stuff once you've finally cleaned it out. A porch that's open and inviting is a porch you'll want to spend time in. A couple of seating areas with side tables and baskets for magazines, knitting, and other diversions will entice people to bring their breakfasts out to enjoy in the serenity of the porch. Add music if you'd like to hear it in that setting.

Don't overdo the art. "Less is more" applies to art, too. You want people to look out, enjoying the view from the porch, so don't clutter walls and surfaces with art. A couple of pieces on the walls and a single *objet* on a table, or a trio on a shelf, are plenty. Remember: You can always rotate them!

Bring out a bookcase. A low bookcase against the porch's back wall or under the windows will hold books and baskets of magazines, crafts, and necessities like tissues and reading glasses. The top can be used for display or be cushioned as a window seat, depending on its placement.

Bank on a bench. As in your home's entryway or mudroom, one of the storage benches that are widely available in home improvement stores and catalogs is a great porch accessory. These benches have cushions for seating and storage space beneath, usually with woven square or rectangular baskets to hold necessities (from books to toys to outdoor gear, if your porch opens to the outside).

Consider a chest. A blanket chest or vintage trunk (painted to match your furniture) also makes a great porch accessory. Used as a coffee table in front

Dear Claire,

My porch is on the north side of the house, so it's cold. And now it's also dark because, since our house was built, the land next door was developed. Now there's a house right next to the porch, casting shade pretty much all day. My porch reminds me of a refrigerator! Can this porch be saved?

—Chilled

Dear Chilled,

Take your lemon of a porch and make a lemon chiffon pie, dear. If it's a screen porch, glass it in, and put venetian blinds on the side where the other house looms over you. Add plush rugs and an additional source of heat (at least a space heater or two; preferably a gas or electric fireplace) and lots of bright, cheerful light. Warm colors and textile accents will help you feel warm, too. Then add comfortable seating and an entertainment center, and you have a lovely entertainment room.

Good luck,
Claire

of a loveseat, it can hold extra pillows and afghans for those chilly mornings (or evenings) or just to accommodate a soothing nap.

Try a tray. Carrying food and drink back and forth from the kitchen to the porch can be a challenge. If you get a few large wooden or wicker serving trays with comfortable handles, it will not only be easier to carry things around, but you can also set the trays on the table and serve from them without having to take all the dishes off the trays, put them out on the table, and then replace them on the trays when everyone's finished.

Or add a cart. A rolling cart can be a great addition to the porch. You can use it like a portable sideboard, to serve food, or use it to house books, toys, crafts, or anything else you'd like to have out there. Just roll it over when you need it and roll it out of the way when you're done. Carts come in a number of styles, from chrome and glass to wicker and wood, so you should be able to match your room's decor.

Add some life. Because a porch is a transitional area between the indoors and the outdoors, it's a great place for plants and animals. A hanging plant by a window, a cage of cheerful finches, a birdfeeder hanging just outside a window—all can enhance your family's enjoyment of the porch. Of course, the porch has to be enclosed and climate-controlled for birds, and you or your family must be willing to take care of any plants and animals conscientiously. Any hanging plants or cages must be well out of the line of traffic. (And caged birds must be out of reach of the family cat!) And you must resist the urge to clutter the porch with plants and animals—a few choice plants, pleasingly displayed and well cared for, and a single birdcage will be far more effective and aesthetic than a collection. And don't forget your four-legged pets! A cozy dog "nest" or cat bed will give them a place of their own where they can enjoy the porch with you.

ONWARD!

Let's sit a while on our cleaned-out porch, deck, or patio with a glass of iced tea and pat ourselves on the back for a job well done. Rest up now, because it's almost time to tackle that famous cave of clutter . . . the garage. Are you ready? Pull on those dirty sneakers and take a deep breath. (Better take that breath *before* you go in the garage!) Now, let's go!

Chapter 15

Cleaning Out the Garage

What do you mean, the cars go in there? For all too many of us, the garage has turned into just another place to stash our excess stuff. It's like the basement revisited. The garage sale "before." The heap of stolen (and unrecognizable) treasure on which Smaug, the dragon in J. R. R. Tolkien's *The Hobbit,* made his lair. But don't panic—whatever your garage looks like now, in this chapter I'll give you loads of ingenious tips to help you turn it into organized, usable space. I guarantee there's more room in there than you think! So read on to find out how to make the most of garage storage, turn your garage into a multipurpose space, *and* park your cars in there. It's all possible—really!

PRIORITIES FOR GARAGES

Before you start setting priorities, ask yourself what you use your garage for now—and what you'd like to use it for once you've kicked the clutter. Try to set goals that are realistic—if they're too pie-in-the-sky, they'll be overwhelming, and the clutter is already overwhelming enough!

Next, as in earlier chapters, start your de-cluttering process by setting some clutter-kicking priorities. To do this, you're going to focus on what matters most to you about the way your garage looks and functions now, and make that your top priority. The best approach is to take a good, hard look at the "before" state of the garage, and then visualize the "after."

A Garage Visualization

To get to your clutter-free "after," you need to start with the "before"—the way things look right now. So get out some paper, or use the "My Garage—Before" form (or make a photocopy of it and write on that). Write down every place there's clutter, and note what that clutter is.

Fortunately, the garage—however overwhelming it may look right now—is really just a room, and usually a room with no major appliances (if you don't count vehicles!), except maybe a second fridge. So even if it's crammed to the rafters with sports equipment, power tools, lawn mowers, and all the other yard equipment, boxes of old appliances, paint, projects, rags, ladders, bikes, newspapers, and mercy alone knows what, it can take only so long to get a good idea of what's going on in there. So back the cars out—if by some miracle they actually fit in the garage at the moment—and take a minute now to write down your "before" so you can get to your "after"!

Once you've taken an inventory of your garage's "before" state, it's time to move on to the "after"—how you want the garage to look when you've finished de-

---

My Garage—Before

_____

_____

_____

_____

_____

_____

_____

_____

_____

_____

My Garage—After

_____
_____
_____
_____
_____
_____
_____
_____
_____

My Garage Priority List

_____
_____
_____
_____
_____
_____
_____
_____
_____

cluttering it. Write it all down on a piece of paper, or in the "My Garage—After" form (or on as many photocopies of it as you need to do it justice).

Think about what you want the garage to _do_ when you've kicked the clutter. To make sure you're being realistic, look at your garage every few minutes while you're taking notes.

5-Minute Fixes for Garages

Stash your trash. Put a trash can by the door to the house and another one beside or under your workbench. The family can toss garbage as they head from the car into the house (rather than leaving it in the car), and you'll be more willing to toss workshop trash if there's a can right there waiting for it.

Put out the welcome mat. If your garage is connected to the house, keep mud and other gunk out of your house by putting a heavy-duty doormat on the garage side of your door.

Keep steps clear. If you have stairs going from the house down into the garage, the steps are *not* the place to keep newspapers for recycling, a spare bag of cat litter, or other clutter. You may not be able to see what's piled there because you're staggering along under a load of groceries or another bulky burden and kids are racing back and forth to get into or out of the car. It's the very definition of a hazard! Get a basket, bin, or hamper to hold things that need to go from the house to the car, but keep it on the house side of the door, not the garage side.

Hang sports balls in mesh bags. Keep basketballs, soccer balls, and volleyballs in sight but not underfoot by storing them in mesh bags hung from hooks on the wall or on a pegboard.

Park the paint. Keep paint cans together in a plastic storage bin on the floor or the bottom shelf of a storage unit. They'll be less likely to spill or get knocked over.

Move (or pitch) the paint. As I noted in the basement chapter, latex paint spoils after 2 or 3 years, or if it's exposed to freezing temperatures (32°F or below). If your garage is unheated and the temperature inside goes down to freezing, dispose of any latex paint you have on hand and find another place to store your paint in the future. (See page 316 for information on disposing of past-its-prime paint.)

Get a knife strip. The magnetic knife strips that are sold as kitchen aids are great in the garage. Use them to hold lightweight tools like screwdrivers, scissors, and pliers.

Your description can be short and to the point: "I'd like all the stuff to be off the garage floor, and I'd like the floor to be clean, not covered with oil spills and stains. I'd like to create a work space where I can create wreaths and other dried-flower projects. I'd like to walk through the garage just once without tripping over bikes and baseball bats. I'd like more wall shelves."

If you like, you can create a more detailed picture of exactly how you'd like your garage to look if it were perfect (for you). Visualize every detail—the storage systems, the work spaces, the floor and wall treatments, the lighting, the vehicles. Write down every detail.

Getting There

Now that you have captured your garage's "before" condition, listing all the specifics, and you've imagined its "after" appearance, you can finally prioritize the steps you need to take to get there from here. Bearing both "before" and "after" in mind, start with what bothers you most about the "before" condition and make that clutter-kicking priority #1. Then work through the clutter issues on your "before" list and use them to create a list of things you will do and in what order you'll do them.

Is your goal simply to fit the cars inside the garage? Or are those moldering piles of bags, boxes, and junk heaped around the walls driving you crazy? Do you dream of a well-lit workshop with a great work space and the latest power tools? Or is your ultimate fantasy of a clean, well-lit, fresh-smelling space with walls of shelves and everything stored neatly in its place?

Note down whatever's driving you to distraction on the "My Garage Priority List" on page 313 (or photocopy it, if you'd prefer) in descending order from most to least maddening. Now you have your priorities straight! Once you've finished the priority list, you can turn to the tips below to find ingenious ways to reclaim your garage.

THE GARAGE TIPS

Dig in. It's unlikely that you could clear out the entire garage all at once, even if you had a whole day (or weekend) to work on it. Instead, pick a wall, or the floor, or a particularly annoying pile, and deal with that one problem. You know the drill by now: Make piles of stuff that should go to the trash, items that need repair, things you want to donate or sell, and stuff that should go back into the garage. Box or bag anything that's not going back right now and label the boxes or bags "Trash," "Salvation Army," "Sale," "Fix," or whatever. Once the clutter is all sorted, stop and take anything that's going out to its final destination. Since your goal is first and foremost to make space, it's more important to clear the stuff out than to go through the entire garage. Schedule another part of the garage for a similar sorting-through on another day, and continue on until you've gone through it all. And as long as you stay focused and tackle the garage in manageable bites, you *will* go through it all! Then the fun can really begin, as you make the garage truly work for you.

Haul off the hazards. Don't let your garage become—or remain!—an accident waiting to happen. Get rid of oily rags; dried-up paint; gunked-up cleaners, oil, solvents, and other fluids and chemicals that have passed their useful lives; old batteries; moldering stacks of old papers and magazines; woodshop leftovers and sawdust; construction scraps; and anything else that could pose a fire or poison hazard. (Call your trash-collection company or municipal waste-disposal office to find out how to dispose of hazardous materials.)

Clear out the tripping traps. While you're at it, get rid of any tripping hazards, too—clear the floor of obstacles. (There are better places for that skateboard or scooter!)

Light it up. Most garages are dimly lit with just one fixture (or—shriek!—bare bulb), contributing to their cavelike atmosphere. Brighten yours up by installing track lighting (available from home improvement stores) so you can finally see what's going on in there! You may want to add shop lights, under-shelf lighting, or even spot lights to give you good working light for your work spaces, but it's a good idea to add bright general lighting as well, and track lighting gives you maximum flexibility, since you can position the lights wherever you need them. Another good idea is to install a motion-sensing light on the wall where you park your car, so you won't have to fumble for a light switch when your arms are full of groceries.

Fix the floor. Once you can actually *see* the garage floor, you may be horrified by its dingy, stained, and generally disgusting appearance. Clean it up! (And see "Love It or Lose It?" for a great way to keep it clean forevermore.) Use a cleaner specifically designed for concrete, such as Quikrete Concrete & Asphalt Cleaner or Behr Concrete Cleaner & Degreaser. Once the concrete's clean, patch any cracks with a concrete patch (available in squeeze-tube and caulk-tube formats). Then give it an upgrade with a concrete stain, concrete paint, or durable epoxy

👍 Love It *or* Lose It? 👎

Want to cover up that concrete garage floor in a jiffy? Try roll-out flooring, such as G-Floor from Better Life Technology (www.bltllc.com), which offers durable poly-vinyl floor mats in six colors and three patterns. Once you've chosen your color and pattern, just roll out the mat and cut to fit with a utility knife (mats will overlap in larger garages). Haul it outside to hose it down when it needs a cleaning. No fuss, no muss! Note that these mats are heavy, since they're sturdy and come in widths up to 10 feet and rolls that are 14 to 22 feet long, so make sure you have plenty of help to install them and move them around. You can also buy a variation of roll-out garage flooring called "Parking Parquet"; it's available in five colors and three sizes from catalogs like Herrington and Improvements (see page 48).

Verdict: Love it!

coating like the Rust-Oleum EpoxyShield Garage Floor Coating system (which comes with its own concrete cleaner, decorative chips, and an instructional video). For a fancy floor, you can get durable colored and patterned high-impact copolymer tiles from RaceDeck (www.racedeck.com), and snap together the stain-resistant floor of your dreams by combining tile colors and patterns.

Clear the paths. If you have an unattached garage, make sure you pick up equipment, tools, garbage, and any other clutter that's lying around along the outside walls. Keep visual clutter minimized by making sure you mow the lawn around the garage and trim the weeds. And maintain walks and entries connecting the garage to the house.

Cart it off. Make it easier to bring things from your unattached garage into the house, instead of letting them pile up, by getting a dolly or upright grocery cart. These make loads easy to move without lifting.

Park smart. Contain slush, snow, mud, water, oil, and other yucky spills with an Under-Car Garage Mat. It's a heavy-duty vinyl mat with snap-on rims that can contain up to 50 gallons of liquid. (But let's hope you don't have to deal with *that* much fluid!) Besides keeping the garage floor tidy and preventing tracking into the house, these mats clearly show where to park so nobody accidentally hits the garage wall. They're available from auto parts and home improvement stores and catalogs like Improvements (see page 48).

Stow the shoes and other wet stuff. The door that connects the garage to the house is also a great place to put one of those rubber "boot trays" to keep wet, muddy shoes on the garage side of the door. They're available at hardware and home improvement stores and from catalogs like Plow & Hearth (see page 47). And don't forget an umbrella rack to keep dripping umbrellas from crying a river on your kitchen floor!

Hang a flashlight. As in the basement, make sure you have a flashlight on hand if the lights go out. Hang a flashlight on the wall by the door into the house. Check it regularly to make sure the batteries are working.

Work your walls. Maximize your garage storage with wall-to-wall shelving. Use metal storage units, or try the vinyl stacking units my boyfriend, Rob, swears by. His are from Rubbermaid and are easy to assemble—you simply snap them together. He put them along an entire wall of his garage and points out that they keep everything dry and off the floor and, despite the fact that they're vinyl, they're extremely strong and durable. (Another friend uses them to store wreath bases and other supplies for her dried-flower business in her garage, and she swears by them, too.) You can also choose from a plethora of wire storage units like the ones made by ClosetMaid, available from home improvement centers and organizing stores.

Go on the grid. Schulte Activity Organizers feature attractive, heavy-duty epoxy-coated steel grids that mount to your garage walls. The 2- x 4-foot grid panels mount horizontally or vertically. Once you've put the basic grid in place, you can attach shelves and organizers to hang tools, sports equipment, even bikes—each grid will hold up to 75 pounds. Look for them at organizing stores and Web sites like All Bright Ideas (see page 48).

Go on the grid (iron). For a more industrial look, try a whole-wall storage system like the Grid Iron system (www.gridironusa.com). Grid Iron makes heavy-duty lipped metal panels that you attach to your wall; sturdy holders for equipment and shelves lock onto the panels' 1-inch rolled-steel channels.

Gear up with GearWall. If you don't want a full-wall covering but like the idea of panels, consider 1- by 8-foot GearWall panels from Gladiator GarageWorks (www.gladiatorgw.com). You can install as many of these heavy-duty plastic panels as you need onto studs or drywall, and their slot-wall system holds all Gladiator and GearBox accessories for tools and excellent, accessible bins for nails and other hardware.

If you're considering making any garage renovations, start by picking up a copy of my favorite garage book, *Popular Mechanics Garage Makeovers* (Hearst Books, 2006, $17.95). Written by Rick Peters, who has been an expert in the do-it-yourself field for more than 20 years (and in that time has written many excellent DIY and woodworking books, in addition to being the former editor of *ShopNotes* magazine), it is absolutely packed with tips, step-by-step directions, photos, and ideas for garage renovations, from creating the perfect pad for your sports coupe to enclosing a carport to converting part of your garage into a dream workshop. Rick and his team have tested every product, built every project, and created all the garage makeovers in the book themselves. If you have garage questions, Rick has the answers in this eye-opening book.

Go with PVC panels. Another option along the same lines is storeWALL PVC panels, available in five colors and a variety of widths and lengths (www.storewall.com). Grooves in the panels hold shelves, cabinets, and other accessories including bike hooks. Look for components for storeWALL systems from The Accessories Group (www.theaccessoriesgroup.com).

Hang it up. For a cleaner look that still gets your stuff off the floor and onto the wall, choose one of the specialty hanger systems like the ones made by Racor (www.racorinc.com). They attach to WallDocks fasteners and will tidily—dare I say attractively?—hold and display everything from bikes, sleds, and golf bags to power tools and shop supplies. You create your own flexible (and easily changeable) storage system to meet your individual needs. Look for them at organizing stores and Web sites like All Bright Ideas (see page 48).

Get on the fast track. Another clean-looking wall-mounting system is FastTrack from Rubbermaid (www.rubbermaid.com). Wall-mounted FastTrack Rails hold numerous types of hooks, holders, mesh bins and baskets, cabinets, and shelves that snap on for flexibility or screw on for more permanent placement. They're durable enough to hold ladders and wheelbarrows as well as tools, power equipment, and sports gear—up to 2,000 pounds per rail.

Raise stuff to the rafters. Use your ceiling space for storage with help from heavy-duty galvanized steel racks, available in single and double widths and capable of holding up to 500 pounds, or the crank-operated Heavy Lift "Garage Elevator," a 4- by 4-foot steel platform that raises and lowers up to 250 pounds. Both are great for storing tires, ladders, lightweight lawn and patio furniture, and other seasonal storage. For lighter ceiling storage, consider Rafter Solutions, which attach to the rafters and have two shelves, each of which holds up to 75 pounds. All three are available from home improvement stores and catalogs like Improvements (see page 48).

Put up some pegboard. If you have a workshop area in your garage or just need a place to hang tools, a pegboard is an excellent choice. The good news is, you don't have to settle for boring brown hardboard pegboard—DPI (www.decpanels.com) makes metallic pegboard panels that will brighten up your work space. You can attach pegboard to furring strips, exposed wall studs, or a pegboard fastening system that provides spacers to hold the pegboard away from the wall so you can hang up the pegboard hooks to hold your stuff. Pegboard is great for tools because it holds them securely—no risk of anything falling off shelves—and all your tools will be displayed where they're easy to find, right where you're going to use them. To make sure you're not missing any, use this idea from my days as an editor at *Organic Gardening* magazine: One of our readers' favorite tips was to put up a pegboard and paint or draw the outline of each of their tools on the board. With a glance, they could see if any tools were missing.

Put it in plastic. Plastic storage containers, available from groceries, pharmacies, hardware stores, home improvement stores—pretty much anywhere!—in a

Tools of the Trade

Store tools in a mobile tool cart, which holds drawers for tools in a wheeled metal frame. Stash paintbrushes, measuring tapes, hand tools, and other essential stuff in the drawers, then just roll the cart wherever you need it. Or you can load it up for a particular project so you have everything you need in one (mobile) place, instead of having to search all over the garage every time you need another tool or piece of hardware to complete a project. Look for carts like this at home improvement centers and hardware stores.

wide range of shapes and sizes, are ideal for garage storage. You can see what's inside so it's easy to find things, and you can buy whatever size you need to fit your shelves or your stuff. No more bits and pieces raining down when you're trying to find something!

Cache it in cabinets. Garage cabinets should be tough, and some are specially manufactured to take abuse and still look great. Try Schulte's freedomRail garage system (www.schultestorage.com) or the good-looking, durable, ready-to-assemble garage wall and floor cabinets from Rubbermaid (www.rubbermaid.com).

Protect your walls (and car doors). Put thick polyethylene wall bumpers along your garage walls at car-door height to protect your car doors and garage walls (once you're actually able to get your cars in there!). They come with wall-mounting hardware for drywall, open studs, concrete, or brick and are available at home improvement stores and catalogs like Improvements (see page 48).

Put sports gear together. If your garage is home to an ever-expanding collection of sports gear, contain it in the Rubbermaid Sports Station Organizer (www.rubbermaid.com), which has compartments and hooks for racquets, bats, and hockey sticks as well as storage space for balls and helmets and a mesh bag for storage or carting off to the game.

Grook your gear. Or hang up your sports equipment on a wall-mounted Grook Tool holder, with rubber loops and hooks to hold gear securely. Find it at The Container Store (www.containerstore.com).

Hang up your bike. The Bike Hoist Pulley System lets you raise a bike into the air and lock it in place by pulling on a cord (just like you lift and lock blinds), and lower it the same way. Brackets hold the bike at ceiling height and out of your way until it's needed. The system is available from catalogs like Improvements.

Add shelves to your studs. For unfinished garage interiors, there's even a special shelving system designed to fit between exposed 16-inch on-center studs. The shelves, which attach with screws, come in $6\frac{1}{2}$- and 11-inch depths, and the system also includes extension-cord hangers. Ingenious! Look for them at home improvement centers and catalogs like Improvements.

Or turn them into storage centers. The Improvements catalog also features two powder-coated steel storage centers designed to mount on 16- or 24-inch on-center studs. The Power Center holds power tools like trimmers, leaf blowers, and chain

SANITY SAVERS

Listen up, guys! A new trend is sweeping across America, and it spells good news for you. It might save more than your sanity—it might save your marriage! It's called the "Man Cave." I read an article about this new phenomenon when I was home in Nashville visiting my father and his girlfriend, Alice. The story told how more and more men were using their garages as hangouts, whether they had grilling parties and 24/7 sports on their home theaters with surround sound or cowboy-themed garage rooms full of Western paraphernalia. Guys hang out in Egyptian-themed "tombs" behind secret doors, English pubs with a pool table and jukebox, theaters complete with popcorn machines, recording studios, and wine cellars guarded by chained skeletons and suits of armor. Home gyms and workshops are common. One Man Cave in Franklin, Tennessee, has a 120-inch projection screen and two 42-inch plasma TVs (so its proud owner and his friends can watch three things at once), as well as a fridge, bathroom, dartboard, foosball table, and popcorn machine. Some Man Caves become neighborhood hangouts, drawing up to 100 guys when they're "open for business." Wives say the "caves" are like fraternities and appreciate the chance for their spouses to get together in a safe place—not to mention the quiet time they get at home while the guys are off doing their thing. Sound good? Look at your garage's possibilities and see what you can come up with!

saws, while the Aqua Center holds garden and coil hoses, sprinklers, and nozzles.

Get creative with car parts. If you happen to have vintage car parts lying around your garage, there's an alternative to hauling them off to the dump or selling them on eBay: Turn them into wall art instead of clutter. I'll never forget how impressed I was when I went to nearby Emmaus, Pennsylvania, to see the home my friends Fern and Tom had bought. The house itself was a typical suburban home, but in the garage, the previous owners had hung a Corvette—or was it a Corvair?—grille with (working!) lights on the wall. You turned on a switch on the wall and the headlights came on. It was *so* cool!

Ban busted appliances. If your garage has become a graveyard for broken kitchen appliances, office equipment, bikes, electronics, and air conditioners, get real, please. Either get it fixed or get it out. Is it cheaper to get a new one, or have you long since replaced the old appliance but are keeping it out there "just in case"? Donate it or toss it. "In case" is never worth the space.

Have a hierarchy. Put the stuff you use most often where it's easiest to reach. Stash the seasonal or "once in a while" stuff higher on the shelves or walls, or hang it from the ceiling, where it's out of your way but easy to get to when you need it.

Group garage stuff. You'll save a lot of time and frustration if you keep like stuff together—sports equipment in one place, workshop supplies in another, auto supplies in yet another, garden equipment in another, and so on. No more endlessly looking for what you need! And it's easier to see if something is missing or needs to be replaced if you know exactly where it should be.

Rent what you don't use often. Why buy—and store—a tool or piece of equipment you use once or twice a year? Rent it instead and save the space (not to mention the upkeep)!

Keep recycling convenient. If you store your recycling bins in the garage, keep them near the door to the house to make it easier for the family to toss cans, bottles, newspapers, and other recyclables into the appropriate bins as they come and go.

Try a T-bar. T-bars hold skis and even lumber off the floor and out of the way.

Corral corrosives. If you keep potentially hazardous materials like pesticides, paint stripper, turpentine, solvents, cleaners, and pool and hot tub chemicals in your garage, lock them up behind closed cabinet doors to keep them from getting spilled and to protect family members and friends from them!

Clip it on. Use this tip from my friend Karen to collect all those to-do and materials lists, project plans, bills, and other papers that can cover your worktable (and

[Tools of the Trade]

Like basements, garages can flood, so I'm repeating this tip here: If you think there's the least chance that water might pool on your garage floor, it's safest to store everything at a higher level. Fortunately, some inventive soul created rust-proof, rot-proof plastic Hi & Dri Storage Pallets to raise garage storage out of harm's way. They come in two sizes and can support 1,000 pounds, lifting your boxes $3\frac{1}{2}$ inches off the floor. If water seeps in, it will just flow underneath the pallets while your stuff stays, well, high and dry. Look for them at home improvement centers and in catalogs such as Improvements (see page 48).

Pet Alert!

If your pets go into the garage for any reason—because the cat door's in there, because the dog gets into the car in there—it is absolutely essential that you protect them from antifreeze spills. Antifreeze is incredibly toxic to animals, but unfortunately, it's apparently also irresistible to them—sort of like Gatorade for pets. But one slurp of the lime-green or brilliant blue liquid and they'll be heading to pet paradise. I don't know why manufacturers don't add a scent or flavoring that's repellent to pets, but until they do, make sure you clean up any spills, pools, or splashes of antifreeze ASAP.

floor) or take up too much wall space: She uses a big spring-loaded clip with a magnetic back to hold everything in one spot.

Minimize cord clutter. Anywhere you use a lot of electrical devices, including the garage, you can accumulate a lot of cord clutter. Confine it to one place with a Squid Power-Outlet Multiplier, which lets you run five electrical devices off one grounded outlet even if each one has a large transformer plug or timer. This ingenious contraption (which does look rather squidlike) is available from home improvement stores and catalogs like Improvements and Herrington (see page 48).

Rack it up. Organizing catalogs and stores like All Bright Ideas (see page 48) also sell wonderful heavy-duty wire grid systems that hang on the wall and hold tools with a series of different hooks and clips made to fit each tool. They can hold anything from picks and sledgehammers to rakes and shovels, so you can customize the rack for the tools you need. The hooks and clips are coated to protect the tools and provide a secure grip.

Put up some clips. You can also clip your tools directly to the wall using the kind of metal clips sold in home improvement and organizing stores and catalogs to hold brooms, mops, and other cleaning equipment on pantry doors.

Hang some hooks. Put up single hooks or two-pronged hooks to hold tools, equipment, birdfeeders, scoops, leashes, and plastic bags you use to pick up after the dog. Hang them where no one will run into them or get their clothes caught.

Set up some shelving. Set up a metal shelving unit along a wall of the garage to hold bags, boxes, plant pots, birdhouses, plastic bins of hardware, and anything else that will fit securely. (It's best to hang hand tools and anything else that could hurt someone if it slid off a shelf.) My boyfriend, Rob, would advise you to get heavy-duty vinyl shelving (such as Rubbermaid's). If you'd like to set up a wall shelving system that's customized to your space rather than a freestanding unit, CabinetMaid makes wire shelving of all types and lengths just for this purpose. All three types are available at home improvement stores.

Bring out the tins. If your garage is where you store grass seed, birdseed, cat or dog food, or anything else that mice might think was tasty, put it in big, mouse-proof metal tins. Pet stores often give them away for free as part of pet-food promotions, and stores that sell wild bird supplies sell an assortment of sizes with beautiful bird-themed art on them. I know home and pet stores and catalogs sell beautiful wooden bins for pet food, but I wouldn't bet on them being mouse- or bugproof. Heavy-duty plastic might work, but tins are safe and convenient (and did I mention they're often free?). Label the lids with the contents so nobody accidentally gives your grass seed to the birds or feeds Clifford's food to Garfield by mistake!

Cars, Cars, Cars

Let's not forget the cars (trucks, SUVs, vans) themselves. Sometimes it seems like they've accumulated as much clutter as the garage! It's astounding how much stuff can be crammed into such a small space. These tips will help you get your car cleaned out and organized.

[Tools of the Trade]

Prevent gasoline spills with a Petro Pump, a 5-gallon gas container with its own pump. No more lifting the container to pour fuel into your lawn mower or other gas-powered equipment—or onto the garage floor! The 4-foot fuel hose gives you a good reach, and you can control the flow, from fast to a trickle. Good idea! It's available from home improvement stores and catalogs like Improvements (see page 48).

Clear out the glove compartment. Admit it: You have no idea what's in there, do you? Is your glove compartment an explosion waiting to happen—crammed with outdated road maps; ancient tissues; fast-food napkins, condiments, and other detritus; hand-written directions on scraps of paper to places you haven't been in years (or printouts to same); a few school papers; an old vet bill; and mercy knows what else? Take 10 minutes and a plastic grocery bag and deal with it. Pull out the stuff, trash everything you can, and try to find better homes for the rest. (You don't really need to keep the map of Virginia in your glove compartment if you go there once every year or two. Put it in a labeled plastic storage bin with your other maps and directions and shelve it in the garage!) Once you've cleaned everything out, treat yourself to a current road map and road atlas. You deserve it!

Empty the console. Consoles also accumulate all kinds of junk—broken sunglasses, dried-out pens, bottle caps. Get rid of all the trash, and leave just a few essentials: a notepad, pen, tire gauge, and flashlight—and maybe a *functional* pair of sunglasses.

Find the floor. Now it's time to tackle the car floor. Can you see it? Or is it buried under bags (what's in them, anyway?), shoes, cartons and other fast-food trash, soda cans, toys, sports equipment, umbrellas, a fleece jacket, tissue boxes, CD cases . . . good grief. You may need a full-size garbage bag for this one! But again, you should be able to clean it all out in just 10 minutes, no matter how trashed it is. Throw out what you can and find homes for the rest in the house or garage. For the stuff that has to stay in the car, get a large canvas tote (like the famous ones from L.L. Bean) or a Cargo Carryall (see "Tools of the Trade" on page 329) and store your stuff safely (and upright) in them. All done? Time for another treat—a trip to the car wash and a vacuum. Then sit back, relax, and enjoy that cleared-out, cleaned-up car!

Tackle the trunk. Do you know what's in your trunk right now? Take a good look. Your trunk should function as an emergency center, with a spare tire, jumper cables, and other auto emergency gear like flares and a "help" sign (see "The Pros Know"); supplies like motor oil, brake fluid, antifreeze, and windshield-washer fluid; a local phone directory; a travel snow shovel; a bag of cat box filler or sand (for traction on ice); and the like. It can also hold dog-walking supplies, picnic gear, car-washing supplies (in a plastic bucket), a tote for umbrellas and rain gear like ponchos, and Cargo Carryalls (see "Tools of the Trade" on page 329) to

One thing it definitely makes sense to carry in your car is a stash of emergency supplies. And who knows more about being prepared than that diva of domesticity, Martha Stewart? She recommends putting a large, rectangular, heavy vinyl catchall in the car and stocking it with supplies like a first-aid kit, auto fire extinguisher, jumper cables, flares, tire repair kit, paper towels, duct tape, and bungee cords. To be prepared for a breakdown, Martha suggests packing a separate bag with a blanket, warm clothing, bottled water, and granola bars.

hold grocery and other shopping bags upright. Everything should be neat and easy to find. If you're using the trunk as a mobile storage area for stuff that has no place in your car, clean out the junk, put the storage where it belongs, and organize what's left for easy access. Then, if there's something that *should* be in the trunk but isn't, you'll have room for it.

Be prepared, part one. Always keep a few essential tools in your car so you'll be prepared for an emergency. You can stash them in a plastic storage container (I like the ones with handles) and put them on the floor in the back or in the cargo area. New inventions have made it easier than ever to have what you need on hand. Besides a vehicle emergency kit (see "The Pros Know"), I recommend a Life Hammer (it can smash car windows and cut jammed seat belts so you can escape from your car; put this gadget where you can reach it if you're in a crash, don't store it in the trunk); a "Sputnik" 7-in-1 screwdriver with an LED flashlight or a 12-in-1 Hammer Tool; a portable Rescue Shovel for snow and a Rechargeable Ice Scraper that charges through your cigarette lighter socket to deal with windshield ice fast; a 4-in-1 Emergency Flashlight that's crank-powered and includes an FM radio, cell phone charger, and emergency siren; and the Car Charger, a battery charger that works through your cigarette lighter socket so you don't have to get out of the car or wait for another vehicle to help you. And, of course, I hope you have an LED miniflashlight (called a Clip-Light) on your keychain! Look for all these wonder tools at auto parts, home improvement, and hardware stores, and in catalogs like Plow & Hearth, Herrington, Solutions, and Improvements (see pages 47 and 48).

Be prepared, part two. My friend Jennifer isn't about to be stuck on the road without a few essentials of a different kind. "I keep my going-away toiletry bag packed and ready all of the time with extra toiletries and a hair dryer inside," she explains. "I keep it in the car just in case I'm ever stuck on the road someplace with car problems or bad weather." Sure beats getting unexpectedly stuck in a hotel without so much as a toothbrush!

Stash the stroller. Jennifer has another tip for making the best use of your car space. "I store my son's stroller in the trunk of my car, where it's handy if we're out someplace and need it," she says, adding the clincher, "and it's not taking up space in the garage."

Bag it up, part one. Jennifer's not the only one who knows how to make the most of her car's storage capabilities. My environmentally conscious friend Chris likes to reuse plastic and paper bags at the grocery store. She stores them in the trunk so they're readily available and she doesn't have to remember to bring some every time she goes to the store.

Bag it up, part two. Of course, Jennifer has her own solution to the bag issue. "I keep two big cloth bags in my car and take them to the grocery store," she says. "I can get most of the groceries into these bags, which makes it easier to get into the car and into the house than carrying a bunch of small bags—and then I don't have to store or get rid of all those plastic bags."

Bag it up, part three. Speaking of bags, make sure you always have a trash bag in the car to collect wrappers, tissues, cups, papers, CD wrappers, and the endless other detritus that seems to accumulate in vehicles. Keep some plastic grocery bags in the glove compartment and pull one out for each trip. When you get home, if there's trash in it, take it inside with you.

Make your cup holder multitask. Get organized with a Cell-Cup, a gray foam container that fits in your car's cup holder and has compartments to hold your cell phone, pen and pencil, change, or sticky notepad safely and in easy reach. It also has an opening in the bottom for your cell phone charger cord. Look for it at home improvement and auto parts stores, and from catalogs and Web sites.

Hang it up. Backseat passengers can stow books, magazines, water bottles, snacks, and other stuff in a pocket organizer that hangs over the back of the front seat.

Say bye-bye to bumper stickers. Don Aslett, in his wonderfully named book, *Clutter's Last Stand*, calls them "junker stickers." And you know he's right. However irresistible the message, a bumper sticker makes a car look cluttered. And a bunch of bumper stickers doesn't just create visual clutter—it distracts other drivers, making fender benders more likely. So do what I do—if you absolutely must have that bumper sticker with Chief Seattle saying, "The earth does not belong to us, we belong to the earth," buy it and tack it up on the garage wall as garage art. If you have a handful of favorites, rotate them. That way, you'll get a boost every time you walk through the garage—without trashing your car.

Ditto for dashboard detritus. I can't tell you how many times I've seen cars with their dashboards covered with bobble-head characters and the rear window completely obscured by stuffed animals. And some dashboards look like out-of-control file cabinets and wastebaskets, several inches deep in papers and paper coffee cups. This is clutter for clutter's sake. It restricts visibility, clutters the car, and could even hit you or your family in the case of an accident or sudden stop. (This goes for long things hanging off the rear-view mirror, too. If you want to hang up a rosary, dream catcher, or whatever on the mirror, keep it tightly wrapped so you don't lose an eye if you have to jump on the brakes.) Get . . . it . . . out.

ONWARD!

Wow! You've kicked out all that garage clutter. You probably feel that you deserve a medal—or a chestful! Instead, how about a little fresh air? If you stroll outside, you're bound to see the subject of our next chapter—the yard and garden. But don't worry: After taking on the garage, de-cluttering those outdoor spaces will seem like, well, a walk in the park! So turn the page and let's head on out there.

Chapter 16

Sprucing Up the Yard and Garden

Maybe you don't *really* need 25 birdfeeders . . . especially when 7 of them have fallen apart and you've positioned 14 of them where you can't even see them from the house. And okay, that garden gnome looked cute, but his accumulated siblings make your front yard look like the home of Snow White and the Seven Dwarfs. In this chapter, you'll find tons of useful tips to help you know when lawn art looks like art and when it just looks like junk; how to keep the yard and gardens looking tidy and inviting; how to tie it all together; and how to combat visual clutter. Plus "5-Minute Fixes" to give your yard that pulled-together look in a flash!

PRIORITIES FOR THE YARD AND GARDEN

At most houses, the front yard and backyard have different purposes. The front yard is a showplace, the part people see from the street. The backyard is the place where outdoor living happens. Because their functions are so different, I suggest you do two separate visualizations, one for the front yard and one for the backyard. You can adopt the "My Yard and Garden—Before" form to make space for both.

As in earlier chapters, you'll start your de-cluttering process by setting some clutter-kicking priorities. The first step in that process is to focus on what matters most to you about the way your front and backyards look by taking a good, hard look at the "before" state of each part of the yard. Then you'll go on to visualize the "after."

A Yard and Garden Visualization

To get to your "after," you need to start with the "before"—the way things look right now. So get out some paper, or use the "My Yard and Garden—Before" form on page 332 (or make a photocopy of it and write on that). Once again, it helps to look at your yard with fresh eyes. Pretend you're a realtor who's come to evaluate the property or, say, your prospective new boss arriving to see if you'd be a good candidate—based on the appearance of your yard. Write down every place on the lawn and in and around garden beds and borders where there's clutter, and take note of what that clutter is. In the case of a yard, untidiness—anything that makes the yard look unkempt—equals clutter, in addition, of course, to clutter itself. So take a minute now to write down your "before" so you can get to your "after"!

Once you've taken an inventory of your yard's "before" state, it's time to move on to the "after"—what you want the yard to look like when you've kicked the clutter. Write it all down on a piece of paper, or on the "My Yard and Garden— After" form on page 332 (or on as many photocopies of it as you need to do it justice). To make sure you're being realistic, look at the yard every few minutes while you're creating your description.

Your description can be short and to the point: "I'd like a lush, green lawn out front, not a weedy mess. I'd like to have something nice under my trees, instead of bare ground. I'd like a neat hedge or fence, not the leafless hedge we have now. I'd like to have a playground for the kids and a cutting garden for myself in the back-yard. I'd like to cut down the tree that's shading the living room."

If you like, you can create an even more detailed picture of exactly how you'd like your yard to look if it were perfect (for you). Picture every lovely detail—the flowerbeds, the rose-covered arbor, the pool or water garden, the luxuriant kitchen or herb garden, the paths, the pergola—everything.

My Yard and Garden—Before

Front Yard:

Backyard:

My Yard and Garden—After

Front Yard:

Backyard:

Getting There

Now that you've captured your yard's "before" condition, listing all the specifics, and you've imagined its "after" appearance, you can finally prioritize the steps you need to take to get there from here. Bearing both your "before" and "after" in mind, start with what bothers you most about the "before" condition and make that your top priority.

Unmowed grass, garden tools lying around, dog toys, balls, bikes, kids' toys, and hoses snaking across the lawn may be making a mess of your yard. Maybe you'd like to turn that unkempt, weedy brush pile in the backyard into a flowerbed or upgrade the falling-down playground equipment and set up a fantastic swing set and fort for the kids. Or turn that shaded bare spot in the back that's just collecting a clutter of sticks and your dog's favorite half-chewed bones into a volleyball court. Or you'd like to haul off the disintegrating compost bins and replace them with attractive new bins—and add some tidy raised beds for your veggie garden, while you're at it. Or you can't take another week with the rotting railroad-tie steps in the front and want to replace them with something that's both attractive and durable.

Write down whatever's driving you to distraction on the "My Yard and Garden

My Yard and Garden Priority List

_____

_____

_____

_____

_____

_____

_____

_____

_____

A Dozen 5-Minute Fixes

You got held up in traffic and your guests are due within the hour. Your boss just called to say she'd be by to drop off some papers in a few minutes. You've been so busy housecleaning before your big date that you completely forgot about the yard. Or you're just intimidated by the size of the cleanup job you're facing. Yikes! What to do? Try these tried-and-true tips to make the yard look presentable fast.

Pick it up. Take a plastic garbage bag and rush around the front yard, collecting any fallen sticks, litter, and other debris. Get it out of sight!

Clear the drive. If there's anything in the driveway—toys, bikes, garbage bins—get them out. Bag the toys and put them, the garbage bins, bikes, sports equipment, and other stuff in the garage (for now).

Sweep the drive. Quick—sweep the drive so it looks its best. Do the sidewalk, too!

Clear the lawn. If you see toys, debris, or anything else on the lawn, get them out of sight ASAP.

Clear out your car. If your car is sitting out in plain sight, rush over there with a plastic garbage bag and dump the trash, random bags, bottles, books, CDs, gym bag, wrappers, and anything else you find into it. Nothing says clutter like a trashed car!

Clean around the mailbox. Weed around the mailbox with gloves, shears, or a weed-whacker. Make it look neat. If you have flowers growing around the mailbox, water them and deadhead (cut off any dead flowers). Pick up any newspapers lying around the mailbox and bring in the mail.

Clear the path. Sweep the walkway, while you're at it, and pull any weeds on the walk, tossing them into a plastic bag en route to the compost or trash. If

Priority List" on page 333 (or photocopy it, if you'd prefer) in descending order from most to least maddening. Now you have your priorities straight! Once you've finished your priority list, you can turn to the tips below to find ingenious ways of dealing with each problem.

you have an overgrown grass path, give it a quick mowing. Make sure there's nothing on the path—no toys or sports equipment, no fallen leaves, seedpods, sticks, or rocks.

Sweep the stoop. Next, sweep the front stoop and steps (if you have any) and shake out and sweep the doormat.

Add a feature. If it's not too cold and you have enough forewarning, run to your local nursery—or even a grocery store—and buy a blooming plant to put by the door. Make sure it's big and colorful enough to make a splash. If it's a hanging basket, set it by the door and tuck the chain discreetly underneath the pot or temporarily detach the plastic or metal hook. (You can always reattach it once your company leaves if you want to hang it up in the backyard.) Buy something you'll enjoy when your guests are gone, or give it to them as a guest gift when they leave.

Add more color. Front yard looking drab? Race around to the deck and see if you have any colorful container plants. Tuck them in beds in the front yard for a burst of instant color.

Light the way. If your guest or guests are arriving after dark, turn on the walkway lights and the light over your front door. No pathway lights? Consider making luminarias. (These are small paper bags with sand in the bottom to hold them open and stabilize them and tea lights or votive candles set in the sand.) When lit, they provide soft, lovely illumination.

Come out to meet them. It's much easier to distract guests from the less-than-perfect state of your front yard if you rush out to greet them, talking enthusiastically while herding them toward the front door before they know what's hit them. Just remember, if it's not dark when your guests leave, you'll also have to accompany them back to their car, chatting enthusiastically all the way.

THE YARD AND GARDEN TIPS

Now that you've gotten your feet wet, let's start in the front yard—the part people see first. Then we'll head around back.

The Front Yard

Manage the mailbox. The mailbox is the first thing people see when they arrive at your house, so take a good look at it yourself. Is it falling down, ancient, dented, rusting, or otherwise dilapidated? Are weeds or grasses reaching for the stars all around it? If so, it just screams to the world, "Slovenly people live here!" So come on, how hard is this to fix? Put up an attractive mailbox. Mow or weed-whack around it to keep the weeds and grass low. And add a decorative vine like a gorgeous clematis to grow up the post and spill over the top with its beautiful starry blooms. Or buy one of those clever planters that fit around a mailbox post and fill it with colorful marigolds, petunias, or other plants of your choice. But don't plant anything if you won't water and maintain it! Better a tidy but bare appearance than a display of crisp, brown, formerly living plants.

Handle the hedge. An overgrown hedge is dark, creepy, and unkempt. And a badly sheared hedge has that hideous fringe effect—a thin layer of leaves on the outside and bare branches inside. If you have a hedge, make it work for you. Keep it pruned and tidy. If you must shear it, shape the hedge like a pyramid, not a box, so light can reach the lower parts more easily. This will help avoid "bare-legs syndrome," where the top is green and the bottom branches are bare because they've been shaded out. If you don't have a hedge but are considering one, or you are ready to really renovate yours, consider a flowering hedge to add more interest and beauty to your yard. Rugosa roses are tough road-, salt-, and weather-resistant bushes. They have beautiful, fragrant flowers, showy red rose hips, and yellow fall foliage, creating a long season of interest. My favorite is 'Alba', with lovely single white flowers. You should also investigate hedge roses like 'Carefree Beauty', widely available from garden centers, nurseries, and plant catalogs like Carroll Gardens (444 East Main Street, Westminster, MD 21157-5540; 800-638-6334; www.carrollgardens.com) and the 'Simplicity' series from Jackson & Perkins (1 Rose Lane, Medford, OR 97501; 800-872-7673; www.jacksonandperkins.com). All of these roses are bred to be tough and disease-resistant, and they stay comparatively low—usually 3 to 5 feet tall—so the only maintenance they require is for you to mow around them to keep them from spreading and to prune out any dead branches. If you want an all-green hedge, two classic plants are privet and, in the Southeast, yaupon holly.

My friend Cole Burrell is a well-known landscape designer. Besides designing landscapes for clients, Cole also teaches landscape architecture, lectures around the country (and sometimes the world), and has written numerous books and myriad articles on plants and garden design. Need I say that he knows a thing or two about how to put a landscape together? Because one of Cole's specialties is designing gardens featuring native plants, his clients often want him to put a prairie garden or wildflower meadow in their front yard instead of a more traditional flower border.

Now, as you can imagine, one concern about putting a meadow in the front yard is the danger that neighbors and passers-by, instead of appreciating the ever-changing beauty of nature at work, might conclude that you'd simply forgotten to mow the grass for the entire season and call city hall to complain. But Cole has a solution for this. When he designs meadows for clients, he frames them carefully to make them look intentional. By surrounding them with a ribbon of very carefully maintained lawn, Cole makes it obvious that this is a garden, not a yard gone wild. And of course the beauty of the flowers and native grasses in bloom reinforces this impression.

So keep the idea of intentionality in mind when you create gardens and features for your yard. A tidy fence, a neat stone or brick edging, or a strip of manicured lawn or mulch can make the difference between perceived clutter and design brilliance!

Focus on your fence. Good fences may make good neighbors, but bad fences make clutter. If your fence is falling down, needs painting, or has weeds coming up around it, it's an eyesore. Unless your front yard faces a really busy street or a hideous view—say, a cluster of stores or your neighbor's junkyard—an open rail fence or a low picket fence is better than a high, impenetrable palisade or panel fence. If at all possible, you want to keep your view open in front, displaying your yard and home like a jewel. As for the weed issue, I'd suggest putting down landscape fabric and mulch in a narrow strip under and around your fence, then planting climbing roses and clematis or honeysuckle through it at regular intervals to foam over the fence, filling the air with fragrance and the eye with color.

Watch the walk. The front walk is one of the most important, and neglected, aspects of your front yard. It should be wide, smooth, and uncomplicated. No pointless meanderings allowed! Instead, it should curve gracefully from the parking area to the front door. If you have a formal landscape, opt for a nice straight walkway, instead. It should be obvious and easy to follow, cleared of debris, snow and ice, and toys or other clutter. If you edge it with plastic edging (which you pound into the ground so it's not visible) or narrow strips of mulch over landscape fabric on either side, it's easy to maintain a weed-free path. Add in-ground lighting so people can navigate at night. If it's paved, the surface should be even, with no bricks or concrete edges sticking up. Make sure you replace chipped or cracked bricks or concrete, and level stepping stones, securing them in the ground. If it's a mulch path, the mulch should be clean and thick, not weedy and uneven. If it's a grass path, keep it neatly mowed and raked. Help people reach your door easily and safely.

Ditto the driveway. A cracked, splitting, discolored, weedy driveway gives an awful impression of the family that owns it. And the same is true of a weed-filled, bumpy gravel drive, where most of the gravel has migrated into the lawn and vice versa. Keep your driveway maintained and picked up. Bikes, trikes, and toys should never be left in the driveway, unless you just happen to enjoy crushing them on your way in or out. And, needless to say, rusting vehicles or auto parts should be hauled off unless your family has an in-home junkyard business.

Love your lawn. An unkempt, weedy lawn tells everyone who sees it that you don't care what state your house is in—you're a slob. And a lawn full of bald spots is even more of an eyesore. Both create visual clutter, too. Keep your lawn mowed, but keep it from browning by setting the mower blades high—2 inches is the usual recommendation—so the grass won't dry out. Whether you have lawn surrounding lush shrub plantings and flowerbeds, a handkerchief-size lawn, or a vast sea of grass, it's important to maintain it. A nice lawn sets the tone for your whole property.

Tame your trees. So often, a tiny yard is dwarfed by giant shade trees. Years ago someone planted maples or weeping willows or looming evergreens in a small front yard, and now they've plunged the whole yard and house into shade, their roots have made it impossible to grow anything in the yard, and they've cracked the sidewalk (and are threatening the driveway). Yikes! You basically have two choices: create a raised walk, like a boardwalk, or have the trees cut down. (Use a professional service for this, both because of the hazards and because you want them to take out the stumps and roots.) Then you can regenerate the soil and start over with trees that will stay small and be decorative. (Remember that some of the showiest small trees, like Japanese maples and crabapples, can create a lot of landscape clutter when their fruit or seed drops—and seedlings start appearing everywhere—so consult a pro before choosing a replacement.)

Go to Fantasy Island. Speaking of trees, if you have trees and shrubs dotting the front yard, instead of fighting weeds beneath them all, why not connect them with island beds? These lovely free-form beds surround the trunks of the trees or shrubs and flow out from them in a naturalistic manner to connect with other trees or shrubs. Plant beautiful shade-tolerant flowering or foliage plants and groundcovers in your island beds (astilbes, hellebores, heucheras, bleeding hearts, ferns, pulmonarias, and hostas are just a few of the landscape choices for shady sites). To avoid a spotty, cluttered effect, connect small island beds into fewer, larger, contiguous ones rather than simply ringing your trees and shrubs. Echo the plant choices in all the beds, whether or not they are connected (though you can vary the flower and foliage colors, if you wish) to create a unified look with no visual clutter.

Go to bed. A flowerbed can brighten a small front yard, and a matching pair adds a low but attractive foundation planting to the front of the house. If you're siting it in the middle of a lawn, a round, oval, or kidney-shaped bed will look more pleasing than a rigidly rectangular bed. Plant groups of three, five, or seven of the same plant rather than one of each, and repeat groupings to avoid a chaotic, cluttered look. If you're choosing your own plants, select types that thrive in your conditions and grow well together. Need help choosing? Check out my friend Cole Burrell's book *Perennial Combinations* for some wonderful suggestions.

Patrol your borders. Flower borders are simply longer versions of beds. Depending on your energy level, enthusiasm, and free time, you can plant borders along your driveway, around the perimeter of your property, around your house, or in a formal garden. Borders are elegant landscape features, but they require a lot of maintenance to look attractive and not unkempt. Unless you're an experienced gardener, work with a landscape or garden designer to create a border that's right for your area, conditions, budget, and the amount of upkeep you're willing to invest in it. Start small—with a single modest border—and add on as your knowledge and enthusiasm grow. (If the plants don't grow well, you won't be looking at a major maintenance nightmare.)

Play ring around the rosy. Dress up light posts, mailboxes—even telephone poles and other vertical features—with a ring of flowers or groundcover plants. Garden centers and catalogs sell semicircular planters designed to fit around the base of a light post or mailbox. These cut down on digging but require daily watering if it doesn't rain. Cut weed cloth to fit beneath the planters, fill them with the annual flowers of your choice, set them on the weed cloth, and voilà! They'll protect your post from the mower and string trimmer, too. Just limit the varieties and colors of the plants so they don't end up becoming visual clutter. Don't forget to water, and remove dead blooms regularly to keep the plants blooming and tidy.

Limit lawn art. I have a friend whose lawn art outnumbers the plants in her yard. Everywhere you look—gnomes, statues, gazing balls, brightly painted tools, and a plethora of other lawn art are peeking at you, looming over you, or about to decapitate you. Or you're about to step on or trip over it. While most yards aren't quite *that* full of lawn art, it's easy to get carried away. Down the street from my house, one old gentleman has filled his driveway with a Mexican and burro with cart, a large Uncle Sam, several deer statues, a standing bear, and an assortment of other statuary. (You should see his Christmas display.) It looks for all the world like a low-end garden center.

Use lawn art where it will create an impact, not clutter. One birdbath, gazing ball, or large urn can make a striking focal point. Don't be afraid to try something different, too: nestling a gazing ball into a garden bed instead of putting it on a pedestal, using an old wrought-iron chair as a sculpture. One of the most magical effects I ever saw was a gazing-ball mobile hanging down from the branches of a huge tree (well above head height, of course); the small silver balls glittered like stars. So have fun and enjoy your lawn art, but use restraint and choose pieces that fit your garden and home style. An ultra-modern abstract sculpture in front of a serene Colonial home is jarring, while a pedestaled sundial is a lovely fit. (And that abstract sculpture would look great in front of an ultra-modern home.)

Don't fixate on feeders. Birdfeeders are delightful additions to the yard—the backyard. But don't put them in the front, where they look like clutter and the dropped seed creates an unsightly mess. The best place for a feeder is off the deck or kitchen where you'll be able to sit and enjoy watching all the birds. And remember—the more feeders, the more clutter, the more mess. Two—or at most, three—feeders are enough for any family, unless you've converted your backyard into a wildlife habitat with trails and viewing spots. Then feeders at intervals along the trail will add interest to your habitat. Maintain your feeders and replace any broken or battered ones immediately to avoid a run-down, junky-looking landscape.

Mulch it. Mulch gives gardens a neat, finished look. Use the same kind and color of mulch everywhere you use it, and remember that the point of mulch is to blend in, not to become a landscape feature in its own right—so for mercy's sake, avoid all those unnatural, screaming mulch colors, and don't mound it on like you're trying to create your very own mountain range.

The Outback

Create a nice view. Remember that you'll be looking into the backyard from the deck, patio, porch, or back windows (such as, in my case, the sliding glass doors off the kitchen). So create a view you want to look at, even if it is in the backyard. That doesn't mean the backyard can't be useful as well—a charming playground with a delightful playhouse you've painted with flowers; a beautifully laid-out kitchen garden full of vegetables, herbs, edible flowers, and berries; or a grouping of flowering shrubs that can be practical as well as beautiful.

Design destinations. Your backyard will work hard for you, and contribute the most to your household, if you design it by breaking it into areas. Think about what you want to put there—a grove of shade trees with gorgeous autumn colors; a greenhouse; the compost bins; a playground; a craft studio; an herb garden; a wildflower meadow; a water garden; a trellised gazebo covered with climbing roses; a mini-vineyard; a little chicken coop; a dog kennel; a raised bed of strawberries; or a few dwarf fruit trees.

Once you've narrowed the list to what you really want, lay out the area on paper, giving each area its logical location, and then do a reality check. Do you have the room, money, and time for all these things? If not, what can you most easily drop (for now)? If so, are the features arranged in a logical, easy-to-access manner that gives them the protection, structures, and lighting they'll need without interfering with other important activities? For example, a playground for the kids sited near a raspberry or blackberry trellis invites cuts and scratches; if it's located near a greenhouse, it could mean broken glass.

Once you've pared down your list to the best options for your present circumstances and income and have laid them out in the most logical and appropriate way for your family and site, you should think about how you, your family, and others will move around the backyard. Will someone haul water to the greenhouse, then feed the fish in the water garden and check the filter before swinging by the veggie garden to water and pick ripe produce, making a final stop at the chicken coop to drop off any spoiled stuff from the veggie garden, feed and water the chickens, and collect eggs? Will the kids engage in a fevered volleyball game, then jump in the pool?

Think about how you and your family will really use your space, and then lay out your paths accordingly. Don't waste time creating elaborate paths that no one will use as the family cuts across the yard instead. Plan paths that reflect backyard traffic flow. Unless your paths reflect real-life traffic patterns, you'll end up with bare-soil paths where people really walk, which creates unsightly visual clutter.

Tame your tools. Neglected, abandoned, rusting tools are landscape clutter—and they're also tripping hazards. Follow the good gardener's rule, and put each tool back in its place at day's end, cleaned and ready to use the following day. A good tip is to paint tool handles with bright fluorescent colors—orange, hot pink, chartreuse, yellow—so it's easy to find them in the yard or garden and bring them back inside. See Chapter 15 (beginning on page 311) for tips on tool storage in the garage.

Fence your vegetables. Many gardeners enjoy growing at least a few homegrown veggies in the backyard garden. But an unfenced vegetable garden invites dogs, cats, raccoons, and we won't even say what else into the garden plot to enjoy themselves, especially after dark. Don't get mad—get even. Bury a wire fence around your garden, sinking it a few inches into the ground to discourage prowlers. Make sure it's tall and secured well enough to discourage climbers like raccoons and jumpers like deer. Don't like the look of wire? Cover it with wooden latticing or grow vining plants like grapes, pole beans, clematis, and hardy kiwis over its surface to soften it.

Perfect your playground. There is no reason for your kids' playground to look junky, ugly, or cluttered. A well-built, well-secured swing set is a pleasure for the whole family. (Try it!) A gym set, slide and tube, merry-go-round, sandbox, tire or rope swing, and other toys can be every bit as much fun. The key is to think of the playground as a public park and to build it to last and to grow with your kids' needs. Check out what's in your local park or your kids' school playground—and which pieces of equipment in the park or school your kids love—before you buy your own playground equipment. Then site it where it's shaded and won't dominate the whole yard, but where you can still keep an eye on the kids. Replace rusty, falling-over playground equipment immediately or, if the kids have outgrown it, donate it, have the stuff hauled off, or place a classified ad and hope somebody will come and get it!

Oust awful outbuildings. Collapsing outhouses, leaning sheds, ancient doghouses—say good-bye to any structure that's no longer usable. Replace what you need with attractive, safe, useful outbuildings, but consign the hopeless cases to the flames or to trash pickup.

Reel in the hose. Don't just leave your hoses lying around the yard or across the driveway; they can be ruined by someone running over them with the lawn mower or driving over them with the car, or *you* can be ruined when someone trips over them and sues you. Put them on a reel cart that keeps them coiled and kink-free when not in use, can be rolled to where you want to use them, and tucks away in the garage or tool shed when you're through with the watering or ready to store the hoses for winter. You'll prolong the life of your hose, and maybe your own, as well!

Move the mowers. Repeat after me: Lawn mowers are *not* lawn art. Don't leave them out in the yard, where they're not just giant eyesores, but will also be wrecked

Love It *or* Lose It?

Faux stones. Know what I'm talking about? Those hollow plastic "boulders" a lot of catalogs and home centers sell to cover up unsightly things like septic pipes and utility boxes. Well, no one would deny that pipes and other metal objects sticking up out of the ground are unsightly. But so are these plastic atrocities! It's bad enough to see all the *real* boulders people toss onto their lawns in misguided attempts at landscaping (they always make me think of "The sky is falling!"), without us now having to stare at hideous plastic ones. (It takes a highly skilled landscape architect to use stones well in a landscape. My advice: Do *not* try this at home unless you have superb professional guidance.) A far better solution is to garden around the eyesore and hide it among the plants.

Verdict: Lose it!

by the weather. Take care of your investment and reduce yard clutter by storing your lawn mowers in the shed or garage when you're not using them.

Put a brake on the bikes. That goes for bikes, trikes, skateboards, and all other mobile devices that kids love but seem incapable of storing. These create visual clutter, get battered by the weather, and create tripping (and mowing) hazards. If the kids are old enough to ride 'em, they're old enough to put 'em away.

Fence the utilities. Garbage cans, central air units, and other large, useful, but unsightly objects are facts of life. But that doesn't mean you (and your guests) have to look at them. An attractive picket fence or lattice screen enclosing the trash cans or AC can make a world of difference. Paint it to match your house (or trim), and make sure one side opens easily for access. True, it won't make the eyesore disappear, but at least it won't be an eyesore any more!

Clear out deadwood. Few things are as unsightly as a brown, dead shrub or hedge—or as unsightly and dangerous as a rotting, fallen tree trunk or branch. Call an arborist and have them hauled away or stacked neatly under cover where they won't be an eyesore but are still convenient for stoking the fireplace or woodstove. Don't leave a hideous tree or shrub in place when it's beyond saving—it will ruin the whole yard, since it will be the first thing a visitor's eye goes to. ("What's that dead brown thing?") Cut it down and haul it off or burn it!

Watch the woodpile. Speaking of burning wood, if you have a woodpile, manage it. Don't ever put it out in the front yard to become an eyesore. Stack the wood neatly in a sheltered location in the backyard, and cover it with a brown (never blue!) tarp to protect it from the elements. Hardware and home improvement stores and catalogs like Plow & Hearth (see page 47) and Solutions (see page 48) offer racks to hold your cut firewood upright and stable, and they also sell tough, durable covers for the piles. These are great ideas. But the best idea is to *use* your wood, rather than letting it sit and rot while waiting for the next "Y2K" to strike. Instead, enjoy it! Replace your stack with more good wood every year, and you'll still be ready if disaster strikes.

Ditto for detritus. Okay, all. Bits and pieces of rusting metal, fencing, cardboard boxes, pallets, stacks of newspaper and tin cans, abandoned lawn mowers and other equipment, burst hoses, old tires, leftovers from ancient do-it-yourself projects, tools that look like they came from a Mayan ruin—gather them up and haul them off. Or have someone else haul them off. Do not leave them lying around the yard creating a tetanus hazard and transforming what could be a pleasant space into an amateur junkyard. There is *no* excuse for this! Get that stuff outta there.

Patrol the pool. Besides making sure your pool is kid- and animal-safe, make sure it looks as good as it can. Inground pools usually look great as long as they're well maintained (especially if they're landscaped), but no pool looks good if moldy towels, flip-flops, pool toys, plates and glasses, suntan lotion, and heaven knows what else are left out there to decompose at their leisure. Pick up all the pool debris after each swim session and put it back where it belongs. (And get your kids involved in dealing with their own pool stuff—taking away pool privileges can be a powerful motivator!) If you have an aboveground pool, try to site it as attractively as you can. Putting a deck around it and adding plants, lattice screening, and attractive deck furniture can help make the pool look like part of your yard, not something that fell to earth from a passing spaceship. If you can connect the pool decking to the house deck, so much the better—it will look more integrated and be easier to get to.

👍 Love It *or* Lose It? 👎

When I started gardening, I didn't have a lot of choice about what sorts of containers to use to haul soil, compost, and fertilizers around in. They tended to be ugly, awkward, and heavy. But these days there are some really wonderful options that are lightweight and colorful as well as capacious. Garden centers and home and garden catalogs like Gardener's Supply Company and Kinsman Company (see page 49) sell sturdy but flexible plastic tubs (called Trug-Tubs) in a variety of cheerful colors. They have handles so they're easy to haul around, and they're attractive enough to keep out on display on your potting bench or under your plant bench, full of potting soil, bulbs, or whatever you'd like.

But that's not all. These companies also sell collapsible, lightweight "pop-up bags" that fold down to 4 inches for storage but open up to 20 inches. They're made of water-resistant woven plastic and are strong enough to hold up to 45 pounds of leaves, soil, spent plants you want to haul from the greenhouse out to the compost, and so on. They also have cushioned handles for comfort and come in an array of cheerful garden-themed patterns.

Verdict: Love them both!

Pet Alert!

Dogs and yards go together. But dog-related clutter—be it a kennel of bare dirt, holes, bones, and scraps, a down-at-heels doghouse, or piles of poop and yellowed rings in the grass—still spells clutter. (And worse. "Neglect" and "disease" are both good words.) If you like to let your dog out unattended, consider putting in an invisible fence instead of a kennel or run.

Make sure your dog's house looks appealing and well maintained. Try to make it match your house's architecture style or color. If you're handy, you can have a lot of fun designing a custom doghouse. See the book *Barkitecture* by Fred Albert, or look to another doghouse style book for inspiration. The same goes for toys, bowls, and any other dog-related paraphernalia: Make sure they're in good shape, replace them regularly, and contain them when your dog's not playing with them. Two or three dog toys and bones are enough; don't litter the yard with them. As with anything else, rotate your dog's favorites instead of letting them all lie out there exposed to the elements. They'll last longer, hold your dog's interest longer, and keep your yard looking better!

Finally—and this should go without saying—pick up after your pet. No one wants to walk through a minefield of poop! And you can pick up parasites if you wander barefoot through a poop-filled yard. Of all the kinds of outdoor clutter, this is the very worst. As for those yellow lawn rings, if you take your dog to a new spot every day and make sure the grass is watered during dry spells, you should be able to avoid them.

Compost what you can. Make free, nutritious fertilizer for your gardens and lawn by putting vegetable and flower clippings, pulled weeds (minus seed heads), kitchen scraps (except for dairy products, oily leftovers, and meat scraps, which can attract vermin), leaves, shredded paper, and grass clippings in a compost bin. Contain the compost in a homemade pallet bin or a ready-made wood or plastic bin so it will look good and not perturb your neighbors. You can get rid of a lot of landscape, kitchen, and paper clutter this way, and feed your lawn and gardens at the same time!

Clean up your gardens. At the end of the growing season, gardens are brown, weedy, overgrown, and unkempt. They are, in short, yard clutter. Cut down the dead stuff and compost it, please. You'll thank yourself every single fall and winter day as you look out at an attractive landscape instead of a jungle of dead plants. And your garden will be ready to go in spring instead of still awaiting cleanup. Worried about sheltering birds and beneficial bugs? The bugs will be fine in the compost pile, which, after all, will hardly be cooking when it's cold outside, and you can put up feeders and houses for the birds.

Recycle plant pots. If you're like me, you buy lots of transplants and container plants every year, and after you set them out in the garden or pot them up, you have a wealth of plastic plant trays, pots, and seedling packs left over. Fortunately, I've discovered that most nurseries will be happy to take them back if you bring them over. If you have cracked and chipped terra-cotta pots, smash those suckers and use the pieces to add drainage at the bottom of good pots.

ONWARD!

Well, congratulations! You've made it through the indoors, the outdoors, and the gray areas where outdoors and indoors meet. You've kicked the clutter out of your house and yard. But now, what do you do with it? In the next section, Trash (Yours) to Treasure (Theirs), you'll find out about the myriad ways you can donate, sell, swap, or just plain get rid of every last piece of (ex-)clutter. Maybe all that stuff will finally pay off—or at least pay you back something for taking up so much of your life for so long.

PART FOUR

Trash (Yours) to Treasure (Theirs)

Chapter 17

Donations and Write-Offs

When you're kicking out clutter, Goodwill, the Salvation Army, and the Society of St. Vincent de Paul can be your best friends. So can homes for pregnant teens and abused families, homeless shelters, missions, and numerous other charities. Here's how to find them, how to tell in advance who'll want what, and how to get a tax break for your stuff without risking Uncle Sam's ire.

GIVING IT ALL AWAY

I don't know about you, but I find few things as satisfying as hauling a bag of stuff off to Goodwill or the Salvation Army. The thrill of seeing all that unused stuff moving out of my house! The thought that perhaps it will be sent to someone in need, or at least find a second home where it will be appreciated! I always have a "Goodwill bag" going, and as soon as I cart it off, I start another one. But these aren't the only places you can take your (former) clutter. Read on for plenty of ways to match your stuff with a charity or other worthwhile nonprofit agency. Just remember to donate responsibly—don't donate stuff that's in such bad shape that it really belongs in the trash.

Think Like an Angel

For the past 7 years, the local paper in my area, the Allentown, Pennsylvania, *Morning Call,* has held a "Be an Angel" campaign for 2 months, from the end of November through the end of January. Its purpose has been to match up nonprofit organizations and their wish lists with local donors. The program has been so successful that last year, the *Morning Call* had 407 organizations involved, each listing three wishes, from cars and cameras to diapers and craft supplies. They ranged from local hospitals, the Red Cross, and Easter Seals to the local ecumenical food bank, adult literacy center, Meals on Wheels, and Crime Victims' Council. Schools, pet shelters, historic societies, museums, churches, fire companies—the breadth of organizations involved was just amazing.

Your community may not have such an organized giving campaign, but you can still locate services and agencies in your area just like the ones where I live. I suggest that you call your favorite nonprofits and ask them if they'd accept donations and, if so, what they need. I was amazed at how many groups wanted things that are typically hard to get rid of, like computers and appliances. And, of course, lots of them wanted household items, clothing, books, toys, TVs, DVDs, video tapes, CDs, and players for those videos and CDs. It's certainly worth a few phone calls to find a *really* good home for your unwanted stuff!

SPECIFIC DONATIONS

Trying to get rid of something in particular? Check the list below to see where you can find an organization that needs your donation. If I haven't listed your item, try contacting the organizations in "The Pros Know" on page 354 for help.

Appliances. If you want to donate a (working) appliance that's no more than 3 years old, contact Habitat for Humanity (www.habitat.org). Or check out Excess Access (www.excessaccess.org) to be matched with a local charity that will come pick up your appliances.

Automobiles. JustGive's Web site has a lot of links to charities that accept cars and other vehicles in a variety of conditions. Check them out at www.justgive.org.

Books. See if your local library will accept donations. Check with your local veterans' home, senior centers, and assisted-living facilities to see if they accept

An Ounce of Prevention

Before 2007, it used to be easy to give stuff to places like Goodwill and the Salvation Army. You handed stuff over, filled out a form listing the items you'd donated and their value, and then pulled out your deduction lists at tax time. (The Salvation Army has a valuation guide for goods of all kinds on its Web site; go to www.salvationarmyusa.org and search for "valuation guide." Goodwill Industries also lists values as guidelines on its Web site at www.goodwillpromo.org.) But beginning with 2007 tax returns, the guidelines are different for taxpayers who choose to itemize their deductions rather than taking the standard deduction.

The IRS now requires that only "usable items" can be deducted—no broken appliances, torn clothing, and the like—and that any item valued at more than $500 must have an official appraisal submitted with the tax form. Should you wish to deduct a large item like a used car, boat, or RV, you may only deduct what the charity actually receives from the sale of the item, as opposed to the "fair market value" that was allowed in the old days. And unfortunately, the valuation guidelines posted by the various agencies are considered a conflict of interest under the new laws. So how do you know what it's legal to deduct? Though there are still no cut-and-dried guidelines as of this writing, you might consider the advice of the New Fairfield Community Thrift Shop in Connecticut, which suggests that its donors deduct 10 percent of the original value of their items. And make sure you check IRS publication 561, "Determining the Value of Donated Property" (www.irs.gov/pub/irs-pdf/p561.pdf).

What caused the change? A congressional study found that, in 2003, Americans who itemized their deductions were writing off pretty eye-popping sums: 4 million households wrote off an average of $1,440 each for clothing donations, and 2.4 million wrote off an average of $1,356 for donated household goods. Now, if you're going to itemize, you're going to have to provide proof that your donations actually measure up to your claims of their value. So make sure you have the receipts and valuations!

books. Local day care centers might appreciate a gift of children's books. You can also donate children's books to BookEnds (www.bookends.org), an organization that provides them to shelters, schools, family literacy centers, and youth organizations. There are also national specialty organizations that accept donated books. You can donate textbooks from elementary school through college level if they're

10 years old or newer, current editions of encyclopedias, and issues of *National Geographic* from 1985 on to Books for Africa (www.booksforafrica.org). Books for America (www.booksforamerica.org) donates books to community organizations, hospices, shelters, and prisons.

Calendars. Sometimes it seems like you can't turn around toward the end of the year without getting a free calendar in the mail, being handed one every time you walk into a store, and, of course, receiving half a dozen as holiday gifts. Don't throw them out or resort to "regifting." Follow my friend Chris's lead: She saves her unused calendars to give to assisted-living facilities.

Cell phones. Donate these to a national organization like Donate a Phone or Collective Good. Find them at Earth 911 (www.earth911.org). Used cell phones can be used to dial 911, and shelters for abused women and children often give them to their clients for emergency use.

Clothing. Make an itemized list and take your used or simply unworn and unwanted clothes to your local Salvation Army (which has receipt forms to fill out inside the drop-off door), Goodwill, or Society of St. Vincent de Paul. Or, if you don't want a receipt for tax purposes (see "An Ounce of Prevention" on page 353) and you don't care what happens to your clothes, simply look for a used clothing drop-off bin. Where I live, these are marked dumpsters located in corners of various pharmacy parking lots. Lillian, one of my fellow Curves members, admits that she always uses these but is a bit concerned because she has no idea what happens to the clothes once she drops them off. I've read that clothing in these bins is often sold by the pound to be recycled into rags for rag rugs and industrial purposes, with the proceeds going to charity, but who knows for sure? The bins always seem to be full, so I guess the convenience is worth the uncertainty for lots of local residents!

the **Pros Know**

Not sure where to donate something? Luckily for us, some organizations specialize in matching donors with nonprofits. Check out the Web site of Earth 911 (www.earth911.org), the "ways to give" area of JustGive's Web site (www.justgive.org), or Excess Access (www.excessaccess.org), which will list your stuff so interested organizations can pick it up.

Other options are to donate clothing to a local homeless shelter or thrift store or to see if your church, temple, or other place of worship has a clothing drive or other suggestion for donating clothing. (Also see "Work clothing" on page 356.)

Computers. If your computer or its components still work and you're just upgrading, contact Share the Technology (www.sharetechnology.org). It will put you in touch with a nonprofit organization that needs computers. If it's fewer than 5 years old, you can also donate it through www.pcsforschools.org or www.techsoup.org/recycle; if it's older, try www.worldcomputerexchange.org. Or check the list of places to donate computers and related technology to at JustGive (www.justgive.org). Just make sure all of your personal information is completely removed from your hard drive—you need to do more than just delete it or put it in the recycle bin.

Eyeglasses. Donate these to the Lion's Club (www.lionsclubs.org). They put containers for donated glasses in local libraries, LensCrafters, Goodwill stores, community offices, and other places.

Food. Find a food bank near you by checking the Yellow Pages or America's Second Harvest (www.secondharvest.org), the national food bank and food-rescue network. Don't even think about trying to donate expired food, though, please! Or you can donate food to a local soup kitchen; look for them in the government section of your phone directory, or ask at your church, synagogue, or other place of worship if they know of a soup kitchen in your area.

Furniture. Your local Salvation Army, Goodwill, and Society of St. Vincent de Paul stores are all good choices for furniture donations, and they may even come pick up your stuff. They do expect it to be in saleable condition, not beat. Or check JustGive's Web site (www.justgive.org), which lists additional places that accept furniture. Or go onto Excess Access (www.excessaccess.org), which will match you with a local charity. Other options include local homeless shelters and shelters for battered women and families, which may be looking for furniture to help families that are starting over.

Gardening tools. Donate gardening tools, hoses, wheelbarrows, and other supplies to your local community garden. Check the Yellow Pages for a community garden in your area, or contact the American Community Gardening Association (www.communitygarden.org).

Hearing aids. Donate hearing aids to Hear Now (www.sotheworldmayhear.org/hearnow), a nonprofit program directed by the Starkey Hearing Foundation.

Pet Alert!

My friend Chris donates old towels and linens to a local animal shelter. Great idea! Some shelters need newspapers, too. If you're like me, well-meaning friends are always giving you pet treats and toys you don't feel are "good enough" for your precious furry friends. Pass them along to the shelter, too. And, of course, if you have extra grooming tools that are in good shape, I'm sure they'd appreciate those! Not sure where to give? Check out Pets 911 (www.pets911.com) for recommendations.

Musical instruments. Check with your local school district to see if they'd be interested in your family's cast-off musical instruments (assuming they're in good shape).

Videos, DVDs, and CDs. Many of the same organizations that accept books (see page 352) will also take video tapes, DVDs, and CDs. Also check with your local libraries, senior centers, assisted-living facilities, veterans' homes, shelters, hospices, blood centers, and childrens' homes and organizations to see if they'd be interested.

Work clothing. Help low-income people get and keep jobs by donating work clothing and accessories. For men, donate to Career Gear (www.careergear.org). For women, check out Dress for Success (www.dressforsuccess.org) or the Women's Alliance (www.thewomensalliance.org), which has the wonderful motto, "Someone's future is hanging in your closet."

ONWARD!

Well, I hope you've been inspired to donate useful items to deserving organizations, whether you choose to itemize your deductions for your tax return or simply enjoy feeling good about doing something positive with your clutter (for a change). But you might be tempted to try your hand at selling some of your stuff, as well. It can be fun and rewarding! In the next few chapters, we'll review the many ways to unload your clutter for cash or credit. In the next chapter, we'll start with secondhand shops.

Chapter 18

Secondhand Shops

From music and bookstores to consignment clothing stores, you can often sell your cast-off stuff for cash or store credit. The tips in this chapter will help you decide when to take the money and run, when to take the credit, how to find the right stores for your stuff, when to donate it instead of sell it, and, of course, how to get the most for each precious piece of clutter.

THE JOY OF SECONDHAND STORES

My mother would have as soon been dead as set foot in a secondhand shop, so it took many years and many miles before I began to patronize them. Admittedly, I had always been a huge fan of used bookstores—especially the giant barnlike ones with floor after floor of hidden treasures. And my whole family was addicted to antiques stores (see Chapter 22—Antiques in Your Attic, beginning on page 429, for more on this). But, thanks to enthusiastic friends like Delilah and Susan, I finally began to appreciate the charm of consignment stores, vintage clothing stores, and thrift shops. Then, when I read an article that pointed out that if no shirts were ever made again, there'd be enough shirts to clothe everyone in the world 'til the end of time, secondhand shops became my favorite clothing stores.

Not that I don't also succumb to clothes from the Orvis and Boston Proper catalogs and the nearest Coldwater Creek store! But for everyday, the thrill of the chase—finding that Laura Ashley, Calvin Klein, or Liz Claiborne piece for $3.50, good as new; or the absolutely best-fitting-ever jean skirt; or perfect, wonderfully colored tee-shirts for under $10 for a huge bagful—simply cannot be beat. I myself am afraid of used shoes—I dread the thought of bringing the fungus among us—but I've gotten wonderful belts and purses (not to mention Hawaiian shirts for my boyfriend, Rob, who has a weakness for them) at secondhand shops.

Then, of course, there are the amazing cooking supplies—pots, pans, dishes, silverware, glass, and appliances of all stripes and types—to be found at stores like Goodwill and the Salvation Army, pretty much all for under $5, many of them vintage and wonderful. (Check out these stores for astonishing heavy-duty cast-iron and grilling cookware at unbeatable prices.) I found a mini–slow cooker there for heating up dips; it cost less than $3 and worked like a charm. And Rob loves old-fashioned drinks like Manhattans, so I've amused myself by looking for interesting, old-fashioned cocktail glasses for him—not to mention actually elegant wineglasses for us. Secondhand stores are also great places to buy Christmas ornaments affordably, as well as linens, towels, bedclothes, and much, much more. (You may remember me raving in an earlier chapter about the wine racks and CD holder I found at the local Goodwill, all for under $5, and I've had equally good luck at the Salvation Army.)

Sometimes, you really can find hidden treasure at secondhand and consignment shops. I once found a Navajo Wedding Basket, worth at least $250, that had been stuffed into a bin of Easter baskets, all priced at $4, at a local consignment shop. And my friend Tom e-mailed me recently to ask if I'd heard that a man had found a copy of the Declaration of Independence worth $250,000 at his local thrift shop!

But wait, aren't we supposed to be talking about *selling* stuff, not buying it? Sorry, I got carried away. Let's head out to some consignment and secondhand shops and see what you can expect.

Consignment versus Secondhand

First of all, what's the difference between a consignment and a secondhand store, anyway? Basically, they're both "secondhand"—that is to say, both deal in previously owned if not previously used items. The difference is in the way they acquire

I Did It!

You'll get the most from your secondhand or consignment experience if you ask the store owner or manager these questions before you simply head over with a trunkful of bags or boxes:

1. Do you have a brochure I could look at?
2. What sort of items are you interested in?
3. How many years have you been in the business? (I was astounded by how many decades most area secondhand and consignment businesses had been operating.)
4. Do you offer cash up front or cash when the item sells (consignment)?
5. What percentage of the sale price will I get?
6. Do you offer a higher percentage in store credit?
7. (If it's a consignment shop) How long do you keep the item?
8. (If it's a consignment shop) Do you discount the price at intervals while it's on display?
9. Do I need to make an appointment to bring items in?
10. Do you have a limit on the number of items I can bring at one time?
11. Do you take seasonal items only, and if so, what are your seasonal time limits?
12. Do you pay in cash or by check?
13. (If it's a consignment shop) Can I pick up any unsold items at the end of the consignment period?
14. (If it's a consignment shop) Will you donate any unsold items to a charity for me?
15. (If it's a consignment shop) Will you give me a donation receipt (for tax purposes) for any items you donate to charity?

their merchandise. A secondhand store buys the stuff from you directly—if they want it, they offer you a price, and you take it, make a counteroffer, or pack it back up and move on.

At a consignment shop, you're basically asking the store owner to sell items for you on commission. Technically, the items are still yours and could come back to haunt you if they don't sell within the time limit the store owner typically sets. The majority of consignment shops, but not all of them, are used-clothing stores, but not all the clothing stores limit their sales strictly to clothing, or even clothing and accessories like jewelry, purses, ties, and shoes.

To add to the confusion, not all consignment stores sell the same way. I have patronized quite a few in my area and have noticed two distinct sales trends. One is the single-price item, which sells for the same price during the entire 90 days (or however long) it's for sale. The other (always enticing for bargain-loving buyers) is the sliding price scale, where an item has three prices on its sales tag—one for the first month, a lower one for the second month, and the lowest for the third month it's on sale in the store.

Though it's great news for patient buyers who are willing to take the chance that their prize may sell for a higher price to someone who's willing to pay it, the sliding scale may not be the greatest news for those of you who are trying to sell your stuff, since you still make a set percentage of the sale price, however low it goes. Still, if your primary goal is to get your clutter out the door and your secondary goal is to make a little money in the bargain, any of these options are exciting. Let's take a closer look at them.

STARTING OUT RIGHT

To get the most for your stuff at a secondhand or consignment shop, you need to do your homework. Once you do, you'll find stores that will take pretty much anything you want to consign, as long as it's in decent shape. (Not 5 miles from my house, the sign in front of the Eagle Arms proclaims, "Cash for Guns!") Taking the time to check out the secondhand and consignment shops near you is definitely worth it.

For example, if I had clothes to consign, I could take them to 20 shops in my area. But if they were designer clothes, I'd get more for them at Designer Re Runs, which specializes in higher-end fashions; if they were clothes for college kids, I'd get the best deal at the Attic, whose clientele is between 15 and 30; and if they were for little kids, Back Again for Kids would be the place to go. The closer the match between your stuff and a shop's specialty, the more you're likely to get for it.

Browse the shops in your city and in nearby towns (trying, of course, to resist bringing home yet more clutter!) and see what they offer. Many consignment and secondhand shops have excellent brochures that spell out their consignment and buying policies; collect as many as you can. Talk to the owners and try to get a feel for the place. Ask how long they've been in business. Ask if they also sell online, maybe on eBay. (Some stores sell the majority of their merchandise online, which can mean a faster turnover.)

Finally, keep your eyes open! What sort of person is shopping while you're in the store? Are there many people coming through? Are they buying? If you have time, go back in a week or two and see if the merchandise has changed noticeably. (I know one extremely busy shop whose merchandise changes daily!)

So find a place that's a good fit in terms of what's being sold and how well the store seems to be doing in terms of business and merchandise turnover. Then, if you're happy with their sales or consignment agreement and terms, make an appointment and bring in your stuff. You're on your way to kicking the clutter!

Above all, be realistic. You're not going to make what you paid for an item. You're probably not going to make half. But usually the store owner has a good idea what the item will sell for—especially if the shop specializes in that type of goods. And remember, if you get anything for your items, you're coming out ahead—doubly!—since you're getting stuff out and bringing cash in.

WHEELING AND DEALING

Let's take a tour of some typical consignment and secondhand shops so you can see the sort of arrangements you'll be likely to encounter when you bring your own stuff in.

Hitting the Books (and Making Music)

Brendan D. Strasser is the proprietor of the Saucony Book Shop in Kutztown, Pennsylvania. Like many used-book stores, the Saucony is a book collector's paradise, with buried treasure piled high to the ceiling in every room, shelves overflowing, and the occasional old map or print enticing you to come over for a closer look. But the Saucony is noticeably lacking the paperbacks that are the bread-and-butter of the used-book trade—the popular fiction, bestsellers, and romances that fill the back rooms of most used-book stores.

That's because Brendan specializes in terms of what he sells, featuring local history, general history, cooking, art, music, and a range of other topics. So when you bring books in for Brendan to look at or you describe them to him on the phone, he's likely to know right away if he's interested. If he's not, he'll direct you to other booksellers who carry the type of books you have, or he'll donate them to a library if you'd just like to get rid of them. He'll also do estate appraisals or come to your home if you have a large collection; otherwise, you can make an appointment to bring books in.

Brendan prefers to buy books outright; he takes a book on consignment only if it's really valuable (as in, worth thousands of dollars). Like many store owners I spoke to, he'll give more store credit for a book than he will outright cash—50 percent of what he sells it for in store credit versus less than half that in cash, your choice.

Brendan prices books based on 20 years' experience in the business and on a sound knowledge of market value: He checks what books are going for on national and international book Web sites and on eBay. And, like many other businesses I checked out, most of Brendan's business—90 percent—is done online, on the six major book sites (like Alibris, which has 60 million books at its disposal); only 10 percent of the books are sold through his bricks-and-mortar store.

A few blocks from the Saucony Book Shop is Young Ones, a fabulously funky used and new music store with an original mural covering the outside wall. In brilliant color, it pays tribute to such legends as Bob Marley, John Lennon, and Jimi Hendrix, with eye-catching, larger-than-life figures of the fallen stars of rock and reggae. It's equally colorful inside, with a tremendous selection of new and used CDs and of used LP records, cassettes, DVDs, and video tapes. Like the Saucony, Young Ones will give you a much better deal if you take store credit rather than cash.

Clearing Out the Closet

Clothes are another thing we all seem to have too many of. Whether our clothes have gone out of style, we've worn them to death, or we just can't fit into them any more (maybe because we've *lost* weight, hooray), we usually find ourselves picking up new clothes and facing a closet stuffed with old ones every season. (And then, of course, those kids do keep on growing. And if you think *you're* style-conscious, ask yourself how many times you've hauled your teen to the mall in the past week!)

Finally, one too many fights with coat hangers, shoe avalanches, drawer volcanoes, or other overstuffed disasters makes you decide you really *have* to whittle down your wardrobe. And now you've taken the worn stuff to Goodwill and still have a bagful of stuff (or two or three) that's in good enough shape to consign. What are your options?

Designer Duds

At Designer Re Runs, an upscale consignment and resale boutique in Allentown, Pennsylvania, owner Kay Chrin provides a helpful brochure with extremely clear guidelines for potential consignees. Kay accepts brand-name women's and junior's apparel and accessories in sizes 2 to plus. She'll accept only seasonal items and advises everyone to "think what you would wear for the 8 weeks your articles will be on consignment" when deciding what to bring in. (She does provide broad seasonal guidelines, too—fall clothes after Labor Day, winter starting October 14, spring beginning February 14, and summer clothes starting April 14.)

Kay wants "gently used" clothing that's freshly washed and pressed or dry cleaned, and she reminds consignees to check zippers, pockets, and seams. She asks that you bring all items on hangers (which will be returned to you) rather than in bags where they could wrinkle. As she says, each item must be in excellent condition and in style—1 or 2 years old. (Her key question: "Would you purchase it?")

Unlike many stores, Designer Re Runs will let you bring in your consignment clothing and accessories without an appointment, 7 days a week, as long as you come in more than an hour before they close. Once Kay accepts an article, she'll keep it in stock for 8 weeks, then you can either pick up your items or Designer Re Runs will donate them to charity. Kay points out that it's your responsibility to keep track of the pick-up date and retrieve your stuff promptly if you want it back. Once the consignment cycle is over, Kay's clients receive 50 percent of the selling price; she mails a check within 15 days.

Across the Board

In the town of Emmaus, Pennsylvania (where my publisher, Rodale Inc., maintains its home office), Once Is Not Enuf has been going strong for 30 years. Once Is Not Enuf sells women's fashions across the board, from evening gowns to jeans, along with a wide selection of purses, scarves, shoes, jewelry, and other accessories.

Like Designer Re Runs, Once Is Not Enuf has a thorough, excellent brochure that spells out exactly what they expect from their consignment clients and what clients may expect from them. But unlike Designer Re Runs, Once Is Not Enuf asks that you call for an appointment and, when you call, indicate the number of items you're planning to bring in, with a limit of 25 per appointment. They accept seasonal clothing only and list their seasonal guidelines, accepting fall clothes in August and September, winter clothes from October through January, spring clothes in March and April, and summer clothes from May through July.

Once Is Not Enuf will accept women's and junior's clothes in sizes 2 through 26, as well as small decorative household items and accessories that they can sell for $10 or more. Their terms for acceptability are identical to those of Designer Re Runs: Clothes must be in style, no more than 1 to 2 years old, and delivered freshly washed and pressed or dry cleaned, wrinkle-free, on hangers, with seams, pockets, and zippers in good repair. They'll also consider some vintage items. Like Brendan Strasser of the Saucony Book Shop, the owner of Once Is Not Enuf sets sale prices for consignment articles based on her 30 years' experience in the business.

Their terms are also a lot like Kay Chrin's of Designer Re Runs: Articles are stocked for 8 weeks, with the items' prices reduced by 20 percent and then another 25 percent at intervals over the 8-week period if they don't sell. (I mentioned that the price reductions seemed hard to come up with, since they were in percentages rather than whole dollars, and the owner noted that there's a computer program that calculates the amounts precisely so they don't have to do all those calculations by hand!) Clients get 50 percent of the sale price, via a mailed check (if you don't want any unsold items) or at store pickup (if you come in to get your other items or it's less than $25). Like Designer Re Runs, Once Is Not Enuf expects you to keep track of your 8-week consignment period and pick up your unsold items within 2 weeks after the end of the period. Otherwise, they'll be donated to a charity.

Vintage and Funk

Closer to my house, Clares Closet in Kutztown, Pennsylvania, sells men's, women's, and vintage clothes on consignment. In addition to their inviting store, which also features locally made accessories and crafts like handbags, soaps, and wooden utensils, Clares has a thriving eBay store and takes items on consignment for it, too. (See Chapter 19, beginning on page 372, for more on the eBay side of things.) One of Clares's co-owners, Janet Brito, sets the prices for consignment items, again based on many years in the business. If your items have designer labels, the prices tend to be higher.

The attitude at Clares is a little more relaxed than at the other clothing consignment stores I patronize, in keeping with their "Fashion and Funk" theme and Kutztown's small-town charm. They technically accept items on consignment for 90 days, but will actually keep them longer, especially if they have confidence that it's something that will sell. "Sometimes a piece just seems to sit there, then one day someone comes in, takes one look, and boom!" Barb, one of Clares's veteran sales clerks, told me. Like the others, they accept seasonal clothes only because of space limitations, unless the item is seasonless (like jeans) or vintage, in which case they'll accept it at any time of year. You can call or drop by to make an appointment to consign.

Clients get 40 percent of the sale price at Clares, but unlike Designer Re Runs and Once Is Not Enuf, sale prices are fixed, not tied to the length of time the item is on sale, so the owner will get just as much if the item sells in 90 days as if it sells the first day it's brought in. If, after the 90 (or so) days, the item doesn't sell, the owner can come and retrieve it, or Clares will donate it to the local Hope Rescue Mission and give the (former) owner a receipt for tax purposes.

Because Clares Closet goes beyond the everyday clothes it carries to specialize in vintage and funky clothes and accessories as well, they sell a lot of clothing for private costume parties and, of course, for Halloween. And local theater groups, as well as the Kutztown University theater department, also check in regularly to see if Clares has gotten in anything they can use in an upcoming production.

The Young and the Restless

Because Kutztown is a college town, the Attic, a secondhand clothing store on the main street, specializes in clothes, vintage apparel and accessories, shoes, collectibles, and jewelry that students can relate to. The mother-daughter co-owners, Linda and Anne Kuronyi, specifically target 15- to 30-year-olds with an arty, vintage layout and a delightful assortment of clothes and vintage accessories, many from the sixties and seventies (buttons, anyone?). Like Clares, they also sell clothes for costumes.

You don't need an appointment to bring things in to the Attic. But unlike the other clothing stores, it's not a consignment shop—it pays cash or gives store credit on the spot for everything it takes (30 percent of their sale price in cash or 55 percent in store credit). "Because we pay cash, we're really picky about what we take," the college-age clerk told me when I stopped in. "Everything has to be in excellent condition." Being picky and buying less means that the Attic will buy clothing for any season at all times and will simply hold merchandise for the appropriate season. If they don't take your clothes and other items, they'll be glad to donate them to local charities. They summarize their business practices and philosophy on a postcard—no mean feat!—and have a great Web site, www.atticclothes.com, that tells you a lot more.

Furniture, Housewares, and All That

Clothes? Check. Books, music, and movies? Check. Household stuff? Still looking for a home. Well, seek and ye shall find. There may not be as many consignment shops for housewares as there are for clothes, but trust me, they are out there. Here are a few of the types you might encounter. As with everything else, try a store that specializes in your type of stuff if you want to get it sold.

Kid Stuff

Maybe my area has a lot of kids, but just driving around running errands takes me past four infants' and children's clothing, toy, and furnishings secondhand and consignment shops, all within half an hour of my house: Bears Repeating in

Consignments for a Cause

You can sell anything you want, from furniture, china, and crystal to jewelry, Christmas ornaments, quilts, and chess sets, at the Elephant's Trunk in Emmaus, Pennsylvania. But the Elephant's Trunk isn't just a consignment shop—it's a consignment shop for a cause. It's operated by volunteers for the benefit of Planned Parenthood of Northeast Pennsylvania. Since 1985, the Elephant's Trunk has raised more than $400,000 in support of Planned Parenthood's services.

And it's not alone. Pat Robertson, the owner of Antiques Etc., a shop in Maxatawny, Pennsylvania, mentioned that in her area, Nova Thrift Shop, which takes both consignments and donations, benefits battered women. Imagine the thrill of consigning your clutter to benefit your favorite cause! Call the causes you support and see if they have a consignment shop in your area. Like other consignment shops, benefit shops take a percentage of the sale.

the Pros Know

"Consignment stores are the perfect place to take unwanted clothing," says Janet Brito, co-owner of Clares Closet in Kutztown, Pennsylvania. If you're considering consignment, take her great advice to make your experience pleasant and profitable.

"Don't automatically pitch outdated clothing or clothes that have been stashed in the attic or basement," says Janet. "There is a huge resale market for retro clothing from the sixties through the nineties. Of course, the clothing has to have flair and not be stained, torn, and so on. Stores like ours will even come to your place and help you sort through it, especially if Mom or Dad passed and the job seems overwhelming to you."

Here's more of Janet's practical advice. "Find a way to monitor your current closet," she says. "One hint that we learned was to hang all hangers one way at the beginning of the season, and then if you wear an item, turn the hanger around. At the end of the season, you can see what you didn't wear and need to part with." What a great idea!

"Sort this unworn clothing into two piles, a donation pile and a consignment pile," Janet says. "Anything that is worn out, stained, mended, from discount stores such as Wal-Mart, pulled, pilled, or just not like new, put in the donation pile. Make a count of the donated items, along with their value (clothing items are worth a few dollars each), and take them to your favorite charity store. Make sure you get a receipt, because you can claim this donation on your taxes. Even if the charity store decides an item's not worth reselling, you can still take a deduction."

The items you have left are the ones Janet and her peers can help you get rid of. "The good-quality, brand-name, like-new items that are clean, wrinkle-free, pet-hair free, and smoke-free will be accepted at almost any reputable consignment store," Janet says. "You can earn a fair amount with these items for your mad money!"

Trexlertown, Rock-a-Bye Baby in Allentown, Once Upon a Time in Emmaus, and Back Again for Kids in Kutztown, Pennsylvania. And I'm sure that's just the tip of the iceberg!

At Back Again for Kids, housed in a huge, imposing old white farmhouse, they have room for a lot of stuff—and they get it. They're so busy that you need to book an appointment about a month ahead to bring in your stuff. They're not a consignment shop—they'll buy your things outright for 40 percent of what they'll price them at or give you 60 percent in store credit.

Like other stores, they accept only seasonal clothes—spring and summer starting in March, fall starting in July, winter clothes in October. But they'll accept "seasonless" clothes (like jeans) all year. They don't accept clothes for infants under 12 months but will take boys' clothes for up to ages 14 to 16. They'll also accept girls' clothes into the teens but are much more discriminating about them because "girls are so picky." And they take kids' stuff as well as their clothes—strollers, portable playards, playhouses, toys—"anything that's not beat up or scratched." These are typical arrangements; the shops take most anything that's in decent shape. Now, that *is* good news!

One caveat, though. My friend Anne advised me that kids' toys and furnishings are tested regularly for safety, and recalls are sometimes issued. It would be considerate and responsible to check into whether there have been any safety recalls on car seats, baby toys, or other items you plan to donate or sell, and refrain from giving any items that have been recalled.

Household Stuff

The cheerful volunteers at the Elephant's Trunk in Emmaus, Pennsylvania (see "Consignments for a Cause" on page 367), greet you as you come in the door. Unlike other consignment shops, the Elephant's Trunk is laid out more like an antiques shop, with plenty of room to walk around and items placed artistically on shelves instead of heaped in an intriguing jumble as if waiting to be discovered. As a result, it lacks the lovable "treasure-hunt" feeling of so many consignment and secondhand shops.

But there are indeed treasures waiting to be discovered! After seeing Christmas ornaments heaped like jewels in clear glass vases and hurricanes in a copy of *Martha Stewart Living*, I thought, "What a fabulous idea for a mantel display!" Then I priced the vases and hurricanes (ouch!). And *then* I headed to the Elephant's Trunk, where for $6 to $8 each I managed to acquire an impressive huge glass vase, a snifter, and a hurricane—and created my best-ever Christmas display. Just this week, I saw a set of marvelous dishes that I'd have loved to own (as if I had room for a second casual set). I'm planning to tell my friend Delilah, who enjoys using just that type of dishware for her outdoor entertaining and has entire cabinets for her china and glassware.

The Elephant's Trunk provides the ultimate brochure on exactly what they'll accept for consignment ("pictures, china, pottery, glassware, collectibles, dinnerware, silver, linens, fine jewelry, costume jewelry, objets d'art, lamps, furniture, antique quilts, kitchenware . . .") and what they won't ("novels, Avon products, clothing, records, used electrical appliances, draperies, computers, luggage . . ."). And they spell out their terms so there's no possibility of misunderstanding.

They have specific hours 4 days a week when you can make an appointment to bring in consignments, and you're limited to 20 items per week. You sign a "consignor agreement" and pay a yearly fee of $10. Items are consigned for a period of 6 weeks and are reduced 20 percent at the end of 4 weeks if they haven't sold. If you want them back after the 6 weeks are up, you can call to have them packed for pickup; otherwise, you can leave them as a donation and receive a receipt for tax purposes. (Items valued at less than $8 are ineligible for consignment but may be left as a donation.)

Clients receive 50 percent of the final selling price for all items, via check mailed the 10th day of the following month; they can also take the remaining 50 percent as a tax write-off. This shop is very specific about the importance of having items clean, polished (in the case of silver and the like), and in working order, with working batteries in items that use them, such as watches and clocks. They also accept holiday items for limited periods of time (for example, Christmas items from October 1 through December 15), and special rules apply to them: They're automatically reduced 50 percent the day after the holiday, and if they haven't sold, they're packed for pickup 2 weeks later.

Back in Kutztown, the 2nd Hand on the Saucony is a more traditional consignment shop, with stuff of all stripes and types loaded up on shelves and spilling onto the floor as far as the eye can see. You feel like you could find absolutely *anything* in there, and you probably could—including the owner's and friends' babies and kids running around or gurgling from the secure circle of their mothers' arms.

They'll take pretty much anything you have, as long as it's not beat up and (where applicable) still works, and you don't have to make an appointment to bring stuff in. There's no limit on the number of items you can bring, and they don't care about seasonality, either. They take housewares, linens, furniture, antiques, books, games, toys, clothing—you name it, it's in there. And their merchandise moves so fast that you don't see the same objects from week to week. (A good Main Street location certainly helps.)

ONWARD!

Now you should know whether consignment or secondhand stores are for you (and, of course, your stuff!). Let me remind you that they are addictive, so try to bear the "it is better to give than to receive" philosophy in mind when you step through those magic doors to sell your stuff.

Now it's time to tackle the big guy—eBay! If you're ready, turn the page and see what the mother of all online auctions has to offer you.

eBay and Other Online Auction Sites

This chapter provides a tour of the ins and outs of eBay. You'll learn how to do your homework without getting sucked in (after all, you bought the stuff once—you don't want to go online and find yourself bidding for more!), how to get the most from an eBay store, how to sell directly on eBay and set up an eBay store of your own, how to use other online sales venues, and the pros and cons of the various online sales options.

ALL ABOUT eBAY

Yes, you really *can* find just about anything (legal) on eBay, with a few exceptions like live animals and, say, your dream date. Recent "top buyer searches" included the Nintendo Wii, Xbox 360, PlayStation 3, iPod, and . . . Britney Spears's hair. (Further investigation revealed that sellers were offering Britney paraphernalia with and without hair, not her actual hair.) I myself have bought a Mark Knopfler guitar pick, a new Le Creuset Dutch oven in Lemongrass, a vintage Gunne Saxe dress, and a one-of-a-kind hand-carved tropical chess set (that I love but my boyfriend, Rob, hates because the two sides are almost the same shade of wood).

Pet Alert!

There are a few things you *can't* sell on eBay, and live animals are one of them. (Shame on you for even thinking of it!) So are animal parts and taxidermy specimens. Other eBay no-nos include guns and other weapons, drugs (including prescription drugs), and human body parts (someone once notoriously offered one of his kidneys on eBay). You can find a complete listing on the eBay Web site (www.ebay.com). Love your pets, love your eBay experience, but don't mix 'em up.

And I've noticed Rob checking the listings for his favorite Markland HO-scale model trains.

All of which is to say that, if you have something to sell, it's probable that at least a few of the more than 200 million worldwide eBayers will want to buy it. The question is, what will they pay for it, and is it worth the trouble? Because yes, it *is* a lot of trouble to sell something on eBay. QuikDrop, one of the many eBay drop-off store franchises, put it concisely in one of the understatements of all time when they said, "Buying on eBay is relatively easy. Selling is more complicated."

Not that it can't be done. I have friends who sell the occasional object on eBay, and well over a million people make their living selling stuff on eBay. But making a living selling lots of stuff for modest returns and making a killing on a single item are two very different propositions, and the latter is a rarity on eBay. (After all, most of us go on eBay looking for bargains, not planning to pay top dollar.)

So please, don't start your eBay sales career thinking you'll sell Great Aunt Rosa's original Ziegfeld Follies program for a million dollars and gain financial freedom. Instead, think of eBay as a great and relatively painless way to get rid of clutter that you can't give to family or friends, and make a profit in the bargain. Then, if something does end up in a bidding war and makes you a lot more than you expected, it will be a thrilling surprise. And if it doesn't, you'll still be bringing money in and kicking clutter out.

What eBay isn't, in my opinion, is a place to try to sell things that you know are actually valuable—fine jewelry, museum-worthy art, rare antiques, or a classic Rolls-Royce, for example. If you're certain what you have is valuable, or you have a suspicion that it is, have it appraised and sell it through an antiques dealer or another appropriate venue. (See Chapter 22—Antiques in Your Attic, starting on page 429, for more on this.)

Look at eBay as a great place to sell off your collectibles, household items, clothing, and other stuff that you might otherwise sell at a yard sale or see at a flea market. The eBay experts estimate that most people have about $2,000 worth of eBay-worthy items (we might be less tactful and call it clutter, or even dustables) lying around their homes. That $2,000 isn't going to make or break you, but it can sure help with the heating bills, car payments, or taxes. (And speaking of taxes, if you make a profit on eBay, you'll need to report it to our good friend Uncle Sam.)

TAKING IT TO THE PROS

To me, the most sensible way to offload your clutter on eBay is to take it to a store that specializes in selling stuff on eBay. They do the work, and you get the check. Maybe it's not as big a check as you'd have gotten if you sold the stuff yourself, but you don't have to do any of the work—and that includes listing the item on eBay, dealing with the buyers, and packing it up and hauling it off for shipping—or learn the ins and outs of eBay selling. If your goal is to get rid of your stuff and any money you make is a bonus, this is a really painless way to go. If, on the other hand, you're counting on making a killing, you may be very distressed to find yourself taking home a comparatively small piece of the pie. (But if that's the case, ask yourself if kicking the clutter is really a priority.)

I've found several types of eBay third-party sellers, and their approaches are all different. If you choose to go this route, scope out your area and see who's doing eBay selling. Check out a few places and see what you think. Then choose the one that works for you.

The "Little Guys"

One option is to go to a local shop that specializes in selling on eBay or sells some of their merchandise in a "bricks-and-mortar" store and some on eBay. It's not

the Pros Know

If you're thinking about turning to eBay to unload your clutter, first turn to the authority on eBay, *eBay for Dummies,* by Marsha Collier (Wiley Publishing, Inc., 5th edition, 2007, $21.99). Marsha, who's been selling on eBay since 1996, is the author of five other *Dummies* books about eBay that have collectively sold more than a million copies. In *eBay for Dummies,* she shares an insider's secrets—plus, of course, all the basics—of online selling on eBay. (And buying, too—but let's not even go there.) You can't go wrong following her advice! Just make sure you buy the latest edition of the book—it looks like they're updating it almost yearly to keep pace with eBay's evolution. Marsha's advice is so comprehensive that it's hard to pick out some pointers to show just how good it is. But I'll give you three favorites that aren't as intuitively obvious as they might seem.

The first is about the importance of timing. It's tempting to put stuff up on eBay as soon as you've decided to get rid of it—and getting rid of stuff ASAP once you've made that painful decision is usually good advice. But as with consignment shops that only accept clothing in season, seasonality can make a big difference in how much you get for an item sold on eBay if that item has a specific season. Sell your dirt bikes in spring and your snowmobiles in fall, not the other way 'round. Ditto for that Tasha Tudor-illustrated copy of *The Night before Christmas* or that fabulous pool float that feels like you're drifting on clouds. And of course, sell coats in winter and sundresses in summer!

The second tip is about getting your feet wet. Marsha suggests—quite rightly—that you shouldn't try to sell on eBay if you've never bought anything on eBay. But you're trying to de-clutter, not add clutter, right? Never fear. She suggests starting by buying *recipes*—which can be had for under a dollar and take up only the space of a sheet of paper. What an idea! But she's right on target; buying a few recipes will get you familiar with the eBay buyer process without costing you a bundle or flooding your house with stuff.

Another great tip is about spelling. Normally, correct spelling is a good thing, but on eBay, it can be a bad thing, if much of the buying population routinely misspells a word. Marsha points out that when buyers search for an object, eBay brings up the items that are spelled exactly the way they've searched for them. That means that if you spell something correctly when most people misspell it, you'll be passed over. (She uses "Caribbean" and "Carribean" as examples. Do you know which is correct?) The solution is to list it both ways, so both bad and good spellers can find it. Great idea!

For thousands of other great tips, get your own copy, or do as I did and have your local library order it for you. You'll be glad you did!

SANITY SAVERS

If you're selling something on eBay or entrusting your stuff to an eBay drop-off store (see page 382) or Trading Assistant (see page 378) to sell it for you, one word matters more than just about anything else: feedback. A seller's eBay feedback rating shows the entire community of buyers, at a glance, how trustworthy he or she is. It's the place on eBay where buyers can rate their transaction experiences as good, bad, or neutral, and leave feedback comments that can encourage buyers to purchase items from that seller or shun them like the plague.

If you want your items to sell on eBay, you want the seller you choose to have an excellent feedback rating (at least 98 percent positive)—and that's true if you sell it yourself, too. When I interviewed Patrick McWilliams about his eBay store, Kutztown OLDIES (see "Beyond Bikes"), his father appeared in the door to tell me that Patrick has a 100 percent positive feedback rating. Clares Closet's eBay store, Clares Closet/Fashion and Funk (see "The Pros Know" on page 368) also has a 100 percent positive feedback rating. Now, that's ideal!

People get good feedback by listing items exactly; maintaining good contact with the bidders and ultimate buyer, including answering questions promptly; making sure all terms are clear; mailing the item out well packaged and quickly—as soon as payment has been received or has cleared; and giving good, prompt feedback to the buyer. (Feedback is a two-way street—sellers can also see a buyer's feedback rating, review the comments he or she received, and decide whether or not to sell to him or her as a result.)

Mind you, a seller can have a 100 percent positive feedback rating but only have a handful of sales, so if you're entrusting your former clutter to someone else to sell on eBay, look for someone who's racked up a lot of sales and *still* has a great rating. Sales are counted as "points" on eBay and are listed in parentheses after the seller's eBay name (user ID). (It's actually more complicated, since—for one thing—sellers only get a point the first time they sell to each buyer, so their actual sales could be much higher than the number of points. But you can be sure the seller has sold *at least* that many items.) Clares, for example, has more than 2,400 points and is an eBay Power Seller. Marsha Collier, the author of *eBay for Dummies*, has more than 5,000 points and a 100 percent positive feedback rating. So start out right and save your sanity by choosing sellers you can trust!

difficult to find one that's selling stuff like yours, even in a small community like mine. I was driving to a friend's house for dinner last month and passed a used-car dealership I'd often seen before. But this time it looked different: They had put up a big sign that said, "Let us sell your used cars on eBay!" At my favorite antiques store (you'll read more about it in Chapter 22), Moyer's Stamps and Collectibles, co-owners Bruce and Karen Moyer sell all sorts of antiques in their shop, but Bruce also sells especially choice stamps and coins on eBay.

Let's take a closer look at another "eBay store within a store."

Beyond Bikes

Patrick McWilliams set up his eBay store, Kutztown OLDIES, in the back of his father's store, Kutztown Bike Shop, in (surprise, surprise) Kutztown, Pennsylvania. Patrick had sold stuff for himself and his siblings and friends on eBay since he got out of high school. After 8 years of that, he had the eBay bug big-time and decided to sell full-time for anyone who needed his services. Initially, he sold—what else?—bikes, but then he expanded into all sorts of goods.

Patrick printed up an informative card that spells out his terms for prospective buyers: Items should have an average sale price of $50. You pre-pay $10 for him to list the item on eBay. This fee includes professional photography, description, and basic research. He also monitors bidding for you. He'll normally list items for 7 days (the standard eBay auction listing), but other time listings are available. If the item is sold, the $10 is credited to you. Patrick's commission is 30 percent up to $1,000 and 20 percent over $1,000. The buyer pays shipping and handling; you pay the eBay and PayPal fees. (Huh? See "Tools of the Trade" on page 384.) Patrick handles packaging and shipping.

When I spoke to Patrick recently, he had some great insights to share about selling on eBay and when you should consider other options. His first piece of advice was to think about what the item can actually get at auction. Patrick stresses that it's not worth it to sell anything that will bring under $40 or $50 on eBay (the usual cutoff for eBay stores), but that, in reality, stuff either sells for way less or way more than that.

I asked Patrick what sells best—and what doesn't sell at all. In the "doesn't sell" category, he said that you don't get much for mass-produced stuff. Don't try to sell stuff like old records on eBay; it's not worth it. (Kutztown's flea market has a specialty shop that sells records, and it would make more sense to sell to the owner.) In Patrick's view, because of shipping costs and hassles, it's not worth trying to sell heavy stuff on eBay, either; he thinks it's better to use Craigslist (see Chapter 20—Clutter in the Classifieds, beginning on page 394, for more on this) or have a yard sale. So what *does* sell? Stuff that's no longer made, from rims for seventies bikes that probably cost $5 back then but can now sell for $250, to BMX bikes from the eighties that can bring in thousands on eBay.

Once you start looking for stuff on eBay, one thing you'll notice right away is that different listings for the same item can, in some cases, have one or two photos and a one-sentence description, while others have tons of photos and a wealth of text, describing in loving detail the glories of the product, its history, and any outstanding features. Ever since I started using eBay, I've wondered if a great description helps the item sell for more or if people couldn't care less and just go for the lowest price. In Patrick's experience, a good description with a history that's intriguing or compelling does help sales. Finally, for those of you providing your own photos, Patrick offers a tip: Upload your own digital photos through ImageShack (www.imageshack.us), an image-hosting service.

Trading Assistants

A different kind of "little guy" who can sell your stuff for you is the eBay Trading Assistant, someone local who already has a lot of experience selling on eBay and who is willing to act as a middleman to sell your items for a fee. You can find Trading Assistants in your area by going on the eBay site (www.ebay.com). All Trading Assistants listed have experience selling on eBay and are in good standing in the eBay community, with a feedback score of at least 100 and at least 97 percent positive feedback. Some Trading Assistants will sell all sorts of things on eBay, while others specialize in one or a few types of items, so make sure the one or ones you contact will handle the kind of stuff you're selling. You can contact Trading Assistants via the information in their Trading Assistant profile. Discuss fees and terms with them and make sure you're comfortable with the arrangement. (You can also ask for references from past clients.)

the *Pros* Know

Janet Brito and her sister, Barb O'Brien, are co-owners of Clares Closet, in Kutztown, Pennsylvania. (You may remember Clares from Chapter 18—Secondhand Shops.) Clares specializes in "Fashion and Funk" for men and women, including great vintage clothes and accessories, and sells both through a bricks-and-mortar store and on eBay. I've found great things at Clares over the years, from tie-dyed cushions and Hawaiian leis for a Jimmy Buffet-themed "Margaritaville" party my boyfriend, Rob, and I wanted to host, to the broomstick skirts I love to wear in summer. And whenever my friend Susan is visiting from Washington, DC, she insists on stopping at Clares to look for black skirts and jeans. I think you'll find Janet's answers to my eBay questions as helpful as I did!

Q: What are the advantages of selling through a professional service or eBay store like yours versus trying to sell on eBay yourself?

A: No matter what people say, it's hard work to sell on eBay. Plus, if you don't know what you're doing or don't look professional, you may not get as many folks looking at your items and you may not get as much as you could if you went to an eBay service. There are lots of tricks to the trade, lots of ways to list things to get attention, and lots of pitfalls if you don't know what you're doing. However, if you have just a few items or things that don't have too much value, it likely doesn't matter if you list them yourself.

Q: Are there things to look for—or look out for—when choosing an eBay store or service to sell your stuff through?

A: I think you need to look for someone who has experience and someone you feel you can trust. My sister, Barb, loves to get signed contracts. I love to work on a handshake. Either way, we need to have people trust us. I also think that you have to realize the actual value of what you have. There are lots of hyped-up stories about people selling things for a fortune on eBay. That's the exception and not the norm.

Q: How do you want people to approach you about an eBay consignment—make an appointment to bring stuff in, send an e-mail, or ask you to come over and see the stuff?

A: We're open to almost any way of folks initially contacting us. Since we have a retail store, many people do stop in. But when it gets down to evaluating their items, an appointment seems to work best.

(continued)

the Pros Know

(cont.)

Q: **What do you think makes a good eBay item—rarity, condition, interesting history—and what makes an unsuitable one?**

A: Rarity and demand are the number one moneymakers. But if you have something rare and no one wants it, then you're out of luck. On the other hand, if you have a more common item but it's in great demand, then you will likely sell your item at a price that you're happy with. And of course, condition greatly affects the price your item will fetch. The tough variables are timing and luck. You can put up an item one week and no one will look at it, no one will bid on it, and you end up with no sale. However, you can turn around and relist the exact same item for the same price just a week later and it will get so much activity you cannot believe it. But remember, the market is really fickle, and the market is sometimes flooded with identical items that you may think are rare and valuable.

Q: **Are there ever times you suggest that people consign the stuff in your shop instead of selling it on eBay, or vice versa?**

A: If we feel it will not do well online, then we simply state that. However, there are lots of times that we tell folks that an item will do better in our bricks-and-mortar store than online. Hands-on impulse buying will generally fetch a higher price for a more common type of item. But there is a trade-off: Online, you have 200 million potential customers. Not so in a retail store. So online selling of a more common item may sell the item faster but fetch a lower price. In the retail store, an item may have to be displayed for months but will eventually sell for more. It's a tricky formula, and we try to do the best we can for our clients. We try to do a combination of keeping an item online as well as in our bricks-and-mortar store.

Q: **What are your terms for selling on eBay for someone? How do you determine a baseline bid? How long do you keep things up for them? What happens if they don't sell?**

A: We have gone through various types of terms and have landed on what we think is the most fair. We normally receive 50 percent of the selling price if and when something sells. If it sells for more than $200 or $300, we will

Like other eBay selling services, Trading Assistants will list the item on eBay, answer bidders' questions, ship or deliver the item to the buyer, collect payment, and send you a check once they've deducted all fees. Some will come to your house take a lower percentage. This business is very labor intensive and our time is valuable, so in order to stay in business, we have to cover our costs. Plus eBay and PayPal take a large chunk of the profit. Some places charge a nonrefundable fee for listing an item, which helps cover the eBay fees if an item does not sell. We do not, since we are trying to select items that will sell. But if an item doesn't sell, then the client is welcome to have it back.

Q: **Have you encountered false expectations from people who bring in stuff to sell on eBay ("I read in a book on ceramics that this was worth $500," or the like), and if so, what's your advice for potential eBayers on keeping their expectations realistic?**

A: Yes, there is a lot of hype about what you can make on eBay! Our advice is fairly simple. Be honest with the clients. It goes back to Economics 101: Supply and Demand. Pair this with a bit of luck, a good-looking listing, and a smart listing strategy, and you will get the most that you can at that moment in time. We never promise anything, but we will honor a minimum price if that is what the person wants, so that if it does not get bid on for that minimum, it does not sell. If a potential client has an unrealistic expectation, then we encourage them to keep the item for another time or reseller.

Q: **Do you have any general or specific tips or wisdom to share with people who are thinking of going the eBay route, either on their own or through an eBay store or service like yours?**

A: Be prepared for lots of work and lots of questions. If you are trying to sell your child's outgrown clothes, or your Longaberger collection, or a set of used tires, and you only want to make a few bucks, you will be fine on eBay. If you want a time-consuming hobby, then you can likely do eBay yourself. However, don't let all the hype about eBay fool you. It's a business—and a big business. There are lots of pitfalls, and with a few simple mistakes, you can end up making nothing or less than nothing. Most of our clients either have a truly collectible, valuable item or simply want the items out of their house and are grateful for whatever they get.

Check out Clares yourself by going to their eBay store: clares_closet, or their Web site: www.shopatclares.com.

to pick up the item initially. If an item doesn't sell, the Trading Assistant will return it to you; some also offer the option of donating it to charity for you.

Be aware that Trading Assistants are in no way a part of eBay; eBay simply provides the listing of Trading Assistants as a service to potential eBay sellers. Make sure you're comfortable with that before you choose to go the Trading Assistant route over an eBay drop-off store. (I'd go with the store, can you tell? But that's just me.)

The Big Guys: Drop-Off Stores

Because eBay is such a phenomenon, eBay drop-off stores that sell people's stuff for them on eBay are one of the fastest-growing franchises in the country. The biggest franchise is iSold It ("Turn old memories into new money with iSold It. It's easy."), followed by QuikDrop ("We sell your stuff on eBay!"). You can probably find several of each in your area. The franchises open in strip malls, so they're in standardized "box spaces" and they have a standard appearance. (iSold It sends its franchisees the entire inside of their stores via truck shipment in what they call a "store in a box.") Owners and employees are also professionally trained by the parent company. What this means is that you know what you'll be getting from any one of the stores—the only surprise is how the merchandise will sell on eBay.

I know a lot more about eBay drop-off stores today than I did last summer, when my friend Delilah and I ventured into one, hoping to make big bucks with our extra stuff. I'd noticed a sign for an eBay drop-off store while driving through Quakertown, Pennsylvania, and gotten all excited. I knew I didn't want to sell

---

Tools of the Trade

Most eBay drop-off stores won't take items that would bring less than $30 (in the case of iSold It) to $50 (for QuikDrop). Instead of hauling a bunch of stuff to the store and being turned away, do your research first the way the store employees do it—through eBay itself. Go online to www.ebay.com and search for your item or something like it. You can use eBay's "Advanced Search" feature to look under "Completed Auctions" and see what like objects have recently sold for. Whether the news is good or bad, you're a winner: Either you may make some money at the drop-off store with your item, or you'll be saved the trouble of taking it.

stuff on eBay myself, but I enjoyed buying things on eBay and had watched the progress of many an auction with fascination, trying to figure out why one item sold for a bundle while the identical item didn't even sell. Here was a painless opportunity to get my feet wet from the seller's side, get rid of some surplus stuff, and make a little money.

Unfortunately, "a little money" turned out to be the defining part of the experience. Delilah, my co-conspirator in all things thrift store and flea market, was all for trying the drop-off store experience. We packed up a little stuff each—since it was just a trial—and headed over to the Quakertown drop-off store. The store experience itself has all the charm of waiting in line for your driver's license photo. But the employees certainly knew their business and knew how to do their research.

After checking us in and taking our data (including photocopies of our driver's licenses, which they stashed in a large notebook of other customers' similar pages), they turned their attention to our stuff. Delilah had brought some Dansk china and blue glassware, while I had a vintage movie poster and a couple of pieces of handmade pueblo pottery. After asking us a few questions about the items, the employees were able to scope out the sales of similar items on eBay. They then rejected my vintage poster, since another one on eBay failed to sell. But they accepted the rest of the items and filled out forms for each item (more on that in a bit), making sure to note down any potential flaws—they were very conscientious about wanting to represent the items exactly as they were. They also went over the terms, which were complex enough to leave both of us reeling. It was all very efficient and very impersonal. We returned to the car feeling shaken and dubious, but hoping for the best.

Things started looking up when we each got an e-mail with links to our items' auction pages so we could follow the auctions ourselves and track how our items were faring. The auction pages looked extremely professional, with great photos of the items. I can't vouch for Delilah, but I'll confess to checking the progress of mine several times a day for the 7 days the auction lasted. They did sell, but not for very much money. But the real sticker shock came when my check eventually arrived—for $7! (I think Delilah got about $38.) After all the fees and charges were taken out, there wasn't a lot left over. Neither of us even began to get back what we'd paid for our stuff, and we both felt that we could have done better elsewhere.

(continued on page 386)

Tools of the Trade

When you're talking about eBay, eBay drop-off stores may be the ultimate "tools of the trade." With 900 franchises and plans to expand to 3,000 in the United States—and more around the world—iSold It is the leading franchise, followed by QuikDrop. The iSold It Web site (www.i-soldit.com) gives a concise overview of how the drop-off process works that is true to my own experience:

"Our experienced staff can conduct some quick online research to help estimate [your object's] value. During the check-in process, our store staff will work with you to capture any key copy points you'd like to make in your eBay listing. Once you've checked in, we place the item in our inventory and hand you a receipt. Then we get to work photographing and listing your item on eBay. Once we've listed your item on eBay, we'll send you an e-mail with a link to the auction, so you can watch all the action as it occurs. Once the transaction is complete, we send you a check. Or, if you prefer, we can send the proceeds to your favorite charity."

iSold It will sell items with an expected value of $30 or more, that weigh less than 150 pounds, and that measure less than 130 inches in length and girth combined. They typically list auctions for 7 days but can shorten that to as little as 1 day for time-sensitive items like concert tickets or tickets to sports events. If an item doesn't sell, they'll send you an e-mail and you can either pick it up within 10 days of the end of the auction or they'll donate it to charity. Sellers can set an opening bid of $9.99 or higher, but they're warned that that can limit bidding activity. Sellers can expect their checks within 30 to 45 days after they drop off an item at the store.

QuikDrop's services are similar. They'll sell items with an expected value of $50 or more, typically list them for 7 days, and give you 15 days to pick up anything that doesn't sell (then they'll donate it to charity). On their Web site (www.quikdrop. com), they note that they provide a gallery photo for all listings. This means that prospective buyers can see the photo when they do an item or category search rather than seeing an annoying camera symbol letting them know that if they click on the entry there will be photos. (Worse still is when there's no symbol, which means there's no photo of the item—bad idea.) QuikDrop also uses bold titles in their listings, which they say gives the items more exposure. Like the other services, Quik Drop tracks each auction, answers questions from prospective buyers, processes payment, packages the item, and ships it to the winner when the auction closes.

Now for the downside: transactions fees. Just how much are they, and why do you have to pay them? Well, get ready to whip out your calculators (though both iSold It and QuikDrop have charts with examples of selling prices and the fees associated with them on their Web sites, so check them out for more details).

First, the why: Well, obviously the store owners have to pay off the $65,000 to $100,000 startup costs for their franchises, not to mention the ongoing operating costs. But, as they rightly point out, they're also doing all the work for you, from researching, photographing, and listing your stuff on eBay to conducting all the transactions, getting your money from the winner, packing and shipping the item, and sending you a check. Plus, they're paying eBay (and often PayPal) listing and payment processing fees. And they're guaranteeing those all-important high positive feedback ratings that will get potential buyers to choose their items over similar objects from sellers with lower ratings. In return for all these services, you're turning over a hefty percentage of your profits.

Both eBay and the drop-off stores base their commissions on a sliding scale. For eBay, the initial listing and gallery photo fee is 75 cents, followed by a commission of 5.25 percent of the first $25, 2.75 percent of the next $975, and 1.5 percent of any amount over $1,000. The typical iSold It commission is 35 percent of the first $500 and 20 percent of the remaining amount over $500, with a minimum commission of $5 per item. For QuikDrop, it's typically 42 percent of the first $200, 34 percent of the next $300, and 25 percent of the remaining amount over $500. Then there are the payment processing fees: iSold It charges $1.05 plus 2.55 percent of the total transaction value (sales price, shipping and handling, and sales tax). QuikDrop charges 2.9 percent for payment and processing fees, plus sales tax.

So how does all this break down? If your item sells for $100 on eBay, you'll get a check for $57 (57 percent of the final selling price) from iSold It; if it sells for $1,000, you'll get $642 (64 percent of the selling price). If you sell an item for $100 through QuikDrop, after eBay's commission of $8.86 and QuikDrop's of $42, you'll get a check for $49.14; if it sells for $1,000, after eBay's commission of $64.36 and QuikDrop's of $311, you'll get $624.64. Again, see their Web sites for more examples.

There are plenty of other eBay drop-off stores to choose from, all of which are run along similar lines. For example, AuctionDrop stores operate out of United Parcel Service (UPS) stores. They'll take items worth over $75 on eBay, as long as they weigh less than 25 pounds. AuctionDrop typically starts bids at $1 and lists for 7 days, but you can pay them a fee of $19.99 that gets you "premium service" and lets you set an opening bid that's higher than $1. (AuctionDrop will credit the $19.99 toward its commission fee if the item sells.) AuctionDrop's commission is 38 percent on the first $200, 30 percent on the next $300, and 20 percent on the remainder over $500. Check them out online at www.auctiondrop.com. For other drop-off store franchises, look online for www.theonlineoutpost.com.

That's not the end of this story, however, or I wouldn't be recommending drop-off stores to you. If I'd had the sense to do some online research or had been more focused on de-cluttering and less on making some money, my attitude about the whole experience—which was fast, painless, and professional—would have been quite different. For one thing, I'd have found out that almost nobody gets the street or book value of an item, much less as much as they paid for it. And I'd have found out about all the fees, so I could have prepared myself for the sticker shock.

As I now see it, the correct attitude is: At these stores, people take your unwanted stuff away and replace it with money! In the words of my ex-father-in-law, "It beats a jab with a sharp stick." All of which is to say, I wouldn't recommend eBay drop-off stores as a way to build your retirement savings or pay off your credit cards—though of course some lucky customers do strike it rich with a big auction price. Don't count on it, though. Instead, bring in your yard-sale stuff, sit back, and enjoy the spare change when those checks come in.

What to Sell

What sells best at a drop-off store? At iSold It—assuming your items are clean and in good condition—the list is long. Their Web site lists antiques and collectibles, appliances and small furniture, cameras and video recorders, designer apparel and accessories, electronics and phones, event tickets, housewares, musical instruments, sports equipment, and vehicle parts. Musical instruments, electronics, and vintage or antique items also move fast at QuikDrop. And both stores will sell your vehicles, too.

What if you're trying to unload something big? They can handle big stuff at iSold It, too, but they'll ask you to leave it at home, take 10 or more photos of the object, fill out an Item Questionnaire, and bring the photos and questionnaire to an iSold It store instead of the object itself (you can find guidelines and the questionnaire on their site, or see "Tools of the Trade" on page 384 for details). Once an item sells, they'll arrange for the winning bidder to pick up the piece at your house or arrange for a freight service to transport it. Some stores also offer a "house calls" service where, for a fee, a store employee will come to your house to photograph your stuff and fill out the questionnaire for you. Check with the other drop-off stores for their policies on large items.

According to iSold It, popular large items on eBay (besides vehicles) include game-room items like jukeboxes, pool tables, and arcade games; pianos and other musical instruments and equipment; luxury name-brand furniture (like Eames) and high-end appliances (like Viking); big screen and plasma TVs; motorized equipment (such as golf carts, wheelchairs, and Rascal scooters); architectural elements and artwork (such as woodwork, flooring, and oil paintings); and large antiques and collectibles. (Again, if your antiques, collectibles, and artwork are really valuable, please read Chapter 22—Antiques in Your Attic, beginning on page 429, before consigning them to eBay.)

GOING IT ALONE

If you decide to take the plunge and sell your own stuff on eBay—you just wouldn't listen to me, would you?—for heaven's sake, do your homework. Get your hands on a copy of *eBay for Dummies* (see "The Pros Know" on page 375) and read it. Check out the eBay site to see if they're holding an eBay University anywhere near you. It's a daylong seminar that, for a mere $59, will show you the ropes of selling on eBay. You can also take the course online for free, so do it! (eBay University also offers an advanced course online for $19.95, or at the local sessions for $59.)

Spend a lot of time on eBay, exploring the "Seller" portion of their site and monitoring auctions. Look at the various listings and see how the sellers have set up their pages. Check out sellers' feedback and see what you can expect. Go to Marsha Collier's Web site, www.coolebaytools.com, which is directed at eBay sellers, and sign up for her free newsletter. Make sure your photography and computer skills are up to snuff.

This is *work*, you all. If you're a seller, you'll be responsible for taking the photos; writing the description; setting the terms; listing the item on eBay; monitoring the auction; answering bidders' questions; determining shipping, eBay, and PayPal fees, as well as sales tax; collecting and processing payment; packing and shipping the item; and tracking and reporting profits to Uncle Sam. About 165 pages in *eBay for Dummies* are devoted to getting you up to speed as a seller—and that's the most basic of the *For Dummies* eBay sellers' books! That doesn't mean it can't be fun, but it does mean that you should learn the ropes before you start, and then start very small.

Before you put a single item up for sale on eBay, you need to register on the site as an eBay seller, with a credit card on file with eBay. Go to the "Seller" area of their site (www.ebay.com) and follow their directions to register. Then fill out your "Sell Your Item" page and you're ready to list your first item and go for it!

What to Show and Say

Take it from the pros when it comes to creating your own listing. You can't do better than what the eBay drop-off stores request from you in the way of photos and descriptions—except, of course, in terms of adding more color to your descriptions and histories, plus a really great title.

In terms of photos, you should take a bunch and choose the best to use in the listing. (eBay allows up to eight, but you have to pay an additional fee for every photo after the first one, which is free.) Make sure the photos are in focus and well lit. Photograph the object from all sides, and take close-up photos of all features, both good (manufacturers' names, design details) and bad (scratches, dents, discolorations, stains). If you don't have a digital camera, have your 35mm photos developed onto a CD-ROM (most photo processing stores can do this).

As for what to say, you should start by choosing a category or categories in which to list your items. Start with the general (antiques) and add what you need to help potential buyers find your item (collectibles, dolls, Shirley Temple dolls).

After the category, you need a title—the thing buyers see (along with the gallery photo) when the list of items they've requested comes up onscreen. It should be descriptive and catchy, so people both know what you're offering and are pulled in. You have only 55 characters (meaning both individual letters and spaces between words), so they all have to count. "Rare Signature MARK KNOPFLER Martin Acoustic Guitar" or "Cool Vintage Spiro Agnew Collectible Tee-Shirt '70s Chic" both tell buyers what you have on offer. For an extra fee, you can add a subtitle to say a few more things about your object, if you need to.

Next, provide a detailed description, including the item's color(s), name, make and model, dimensions (height, length, and width), weight, accessories, age, and anything else you can think of to enhance the item's appeal to a buyer (as long as it's accurate). "Original 1976 Diane von Furstenberg silk wrap dress, size 8, white with blue and gold paisley design, mint condition, vintage designer couture collectible" tells potential buyers a lot more than "White wrap dress with blue and gold design, size 8," don't you think? Whatever it is, describe it lovingly.

Note any flaws in your item and show a close-up photo of the flaw in your listing to make sure buyers know exactly what they're getting and can happily report that the item was as described. (Protect your feedback rating!) Better to note that your rare vintage Lys acoustic guitar has a small scratch by the soundhole than risk endless grief when the buyer gets it in the mail.

Moving beyond drop-off store basics, it's time for the cream, the stuff that hooks an already-interested buyer in your particular item, as opposed to just anybody's. In the case of the dress, you could give some background on Diane von Furstenberg: talk about her rags-to-riches story, colorful life, and appointment as head of the Council of Fashion Designers of America in 2006, making her arguably the most powerful woman in fashion. You could talk about the stellar success of the wrap dress design—one of Ms. von Furstenberg's is on display in the Metropolitan Museum of Art—and its current revival. You could position your particular dress in its history—did it come out the first year Ms. von Furstenberg created the style? (The first year was actually 1973, so no luck on that one.) And you could add some personal history, such as how and why you got it. ("I wore it on my honeymoon in Paris," or "Mom bought it and wore it to see her first play in New York.")

In the case of the Lys guitar, you could give a history of its creator, Robert Godin, who began with the Lys line in Canada in the sixties and went on to found Godin Guitars, with six different highly successful lines. You could discuss the rarity of Lys guitars today, their collectibility, their great sound. Give the history of your guitar. Give a few examples of famous musicians who play Godin guitars today.

Whatever your item is, see what other people are saying about it on eBay by searching for it in other auctions. If what they're saying is both compelling and accurate and refers to the brand as a whole, not just their individual item, consider adding it to your description (in your own words, of course). Check out companies, designers, and well-known objects on Wikipedia (www.wikipedia.com). Search for them at www.google.com to see what you can find for your listing. Go to the companies' or designers' own Web sites. The more you know, the better your listing can be.

However: You *don't* want to drone on and on about your object, numbing the prospective buyer, and you don't want to give a bunch of meaningless verbiage. Make sure what you say is interesting and informative, and that it would appeal to you as a buyer.

Other Essentials

What else matters when you list something on eBay? Auction terms, auction time, shipping (and handling), and methods of payment. As far as auction terms, you can set a low opening bid, a higher opening bid, a reserve, and/or a "Buy It Now" price. Low opening bids—as in a dollar or less—tend to attract bargain-hunting buyers. But what if somebody actually *buys* President Lincoln's mother's sister's bird's-eye maple dresser for $1? Horrors! But it ain't necessarily so.

Obviously, you can set the starting bid at the lowest price you'd be willing to accept, but eBay insiders have found that that discourages bidders. So they often get around the low-low opening bid by setting a reserve price for the item—which is usually also the lowest price they'd be willing to accept. Potential buyers will be attracted by the low opening bid, but will see that there's an undisclosed reserve price, and will also see whether or not the reserve has been met. (If it hasn't been met by the end of the auction, you don't have to sell the item.) Items with reserves are intimidating to bargain hunters—who knows how much the seller is expecting?—so given a choice between an item with a reserve and a similar one that broadcasts "NR" or "no reserve" in its title, they'll gravitate toward the one without a reserve. You can try to counteract that by putting "low reserve" in your title, or telling bidders right in the description what the reserve is and why you've set it. That way, they'll know if your object is within their financial reach.

There's also the optional "Buy It Now" feature. It's another way to offer bidders the option of buying something they really want at a price you're willing to accept (always higher than the opening bid, but, depending on the bid, not necessarily much higher). This is a gamble on your part—if a buyer takes you up on it, you might make less than you would from an auction. But if bidding doesn't get as high as the "Buy It Now" price, you'd have been better off if someone had taken you up on it. In any case, if anyone places a bid, your "Buy It Now" option disappears (unless you've set a reserve, in which case it will disappear once a bidder meets the reserve price), and then anything goes.

Auction time is a factor because eBay, which is based in San Jose, California, runs its auctions on Pacific Standard Time. And since most bidders monitor auctions closely as they near their end, you don't want them to end at some ungodly hour when many of your would-be buyers are asleep. (eBay's peak hours of operation are 5:00 p.m. to 9:00 p.m., and that's probably true of 5:00 p.m. to 9:00 p.m. in your time zone, too, whatever time it is on the West Coast.) eBay ends its auctions 7 days from the exact same time that they started, so you'll know when they'll end an auction based on when you begin it.

You choose when to start your auction, so make sure it will end at a reasonable time for people in your part of the country. Why? Because given a choice of several of the same item in different locations, people are more likely to bid on objects closer to them, since—all else being equal—the shipping will be lower. (Marsha Collier has a free eBay time calculator to help you with this; look for it on her Web site, www.coolebaytools.com.) And speaking of timing, sellers' wisdom says to run auctions over holidays if you can, since people are at home and online then. Marsha advises that you run the auction so it ends the Tuesday after the holiday Monday.

Because you've measured and weighed your object carefully, you can calculate and list shipping charges so the buyer knows what to expect. (You can also put an automatic shipping calculator in the listing so a would-be buyer can calculate the cost for him- or herself.) This matters, since the winner will pay for shipping. If you don't list shipping costs, lots of buyers will pass over your listing in favor of someone else who has a similar item and does list shipping. Specify where you're willing to ship—the continental 48 states, all 50 states, the United States and Canada, internationally?

The US Postal Service has partnered with eBay to provide a wide array of shipping services online, including one-price shipping anywhere in the United States if the item will fit in a Priority Mail flat rate box, plus free carrier pickup. Go to http://pages.ebay.com/usps/home.html to check out all the options.

If you'll allow the winning bidder to pick up the object in person, as opposed to paying shipping, it might attract even more bidders. (But that means meeting people someplace or letting them come to your house, so you'll need to decide if you're comfortable with that.) In addition to the shipping charges, note whether you require insurance for the package and how much, if anything, you'll charge for "handling" (acquiring packing materials, packing up the item, and hauling it off to be shipped). I'd say make this number as small as possible, or waive it altogether and include those costs in your opening bid or reserve.

Then there's that little matter of payment. Let your hopeful buyers know what forms of payment you're willing to accept—and the more forms, the better. Options include eBay's own online payment service, PayPal (www.paypal.com), which allows money to be transferred from one bank to another electronically, like magic, and also handles credit card transactions so you don't have to deal with them. PayPal does assess fees to sellers, but not to buyers, and its convenience to both makes it a popular option. Lots of sellers also accept personal checks, cashier's checks, and money orders, for folks like me who'd rather put the check in the mail. Be very clear about your terms: how soon after the end of the auction you expect payment; that you won't mail out an item until a personal check clears (usually within 7 to 10 business days); and if you'll charge the buyer sales tax if he or she lives in your state and, of course, if your state has sales tax. (Needless to say, if you sell to an in-state buyer in a sales-tax state and you don't charge the sales tax to the buyer, you'll have to pay it, but offering to do so is another possible sales tactic.)

Once you've collected the money—and kept the documentation for those potentially pesky IRS auditors—you'll need to remit the fees you owe to eBay and PayPal (if you use it). Remember all those fees I talked about in the drop-off store section?

Well, you'll need to calculate the 20 cents to $80 listing cost and 2 to 8 percent of the final price that you owe eBay, plus any additional fees from PayPal.

What happens if your high bidder defaults on the payment? Luckily, eBay lets you contact the second-highest bidder with an exclusive "Second Chance" feature that offers them the opportunity to buy the item at their highest bid. And if they decline, and you want to, you can continue to offer the "Second Chance" to other bidders until you get a buyer.

ONWARD!

Obviously, this is just the tip of the eBay iceberg. But I hope it's been enough to give you a good idea of your options and to decide what you'd like to do as far as selling your stuff on eBay or another online auction site. Now it's time to move on to a more old-fashioned and local (but nonetheless effective) technique, the good old classifieds and their online descendant, Craigslist. Grab a paper—or turn on your computer—and let's go!

Chapter 20

Clutter in the Classifieds

Extra, extra! Local woman makes a tidy profit off her former clutter while creating space she never knew she had! In this chapter, you'll learn your online and in-print options, from newspapers to Craigslist, as well as how to write an ad that will sell your stuff, tailor ads to the sales venue, evaluate buyers and their methods of payment, and make the exchange after you've made the sale.

THE CLASSIFIEDS: READ ALL ABOUT IT!

Despite the advent of Internet sales venues, many people still sell their stuff through classified ads in their local papers or in special "bargain" papers like my own area's *Merchandiser* and *Penny Pincher,* both of which are ads- and classifieds-only publications. With classifieds, you're limiting your market not just locally, but to readers of the paper or publication where you place the ad. However, if you live in an area with cheap (or even free) ad rates or you're advertising a more expensive item, it makes sense to advertise in one of these papers because it requires almost no effort on your part, it attracts the people most likely to come to your home to haul off the stuff while paying you for the privilege, and an item that sells for a lot of money will more than cover the cost of a cheap ad.

What to Say

As in any other sales venue, your classified ad is competing with pages of other ads for the attention of busy, distracted readers. Your goal is to make your ad jump out at a reader who might want your stuff. How can you tell what will catch somebody's eye? Look at your local paper's classifieds and see which ads catch yours, and why. If one of them makes you want to actually *buy* something, then you know you're on to something. Study it closely and see why it's so intriguing.

The hook for your ad may be the title or capitalized first few words, but the core of your ad is the description you write of the item or items you're offering for sale, so make it as vivid and inviting as possible. Look at various ads for the same thing—say, golden retrievers or exercise equipment or bedroom sets or Harleys—and see which ones paint the best and most inviting picture. That's your goal, too. For example, "beautiful warm cherry" sounds a lot better than "cherry finish," doesn't it?

A great ad I saw recently for a dining-room table read like this: "DINING TABLE beautiful AICO brand, w/8 chairs, exquisite detail, inlaid bird's-eye maple, heavy, high-quality estate piece, 1 yr old, flawless, must see! Can e-mail photos." Just above it was an ad that said "DINING ROOM TABLE with chairs." You choose!

Remember, when you place a classified ad, you're paying by the word or line, and classified columns are just 28 spaces per line, so you want to say the most possible in the fewest words. How can you do that? Start by writing down *everything* you want to say about the item you're selling. Once you've gotten it all down, take a good look at what you've written and see what you can get rid of (because it's not going to increase sales), what you can combine (when you've said basically the same thing in different ways), and what you need to keep. The *Express-Times* puts this best in their tip on editing your ad: "Remove nonessential information and insert more benefits for prospective buyers."

Note the abbreviations in the sample ad above. Abbreviations cut down on lines—a good thing, as long as they're easy to understand and there aren't so many of them that a buyer feels like he or she is reading HTML. (Some papers, like the Nashville *Tennessean*, recommend against using abbreviations because not everyone knows what they mean.)

Tools of the Trade

Wondering how to make your classified ad stand out in a sea of ink? Here's a checklist of ways to get buyers' attention.

❋ Put the first few words in bold type to get your readers' attention.

❋ Make sure the words you put in bold type are attention-getting. You can say something startling ("BETTER-THAN-NEW JOHN DEERE RIDING MOWER is guaranteed problem-free."), or something unexpected ("JOHN DEERE MOWER. FREE up your time. Switch to a riding mower."). "HUGE SALE!" and "BIG SALE!" are also attention-getters if you're selling a number of items. Others to think about: "GREAT DEAL!" "HERE IT IS!" "LIMITED EDITION!" "NEVER USED!" (if that's true) "REAL BARGAIN!" "CHECK IT OUT!"

❋ Don't forget to say what the item is as part of the bold listing, so it will be listed with its competition and people scanning the ads for, say, a piano, will see it with the other pianos.

❋ Follow the heading with a benefit. Why does a buyer need your stuff? ("Stop sweating behind a push mower." "Save 75 percent over a new mower.")

❋ What's unique about your item? How is it better than or different from similar items that will have ads running alongside yours?

❋ If you have room, such as in a Craiglist ad where you can write as much as you want for free (see page 398 for more on Craigslist), add a statistic to reinforce the value of what you're selling. ("This model John Deere riding mower was rated #1 for its year by *Consumer Reports*." "I just checked the cost of metal pillar candle molds like the ones I'm offering, and you can buy my three bins of candlemaking supplies—*including* 10 metal pillar molds—for less than it would cost to buy five new molds!" "This Braun coffee maker got top user ratings by Amazon reviewers.")

❋ Give your description oomph by adding attention-getting words (if they're true): "excellent condition," "limited edition," "new in box," "still in plastic," "first edition," "never used," "original," "designer," "vintage," "antique," "high quality," "mint condition," "exquisite," "valuable," "precious," or "adorable." You get the idea. And you can mix and match them as you describe the item.

❋ Add a call to action at the end of the ad. ("Like-new condition, won't last. Call today." "Don't wait at this price. Respond now.")

If you look at a paragraph or page of text and want to keep it all, put it aside for a day and look again when you're more detached, or give it to your spouse or a friend and ask them to read it and "edit" it for you. Make every word count. Above all, make every word accurate. Make sure you're not (even accidentally) misleading potential buyers.

Now you're almost done. After the description, you still need to list the price you're asking for the item. Follow that with your contact data (phone number or numbers and/or e-mail address) so buyers can reach you. The *Express-Times* notes, "Many sales are lost because the advertiser was just too difficult to reach." Add that "call today" closure if you want to. That's it!

How to Do It

Check your local paper's classified ad guidelines to see their directions and charges. When I looked up how to place a classified ad at my local paper's Web site (www.mcall.com), it couldn't have been easier. It uses a software service called Advertise123.com by AdStar that walks you painlessly through the process. Once you tell them that you're a private-party advertiser (as opposed to a business), it takes you through its "Ad Placement System," which helps you place the ad in the right category, compose the ad, and schedule it, and even provides tips to help your ad stand out! I also checked the Web site of my hometown paper, the Nashville *Tennessean* (www.tennessean.com), and found that they used AdBaseE software to create a very easy-to-use system that also walks you through the process. (They also provide ad-writing tips, and so did the paper my boyfriend, Rob, used to work for, the *Express-Times;* check out their Web sites at www.pennlive.com and www.nj.com.)

So what does it cost? For my paper, the *Morning Call,* the rates are by the line rather than by the word. For a weekend (Saturday and Sunday) ad in both the paper and on its Web site, the rate is $39.44 for four lines and $7.11 for each additional line. For 5 days (Monday through Friday), it's $68.44 for four lines and $14.36 for each additional line. For 7 days, the rate is $91.58 for four lines and $20.14 for each additional line. Every ad gets a full 7 days on the paper's Web site, and weeklong ads also get placed in the paper's extra weekend edition, *The Chronicle,* and on the *Chronicle* Web site for 7 days.

In Nashville, the *Tennessean*'s rates are a lot friendlier, and they vary by type of item. In fact, if you're selling stuff for less than $50, you can place a five-line ad in Saturday's *Tennessean* and on its Web site (www.tennessean.com) and upload up to 10 photos online for FREE (as they'd say in the classifieds). Additional lines cost just $1 each. For stuff over $50 and under $250, the rate is five lines for $19.50, additional lines for $1 each. Again, you can upload up to 10 photos, and you can also list multiple items, as long as the total price is under $250. You'll also get your ad in their weekend special, the *Rage*. Stuff over $250 is $26 for five lines and $3 for each additional line. If you're selling a cheap car ($1,000 or less), you can place an ad in the *Tennessean,* the *Rage,* and online on www.cars.com for just $10 for five lines and 50 cents for each additional line; for more expensive cars, the rate is $40.25 for five lines and $2 for each additional line. All ads run for 7 days.

As you can see, a classified ad may not compare to the cost of a "real" ad, but, depending on where you live, it may not be cheap, either. That's why most classifieds are for higher-priced items like pianos, home gyms, mattresses, large equipment and power tools, large furniture, good jewelry, and collectibles, rather than yard-sale stuff. (That bird's-eye maple dining table and chairs I mentioned earlier were offered for a firm $3,000, for example.) It's also why, if you do see less expensive items, they're often grouped together in a single ad. Before you place a classified ad (unless, of course, it's free), make sure you'll get enough for your item to make it worth the cost.

CRAIGSLIST: THE "OTHER" CLASSIFIEDS

Craigslist, which started out in 1995 in San Francisco as a sideline hobby for a guy named—guess what?—Craig, has become the eBay of classified ads. You can find it in more than 450 cities worldwide, and more than 10 million people use it a *lot*—it gets over 5 billion page views per month, making it the eighth-ranked Web site in the United States. It's also the leading classified ad service, with over 10 million new ads posted each month.

Obviously, if you post a classified ad on Craigslist, you'll have a lot of competition. But you'll also have a lot of potential buyers. It's free to list an ad on Craigslist, and listings are posted for 45 days. You have nothing to lose by trying—except your clutter!

the **Pros Know**

Craigslist is huge and user-driven, with minimal regulation, so it's vulnerable to abuses. The site's owners warn you upfront when you place an ad that there are scammers out there who will send you counterfeit money orders and cashier's checks. Craigslist provides a link to their "current scams page," so you can see what unscrupulous scammers (aka thieves and forgers) are trying to pull off now. But to be on the safe side, they offer the following excellent advice: "Avoid scammers by dealing locally with buyers you can meet in person!"

Checking Out Craigslist

To see how it worked, I went to the Craigslist home site (www.craigslist.org), then clicked on "Pennsylvania" to see what was available in my area. (You could click on individual states, large US cities, or countries.) A page appeared asking me to choose the city or area nearest me, so I selected "Lehigh Valley." This opened up the Allentown listings. So far, so easy.

A pageful of categories appeared on the screen, so I clicked on "collectibles" and found listings by day, with today's date at the top. I could choose from a Bethlehem Steel jacket, candlemaking supplies, a collection of 45 rpm records, a circa-1900 clawfoot bathtub, a Longaberger pie plate, a Hotwheels service center or garage, an antique men's shaving mirror, the "entire Hess truck collection," a photo of Dorney Park (a local amusement park) taken in 1902, and a 10-gallon aquarium with light lid, all listed (with other stuff that I'll spare you) the first 3 days of this week. Prices ranged from "make offer" (for the Dorney Park photo) to $950 (for the Hess trucks), though most were in the under-$50 range.

The one that jumped out at me had the heading "Want to sell snake skins—$10!" (I am *not* making this up.) Sure enough, when I clicked on it, it turned out that some guy was offering his pet snakes' shed skins to interested Craigslisters. He included a short and heartfelt sales pitch, noted that he "has a very pretty corn snake at the moment who sheds perfectly," and added the clincher: "Beautiful collectibles if you are interested." If you happened to collect Hess trucks instead of snake skins, the Hess ad offered nothing but the years of the trucks and number per year—not much for your $950, to my way of thinking, but I guess it told fellow enthusiasts all they needed to know. The person who put the Longaberger plate up for sale knew more about advertising—her headline read, "Longaberger Pie Plate Brand New in Box—$20."

Then there were the owners of the candlemaking supplies. When I clicked on their listing, it took me to a couple of pages of copy, very chatty and personal, but also quite informative, about how they were moving and were trying to sell three Tupperware bins full of candlemaking supplies that had been used and needed some cleaning and were currently in their basement. (To quote their ad, "Note: Items have been used and are a bit messy. If you don't want to dig through and get your hands dirty, this isn't the deal for you.") They carefully listed the stuff—an extensive list—with descriptions of each item, quantity and other specs, condition, and so forth. And they added some strong hooks to interest potential buyers: "I have a great deal for you! It's a candlemaking 'grab-bag' of sorts. Most likely, there's even more stuff than I've listed, but I can say that there's a lot of stuff." After itemizing the stuff included in the deal and adding that anything that they'd forgotten to list in the Tupperware bins was also part of the sale, they added some compelling statistics (what even a fraction of the stuff sold for when new), pointing out that just a couple of items would make it worth the trip to get the supplies. And they remembered to thank potential buyers for looking.

By contrast, the owner of the fish tank's ad simply read "10-gallon fish tank with light lid $7 may e-mail or call me thanks." And the guy who offered the collection of 45 rpm records mentioned at the end of the ad that he'd throw in his 45 record player as part of the deal! ("I will include 45 record player which has been sitting here also. I am not sure what kind of shape the player is in." Hmmm, after reading *that,* I'd bet I could guess what kind of shape it was in!)

So the ads are really all over the place, from barest of bare bones to fullest of full disclosure. Read some in your area, then go for the style that you find most appealing. It's free and you've got all the room in the world, so you can say what you want. But follow the basic rules for writing a classified ad (see page 396): Tell the readers what they need to know about the item—description, dimensions, date of manufacture, color(s), condition. You can add distinctiveness and appeal to your ad with some history or anecdotes, but remember not to bore your buyers or waste their time. They're trying to shop, not read, after all! I myself liked the snake guy—talk about an eye-catching ad!—and the candle people, though their ad could have been a couple of paragraphs shorter without losing anything.

Placing Your Ad

By now you've nailed your style and it's time to place your ad. You access the Craigslist site (www.craigslist.org) and find the list nearest you, then click on the link to it. Next, click on the "create posting" link. You'll be sent to a page that asks you to choose a posting category. (Like me, you'll probably choose the "for sale/wanted" category, since you're trying to sell your stuff.) Click that link and you'll be sent to a page that asks you to choose a category (once again, I chose "collectibles"). Now, you're sent to the actual listing page, where you fill out all the data about your object—title, description, price, and location. You can also attach and edit photos.

Craigslist will assign you a numerical e-mail address so responders can't see your actual e-mail address but can still contact you by e-mail, and of course you can list a phone number as well. (Don't forget to check the little box at the bottom that tells potential spammers and the like that no, it's not okay for people to contact you about other products or services.) When you've finished filling everything out, click "continue" and you're on your way!

Does Craigslist work? Absolutely. When my friend Susan's colleague Lisa switched jobs and moved across country, she persuaded the former owners of her new house to sell her their futon so she'd have a place to sleep until her furniture arrived. But futons are notoriously uncomfortable, and this one was no exception, so once her bed arrived, Lisa posted the futon on Craigslist. "A few days later, someone e-mailed me about it," she says, "and that resulted in a nice young couple coming by my house with a pickup truck, handing me $200, and driving off with the futon. Voilà! I love Craigslist."

Does Craigslist always produce results? No. My father's girlfriend, Alice, tried to sell a "designer" custom-made fence and lighting system for her tennis court on Craigslist, to no avail. It also might not be available—at least not yet, but keep checking—in your area. But if it is available, it's free, it's easy, and it's worth a try! Free is good, and it's also good ad-writing practice. If you're in no hurry to sell, you might list something on Craigslist first, then move on to a (paid) newspaper classified ad if you don't get a buyer through Craigslist. If the newspaper ad is also free or you have to get the item out *now,* list it in both.

SEALING THE DEAL

No matter which method successfully sells your stuff, be sure to use common sense when screening buyers, and stay within your comfort zone when handing over your item. Bear in mind that, if you're selling something, people will probably want to come over to your house to look it over before agreeing to pay for it. Unless you have a houseful of Rottweilers, it makes sense to have one or more other people around when prospective buyers come over. You might ask the neighbors to do a few yard chores or otherwise make their presence known when you let them know a buyer is expected. Don't let buyers come over at hours that strike you as unreasonably late.

Then there's the matter of payment. Ask prospective buyers how they plan to pay, and choose the one whose terms suit you best. Cold, hard cash is always appealing for less-expensive items. (If somebody can't withdraw $40 from their checking account and hand it to you, I don't know about you, but I'd be a little leery of accepting their personal check.) If they want to pay by check for a more expensive item like a piano or piece of furniture, remember that even eBay lets their sellers wait until the check clears to ship an item. You should make it clear that you'll do the same. If you'll accept a money order or cashier's check, let buyers know that. As with every part of a transaction, the clearer you can be about your terms and expectations, the easier and more pleasant it will be for everyone involved.

Speaking of shipping, make sure you and the buyer agree on how large items will be transported. Will they come to your house with a truck or U-Haul and cart it off? Will they arrange for third-party transport? Are you prepared to haul it to their house?

For small items, you can let the buyer come and get them, take them to the buyer, ship them to the buyer (make sure it's clear who's paying the shipping and what those costs will be), or meet at a convenient midpoint. My friend Delilah once bought some (live) ducks from a seller about 100 miles away, and I went with her to pick them up. Rather than have us try to find their farm, the couple met us at a McDonald's just off the highway at the exit nearest them, bearing a box of quacking ducks in the back of their truck. I can tell you, the ride back was like traveling with the Marx Brothers!

ONWARD!

What about that old-fashioned fair-weather weekend event, the yard (aka tag) sale, and its foul-weather twin, the garage sale? We'll take a stroll around the yard (sale) in the next chapter. And we'll also look at some fun ways to get rid of stuff you don't want to or don't think you can sell. So start your engines and look for those yard-sale signs. . . .

Chapter 21

Yard Sales, Swaps, and Giveaways

Call 'em yard sales, garage sales, tag sales, or rummage sales, what's really for sale is your clutter. Here's how to set one up, how to display and price your stuff, whether to organize a block party or go it alone, how to make the sale, when to hold your sale, and, most importantly, what *not* to do. You'll also get a primer on the good old-fashioned art of bartering—who to approach, how to approach them, what's a fair swap, and what to expect. Plus: Great ways to persuade total strangers to come pick up your junk, take it away, and love it!

OUT IN THE YARD (OR IN THE GARAGE)

My friend Tom's idea of heaven is an endless weekend of yard and garage sales. Every weekend, he cruises around his neighborhood and scans the classifieds looking for promising sales. Does he need anything? No. Is he looking for anything particular? No. But to Tom, it's an entertaining way to spend free time (with an emphasis on "free"—it costs nothing to attend yard sales, after all), a treasure hunt that might yield a really great bargain or a one-of-a-kind jackpot—or just some useful stuff at a reasonable price.

Tom's not alone in his passion for yard sales. Despite the popularity of eBay and other online venues like Craigslist, more than 60 million people go to yard sales in the United States each year. One of them could be yours!

Three Kinds of Yard Sales

In my area, there are three kinds of yard sales. First are the ones that people have because they're moving, or because it's spring and they're trying to unload some stuff as part of spring-cleaning, or because they just ended up with a whole bunch of stuff when their parents moved to a retirement home or died. Those are the "once-in-a-while" sales, the kind where you see the little handmade signs by the road as you're driving around.

Next, there are what I'd call the "professional yard salers." These people have the long folding tables, the plastic covers, the folding chairs, sometimes even tents—the whole shebang. And every weekend from early spring through fall, those tables are set up and covered with stuff. These people tend to have homes on busier roads, and they don't bother with signs—people know where to find them or see them as they drive by. They're sort of halfway between a yard sale and a flea market. Clearly, they get stuff from other sources—maybe from "once-in-a-while" yard sales—and resell it at their sales.

Finally, there are the neighborhood yard sales, where two or more families pool their resources and hold a big sale, again hoping to clear out their collective clutter. These are "once-in-a-while" sales on a bigger scale and are held in the flattest yard or the one with the most on-street parking or the one that's easiest to see from the main road (or, in bad weather, at the house with the biggest garage). If you mention the multi-family angle in your advertising ("Block Sale!" "Neighborhood Yard Sale!" "Monster Multi-Family Garage Sale!"), you'll almost certainly attract more people, since there's the promise of more to check out.

GETTING YOUR YARD SALE NOTICED

By now, you probably know that there are four keys to really successful sales: good merchandise, good advertising, good pricing, and good selling (customer) technique. It's true of every sales venue, from classified ads to eBay, and it's certainly

the **Pros Know**

Did you know that there are professionals who can hold your yard sale for you? Like auctioneers and eBay drop-off stores, they'll take a commission on sales (usually 20 to 30 percent). But in return, they'll handle all the advertising, pricing, display, and actual sales of items, and they'll even deal with the customers. These people are pros at selling housewares and collectibles. They know what prices they can get, and some of them have client lists, so they can contact buyers if you have stuff of interest to them.

Of course, professionals won't think it's worth their while to spend a day or a weekend in your yard if what you have to sell is worth pocket change. But if you have some good stuff (furniture, silver, crystal, china, better collectibles, electronics) and you really don't want to do all that work yourself, or you don't feel confident about pricing or selling, contact area professionals and find someone to do it for you. Look for them in your local classifieds under "Yard Sales," "Garage Sales," or "Merchandise."

true of yard and garage sales. (There's a fifth key, too. It's called "luck" and typically involves the weather and location.) Making *your* yard sale the must-see sale of the weekend is your goal, and to do that, it has to stand out from the competition.

[There are four keys to successful sales: good merchandise, good advertising, good pricing, and good selling technique.]

Here are some ways to get your sale some attention:

❑ Post notices on bulletin boards at local libraries, markets, and other community bulletin boards. Print them out on a full-size 8½ x 11-inch sheet (copier-paper size). Use big, bold type that's easy to read and add plenty of color. (Just make sure the type itself is dark enough to read easily.) Add digital photos of some of your more appealing items with a brief description under each photo. If you want, add balloon icons, borders, or stickers to remind people to look for the balloons on your mailbox.

- Put classified ads in local papers; they'll typically also put them up on their Web sites' classified sections. (See "Placing Your Ad" on page 409.)
- Post a notice on the garage sale section of your area's Craigslist Web site (www.craigslist.org) and other community Web sites.
- Use words and phrases that help your ad stand out: "1-Day-Only AMAZ-ING Garage Sale!" "Mother of All Yard Sales!" "AWESOME Garage Sale!" "Grandma's OVERFLOWING Attic Sale!" "Basement BLOWOUT Sale!"
- In the item descriptions, list the biggest and most interesting items first.
- If your sale has items that are surefire crowd magnets, like vintage clothes, baby clothes and equipment, kids' clothing and toys, costume jewelry, dolls, and tools, feature them prominently in your ad. Then make sure you draw attention to them at the sale itself by grouping them together and putting up a large display sign (like a lavender sign that says "Vintage Clothing!" in flowery Victorian lettering, with a hand icon pointing down at the table).
- Good signage makes good sales. Hang big signs over your tables telling what's on them in bold, easy-to-read letters that can be seen across the yard.
- People love food, so if you have the manpower to deal with a small refresh-ment table set somewhat apart from the rest of the sale, take a tip from church sales and offer (or sell) treats like mini chocolate-chip cookies and doughnut holes and small paper cups of water, lemonade, or iced tea at your sale. Don't sell anything gooey, and set big trash cans near the table so people can gulp their treats and dump the cups and plates before heading back to the sale tables. Of course, put up a big "Refreshments" sign over the table. If you don't want to charge for them, consider setting a glass jar with some coins in it on the table to encourage people to toss in a quarter or two for their treats. Don't forget to mention the refresh-ments in your ad! If you do offer them, be aware that you may get some spills and crumbs on your stuff. But it will definitely set your yard sale apart!
- Have a bargain or grab-bag table (or combine both at one table, with signs over the table for bargains and grab bags). Sell your bargains for $1 and under and your grab bags for 50 cents, and note that prominently on the signs. If you set out boxes of costume jewelry or other little items on this

table, have signs on each box listing the per-item price ("Anything in this box is $1!") and also, if you want, a multiple-item price ("Any three for $2!"). This kind of pricing also lets you move stuff over to the bargain table toward the end of the sale if you see it isn't selling.

❏ Don't put out anything you aren't prepared to sell, with the exception of the display tables, folding chairs for sellers, cash box, bins for tags, and boom box (and hide that under a table beside a seller). Don't be surprised if people want to buy them, too. If you put bright tablecloths, sheets, or other textiles under your stuff to "set it off," someone will inevitably want to buy the textile and end up feeling disgruntled when you won't sell it (or you'll end up disgruntled if you decide to oblige and have to pull off all the stuff on top of it, then put it all back). Worse, the pattern in the textile will distract people from the stuff that *is* for sale and make it harder to see it, too. So use plain white sheets or leave the tables clean and bare.

❏ Give your sale an inviting "block party" feel by adding some music—salsa, Jimmy Buffet, something upbeat and inoffensive. Don't crank up the volume—you want to hear buyers easily, you want couples to be able to confer with each other, and you don't want to disturb the neighbors! But don't make it so soft that it doesn't contribute to a happy atmosphere.

❏ When people arrive, act like you're glad to see them. Don't sit there sulking (or hiding) behind your table. Smile, come up and greet people, thank them for coming, ask if there's anything special they're looking for. (If they say they're looking for something you don't have, do not just say "I don't have that." Instead, say something along the lines of, "If we have one of

the **Pros Know**

Want to learn more about holding a yard sale? The undisputed yard-sale queen in America is Cathy Pedigo, author of *How to Have Big Money Garage Sales* (Winning Edge, 2002, $10.95) and coauthor with Sonia Weiss of *The Pocket Idiot's Guide to Garage and Yard Sales* (Alpha, 2003, $9.95). Check out her Web site (www.win-edge.com/GarageSale.shtml), where you can order her book—which she promises will more than triple your garage or yard sale income—or get a downloadable version for $8.95 (or both for $12.95).

those, it would be on that table/in that bin over there," or "I don't think we have one, but you might be interested in. . . ." Once they start looking at something else, you have a good chance of making a sale.)

Placing Your Ad

My boyfriend, Rob, was for years an editor at the *Express-Times*, which serves both the Easton, Pennsylvania, area and parts of New Jersey. I decided to look there for good yard sale ads. I noticed immediately that the *Express-Times* categorizes sales as "Estate & Tag Sales," "Garage/Yard Sales," and "Yard Sales," a rather mystifying set of distinctions, since the ads seem to be identical. Each ad gave the town, street address and directions, date(s) of the sale, and time of the sale (8:00 a.m.–2:00 p.m., 9:00 a.m.–?).

After listing the basics, some ads managed to be both concise and enthusiastic ("Yard/Moving Sale! Housewares, antiques, furniture, tools, gardening items, camping equipment, 1,000 items and more!"). Some were quite specific ("Leather pull-out sofa, mahogany 4-poster bed, iron & glass table/chairs, cherry desk/chair, baker's rack, piecrust table, Waterford, Lenox, grandfather clock, housewares"). Some listed quite a bit more. Others threw in catch phrases like "Everything must go!" "Rock-bottom prices!" "Plus much more," "Parents moving," and "Too much to list."

In the Nashville paper, the *Tennessean*, the garage- and yard-sale ads were even more exuberant. The paper provided eye-catching headings if you wanted to list your sale as a moving sale, kids sale, or estate sale. A quick scan of the ads themselves showed me hooks aplenty, including "New & used items!" "Tons of new stuff!" "LOTS of stuff!!" "Rain or shine!!" "Super Estate Sale!" "All must go today!!" "Fabulous Finds!!!" "Something for everyone!" and my favorite, "Y'all Come!"

Churches and bigger sales added the lure of food to their yard sales ("Bake sale with hot foods," "Cake and refreshments will be sold"), which I thought was a great idea. And one of them threw in a cool bargain element ("Bag day will be Saturday") to add even more appeal.

Note that, unlike classified ads for individual items, the goal of a yard-sale ad is to cover as much ground as possible—to entice buyers with popular categories of items (like vintage clothing) and with the breadth of the offerings (1,000 items) rather than descriptions of individual items. Note, too, that they start with the big-ticket stuff (antiques, leather pull-out sofa), then move on to the small potatoes.

What Does It Cost?

Like placing a classified ad for one or more individual items, the cost of placing an ad for a yard or garage (or tag) sale varies with the paper. In the *Tennessean,* it costs $31 to place five lines for a garage sale listing and $2 for each extra line. The paper also offers a free garage sale kit if you advertise and lets you advertise the leftovers from your sale for just $5. The *Express-Times* boxes their garage sale ads, so you're paying for a 2-inch-deep box rather than individual lines. They charge $46.50 to run your ad for 4 days (Thursday through Sunday), or $43.50 to run it for your choice of any 3 of the 4 days. In either case, your ad will also be featured online at www.nj.com and www.pennlive.com for 30 days, included in the cost, and you'll get a free kit from them, as well.

In my local Pennsylvania *Merchandiser,* an all-ads community paper with two special editions and a Web site, you can run a garage/yard sale ad for $4.20 for up to 20 words and 10 cents for each additional word per issue per week. Ads can run up to 12 weeks in one or both editions and will automatically be featured on their Web site. They'll run a "super ad" in all-bold type for $6.05 per ad, per week, per publication.

So check the Web sites of your local papers for pricing (or call the classifieds departments of the papers and speak to a sales rep). And remember, it's smart to advertise in *all* your local papers, as long as it won't cost you so much it will eat away your yard-sale profits. (If that's the case, see which one or ones have the most garage/yard sale ads and go with it or them.)

How Does It Work?

All the newspapers I checked have forms on their Web sites, making it as easy to create an ad for a garage or yard sale as it is for a classified ad. You just fill in the blanks! Some, like the *Express-Times,* have a different form for a garage sale than for a single- (or multiple-) item classified, while others, like the *Merchandiser,* use the same form for both kinds of ad. See Chapter 20—Clutter in the Classifieds, beginning on page 394, for more tips on ad writing.

COUNTDOWN TO THE SALE

Okay, you've checked it all out and decided to try a yard or garage sale for yourself. Congratulations! Here's what you should do as you plan your yard sale.

1. **Get permission.** Check with your township or city hall to see if there are regulations governing yard sales or if you need a permit to hold a yard sale in your area. If so, make sure all the paperwork's in order before you place your ad. While you're at it, if you live in a state that charges sales tax, check to see if you'll need to collect it at your sale. (In most states, that's not necessary if you hold four or fewer yard sales a year, but be sure to check—better safe than sorry!)

2. **Collect your stuff.** Gather everything you want to sell, bearing in mind that seasonality might count—in spring, people will be more likely to be looking for lawn mowers than snow blowers. You could divide up the stuff into spring/summer, fall/winter, and "anytime" piles, and hold two yard sales, one in spring and one in early fall, assuming you have someplace to store the off-season stuff in the meantime. Put the "anytime" stuff out with both sales. Don't be too hasty to assume something's too junky or broken to sell. As yard-sale whiz Jackie (see page 422) reminds us, one man's trash really is another man's treasure. "People will buy *anything*," Jackie says, "even empty hat boxes." You can always donate it, put it out for the trash, or have it hauled off afterwards if it doesn't sell.

3. **Talk to the neighbors.** See if any of your neighbors are interested in participating in the yard sale with you. Bigger yard sales draw more buyers, and you can split the costs of advertising; the setup work; cost of hiring a professional (if you all decide to go that route); and actual work of monitoring tables, talking to customers, taking money, making change, bagging or boxing up purchases, and other tasks. If several families agree to participate, choose the largest, most visible yard (with the best on-street parking) for the sale, or, if there's lots of stuff and the houses are adjacent to each other, you can have stuff on display in every yard to create the

impression of a *really* big sale. If your neighbors (or your relatives, for that matter) do go in on a joint sale with you, make sure all the arrangements are spelled out, including what will be done with the stuff that doesn't sell by the end of the sale. Even if your neighbors aren't interested in participating, they may offer you some of their clutter to add to your sale— or they may come over and buy some of yours!

4. **Call in the pros.** If you're planning to hire a professional, now is the time to find one and have him or her come over and evaluate your stuff (and your neighbors', if you're having a group sale). If you do bring a pro on board, this is pretty much your last step—they'll usually take it from here, even down to cleaning and polishing your stuff. (See "The Pros Know" on page 406 for more on hiring a yard-sale pro.)

5. **Clean up your stuff.** You'll be less stressed if your stuff is clean and ready to sell before you set your sale date. Make it look as good as it can. Sort clothes by type (tee-shirts, jeans, skirts) and size; separate men's, women's, boys', and girls'. Sort junk, like a collection of rusty small tools; odd batches of screws, nails, and hooks; sewing odds and ends; and other little things into grab bags or boxes. Put marbles, buttons, and other potentially decorative junk into glass canning jars. If you're trying to get rid of extra sewing or quilting fabric, tie several complementary pieces together with ribbon, like they do in quilting shops, and sell them as a bunch.

6. **Watch the weather.** Try to hold your yard sale on a nice day. You can monitor weather in your area up to 10 days in advance on sites like Weather. com (www.weather.com) and Weather Underground (www.wunderground. com), or check the local paper for a 5-day forecast. NOAA weather radio also gives extended forecasts. No forecasting system is perfect, but it's better to wait if bad (especially severe) weather is predicted, and hold your sale another weekend. Decide if you can hold the sale in your garage (or a neighbor's) if the weather turns bad despite your efforts, and if not, set (and advertise) a rain date.

7. **Finalize the timing.** Jackie, Nashville's yard-sale queen (see page 422), recommends holding a yard sale when there's a big flea market in town, since people will come from all over for the flea market, and many of them scour the area for yard sales while they're visiting. In their excellent book

Scaling Down, authors Judi Culbertson and Marj Decker suggest holding your yard sale between July and September if you live in an area that attracts tourists. There's also the question of how many days the sale should last. Jackie suggests holding a 2-day sale on Friday and Saturday, unless you have only a small amount of stuff, in which case it should be a 1-day sale on Saturday. Judi and Marj recommend always holding a 1-day sale (they also recommend Saturday), regardless of the size; they don't think second days are worth it. Other experts, like Michael and Pam Williams (see "Price your stuff," on page 414), claim that 3-day sales from Friday through Sunday are the most successful. (Yard-sale veterans refer to the "usual after-church crowd.") You decide, or try it two or all three ways (if you hold several sales) and see which works better for you. Marj and Judi advise against holding a yard sale over a major holiday weekend, since people will be having family gatherings and are less likely to head out to a sale. Time of day also matters. People won't buy what they can't see, so unless you have exceptional outdoor lighting or are holding your sale in a well-lit garage, make sure the sale ends before dark.

8. **Write your ad.** See "Getting Your Yard Sale Noticed" on page 405 for more on this. You can also check out Chapter 20—Clutter in the Classifieds, beginning on page 394, for ad-writing tips from the pros, and check your local papers' Web sites' classifieds sections, since they often provide ad-writing tips. Make sure your ad says what you're selling, when you're selling it (days and times), what your address is and how to get there, and includes a rain date if you decide to have one.

9. **Place your ad.** Put your ad in all the local and area papers, including special marketing papers like (in my part of Pennsylvania) the *Merchandiser* and the *Penny Pincher.* If you have special-events papers (the Nashville version is called the *Scene*), advertise in those, too. Post your sale on Craigslist and other community Web sites. (See "Placing Your Ad" on page 409 and Chapter 20—Clutter in the Classifieds, beginning on page 394, for more on placing ads in the paper and on Craigslist.) Tack up notices on community bulletin boards at local libraries and markets. When you place an ad in your local paper's classified section, if you have an option as to how long it runs, I'd opt for starting it the day before the sale and running

it each day of the sale; Jackie, who certainly knows her business, suggests running it the days of the sale. Some papers simply run the ads for a week. Whatever the case may be, find out by calling the classified department several weeks before your sale. The last thing you want is to place your ad too late for it to make the paper in time!

10. **Price your stuff.** Decide on a price for each item or box or bag of items. Do your research! Check out pricing at local yard sales and see what other people are asking. Go to local flea markets, where the sellers are pros, and see not only what they're selling their stuff for (assume you'll get less), but how they tag or otherwise show the prices of their stuff. In their book *Garage Sale Magic!,* authors Michael and Pam Williams suggest pricing items at 25 percent of retail cost, but discounting clothes and outdated electronic items much more. Books and magazines are other items that won't sell unless they're deeply discounted. But it's still possible to make a profit, even if you have a whole table of 25-cent stuff. In fact, most of the big-money garage salers who made hundreds and even thousands of dollars and bragged about it on yard-sale diva Cathy Pedigo's Web site said upfront that they had only two or three $25–$50 items, and most of what they sold was priced at 25 cents to $15. Judi Culbertson and Marj Decker recommend pricing everything in 25-cent increments, so you don't need to keep dimes, nickels, and pennies on hand for change. Make sure you tag every item with a price (in large, easy-to-read, waterproof ink, please) and attach the tags where buyers can see them. No staples, please! I don't like having to pry a stapled price tag off a piece of clothing and risk pulling threads (or worse), and I'm sure you don't, either. If you're having a multi-family sale, take a tip from the pros and give each family its own color of tags so you can tell who's made what at the end of the sale. Getting all the prices figured out, written out, and attached in advance will really cut down on stress on sale days!

11. **Get your setup assembled.** Don't wait 'til the last minute to gather all the tables, rolling clothes racks, bins, chairs for you and your family to sit in, signage, cash box or money belt, and other necessary supplies, or your yard sale will be a disorganized mess. You'll be most successful if your stuff is neatly displayed and you have plenty of room between tables and displays. Make sure you have enough table and bin space to display every small item

and enough floor or yard space to set up clothes racks, large stuff, and tables (and your chairs), and still leave plenty of walking room between tables or objects. (Again, you can learn a lot by checking out other people's yard sales and flea market setups—both what to do and what *not* to do.) Practice setting out the stuff. If your sale is in the garage (What? You have room for it in the garage!), it will be easy to do a practice setup and make any needed adjustments to make the layout work. If it's in the yard and driveway, set up a table in the house and practice displaying the stuff on it. (Needless to say, folding tables and chairs work best for yard sales, even if you have to beg everyone you know to lend you some for the weekend.) Eyeball the tables and large stuff and your yard space until you're sure you have enough room for everything *and* for, at times, 30 or more browsing buyers. Make sure you have tarps or big plastic sheets (and a secure way of anchoring them!) to put over everything if it's a yard sale and you plan to set up the night before or keep everything set up over 2 or 3 days.

12. **Buy some balloons.** You'll need some big, bold, colorful balloons on your mailbox to help buyers find you on the big weekend.

13. **Decide where to put your signs.** You'll need to know this before you actually make the signs, since where you'll put them will determine the driving directions you write on each sign as well as how many signs you'll need. You'll want to put them at all major intersections near your home, at both ends of your road, and along the road (these will just require the address and arrows, not directions). Put a big, bold sign in the yard itself ("Here It Is!!!"), and make sure it can be seen from the road.

14. **Make your signs.** You want your signs to stand out, but it's even more important that they be easy to read. I love color, but have you ever seen signs posted along the road on paper that was such a dark pink, red, or whatever that you couldn't read what was on them? Remember that people will see these signs while they're driving past at 25 to 55 miles an hour, so you need to make them as easy to see as possible. A pale shade of a bright color (like pink, yellow, or orange) might work if the ink is really bold and black. Try it and see! Make sure the sign is big enough to actually read, which is probably going to be a lot bigger than you think. Use paper or cardboard that's stiff enough that the signs will not fold, bend over, or wrap around a telephone

pole in the wind and thus be unreadable. Practice writing your signs until the lettering is huge, dark, and easy to see (or create it on your computer using the same criteria). Waterproof ink, please! Don't forget stakes, staples, tape, and anything else you'll need to actually put up your signs. Once you think you've got it down, put up one of your signs, then drive by and see if you can read it. If you can't, fine-tune it until you've nailed it.

What should you put on your sign? Start with a headline. Why say "Yard Sale" or "Garage Sale" when you can say "Mother of All Garage Sales!" or "Basement Blowout Sale!" Tell folks when it is (days and times), where it is (address and simple directions), and the rain date (if there is one). Don't forget directional arrows, which can be a different color (like red) to add an eye-catching touch. (Remember that the directions and the way the arrow points will be different for the different streets where you put the signs—don't write the same thing on every sign.) Add a drawing of balloons or some colorful, big balloon stickers to remind people to look for the balloons at your house, or, when it's time to put up the signs, attach actual balloons to the signs themselves. Judi Culberston and Marj Decker recommend that you also make signs to post downtown if you live in an area that gets lots of tourists.

15. **Clean up the yard.** Or the (gasp) garage, if you're holding the sale inside. It's very important to make a good impression on prospective buyers—you want them to have confidence in you and your stuff. A neat, tidy yard (or garage); an attractive front door; and well-organized, attractively displayed merchandise (hey, it's no longer "stuff"—it's for sale!) can work wonders in boosting both stops and sales. For tips on how to neaten up, see Chapter 16—Sprucing Up the Yard and Garden, beginning on page 330, and Chapter 15—Cleaning Out the Garage, beginning on page 311.

16. **Put out your signs.** Put up your signs the morning before your sale begins (Thursday morning if the sale starts Friday), so people can plan their weekend accordingly. I've seen signs go up in my area even earlier.

17. **Get small change.** Stock up on cash and change so you'll be ready for your customers. They'll probably arrive with $20 bills from the ATM, so you'll want to have plenty of tens, fives, and ones on hand, as well as loads of quarters. Because people like to bargain, I think it makes sense to have small change on hand, too—if somebody offers you 20 cents for that 25-

cent paperback, are you really going to turn them down? Once you have the money, practice using the money belt or cash box so you (and anyone else who's using it) will be comfortable.

18. **Get refreshments and supplies.** If you're selling (or offering) refreshments like doughnuts, cookies, bake-sale items, lemonade, iced tea, or water, get your supplies together. Do you need napkins, paper plates, little paper cups? How about plastic wrap (if you're selling the stuff)? Do you have a couple of trash cans for the cups and food wrappers? If not, can you borrow some? Do you have enough bags and newspaper to bag or wrap up all your stuff? If not, now's the time to bug friends and neighbors to fork over their extras. (You can offer them a doughnut and some lemonade in exchange!)

19. **Set it up.** If it's a garage sale or a big yard sale, unless you want to be out there at 3:00 a.m. stumbling around in the dark, set everything up the afternoon before the sale. That way, there's still time to borrow an extra table, rearrange the display, or run off for some additional supplies if you realize things are missing. Put up your signage and make sure it's secure so folks can actually read it. Double-check to make sure several people can walk abreast between tables and displays. Set out bigger stuff to double-check the display, but take rolling clothes racks, furniture, and other portable items back inside for the night and bring them back out on the mornings of sale days. Obviously, keep your cash box in the house! Put out the balloons on your mailbox, keeping some in reserve in case of vandals. Look everything over and make sure you're pleased with the way it all looks.

Yard-sale veterans recommend putting some of the bigger, higher-priced items in the front of the display to attract more buyers. Go out to the road and make sure that what you see looks inviting, abundant, well organized, and intriguing. And make sure you can see your sign. To make things even more inviting, you can set pots of colorful flowers at the base of your sign and on the cashier's table—but if you do, be prepared to sell them!

20. **Keep your focus.** People go to yard sales for fun. Do what you can to make it a fun experience for them *and* for you. Remind yourself and all involved that your goal is to get rid of stuff, not to haggle and try to make a huge profit. Yard-sale diva Cathy Pedigo recommends having music playing. Laugh, chat, be cheerful, have a good time!

21. **Go for it!** It's finally the big weekend. Make sure you're up and out early. Set out refreshments (if you're having them), get everybody in position, and make sure everyone knows what they're supposed to be doing. Set out the big stuff and remove the tarps or plastic from the tables. Make sure all signage is still in position. Finally, lock the doors to the house and you're ready to roll. Good luck!

Troubleshooting

There are a few precautions you can take to prevent the most common mishaps from striking your yard sale. I'm going to assume that you've already checked with your township or city hall, gotten any necessary permits, and followed any regulations. I'll also assume you've been clear with your neighbors about everyone's roles and responsibilities, and if you've hired a yard-sale professional, you're clear on what they're offering (and taking in return). And I'm going to assume you have a Plan B for bad weather. Here are some other things to watch for and what to do to keep them from happening (or at least, getting out of hand).

- ❑ **Haggling.** People love a bargain, and they love trying to get a lower price. And for a lot of people, that's what yard sales are all about. Expect to hear variations on, "Is this your best price?" "Can you do better on this?" and "I'll give you X for this." Judi Culbertson and Marj Decker suggest that you price slightly higher so you can come down and help people feel like they're getting a bargain. (Emphasis here on "slightly"—several yard-sale pros note that if someone thinks one item is overpriced, they're likely to conclude that everything is and leave without buying anything.) If their offer is too low, you could always offer to throw in something—a second paperback, another toy. But remember that your object is to offload the stuff! No matter what— even if someone tries to bring down a price by saying awful things about the item they want to buy—remain pleasant, cheerful, and courteous. You owe it to yourself. And other buyers are listening!

❑ **Stealing.** The best ways to keep someone from making off with stuff is to have it all well organized and displayed, with plenty of room between tables, and to have enough people manning the sale that anyone who arrives and lingers will be asked very pleasantly, "May I help you find something?" It's a lot easier to take stuff when the stuff is all piled and jumbled in a chaotic mess or there's one lonely person trying to deal with a line of paying customers.

❑ **Unwanted visitors.** Speaking of thieves, while you're out in the yard, it's possible that an uninvited guest is in your house. And besides simply snooping or trying to buy your everyday china, someone could be casing the house or stealing something. It's one thing for a light-fingered passerby to make off with a piece of costume jewelry and quite another for a thief to remove your spouse's Rolex or your diamond earrings. I don't know about you, but I'd make sure all doors to the house were locked and all downstairs windows closed and locked. (If one of your family or the sales group needs to get inside, you can give them the key.) Of course, if you have professionals handling the sale, you can be inside keeping an eye on things—but I'd still lock the doors.

❑ **Early birds.** Veteran yard salers start early because, like the early bird, they want that worm. That means that, if you advertise a sale starting at 8:00 a.m., you might look out your windows bleary-eyed at 6:00 a.m. and find people pulling up to the curb and pawing through your stuff. There are two ways to deal with this—advertise the sale as starting at 9:00 and get out there at 7:00, or do as a number of folks did in the Nashville *Tennessean* and say "NO EARLY BIRDS!" in your ad. (I'd opt for the first approach to avoid turning away customers, but if you're not an early bird

(continued on page 422)

the Pros Know

I was lucky enough to be writing this chapter while visiting my father and his girlfriend, Alice, down in Nashville. When I mentioned it to them, Alice pointed out that a friend of theirs, Jackie, was the yard-sale queen of Nashville. So of course I got on the phone with Jackie and asked her to tell me all about it. Read on for an insider's view of all things yard sale!

When Jackie started holding yard sales, she did it all herself, and she still recommends that approach if you have just a small amount of stuff or none of it is worth very much. But if you have a lot of stuff, or you're going in with some neighbors, or you have some valuable pieces—"if you're unloading your house, not just your basement," as she put it—do as Jackie did and hire a professional to handle your yard sale. (Jackie found hers through word of mouth; see "The Pros Know" on page 406 for other options.) She points out that professionals are interested in the bigger and better stuff, like dining room sets, and are very selective about taking on yard sales.

But if you have the goods, a professional is fabulous: For 25 percent of the take (in Jackie's case), Ron, the professional she works with, comes over with a team of two to three assistants. They evaluate the stuff and ticket every item. If several families are holding a joint sale, they'll use different-colored tickets for each family so it's easy to tell who's made what at the end of the day. Ron creates a great ad and places it in the local paper and anywhere else he thinks will help draw a crowd. They set out signs on critical corners.

On sale days, one of the assistants acts as cashier while the others monitor the crowd, guard the house (unobtrusively, of course), collect the money, wrap or bag items for buyers, and are generally helpful. Throughout the process, they keep meticulous records. At the end of the sale, Ron looks over what didn't sell, then takes any pieces he thinks he can sell at his flea-market stand and gives Jackie the money when each item does sell. What about the items he doesn't want to take? "He gets somebody to come out with a truck and haul it all away, and then they send me a check," Jackie says. No fuss, no muss!

Does it pay off? "My biggest sale made $4,000 over one weekend," Jackie said. Wow. That's more than most of us could hope to get from even a big yard sale—usually anything over $1,000 is considered fantastic, and if it's a small sale, you should be happy to make a few hundred. Whatever you make is good. "After all," as Jackie says, "it's found money, from stuff that's just lying around."

At the end of it all, even somebody as successful at yard saleing as Jackie isn't really in it for the money. "I do it for the challenge of it," she says.

Yard Sale Specifics

I asked Jackie to share some insights with all of us, and she generously agreed. Here are some tips you can use to make your yard/garage/tag sale a winner:

✳ **When to have the sale.** Jackie says you should hold your yard sale on a Friday and Saturday, unless it's really small, in which case do a 1-day sale and hold it Saturday. She always aims to hold sales when there's a big flea market or antiques event in town. "People come from all over to attend these events," she says. "They bring the paper along and go from yard sale to yard sale as well as the flea market."

✳ **When to expect the crowds.** Jackie says the most people will come early, especially on the first day. "If you advertise that the sale starts at 8:00, they'll be lined up in your driveway at 6:00," she warns. (This is another case where those yard-sale professionals can come in handy.) She says activity will continue to be heavy through the morning and early afternoon, then start tapering off around 3:00 p.m.

✳ **When to advertise.** Advertise on the days you hold your sale, Jackie advises. If you're planning a 2-day sale starting on Friday, place your ad to come out on Friday and run again on Saturday.

✳ **Where to put up signs.** Jackie says to put up signs at the principal intersections in your area, as well as at the turn-offs to your road, and, of course, in front of your house. Announce that it's a yard, garage, or tag sale (depending on what it's called in your area); give days, times, and the address; and add an arrow pointing in the direction of the sale.

✳ **What to expect.** Surprises, according to Jackie. "Stuff that means the least to you is the stuff that sells first," she says. She also warns that you need a thick skin when you're selling off things you care about. "You may have loved that painting, and you'll be shocked by the unkind comments you hear about it."

✳ **Who to expect.** "The dealers come first," Jackie says. They'll snap up the things they think they can sell, then resell them at their flea-market stands. Once they've picked over your stuff, the yard-sale enthusiasts (like my friend Tom) are likely to show up. These are the people who love yard sales enough to get up early on a weekend and turn out for them when they could be sleeping or lounging around in their pajamas drinking coffee. Finally, the general public drops by.

(continued)

❋ **What sells.** Tools, costume jewelry, vintage clothing, dolls, books, baby clothes and equipment, kids' stuff, kitchenware, glassware, and linens all do well. "If you've moved to a condo and no longer garden, get rid of those tools," Jackie advises. She says people are always looking for dolls and baby stuff. People love costume jewelry, and lots of people make stuff out of it, including other jewelry. Vintage clothing is so popular that "it's like the running of the bulls" when Jackie advertises it in one of her yard sales. Grandparents who've long since gotten rid of all the kid stuff in their homes often shop yard sales for games, toys, and equipment like trikes and bikes once the grandkids start visiting. I was surprised to hear that books did well, but Jackie says as long as you don't want much for them (you might have to sell three or four paperbacks for a dollar), both paperbacks and hardcovers sell well. And, as Jackie points out, urging us all to cull our collections regularly, "How many books can your bookshelves hold?" Other strong sellers—both surprises to me—were artificial flowers and bric-a-brac.

❋ **What doesn't sell.** Outdated technology, for the most part. "I could not give away a typewriter, no matter how good or expensive it was," Jackie laments. On the other hand, old camera equipment is often bought by collectors, and people sometimes buy old Mixmasters and other kitchen equipment as decorations if they want to create a vintage or period look in their

yourself, you might want to go for the other. But don't be surprised to see a few vultures circling even if you do put the warning in your ad.)

❑ **Parking.** On-street parking is good; blocking your driveway (and potentially crashing into other cars while pulling in and out) is bad. Keep it from happening by setting up display tables, clothes racks, or on-sale equipment or furniture in the driveway, far enough toward the street that no one can pull into the drive.

❑ **Accounting.** As people pay for each item, remove the tag and put it in a small plastic storage bin. (If you accept a different price than the one on the tag, cross out the original price and write the new one on the tag before you toss it in the bin.) This is another reason not to staple on tags—you need them for your records, so they should be easy to remove. If several families are involved, have a separate small bin for each color of tag, so kitchens. Yard sales are also one venue where designer clothes do not bring a premium. "My daughter tried to sell some expensive designer clothes at a yard sale, and they brought only $4 to $5 apiece," Jackie says.

❊ **What to do first.** Make sure you look carefully at everything you're setting out. Jackie points to the time she'd put out a box of costume jewelry and a conscientious customer brought her a heavy gold man's bracelet that had a broken catch and had been tossed into the box years before and been long forgotten. She wasn't as lucky the time she mistakenly put her new weed eater into the yard sale instead of the broken one and sold it for $2. When she realized her mistake, Jackie contacted the buyer, but he refused to give it back. And then there was the time she was selling a golf bag. The prospective buyer looked in a pouch and discovered a pair of her husband's underwear! (He bought the golf bag anyway.)

❊ **What to watch out for.** If you let buyers into your home, it's every man for himself. When her mother died, Jackie held an estate sale at her mother's home. Her yard-sale professional, Ron, and his team had roped off most of the house, but had let people into the den and the kitchen. Though nothing inside the house was supposed to be for sale, Jackie watched one couple buy the kitchen cabinets right off the wall and haul them away (she was planning to renovate the kitchen anyway) and another woman slip under the barricade and return demanding to buy the living-room curtains, rods and all.

that, at day's or sale's end, it's super-easy for each family to add up their sales and take their share of the profits.

FINDING STUFF A HOME

Not everyone has what it takes to hold a yard or garage sale. Maybe you don't want zillions of people coming to your home. Maybe you don't think your stuff is good enough to sell. Maybe, like me, you live on a death-defying road that curves right before your house and has absolutely no curb between the lawn and the road. (Drat! But I haven't given up hope. Rob and I are scheming to hold a group yard sale with our friends from our Friday Night Supper Club. Now we just have to let them know.) Or maybe you just don't want to be bothered. But you'd still like to unload some stuff.

Never fear! There are some really fun things you can do to get rid of stuff you don't want—and maybe get stuff you need, in the bargain.

The Freecycle Network

A great resource is the Freecycle Network (www.freecycle.org). Like Craigslist, the Freecycle Network started as a small idea in 2003—a way to keep stuff out of Tucson landfills—and grew into a network of almost 4,000 local groups. That's because the idea is so easy and great. You sign up with your local Freecycle group, and you can view all the free stuff they're offering online, or post your own stuff. There are just three restrictions—that anything offered be free, legal, and appropriate for all ages. Their motto is, "Think globally, recycle locally."

This is a great way to get rid of stuff you might otherwise have to contact someone to have it hauled off. My friends Jeff and Nitya, who purchased a home in rural Pennsylvania, wanted to get rid of a falling-down garden fence. So they put it on Freecycle. To their amazement, a Yuppie guy contacted them about it, then arrived to haul it off, explaining that his wife was redecorating one of their bathrooms and wanted to use the decrepit fence to give the bathroom walls a rustic look!

Meanwhile, in Washington, DC, my friend Susan's condo tenant broke up with her boyfriend, who decamped with some of her stuff but left his bed behind. Sure enough, she listed it with Freecycle and someone carried it away (for free!). No more bad memories for her!

Susan herself signed up for Freecycle and was able to find people to come pick up a bag of books she'd been carting around in her car for months (meaning to donate them to the library but never managing to do it) and some cans of Science Diet salmon cat food, a flavor her boyfriend's cat had refused to eat. Within 2 hours of posting them, she had offers for both. (You get to choose who to give your stuff to from the respondents; she chose first-come, first-served.) She sent directions, put the stuff out on the porch, went out to run errands, and by the time she got back, poof! They were gone!

Susan was just amazed to see what her local group was listing (and asking for). Among the listings were a bag of plastic coat hangers someone had rescued from the trash, a working television, size 6 shoes, a set of flash cards for calculus, a food processor, and a whiteboard. On the "want" side, someone was looking for empty pillboxes for an art project. As she says, "All of a sudden, de-cluttering began to feel more like a stroll through a flea market." (But don't get any ideas—remember, you're trying to offload stuff, not haul it off to your home!)

It's super-easy to navigate the Freecycle Network site and to find your local group and sign up. You do need moderator approval, though, and to get it you have to explain why you want to join the group. My local group had 485 members when I signed up!

Just for Books

Want to get rid of some books and have fun at the same time? Check out Book-Crossing (www.bookcrossing.com). It's based on "Where's George?" (www.wheresgeorge.com), a tracking system for dollar bills that lets people who find specially stamped bills log onto a Web site and note where that particular bill has turned up. Started by a software and Web site developer and his wife in 2001, the nonprofit BookCrossing now has more than 500,000 members internationally.

To "read and release" books, you register on the BookCrossing Web site. Then they send you book labels that you put in the book you want to pass along. You leave it somewhere, and when the next person picks it up, they go to the Web site and log where they found it—and what they thought of it. Then they pass it on.

My friend Susan was very excited to discover BookCrossing and couldn't wait to try it. She signed up, got the bookplates, and left her first book in a café in Greenbelt, Maryland. Then she began obsessively checking to see if anyone had picked it up. Unfortunately, it was a physical anthropology text on hominids, so she had a longer wait than most, but sure enough, one day she received an e-mail from BookCrossing with a post from the next person who'd picked it up and her review of it. (She enjoyed it and was looking forward to the sequel.)

Good Old Barter

Don't forget that primordial trade technique, swapping. You can always offer goods for services or goods for goods. My little farmette of six heirloom chickens lays more eggs than Rob and I can eat, so I often take a six-pack (a half-egg carton) or two of delicious, organic eggs to the weekly gathering of my Friday Night Supper Club. In return, I'll get homegrown produce, fresh herbs, baked goods, jams and jellies, or whatever anyone has on hand. It's an informal arrangement that works well for all of us.

My friend Carolyn swaps pet-sitting duties for eggs from our friend Nitya's small-farm enterprise. My friend Delilah will exchange her unwanted kitchenware and collectibles for items she does want or store credit at local antiques stores and flea markets. (I'm sure this wouldn't work everywhere, but I've never heard of a vendor turning her down, and I've been present at some of these exchanges.) Delilah and I swap extra plants, and there's a whole group of us who exchange extra seeds each spring. My neighbor had a tree removed in exchange for giving the arborists the wood.

If you know of someone who wants some of your stuff and you'd like something of theirs (or some kind of service, like lawn mowing), give it a try and see what you can do. It's fun, it's a great feeling to know you're giving someone something they want, and it's wonderful to get stuff and services you actually want in exchange for your clutter.

Barter at Work

If your co-workers are up for it, arrange to unload your stuff at an office swap. Have people bring a limited number of items (say, a maximum of five) and set them out on a table in the employee break room or somewhere else out of sight of clients and bigwigs. Either let people take what they want, have everyone gather at a set time and take turns, or draw numbers and choose based on the order in which their numbers came up—1 goes first, 2 goes second, and so on. (Bear in mind that you are trying to kick your clutter and don't have to take *anything* unless you actually need it!) If everyone enjoys the experience, you could have "swap day" once a month.

Make sure your colleagues agree about what to do with the stuff once the swap is over. Will everyone take home their stuff if it wasn't chosen? Will it be left on the table for a certain (predetermined) amount of time with a "Free" sign in case someone comes by and wants something? At the corporation where I worked, there was a small snack kitchen on my floor, and it was understood that any employee who had something to give away would leave it on the table in that room, and anyone who wanted something could take it. I'll confess that I found a few good books there, and left a few, too!

If your neighborhood is close-knit, there's no reason why you couldn't hold neighborhood swaps, too. Every year, I give my neighbor extra plants from my water garden (mine's small, so the plants are always spreading too much, and his is bigger and can hold them) in exchange for snow shoveling in winter. If you'd like to involve several neighbors or even the whole block, you should set it up like a yard sale. ("My Trash, Your Treasure! Neighborhood FREE Yard Sale!") Have everyone bring stuff to the most convenient yard and put it on display tables.

Make sure everybody knows when the swap will happen (day and time) and what to expect in terms of bringing and taking stuff. They should bring their own bags and boxes to haul stuff off in and should return at the end of the day to take back any of their stuff that wasn't claimed. Providing cupcakes, doughnuts, cookies, or other snacks would be a nice touch. Just don't be surprised if strange cars start pulling up when they see stuff on tables!

Barter Online

If you find you enjoy bartering or you want something your friends and family can't give you, you can go online. Craigslist (www.craigslist.org) lists a barter category in its classifieds. In the Allentown area, I saw ads from a guy seeking to exchange painting or drywall work for a dirt bike, boat, motorcycle, car, or truck in any condition; someone wanting to exchange computer work for tattoo work; someone offering to do tattoos in exchange for a digital camera; a Harley mechanic who would trade work on your bike for tools or electronics; someone who wanted to trade his dirt bike for an old manual truck; someone offering to give flying lessons in exchange for Web and graphics work; and someone who would paint your home for a piano, to name just a few.

There's also a service called Trashbank (www.trashbank.com) where you register, list your item (with description and photo) in the appropriate category—antiques, jewelry and watches, toys, sports, books, collectibles, computers, music, movies, and so forth—and then can offer to swap it for another item or service or sell it. It's free to register, post your item, and request trades (there are no fees or charges). As they succinctly put it, "Barter, Swap, Trade, Buy, or Sell Online Absolutely Free!"

Other Unloading Options

Still trying to find free homes for your stuff? Craigslist (www.craigslist.org) lets you post stuff that's free on its Web site. (See Chapter 20—Clutter in the Classifieds, beginning on page 394, for more on Craigslist.) Or you could do what tons of people in my area do—set the stuff out on the curb (when dry weather's predicted, please). I've seen more sofas and mattresses on area curbs than I could ever imagine. Some put "Free" signs on their stuff; others assume people will figure it out for themselves. Either way, I'm always amazed at how soon that stuff disappears!

Of course, you could call your local sanitation service and arrange for pickup, especially if you're really trying to dispose of trashy stuff. Or contact a local franchise of a junk-removal service like 1-800-GOT-JUNK (www.1800gotjunk.com), TrashBusters Garbage and Trash Removal Service (www.trashbusters.com), or Junk It! Garbage Removal Service (in Canada; www.junkit.ca). There are plenty of local services that will come clear out your basement, attic, garage, or shed; check the classifieds under "Services." (One in my area has the great slogan, "If you call, I'll haul.")

And don't forget all those donation options we discussed in Chapter 17—Donations and Write-Offs, beginning on page 351. Where there's a will to kick the clutter, there's a way!

ONWARD!

Yard sales, eBay, classifieds, and giveaways are great when you have less-valuable clutter to kick. But what if you have Uncle Edmond's original Arts and Crafts bookcases, or Grandma Stella's Tiffany lamp, or a platinum-and-diamond cocktail ring that's come down in your family, and you don't want them? It's time to turn to the next chapter and head for your very own antiques roadshow. So let's hit the road!

Chapter 22

Antiques in Your Attic

If your clutter is actually valuable (to someone, anyway)—for example, you've inherited Great Aunt Sophie's cherished Sèvres collection, or a Cubist painting, and you don't like it—the best way to sell it may be through an antiques store or specialist. But how do you find the right one, and how much can you expect to get? Should you contact a museum or head to the local flea market? This chapter tells you how to match your stuff to the appropriate dealers, how to get their attention, what to expect, pitfalls to avoid, and more.

WHAT TO EXPECT AT AN ANTIQUES STORE

Like my parents, I've always been an avid antiques hound. I love going to antiques stores and flea markets, and also to museums and historic houses that are open to the public. But, though I've bought many antiques over the years, I've never tried to sell them. So when I wanted to get the scoop for this chapter, I went to the pros.

One of my favorite antiques stores is Moyer's Antiques and Collectibles in the picturesque village of Monterey, Pennsylvania. I decided to begin my investigations there, with owners Bruce and Karen Moyer. Karen and Bruce buy lots of their stuff from people like you and me who just drive up and bring things in from their cars or who call for an appointment to show their heirlooms.

Karen told me right away that people often have unrealistic expectations because of what I call "*Antiques Roadshow* Syndrome." They see an episode where someone's blackened flowerpot turns out to be an original Paul Revere sterling silver punchbowl worth a bazillion dollars. (Remember the story in Chapter 18—Secondhand Shops, about the guy who went into a thrift store with a few dollars and came out with a copy of the Declaration of Independence worth $250,000?) So they think, "Gee, I have some old stuff. It must be worth a bazillion dollars, too!" Or they collect a particular type of vintage ceramic or coin. They buy a book called a price guide that gives the value of every known style of that kind of ceramic or coin. Then they bring a piece in to a dealer and are dismayed when the dealer offers less than "book value."

It's a hard lesson for all of us, especially if, like me, you are an enthusiastic collector and have spent time and money acquiring pieces that you can't sell for close to what you paid for them, much less at a little profit. But the takeaway lesson is this: For the antiques dealer, the bottom line is not what the piece is "worth." It's what they can get for it. And of course, they need to make a profit on the sale, so what they'll offer you is still less.

Karen has some advice to help you avoid disappointment when you bring your stuff to a shop: Do some research first. Go on eBay and look for similar items. (Remember how to do that? Go to www.ebay.com, then type in the name or keyword of the item you want to find in the title search field. Select the "Completed Items Only" check box. Click "Search," and it will show you what the item actually brought at recent auctions.) You can also check out local antiques stores; if you can find someone selling the same object, you'll see what they're asking for it. (Remember, you'll probably be offered less.) Once you're better prepared, you'll be less likely to be disappointed.

Mind you, if you happen to have the exact same object that was just featured on *Antiques Roadshow* and appraised for a gadzillion dollars, then maybe you've found that pot of gold. Good luck!

Antiques Store Checklist

This checklist should help you get the most from your antiques store experience. Look it over, and do your homework before you bring your stuff to the store.

1. **Keep a clutter-kicking mind-set.** Remember why you're getting rid of this stuff—to get rid of it. If someone offers you $25 for a piece you thought was worth $250, or $250 for a piece you hoped might bring $2,500—and you've done your homework and know you can't get a better offer elsewhere—it's still money you didn't have before, and it's one less piece of stuff taking up space in your home.

2. **Be realistic.** Remember that what an item will bring on the market isn't usually as much as it's worth—and often, it's not even close. Find out what items like yours are selling for in your area and on eBay or other online auction sites (see page 392 for a list of Web sites). Then bear in mind that the dealer has to get a percentage, so you'll actually get less than the sale price.

3. **But be aware of what you have.** If you have something that you feel or know is really valuable, for mercy's sake, get it appraised. (See pages 435–36 for more on this.) You do *not* want to be the person who dropped off that copy of the Declaration of Independence at the thrift store! And you probably don't want to sell it through a local shop, either, unless that shop specializes in what you're selling or is very high-end. Which brings us to . . .

4. **Pick the right shop.** If a shop specializes in vintage comic books and sports cards, you are not likely to have much luck selling them your jardiniere or Bakelite jewelry. Even if they took it, it's not likely that they'd pay more than a pittance. But if you took your jardiniere to a shop that specialized in garden antiques or your Bakelite to a shop that specialized in vintage jewelry and accessories *and* had a good selection of Bakelite, you'd be more likely to make a good sale. Of course, if the store already had 5 or 10 identical pieces, they might not want yours, too—at least not right now. In that case, you could ask them to recommend another store that might want your item, or ask them to call you if they sold the ones in the shop and needed more. You could also simply check back every few months to look over their inventory. A shop that sells a variety of antiques and collectibles, like Moyer's Antiques and Collectibles, is also a good choice. A generalist might not offer as much as a specialist, but they'd be likely to take the piece if they thought they could sell it.

5. **Comparison shop.** It's perfectly fine to say, "Thanks, let me think about it," if you don't like the price you're offered for a piece. Then you can take

it to a few more shops and see if you can get a better deal. What's *not* fine is to argue with a store owner about the price they offer. You may know everything about the piece, but they know their market. Take it or leave it, but mind your manners.

6. **Don't forget antiques malls and flea markets.** I live in an antiques-rich area, and there are huge antiques malls in several communities near me with both general and specialty shops. There are also lots of established weekend flea markets with regular vendors. When you're scouting around for a good fit for your stuff, don't overlook them—you might find the perfect match. Flea markets are usually a better choice for less-valuable collectibles (Disney figures, Hallmark ornaments, Matchbox cars) and old rather than antique furniture—stuff that might be too good for a yard sale but not good enough for an antiques store. But you never know!

UP FOR AUCTION

At Antiques Etc. just down the road from me in Maxatawny, Pennsylvania, owner Pat Robertson has a different take on how you should sell your antiques. "Sell them through an auction," she told me. That's where she buys the vast majority of the antiques she features at Antiques Etc. and in her two other antiques stores.

Pat says it's easy to find auctions online through sites like AuctionZip and Auction Guide. (See "Tools of the Trade" for more on them.) Once you've found them, she reminds you to do your research! Choose an auction that sells what you have. For example, if you lived in my part of Pennsylvania and had art to sell, Pat says, you should take it to Alderfer's Auction Company in Hatfield, Pennsylvania, which is known for its art auctions.

Like seasonal goods at consignment shops, auctions have their seasons. Pat says that winter's a bad time to try to sell something at auction, but anytime from spring through fall is good.

Speaking of consignment shops, Pat's a big believer in taking things there. (See Chapter 18—Secondhand Shops, beginning on page 357, for more on them.) Her advice is, once again, to match your stuff with the shop. For example, if you have nicer things, you should try a more high-end store. Pat recommended Select Consignments in Quakertown, Pennsylvania, as an example; it's now on my agenda for an upcoming visit with my thrift-shop coconspirator, Delilah. Or put your stuff where you feel it can do the most good. Pat gives her things to the Nova Thrift Shop, which benefits battered women and accepts both item donations and consignments.

Auctioning Off Your Stuff

If you've ever been to an auction but aren't a devotee, you know how intimidating they can be—the auctioneer pattering away at a mile a minute, items flying across the stage, people bidding all around you. (Or are they? And what is that auctioneer saying, anyway?) Luckily, if you're selling something, you don't need to know the ins and outs of bidding. But if you're curious, attend a few live auctions, or check

the **Pros Know**

The Web site www.guidetoauctions.com has links to a lot of auctions and auction sites. Go to their home page, then search "Related Topics" for "Antiques Auctions," click, and check out the links. (They even provide a history of live auctions from ancient Babylon to the present!)

They also feature two valuable tips for people who are thinking about selling their antiques at auction. The first is to sell your antiques when they're hot, since items that are in demand will get more and higher bids. For example, it would have been a good time to sell a Louis XVI chair after the movie *Marie Antoinette* came out, or a vintage Indian motorcycle after the movie *The World's Fastest Indian* revived interest in the brand. Their other great tip is to resist the urge to monkey with, modernize, or "improve" your antiques. An antique in original condition can be worth hundreds or even hundreds of thousands of dollars more than one that's been refinished or painted. Both these tips hold true if you're trying to sell your antiques to a store, too.

out the run-through on the Auction Guide site (www.auctionguide.com). (See "Tools of the Trade" on page 433 for more about this.) In fact, once you've turned your stuff over to an auctioneer, you should follow the pros' advice and *stay home* while it's being auctioned—otherwise, you might find yourself bidding on it and paying for it twice!

Instead, find an auctioneer or auction house that meets your criteria, either online, via the Yellow Pages, by a referral from an antiques dealer or museum, or in your local paper. (My own local paper, the Allentown *Morning Call*, recently featured a prominent ad from Tom Hall Auctions, Inc., under the headline "Something to sell? Auction is the answer!" with the announcement, "Sell your fine antiques and heirlooms to the highest bidder in our Internationally Advertised Auction." If this weren't inducement enough, besides providing contact data, they note "28 Years' Experience—Over 10,000 Satisfied Customers.")

Auction houses typically work like this: You contact them, and they call you and try to make sure the sort of things you have are things they want to (and can) sell. If so, they'll come to your house and decide what they want. Then they'll arrange for pickup and schedule your stuff in one of their auctions (probably several months out). They'll send you a list of the items, with their estimates of what they expect each piece to bring. (Note that these are *estimates* based on their experience. Don't get your hopes up too high.) Finally, auction day arrives and the items (hopefully) sell. Within 30 days of the auction, you'll receive a listing of what each item sold for and a check for your part after the auction house deducts its commission (usually 30 percent) and any transport fees. As with anything else, ask about fees up front so you'll be prepared for the auction house bite.

GETTING AN APPRAISAL

When I moved to Pennsylvania and rented my first apartment, my parents gave me a framed Toulouse-Lautrec that my mother thought "might be something." The small artwork of a couple enjoying a country drive in their carriage had come from a shop in Nashville, and my parents considered it quite a find.

Not long after my move, I saw that the Allentown Art Museum was having an antiques appraisal event, where for a small fee you could have professional appraisers from one of the big houses—Sotheby's or Christie's, I can no longer remember which—look at your treasures and tell you if they were trash or the real thing.

Clutching my Toulouse-Lautrec, I joined the long line of other hopefuls with their vases, lamps, furniture, jewelry, art, and other heirlooms. My hopes began to dim as I saw the bored looks on the appraisers' faces and the demoralized expressions of the disappointed appraisees.

Finally, it was my turn. As I placed the Toulouse-Lautrec on the table, the appraiser suddenly became animated. My heart pounded as he excitedly called his colleagues over for a look. They turned the frame over, conferring quietly. Then the others returned to their stations and the original appraiser turned back to me.

"Is this the frame your parents bought this in?" he asked. I replied that it was.

"Then I'm afraid it's just a print and has very little value."

Visions of financial security drained from my sight as I crawled away. I still have—and still enjoy—my Toulouse-Lautrec. But, like most of my lottery tickets, it wasn't a winner.

Nonetheless, if you have art or antiques that you think (or know) are truly valuable, and you want to sell them, you need to get them appraised. (There are lots of ways to do that; see "The Pros Know" on page 436 for some of the best.) Read on to find out how to take *your* antiques on the road.

the Pros Know

As it happens, my father's girlfriend, Alice, was a renowned art-gallery owner in Nashville for many years, so when I wanted to know about getting something appraised, I turned to her. I wasn't disappointed with her advice! Her tips can help you as well, whether you have art or antiques that you need to have appraised.

Alice said the first thing she'd suggest would be to take the work back to the gallery where you bought it and have it appraised there. (They might buy it back or even suggest potential buyers.) She said that you could also call Sotheby's or Christie's, the two auction giants, and find out what similar works had sold for recently. (This service is free.) If it's a very valuable item, Alice recommended that you consign it to Sotheby's or Christie's for sale.

Other options? Alice suggested that you look online or in the Yellow Pages for an appraiser who is registered with a reputable national or regional professional association like the American Society of Appraisers, Appraisers Association of America, or New England Appraisers Association. You could also call a local museum and ask them to recommend appraisers to you. (Tell them what you have so they can make an accurate referral.) Or do as I did and take your heirloom to a museum appraisal event. (Call your museum to see if and when they have them.)

Your Own Antiques Roadshow

Antiques Roadshow, PBS's Emmy-nominated antiques appraisal show, is beloved by all of us who hope Grandma's cream pitcher is worth thousands—or even hundreds of thousands—of dollars. But the long-running program inspires both love *and* hate in antiques dealers. Love, because it's done so much to raise public awareness about antiques, and that's great for business. Hate, because the show's "jackpot" approach has created *"Antiques Roadshow* Syndrome," where everyone selling something old to a dealer thinks it's surely worth its weight in gold—at least. If you've ever enjoyed watching an episode or are an *Antiques Roadshow* addict, you know what I mean.

But whether you watch the show, want to be on the show, or couldn't care less about the show, if you have antiques to sell, *Antiques Roadshow* is your friend. That's because of their wonderful companion Web site, Antiques Roadshow

Online (www.pbs.org/roadshow). It has, of course, features about the show, tips from the show, and a great list of terms used in the antiques world and to describe antiques, called "Antiques Speak."

If you'd like to attend one of the six yearly appraisal events hosted by *Antiques Roadshow* and held in cities across the country, you can apply online or via post-card and hope that yours is one of the applications randomly selected for a free ticket. If you get one, you're entitled to show up at the event with two objects that will be appraised by one of the 70 to 80 appraisers who attend each event. The appraisals are also free. Go to their site's FAQ (frequently asked questions) for application and event details.

But the real beauty of the site, in my opinion, is its list of appraisers and auction houses that are affiliated with the show. You can go to their appraisers index and look up appraisers alphabetically or by specialty. (For example, if you collect pueblo pottery, as I do, you'd search the listing of appraisers under American Indian/Ethnographia. You'd get a listing of appraisers who work in this specialty. I was astounded to find one in Franklin, Tennessee, just down the road from my family home!) There's a profile for each appraiser and contact data, so you can contact them directly. There's also a section on auction houses affiliated with the show (including all the big guys, like Sotheby's, Christie's, and Skinner's), with summaries of their history, what they sell, appraisal practices, and contact data. (Where contact data isn't provided, you can access them easily through a Google search.)

Going on the *Antiques Roadshow* Web site is like gaining access to your own personal cache of appraisers and auction houses. So if you haven't already done so, make friends with *Antiques Roadshow* today!

ONWARD!

You've almost done it. You've cleared out the clutter from every part of your house and yard—even the car—and you've hauled it off, donated it, sold it, swapped it, or given it away. There's just one thing left: Keeping it from coming back. And that's the subject of the next section, Controlling Clutter Creep. Before your clutter has a chance to sneak back, turn the page and read about how you can finally kick your clutter out forever!

PART FIVE

Controlling Clutter Creep

Chapter 23

Kicking the Clutter Habit

Okay, you've gotten it out. But like with losing weight, where getting the excess poundage off is just half the battle, getting rid of the clutter is only half the solution. Now, you have to keep it out—or, just like the diet gurus are always telling you, you'll gain it all back and then some! But by now we've given you some great techniques for de-cluttering every part of your house and yard, so you're prepared to clear the clutter as soon as you see it creeping back. And in this chapter, you'll find a smorgasbord of effective ways to catch yourself (and others) before the old habits—and new clutter—start taking hold.

IT'S BA-A-A-ACK!!!

Has this happened to you? You go on a cleaning frenzy and empty the house of all the clutter and junk. Whew! What a triumph! As you survey your domain, you can't see a single piece of clutter taking up space. You think, "Well! Thank heavens *that's* over!" and go back to your usual occupations. One day—maybe 6 months from that triumphant moment—you look up and see . . . clutter. Wait a minute—how did that happen? You don't even remember bringing all that stuff back in.

Like weight, clutter has a sneaky habit of creeping back up on you the second you think you've got it licked. You think you might need your "fat" clothes again sometime, so you stuff them in the back of the closet. That three-for-one sale at the local shopping club was too good to resist. Your sister-in-law had a few pieces of furniture she didn't need but was convinced you'd love. You upgraded your coffee maker but kept the old one, "just in case." Your husband promised to replace the deck railing, but somehow all the materials ended up in the garage. Before you know it, your home starts to look junky and crowded all over again. And you'd worked so hard to clean it out!

Don't panic. Here are some ways to recognize when clutter's creeping in through the back door and kick it out *before* it becomes an issue.

[The easiest way to keep clutter out is not to bring it in.]

Use It or Lose It

"Try to find a place or use for everything," advises my friend Chris. "If you don't have an immediate use for it, don't buy it or get rid of it." If only it was that easy! But try to keep Chris's advice in mind when you're thinking about whether or not to buy something, and use it to cull objects you already have whenever you can.

Avoid Temptation

Just as you'd avoid the pizza or ice-cream parlor if you were trying to lose weight, if you can't resist buying when you go into stores, find other ways to shop.

"I try to avoid looking at catalogs or going to the mall so I don't buy things I don't need or have space for," says my friend Jennifer.

Jennifer has another excellent tactic for buying what she needs without being tempted to buy anything else. "I buy things online whenever possible, especially if the store offers free shipping," she says. "That way, I save gas and time, and I avoid seeing—and buying—extra things I don't need or have space for."

Know Your Limits

Your space limits, that is. When stuff starts overflowing its allotted space, it creates both visual and actual clutter.

"I allocate space in my home for categories of things—such as a bookcase for my books and a cabinet for my glassware," my friend Jennifer says. "Once I exceed that space, if I bring another item home, I have to get rid of one."

And don't forget the advice of Diane, one of my colleagues at the Kutztown Curves (you met her in Chapter 1): Her rule is, if one item comes in, *two* have to go out. If you can manage that, you'll not only keep clutter from coming into your home, you'll reduce the amount of stuff you have over time.

Take Five (or One)

Keep your clutter in check by constantly culling your stuff. If you can find a few items to put in a donation bag for your local thrift store each day, you'll be amazed at how soon things get back under control. I do this with my dressers, closets, and cabinets, taking it a little at a time. When my bag is full, I drop it off at Goodwill or the Salvation Army and start a new bag. Easy does it!

Toss the Little Stuff

Be ruthless with worthless junk-drawer clutter like twist-ties, rubber bands, bottle caps, and paper clips. If you must, keep just enough to fill a sandwich-size zipper-lock bag and toss the rest. You'll have plenty for any household needs, you'll be able to get them when you need them, and they won't take over the drawer. Get rid of restaurant packets that come with take-out orders. Cull coupons regularly, and clip only the ones you'll use—don't clip coupons for every item that looks like it might be worth trying someday.

Find Better Things to Do

Shopping is entertaining—certainly for me, probably for you. But when shopping results in buying, clutter will be coming in the door with you every time you return from a shopping trip. Escape this trap by planning outings that don't produce clutter: Go for a walk, go to the movies, go to a concert. Research and plan vacations (even if you never take them, it's fun to think about your dream vacation locations and put together the perfect weekend, cruise, spa trip, or the like). Check out the books, magazines, CDs, and DVDs or video tapes at your local library. Get a subscription to Netflix. If you simply *must* shop, indulge your shopping habit by going to the most upscale stores you can imagine—jewelry, antiques, fashion, furnishings—where you *know* you won't be tempted to buy anything but can enjoy looking at the best.

Trade Up

Remember the concept of trading up from Chapter 1? It's another take on "one in, two out" that's especially helpful for Collectors like me. Take a handful—or armful, or carful—of less-good stuff from your collection and sell it, then use the money you make to buy just one very good (or at least, much better) thing. You could get rid of a box of so-so jewelry and get the piece you've had your eye on all season, or exchange your starter woodworking equipment for the router you've been drooling over. Take a box of books to the used-book store and use the store credit to buy one or two really nice books. In the case of art and collectibles, sometimes the store or gallery where you bought the pieces will take them back (don't expect to get what you paid for them, though). Then you can apply whatever money you make to the price of the piece you want to buy.

Take Small Steps

Any time you think clutter is starting to get a foothold again, turn back to Chapter 4—Five Simple Steps to Kick Your Clutter, beginning on page 54. Review the steps and see if you should be using one or more of them more often. The sooner you act, the faster you'll bring the clutter under control and get your house back to where you want it.

Take a Picture

Give yourself a clutter-fighting chance by taking photos of each room or area of your house and yard after you've gotten the clutter out of it. If clutter starts creeping back, take out the pictures and see how great everything looked. You'll be inspired to get the space cleared out again.

Review Your Visualizations

Another good way to bring clutter creep to a screeching halt is to look at the "After" visualizations you wrote down in Parts Two and Three of this book. If the family room is starting to look shabby or the front yard is getting away from you, reread that visualization and once again picture your dream space. It will motivate you to kick the clutter back where it belongs. Review the tips in the relevant chapter to remind yourself of all the ways you can show clutter the door.

Try Some Tools

The right tools can make all the difference in any task, and clutter-control is no different. If you haven't tried any of the tools I recommend in Chapter 3—Tooling Up (beginning on page 35), go back and look them over. Pick one thing—even if it's a single storage container or a showerhead bottle holder—and treat yourself. It really makes a difference! Or go to an organizing store in your area or online, and see how many ideas you get just from looking around. It's inspiring!

Enjoy Yourself

As I hope you've found out by now, lots of the ways you can use to get rid of clutter are actually fun! Whether you have been bitten by the eBay bug, feel like you've finally mastered the art of yard-saleing, have made a little cash on consignment, or just enjoy hauling bags and boxes to the thrift store, remember the fun part when you see clutter start to creep back. Figure out what you're going to do with each type of clutter—have another yard sale next month, put it on Craigslist or Freecycle, take it to the eBay store. Choose the option you'll enjoy most, and go for it!

Don't Give Up

You've worked hard to get the clutter out. But if there are things still lying around that you can't figure out how to get rid of, don't despair. Even if you have to call

Dear Claire,

My kids are clutter hogs—or maybe they're just hogs. I worked all month to get our family room shoveled out, and by the next weekend, the kids had totally trashed it. I didn't even get to enjoy it! I know it's not really as bad as it was, but it will be soon if something doesn't happen. What can I do?

Hog-Wild in New Haven

Dear Hog-Wild,

How do you get your kids to do their homework, chores, and other social obligations? Choose the incentives (or punishments) that have worked in other situations and apply them here. Tell them that they're free to trash the family room as much as they please as long as they're in there, but that everything must be taken to their rooms or put in its place when they leave the room. And, dear, before you start meting out punishments, make sure that when you took out the clutter, you remembered to put in lots of storage solutions. If you forgot this vital part of the de-cluttering process, do it now, and then explain to the family what you expect from them. Show them where to stow their stuff, *then* lay down the law.

Good luck,
Claire

in a hauling company and pay them to cart stuff off, it beats continuing to live with it.

As Pat Robertson of Antiques Etc. (see page 432) put it, "If you want to get rid of your stuff, there's a way."

ONWARD!

Just two things left to read and you've done it! The first is Chapter 24—The Top 10 Clutter Traps, starting on the next page. It's an at-a-glance guide to the most common ways clutter can creep back into your home. Last—but far from least, for most people—is Photo Finish, beginning on page 450. As you might guess, it's a guide to all the ways you can (finally) bring your photo clutter under control.

The Top 10 Clutter Traps

I'll leave you with a checklist of the most common ways clutter can creep back into your house . . . and your life. You might want to photocopy them and post them on the fridge as a reminder. But then again, you might decide that's just more clutter!

1. **Buying in bulk.** Yes, buying 24 rolls of toilet paper instead of four might save you money. But if you don't have room to store the 24 rolls, you're creating clutter. And an attractive, uncluttered home is worth more than the few cents (or even dollars) you'll save by buying in bulk!

2. **Getting free stuff.** "Buy one, get one free!" "Free matching purse with this raincoat!" Free stuff sells stuff, as canny marketers know. But unless you actually *need* the free stuff, it's just clutter. Turn it down or donate it.

3. **Keeping unwanted gifts.** Aunt Jane gave you that urn as a wedding present. Your parents generously bestowed that sofa on you when you left home. Whatever it is, you never liked it, but you're afraid you'll hurt someone's feelings if you get rid of it. But who's getting hurt because you're keeping it? You and your family, that's who. Unload it. (See Chapter 1 for ways to do it discreetly.)

4. **Keeping stuff you don't like because you paid for it.** I know you spent good money on that orange-eucalyptus herbal tea or the dress that was just like the one that looked so wonderful on Angelina Jolie. But you can't stand the tea, and when you put on the dress, your bratty teen asked if you'd

decided to go to a costume party dressed as a hippo. Know what? If you don't like something now, you're not going to decide you love it months (or years) from now. And meanwhile, it's taking up space. Take the tea to the office and set it out with a "free" sticker. Sell the dress through a consignment shop and make back some of your money. Mistakes happen, and they do cost money. But don't compound your original mistake by letting it turn into clutter.

5. **Keeping stuff too long.** I'm as guilty of this as anyone. I wear shoes I love until the heels have practically worn off and have been known to wear my favorite tees until they're so threadbare holes actually appear in them. But deep down, I know—and you know it, too—that keeping clothes, appliances, food, you name it, past its prime is doing you no favors. The hairdryer that takes three times as long to dry your hair as it did when it was new is wasting three times as much of your life every single morning (and probably wasting electricity, too). Worn-out clothes, however beloved, are *not* becoming. Treat yourself (and your wardrobe) with some respect, and replace worn items before strangers start offering handouts!

6. **Letting paper pile up.** Don't have time for the paper? Magazines, catalogs, and bills spilling off the coffee table, kitchen counters, and dining table? Paper is one of the worst clutter traps because every family member has his or her own, and nobody likes to get rid of it. ("Don't throw out my magazine!" "I haven't read that section yet." "I might want to try that recipe.") Getting tough on paper pileups will save you a lot of clutter headaches in the long run. Set strict deadlines about how long different kinds of paper can stay in the house before they're recycled, and stick to them. Consider reading the paper online if it looks like nobody's reading the print version. If someone wants to hang onto their guitar or cooking magazines, they should be shelved neatly in magazine files. No room on the shelves? Either they or something else up there's gotta go.

7. **Keeping your kids' stuff.** The kids are in college . . . they've got their first apartments . . . they're married and haven't lived at home for 15 years. But somehow, their stuff is *still* living there, because however long they've been gone, there's always some reason why they can't take it. Call a halt. Tell them they have 3 weeks (or 3 months) to get over to your place and take

what they want—or it's going to Goodwill. Nurturing them was one thing; nurturing their clutter wasn't part of the deal. Tell them your home isn't a self-storage unit, and they're welcome to rent one if they need to.

8. **Getting the whole set.** Collector, know thyself! Why have just one or two (or ten, or . . .) shells, marbles, Barbies, Sting albums, Ansel Adams prints, or first editions when you know there are more—so many more—waiting somewhere out there just for you? When you can't see or store your stuff, it's stopped being a collection and become clutter. Cull it, and start enjoying your treasures again. Sell off the ones you like less and invest in one you've always wanted. It may feel like a big sacrifice at the time (and I know whereof I speak here), but it really won't kill you not to buy every single one, or even the next one. Think of what else you could do with your money, like paint the house or replace those ancient shoes. This goes for getting more china, crystal, and silverware than you need. In the days when families were large and family gatherings were even larger, 16-piece place settings were the norm. But if your family is small and your dinner parties are modest, don't buy 12 glasses when you need 6 . . . or 2. Save your money and your space.

9. **Keeping "extras."** You bought a new coffeemaker to replace the one that went on the fritz, but the old one ended up in the basement, "just in case." The old lawn mower's still in the garage. You have all three electric can openers you got at your bridal shower. Pick the best and toss, recycle, sell, or donate the rest. The space you save will be your own.

10. **Keeping stuff for "someday."** The sewing machine you got a great deal on when you decided to make your own clothes (but never did). The black walnut boards you were going to make into a table. The older we get, the more stuff like this we have. No, we didn't end up taking up painting, or the trumpet, or model-building after all. But we might, someday, so we hang on to all our supplies, even if we can't remember where, or even what, they are. Well, here's a little secret: If "someday" really *does* come, you can buy the stuff again. Meanwhile, stop letting it clutter up your home. Sell it, donate it, give it to someone else who's actually doing the craft, art, or work. Perhaps in return they'll give you a finished project that you can display and enjoy!

Photo Finish

Because so many people have a lifetime of photos, negatives, and envelopes stuffed all over the house, I decided to break this section out as a special appendix to make it easy to find. Read on for ways to corral, catalog, and curb your photo clutter!

Let's start with the printed photos, negatives, and associated clutter. (We'll get to the digital versions in a minute.) Follow these steps to make them manageable.

1. **Collect your photos.** You probably have them stashed everywhere—in drawers, boxes, maybe even (gasp!) albums. You can tackle the entire assortment at one time, which will make it easier to figure out what you actually have and, thus, what you'll want to keep. Or, if that's just too much to deal with, you can take on a single box, drawer, album, or envelope at a time and work through the mountain of photos bit by bit.

2. **Toss what you can't see.** This step should be easy, but I know too many people who can't seem to part with any photo, however abysmal. *Please* don't let yourself get stuck here. Unless it's the only known photo of Great-Great-Uncle Leo or it's a pioneer photo or rare shot of your Civil War ancestor in uniform, if it's too dark or out of focus, toss it.

3. **Vanquish the vampires.** Red eyes, grimaces, half-headed monsters (this one's my specialty, alas). If someone doesn't look good in a photo, for whatever reason, unless it's a vintage shot and you can't take another photo

of that person, throw that photo out. Think about how you'd feel if it were a photo of you, and be kind!

4. **Ditch duplicates.** If you've inherited (or are yourself guilty of taking) 1,000 identical or nearly identical shots of the Eiffel Tower, London Bridge, or your dog Milton, give it a rest. (Father, cover your ears, please.) Pick the best shots for your own collection. If you have duplicates of the best shots, set them aside for your kids, friends, traveling companions, or relations—*if and only if* you know they'd be interested. (And don't forget that you can pick up the phone and ask them!) Put those in envelopes marked with each recipient's name. Then toss the rest.

5. **Don't save strangers' photos.** No idea who's staring back at you from that old photo? Don't make yourself a hostage to ancient clutter. If you think it's an ancestor or relative, send or take it to the family historian or an older relative for an ID. You might discover that it's your mom's college roommate! Can't remember the name of your BFF from sixth grade? Say good-bye. Same for your granddad's colleagues from the mill. If you get an ID and the photo is of someone who matters to you, label it and save it. If you've ID'd Great-Uncle Al and couldn't care less, send it to his kids or grandkids. But if nobody has a clue who it is and you don't really care, throw it out. (If it's a nice old photo, you might be able to sell it to an antiques store.)

6. **Ditto for strange places.** If you don't have a clue what that scenic photo's showing, it might be of some obscure place your grandparents visited during the Depression. Unless it means something to you or someone you love, throw it out. (Or again, if it has that vintage look, take it to an antiques store.)

7. **Label everything.** Once you've pared everything down, if the people, place, occasion, and date aren't already on the back of the photo, write them on or write the data on a label and attach it. You don't ever want to go through this again—or put your kids through it, either! If you don't know the date, give an approximation with a question mark.

8. **Store them together.** Stash the photos you've decided to hang on to in photo albums by family member, place, theme (such as Christmas or pets), or time frame. (Or choose your own organizing theme. I have an album of photos documenting the construction and contents of my greenhouse.)

Paste a label on the spine of each photo album so you can see what's in it at a glance, and keep them all together on a shelf for easy retrieval.

Besides those basic principles, here are some additional tips for photo storage:

Know where they are. If you're like me, family photos are one of the top things you'd try to save in case of a fire, along with your pets, purse, and best jewelry. Make sure you know the exact locations of the albums and framed photos that matter to you most. Keep those precious albums closest to the door. Drill yourself and your family to see how fast you can grab the must-keep photos off walls and shelves and take them outside to safety.

Use acid-free paper. Photos are fragile and react quickly and sometimes dramatically to their environment. If you're storing them in photo boxes or scrapbooks (available from crafts or scrapbooking stores and Web sites), make sure you choose acid-free paper to protect them. The same sources sell acid-free labels to use as IDs on the backs of photos.

Keep them out of the basement. That goes for the attic, too. Store photos in a dry, climate-controlled room—one you'd be comfortable in yourself.

Repair the damage. If you find a precious family photo that's nicked, cracked, splotched, or otherwise damaged (I told you to keep them out of the basement!), you can have it professionally restored thanks to the wonders of modern technology—call a photo shop near you. Or, if you're up for it, you can do it yourself with a program like Adobe Photoshop LE and a scanner.

Peel 'em off. Apparently, stick-on photo albums were all the rage in the seventies—and, as you might expect, the sticky stuff did no one's photos any favors. If you happen to have any of these albums lying around, extract your photos and put them in today's archival-quality sleeves.

Show them off. Look through your stash for photos that are especially evocative. If you find some good ones, have them enlarged and frame them for display. In their living room, my friends Gary and Carolyn have a marvelous black-and-white photo of their daughter Michelle holding a goose. My boyfriend, Rob, framed some wonderful shots of his road trips to Utah, Wyoming, Colorado, and the Four Corners area of New Mexico, and he displays them in his office at the college where he teaches. Why have photos if you don't look at them?

Box 'em up. If you decide to store photos in an archivally sensitive acid-free photo box, add tabbed dividers to sort photos by topic (pets, vacations, Grandma's house, birthdays, Christmas, whatever). You can find them at stores like West Elm (www.westelm.com) and, for larger prints, Exposures (www.exposuresonline.com).

Make some memories. Photos and scrapbooking just seem to go together. As you create a scrapbook around a given theme, whether it's Christmas or that never-to-be-forgotten trip on Route 66, add some photos to bring your multi-media treatment to life. It's a great way to preserve your photos as well as your memories!

Keep up. Whenever you get printed photos—from the pharmacy or from your printer—immediately write who, what, where, and when on the back of each photo you choose to keep. Don't put off this vital step! If you cared enough to take the photo, you care enough to document it. And please, toss the bad shots as you go through.

Try compact options. Catalogs like Solutions (www.solutions.com) offer ways to store lots of photos in small spaces. They allow you to display 100 photos, 4 by 6 inches each, in a single wooden frame that lets you flip through the photos to display your favorites; or organize 400 of your 4- by 6-inch photos in six-compartment photo storage boxes. You can group them by theme or person, whatever works for you.

Nix the negatives. I know this is heresy to lots of people, but in these days of photo scanning, when anyone can reproduce their photos ad infinitum and any pharmacy or photo shop can duplicate a photo from the original photo, negatives seem pointless to me. Unless you're a professional photographer, they're just anachronistic photo clutter. I recommend tossing your negatives—you (and your photo library) can live without them.

Or keep them close. If you can't bear to toss your negatives, I suggest storing them in envelopes attached to the inside back of the album where the photos contained in them are displayed. That way, they're at hand if someone asks for a copy while thumbing through the album, and you always know where they are.

Get some ammo. My friend Susan says her cousin Chuck has discovered a great way to store negatives. "Chuck bought a bunch of army surplus ammo boxes for storing negatives and other family treasures," she says. "The ammo boxes, he says, are designed to keep things from getting damp."

Buy a bin. For a more professional option, you can buy a special negative-storing box designed to store more than 2,000 negatives (35mm format). It's a steal from www.mvconservation.com.

Keep them safe. Some organizing experts, like Linda Koopersmith, the Beverly Hills Organizer, recommend storing your negatives in your safe deposit box. That way, if your actual photographs are lost in a fire, flood, or other disaster, you'll still have the negatives. If you choose this option, you might want to consider getting a light-resistant, protective storage case made especially for negatives. You can get an inexpensive one that holds 2,000 negatives from www.mvconservation.com.

Label your negatives. Write the date and content of your negatives on each envelope so you can identify the contents at a glance.

Pass them on. Do you have framed photos of your son's ninth-grade soccer team, your daughter's riding trophy, the twins' wrestling medals? Yow. Pass them on to the child concerned; it's his or her history. Ask yourself, do I *really* want this?

Digital Dilemmas

Just because digital cameras don't (necessarily!) leave a paper trail, that doesn't mean you can just ignore digital photo clutter. Here's some advice to help you reduce and organize the digital photo flow.

Ditch digital duds. They may not be piling up around the house like printed photos and negatives do, but those digital dupes and "oops" are still filling up your memory card. My boyfriend, Rob, loves his digital camera, and he tends to go overboard whenever he's taking photos of pets, family, or scenery from one of his famous road trips to the Southwest. To make sure he always has plenty of space for new shots, he's diligent about deleting duplicates, fuzzy shots, and anything he doesn't absolutely love as soon as he finishes a shoot.

Shop for software. Software programs like Adobe's Photoshop Album (www.adobe.com), Paint Shop Photo Album (www.corel.com), Google Picasa (www.picasa.com), Apple iPhoto (www.apple.com), and Photo Mechanic (www.camerabits.com) let you sort and store digital photos by subject, event, or date. Picasa is free, and the others have free trial versions that let you test them before you buy.

Use your e-mail. E-mail systems like Yahoo! have free online photo storage sections ("My Photos," in the case of Yahoo!) that let you archive and e-mail favorite photos.

Download onto CDs. Not only does downloading digital images to CDs (or DVDs) free up your photo card, it also gives you great archives and gifts. (Just make sure you edit all those digital photos rather than mindlessly dumping them all onto CDs!) Many image-editing software packages feature a contact-sheet option that lets you create customized CD case covers with choice images from the shoot that's on the CD.

Label your CDs. For what strikes me as a rather hefty initial investment, you can buy a CD/DVD title printer that will print a professional-looking title on your photo CDs. You can buy a compact printer with five type fonts, 14 languages, and 650 symbols from catalogs like Hammacher Schlemmer (www.hammacher.com) for $129.95.

Store your CDs. Stash those photo CDs in soft plastic CD photo sleeves from the Container Store (www.containerstore.com). The inexpensive CD storage pages keep four photo CDs safely stowed on each side.

Box 'em up. If you have a lot of photo CDs or DVDs, check out Atlantic Inc.'s super-affordable CD File Box, which holds up to 80 CDs or DVDs in protective hanging file folders in a blue fabric cube. Get it from www.atlantic-inc.com.

Frame your digital photos. Wood meets electronics in a digital photo frame from Solutions (www.solutions.com). The 6- by $3\frac{1}{4}$-inch framed view accepts your digital camera's memory card and shows your photos like a slideshow or one at a time.

Put them on a chain. Catalogs like Solutions (www.solutions.com) offer key chains with viewing capacity for up to 56 digital photos on a 1.4-inch screen. Software for both Macs and PCs lets you edit photos on your computer, then download them to the key chain.

INDEX

Underscored page references indicate boxed text.

H

Home offices *(cont.)*
    printers, computer, 236, 239–40
    prioritizing, 227, 229, 231, <u>231</u>
    the Pros Know, <u>234</u>
    resources for de-cluttering, 47
    rolling carts, 233–34
    Sanity Savers, <u>239</u>
    shelves, 235–36
    tax materials, 246–48
    trash, 236
    visualizing, 229, <u>230</u>
    warranties, 236
    wireless technology, 232–33
Hooks
    bathroom, 136–37
    bedroom, 205
    closet, 205, 224
    garage, 324
    for hats, 205
    mug, 93
    ornament, 287
    for purses, 205
Hoosier cabinets, 111
Hope chests. *See* Blanket chests
Hoses
    outdoor watering, 343
    washing machine, 258
Host(ess) clutter-attracting type, 14–15
Houseplants, 157, 191, 240, 274, 309–10
Housewares and secondhand shops, 367–71. *See also specific household items*
Hutches, 174

I

Ikea, 46, 307
Improvements (catalogs), 48, 110, 188, 195, 215, <u>245</u>, <u>256</u>, <u>263</u>, 267, 287–88, <u>301</u>, 303, 317, <u>317</u>, 321, <u>323</u>, 324, <u>325</u>, 327

"In-and-out" boxes, 238
Inflatable air mattresses, 163, 194–95, 222
Inheritor clutter-attracting type, 8–10
Internal Revenue Service (IRS), <u>353</u>
Internet Auction List, 51
Ironing boards, fold-down, <u>256</u>
IRS, <u>353</u>
Islands, kitchen, 109–10
iSold It, 51, <u>382</u>, 384, 386–87

J

Jackson & Perkins, 336
Jars, apothecary, 139
Jewelry, 188–89
Jewelry boxes, 188
Junk It! Garbage Removal Service, 428
Junk removal, resources for, 49–50
JustGive, 49–50, <u>354</u>, 355

K

Keep It–Toss It Spectrum, <u>30</u>, 31
Keys, storing, 77, <u>77</u>
Kids' rooms
    armoires, <u>213</u>
    art, 214–16, 219
    baskets, 214
    beds, 212, 222
    blanket chests, 212–13
    blanket or hope chests, 212–13
    bookcases, 213
    boxes, 214–15
    bulletin boards, 215
    cabinets, 222
    chalkboard walls, 210–11
    closets, 223–26
    clothing, 218, 223, 225–26
    computers, 211–12
    desks, 215

    doodads, 218
    dressers in, <u>219</u>
    5-Minute Fixes, <u>212</u>
    furniture and furnishings, 211–12, 221–22
    hair accessories, 217–18
    laundry hampers, 215
    lighting, 211
    lockers, metal school, 222
    Pet Alert!, <u>220–21</u>
    prioritizing, 207–8, 210, <u>210</u>
    the Pros Know, <u>216</u>, <u>219</u>
    reading materials, 216
    rolling carts, 222
    Sanity Savers, <u>211</u>
    shelves, 213–14
    sleeping bags, 222
    stools, 214
    storage, 212–16, 220–23
    stuffed animals, <u>212</u>, <u>217</u>
    suitcases, 220–21
    trains, 216–17
    trash, 214
    visualizing, 208, <u>209</u>
    walls, 210–11
Kids' stuff
    in attics, 10–11, 281–83
    in dining rooms, <u>177</u>
    in entryways, <u>79</u>
    in home offices, 236
    in kitchens, 96
    porch furniture, 307
    secondhand shops for selling, 367–68
Kinsman Company, 49, 303, <u>345</u>
Kiplinger's Taming the Paper Tiger, 47
Kitchen Accessories Unlimited, 46
Kitchens
    appliances and gadgets, 85, 99–102
    armoires, 111
    bags, 89, 96
    baskets, 102
    benches, 125
    bookcases, 108–9
    breakfast nooks, 119

Y